DEAD SOULS

Nikolai V. Gogol

DEAD

SOULS

*Translated from the Russian,
and with a Foreword, by*

Bernard Guilbert Guerney

THE MODERN LIBRARY

NEW YORK

1997 Modern Library Edition

Biographical note copyright © 1997 by Random House, Inc.
Copyright © 1965 by Bernard Guilbert Guerney
Copyright renewed 1993 by Bernard Guilbert Guerney, Jr.

Jacket portrait courtesy of Culver Pictures

LIBRARY OF CONGRESS CATALOGING-IN-PUBLICATION DATA
Gogol', Nikolaĭ Vasil'evich, 1809–1852.
[Mertvye dushi. English]
Dead souls/Nikolai V. Gogol; translated from the Russian, and
with a foreword, by Bernard Guilbert Guerney.
p. cm.
ISBN 0-679-60265-8
I. Guerney, Bernard Guilbert, 1894–1979.   II. Title.
PG3333.M4   1997
891.73'3—dc21   96-29784

Modern Library website address:
http://www.randomhouse.com/modernlibrary/

Printed in the United States of America on acid-free paper

2   4   6   8   9   7   5   3   1

NIKOLAI V. GOGOL

Nikolai Gogol, a writer whose imaginative, satiric work ushered in the naturalist movement in Russian literature, was born in the Ukrainian town of Sorochintsy on April 1, 1809, into a family of ancient and noble Cossack lineage. His father was a minor official, amateur playwright, and gentleman-farmer who presided over Vassilyevka, an estate of some three thousand acres where Gogol grew up in an atmosphere of relative affluence and parental indulgence. In 1821, at the age of twelve, Gogol left Vassilyevka and entered the School of Higher Studies at Nezhin; there he developed an unbridled passion for theater and poetry. After he graduated in 1828 he attempted to find work as an actor but also published *Hans Kuechelgärten* (1829), an epic poem that received only negative reviews. He secured a post with a government ministry in St. Petersburg and began writing a series of folk tales set in his native Ukraine.

The appearance of *Evenings on a Farm near Dikanka* in 1831 brought Gogol immediate acclaim. "I have finished reading *Evenings,*" wrote Alexander Pushkin to a friend. "An astounding book! Here is fun for you, authentic fun of the frankest kind without anything maudlin or prim about it. And moreover—what poetry, what delicacy of sentiment in certain passages! All this is so unusual in our literature that I am still unable to get over it." A second collection of *Evenings* came out in 1832, and in 1835 Gogol published two more volumes of Ukrainian tales, collectively entitled *Mirgorod,* as well as *Arabesques,* a series of extraordinary stories about St. Petersburg.

Gogol's association with Pushkin soon inspired two of his greatest works: the play *The Inspector General* and *Dead Souls.* A comedy of mistaken identity that is a satiric indictment of Russian bureaucracy, *The Inspector General* set all of Russia laughing when it was staged in 1836. "Everyone has got his due, and I most of all," Tsar Nicholas I reportedly remarked. *"The Inspector General* happened to be the greatest play ever written in Russian (and never surpassed since)," judged Vladimir Nabokov. "The play begins with a blinding flash of lightning and ends in a thunderclap. In fact it is wholly placed in the tense gap between the flash and the crash. . . . Gogol's play is poetry in action."

Stung by criticism of *The Inspector General,* Gogol moved to Italy in 1836, and except for two brief visits home he remained abroad for twelve years. Much of this time was devoted to writing *Dead Souls.* Published in 1842, the novel revolves around Pavel Ivanovich Chichikov, a mystifying swindler who travels through provincial Russia trafficking in "souls"—those serfs who, despite being dead, could still be bought and sold.

The same year marked the appearance of Gogol's famous short story "The Overcoat," in which a buffoonish clerk is robbed of a symbolic garment that represents all his hopes and dreams. "We all came from Gogol's 'Overcoat,' " said Dostoevsky in acknowledgment of Russian literature's vast debt to Gogol. And Vladimir Nabokov noted: "When, as in his immortal 'The Overcoat,' Gogol really let himself go and pottered happily on the brink of his private abyss, he became the greatest artist that Russia has yet produced." But *Selected Passages from Correspondence with My Friends* (1847), a reactionary work reflecting the writer's growing religious and moral fanaticism, virtually ended his career.

Gogol spent his final years struggling in vain to finish the second part of *Dead Souls:* a sequel in which he intended to depict Chichikov's moral conversion. The effort helped propel him into insanity, and he burned the final version of the manuscript shortly before his death in Moscow, following weeks of fasting, on the morning of March 4, 1852. Commenting on the crowd at Gogol's funeral, a passerby asked: "Who is this man who has so many relatives at his funeral?" A mourner replied: "This is Nikolai Gogol, and all of Russia is his relative."

*This new (and revised) rendering
of a Russian masterpiece and a
world classic is rededicated to*
DR. VIRGIL JORDAN
*in sincere acknowledgement of a
gracious service done to the
translator, which the latter has
found, during something like half
a century, not only unprecedented
but unparalleled.*

TRANSLATOR'S FOREWORD

A creative work unencompassably artistic in its cast of characters and details of the Russian way of life—and at the same time social, societal, historical, of profound thought. . . . In *Dead Souls* the author has taken so great a stride that all he has written hitherto seems feeble by comparison.

—BELINSKY

A clinical history of a disease, penned by the hand of a master.

—HERZEN

When *Satyricon,* that fabulous Russian weekly, was revived in Paris in 1931, its first cover showed a bewildered émigré *intelligent* with a samovar and a portfolio of the Tretyakovskaya Gallery prints close by on the trottoir. But what was this storm-buffeted starveling hugging to his drab and raggedy bosom? Pushkin and Gogol, each complete in one volume. And, although the montage background of sky was studded with nothing more gemmary than the Eiffel Tower and the silhouette of a giant gendarme with baton raised, and the only approach to a vocalizing angel was Josephine Baker, the quotation-caption made it poignantly Russian: "We shall rest, Uncle Vanya! We shall behold the sky studded with gems, we shall hear the angels singing over our heads!"

Pushkin is understandable: no literate Russian would think of being marooned without his greatest poet. But why Gogol, out of all of Russia's galactic prosateurs? As one fortunate enough to have been born not only in Russia but in Gogol's own Ukraine, the present writer will try to share some of the delight a Russian derives from his Gogol—but the barebones of biography must be dealt with first.

Nicholai Vassilievich Gogol-Janovski (he eventually dropped the Polish name; *gogol* is a species of wild duck, and the Russian equivalent of *strutting* is *to walk like a gogol*) was born in 1809—on the first of April, and if that be significant, make the most of it—into a family of Ukrainian squireens. His formal education began at seven in a provincial private school; at twelve he entered the Gymnasia of the Higher Sciences at Nezhin, another Poltava town as ensorcelled though not quite as small as his birthplace of Sorochintzy, graduating when he was about twenty. As a student he was bright and . . . resourceful, rather than assiduous, impossible in mathematics and, in languages, hopelessly xenophobic: he was nicknamed Universum Mundus, after the introductory phrase in a Latin chrestomathy, which phrase remained the Ultima Thule of his Latinity; he could not read the easiest French without a dictionary; Goethe and Schiller, he maintained, could not possibly have written in so vile a tongue as German; English was (literally and not slangily) strictly for the birds, not only vocally but because of the facial contortions it demanded—and, like Chehov after him, he contrived to get poor marks even in Russian. He excelled, however, in composition, draftsmanship (in which he was the peer of Thackeray, if not of Du Maurier), music, elaborate acrostic pasquinades, practical jokes (once feigning madness for two months to gain time for writing and correspondence) and, above all, in school theatricals.

The years from 1828 to 1836 constitute his St. Petersburg period. At one point he sank to the penultimate circle of the impecunious *intelligent*'s hell: tutoring the blubbery progeny of the greasy merchantry. (The nethermost circle was plumbed by Belinsky: writing a Russian Grammar; Gogol, unlike Dostoevsky, could not qualify for the third circle from the bottom: that of Translation.) He had studied law but never practiced it; he was in civil service (1830–32), which he entered brimming over with idealism and left drained of everything but disillusionment. He was, admittedly, no Keats, but his first book* was reviewed as scathingly as *Endymion* and, yanking back all the copies he could from the booksellers with whom they had been left on consignment, he took a hotel room with a fireplace for the specific purpose of burning them.

He tried teaching: twice. First in a finishing school for young ladies but, although he was young and not at all unprepossessing (even though he was able to duplicate the feat of Morimoto, the great facial contortionist, of covering

---

* *Hans Kuchelgarten, an Idyll in Tableaux,* by V. Alov (*ca.* 1827). *The Poems of Joseph Olov* may have been Gogol's second attempt to win recognition as a poet. According to a well-known St. Petersburg bookseller this 32mo with a multitude of vignettes had been left with him on consignment by Gogol and subsequently withdrawn. It may well have met the same fate as *Hans:* the book is of extreme scarcity.

the nose with the lower lip), the young ladies did not cotton to him. His second assignment was as Assistant Professor of History at the University of St. Petersburg. His opening lecture was a pyrotechnical display of scholarship and showmanship; the succeeding ones, owing to lack of preparation, were duds. Gogol shammed toothache, bound cheek and all, to avoid speaking and, instead of lecturing, passed around old historical prints among his hearers—of whom Turgenev, then unknown, was one. The administration—apprehensive of unseemly pranks by the students—brought Gogol's pedagogical career to a close.

That he should consider going on the stage was inevitable. He had been trained from childhood in observation, improvisation and all the arts of the theatre by his father (a theatromane, two of whose comedies hold a high place in Ukrainian literature); in school theatricals Gogol not only acted (comic characters, with enormous success) but took over every detail of production, from painting scenery to lighting and music. He was as superb a reader and nonprofessional actor as Dickens but, unlike Molière and Shakespeare, he never became a player. Accounts of his tryout for a state theatre vary. According to one, Gogol had an attack of stage fright before the luminaries on the hearing committee, dried up on his lines when he did not mumble them, gave a "wilted" performance and, at best, would have been considered only for rôles just a frog's whisker above walk-ons. According to another source his acting was "expressive, masterly and absolutely natural," and since it ran counter to the artificiality and affectation prevalent at that time he would hardly have been found acceptable by the "theatrical aristarchs." At any rate he did not bother to return for the verdict on his audition.

It was only with the publication, in 1831, of his *Dikanka Nights*, a collection of fantastic stories in a fresh genre, that Gogol won recognition, comparative success and, most important of all, the friendship of Pushkin, Zhukovsky and other literary lights.

Gogol was, definitely, afflicted with Cossack wanderlust (the reader can determine this for himself from the magical passages on the open road and on the troika) and has confessed to his "elemental urge to escape." In 1829 he actually started out for the "American States" with the intention of settling there but, on reaching Hamburg, he simply turned around and headed back for Russia.

Gogol was not alone in finding it hard to write about Russia unless he was out of it. His wander-years began in 1836 with his flight from the commotion caused by the production of *The Inspector General*. Vevey, on Lake Geneva, became the first of his "beautiful far-off places"; there he began work in earnest on Volume One of *Dead Souls*. In 1836–37 he wrote a great deal of it in Paris; from 1837 to 1839 he worked both on *Dead Souls* and *The Overcoat* in Rome; in the winter of 1839–40 he visited Russia but in the latter year he returned to Rome and remained there until 1841 to complete both *Dead Souls* and *The Overcoat*; 1841 found him in Russia again and, in 1842, he published the first part of his greatest work.

His wanderings, throughout which he kept working on the second (and very conjecturally on a third) part of *Dead Souls*, were to last until 1848 when, in search of spiritual consolation, he undertook a pilgrimage to the Holy Land. Actually, this final journey proved as pointless as his first. From 1849 his sojournment in Moscow was to remain unbroken, save for a visit during the winter of 1850–51 to Odessa, where he was engaged to read the play to the actors and to direct them in a production of Molière's *School for Wives*.

Apparently all artistic creativity is little more than a form of spiritual exhibitionism. The artist, Leonardo asserted, keeps limning his own soul throughout his life. What is practically all of Dostoevsky's bepraised psychologizing except self-revelatory finger-painting? It would not be too difficult to maintain the thesis that Turgenev's Superfluous People were self-portraits, and Goncharov admitted that he sat as model for his Oblomov. Gogol confessed that in his youth he had found relief from black melancholy (inexplicable, except most probably by his valetudinarianism) by inventing the funniest of characters and placing them in most preposterous situations. It was to this catharsis that he traced the origin of all his early published works. From that to scabies of the psyche is just a step away. "Why was I designated," he complained, "to acquire knowledge of the soul of man not otherwise than through a strict analysis of my own soul?"

There is perhaps no more horrendous example than Gogol of the elemental and inexorable law that no creative artist ever contracted religion without a concomitant atrophy of his talent or genius. In the mid-1840's Gogol fell under the influence of Father Matthew: it is open to doubt if this fanatical lout of a country *pawp*, exceptionally ignorant even for an Orthodox priest, could, even by stretching up to touch bottom, have attained to the stature of one of our own cotton-pickin' Savannahrolas: yet he became the spiritual father—and evil genius—of Gogol. Pushkin, to Father Matthew, was a sinner and a pagan; all writing—but Gogol's most of all—was inspired by Satan; this Father it was who fanned Gogol's smouldering mysticism into blazing religious mania.

In 1848 Gogol brought out his expiatory *Choice Passages from Correspondence with Friends*—a work so ghastly in its obfuscation and reactionism that gogolators shudder and avert their eyes at the mere mention of it. Its only values lie in its pathological revelation of genius in debacle and in having aroused Belinsky to pen his vitriolic *Letter to Gogol:* for merely having been present at a reading of which *Letter* Dostoevsky came within thirty seconds of execution and lost ten of his best years in the Siberian House of the Dead, but of which Turgenev was to say: "Belinsky and his *Letter* constitute all my religion"—and not of Turgenev alone, but every honest and decent Russian for the next seven decades.

Messianism swamped Gogol. He would not only expiate such of his sins as *The Inspector General* and *The Overcoat* but atone for *Dead Souls* by reforming his rapscallion Chichikov and saving all of his beloved Russia. With hardly astonishing originality he decided that all-round salvation lay in peddling the same Operation Bootstraps panacea which was to be discovered and peddled by Dostoevsky, that half-Prometheus, half-burgher, by that self-made mouzhik, Count Leo Tolstoy, and by Merezhkovsky, the pagan-haunted Christian. Instead of seeking a sunnier clime and drinking beef-and-iron tonic, Gogol took to fasting and mortifying whatever was left of his flesh and put himself on a strict regimen of prayer and Father Matthew's theology. To set his chubby soul-snatcher's feet on the path of Honest Acquisition he dreamed up a businessman-farmer of unearthly rectitude—and, of all things, a Turk; as Chichikov's spiritual guides he created two unique monstrosities: a saintly millionaire tax-farmer and a grandee of such incorruptibility that the world has not seen his like since High Office begot Nest-Feathering out of Complicity on Noah's Ark. There is inferential yet sound evidence that Chichikov, deskunked of his hankerings for a substantial landed estate, worked by flesh-and-blood serf-souls, a sweet-dough Chichikova and a brood of Chickchickovs, was slated to wind up in the full Chanel No. 5 of sanctity as the darlingest of little anchorites in a snug little Siberian hut of somewhat monastic architecture, plinking away on a psaltery and psnuffling Psalms.

As for poor Russia, she was to be saved by giving the go-by to sugar, books, bibelots, playing cards and French restaurants and, on the positive side, by plain but nourishing meals, cooked at home from thriftily shopped local produce and provisions, by wearing clothes (plain and cheap) until there wasn't another stitch of wear in them, by more assiduity in quill-driving and easing up on official grafting—and, of course, lots and lots of Bible-reading. And, also of course, Gogol's redemptionary efforts were crowned with precisely the same success as those of all other messiahs.

In a final blinding flash of sanity Gogol perceived the impossibility of reconciling his genius with his religious madness. On February 11, 1852, at three in the morning, after strict fasting and protracted praying, he burned, among others, the manuscripts of the second (and presumably the conjectural third) part of *Dead Souls:* an auto-da-fé which, among the many tragedies of literature, is approached in poignancy only by the suicide of Chatterton. In the daylight, on what was to be his deathbed, he repented his act and attributed it to the instigation of the Evil One. If one bears Father Matthew in mind, poor Gogol, even though quite unintentionally, was right.

Gogol remained deaf to all pleas concerning his health: he wanted to die—and did, at eight on the evening of March 4, calling out "The ladder! The ladder!" This, with deathbeddish patness, has been taken for delirium; most probably it was no more than a quotation from Jeremiah in a translation based not on the original Hebrew but a version from the Greek. He was buried three days later—perhaps in deference to his wish that his body was not to be interred until the first signs of decomposition appeared. Another of his testamental wishes was disregarded: a monument was not only put up over his grave but inscribed with an utterance also attributed to Jeremiah: "At my bitter words I shall laugh."* One of his last jottings might have been better: "Be ye living souls and not dead souls!" Or, best of all, his warning in *An Author's Confession* (1847): "One must be careful with laughter."

The coffin, followed by vast throngs, was borne by students all the way to the cemetery, a distance of almost five

---

*This may be another translation from the Greek rather than the original Hebrew. Apparently there is no corresponding passage in the King James version; any information will be appreciated.

miles. A not necessarily apocryphal story has it that when a passer-by asked: "Whom are they burying? And are all these people blood kindred of the departed?" he was told: "It's Gogol they're burying and we're all blood kindred of his—and all of Russia along with us." There is absolutely nothing apocryphal, however, about Dostoevsky's* dictum on Russian writers: "We have all issued from under the *Overcoat*," and, in addition to Dostoevsky himself with his funeral mantle, the glorious roster includes Turgenev, Leskov, Ostrovsky, Nekrassov, Goncharov, Shchedrin-Saltykov, Uspensky, Garshin, Korolenko, Gorki, Chehov—from under whose dove-gray cloak so many near-Chehovs have unfortunately emerged, especially (and so disastrously) among the marinated prosateuses in England.

All of Russia mourned—all, that is, except its upper crust. Autocracy, aristocracy, bureaucracy, slavocracy, plutocracy—the military, the propertied and the privileged—were not slow to perceive what Gogol himself failed to see: the possibly unintentional yet decidedly great danger he represented to the Mafia of their Russia. After *The Inspector General* they lost no time in tagging Gogol as a "filthy scribbler," and he was not to escape their consistent hatred of all writing fellows. They had rejoiced at the assassination-by-duel of Pushkin; "A dog's death," they had said on hearing of Lermontov's death in a duel with a Mohock,† "befits a dog," and one most influential grandee was merely voicing

---

* However, a fairly recent issue of the *New York Times Book Review* attributed this famous mot, for some epoptic reason, to Turgenev.

†Mohock=Mohawk=an aristocratic Apache.

the general sentiment of his fellows in wondering why any-body should want to make a fuss over the death of "such a flunkyish writer as Gogol."

However, it was another aristocrat who was also a writing fellow who saw to it that the end of a great writer should not, with Gogolian grotesquery, be passed over in silence. Gogol had circumvented the Moscow censors by publishing *Dead Souls* in St. Petersburg; Turgenev stole a march on the St. Petersburg censors by sneaking into the *Moscow News* his necrologue on "Gogol . . . this man whom we now have the right to call great, the bitter right granted to us by death; a man whose name signalized an epoch in our literature, a man whom we are proud of as one of our geniuses. . . ." Which necrologue led, inevitably, to the jailing of the necrologist, his house-arrest in the country for two years, and a narrow escape from suppression of his *Hunting Sketches.*

Gogol had, undoubtedly, the photographic eye, the stereophonic ear—yet that eye had a blind spot, that ear had a deaf field. He had been given the theme for *The Inspector General* by Pushkin and his avowed aim was "to pile up in one heap everything vile in Russia"—yet although autocracy was in that heap it was there without the author perceiving it. The theme of *Dead Souls* had also been given to him by Pushkin, who had at first thought of using it himself. Serfdom is the leitmotif of the magnificent opera—yet its composer was the only one who could not discern it.

It is this blind spot, this deaf field, which constitute the paradox of Gogol, the first of Russia's realists, one of Russia's (and the world's) supreme sardonicists.

All talk of any foreign influences on Gogol—by Sterne,

by Hoffmann, by Molière—can be dismissed as professorial poppycock, pedantic pigeonholing and pseudo-critical ramming of square pegs into round holes. He was influenced, primarily, by the sun, skies, springs, summers of Little Russia, its moonlight, black loam and folk-poetry, by Ukrainian buckwheat grits and Poltava white bacon, by the fogs and white nights of St. Petersburg, the vistas of Moscow under snow, the land-seas of the steppes. Gogol, the great wayfarer, was the most Russian of the Russians.

There are so many comparisons, so many contrasts! Rabelais? Both the Tourainian and the Ukrainian share a love for exuberance, richness, raciness, robustness in speech, for folk-diablerie, for exaggeration as a humorous device, for curious cataloguing, for lyricism; each wields stiletto or slapstick with the same deftness, and both have the same gusto for good food, that poetry of earthy man, spanning the ages in this to shake hands with another Southerner, Thomas Wolfe. Molière? It would be as unfair to style Gogol the Slavic Molière as to call Molière the Gallic Gogol. Each has his magnificent stageful of deathless characters, but there they part company. The satyricon of the Russian is full-bodied, blood-red; the satyricon of the Frenchman is dry, glaucous. Harpagon is superb, yet not without a whiff of mummy; Pliushkin is but skin-and-phlegm, but the phlegm courses under the skin, his tread is heavy, solid upon the earth.

Swift? The world has two alpimalayan peaks of sardonicism: the Dean's *Modest Proposal* and the scene in which Chichikov, the zombie dealer, is haggling for dead serfs with Korobochka, the immortal widow-woman. There is no *reductio ad absurdum* in either case; rather, each master takes a social condition, as idiotic as it is appalling yet universally tolerated and, through remorseless logic, writes *Q E D* after a presentation which humanity cannot accept. And Gogol goes Swift one better, throwing in the bit about playing for dead souls—not with dice, not with cards, but at... however, let the reader discover that game for himself.

One aspect must be dealt with: the Gogolian detail. He could create a character with a single stroke of his pen, often with no more than a name (Leo Tolstoy, together with the burlesque touch, took over the trick—but preferred to use the adz); the most characteristic, however, was the deceptively casual detail. So subtle is this sleight that I must, with the help of italics, reduce it to slow motion. Porphyry is little more than a walk-on, the property of one of the stars of the piece, Nozdrev, bully, braggart and liar. At his orders Porphyry has brought in an amazing puppy, a recent acquisition, and placed it on the floor for Chichikov's inspection.

"There's a pup for you!" said Nozdrev, *picking it up with one hand by the loose skin on its back.* The puppy let out a rather piteous whimper.

Nozdrev examines the puppy and proceeds to accuse Porphyry not only of having disregarded orders to rid the puppy of its fleas but of having added a host of his own fleas thereto and, paying no heed to the serf's protestations, orders him to take the dog out.

Porphyry, *picking up the puppy under its belly,* bore it off to the carriage.

There you have it: a confrontation of two castes, more effective in its unobtrusiveness than a multi-volumed sociological tractate: the master who cares nothing about the feelings, physical or spiritual, of his living chattels, and the slave, with the understanding of one domestic animal for another.

It would seem only natural that Russia, with her oceans of land, should produce more picaresques than even Spain, with no dearth of adventure, of course, but with the emphasis, somehow, on characterization. Of the stellar rogues Gogol has produced two (three, if one counts Iharev, the biter-bit card-mechanic of *The Gamblers*). Obviously, Chichikov towers over Hlestakov; there was nothing Hlestakovian about Chichikov in his youth, but a maturing Hlestakov (that is, if one can imagine a Hlestakov ever attaining maturity) would undoubtedly have profited by taking on some of Chichikov's business sense and ethics. After all, whom did Chichikov injure except his own ill-starred self? The landowners whom he diddled out of their dead serfs? Why, he actually benefited them. The government? It goes without saying that no Englishman or American would as much as think of horn-swoggling his extra-intelligent and utterly incorruptible government; but what Frenchman, what German, what Patagonian would give a second thought about trying to get something of his own back from his officialdom? And, when you come right down to it, what's so wrong with that little ruggedly individualistic free enterpriser Chichikov? Mortgaging dead souls or putting up deliquescent manure fertilizer in ethereal tanks as collateral—what's the odds, as long as a man wins status? Naturally, those inexplicable and contrary Russians would shoot Chichikov out of hand today—if he were caught. But in what sane, workable, normal social order would he not be honored and emulated—even if he were caught?

The mention of Cervantes is inescapable. Cervantes did influence Gogol—but only indirectly, through Pushkin, who held up the Spaniard as an outstanding example of a writer who would never have amounted to a hill of beans if he had not abandoned turning out trifles in favor of producing a major work. The dust raised by literary campfollowers has long since settled: Cervantes and Gogol stride through time side by side as satirists of the same stature. Yet their heroes can never be reconciled. Don Quixote is a knight-errant, seeking windmills to fight; Chichikov is a *chevalier d'industrie,* to whom all is grist that comes to his mill. Nevertheless you may be sure that Assessor and the two others of the timeless troika are pastured in the same Elysian field with Rosinante and Dapple, and that Sancho Panza is tippling near-nectar with Seliphan and Petrushka in a Milky Wayside pothouse not too far off.

Dead Souls should by no means be considered the Russian *Uncle Tom's Cabin.* That distinction goes to the *Hunting Sketches* of Turgenev, first brought out in book form in the fateful year of 1852, also marked by the first publication of Mrs. Stowe's book.*

The publishing history of Gogol's masterpiece is not without some touches as grotesque as any in the book itself.

---

* The White Negroes of Russia were emancipated (and that without any internecine war) almost two years before the black ones in the U.S.A. However, the Americans were almost ten years ahead of the Oblomovian Russians in assassinating their Emancipator.

Rabelais had to flee France to save his ears from being cropped by censorious theologues for having ventured to pun on *âme* (soul) and *âne* (ass). Gogol had to shift the publication of *Dead Souls* to St. Petersburg to save the book from being banned by the theological censors in Moscow because of the pun inherent in *dooshee*, which can mean either *souls* or *serfs*. A serf-soul could, with all legality (and propriety), be bought, sold and even mortgaged, whether the serf was living or dead; the soul-soul, however, was considered immortal and it was not only improper but blasphemous to speak of it as dead. But even in Czar Peter's Town the author could save his original title only as an alternate one: Volume One was brought out (1842) as *The Peregrinations* (or *Expeditions*, or *Campaigns*, or even *Adventures*, but hardly *Journeys*) of *Chichikov, or, Dead Souls*.

The bizarrerie of the book's first appearance in English, however, out-Gogols Gogol. Strictly speaking, it was not until the fairly early 1880's that the prospecting British really discovered that the mouzhiks actually had a Klondike of something very like a literature which would assay as not too low grade even by Victorian standards. (The first to be worked, however, was—most regrettably—the Dostoevsky Lode.) Since then the vast yield of translations (preponderantly into British) can hardly be described (unless one's soul is filled with nothing but extreme charity and absolute ignorance of Russian) as anything but ersatz, occasionally highly polished yet still as phony as a seven-dollar bill. But *Dead Souls* has the comparatively rare distinction of owing its introduction into English to an out-and-out hoax. The permutations of the bright shards in a kaleidoscope are, I understand, incomputable—in contradistinction to the repetitiveness of the shabby patterns of history. The year was 1854; the Crimean War was on, the Russians were regarded then, even as now, as "our ancient allies and present foes"; the London publishers, not at all improbably, must have regarded Chichikov as the grandpappy of all the Doctors Zhivagos and trotted him out as *Tschitschikoff's* [sic] *Journeys; or, Home Life in Russia,* by a Russian Noble, Revised by the Editor of *Revelations of Siberia*—and so on. "Was that nobleman called Hlestakov?" Vladimir Nabokov asks in *Nikolai Gogol.** "Was it Chichikov himself?" At any rate this enterprising aristocrat anticipated the British literary sourdoughs and was not only a Pioneering Father of what was to become known as Kremlinology but the first to cut the deliciously horripilant pseudo-political stencil which the overwhelming majority of Russian refusees use to this day: his Publishers blurbed their inability to mention his name, "but . . . the writer . . . is perfectly well aware that the avowal of his handiwork . . . will not serve as a special recommendation except possibly as a passport to the innermost regions of the Siberian wilds." Apparently the Publishers were not perfectly well aware that prisons for debtors and not-overcautious entrepreneurs were not in short supply in cis-Siberian Russia.

Some of the evil that Russian Noblemen do lives after them: the spuriousness of the 1854 British title persisted until the 1940's. It is heartening to feel that modern read-

---

* One of the best pieces of Gogoliana in any language—and, in English, the only one worth reading.

ers, who can stomach a *Naked Lunch,* let us say, will not turn queasy at the implication of d——th and, clutching their book-pennies in their hot little fists, flee in a panic from the simple and forthright title of *Dead Souls* by which a great work has been known in its country of origin for well over a century.

——

Pouteouatamiouec. . . . I doubt if even a pedant nowadays would cling to this hoary form of a name so simple as Potomac. Scholars have long since singled out *Shakespeare* as the most acceptable of the thirty-three variants of the name, but there are still thirty-two different spellings in English (another actual tabulation) of Turgenev. The Epileptic Genius, who hated Jews even more than he detested Frenchmen, Germans and Poles, keeps right on bobbing up as Dostojewski. I have yet to see Hercules transliterated into English as *K*hera*k*les but Chehov, probably in the simple-minded belief that spiking anything Russian with enough *k*'s by way of monosodium glutamate will bring out that delectably kwaint Slavick savor— Chehov will still be albatrossed as Che*k*hov (invariably— and shuddersomely—pronounced as Check-off) through generations yet unborn. *Tsch-, Tch-, Cz-, -koff, -kowff, -kow, -owski, -oeuieffski, -owicz, -itsch* and, most insufferable, *-itch:* all these rawhead-and-bloody-bones ghoulashes were originally concocted because of the early exigencies of transliterating (and translating) not from the original Russian but from translations into German, French, Polish, Tagalog, and are kept simmering by the mortmain of sundry Societies, Councils and Institutes of pseudo-scholarship and by tongs of Mandarin learning, at all of which the reader, I am sure, can be trusted to turn up (or better still thumb) his or her nose.

Diacritical marks will do nothing for the reader except flyblow the fair printed page, and accents are equally utile. However, there are two suggestions, utterly empiric and unscholarly, yet which will work eight or nine times out of ten. Russian can be harsh, of course, but on the whole it is gentle and charming; if you want to say something in Russian you'll rarely err in dumping the gravel out of your voice. Secondly, in pronouncing a Russian name stress it exactly contrary to the way you feel like stressing it: you may want to say Nata*sha*—make it Na*ta*sha and you'll do better than all the top-notch American, British, Gallic, Teutonic and Paranomasian stars of stage, screen and television. Oh, yes—Ivan is not *Eye*van but Ee*van*.

The *sky* ending (rhyming with *key*) is beautifully concise and connotative; Alexander *Nev*sky is Saint Alexander, Victor in the Battle against the Swedes at the River *Neva*, Victor in the Carnage of the Sword-Bearing Teuton Knights on the Ice of Lake Chudskoe, Prince of Novgorod, Grand Duke of Vladimir, and so on. Russian names are rarely meaningless; the Russians take Longfellow in their stride, and there is really no need to shrug off Tolstoy (Stoutfellow) as merely outlandish. However, should any name in this book strike the reader as funny he or she has not only my dispensation but the author's to laugh at it freely: Gogol has noted the Russian's aptness at names and, like so many others of the better-writing Russians, was a master of the rich (at least in Russian) device of characterization by playing with (and upon) proper names.

The Russians, along with other folk, cling to the quaint

yet charming courtesy of the patronymic. The suffixes *-ovich, -ievich* (or even *-ych*) correspond to such prefixes as Mac, Mc or O'. Andrei Andreievich Andreiev is Andrew McAndrew Andrews. *-ovna, -evna* (or even *-ishna*) are feminine: Tatiana Alexeievna is Tatiana, daughter of Alexei. The *a* ending is generally feminine (even though Constance Garnett calls Anna's husband Karenina instead of Karenin), but I wouldn't bank on that if I were you. Gogol, to his mother, was Nickosha; the *ka* ending can make a masculine name sound very familiar or even contemptuous: Ivashka=Jack, and there's still another curious but nonderogatory application of this *a* to masculine names given in "The Office," one of the *Hunting Sketches* of Turgenev.

Only a handful of Russian words has been used throughout, but they are so familiar and current that it would have been feeble to approximate them in English. Measurements and weights have been ruthlessly computed into our own equivalents; on the other hand, since it would have been downright silly for the mouzhiks to be dealing in farthings or pence, or even cents and dimes, I have been benign enough to allow them to stick to their own currency: a ruble was worth, in silver, 49¢ and, in depreciated paper money, nearly 17¢; a kopeck was, and still is, a hundredth part of a ruble.

Also, at this point, I must acknowledge, and hereby gratefully do, my indebtedness to a decidedly younger but much more orthodox scholar than I, Susannah Beth Fine, Ph.D., for her unstinted assistance in extremely pernickety research.

For Volume One (the translation of which is here revised for the second time) I have, in the main, followed the second edition, but have added considerable (and significant) passages from the first.

Gogol can scarcely be accused of that sloth in which Ukrainians take such a pejorative pride. In one of his relaxed moods he explained his writing habits and confessed: "Others may turn out a book in six drafts or in eight—I have to do it in seven." Two truncated drafts of Volume Two escaped the final holocaust (there had been previous burnings): an early one and a later. I preferred the latter (the translation of which is now first revised), but have not overlooked certain significant passages from the earlier version. I have also, in order to fill in the gaps insofar as that is possible, included supplementary addenda from secondary sources, as well as from Gogol's own fragments and even scrapiana—material hitherto unorganized and untranslated, to the best of my knowledge. Whatever its defects, I feel and believe that the present version is the nearest approach to a complete one—in any language.

As for those finicky souls who disparage all sequels, I can say only that even the unfinished work of a genius is better than the best finished work of a second-rater, and that the reader will find Volume Two richly rewarding; it has plenty of the old Gogol in it, plenty of those characters, details, scenes, situations which no one but Gogol could create. Why, meeting Petuh alone ought to suffice!

The opportunity for a definitive revision of a translation which has found favor for more than twenty years not only with critics but, above all, with the public, is an exceptional one, and full advantage has been taken of it to correct all such errors as time may have laid bare to the eye. I have always regarded such revisions as collaborations between a younger man for whose élan something not altogether derogatory might be said, and a somewhat more mature one whose comparatively greater skill in literary carpentry may compensate to some extent for an élan that may have become quite curly around the edges. In short, I have tried to temper whatever liking and admiration I may still have for my younger colleague by means of such judgment as may have come with the years. It is sobering to think that, with proper attention to copyright renewal, the present version may last *(strontium volens)* until the year 2020. . . . In which case it should, like all translations which have managed to last, be revised again. Nevertheless I cannot help cherishing the poltergeistish hope that the future editor will for the most part content himself with quickening the pulse of this Englishing of *Dead Souls* to beat more closely to the tempo of his day, yet not without showing the same consideration for both Guerneys which I have shown for the younger one.

—

After all, there are but two classes of books: books and Books. Reader, this is a Book.

Ee tak, droozya moee, pirshistvooite—rad as Vami podelitsya!

BERNARD GUILBERT GUERNEY
At the Sign of the Blue Faun
1942; 1948; 1964.

CONTENTS

Volume Two

VOLUME ONE

CHAPTER ONE

A rather handsome light traveling carriage on springs rolled into the gates of an inn in a certain provincial capital, the kind of carriage that is favored by bachelors: retired lieutenant colonels, second captains, landowners possessing a hundred souls or so of serfs—in a word, all those who are called the fair-to-middlin' sort. The gentleman seated in this carriage was no Adonis, but he wasn't bad to look at, either; he was neither too stout nor too slim; you couldn't say he was old, but still he wasn't what you might call any too young, either. His arrival created no stir whatever in the town of N—— and was not coupled with any remarkable event; all the comments it called forth came from two indigenous muzhiks standing in the doorway of a pothouse across the way from the inn, comments which, however, had more to do with the carriage itself than with the man sitting in it.

"Look at that, will you!" said one muzhik to the other.

"What a wheel! What think you—would that wheel make it to Moscow, if need be, or wouldn't it?"

"It would," answered the other.

"But it wouldn't make it to Kazan, I'm thinking—or would it?"

"Not to Kazan, it wouldn't," the other answered.

And with that the discussion ended.

Also, as the carriage drove up to the inn it encountered a young man in white dimity trousers, quite narrow and short, and a swallow-tailed coat that made a brave attempt at being in the mode, revealing a dickey fastened with a brummagem stickpin of bronze, in the shape of a pistol. The young man turned back, looked the vehicle over while clutching at his cap, which had been almost carried away by the wind, and then went on his way again.

As the carriage drove into the yard, its occupant was met by one of the tavern help (or *servers,* as they are called), so very lively and spry that it was downright impossible to make out what sort of face he had. He dashed out nimbly, napkin in hand—a long figure himself and wearing a long frock coat of linsey-woolsey, its back so high that it reached almost to the very nape of his neck—tossed back his hair and nimbly led the gentleman up and along the entire wooden outside gallery to show him the chamber that God had provided for him. The chamber was of a familiar kind, inasmuch as the inn was also of a familiar kind—that is, precisely like all inns in provincial capitals, where for two rubles a day the transients receive a restful bedroom with cockroaches peeking out of every corner like so many black plums and with a door, always barricaded with a bureau, leading to an adjoining apartment, which apartment is always taken by a fellow guest who is taciturn and placid yet exceedingly inquisitive, interested in knowing all the details about the latest transient. The façade, or exterior, of the inn corresponded to its interior; it was a very long building, of two stories; the lower one had not been stuccoed and exposed its small dark-red bricks, which, while they had grown still darker from the cruel changes of weather, were nevertheless rather grimy in their own right; the upper was painted yellow, of a never-varying tint; below were shops stocked with horse collars, ropes and hard, brittle cookies. The corner one of these shops—or, to put it better, its window—was occupied by a vendor of hot mead, with a samovar of ruddy copper and a face as ruddy as his samovar, so that from afar one might think that there were two samovars standing in the window, if only one of them were not sporting a beard as black as pitch.

While the transient gentleman was inspecting his room, his belongings were carried in; first and foremost, a small trunk of white leather, somewhat scuffed, indicating that this was not the first time it had been out on the road. The small trunk was brought in by Seliphan, the coachman, a squat little fellow in a short sheepskin coat, and by Petrushka, a flunky, a lad of thirty in a loose much-worn frock coat, evidently a hand-me-down from his master's shoulders, a lad somewhat austere at first glance, whose lips and nose were on a very large scale. After the trunk, they carried in a small casket of mahogany with marquetry of Karelian birch, a pair of shoe trees, and a roasted chicken wrapped in blue paper. When all these had been carried in Seliphan the coachman set out for the stable to see to the horses, while Petrushka the flunky began settling himself in the tiny anteroom, a very dark cubbyhole, whither he had already brought his overcoat and, together with it, a certain odor all his own, which had been also imparted to the bag he brought in next, containing sundry flunkyish effects. In this cubbyhole he set up against the wall a small and narrow cot with only three legs, putting on top of it a skimpy simulacrum of a pallet, as lumpy and flat as a pancake (and, perhaps, just as greasy), which he had succeeded in wangling out of the owner of the inn.

While the servants were arranging things and fussing about the gentleman went down into the common room. What these common rooms are like every transient knows well: there are always the same calcimined walls, darkened at the top from chimney smoke and glossy below from the backs of sundry travelers, but still more from those of the indigenous traders, inasmuch as the merchants came here on market days in their sixes and their sevens to imbibe their well-known glass or two of tea; the same sooty ceiling; the same hanging chandelier dingy from smoke, with a multitude of pendent bits of glass that leapt and bounded and tinkled every time a waiter dashed across the worn-out linoleum, deftly swinging a tray on which was perched as great a host of teacups as you might find of birds on a shore; the same pictures, covering an entire wall and done in oils—in a word, everything the same as you would find everywhere; the sole difference was that one picture depicted a nymph with such enormous breasts as the reader, in all probability, has never beheld. Such a sport of nature, however, occurs in various historical pictures, although no one knows at what period, or whence, or by whom they were imported among us in Russia—now and then, perhaps, by our grandees, those lovers of the arts, who must have bought them up in Italy upon the advice of the couriers who had driven them about.

The gentleman threw off his cap and unwound from around his neck a woolen, tricornered neckerchief of all the hues of the rainbow, of the sort that is folded for married men by their wives, with their own fair hands, to the accompaniment of prudent counsels on how they ought to muffle themselves; as for who performs that office for bachelors I cannot say with any certainty—God knows what shifts they are put to!—I never having worn such neckerchiefs. Having unwound it, the gentleman ordered his dinner. While the various dishes usual to taverns were being served up to him, such as cabbage soup with small dumplings of puff paste (the latter purposely preserved for weeks at a stretch for the particular benefit of transients), brains with peas, sausages and sauerkraut, a roast pullet, dill pickles, and the eternal sweet pastry of layered dough, which is always at your service—while all this was being served to him, either warmed over or simply cold, he made the tavern waiter retail to him all sorts of small talk concerning such things as who had kept this tavern before and who was keeping it now, and whether it yielded much income, and whether the host were a great scoundrel, to which the waiter made the usual answer:

"Oh, he's a great hand at a swindle, Sir!"

Even as in enlightened Europe, so in enlightened Russia as well there are at present many worthy persons who can never dine in a tavern without having a chat with the waiter and at times even having a bit of fun at his expense. However, not all the questions this transient gentleman put were idle ones; he inquired, with the utmost particularity, about the officials in the town: who was the Governor of the province, who was the Chairman of the Administrative Offices, who was the Public Prosecutor—in short, he did not pass over a single bureaucrat of any importance; but with still greater particularity, if not downright concern, did he make inquiries about all the prominent landowners: how many souls of serfs each one owned, how far out of town he lived, even what his character was like and how often he drove into town; he inquired closely about the state of the region—whether certain diseases weren't prevalent in that province, such as epidemic fevers, deadly agues of one sort or another, smallpox and things of that sort, and all this he asked in such a way and with such particularity as to indicate that his interest was more than mere curiosity.

There was something substantial about the ways of this gentleman, and whenever he blew his nose he did so exceedingly loudly. No one knows just how he did it, but all the same his nose resounded like a trumpet. This point of merit, apparently a perfectly innocent one, won, nevertheless, a great deal of respect for him on the part of the tavern server, so that every time he heard this sound he would toss back his hair, straighten up with greater deference, and, inclining his head from the heights, ask was the gentleman wishin' somethin'.

After dinner the gentleman partook of a cup of coffee and seated himself on a divan, resting his back on one of the cushions (which in Russian taverns are stuffed with broken bricks and cobblestones instead of resilient wool). At this point he took to yawning and asked to be shown to his room where, lying down for just forty winks, he fell asleep for a couple of hours. Having had his siesta, he wrote on a slip of paper, at the request of the tavern waiter, his rank as well as his first name and his last, for reference to the proper quarters: the police department. As the server went down the stairs, he spelled out the following on the slip of paper:

"Collegiate Councilor Pavel Ivanovich Chichikov, landowner, traveling on private affairs."

While the server was still spelling out the note, Pavel Ivanovich Chichikov himself set out to look the town over, and, it would seem, was quite satisfied with it, since he found that it in no way yielded to the other provincial towns—the paint on the stone houses was the usual yellow and just as hard on the eyes, while the paint on the wooden houses showed as a modestly dark gray, quite unexceptional. The houses were of one story, of two stories, and of a story and a half, with the everlasting mezzanine which, in the opinion of the provincial architects, is ever so handsome. In some places these houses seemed lost in the midst of a street as wide as a field and among never-ending wooden fences; in others they got into a huddle, and in such places one could note a greater movement of people and greater animation. One came across signs that were all but washed off by the rains, showing pretzels and boots; occasionally these signs depicted blue breeches and the signature of some tailor or other who hailed from 'Arsaw; here was a store with caps and forage caps, and the inscription: "Vassilii Fedorov—from Abroad"; over there, a depiction of a billiard table with two players, togged out in the sort of frock coats worn in our theatres by those guests who come on the stage in the last act. The billiard players were portrayed taking aim with their cues, their arms twisted backward somewhat, and with bowlegs, for all the world as though they had just cut a caper in the air. Under this was inscribed: "This Way to the Academy."

Here and there, right out on the street, stood stalls with nuts, soap, and cookies that looked like soap; occasionally one came on a cookshop, with a depiction of a rotund fish with a fork stuck in it. But most frequently of all one noted the time-darkened two-headed imperial eagles, which by now have been replaced by the laconic inscription: "Liquors at Retail." And the pavement was rather poor everywhere.

Chichikov also looked in at the town park, consisting of the puniest of trees, which had taken but poorly to the soil, with props at the bottom, placed in triangles and very handsomely painted in a glossy green. However, although these trees were no higher than reeds, the newspapers, in describing certain gala illuminations, had said of them that, "Our city has been graced, thanks to the solicitude of the Municipal Director, by a park of shady trees whose spreading boughs provide coolness on a sultry day," and that, during the ceremonies, "it was most touching to observe how the hearts of the citizens throbbed in an excess of gratitude and torrents of tears streamed forth as a mark of appreciation for His Honor the Mayor."

Having minutely questioned a policeman on post in a sentry box as to what was the nearest way of going, if need be, to the cathedral, to the government offices, to the Governor's, Chichikov set out for a look at the river which flowed through the middle of the town; on his way thither he tore off a poster tacked up on a post, so that, upon his arrival at home, he might give it a thorough reading; eyed closely a lady who was not at all hard to look at as she passed over the wooden sidewalk, followed by a boy in the uniform of a military school with a small bundle in his hand; and after once more casting an eye over everything, as though to memorize well the lay of the land, he set out straight for home and his room, being deferentially helped up the stairs by the tavern waiter.

Having regaled himself with tea, he seated himself at a table, called for a candle to be brought to him, took out of his pocket the poster, and, holding it close to the candle, fell to reading, puckering his right eye just a trifle. However, there wasn't a great deal of anything remarkable in the broadside: a drama by Kotzebue*[1] was being presented, Rollo to be played by one Poplevin, Cora by Mlle Zyablova, while the other personae were even less outstanding; however, he read the names of the whole cast through, getting down even to the tariff on parterre seats, and also learned that the poster had been printed at the printing press of the Administration of that province; next he turned the sheet over, to find out if there might not be something on the other side as well, but, finding nothing, he rubbed his eyes, folded the sheet neatly, and put it away in his traveling casket, wherein it was his wont to store everything that came to his hand. The day was (unless I am mistaken) brought to a close by a portion of cold veal, a

---

*All notes indicated by superior numbers are to be found on pp. 671–674.

bottle of beet cider, and sound slumber, with the air pump going full blast, to use an expression current in certain localities of our widespread Russian realm.

The whole of the following day was dedicated to paying calls. The new arrival set out to call on all the high officials in town. He paid his respects at the office of the Governor, who, it turned out, was just like Chichikov, in that he was neither stout in body nor thin, who wore the decoration of Anna about his neck, and concerning whom it was even being hinted that he would be proposed for a Star; he was, however, a goodhearted fellow and even occasionally embroidered fancywork on tulle with his own hands. Next Chichikov set out for the Vice-Governor's; then he called on the Public Prosecutor, on the Chairman of the Administrative Offices, on the Chief of Police, on the tax farmer, on the superintendent of the government manufactories. . . . It's a pity that it's somewhat difficult to mention all the mighty ones of this earth, but it will suffice to state that the newcomer evinced an unusual activity in the matter of calls: he put in an appearance to attest his respects even to the Inspector of the Board of Health and the Town Architect. And after that he still sat for a long time in his light carriage trying to call to mind to whom else he ought to pay a call, but it turned out that there were no more bureaucrats in that town. In his conversations with these potentates he was most artfully able to flatter each one. To the Governor he hinted, as though by the bye, that when one entered his province it was as if one were entering into a paradise: the roads might have been lined with velvet, they were so smooth, and that those governments which appointed wise dignitaries were deserving of great praise. To the Chief of Police he said something most flattering in regard to the policeman on post; while in his chats with the Vice-Governor and the Chairman of the Administrative Offices, who were still only state councilors, he addressed each a couple of times, in error, as Your Excellency, which proved very much to their liking. The consequence of all this was that the Governor extended him an invitation to attend an evening-at-home he was having that very night; the other bureaucrats, for their part, extended their invitations—this one to dinner, that one to a round of boston, a third to a dish of tea.

The newcomer, it appeared, avoided saying much about himself; if he did say anything, it was in general terms, with a perceptible diffidence, and his speech on such occasions would take a somewhat bookish turn as he explained that he was the most insignificant worm in this world and unworthy of arousing much concern; that he had gone through a great deal in his day; that he had endured much for the sake of righteousness while in the service of his country; that he had many enemies, who had even made attempts at his life; that now, desirous of finding peace and quiet he was seeking a choice spot where he might settle down at last, and that, upon his arrival in this town, he deemed it his bounden duty to attest his respect before its foremost dignitaries. And there you have everything that the town found out about this new person, who very shortly thereafter did not fail to show himself at the Governor's evening-at-home.

The preparations for this evening-at-home took up two hours and a bit over, and in this matter likewise the newcomer evinced an attentiveness in grooming such as is hardly to be met with in general. After a brief after-dinner snooze he ordered water and a wash basin to be brought, and for an exceedingly long time scrubbed both his cheeks with soap, thrusting them out from within with his tongue; next, after taking a towel from the shoulder of the tavern waiter, he wiped his full face thoroughly, beginning with the back of his ears, but only after first snorting a couple of times in the tavern waiter's very face; next, he put on a dickey in front of the mirror, plucked out with tweezers a hair or two that stuck out of his nose, and immediately thereafter was clad in a frock of scintillating bilberry-red hue. Having thus clothed himself, he drove off in his own carriage, rolling along through streets infinitely broad yet lit only by the scanty light from windows glimmering here and there.

The Governor's residence, however, was illuminated as if for nothing less than a ball; there were carriages with lamps, a brace of gendarmes before the driveway, postboys calling in the distance—in a word, everything was just right.

Upon entering the main hall Chichikov was compelled to narrow his eyes for a minute or so, since the brilliance of the candles and lamps and the ladies' gowns was terrific. Everything was flooded with light. Everywhere one looked black frock coats flitted and darted by, singly and in clusters, as flies dart over a conical gleamingly white loaf of refined sugar in the summer season, on a sultry July day, as an aged housekeeper standing at an open window cleaves and divides the loaf into glittering, irregular lumps: all the children, having flocked together, are looking on, curiously watching the movements of her roughened hands as they lift up the maul, while the aerial squadrons of flies, held up by the buoyant air, fly in boldly, as if they owned the whole place and, taking advantage of the crone's purblindness and of the sun that bothers her eyes, bestrew the dainty morsels, in some places singly, in others in thick clusters. Sated with the riches of summer, which spreads delectable repasts at every step even without such windfalls as this, they have flown in not at all in order to eat but merely to show themselves, to promenade to and fro over the mound of sugar, to rub either their hind- or their forelegs against each other, or to scratch with them under their gossamer wings or, having stretched out their forelegs, to rub them over their heads, and then once more turn around and fly away, and once more come flying back with fresh harassing squadrons.

Chichikov had hardly had time to look about him when his hand was already seized by the Governor, who presented him on the spot to his good lady. Here, as well, the newly come guest did not fail to keep up his end: he delivered himself of some compliment, quite suitable for a man of middle age whose rank was neither too great nor too low. When the dancers who had paired off for the evening crowded everybody to the walls he, with his hands clasped behind him, contemplated them very attentively for a few minutes. Many of the ladies were gowned well and in the latest mode; others had put on whatever the good God may have apportioned to a provincial capital. The men here, even as everywhere, were of two kinds: one consisted of those who were as slim as slim could be, who were forever fluttering about the ladies; some of these gallants were the sort that one could only with difficulty tell apart from the dandies of St. Petersburg, having much the same side whiskers, combed with quite a deal of thought, although the faces of some, while comely and oval, were quite smooth-shaven; they all seated themselves next to the ladies just as airily as the true dandies, spoke French just as the others did, and, just like the others, made the ladies laugh: everything was done just the way it is in St. Petersburg. The other sort consisted of stout men, or of such men as Chichikov—that is, not what you might call any too stout, but by no means slim, either. These, in contrast to the others, eyed the ladies askance and backed away from them and were constantly looking this way and that, to see if one of the Governor's servants was not setting out the green-baize tables for whist. Their faces were full and round, some of them even with moles, while here and there one came across a fellow who was pock-marked as well; they did not dress their hair either in topknots or in curly locks, or in the "may-the-devil-take-me" mode, as the French put it; their hair was either cropped short or slicked down, while their facial features were for the most part rounded out and strong. These were the officials, the bureaucrats, highly regarded in the town. Alas! The stout ones are able to manage their affairs in this world better than the slim ones can manage theirs. The slim ones work for the most part on special missions or are merely carried on the rolls and gad about hither and yon; their existence is somehow all too easy, ethereal, and altogether insecure. But the stout ones never take up posts that are off to one side but always those that are right in line, and once they come to roost anywhere, they will roost securely and fast, so that though the perch may crack and bend under them they will never fall. They are not fond of outward glitter and show; the frock coats upon them are not so deftly cut as are those of the slim ones; but then they do have God's own plenty in their little tin boxes. A slim fellow won't have, in space of three years, a single serf-soul that isn't mortgaged; the stout man plods along, slow but sure and, lo and behold ye, somewhere at the end of the town a house has appeared, bought in his wife's name; then, at the other end of the town, another house; then, a little way out of town, there's a hamlet, and after that even a country seat, with all the adjuncts of landed property. Finally the stout man, having served God and sovereign, having earned the respect of all, leaves his service, moves to a new place, and becomes a landed proprietor, a fine Russian squire, noted for his hospitality, and not merely lives but lives gloriously. And after him his slim heirs again try to see how fast they can let all the paternal effects go down the drain.

It would be impossible to conceal that reflections of almost this nature were occupying Chichikov while he was looking over the social gathering, and the consequence was that he at last joined the stout ones, among whom the personages he encountered were nearly all familiar ones: the Public Prosecutor, whose eyebrows were quite black and bushy and whose left eye had something like a habitual wink, just as though he were saying: "Let you and me, brother, go into the next room—there's something I want to tell you"; but a fellow who was, nevertheless, serious and taciturn; the Postmaster, a short little man to look at, yet a wit and a philosopher; and the Chairman of the Administrative Offices, quite a judicious and amiable man. All of them welcomed Chichikov as an old acquaintance, to which welcome he responded with bows, done somewhat to one side but on the whole not without an agreeable air. It was among them that he made the acquaintance of a quite obliging and affable landowner by the name of Manilov and of a certain Sobakevich, who seemed somewhat clumsy at first glance and who began the acquaintanceship by stepping on Chichikov's foot and then begging his pardon. Here, too, a place card for a whist table was thrust into his hand, which card he accepted with his unvaryingly polite bow.

They seated themselves at the green-covered table and never got up until supper. All talk ceased abruptly and utterly, as is always the case when people dedicate themselves to some really worth-while occupation. Although the Postmaster was quite loquacious, even he, once he had picked up his cards, immediately made his face assume a cogitative expression, sucking his lower lip under the upper and keeping it there all the time the game was on. When playing a court card he would slap the table hard with his hand, adding, if the card was a queen: "Get along with you, you old shrew!" and, if it were a king: "Go on, you Tambov muzhik!" As for the Chairman of the Administrative Offices, he would add: "Why, I'll knock his mustache off! I'll knock his mustache off!" At times, as the players slammed their cards down on the table, certain expressions would escape them: "Ah, come what may—might as well play diamonds if there's nothing else"—"Spades, dig in!"—or simply exclamations denoting the various diminutives and pet names with which they had rechristened the four suits within their own circle.

At the conclusion of the game they disputed, as is the

wont, quite loudly. Our newly arrived guest disputed as well, but with an extreme finesse, so that all perceived that while he was disputing he was at the same time doing so most agreeably. Never did he say: "You led," but: "You were pleased to lead; I had the honor of covering your deuce," and the like of that. In order to win his opponents over still more concerning some point or other he would, at every opportunity, offer them a pinch from his silver-and-enamel snuffbox, at the bottom of which they noticed two violets, placed therein to impart their fragrance to the snuff.

The attention of the newcomer was especially taken up by Manilov and Sobakevich, who have been mentioned above. He immediately made inquiries about them, calling the Chairman of the Administrative Offices and the Postmaster a little to one side. The few questions he put demonstrated that this visitor possessed not merely curiosity but judiciousness as well, for first of all he asked how many serf-souls each one of them owned and what condition their estates were in, and only after that did he ascertain their names and patronymics. In a short while he succeeded in absolutely enchanting them. The landowner Manilov, still not at all an elderly man, with eyes that were as sweet as sugar, and who puckered them up every time he laughed, lost his head over Chichikov. He shook his hand for ever so long and begged him most convincingly to honor him by coming to his village which, he said, was only some ten miles from the city limits, to which Chichikov replied, with quite a polite inclination of his head and a sincere handclasp, that he was not only ready and very willing to, but would even consider it his most sacred obligation to do so. Sobakevich also said, somewhat laconically: "I beg of you to come to my place also," with a scrape of his foot, shod in a boot of such gigantic proportions that its equal was hardly to be found anywhere, especially in these times, when doughty wights are beginning to die out even in Russia.

The following day Chichikov set out for a dinner and an evening at the home of the Chief of Police where, three hours after dinner, everybody sat down to whist and played until two in the morning. There, among other things, he made the acquaintance of Nozdrev, another landowner, a man of about thirty and a sprightly fellow who after an exchange of three or four words began *thou*-ing him. He was likewise on thou-ing terms with the Chief of Police and the Public Prosecutor, and treated them as close friends, but just the same when they sat down to play for big stakes the Chief of Police and the Public Prosecutor scrutinized the tricks he took with the utmost attentiveness and kept an eye on almost every card he played.

The evening of the day after that Chichikov passed at the home of the Chairman of the Administrative Offices, who received his friends in a dressing gown that was somewhat greasy, even though there were two ladies (let us call them that) among the guests. Subsequently Chichikov was at an evening given by the Vice-Governor, at a grand dinner at the tax farmer's, at a modest dinner at the Public Prosecutor's (which, however, had cost as much as the grand one); at the Mayor's after-mass cold buffet luncheon, which was likewise worth any dinner. In short, he did not have to remain at home for a single hour, and he would come back to his room only to sleep. The newcomer had a never-failing presence of mind, somehow, and showed himself to be an experienced man of the world. No matter what the conversation might be about he always knew how to keep it going; if the talk was about a stud, he would speak of a stud; if they happened to speak of thoroughbred dogs, he would impart very sound observations on that subject; if the conversation had to do with an investigation being carried on by the Treasury Department, he demonstrated that juridical quiddities were likewise not unknown to him; if the discussion was about the game of billiards, he did not let his auditors down in that game, either; if they happened to speak of virtue, he would discourse about virtue too, and discourse exceedingly well, so that tears actually welled up in his eyes; if the talk was of the distilling of hard spirits, he knew what was what in hard spirits also; if of customs inspectors and clerks, why, he passed judgment about them too, as though he himself had been both a clerk and an inspector. But it was remarkable that he was able to clothe all this with some sort of sedateness, that he was able to conduct himself well. He spoke neither too loudly nor too low, but in a manner that was just what it should be.

In a word, no matter which way you looked at him, he was a very decent fellow. All the officials were pleased by the arrival of this new personage. The Governor expressed himself clearly on the subject, that he was a well-intentioned man; the Public Prosecutor said that he was a man of affairs; the Colonel of Gendarmes, that he was a learned man; the Chairman of the Administrative Offices, that he was an experienced and meritorious man; the Chief of Police, that he was a meritorious and an amiable man; the wife of the Chief of Police, that he was the most amiable and the most courteous of men. Even Sobakevich himself, who rarely spoke well of anybody, after arriving rather late from town and having already completely undressed and got into bed by the side of his gaunt wife, said to her: "I had supper at the Chief of Police's evening-at-home and made the acquaintance of a collegiate councilor by the name of Pavel Ivanovich Chichikov—a most pleasant fellow!" To which his spouse answered "Hmm!" and gave him a kick.

Such was the general opinion, quite flattering to him, which was formed concerning the newcomer in that town, and it was maintained until such time as a certain strange characteristic of his, as well as an enterprise (or, as they put it in the provinces, an "escapade") that he embarked on, both of which the reader will soon learn about, threw almost the whole town into utter bewilderment.

CHAPTER TWO

The newly arrived gentleman had been living in the town for more than a week by now, driving about to attend modest evenings-at-home and dinners, and in that manner passing his time, as the expression goes, very pleasantly. Finally he decided to extend his visits beyond the town and to call on Manilov and Sobakevich, the landowners to whom he had given his word he would. Perhaps he was urged to do so by another, more essential reason; a matter more serious, nearer his heart. . . . But concerning all this the reader will find out by degrees and in its own due time, if he will only have the patience to read the narrative offered him—a very long one, which has yet to expand more sweepingly and broadly as it draws to that end which crowns the matter.

An order was issued to Seliphan the coachman to harness the horses in the familiar carriage early in the morning; Petrushka the flunky was ordered to stay at home, to keep an eye on the room and the small trunk. It would not be superfluous for the reader to make the acquaintance of these two bondmen of our hero's. Even though, of course, they are not such very prominent personae and belong to what is called the secondary or even the tertiary category, and even though the chief actions and mainsprings of this epic are not based upon them, and may concern and implicate them but lightly here and there, yet the author is exceedingly fond of being circumstantial in all things, and even though he himself is a native of Russia, he wishes, in this respect, to be as thoroughgoing as any German. This, however, will not take up very much time and space, since it will not be necessary to add a great deal to that which the reader already knows—to wit, that Petrushka walked around in a loose brown frock coat that was a hand-me-down from his master, and that he had, as is usually the way among people of his calling, a nose and lips done on a large scale. He was by temperament taciturn rather than talkative; he even had a noble impulse toward enlightenment—i.e., the reading of books, the contents of which presented no difficulty to him whatsoever; it was all one to him if the book dealt with the adventures of an enamored hero or whether it was simply a dictionary or a prayer book—he read everything with the same attentiveness; if a handbook on chemistry were to be thrust under his nose he wouldn't have spurned it either. It wasn't what he read that pleased him, but more the reading itself or, to put it better, the very process of reading—look and behold ye, some word or other inevitably emerged from out the welter of letters, even though, at times, the Devil alone knew what that word meant. This reading was generally performed in a recumbent position, in the entry, on his cot and pallet; the latter, owing to this circumstance, had become as flat and thin as a wafer. Besides his passion for reading he had two more habits that comprised his other characteristic traits: that of sleeping without undressing, just as he was, in that very selfsame frock coat, and of always having about him a certain atmosphere that was peculiarly his own, somewhat redolent of quarters that had been long lived in, so that it sufficed for him merely to set up his cot somewhere, even in a room that had not up to then been lived in, and to drag his overcoat and worldly goods into it, and it would immediately seem that people had been living in that room for ten years or so. Chichikov, being quite a sensitive man, and even in certain cases downright squeamish, upon drawing in a whiff of the air in the morning, through a nose refreshed by slumber, could but make a wry face and say, after a shake of his head: "The Devil alone knows what you're up to, brother; you're sweating, or something. You ought to go to a public bath, at least." To which Petrushka would make no reply and try to busy himself with some immediate task: he would either pick up a clothesbrush and go to where his master's frock coat was hanging, or simply begin tidying up something or other. What were his thoughts the while he went silently about his tasks? He may have been saying to himself: "You're a fine fellow, too; you never get bored with saying the same old thing over and over and over. . . ." God knows, it is hard to know what a slave servant thinks about while the man who owns him gives him a lecture. And there, for a start, you have what can be told about Petrushka.

Seliphan the coachman was an altogether different sort of man. . . . However, the author is quite conscience-stricken about taking up the time of his readers for so long with people of a low class, knowing by experience how unwilling they are to be introduced to the low strata of society. For that's how the born Russian is: he has an overwhelming passion for scraping up an acquaintance with him who may be but a single step above him in rank, while a nodding acquaintance with a count or a prince is for him a better thing than to be on the most intimate terms with a real friend. The author actually feels dubious about his hero, who is only a mere collegiate councilor, after all. There is a likelihood that court councilors, say, may condescend to know him; but as for those who have already clambered up the rungs of General This and General That, these, God knows, may even bestow upon him one of those contemptuous looks which man proudly bestows upon anything that may be crawling like vermin at his feet, or, which would be still worse, will pass him by with an unconcern that would be lethal for the author.

However, no matter how exceedingly grievous either the one course or the other would be, we still must come back to our hero. And so, having issued the necessary orders the evening before, after awaking very early in the morning, after a wash-up and a sponge bath from head to foot (something that was ordinarily gone through only on Sundays, and this day happening to be a Sunday), after shaving himself so closely that his cheeks became truly satin-like, as far as smoothness and glossiness were concerned, and donning his frock coat of scintillating bilberry hue, and then a greatcoat lined with choice bearskins, he at last descended the stairs, supported now on this side, now on that, by the tavern servant, and seated himself in his light carriage. The said carriage thundered out of the gates of the inn and into the street. A priest who was passing by doffed his hat; several street urchins in thoroughly soiled shirts held out their hands, to a chorus of "Kind Sir, give something to a poor orphan!" The coachman, having noticed that one of them had a great fondness for hitching on behind, lashed him with his whip, and the carriage was off, bouncing over the cobbles.

Not without joy did Chichikov behold the striped toll-gate in the distance, informing him that the paved way, like every other torture, would soon be at an end; and, after having hit his head quite hard a few more times against the body of the vehicle, he was at last rolling along on soft earth. Hardly had the town receded when (quite the usual thing among us) there unrolled on both sides of the road vistas of a wild preposterousness: hummocks, fir groves, small, squat, sparse undergrowths of young pines, charred stumps of old ones, wild heather and suchlike stuff and nonsense. One came upon villages all strung out in a single line, with huts that looked like weather-beaten wood-piles, covered over with gray roofs, the wooden fretwork decorations underneath them resembling draped towels with embroidered designs. A few muzhiks whom they chanced to come upon, Chichikov and his coachman, they squatted on benches placed before the gates; countrywives, with stout faces and their breasts caught up by shawls, were looking out of the upper windows; out of a lower window a calf would peer, or a sow might be poking out its unseeing snout. In brief, the sights were of a thoroughly familiar nature. Having passed the tenth mile, Chichikov recalled that, according to Manilov, his village must be thereabouts, but the eleventh mile flew by as well and yet the village was still not to be seen, and, had it not been for two muzhiks whom they chanced to come upon, Chichikov and his coachman would hardly have hit upon the right direction.

In response to the query whether the village of Zamanilovka was far off, the muzhiks doffed their hats, while one of them, who was brighter than the other and adorned with a beard shaped like a wedge, answered: "Is it Manilovka, mebbe, and not Zamanilovka?"

"Well, yes, Manilovka."

"Oh, Manilovka! Why, soon as you drive on for a mile more you'll come smack on it—that is, sort of straight to the right."

"To the right?" the coachman echoed him.

"To the right," said the muzhik. "That will be your road to Manilovka; as for Zamanilovka, there ain't no such place whatsoever. That's what it's called—it goes by the name of Manilovka, that is; but there ain't no Zamanilovka hereabouts at all, at all. When you get there, you'll see a house up on a hill, of stone, two-storied—the manor that is, where the squire himself lives. And that there is your Manilovka; but as for Zamanilovka, there ain't no such place whatsoever hereabouts, nor ever has been."

They set out in search of Manilovka. Having driven for well over a mile they came to a turn in a country road; but they covered another mile, then two and three, it seemed, yet there was still no two-story house of stone to be seen. At this point Chichikov remembered that when a friend invites you to call on him in his village, only ten miles out of town, it means that it must certainly be twenty miles distant.

The village of Manilovka could hardly lure many people by its location. The manor house stood by itself on a knap, an elevation, that is, open to all the winds of heaven that might chance to blow; the steep slope of the hill upon which it stood was covered with closely clipped turf. Two or three flower-beds with lilac bushes and yellow acacias were scattered over it, in the English manner; birches, in small groups of five or six, reared their small-leaved, rather scanty tops here and there. Under two of these one could see an arbor with a low green cupola, blue wooden columns and an inscription reading: "A Temple for Solitary Meditation"; somewhat lower was a pool covered with green scum, which, however, is no great matter of wonder in the English gardens of Russian landowners. At the foot of this hill, and partly up the slope itself, crisscrossing and showing darkly, stood gray little log huts which our hero, for some reason unknown, fell to counting that very moment, and of which he counted more than two hundred. Nowhere among them was there the smallest tree growing, or any sort of greenery; everywhere there were only logs to be seen. The view was animated by two countrywives, who, with their smocks raised and tucked in all around, were wading up to their knees in the pond, dragging by two wooden grapples a torn dragnet wherein one could glimpse a couple of entangled crayfish and the gleam of the captured dace; the women, apparently, were at odds and having high words over something. Showing darkly, somewhat at a distance and to one side, was a pine forest of a depressingly bluish tint. Even the very weather had quite fittingly put itself out: the day was neither clear nor cloudy, but of that dove-gray tinge, such as you can find only upon the much-worn uniforms of soldiers in garrison, those troops that are peaceful, on the whole, but never entirely sober of Sundays. To round out the picture there was not lacking a rooster, that harbinger of changeable weather who, disregarding the fact that his head had been pecked through to the very brain by the beaks of other roosters over certain affairs of gallantry, was clamoring at the top of his voice and even beating his wings, as bedraggled as old straw matting.

As he was driving up to the courtyard Chichikov observed the master himself standing on the porch, in a coat of green Châlons cloth, with his hand at his forehead, cupped over his eyes as a sunshade, the better to see the approaching vehicle. As the light carriage neared the porch, his eyes grew merrier and merrier and his smile expanded more and more.

"Pavel Ivanovich!" he cried out at last, as Chichikov was alighting from his carriage. "So you have at last managed to remember us!"

Both friends kissed each other most heartily and

Manilov led his guest inside. Although the time during which they will be passing through the entry, the anteroom, and the dining room is somewhat brief, nevertheless let us try if we can't somehow utilize it to say a thing or two about the master of the house. But at this point the author must confess that such an undertaking is a very difficult one. It is considerably easier to depict characters that are on a grand scale: there you just slap the pigments onto the canvas with a full sweep—black blazing orbs, beetling eyebrows, a forehead furrowed by a deep crease, a black cape (or one as scarlet as fire) tossed over the shoulders—and your portrait is done; but you take all these gentlemen, now, of whom there are so many in this world, who are so very much like one another in appearance, and yet at the same time, when you take a close look, will be seen to have many exceedingly elusive peculiarities—why, these gentlemen are dreadfully difficult to do in portraits. Here you will have to strain your observation hard, until you compel all the fine, almost imperceptible traits to emerge before you and, in general, you will have to force your eye, already well exercised in the science of prying, to penetrate as deeply as possible.

God alone, perhaps, could tell what sort of character Manilov's was. There is a species of men labeled as "so-so, neither here nor there," or, in the words of the proverb, "neither fish nor flesh nor good red herring." Perhaps Manilov ought to be included in their number also. He was a striking man, to look at him; the features of his face were not devoid of amiability, but there was apparently far too great an overdose of sugariness about it; in his ways and turns of speech there was something that wheedled for your good graces and friendship. He smiled ingratiatingly and was blond in an ashen sort of way, with blue eyes. During the first minute or so of a conversation with him you could not but say: "What a pleasant and kindhearted man!" The minute after that you would not say anything at all, while the third minute you would say: "The Devil knows what's going on here!" and walk away as far as ever you could; if you didn't, you'd feel a deathly spell of the blues coming on. You could not, no matter how long you bided your time, ever get an eager word out of him or, for that matter, even a challenging one, such as you may hear from almost anybody should you broach a matter that touches him to the quick. Every man has his own ambition: one may fancy himself a judge of wolfhounds; to another it seems that he is a great lover of music and amazingly sensitive to all its profound passages; a third may be a great hand at putting away a huge dinner; a fourth feels that he can play a better part in this world, even though that part be but a smidgen above the one assigned to him; a fifth fellow, whose aspiration is more circumscribed, sleeps and dreams of how he might promenade on a gala occasion with some aide-de-camp, showing off before his friends, his acquaintances, and even those who aren't acquainted with him; a sixth may be gifted with a hand that feels a preternatural urge to knock the spots off some big fellow; while the hand of a seventh simply itches to set things to rights wherever he may happen to be, to get under the skin of a station master or of stagecoach drivers. In short, everyone has something all his own, but Manilov had nary a thing. At home he spoke very little and for the most part gave himself up to meditation and thought, but what he thought was, likewise, known only to God—maybe. It could not be said that he busied himself about the estate—he never so much as drove out into the fields; the estate got along of its own accord, somehow. When his steward would tell him: "It might be a good thing, master, to do so and so," he would usually answer, "Yes, that's not a bad idea," as he puffed away at his pipe, pipe-smoking being a habit he had formed at the time he had served in the army, where he had been considered the most modest, the most considerate, and the best-educated of officers. "Yes, just so, that's not a bad idea," he would repeat. When some muzhik would come to him and, scratching the nape of his neck, would say: "Master, give me leave from my work, so's I can earn enough for the taxes."—"Go ahead," he would say, puffing away at his pipe, and it never even entered his head that the muzhik was going off on a bender.

At times, as he looked down from the front porch on the courtyard and the pond, he would get to talking about what a good thing it would be if one were to up and tunnel an underground passage leading out of the house, or build a stone bridge across the pond, on both sides of which there would be shops, and have merchants sitting therein and selling all sorts of small wares that the peasants needed. As he spoke thus his eyes would become exceedingly sweet, while his face assumed the most contented expression. However, these projects ended as they had begun—in mere talk. In his study there was always some book lying about, with a bookmark laid in on page 14, which he had been steadily reading for two years by now. There was perpetually something lacking about his house: the furniture in the dining room was splendid, upholstered with the smartest of silk materials, which had certainly cost quite a bit; but there had not been enough of it for two of the easy chairs, and those two chairs stood there upholstered in ordinary matting; however, the master, for several years at a stretch, kept warning every guest with the words: "Don't sit down on those chairs; they aren't ready yet." In some of the rooms there was no furniture whatsoever, even though there had been talk of it during the first days after his marriage: "We'll have to see to it tomorrow, my pet, and have some furniture placed in this room, if only temporarily." Toward evening an exceedingly exquisite candlestick of patinated bronze, with the three Graces of antiquity and an exquisite escutcheon of mother-of-pearl, would be brought in and placed on the table, and right alongside of it would be put some invalid of common copper, lame, all lopsided and covered all over with winding sheets of tallow; the incongruity of this, however, struck neither the master of the house, nor its mistress, nor the servants.

His wife . . . however, they were perfectly content with each other. Despite the fact that more than eight years had elapsed since their marriage, each one of them still kept bringing to the other either a slice of apple, or a bonbon, or a nut, and would say in a touchingly tender voice: "Open your little mouth wide, dearest, and let me put this tidbit in it." It goes without saying that the little mouth was on such an occasion opened very gracefully. When a birthday was due, surprises would be prepared—some sort of tiny beaded pocket case to hold a toothpick. And quite often as they sat on the divan, suddenly, for no known reason on earth, he abandoning his pipe and she whatever she may have been working on (if it happened to be in her hands at the time, of course), they would impress so languishing and prolonged a kiss upon each other's lips that one could, while it lasted, smoke a small cheroot to the end. In a word, they were what is called happy. Of course, it may be remarked that there are many other things to be done about the house besides preparing surprises and indulging in prolonged kisses, and one could ask a great many questions. Why, for instance, was the kitchen run so stupidly and shiftlessly? Why was the larder rather empty? Why was the housekeeper such a thief? Why were the servants slovenly in person and such drunkards? Why did all the house help sleep so outrageously long, and carry on dissolutely all the rest of the time? But all these are low matters, whereas Mme Manilov had been well educated. And a good education, as everybody knows, is acquired at boarding schools; and at boarding schools, as everybody knows, there are three major subjects which constitute the basis of all human virtues: the French language, indispensable for domestic happiness; the pianoforte, to afford pleasant moments to one's spouse; and, finally, that which really pertains to domestic science: the knitting of purses and other such surprises. However, there do occur sundry refinements and variations in methods, especially at the present time; it all depends for the most part upon the good sense and the capabilities of the boarding-school headmistresses themselves. In other boarding schools the major subjects may be given in such order that the pianoforte comes first of all, the French language next, and domestic science only after that. And at times it may even so happen that the first in order is domestic science—i.e., the knitting of birthday surprises—then the French language, and the pianoforte only after that. The methods vary. It might not be out of the way to make one more remark ... but, I confess, I am very much afraid to talk about the ladies, and besides it is high time I returned to my heroes, who have been standing for several minutes now before the doors of the drawing room, each requesting the other to enter first.

"Don't disturb yourself for my sake, if you please," Chichikov was saying. "I shall follow you in."

"No, Pavel Ivanovich, no—you are my guest," Manilov was saying, indicating the door with a wave of his hand.

"Don't put yourself out, please—don't put yourself out; do go in, please."

"No, really, you must excuse me; I would never allow such a pleasant, cultured guest to go in after me!"

"You have too high an opinion of my culture.... Please go in!"

"Well, now, do be kind enough to go in first."

"But why?"

"Well, now, just so!" said Manilov with a pleasant smile.

Finally both friends sidled through the door together, crowding each other somewhat.

"Allow me to present you to my wife," said Manilov. "My pet, this is Pavel Ivanovich!"

It was only now that Chichikov observed a lady whom he had utterly failed to notice while he had been so busily scraping and bowing to Manilov in the doorway. She wasn't bad to look at, and becomingly dressed. A negligee of some finely woven silken material, pale in hue, sat well upon her; a slender, small hand hurriedly tossed something on the table and clutched a cambric handkerchief with embroidered corners. She rose from the divan on which she had been sitting. It was not without pleasure that Chichikov approached to kiss her tiny hand. Mme Manilov assured him, even lisping somewhat, that he had made them very happy by coming, and that not a day passed without her husband's calling him to mind.

"Yes," Manilov proclaimed, "she even used to ask me all the time: 'How is it your friend does not come?' 'Wait, my pet,' I would tell her, 'he'll come.' And so at last you've actually honored us with your visit. Really, now, you've afforded me such delight . . . like a day in May—a birthday of the heart—"

Chichikov, hearing that matters had already reached the stage of a birthday of the heart, actually became somewhat embarrassed and modestly protested that he had neither a renowned name nor even a distinguished rank.

"You have everything," Manilov interrupted him with the same pleasant smile, "you have everything—and even a bit over."

"How did our town strike you?" asked Mme Manilov. "Have you spent your time pleasantly there?"

"A very fine town, a splendid town," Chichikov responded, "and I have spent my time very pleasantly; the society there is most cordial."

"And how does our Governor strike you?" Mme Manilov persisted.

"A most estimable and amiable man, isn't he?" Manilov put in.

"Perfectly true," said Chichikov, "a most estimable man. And how he has put his very heart into his work—what a grasp he has of it! One can only wish that there were more people like him."

"How adroit he is, don't you know, in receiving anybody, in observing delicacy in all his actions." Manilov contributed his bit with a smile and, in his delight, all but closed his eyes, like a tomcat when you tickle him lightly behind his ears.

"A most obliging and pleasant person," Chichikov went on, "and what a clever, artistic chap! I could never even suppose such a thing, but how well he embroiders all sorts of designs for the house! He was showing me a purse, his own handiwork—there's hardly a lady who could have embroidered it as cleverly as he did."

"And the Vice-Governor, now, what an endearing chap he is, isn't he?" asked Manilov, again puckering up his eyes somewhat.

"A most worthy person, most worthy!" Chichikov responded.

"And, if I may ask, what did you think of the Chief of Police? A most pleasant person, isn't he?"

"Extremely pleasant, and what an intelligent, what a well-read man! We played whist at his place together with the Public Prosecutor and the Chairman of the Administrative Offices until the last roosters left off crowing. A most worthy person, most worthy!"

"Well, now, and what is your opinion of the Chief of Police's wife?" added Mme Manilov. "A most pleasing woman, isn't she?"

"Oh, she is one of the worthiest women I know of!" Chichikov rose to the occasion.

Following this, they did not omit the Chairman of the

Administrative Offices, nor the Postmaster, and in such fashion went over nearly all the officials in the town, who all turned out to be the most worthy persons.

"Do you spend all your time in the village?" Chichikov at last put a question in his turn. "Yes, for the most part," answered Manilov. "Occasionally, however, we drive into town for the sole purpose of seeing some cultured people. You'd become rusticated, you know, if you were to lead a cloistered life all the time."

"True, true," said Chichikov.

"Of course," Manilov went on, "if only one had some good neighbors; if, for instance, one had some such person as one might chat with about the amenities of life, about good usage, or if one had some scientific pursuit or other that would kind of stir the soul, lend one wings to kind of soar with, as it were—" At this point he wanted to express something additional but, perceiving that he had become all tangled up in verbiage, merely fluttered his hand in the air and went on: "In that case, of course, village life and solitude would have very many pleasant points. But there is absolutely no one. All one can do is dip now and then into the *Son of the Fatherland*."

Chichikov evinced utter agreement with this, adding that there could be nothing more gratifying than living in solitude, taking delight in beholding Nature's pageantry, and occasionally reading some book or other.

"But do you know," Manilov added, "that everything, if one has no friend to share it with—"

"Oh, that is true, that is perfectly true!" Chichikov interrupted him. "What do all the treasures in the world signify in that case! 'Do not treasure money; treasure the company of good men,' as a certain sage has said."

"And do you know, Pavel Ivanovich," said Manilov, making his face assume an expression that was not only sweet but actually cloying, like the sort of mixture which an adroit worldly doctor has laced unmercifully with saccharine, imagining that he will gladden his patient thereby, "that in such a case one feels a certain spiritual enjoyment, in a kind of a way.... As, for instance, now, when chance has afforded me the happiness—a rare, exemplary happiness, I may say—of chatting with you and of enjoying your pleasant conversation—"

"Come, what sort of pleasant conversation am I capable of? I am but an insignificant person, nothing more," Chichikov protested.

"Oh, Pavel Ivanovich! Allow me to be frank—I would joyfully give up half my property to have but a part of those good qualities which are yours!"

"On the contrary, for my part I would consider it the greatest—"

No one knows to what lengths this mutual outpouring of sentiments on the part of these friends would have gone if a servant had not entered and announced that dinner was waiting.

"Pray go in," said Manilov. "You must excuse us if our dinner isn't of the sort that's served in parqueted banquet halls, in capital cities; we do things in a simple fashion, after the Russian way—nothing but cabbage soup, yet offered with an open heart. Go in, please."

Here they disputed for another spell as to who was to

go in first, and at last Chichikov edged into the dining room.

Two little boys were already standing in the room—Manilov's sons, who had reached the age when children are already allowed to sit at the family table, but still in high chairs. Their tutor, who was hovering over them, made a polite bow and smiled. The hostess took her seat behind the soup tureen; the guest was seated between the master of the house and its mistress; a servant tied napkins about the necks of the children.

"What darling little children!" said Chichikov, after one look at them. "And how old may they be?"

"The elder is eight, while the younger passed his sixth birthday only yesterday," Mme Manilov informed him.

"Themistoclius!" said Manilov, turning to the elder, who was striving to free his chin, which had been tied up in the napkin by the servant. Chichikov raised his eyebrows somewhat upon hearing such a name—only partially Greek, inasmuch as Manilov, for some unknown reason, had given it the *ius* ending—but made an immediate effort to resume his usual expression. "Themistoclius, tell me, which is the finest city in France?"

At this point the tutor turned his full attention on Themistoclius and it seemed as if he wanted to penetrate into the boy's very head through his eyes, but finally he became perfectly reassured and nodded when Themistoclius answered: "Paris."

"And what is our finest city?" Manilov asked again.

The teacher again became all attention.

"St. Petersburg."

"And what's another great city?"

"Moscow," answered Themistoclius.

"What a clever little darling!" Chichikov commented on this "I must say ..." he went on, at once turning with a certain air of amazement to the Manilovs. "Of such tender years, and yet already possessed of such knowledge! I must tell you that this child will have great abilities!"

"Oh, you don't know him yet!" Manilov responded. "He has an extremely keen wit. You take the younger, Alcides, he isn't so apt; whereas this little chap, the minute he comes across anything—some tiny insect, some little bug—why, his eyes simply light up all of a sudden and start darting to and fro; he'll run after it and draw your attention to it at once. I intend to have him go into the diplomatic corps. Themistoclius," he went on, turning to the boy anew, "do you want to be an ambassador?"

"Yes, I want to," answered Themistoclius, munching bread and letting his head loll right and left.

At this juncture the servant who had been standing behind him wiped the ambassador's nose, and it was very well he did so, otherwise a most considerable blob of foreign matter would have plopped into the ambassador's soup. The table talk began: about the pleasures of a tranquil life, interspersed by comments from the lady of the house concerning the theatre in town and the actors there. The tutor looked at the speakers most attentively, and as soon as he noticed that they were about to smile he would open his mouth at the precise moment and laugh assiduously. Probably he was an accommodating fellow and wanted in this manner to repay the master of the house for good treatment. Once, however, his face assumed a stern look and he rapped sternly on the table, fixing his eyes on the children seated across the table from him. This was really called for, inasmuch as Themistoclius had bitten Alcides' ear, and Alcides, having shut his eyes and opened his mouth, was all set to begin bawling in a most piteous manner, but, sensing that this might easily lead to being deprived of a course, he restored his mouth to its previous state and, with tears in his eyes, fell to gnawing at a mutton bone, which made both his cheeks glisten with grease.

The hostess very often turned to Chichikov with the words: "You aren't eating a thing; you have helped yourself to very little—" to which Chichikov would answer every time: "Thank you very much—I am full. Pleasant talk is better than any course."

By and by they got up from the table. Manilov was in an exceedingly benign mood and, with one arm protectingly about his guest's shoulders, was about to steer him thus into the drawing room when the latter suddenly declared, with quite a significant air, that there was a certain urgent matter he had intended to discuss with him.

"In that case allow me to invite you into my study," said Manilov, and led him off to a small room, one of its windows looking out on the blue-tinged forest.

"This is my den," said Manilov.

"A pleasant, cozy room," said Chichikov, having cast his eye over it. And the room really wasn't devoid of a pleasant atmosphere; the walls were done in some charming bluish tint, on the grayish side; there were four chairs, one easy chair, a table on which a book was lying, with a bookmark inserted therein, which we already have had occasion to mention, and several papers covered with writing; but there was more of tobacco there than of anything else. It was there in all shapes and forms: in paper boxes, in a tobacco jar, and, finally, simply strewn in a heap on the table. Also, lying upon both window sills, were little mounds of ashes knocked out of pipes and so disposed, not without pains, as to achieve very handsome little rows. It was obvious that, on occasion, this must have constituted a pastime for the master of the house.

"I would ask you, if you will allow me, to make yourself comfortable in this easy chair," said Manilov.

"I'll take a plain chair, if you will allow me."

"Allow me not to allow you that," said Manilov with a smile. "I keep this easy chair especially for any guest of mine; you must take it, whether you like it or not."

Chichikov took it.

"Allow me to treat you to a small pipeful—"

"No, I don't smoke," Chichikov answered affably and with an apparent air of regret.

"But why?" asked Manilov, likewise affably and with an air of genuine regret.

"I haven't formed the habit, I'm afraid; they say that pipe-smoking gives one asthma."

"Allow me to inform you that that is a prejudice. I even believe that to smoke a pipe is far healthier than to take snuff. We had a lieutenant in our regiment who never let a pipe out of his mouth, not only at table but even, if I may be permitted to say it, in all other places. And now he is forty and over but, God be thanked, he is in such good health that it couldn't be better."

Chichikov observed that things like that did happen,

most certainly, and that there were many things to be found in nature which were inexplicable for even the broadest mind.

"But first allow me to make one request—" he uttered in a voice about which there was a suggestion of a certain strange (or almost strange) intonation, and immediately thereafter, for some unknown reason, glanced over his shoulder. Manilov also, for a reason just as unknown, looked over his shoulder. "How long ago was it your pleasure to submit a tally of your serfs to the Bureau of Audits census?"

"Why, a long time ago, by now; or it might be better to say that I can't recall when."

"How many of your people have died since the last time you submitted a tally?"

"Why, I can't tell; it would be necessary to ask the steward about this, I suppose. Hey, there, fellow! Summon the steward here; he ought to be around today."

The steward appeared. He was a man of under forty, clean-shaven and used to wearing a frock coat and, apparently, one who led a tranquil existence, inasmuch as his face had a sort of puffily full look, while the yellowish tinge of his skin and his little eyes indicated that he knew only too well what comforters and beds stuffed with down were like. One could see right off that he had gone through his career much the same as all seigniorial stewards do: he had been formerly simply a lad about the house who knew how to read and write; then he had married some Agashka or other, a housekeeper who was her mistress's favorite; had become a manager in his own turn, and after that actually the steward. And having become steward he acted, of course, as all stewards do: he hobnobbed with and acted as godfather to the children of those folk in the village who were better off, and added to the burdens of those of the poorer sort; he awoke when the morning was going on nine, and then took it easy till the samovar came and he had his tea.

"I say, my good fellow, how many of our people have died since the time we submitted the figures for that last census?"

"Why, how do you mean, how many? There's been many dying off since then," said the steward, and hiccupped at the same time, shielding his mouth by slightly cupping his hand over it.

"Yes, I admit I was thinking the same thing myself," Manilov chimed in with him. "Very many have been dying since then—precisely!" Here he turned around to Chichikov and added once more: "Exactly so—very many."

"But what, for instance, would their number be?" Chichikov inquired.

"Yes, how many do they number?" Manilov chimed in.

"Why, how is one to say what their number is? For no one knows how many of them died off; nobody kept any count of them."

"Yes, precisely," said Manilov, turning to Chichikov. "I also supposed that the mortality had been great; there's absolutely no knowing how many have died off."

"You will count them over, please," said Chichikov to the steward, "and make a detailed list of them, with their names."

"Yes, all of them, with their names," echoed Manilov.

"Right, Sir!" said the steward, and went out.

"And for what reason do you need this?" asked Manilov when the steward had taken his leave.

This question, it seemed, was a difficult one for his guest; a sort of strained expression appeared on his face, actually making it turn red—a straining to express something that it was not entirely easy to put into words. And truly, Manilov at last heard such strange and extraordinary things as human ears had never heard before.

"For what reasons, you ask? Here are the reasons: I would like to buy some people—" said Chichikov, then stammered and did not finish what he was saying.

"But allow me to ask you," said Manilov, "how would you wish to buy these people: with land, or simply to take them with you—without land, that is?"

"No, it isn't the actual peasants I am after," said Chichikov. "What I wish to have is the dead ones—"

"What, Sir? Pardon me . . . I am somewhat hard of hearing; I thought I heard a most peculiar word—"

"I propose to acquire the dead people, who, however, would be designated as alive in the Bureau of Audits," said Chichikov.

Right then and there Manilov let his chibouk crash to the floor, long stem, red clay bowl, and all, and for several moments remained with his mouth still gaping. Both friends, who had so recently discussed the pleasures of a life of friendship, remained without motion, staring into each other's eyes, like those portraits which in the old times used to be hung facing each other, one on each side of a mirror. At last Manilov picked up his chibouk and, as he was bending down, looked up into Chichikov's face, trying to catch a possible smile or something of the sort on his lips, to see if he weren't jesting; but there was nothing of the kind to be seen—on the contrary, Chichikov's face seemed to be even more dignified than ever. Then it occurred to Manilov that perhaps his guest might have gone out of his mind by some chance, and he looked at him intently, with fear. But his guest's eyes were perfectly serene; there was no wild, restless fire in them, such as darts through the eyes of a mad person; everything was seemly and proper. No matter how hard Manilov tried to consider how he was to act and what he had to do, he still could not think of anything better than letting the smoke dribble out of his mouth in a very tenuous stream.

"And so I would like to know if you could let me have such people, who are not actually living, yet are alive in so far as legal form is concerned, by transferring them to me, or ceding them, or in whichever manner may be best to your way of thinking."

But Manilov became so confused and muddleheaded that he merely kept staring at him.

"It seems to me that you find the matter a difficult one?"

"I? ... No, that's not it," said Manilov. "But I can't grasp ... pardon me ... I, of course, was unable to receive such a brilliant education as is, so to say, to be perceived in your every movement; I do not possess the high art of self-expression. ... Perhaps in this case ... in the explanation which you have just now put forth ... there is concealed some other ... perhaps you were pleased to express yourself thus for the sake of a good style?"

"No," Chichikov caught him up, "no, I mean the matter to be taken just as it is—that is, I am referring to those souls who are now definitely dead."

Manilov was utterly at a loss. He felt that there was something that he had to do, some question that he had to put, but what that question was the Devil alone knew. He wound up, at last, by again letting the smoke out, this time not through his mouth, however, but through his nostrils.

"And so, if there is nothing in the way, we can with God's grace get down to making out the purchase deed," said Chichikov.

"What—a purchase deed to dead souls?"

"Oh, no!" said Chichikov. "We will write down that they are alive, just as they are actually entered in the census of the Bureau of Audits. I have made a habit of not deviating in any way from the civil legal code; even though I have had to suffer on that account when I was in the Civil Service, yet you must excuse me: an obligation is to me a sacred thing; as for the law, I stand in reverent awe before it."

The last words proved to Manilov's liking, but he still could not, no matter how he tried, penetrate the gist of the matter itself and, instead of replying, took to sucking away at his chibouk so hard that, at last, it began to gurgle like a bassoon. It seemed as if he were trying to draw out of it an opinion concerning such an unheard-of situation; but the chibouk merely gurgled and emitted its death rattle and nothing more.

"Perhaps you are entertaining certain doubts?" asked Chichikov.

"Oh, I wouldn't want you to think so—not in the least! What I am saying has nothing to do with my having any prejudgment concerning you—any critical attitude, that is. But allow me to put this to you: won't this enterprise—or, to use a more comprehensive expression, as it were—won't this negotiation, then, be out of keeping with the civil regulations and the ultimate welfare of Russia?"

At this point Manilov, lifting his head somewhat, looked very significantly into Chichikov's face, exhibiting on every feature of his own and especially on his tightly compressed lips an expression so profound that, in all probability, its like was not to be seen on any human countenance, with the possible exception of some far too clever prime minister and, even so, only at a moment when he was engaged in some particularly brain-racking affair.

But Chichikov merely remarked that such an enterprise, or negotiation, would in no way be out of keeping with civil regulations and the ultimate welfare of Russia, and a moment thereafter added that the Treasury would actually derive benefit therefrom, since it would receive the legal stamp duties.

"Do you really think so?"

"I think that it will be a good thing."

"Ah, if it's going to be a good thing then it's an entirely different matter; I have nothing against it," said Manilov, and became utterly reassured.

"All that remains now is to agree on the price—"

"What—did you say anything about a price?" Manilov was off again, and then paused. "Can you possibly suppose that I am going to accept money for souls that, in a kind of a way, have done with their existence? Since you have already gotten such a, so to say, fantastic whim, then for my part I assign them to you without any financial interest in the matter and will take the costs of the purchase deed upon myself."

It would be a great reproach to the historian of the

events recorded herein if he omitted to state that after hearing Manilov utter such words his guest was overcome with pleasure. No matter how dignified and judicious he may have been, nevertheless at this point it was all he could do to keep himself from actually cutting a caper in the air, something like a goat's, which, as everybody knows, is something that is done only under the strongest impulses of joy. He turned so hard in the armchair that the woolen material of the cushion burst apart; as for Manilov, he was regarding him with a certain perplexity. Chichikov, prompted by gratitude, instantly poured out such a flood of thanks that the host became embarrassed, turned all red, went through a deprecatory gesture with his head and, only at long last, declared that all this was really nothing, that he would actually like to prove in some real way the inclination of his heart, the magnetism of his soul; but as for giving away the dead serf-souls, they were, in a kind of way, so much trash.

"They are far from being trash," said Chichikov, squeezing Manilov's hand.

At this point a very deep sigh escaped him. He was, it seemed, in a mood for heartfelt effusions; it was not without feeling and expressiveness that he uttered, at last, the following words: "If you but knew what a service you have rendered by giving this apparent trash to a man of no lineage or breeding! And really, what haven't I endured? Like some bark or other, tossed amid the ferocious waves. . . . What oppressions, what persecutions have I not experienced, what woe have I not had a taste of! And for what? For that I kept to the ways of righteousness, for that my conscience was clear, for that I extended the helping hand both to the homeless widow and to the poor, wretched orphan! . . ."

At this point he himself had to dab away with his handkerchief at a tear that coursed down his cheek.

Manilov was touched, but utterly. Both friends kept squeezing each other's hand for a long spell, and for a long spell gazed in silence into each other's eyes, in which the welling tears could be perceived. Manilov simply did not want to let go of his friend's hand and went on squeezing it so ardently that the latter by now did not know how to rescue it. Finally, having imperceptibly yanked it away, he said that it might not be a bad thing to put through the purchase deed as soon as possible, and that it might be a good thing if he himself were to see what was going on in town; then he picked up his hat and fell to bowing and scraping in farewell.

"What? You wish to go already?" asked Manilov, suddenly coming to himself and becoming almost frightened.

At this juncture Mme Manilov entered the study.

"Lizanka"—Manilov turned to her with a somewhat plaintive air—"Pavel Ivanovich is leaving us!"

"It must be because we have wearied Pavel Ivanovich," Manilova answered him.

"Madam! Herein," said Chichikov, "herein, right here"—at this point he placed his hand on his heart—"yes, herein shall always dwell the pleasant time I have passed with you! And, believe me, there would be no greater bliss for me than to live with you, if not in the same house with you, then, at least, in the closest proximity to you."

"But do you know, Pavel Ivanovich," said Manilov, to whom such an idea appealed very much, "that it would really be a fine thing if we were to live thus together, under the same roof; or if, in the shade of some elm or other we were to philosophize about some subject or other, were to go in for something profound!"

"Oh, that would be living in paradise!" said Chichikov, with a sigh. "Good-by, Madam!" he went on, approaching Manilova to kiss her tiny hand. "Good-by, my most esteemed friend! Do not forget my request!"

"Oh, you may rest assured," Manilov told him. "I part with you for no more than two days."

They all went into the dining room.

"Good-by, my darling little ones!" said Chichikov, catching sight of Alcides and Themistoclius, who were preoccupied with some little wooden hussar or other, who by now lacked both an arm and his nose. "Good-by, my dear tots! You must excuse me for not having brought you a present, for I must confess I did not know that you were on this earth; but now, when I come, I'll bring you something, without fail. For you, Themistocles, I'll bring a sword. Do you want a sword?"

"I do," answered Themistocles-Themistoclius.

"And for you a drum. A drum for you, eh?" Chichikov went on, bending toward Alcides.

"Yeth, a trum," Alcides lisped in a whisper and with his head bent down.

"Very well, I'll bring you a drum, and what a glorious drum! It will always be beating boom-boom! boom-boom-bang!... Good-by, my little pet—good-by!" Whereupon he kissed the boy's head and turned to Manilov and his spouse with restrained laughter, such as is always turned on for the benefit of parents, thus letting them in on how innocent the desires of their children are.

"You ought to stay, Pavel Ivanovich, really," Manilov remarked when they had already come out on the front steps. "Just look at those clouds!"

"They're only small clouds," was Chichikov's reply.

"But do you know the way to Sobakevich's?"

"That's the very thing I want to ask you."

"If you'll allow me, I'm going to tell your coachman right now." Whereupon, with his unvarying courteousness, Manilov told the coachman how he was to go, and even used *you* once, instead of *thou* in talking to him. The coachman, upon learning that he would have to pass two turns on the road, and turn in only at the third, said: "We'll find the way. Your Honor," and Chichikov was off, to the prolonged accompaniment of bows and much waving of handkerchiefs on the part of his hosts, who finally had to raise themselves on tiptoes to watch their departing guest.

Manilov remained standing on the front staircase for a long time, his eyes following the receding carriage; even when it was altogether out of sight he still stood there, puffing away at his pipe. Finally he went indoors, sat down on a chair and gave himself up to meditation, his soul rejoicing because he had afforded a slight gratification to his guest. After that his thoughts passed on imperceptibly to other matters and wound up God knows where. He was thinking of the felicity of a life of friendship, of how fine it would be to dwell with one's friend on the bank of some river or other, after which his imagination began building a bridge across this river, then a most enormous house, with so lofty a belvedere that one might see even Moscow from it, and he also thought how fine it would be to quaff tea there of evenings, out in the open air, and to discourse on pleasant subjects of one kind or another; after that he imagined that he and Chichikov had arrived in fine carriages at some social affair, where they were enchanting all and sundry with the affability of their behavior; next, the Sovereign, apparently having learned of so great a friendship as theirs, had elevated them to the rank of Generals, and, after that, in the very end, his daydreams were of God knows what—things that he himself could make neither head nor tail of, no matter how hard he tried. Chichikov's strange request put a sudden end to all his reveries. The thought of it refused, in some peculiar way, to jell in his head; no matter how he turned it over and over in his mind he could not make it clear to himself as he sat there all this time and puffed away at his pipe, which occupation lasted until it was high time for supper.

CHAPTER THREE

Chichikov, in the meantime, in a mood of contentment, lolled in his carriage, which had long since been tooling along a highroad. From the preceding chapter it is apparent by now what constituted the main trend of his likings and inclinations, and therefore it is little to be wondered at if in a short while he surrendered thereto, body and soul.

The projects, calculations, and schemes, indications of which strayed over his face, must have been most pleasant, evidently, inasmuch as at every moment they left their traces in a contented smile. Absorbed in them, he paid no attention whatsoever to the fact that his coachman, who was likewise gratified with the reception he had received from Manilov's domestics, was making quite sound observations to the dappled off-horse harnessed to the right. This dappled horse was powerful sly and was merely putting on a show of pulling his load, whereas the shaft-horse, a sorrel, and the other off-horse, a light chestnut in color, who was called Assessor because he had been acquired from some tax assessor or other, put all their hearts into their work, so that one could actually note in their eyes the pleasure they derived therefrom.

"Keep on being foxy, just keep right on! But watch out I don't outfox you!" Seliphan was saying, rising a little and giving the sluggard a taste of his whip. "Just keep your mind on your work, German breeches-maker! You take the sorrel horse, there's a horse to look up to; he does his duty; I'll give him an extra measure of oats right willingly, because he is a horse you can look up to; and Assessor, now, he's a good horse, too. . . . There you go, there you go—what are you twitching your ears for? You just listen, you fool, when someone's talking to you! I ain't a-goin' to teach you nothin' bad, you ignoramus! Look at where he's crawling to!" Here he again gave him a taste of his whip, adding: "Ugh, you barbarian, you! You damned Boneyparte, you!" Then he shouted at all three: "Hey, there, my darlin's!" and flicked all three, no longer as a form of chastisement but just to show them that he was satisfied with them. Having given them that pleasure, he again directed his lecture at the dappled horse: "You've got a notion you can hide from me the way you're carrying on. Oh, no, you've got to live accordin' to the ways of righteousness if you mean to be looked up to. There, over at the squire's where we was just now the people are a fine lot. I take pleasure in conversing, if there's some fine person to converse with; I'm always good friends with a fine person—right friendly; whether it comes to drinking a dish of tea or having a snack, I'm right willing, if it be with a fine person. Everybody looks up to a fine person. There, our master is looked up to everywhere because—do you hear me?—because he done his duty in serving the government, he's a collidjit councilor, he is—"

Discoursing thus, Seliphan at last got off into the most remote abstractions. If Chichikov had lent an attentive ear he would have learned many particulars referring to him personally; but his thoughts were so taken up with their main theme that it was only a deafening thunderclap which forced him to come to himself and look about him: the whole sky was overcast with clouds and the dusty post road had become spattered with drops of rain. Finally a thunderclap pealed a second time, louder and nearer by now, and the rain burst suddenly, as if out of a bucket. At first, taking an oblique direction, it lashed one side of the carriage, then the other; next, changing its method of attack and becoming perfectly vertical, it drummed right on the carriage top; the drops, finally, began pelting the occupant's face. This made him screen himself by pulling down two leather curtains with two round little windows—intended for the contemplation of the views along the road—and give orders to Seliphan to drive faster. Seliphan, who had also been interrupted in the very midst of his harangue, realizing that this certainly was no time to dally, immediately dragged out from under his box some sort of wretched garment of drab cloth, threw it over himself, grabbed the reins and shouted to his troika, who were barely putting one foot in front of another, for they felt a pleasant enervation after the instructive discourses they had heard. But Seliphan, no matter how hard he strove to do so, could not recall whether he had passed two turns in the road or three. Having considered, and recalling the road to some extent, he surmised that the turns had been many, all of which he had let slip by. Since a Russian will always promptly find a course of action at decisive moments, even though it be without considering very far ahead, Seliphan consequently turned to the right at the first crossroad he came to, shouted to his horses: "Hey, there, my honored friends!" and started off at a gallop, giving but little thought to where the road he had taken might bring him.

The rain, however, seemed to have set in for a long spell. The dust lying on the road was rapidly churning into mud and it became harder and harder with every minute for the horses to draw the carriage. By this time Chichikov was beginning to worry seriously, since such a long time had passed without his seeing Sobakevich's village. According to his calculation it was high time for him to have gotten there. He kept looking out on this side and that, but the darkness was such that one might as well have been blind.

"Seliphan!" he said at last, thrusting his head out of the carriage.

"Yes, Master?" Seliphan answered.

"Look around now—maybe the village is in sight."

"No, Master, it's nowheres in sight!"

After which Seliphan, swinging his whip from time to time, launched into a song—well, you couldn't call it a song, exactly, but it was something so long-drawn-out that there was never an end to it. Anything and everything had gone into it: all the encouraging and urging cries which horses are regaled with all over Russia, from one end of it to the other; all sorts of adjectives without the least discrimination, but just as they came to the tip of his tongue. Thus things reached such a pass that he began to call his horses, at last, his "secretaries."

Meanwhile Chichikov began to notice that the carriage was swaying every which way and dealing him the most violent of jolts, which enabled him to sense that they had turned off the road and were, in all probability, straggling over a freshly furrowed field. Seliphan, apparently, had surmised as much himself, but wasn't saying a word.

"Why, you scalawag, what road are you taking?" asked Chichikov.

"Why, Master, what is one to do at a time like this? It's so dark there's no seeing the whip even!" Having said this he made the carriage career so that Chichikov was forced to hold on with both hands. It was only then that he noticed that Seliphan was rather fuddled.

"Hold her, hold her—you'll turn the carriage over!"

"No, Master, how could I ever turn it over?" Seliphan protested. "That's not the right thing to do, to go turning a carriage over, I know that right well of my own self; why, I'd never even think of turning it over, nohow." Thereupon he began to turn the carriage a little, and kept on turning and turning it, until at last he had turned it over entirely on its side. Chichikov went smack into the mud on his hands and knees. However, Seliphan managed to halt the horses, although they would have halted even of themselves, because they were much spent. Such an unforeseen occurrence utterly amazed him.

Having clambered down from his box he took his stand in front of the carriage, placed his arms akimbo, and while his master was wallowing in the mud and striving to scramble out of it, he pronounced, after due deliberation: "Look, now, if it didn't go and turn over after all!"

"You're as drunk as a cobbler!" Chichikov told him.

"No, how could it ever happen that I should be drunk! I know it isn't the right thing to be drunk. I did have a chat with a friend of mine, because one can chat with a fine person, there's nothing bad about that; and we had a bite together. A bite isn't a thing that does anybody any harm; one can have a bite with a fine person—"

"And what did I tell you the last time you got drunk, eh? Or have you forgotten?" Chichikov asked him.

"No, Your Honor, how could I ever forget? I know my duty by now. I know that it isn't the right thing to be drunk. I just had a chat with a fine person, because, you see—"

"Why, I'll take and flog you so that you'll know what it means to chat with a fine person!"

"Just as Your Grace wishes," answered Seliphan, who was ready to agree to everything. "If I've got to be flogged, then let me be flogged; I am not at all against it. Why not be flogged, if one deserves it? That is as the master wills. Flogging, now, is a needful thing, for otherwise the muzhik would get spoiled; order must be maintained. If one deserves it, then go ahead with the flogging—why not?"

To such reasoning the master was utterly at a loss for an answer. But at this juncture it seemed as if fate itself had decided to have compassion upon him. Barking was heard in the distance. Chichikov, heartened thereby, ordered the coachman to give the horses the whip. The Russian driver has good intuition which he uses instead of eyes; it is because of this that there are occasions when, shutting his eyes tight, he will merely jolt along with might and main yet will always fetch up somewhere in the end. Seliphan, without seeing a thing, set his horses in such a straight line for the village that he stopped only when the shafts of the carriage ran right up against a fence and there was absolutely nowhere else to drive. The only thing Chichikov observed through the thick pall of the driving rain was something that resembled a roof. He sent Seliphan off to seek out the gate, which search beyond a doubt would have lasted for a long time if, in Russia, in place of doormen, savage dogs were not employed, who announced him so resonantly that he had to stick his fingers into his ears. A light gleamed in a small window and reached in a misty beam to the fence, indicating the gate to our wayfarers. Seliphan took to pounding upon it and in a short while some sort of figure, swathed in a peasant's drab overcoat, opened a wicket and thrust itself out from it, and the master and his serving man heard a countrywife's hoarse voice: "Who's that knocking there? What are you carrying on like that for?"

"We've just come, mother; let us stay the night," Chichikov informed her.

"Look, what a nimble-footed fellow," said the old

woman, "and what a time to come! This ain't no wayside inn for you; there's a landed proprietress livin' here."

"What are we to do, then, mother? We've lost the way, you see. Surely one can't sleep out in the open fields on a night like this."

"Yes, it's a dark night, and a bad one," Seliphan put in.

"Keep still, you fool," Chichikov told him.

"But who might you be?" asked the old woman.

"I am of the gentry, mother."

The phrase "of the gentry" apparently made the old woman pause and think a while.

"Wait a bit, I'll tell the mistress," she announced, and a minute or two later returned with a lantern in her hand. The gate was unlocked. A small light gleamed in still another window. The carriage, having been driven into the courtyard, came to a stop before a small house which, owing to the darkness, it was difficult to have a good look at. Only one-half of it was lit up by the light issuing from the windows; one could also see a puddle before it, directly in the light from the same windows. The rain beat loudly upon the wooden roof and ran down in gurgling streams into a barrel placed below. In the meantime the hounds were chorusing in all sorts of voices; one of them, with his head thrown back, brought his notes out in such a drawn-out way and with such zeal that it seemed as though he were receiving God knows how high a salary for doing it; another was chopping his notes hastily, like a village sexton; among them tinkled, like a jingle bell on a mail coach, an indefatigable treble, probably that of a young puppy; and all this, finally, was topped by a bass, probably an old fellow, endowed with a stalwart canine nature, inasmuch as he rumbled in his throat, the way a canorous basso profundo rumbles when a choir recital is at its very height: the tenors rise up on their tippity-toes from their strong desire to bring forth a high note, giving out with their all and letting that all escape and soar to the rafters as they throw their heads back, while he alone, thrusting his unshaven chin deep into his cravat, squatting and sinking almost to the ground, lets his note come forth from there, which note makes the windowpanes rattle and emit a jarring tinkle. Judging by the canine chorus alone, made up of such superb musicians, one could have supposed that this small village was quite a considerable one; but our drenched and chilled hero had no thought for anything but a bed. The carriage had barely come to a full stop when he had already jumped out on the small porch, swayed, and almost fallen. Again some woman or other came out on the porch, somewhat younger than the one before but resembling her very much. She led him indoors.

Chichikov took a cursory glance or two about the room: it was done in rather old and poor striped wallpaper; there were pictures, showing some nondescript birds; between the windows were small, antiquated mirrors, with dark frames in the form of curled-up leaves; each mirror had either a letter, or a pack of cards, or a stocking tucked away behind it; there was a wall clock, with flowers painted on its face . . . it was beyond his strength to notice anything more. He felt that his eyes were becoming stuck together as if somebody had smeared them with honey. A minute later the mistress of the house entered: an elderly woman, in some sort of nightcap hastily put on, with a piece of flannel about her neck; one of those motherly creatures, petty landed proprietresses who are forever complaining tearfully about poor crops and their losses as they keep their heads somewhat to one side, yet who at the same time accumulate, bit by bit, their tidy little hoards of money, in little moneybags of bright ticking, tucked away in various chests of drawers. In one little bag they'll put by themselves all the silver rubles; in another the dear little half-ruble coins, and in a third the quarter-rubles, even though it may seem, when one looks there, that there's nothing in the drawers save linen and sleeping jackets, and skeins of thread, and a cloak with the seams ripped apart, destined for a subsequent transformation into a dress, if the old dress should burn through somehow during the baking of cookies and the frying of all sorts of fritters for the holidays or should become utterly threadbare of its own self. But that dress will never burn through and it will not become utterly threadbare of itself; thrifty is the little crone, and the cloak is fated to lie long thus in its ripped state, and then come down, through a last will and testament, to the niece of a second sister, together with all sorts of other rubbish.

Chichikov made excuses for having disturbed them by his unexpected arrival.

"Not at all, not at all!" said the hostess. "What a night for God to bring you to us! Such a nasty storm out. . . . You ought to have a bite of something after your travels, but it's so late at night I can't cook anything for you."

The hostess's words were interrupted by a strange hissing, so that the guest was frightened at first: the noise sounded as if the whole room had become filled with serpents; but after a glance upward he became reassured, inasmuch as he surmised that the wall clock had gotten a notion to strike. The hissing was immediately followed by a death rattle, and at last, summoning all its forces and making a supreme effort, it struck two, which sounded as if someone were walloping a cracked pot with a stick, after which the pendulum started off again clicking away calmly as it swung to the right and to the left.

Chichikov thanked his hostess, saying that he did not need anything, that she should not put herself out in any way, that outside of a bed he did not ask for anything, and wanted to know only what locality he had strayed to, and whether it was far from here to the village of Sobakevich, the landowner, to which the old woman replied that she'd never even heard such a name, and that there wasn't any such landowner.

"Do you know Manilov, at least?" asked Chichikov.

"And who might Manilov be?"

"A landowner, mother."

"No, I never happened to hear of him; there isn't any such landowner."

"What landowners are there hereabouts, then?"

"Bobrov, Sviniin, Kanapatiev, Harpakin, Trepakin, Pleshakov."

"Are they well-to-do or not?"

"No, father o' mine, there's none that is any too well off around here. This one might have twenty souls, that one thirty, but as for those who might have a hundred or so, you'll find none of that sort hereabouts."

Chichikov perceived that he had come to the backwoods for fair.

"Is it far to town, at least?"

"Why, that will be forty miles or thereabouts. I feel so sorry that I haven't anything for you to eat! Would you care for some tea, Sir?"

"Thank you, mother. I need nothing except a bed."

"True enough; after a trip like that one needs to rest— very much so. So you just dispose yourself right here on this divan, Sir. Hey, Phetinia, fetch a featherbed, some pillows and a sheet! What a night God has sent us, what thunder! I've had a taper burning before a holy image all night long. Eh, father o' mine—why, your whole back and one side is caked with mud like a boar's; wherever did you manage to get yourself so muddy?"

"Glory be to God that getting muddy was all I did; I ought to render thanks to Him because I didn't break all my ribs."

"The blessed saints, what you must have gone through! But maybe you ought to have your back rubbed with something?"

"Thanks, thanks! Don't put yourself out; the only thing is, you might order your wench to dry out and clean my clothes."

"Do you hear that, Phetinia?" said the mistress of the house, turning to the woman who had first come out to the travelers and who by this time had already managed to drag in a featherbed and, having plumped it up with her hands on both sides, had loosed a veritable cloudburst of feathers all over the room. "You take this gentleman's greatcoat together with all his other garments and after first letting all of them dry out in front of a fire, as we used to do for the late master, you can then brush and beat them out well."

"Right, Ma'am!" Phetinia kept saying, as she spread a sheet over the featherbed and placed the pillows.

"There, now, there's your bed, all ready," said the hostess. "Good-by, dear Sir; I wish you good night. But maybe there's something else you might be needing? Maybe, father o' mine, you're used to having somebody scratch your heels at bedtime? My dear departed husband could never fall asleep without that."

But the guest passed up even having his heels scratched. The hostess went out and he at once hurried to undress, giving Phetinia all his doffed panoply, greatcoat as well as all the other garments, and Phetinia, having wished him good night in her turn, dragged off all this sodden gear. It was not without pleasure, when he was left alone, that he eyed his bed, which reached well-nigh up to the ceiling. Phetinia, it was evident, was a past mistress of the art of fluffing up featherbeds. When, by standing up on a chair, he clambered into the featherbed, it sank under him almost to the floor, and the feathers, crowded out of their confining covering, flurried to every corner of the room. Putting out the candle, he covered himself with the calico comforter and, curling up into a pretzel under it, fell asleep in a split second.

When he awoke the morning was already rather far gone. The sun was shining through the window right into his eyes, and the flies that had been peacefully slumbering on the walls and ceiling the night before now all turned their full attention upon him: one perched on his upper lip, another on his ear, a third was maneuvering to settle on his very eye; as for one that had been incautious enough to squat near a nostril he, being half asleep, drew it up his nose, which made him sneeze hard, a circumstance that was the cause of his awakening. Casting an eye over the room, he now noticed that the pictures were not all of birds; among them hung a portrait of Kutuzov, that most popular commander,[2] while another, done in oils, was that of some old man or other, with red cuffs on his military uniform, the sort that were sewn on at the time of Czar Paul I.

The wall clock again emitted its hissing sound and struck ten; a feminine face looked in at the door and disappeared at the same moment, since Chichikov, having wished to sleep comfortably, had thrown off absolutely everything. The face that had looked in seemed to him somewhat familiar. He began cudgeling his brain as to who she might be, and at last recalled that this was his hostess. He put on his undershirt; his clothes, dried out and cleaned by now, were lying near by. Having dressed, he walked up to the mirror and sneezed once more, so loudly that a turkey cock who had strolled up to the window—for that window was very close to the ground—began gobbling something at him suddenly and very rapidly in his odd speech; probably it was "God bless you!"—which Chichikov acknowledged by calling him a fool. Having approached the window, Chichikov fell to contemplating the sights it offered; the window looked out practically on the poultry yard—at least the narrow little yard before the window was densely populated by poultry and all sorts of domestic animals. Of chickens and turkey hens there was no end; among them a rooster promenaded with measured strides, tossing his comb and turning his head from side to side, as though he were trying to lend an attentive ear to something; a sow and her family also bobbed up right on the spot, and right on the spot, while rooting through a midden hill, she gobbled up a chick in passing and, without perceiving this, went on putting away watermelon rinds in a systematic sort of way.

This small barnyard, or poultry run, was bounded by a board fence, beyond which stretched away extensive truck patches planted to cabbages, onions, potatoes, sugar beets, and other such domestic produce. Apple trees and other fruit trees were scattered here and there over the truck patches; these trees were covered over with nets as a protection against the magpies and sparrows, the latter flitting from place to place in downright oblique clouds. For the same reason several spread-armed scarecrows had been put up on long poles; one of them was sporting a nightcap that had belonged to none other than the mistress of the house herself.

Beyond the truck gardens came the huts of the serfs, which huts, although they had been built helter-skelter and were not restricted to regular streets, nevertheless indicated, as Chichikov had noted, the well-being of their dwellers, inasmuch as they were properly looked after: the deal on the roofs, if it had become too weather-beaten and timeworn, had everywhere been replaced with new; nowhere were the gates or wickets hanging askew; while in each of those covered sheds that faced him he noted a cart standing, almost new and kept in reserve; in some sheds there were actually two of these carts.

"Yes, this hamlet of hers isn't at all such a small one," he said to himself, and proposed right then and there to have a good talk with the owner of all this and to make her closer acquaintance. He looked through the crack of the door through which she had thrust in her head, and, seeing her seated at a tea table, entered her room with a cheerful and amiable air.

"Greeting, my dear Sir. How did you sleep?" inquired his hostess, rising a little from her seat. She was dressed somewhat better than yesterday, in a dark dress, and was now minus her sleeping cap; but there was still some sort of rag bound about her neck.

"Fine, fine!" said Chichikov, taking an easy chair. "And what about you, mother?"

"I slept but poorly, father o' mine."

"How is that?"

"Sleeplessness. The small of my back keeps on aching without a letup, whilst my leg, from the ankle up, has a nagging pain all the time."

"That will pass, that will pass, mother. You mustn't mind it."

"May God grant that it pass. I rubbed on lard, now, and put on a compress with turpentine, too. And what would you like to have with your tea? There's some fruit brandy in that flask."

"Not a bad idea, mother; guess we'll try a little of the fruit brandy, too."

The reader must have noticed by now, I think, that Chichikov, despite his amiable air, was nevertheless quite more free and easy of speech with her than he had been with Manilov and did not at all stand on ceremony. It must be said that if we Russians haven't yet caught up in a thing or two with the natives of other lands, we have on the other hand got far ahead of them in social behavior. There's no enumerating all the shades and refinements of our behav-

ior. The Frenchman or the German could never in a lifetime either surmise or comprehend all its peculiarities and
nuances; he will use almost the same tone and the same
language in speaking both with the moneybags worth millions and the man who keeps a tiny tobacco shop, even
though at soul he will, of course, crawl and cringe and fawn
enough before the former. But that's not the way we do
things: we have men so wise and adroit that they will speak
to a landowner possessing but two hundred serf-souls in a
way altogether different from that in which they will to one
who possesses three hundred of them; while to him who
possesses three hundred of them they will again speak not
in the same way as they would with him that has five hundred souls; while with him that has five hundred souls the
manner of their speech will again differ from that used
with him that has eight hundred; in brief, even if you were
to go up to a million, you would find different shadings for
each category. Let us suppose, for instance, that there is a
certain chancellery in existence—oh, not here, but in some
Never-Never Land; and in this chancellery, let us suppose,
there exists a Director of the Chancellery. I ask you to have
a look at him as he sits there among his subordinates—why,
out of awe you simply wouldn't be able to let a peep out of
you. Hauteur and noblesse ... and what else doesn't his face
express? Just pick up a brush and paint away: Prometheus,
Prometheus to the life! His gaze is that of an eagle; he am-
bulates with a smooth, measured stride. But that selfsame
eagle, the moment he has stepped out of his office and
nears the study of his superior, flutters along like any par-
tridge, with all his might and main, a sheaf of papers tucked

under his arm. In society or at some evening-at-home, provided that all those present are not so very high in rank, Prometheus will even remain Prometheus to the very end: but let there be present someone ever so little above him, such a metamorphosis will overtake our Prometheus as even Ovid himself could never think of: he's a midge, even smaller than any midge; he has been transmogrified into a grain of sand; "Why, this just can't be our Ivan Petrovich!" you say to yourself as you look at him. "Ivan Petrovich is ever so tall, while this is not only such a squat little fellow but such a scrawny one, too; the other one speaks loudly, booming away in his bass and with never a laugh out of him, whereas the Devil alone knows what this one is up to: he pipes like a bird and keeps on laughing with never a stop." You walk up nearer and take a closer look—and sure enough, if it isn't Ivan Petrovich! "Oho, ho, ho!" you think to yourself. . . .

However, let us get back to the actors in our drama. Chichikov, as we have already seen, had decided not to stand on any ceremony whatsoever and therefore, picking up his cup and lacing his tea with the fruit brandy, led off with: "That's a fine hamlet you've got, mother. How many souls are there in it?"

"There's a little short of eighty souls in it, father o' mine," his hostess informed him. "But the trouble is that times are hard: there, last year, too, the crops were so poor that may God preserve us from their like again."

"However, your muzhiks are a sturdy lot, to look at 'em; their huts are strongly built. But allow me to ask your name. I was so absent-minded—arriving so late at night—"

"Korobochka—relict of a collegiate secretary."

"Thank you very much. And your first name and your patronymic?"

"Nastasia Petrovna."

"Nastasia Petrovna? A fine name, that, Nastasia Petrovna. I have an aunt, my mother's sister, who goes by that name."

"And what is your name?" asked the landed proprietress. "Why, you must be a tax assessor, I guess?"

"No, mother!" Chichikov answered with a smile. "I guess I'm no assessor, but just traveling on my own little business affairs."

"Ah, so you're a commission buyer! What a pity it is, really, that I sold the honey so cheaply to the traders, for now, father o' mine, you'd surely have bought it off me."

"There, now, honey is just what I wouldn't have bought."

"What else, then? Hemp, maybe? But then I've but little of it now, either dressed or raw—only twenty pounds or so in all."

"No, mother, it's a different sort of goods I'm after. Tell me, have any of your peasants been dying off?"

"Oh, father o' mine, eighteen of them!" said the old woman, with a sigh. "And those that died were all such good folk, all fine workers. There's been an increase since then through births, true enough, but what's the good in 'em? They're all such small fry. And then the Tax Assessor came along. 'The tax, now,' says he; 'pay so much for each soul.' They've died off, yet you've got to pay the tax on 'em the same as if they were alive. Only last week my blacksmith burned to death—what a skilled blacksmith he was, and a master locksmith, to boot."

"Why, did you have a fire, mother?"

"God saved me from that calamity; a fire would have been still worse. No, he burned up of his own self, father o' mine. Something caught fire within him, somehow—he'd been drinking overmuch—there was just a small blue flame coming out of him; he kept on smoldering and smoldering all over, and then turned all black, like charcoal—and yet what an awfully skilled blacksmith he was! And now I've nothing to ride out with—there's no one to shoe the horses."

"God's will is in all things, mother!" said Chichikov with a sigh. "One mustn't say anything against the wisdom of God.... Let me have them, now, Nastasia Petrovna!"

"Whom, father o' mine?"

"Why, all these souls that have died off, now."

"But how could I let you have them?"

"Why, just so. Or, if you like, sell them to me. I'll give you cold cash for them."

"But how can one do such a thing? Really, I can't make head or tail of this. Or is it that you'd be after digging them up out of the ground?"

Chichikov saw that the old woman had strayed far afield and that it was absolutely necessary to make clear to her just what was what. In a few words he explained to her that the transfer or purchase would be merely a paper transaction and that the souls would be listed as living.

"But whatever would you want them for?" asked the old woman, staring at him with her eyes popping out.

"That, now, is my own affair."

"Yes, but they're dead now."

"Yes, but who's saying that they're alive? That's the very

reason why they're a loss to you, because they are dead; you keep on paying taxes on them, whereas I now rid you of all bother and of having to pay those taxes. Do you understand? And not only do I rid you of that but I will give you fifteen rubles to boot. There, is it clear to you now?"

"Really, I don't know," the hostess uttered hesitatingly. "After all, I've never sold any dead souls."

"Naturally! It would have been rather something like a miracle if you had sold them to anybody. Or do you think that there's really some good to be got out of them?"

"No, I don't think that! Of what good can they be? No good of any sort. But that's the very thing that troubles me, that they're dead now."

"My, but she seems to be a hardheaded hag and set in her notions!" Chichikov thought to himself. Then: "Look, mother! Do but consider this well—why, you're ruining yourself, paying a tax on a dead serf as if he were alive—"

"Oh, father o' mine, don't even talk of it!" the landed proprietress caught him up. "Only three weeks ago I paid in more than a hundred and fifty rubles, and gave the assessor some palm oil as well."

"There, you see, mother! And now take into consideration merely the fact that it will no longer be necessary for you to give palm oil to the assessor, for now it will be I who'll pay taxes on these dead souls—I, and not you; I take all the liabilities for taxes upon myself; I shall even execute the purchase deed at my expense, do you understand that?"

The old woman went into deep thought. She perceived that the deal certainly seemed an advantageous one; only it was far too novel and unusual, and for that reason she began to entertain strong fears lest this purchaser might take her in, in some way; for he had come God knows whence, and in the dead of night, at that.

"Well, what is it, mother, shall we shake hands on the bargain, eh?" Chichikov was saying.

"Really, father o' mine, I've never yet had occasion to be selling dead folk. I did let some live souls go to Protopopov, something like three years back, it was—two wenches, at a hundred rubles each—and he was right grateful; they turned out to be such splendid workers that they can weave napkins by their own selves."

"Yes, but it isn't live souls we're talking about, God be with them! It's dead ones I'm after."

"Really, I'm afraid, since it's the first time I'm doing such a thing, lest I take a loss, somehow. Maybe you're fooling me, and they are . . . now . . . they're worth more, like."

"See here, mother . . . eh, how can you be like that! What can they be worth? Look at it this way: why, they're nothing but dust. Do you understand, now? They're simply so much dust. You take any worthless thing, any least thing at all, now, a common rag, for instance, and even that rag has a value; it will, at the very least, be bought for a paper mill; but this dust, now, is of no use on earth. There, tell me yourself, of what use is it?"

"Well, now, that's true enough. Yes, it's of no use whatsoever; but there's only one thing that stands in my way—that they're dead, after all."

"May the Devil take her! What a blockhead—her head must be made of oak," said Chichikov to himself, by now beginning to lose his patience. "Try and come to terms with her! She's making me sweat, the damned old hag!" Here, taking out his handkerchief, he fell to mopping the sweat that was now actually beading his forehead. How-ever, it was in vain that Chichikov was getting worked up about her: at times you'll come across a man who is highly respected, and is even in government employ, yet when it comes down to doing business with him he will turn out to be a perfect Korobochka. Once such a man gets a notion into his head there's no earthly means of your overcoming him; no matter how many arguments that are as clear as day you may present to him, they will bounce off him the way a rubber ball bounces off a wall. Having mopped off his sweat Chichikov decided to try if there weren't some other way of setting her on the right path.

"Mother," he said, "you either don't want to understand what I'm telling you, or you're purposely talking the way you are just to hear yourself talk. . . . I'm giving you fifteen rubles cash, in government notes, do you understand that? Why, that's money. You won't pick that up in the gutter. There, now, own up, what price did you sell your honey at?"

"At twelve rubles for each thirty-six pounds."

"You're taking a small sin on your soul, mother. You never sold it at that price."

"I call God to witness I did!"

"There, you see? But it fetched that price because it was honey. You'd been storing it up for nigh unto a year, maybe, having to work hard and being put to all kinds of trouble and a lot of bother; you had to drive about, rob the bees of the fruit of their labor, and then feed and keep them the whole winter through in your cellar, whereas dead souls are not of this world. Here you applied no effort on your part; it was God's will that they leave this world, causing a loss to your estate. So you received for your toil, for your effort, a matter of twelve rubles, but here you get something free and for nothing, and not merely twelve rubles, mind you, but fifteen, and not in silver, but all in lovely blue government notes."

After such potent persuasions Chichikov hardly doubted that now the old woman would, at last, give in.

"Really, now," answered the landed proprietress, "mine is but a poor widow woman's lot! It would be better if I mark time a bit; maybe the merchants will come riding this way, and I'll see what prices dead souls are fetching nowadays."

"This is a disgrace—a disgrace, mother! This is simply a disgrace! There, now, whatever are you saying? Just stop and think it over for yourself! Whoever is going to buy them from you? There, what use could such a purchaser put them to?"

"Well, maybe they can come in handy around the place somehow or another, by some chance—" contradicted the old woman, but never finished her speech, letting her jaw drop and staring at him almost with fear as she waited anxiously for what he might say to that.

"Dead folk around the place! So that's where you've fetched up! Going to scare the sparrows off with them of nights in your truck garden, perhaps, or what?"

"The power of the Cross be with us! What dreadful things you're saying!" the old woman let drop, crossing herself.

"What other work would you like to put them to, then? But that doesn't matter, really, for the bones and the graves all remain with you: the transfer is only on paper. Well, what is it going to be? What do you say? Let's have your answer, at least."

The old woman again went off into deep thought.

"Well, what are you thinking of, Nastasia Petrovna?"

"Really, I still can't decide what I am to do; I think I'd better sell you the hemp."

"But what has hemp to do with it? Good heavens, I am asking you about something else entirely, yet you shove hemp at me! Hemp is all right in its own way; if I come another time I'll take the hemp off your hands as well. Well, what is it going to be, Nastasia Petrovna?"

"Honest to God, this is such a strange commodity, so unusual!"

At this juncture Chichikov lost every last shred of patience, picked up his chair, banged it down in exasperation, and hoped the Devil would take her.

The landed proprietress became inordinately frightened of the Devil. "Oh, never mention him, God be with him!" she cried out, turning all pale. "It was only three days ago that I dreamt of him all night long, the accursed one! I got a notion before bedtime of telling fortunes by cards, after saying prayers, and so, evidently, God must have sent him as a punishment. How vile he appeared! Why, his horns were longer nor a steer's."

"What I wonder at is that devils don't come to you in your dreams by the score! I wanted to do this solely out of mere Christian love of humanity. Here I saw a poor widow woman working herself to death, enduring poverty. . . . Why, may you drop dead and fall through the ground, you and your whole confounded village!"

"Oh, what dreadful curses you're bringing down on a body!" said the old woman, looking at him with fear.

"Why, one can't find words bad enough for you! Really, and without meaning the word in a bad sense, you're like a dog in a manger; it can't eat the hay itself and it won't let others eat it. I was about to buy up your farm produce, of whatever sort, inasmuch as I also supply the government on contracts—" Here he lied a bit, and even though he did so in passing and without any ulterior consideration, he nevertheless met with unexpected success. Those government contracts had a strong effect on Nastasia Petrovna; at any rate, when she spoke it was already in a conciliatory tone.

"Why, whatever did you get so all-fired angry for? If I'd known beforehand that you're so apt to get angry I never would have argued with you at all."

"As if there were something to get angry about! The whole thing isn't worth a tinker's curse, and you think I'm going to get angry over it!"

"Well, if you like, I'm ready to give them up for fifteen rubles in government notes! Only look you, father o'mine, about those contracts, now: should you have occasion to get flour, either rye or buckwheat, or any groats, or any dressed meat, don't you take advantage of me, please, in that case."

"I won't, mother," he told her, but in the meantime was brushing off with his hand the sweat that was coursing in whole streams down his face. He inquired of her if she didn't have some trusted agent or acquaintance in town whom she might empower to put through the purchase deed to the dead souls and do whatever else might be necessary.

"Why, of course! The son of Father Cyril, the Dean,

works in the Administrative Offices," said Korobochka. Chichikov asked her to write him a letter of authorization and, in order not to put her to any extra trouble, even undertook to compose it.

"It would be a good thing," Korobochka was thinking to herself meanwhile, "if he were to take my flour and cattle for his government contracts. I ought to get on the right side of him; there's still some dough left over from yesterday, I might as well go and tell Phetinia to make some pancakes. It might also be a good thing to bake an unleavened turnover with eggs; they bake turnovers well in my kitchen, and it doesn't take much time, either."

The hostess left the room to put into execution her idea about the turnover and, probably, also to round it out with other creations of home baking and cookery, while Chichikov walked into the parlor where he had spent the night, in order to take the necessary papers out of his casket. Everything had long since been tidied up in the parlor; the luxurious feather bed had been carried out and a table, with a cloth on it, had been placed in front of the divan. Placing his casket thereon he rested a while, inasmuch as he felt that he was bathed in sweat, as if he were swimming in a river; every stitch he had on, from his undershirt to his stockings, was wringing-wet.

"Eh, but that damned old woman has well-nigh killed me!" said he, having rested a little, and opened the casket. The author feels that there are readers so inquisitive that they wish to know even the plan and the interior arrangement of this casket. By all means, why not gratify them? Here it is, the interior arrangement: in the very middle was a soap dish; behind the soap dish six or seven very narrow divisions to hold razors; then square receptacles in the corners for a sand shaker and an inkpot, with a boat-like, hollowed-out little ledge to hold quills, sticks of sealing wax, and whatever articles might be quite long; then all sorts of little partitioned receptacles, with lids and without, for objects that were rather short; these were filled with cards—visiting cards, funeral announcements, old theatre tickets and the like, which had been put away as souvenirs. The entire upper tray, with all its partitioned compartments, could be lifted out, and underneath it one came upon a space taken up with piles of paper, in folio; then came a small secret money drawer, which while it had no perceptible opening, could nevertheless be pulled out from one side of the casket. It was always so hastily pulled out and pushed back by the owner all within the same minute that one could never tell with certainty how much money there was in it.

Chichikov immediately bestirred himself and, having trimmed a quill, fell to writing. It was at this point that his hostess entered.

"That's a fine chest you've got there, father o' mine," said she, sitting down near him. "Bought it in Moscow, I guess?"

"Yes, in Moscow," answered Chichikov, writing away.

"I just knew it; everything there is made well. Three years back my sister brought me back some warm little boots for the children, such well-made stuff that they're wearing them to this day. My goodness, what a heap of stamped paper you've got there!" she went on, after a peep into his casket. And really, there was quite a bit of stamped paper on it. "You might make me a present of just one teeny sheet! For that's the very thing I lack; I might have to petition one of our courts, and yet not have anything to write it on."

Chichikov explained to her that this paper was not of that sort; it was intended for the execution of purchase deeds and not for petitions. However, in order to pacify her, he gave her some sheet or other with a ruble stamp on it. Having written the letter, he gave it to her to sign and asked for a short list of the dead serfs. It turned out that this landed proprietress kept neither records nor lists of any kind whatsoever, but she did know the names of almost all her serfs by heart. He made her dictate these to him right then and there. Certain of the peasants amazed him by their family names, but still more by their nicknames, so that every time he heard them called out he had to pause before writing them down. He was especially struck by a certain Petr Saveliev Neuvazhai Koryto (No-Respect-for-the-Pig-Trough), so that he could not help saying: "What a long name!" Another had appended to his name Korovii Kirpich (Cow-Dung Brick); there was one who turned out to be simply Kolesso Ivan (John the Wheel).

As he was finishing his writing he sniffed the air slightly and caught the enticing aroma of something hot, made with butter.

"I beg of you to have a bite," said his hostess. Chichikov looked around him and beheld, already standing on the table, small mushrooms, patties, hasty pudding, scones, tarts, pancakes, and wafers with all sorts of baked additions—baked chopped onion, baked poppyseed, baked curds, baked clotted cream—and Heaven alone knows how many other things were there.

"This is an unleavened turnover with eggs!" the hostess informed him.

Chichikov drew up to the unleavened turnover with eggs and, after speedily eating half of it and a bit over, duly sang its praises. And, really and truly, although the turnover was savory of itself, yet after all the fuss and fret he had had to go through with the mistress of the house it seemed still more savory.

"And won't you have some pancakes?"

In answer to this Chichikov rolled up three of the pancakes together and, having dipped them in melted butter, dispatched them into his mouth, after which he had to wipe his lips and hands with a napkin. Having gone through this performance three times, he asked his hostess to order his carriage harnessed. Nastasia Petrovna immediately sent off Phetinia, giving her orders at the same time to fetch some more hot pancakes.

"Your pancakes are right tasty, mother," said Chichikov, buckling down to the hot ones as soon as they were brought in.

"Yes, they make them well in my kitchen," said the hostess, "but here's the trouble: the crop was poor; the flour isn't what it might have been. . . . Why, father o' mine, why are you in such a hurry?" she asked, seeing that Chichikov had already picked up his hat. "Why, your carriage isn't harnessed yet."

"They'll harness it, mother, they'll harness it. They harness it fast when I'm around."

"Well, then, if you'll be so kind, don't forget me when it comes to filling those contracts."

"I won't, I won't," Chichikov kept saying, stepping out into the entry.

"And aren't you buying any lard?" asked the mistress of the house, following him out.

"And why not? I do buy it, only that will have to come later."

"I'll have lard too, around the Christmas holidays."

"We'll buy, we'll buy, we'll buy everything, and we'll buy lard as well."

"Maybe you'll be after needing feathers. I'll be having feathers, too, about St. Philip's Fast."

"Fine, fine!" Chichikov kept saying.

"There, you see, father o' mine, your carriage isn't ready yet, just as I said," his hostess remarked as they came out on the front steps.

"It will be ready, it will be ready. Do but tell me one thing—how does one get out on the main road?"

"Now, how am I ever to do that?" the hostess wondered. "It's such a complicated thing to explain, there's such a lot of twists and turns, unless I was to send a little wench with you, to show you the way. For I guess you've got room up on the box where she might sit—"

"How else!"

"Yes, that's what I'll do, I'll let you take a girl along—that little wench of mine knows the way. Only, look you, don't you go and carry her off; some traders have already carried one off from me."

Chichikov assured her that he would not carry off the little wench, and Korobochka, set at rest, now began overseeing everything in her yard: she stared hard at the housekeeper, who was carrying a wooden dipper of honey out of a storeroom; at a muzhik who had bobbed up at the gate; and little by little withdrew entirely into the life of her household. But why busy ourselves so long with Korobochka? Whether it be a Korobochka, or a Manilova, whether the mode of life be domestic or not, let us pass these things by. For isn't everything in the world arranged with wondrous whimsicality? The gay can in an instant turn into the sad, if one stand and contemplate it overlong, and then God knows what odd notions may not stray into your head. Perhaps you may even take to thinking: "Come now, does Korobochka really stand so low on the infinite ladder that leads humanity to perfection? Is the chasm so great that divides her from her sister, who is so inaccessibly immured within an aristocratic mansion, with goodly odors floating over its cast-iron staircases, a mansion gleaming with brass and glossy with oriental rugs; her sister who yawns over an unfinished book until such time as she starts out for a visit to some witty social gathering which will furnish her with an arena where she may brilliantly show off her intelligence and express thoroughly rehearsed ideas, ideas which, according to the laws of fashion, will amuse the whole town for a week; ideas having nothing to do with what is going on in her house and on her country estates, both household and estates being in utter confusion and going to wrack and ruin, thanks to her ignorance of domestic science, but ideas having to do with whatever political upheaval is brewing in France, with whatever direction modish Catholicism may have taken?" But let these things pass, let them pass! Why talk of all this? But why, then, amid thoughtless, gay, carefree moments, does another, wondrous strain of thought flash of itself within us? The laughter has not yet had time to fade completely off your face and yet you have already become a different person in the midst of the very same people, and your face has already become illumined with a different light. . . .

"And here's the carriage, here's the carriage!" Chichikov cried out, catching sight, at last, of his carriage driving up. "What were you fussing about so long, you blockhead? Your head hasn't cleared of yesterday's drink yet, it seems."

Seliphan had no answer to this.

"Good-by, mother! Well, what about it, where's that little wench of yours?"

"Hey, there, Pelagea!" the landed proprietress called out to a little girl of eleven who was standing near the front steps, in a dress of some homespun material, dyed and glossy, with bare feet which from a distance might have been thought shod, so plastered with fresh mud were they. "Show the gentleman the way."

Seliphan helped the little wench to clamber up on his box, which she did after first making the step intended solely for the owner's foot all muddy with her own and only then scrambling up to the high perch and settling down there near the driver. After her Chichikov himself put his foot on the step and, making the carriage tip to the right, inasmuch as he was rather on the heavy side, finally settled down himself, saying: "Well, now everything's set! Good-by, mother!"

The horses started off.

Seliphan was morose all the way and, at the same time, very attentive to his work, which was always the case with him whenever he had done something wrong or had been drinking. The horses were wonderful to behold, they were so well curried and groomed. The collar upon one of them, which up to now had almost always been put on with such a rent that the oakum peeped out of the leather, was now skillfully mended. During the whole way Seliphan was taciturn, merely lashing out with his whip from time to time, and not addressing any diatribes to the horses, although the piebald horse would have liked, of course, to lend an attentive ear to something instructive, inasmuch as at such times as these the reins always dangled somehow listlessly in the hands of the usually loquacious driver and his whip strayed only *pro forma* over their backs. But all that could be heard issuing from the grim lips on this occasion was monotonously unpleasant outcries, such as "There, now, you crowbait, there! Keep on gaping, keep it up!" and nothing more. Even the sorrel himself and Assessor were dissatisfied, not having heard themselves called, even once, either "darlings" or "Your Honors." The piebald felt most unpleasant lashes on his fuller and broader parts. "Look you, how worked up he is," thought the piebald to himself, cocking up his ears somewhat. "He sure knows where to whip you! He won't lash you straight across the back, but picks out just the very spot that's most sensitive, flicking your ears or lashing you under the belly."

"Do we go to the right now?" Seliphan turned to the little girl seated beside him, putting the question in the driest of tones and pointing out to her with his whip the road, darkened from the rain, between the vividly green and rain-freshened fields.

"No, no, I'll show you when we come to it," answered the little wench.

"Which way do we go now?" Seliphan asked, after driving on for some time more.

"Why, that way," answered the little wench, pointing with her hand.

"Oh, you!" said Seliphan. "Why, that *is* to the right; you don't know your right hand from your left!"

Although the day was a very fine one, the ground had become miry to such a degree that the carriage wheels, churning it up, soon became wholly covered with mud, as if with felt, which slowed the carriage down considerably; in addition to that the soil was clayey and unusually clinging. Both the one and the other were the reasons for their having been unable to get out of the maze of crossroads before noon. Without the little wench it would have been difficult to accomplish even this, inasmuch as the roads crept off in every direction, like a catch of crayfish when you dump them out of a sack, and it would have been Seliphan's lot to drive about at random, this time through no fault of his own. In a short while the little girl pointed with her hand to a structure showing darkly in the distance and said: "And there's your highroad!"

"And what's that there building?"

"That's an inn," said the little wench.

"Well, now we'll make the rest of the way by ourselves," said Seliphan. "You get along home."

He stopped the carriage and helped her get down, muttering through his teeth: "Hey, you black-footed little thing!"

Chichikov gave her a copper coin, and she ambled off on her way, contented with merely having sat up on the driver's box.

CHAPTER FOUR

As he was driving up to the tavern Chichikov ordered Seliphan to stop for two reasons: on the one hand, to give the horses a chance to rest and, on the other, to have a bite of something and fortify himself as well. The author must confess that he is quite envious of the appetites and stomachs of this sort of people. All the top-notch people living in St. Petersburg and Moscow mean absolutely nothing to him—people who spend their time in thoughtful planning of what they may eat tomorrow, and what sort of dinner to contrive for the day after, and who sit down to this dinner not otherwise than after having popped some pills into their mouths, people who gulp down oysters, sea-spiders and other such wondrous cates, and eventually wind up with having to go to the baths at Karlsbad or to take the medicinal waters in the Caucasus. No, these gentry have never aroused any envy in me. But you take some of these fair-to-middlin' gentlemen, who will call for ham at one stage post, a suckling pig at a second, and at a third for a slice of sturgeon, or some sort of sausage baked with onions, and then, as if they hadn't eaten a thing all day, will sit down at a full table, at any hour you like, and tackle sterlet chowder, with eelpouts and soft roe, so hot it hisses and burbles as they take it into their mouths, followed, as a sort of chaser, by a fish pie with millet porridge, or cabbage dumplings, or a pie baked of young catfish, so that even an onlooker must needs work up an appetite—now, these gentlemen really are enjoying an enviable gift from heaven!

More than one top-notch gentleman would sacrifice in a moment half the number of serfs he possesses and half his estates (mortgaged and unmortgaged, with all the improvements both foreign and domestic), just to have such a stomach as the fair-to-middlin' gentleman possesses. But that's where the trouble lies, that one cannot acquire, either for any sum of money or for any estate (either with improvements or without), such a stomach as you will find a fair-to-middlin' gentleman possessed of.

The wooden, time-stained inn received Chichikov under its shed, narrow and small but hospitable, supported by short turned columns of wood that looked like antiquated church candlesticks. The inn was something in the nature of a Russian hut, only on a larger scale. Cornices of fresh wood, with fretwork designs, under the roof and around the windows, stood out in sharp, lively and motley contrast against its dark walls; pitchers with flowers were daubed on the shutters. Having clambered up the narrow wooden steps Chichikov made his way into a spacious entry, where he was met by a door opening with a creak and a stout old woman in bright calico who said: "This way, if you please!" Within the main room he came upon all the old friends everybody meets in modest wooden inns, of which there are not a few erected along our waysides, to wit: a samovar covered with a hoarfrost-like patina, walls of smoothly adzed pine, a three-cornered cupboard with teapots and teacups in one of the corners, small porcelain eggs, gilt, hung up on blue and red bits of ribbon before the holy images, a cat that had recently had kittens, a mirror that reflected instead of two eyes twice that number and, instead of the face, some sort of wafer or other, fragrant herbs and cloves, stuck around the images in bunches so dried up that he who wanted to sniff them was forced to sneeze for his pains.

"Have you got a suckling pig?" was the first question Chichikov addressed to the countrywife standing before him.

"We have that same."

"With horse-radish and sour cream?"

"With horse-radish and sour cream."

"Bring it on!"

The old woman began bustling about and fetched a plate, a napkin that was starched so much that it buckled like dried tree bark, then a knife the bone handle of which had turned yellow and the blade of which was as thin as that of a penknife, a two-tined fork, and a salt cellar which it was impossible to set upright on the table.

Our hero, as was his wont, immediately entered into conversation with her and questioned her thoroughly: whether she herself ran the inn or if it had another owner, and how much income the inn brought in, and whether her sons lived in the inn, and was the eldest son a single or a married man, and what sort of wife had he taken unto himself, had her dowry been large or no, and had the bride's father been satisfied, and hadn't he been angry because there had been but few presents at the wedding—in fact, there wasn't a thing that he passed over. It goes without saying that he was curious enough to learn what landowners there were to be found thereabouts, and learned there were all sorts of landowners: Blokhin, Pochitaev, Mylnoi, Cheprakov (a Colonel, he was), and Sobakevich.

"Ah! You know Sobakevich?" he asked, and heard, right

then and there, that the old woman knew not only Sobakevich but Manilov as well, and that Manilov was a bit more
refined, like, than Sobakevich was: he'd order a chicken to
be cooked at once, and would ask for a bit of veal also, and
if they happened to have any sheep's liver he'd ask for
sheep's liver as well, yet would only take a taste of everything; this Sobakevich, on the other hand, would order only
one dish, but then he'd eat up all of it and even ask for an
extra helping for the same price.

As he was thus conversing over his suckling pig, of
which only the least morsel remained by now, he heard the
rattling wheels of some vehicle that had driven up. Looking out of the window he saw, halted before the inn, an exceedingly light carriage; it was harnessed with a team of
three good horses. Two strangers were clambering out of it;
one was flaxen-fair, of tall stature; the other was somewhat
shorter, of a dark complexion. The flaxen-fair fellow had
on a dark-blue Hungarian jacket with frogs; the one with
the dark complexion simply a short, striped Tatar kaftan,
fastened with hooks. Another carriage, a most wretched
and small affair, was dragging along at a distance, empty,
and drawn by some sort of shaggy team of four, their collars all rent and tattered and their harness of odds and ends
of rope and haywire. The flaxen-fair man at once started
up the steps, while the swarthy fellow stayed behind, groping for something in the carriage, talking with a servant
near by and at the same time motioning with his hand to
the carriage ambling behind them. His voice seemed somehow familiar to Chichikov. While Chichikov was looking
the swarthy man over, the flaxen-fair fellow had already
managed to find the door by groping and to open it. He was

tall of stature and gaunt of face (or what they call shop-worn), with a small, reddish mustache. By his sunburned face one could conclude that he knew what smoke was—if not that of cannons, then that of tobacco pipes, at least. He made a polite bow to Chichikov, to which the latter responded in kind. Within a few minutes they would have probably got into conversation and become well acquainted with each other, since a beginning had already been made and both, almost at one and the same time, evinced satisfaction because the dust along the road had been completely beaten down by yesterday's rain and now it was both cool and pleasant to travel, when the flaxen-fair man's dark-complexioned friend entered, tossing the cap off his head onto the table and running his hand through his thick black hair, rumpling it up with a "may-the-devil-take-me" gesture. He was a fine lad of medium height, very far from being badly made, with full rosy cheeks, teeth as white as snow, and side whiskers as black as pitch. His skin was clear and glowing, his coloring high; his face seemed simply to exude health.

"*Ba, ba, ba!*" he cried out suddenly, flinging his arms wide at the sight of Chichikov. "What fates bring you hither?"

Chichikov recognized Nozdrev, the same Nozdrev together with whom he had dined at the Public Prosecutor's and who, in the space of a few minutes, had got on such an intimate footing with Chichikov that he had begun calling our hero *thou*, even though the latter had given him no reason whatsoever to indulge in such familiarity.

"Where have you been traveling to?" Nozdrev was saying and, without having waited for an answer, went on: "As for me, brother, I am coming from the fair. Congratulate me: I have lost my shirt at cards. Would you believe it, never in my life have I had such a losing streak. Why, I arrived here on something I had to hire from the natives hereabouts! There, just for the fun of it, take a look through the window!" Here he himself bent Chichikov's head down, so that the latter almost hit himself against the window frame. "See what trash that is? They barely managed to drag me here, the damned crowbaits; then I shifted over to that fellow's carriage." Saying this, Nozdrev pointed a finger at his friend. "Why, haven't you made each other's acquaintance yet? This is my brother-in-law, Mizhuev! We were talking about you all morning. 'You just watch and see,' I says to him, 'if we won't meet up with Chichikov.' Well, now, brother, if you but knew how I was cleaned out! Would you believe it, not only have I gotten rid of four trotters, but of everything. Why, I have not only no watch on me, but not even as much as a chain—"

Chichikov glanced at him and saw that the other certainly had no watch nor chain on. It appeared to him, even, that one of his side whiskers was shorter and not so luxuriant as the other.

"And yet, if I had but twenty rubles in my pocket," Nozdrev went on, "just that, and no more, I would have won everything back—or rather, besides winning back all my losses, I would have—there, as I am an honest man!—I would have put thirty thousand in my wallet, on the spot."

"However, you said that even at the time," the flaxen-fair fellow answered him, "but when I gave you fifty rubles you sent them after the rest—on the spot."

"Oh, I never would have! By God, I never would have! If

I hadn't myself done a foolish thing, I'd never have done it, really! If I hadn't come a cropper by doubling my stake on that damned seven after the others had doubled theirs I would have broken the bank!"

"Just the same, you didn't break it," said the flaxen-fair man.

"I didn't break it because I didn't bet double on that seven at the right time. And do you think that major of yours is such a good player?"

"Whether he is a good player or no, he trimmed you just the same."

"He isn't so great!" said Nozdrev. "If I were to pull some of his stunts, I could trim him too. Oh, no; just let him try to double, then I'll see. I'll see then what sort of a gambler he is! But then, brother Chichikov, what a high time we had during the first few days! The fair was certainly a most excellent one. The merchants themselves say that never before had so many people come together. Everything I had brought from the village was sold at most advantageous prices. Eh, dear brother, did we have ourselves a good time! Even now, when one thinks of it ... the Devil take it! I mean, what a pity it is you weren't there! Just imagine, there was a regiment of dragoons stationed a couple of miles from town. Well, would you believe it, all the officers—and there must have been at least forty of them—were in town, to a man. When we started in to drink, brother dear. . . . Second Captain of Cavalry Potseluev, what a glorious fellow he was! What a mustache, brother dear! He never called Bordeaux anything but plain slops. 'Brother,' he'd say to the waiter, 'bring us some slops, now!' Lieutenant Kuvshinikov

... ah, brother o' mine, what an infinitely charming fellow! There, now, is what one would call a fullblown profligate! He and I went around together all the time. And what wines Ponomarev let us have! You must know he is a great swindler and you can't get anything decent in his shop; he always mixes all sorts of rubbish into his wines—sandal-wood, burnt cork and, the scoundrel, he even rubs alder-wood into it; but then, if he does at last drag some little bottle or other out of his furthest room, which is called the Special Room in his place, well, brother o' mine, then you simply float in the empyrean. The champagne we had was such that ... well, what would the Governor's be beside it? Why, nothing but ordinary bread cider! Just imagine, it wasn't Clicquot, but some sort of a Clicquot-Matradura; that means it's double Clicquot. And he also got out a bot-tle of French wine, by the name of Bon-Bon. Bouquet? A posy of roses and everything else you wish. Oh, we sure did have ourselves a good time! Some prince or other who ar-rived in town after we did sent to Ponomarev's shop for champagne—the officers had drunk it up, every last drop of it. Would you believe it, I alone drank up seventeen bot-tles of champagne at one dinner!"

"Well, now, you could never drink seventeen bottles," remarked the flaxen-fair man.

"As I'm an honest man, I'm telling you I did drink that many," answered Nozdrev.

"You can say whatever you like, but I'm telling you you won't drink even ten."

"Well, do you want to make a bet I will?"

"Why bet on a thing like that?"

"There, you stake the gun you bought in town."

"I don't want to."

"Well, just stake it—see what'll come of it!"

"I don't want even to try."

"Why, you'd be shy a gun just as sure as you're standing there. Eh, brother Chichikov, I can't tell how sorry I felt you weren't there. I know that you and Lieutenant Kuvshinikov would have become inseparable. How well we'd have gotten along together! This isn't the same thing as the Public Prosecutor and all the provincial skinflints in our town, who simply shiver in their boots over every copper. This fellow, brother o' mine, will go for faro or banker, and for anything and everything you like. Eh, Chichikov, how would it have put you out to come? Really, you're a swine not to have done it, you cattle breeder, you! Kiss me, my soul, I'm no end fond of you! Look you, Mizhuev, fate itself has brought us together! There, now, what is he to me, or I to him? He has come God knows whence, and I happen to be just a fellow living hereabouts. . . . And how many carriages there were, brother, and all that *en gros*, on a grand scale. I had a whirl at the wheel of fortune, too, and won two jars of pomade, a porcelain cup, and a guitar; then had one more go and, deuce take it, lost everything and six silver men on top of that. And if you but knew what a man Kuvshinikov is for a petticoat! He and I were at almost all the balls. There was one fair creature at one of them dressed to kill, all frills and furbelows, and the Devil alone knows what else she didn't have on. . . . All I do is to think to myself: 'May the Devil take me!' But Kuvshinikov, now, what a scoundrel he is! He sits down near her and starts dishing out compliments to her in French, and what compliments! Would you believe it, he wouldn't let even common countrywives pass by him. 'Helping oneself to strawberries,' he calls it. There were some wonderful fresh fish and salted sturgeon steaks brought to the fair. I managed to bring a dried and salted sturgeon with me—good thing I bethought myself of buying it while I was still in the money. Where are you bound to now?"

"Why, I just have to see a certain party," Chichikov told him.

"Oh, what does that certain party matter? Drop him! Let's go to my place!"

"Can't, can't; there's a certain business I must attend to."

"There, now it's business! Now you've even thought up a business matter! Oh, you Quacksalve Ivanovich!"

"Really, there is a business matter and an urgent one, at that."

"I'm laying odds you're lying! There, now, just tell me whom you're going to see!"

"Well, it's Sobakevich."

Here Nozdrev burst into that ringing laughter which only a vigorous healthy male peals forth who can show every tooth in his head, and each of those teeth as white as refined sugar, whose cheeks quiver and shake, while a fellow lodger, behind two doors and in the third room from his, jumps up from his sleep, with his eyes starting out of his head, and says: "Something sure must have struck that fellow as funny!"

"Well, what's so amusing about that?" asked Chichikov, somewhat nettled by such laughter.

But Nozdrev went on with his full-throated laughter as he kept on saying: "Oh, have mercy! Honestly, I'll burst from laughing!"

"There's nothing amusing about it; I gave him my word."

"Why, you'll be sorry you were ever born when you come to his place—that fellow can simply milk a billy goat into a sieve! Why, I know your character, you'll come a bad cropper if you think you'll find a good game of banker there and a good bottle of Bon-Bon or something like that. Listen to me, brother o' mine, you just send that Sobakevich packing to the Devil, now! Let's you and me go to my place! What salted sturgeon steak I'll treat you to! How Ponomarev, the low-down beast, scraped and bowed as he told me: 'It's only to you I'd sell it; you could search the whole fair through,' he says, 'and never find the like of that sturgeon.' He's a terrible rogue, just the same. I told him as much to his face. 'You,' I told him, 'and our tax farmer are swindlers of the first water.' He laughed, the low-down beast, and just stroked his beard. Kuvshinikov and I breakfasted at his place every day. Ah, brother, here's what I forgot to tell you—I know you'll pester the life out of me after you see it, but I won't give it up to you, not for ten thousand I won't, I'm telling you that beforehand. Hey, there, Porphyry!" he began shouting, walking up to the window, calling his servant who was holding a small knife in one hand and in the other a crust of bread with a piece of dried and salted sturgeon which he had had the luck to snip off as he had been taking something out of the carriage. "Hey, there, Porphyry!" Nozdrev shouted. "Fetch that pup, now! What a pup!" he went on, turning to Chichikov. "It's a steal; its owner would rather have given up his own life than give up that pup. I promised him the light-chestnut mare—you remember, the one I got in a swap from Hvostyrev—"

Chichikov, however, had in all his born days never laid eyes either on the mare or on Hvostyrev.

"Wouldn't you like to have a bite of something, Sir?" said the old woman at this point, walking up to Nozdrev.

"No, I'm not having anything. Eh, brother, did we have ourselves a good time! On second thought, let me have a glass of vodka. What sort have you got?"

"Anise," answered the old woman.

"Very well, then, let's have the anise," said Nozdrev.

"Let me have a glass while you're at it," said the flaxen-fair man.

"There was an actress at the theatre, the little rogue, who sang like any nightingale! Kuvshinikov, who was sitting next to me, says: 'There,' says he, 'brother, are some strawberries to help oneself to!' There must have been half a hundred show booths alone, I'm thinking. Fenardi somersaulted and whirled like a mill for four hours at a stretch." Here he took the glass from the hands of the old woman, who made him a low curtsy in return. "Ah, let's have him here!" he cried out, catching sight of Porphyry, who had entered with a puppy. Porphyry was dressed in the same style as his master, in some sort of short Tatar kaftan fastened with hooks and quilted with cotton but somewhat more soiled.

"Let's have him—put him down on the floor!"

Porphyry put the puppy down on the floor and, with all its four legs sprawled out, it fell to sniffing the ground.

"There's a pup for you!" said Nozdrev, picking him up

with one hand by the loose skin on his back. The puppy let out a rather piteous whimper.

"However, you haven't done what I told you to do," remarked Nozdrev, turning to Porphyry and examining the puppy's belly painstakingly. "You didn't even think of combing him out?"

"No, I did comb him out."

"Why has he got fleas, then?"

"I wouldn't be knowing. Could be that they'd crawled onto him out of the carriage, maybe."

"You lie, you lie—you didn't as much as give a thought to combing him out; I'm thinking you've even let some of your own on him in addition, you fool. There, take a look now, Chichikov, what ears he has; there; run a hand over them."

"What for? I can see even so; he's of a good breed," Chichikov answered him.

"No, do take him, just you feel his ears."

Chichikov, just to please him, felt the pup's ears, saying: "Yes, he'll turn out a good hound."

"And the nose, now, do you feel how cold it is? There, just touch it."

Since he did not want to hurt the other's feelings, Chichikov felt the puppy's nose as well, saying: "He has a keen scent."

"A real pug," Nozdrev went on. "I must confess I've been hankering for a pug for a long time. There, Porphyry, take him away."

Porphyry, picking up the puppy under its belly, bore it off to the carriage.

"Listen, Chichikov, you must come to my place right

now, without fail; it's only three miles and a half or so to it. We'll make it in one spurt and after that, if you like, you can even go on to Sobakevich."

"Well, and why not?" Chichikov thought to himself. "Guess I'll really drop in at Nozdrev's. In what way is he worse than the others? Just as human as they, and on top of that he's lost his shirt gambling. He's ready for anything and everything, apparently; therefore one may wheedle a thing or two out of him for a song."

"Let's go, then, if you like," said he. "But I warn you, don't detain me; time is precious to me."

"There, that's the way, my friend! That's good! Hold on, now, I'll kiss you for that!" Here Nozdrev and Chichikov kissed each other. "That's just glorious—the three of us will go tooling along together."

"No, you'll really have to let me off, now, please," said the flaxen-fair man. "I have to be getting home."

"Nonsense, nonsense, brother; I shan't let you off."

"Really, my wife will be angry with me. Why, now you can just shift to his carriage."

"Never, never, never! Don't even think of such a thing!"

The flaxen-fair fellow was one of those people whose character evinces, at first glance, a certain streak of stubbornness. You hardly have time to open your mouth when they're already all set to argue and, it seems, under no circumstances will they ever consent to that which is obviously contrary to their way of thinking, or consent to call that sensible which is stupid and, in particular, never consent to dance to another's tune; and yet it will always wind up by a certain soft spot in their make-up coming to the fore, by their consenting to precisely that which they had been rejecting; that which is stupid they will call sensible, and will thereafter set off to dancing to another's tune in a way that could not be bettered—in short, they'll start off smoothly and end up uncouthly.

"Bosh!" said Nozdrev in answer to one of the objections of the flaxen-fair man, put the cap on his flaxen-fair head, and the flaxen-fair one trotted off at their heels.

"You haven't paid for the tots of vodka yet, Sir," the old woman reminded Nozdrev.

"Ah, right you are, right you are, mother! I say, brother-in-law, dear, you pay for me, please! I haven't got a copper in my pocket!"

"How much is coming to you?" asked the brother-in-law, dear.

"Why, how much should it be, father o' mine? Twenty kopecks, all in all," said the old woman.

"You lie, you lie! Give her half, that will be more than enough for her."

"Kind of little, Sir," said the old woman; however, she accepted the silver coin with gratitude, and even made a headlong dash to hold the door open for them. She was not really out anything, inasmuch as she had asked four times as much as the drinks were worth.

The wayfarers seated themselves. Chichikov's carriage rode side by side with that of Nozdrev's brother-in-law, and therefore all three could freely converse among themselves during the whole way. Nozdrev's small wretched calash, drawn by the hired skin-and-bones nags, trailed after them, continually falling behind. It was occupied by Porphyry and the puppy.

Inasmuch as the conversation which the travelers were

carrying on among themselves is of no great interest to the reader, we will do better if we say something about Nozdrev himself, whom, perchance, it may befall to play by no means the least rôle in our epic.

Nozdrev's face is by now most probably familiar to the reader. There isn't a man but has had to encounter not a few individuals like him. They're called free-and-easy chaps, have the reputation, even during their childhood and schooldays, of being good friends, and yet, with all that, are quite painfully beaten up from time to time. Upon their faces is always to be perceived something frank, direct, audacious. They make your acquaintance quickly, and you hardly have time to turn around before they're already *thou*ing you. When they form a friendship, you might think it is forever and a day, but almost always things so fall out that he who has become friends with one of these individuals will have a fight with him that same evening at a friendly drinking bout. They're always great chatterers, revelers, dashing horsemen—folk that strike your eye. Nozdrev, at thirty, was absolutely the same as he had been at twenty and at seventeen—a great hand for having a good time. His marriage had not changed him in the least, inasmuch as his wife had soon passed on into another world, leaving two urchins behind her, of whom he had absolutely no need. However, there was a rather comely nurse to look after the children. He could not, somehow, stay at home for more than a day at a time. His keen scent could smell out even at a distance of a few score miles where a fair might be going on, with all sorts of assemblies and balls, and, as fast as you could blink an eye, he'd be there, argufying and creating a rumpus at the green-baize tables, inasmuch as he had, like all his kind, a low-down passion for the Devil's prayer book. When it came to turning the leaves of this prayer book he was, as we have already seen from the first chapter, not altogether without sin, nor entirely fair and square, being wise in many and sundry palmings and other refinements of trimming, and for that reason the game would often wind up with another sort of game: either they drubbed and stomped him, or else went in for palming and trimming his thick and very good-looking side whiskers so that at times he would come home with only one and that one quite scanty. But his healthy and full cheeks were so well constructed and held such a power of growth that the side whiskers would soon sprout anew, and even more lux-uriantly than the preceding crop. And—which is the strangest of all, which can happen in Russia alone—after a lapse of some time he would again meet those friends who had given him a shellacking and, at that, meet them as though there had never been a thing between them; he paid it no mind, as the saying goes, and they paid it no mind ei-ther.

Nozdrev, in a certain respect, was a man of affairs. There was nary a gathering at which he was present where things got along without an affair. Some affair or other was in-evitably bound to arise: either the gendarmes would lead him by the arm out of the hall, or none other than his own cronies would be compelled to give him the heave-ho. But if such an affair didn't befall, then nevertheless there would be some such thing as could never befall anybody else: ei-ther he would become so quiffy at the buffet that he would be able to do nothing but laugh, or else he would lie such a blue streak that he himself would become conscience-stricken. And he would tell a pack of lies utterly without any need: he would suddenly relate that he had a horse with some kind of blue hide, or pink, and suchlike poppycock, so that his auditors would, to a man, walk away from him at last, saying: "Well, brother, you're laying it on thick for fair, it looks like!"

There are certain folk who have a low-down passion for playing some vile trick on their fellow man, at times without any earthly reason for it. One, for instance, a man who has even attained to high rank, with a noble appearance, with a star gracing his bosom, will be clasping your hand as he discusses with you profound subjects which call for meditative reflection; yet later on, right on the spot, you look and before your very eyes he will pull some vile stunt at your expense, and will pull it in such a way as a common collegiate registrar might, and not at all in the way a man with a star gracing his bosom would who discusses subjects that call for serious reflection, so that you can but stand there and wonder, with a shrug, and there isn't a thing else on earth you can do. Just as strange a passion did Nozdrev have. The more intimate anybody became with him, the more willingly would Nozdrev put the skids under him, of all people; he would spread some wild tale, so silly that it would be difficult to think up a sillier to top it; he would break up a marriage or a business deal, yet would not at all consider himself your enemy; on the contrary, if chance ever led him to meet you again, he would treat you anew as a close friend and would even say: "Why, you're such a low-down fellow, you never drop in on me!"

Nozdrev, in many respects, was a many-sided man—that is, he was ready to try his hand at anything. In the same breath he would propose to go with you wherever you wished—to the end of the earth, even—would propose entering with you on any enterprise you like, to swap everything in the world for anything you like. A gun, a dog, a horse—anything could form the basis for a swap, but not at all in order to gain anything: the swap was undertaken only from some sort of turbulently indefatigable impetuosity and liveliness of character. If, at a fair, he had the good luck of coming upon a simpleton and trimming him, he would buy up a mountain of whatever things happened to meet his eye first in the shops: horse collars, incense pastilles, neckerchiefs for the nurse, a stallion, raisins, a silver wash basin, Holland linen, farina, tobacco, pistols, herrings, pictures, a turning lathe, pots, boots, faïence dishes—as long as his money lasted. However, it but rarely happened that these things reached home: almost the same day they would be lost to some other, luckier gamester, at times even his own pipe, with tobacco pouch and amber mouthpiece, would be added to the other things and, on occasion, his whole team of four horses and everything that went with it—not only calash but the coachman as well—so that the master himself would have to set out in a bobtailed, wretched frock coat, or a short Tatar kaftan, to seek out some friend of his, to get a lift home in his vehicle.

That's the sort of fellow Nozdrev was! Perhaps people will call him a hackneyed character, will start saying that there is no Nozdrev in existence nowadays. Alas, those who are going to say such things will be unjust. Nozdrev will not die off this earth for a long time yet. He is everywhere in our midst, merely walking about in a coat of a different cut, it may be; but men are frivolously unperceptive and a fellow in a coat of a different cut will look to them like an entirely different fellow.

In the meantime the three vehicles had already rolled up to the front steps of Nozdrev's house. There had been no preparation whatsoever for their reception within. In the middle of the dining room stood wooden trestles, and two muzhiks, standing on them, were whitewashing the walls, chanting some endless song; the floor was all spattered with the whitewash. Nozdrev immediately ordered the muzhiks to clear out and take the trestles with them, and dashed off into another room to issue additional commands. His guests heard him giving orders for the dinner to the chef; Chichikov, who was beginning to feel his appetite somewhat, taking everything into consideration perceived that they would not sit down to the table before five. Nozdrev, returning, led his guests off to inspect everything he had in his village and, in a little over two hours, showed them absolutely all, so that there was nothing left to show! First of all they went to inspect the stable, where they beheld two mares, one a gray piebald, the other a light chestnut; then a bay stallion, not much to look at, but for whom Nozdrev swore he had paid ten thousand.

"You didn't give any ten thousand for him," remarked his brother-in-law. "He isn't worth even a thousand."

"By God, I did so give ten thousand!" Nozdrev maintained.

"You can swear by God till you're blue in the face," his brother-in-law commented.

"There now, would you like to lay a bet on it?" asked Nozdrev.

But his brother-in-law didn't want to lay a bet.

After that Nozdrev showed them empty stalls which had previously been occupied by other thoroughbreds. In the same stable they beheld a goat which, according to the ancient belief, it was necessary to keep with the horses, which goat, apparently, lived on good terms with them and strolled about under their bellies as if he were perfectly at home. After that Nozdrev led them off to have a look at a wolf whelp, which was kept on a tether.

"There's a wolf whelp for you!" he said. "I purposely feed him raw meat. I want him to be a perfect brute."

They went for a look at the pond where, if Nozdrev's words were to be believed, fish were to be found so big that it was all two men could do to drag one of them out—which, however, was something that his relative did not fail to express his doubts about.

"Chichikov," said Nozdrev, "I'm going to show you a most excellent pair of dogs; the firmness of their black bodies will simply amaze you; they have hackles like needles!" And he led them to a very handsomely constructed little building, surrounded by a yard that was fenced in on all sides. When they entered the yard they saw all sorts of dogs there, shaggy as well as smooth-coated, of all possible colors and breeds: tan, black with markings of white, liver-colored-and-skewbald, tan-and-skewbald, red-and-skewbald, black-eared, gray-eared. . . . Here were all the nicknames, all the imperative tenses: Shoot, Scold, Flit, Scrape, Pester, Get Hot; Fire, Sloper, Northerner, Darling, Reward, Lady Guardian. Nozdrev in their midst was absolutely like a father in the midst of his family; all of them at once, turning up their tails—which dog-keepers call *rudders*—dashed straight at the guests and began to get acquainted. Half a score or so of them placed their forepaws on Nozdrev's shoulders. Scold evinced the same sort of friendship for Chichikov and, getting up on his hind legs, licked him right on the lips with his tongue, so that Chichikov had to spit without much ceremony. They looked over the dogs, the firmness of whose black bodies would amaze you—and good dogs they were, at that. Then they set out to look at a Crimean bitch, who was blind by now and, according to Nozdrev's words, due to peg out shortly, but, only two years back, she'd been a very fine bitch. So they looked this bitch over as well, and the bitch, sure enough, was blind. Then they set out to look over the watermill, which lacked the part whereon the upper millstone rests as it quickly revolves on a shaft—the part called the *flutterer,* according to the wondrously apt expression of the muzhik.

"And now we're coming to a smithy," said Nozdrev. And, believe it or not, after going on a little way, they saw a blacksmith's shop. They looked the blacksmith's shop over as well.

"On that field there," said Nozdrev, pointing his finger at a field, "there's such an awful lot of winter hares that you can't see the ground for them; I myself caught one by his hind legs with my bare hands."

"Well, now, you'll never catch a winter hare with your bare hands," remarked his brother-in-law.

"But I tell you I caught one; I deliberately caught one!" Nozdrev answered him. "Now I'm going to take you"—he turned to Chichikov—"to see the boundary line where my land ends."

Nozdrev led his visitors through a field that, in many

places, consisted of tussocks. They had to make their way between fallow lands and furrowed corn fields. Chichikov was beginning to feel fatigue. In many places their feet made water spurt forth, so low-lying was this bog. At first they were cautious and set their feet down with care, but then, seeing that this was of no avail, they slogged right on, without choosing between the deeper or the shallower mire. Having gone a considerable distance they beheld, believe it or not, the boundary line, consisting of a short round wooden post as a marker and a narrow trench.

"There's the boundary!" said Nozdrev. "Everything that you see on this side is mine, all of it, and even on the other side, that whole forest that shows so blue over there, is mine, as well as everything beyond the forest—it's all mine too."

"But whenever did that forest become yours?" his brother-in-law questioned him. "Why, did you buy it recently? For it wasn't yours before."

"Yes, I bought it recently," answered Nozdrev.

"How did you ever contrive to buy it so quickly?"

"Oh, yes, I bought it three days ago, and, the Devil take it, I gave a high price for it."

"But you were away at the fair at that time—"

"Oh, you yokel! For can't one be at a fair and yet buy land? Very well, so I was at the fair, but my steward up and bought it without my being present."

"Oh, well, the steward could have bought it," said his brother-in-law, but even then he had his doubts and shook his head.

The visitors returned by the same vile route to the house. Nozdrev led them off to his study in which, however, there were not to be found any traces of that which is usual to studies—books and papers, that is; all they saw there in the way of adornment was two swords and two guns—one of the latter had cost three hundred rubles and the other eight hundred. Nozdrev's brother-in-law, having looked them over, merely shook his head. After that the host exhibited to them genuine Turkish daggers—one of which, however, through some error, was engraved with *Made by Savelii Sibiriakov.* Following this a hurdy-gurdy was exhibited to the guests. Nozdrev, right then and there, ground out a thing or two for them. The hurdy-gurdy played not unpleasingly but, apparently, something must have happened to its innards, inasmuch as a mazurka wound up with "Malbrouk to the Wars Has Gone," while "Malbrouk to the Wars Has Gone" was unexpectedly terminated by some long-familiar waltz. Nozdrev had long since quit grinding, but the hurdy-gurdy had one particularly lively reed that would not quiet down, and for a while thereafter it kept on tootling of its own accord. Then came a display of tobacco pipes: of brier, of clay, of meerschaum, broken-in and new, in chamois purses and without chamois purses, a chibouk with a mouthpiece of amber, recently won at play, a tobacco pouch embroidered by a certain countess who, at some stage post or other, had fallen head over heels in love with him and whose minim hands, according to his words, were the most subtle *superfles*—a word that, for him, probably signified the very acme of perfection.

After a snack of salted sturgeon they sat down at the table about five. The dinner table, evidently, did not con-

stitute for Nozdrev the main thing in life; the courses did
not play a great rôle in the dinner; this dish or that was actually burnt; this dish or that hadn't even been thoroughly
cooked. It was evident that the chef was guided for the
most part by some weird inspiration and would pop into
the pot the first thing that came to his hand; if the pepper-
pot happened to be standing near by he would sprinkle in
the pepper; if cabbage came handy, he would shove in the
cabbage; he slopped in milk, ham, peas—in short, slap,
dash, as long as it was hot, and as for the taste, well, some
sort of taste would probably emerge in the end. But to
make up for all that Nozdrev leant heavily on wine: even
before soup was served he had poured out for each guest a
large glass of port and another of Haut Sauterne, inasmuch
as in provincial capitals and district towns there is no such
thing to be found as ordinary Sauterne. Next Nozdrev ordered a bottle of Madeira to be brought, "And not even the
Field Marshal himself has ever drunk a better." The
Madeira, to be sure, actually burned one's mouth, inasmuch as the wine merchants, knowing well by now the
taste of the landed proprietors who were fond of good
Madeira, hocussed it unmercifully with rum, and on occasion even poured into it vodka as well, the kind called
Czar's vodka, the most ferocious of all, trusting that Russian stomachs would stand anything and everything. Then
Nozdrev also ordered a certain particular bottle to be
fetched which, according to his own unorthodox terminol-
ogy, was both a Bourgognion and a Champagnion, all in
one. He was most zealous in pouring the drink into the
glasses to his right and left, both into Chichikov's and into
his brother-in-law's; Chichikov happened to notice, how-

ever, that he did not add a great deal to his own glass. This compelled him to be cautious and, as soon as Nozdrev would happen to become absorbed in talk or would be filling up his brother-in-law's glass, Chichikov would on the instant tip his glass over into his plate. After a brief interval a cordial made from rowan berries was brought in and placed on the table, which cordial, according to Nozdrev's words, tasted exactly like cream, but in which, amazingly enough, one could perceive moonshine in all its potency. Then they drank balsam of some sort, bearing a name that was hard to remember, and even the host himself gave it another name when he had occasion to mention it a second time.

The dinner had long since ended and all the wines had already been tasted, yet the guests still sat on at the table. Chichikov under no circumstances wished to broach his main object to Nozdrev in the presence of his brother-in-law; after all, his brother-in-law was an outsider, whereas the object demanded a private and friendly talk. However, Nozdrev's brother-in-law could hardly have been regarded as a person to feel apprehensive about, inasmuch as he had, apparently, taken on a sufficient load and, seated in his chair, kept going off to sleep every minute or so. Perceiving himself that he was in a rather precarious state he began, at last, begging to go home, but in such a drawling and listless voice as if, according to the Russian expression, he were putting a collar on a horse with a pair of pincers.

"Oh, never, never! I'm not going to let you go!" said Nozdrev.

"No, don't you be takin' advantish of me, m'friend—really, I'm goin'," his brother-in-law was saying. "You mean to take a great advantish of me."

"Nonsense, nonsense! We're going to make up a game of banker right now!"

"No, brother, you go 'head and make it up by yoursheff, but I can't take a hand in it: my wife will be ver', ver' angry with me, really; I've got to tell her everythin' 'bout the fair. I've got to, brother, really, I've got to give her that pleasure. No, don't you be keepin' me back."

"Eh, send your wife to . . . Really, one could think you two were going to do something mighty important together!"

"No, don't say that, brother! She's sush a good wife to me! That's a positive fact—she's a model wife, sho worthy of eshteem and sho true! She does sush things for me . . . would you believe it, it makes tears come to my eyes. No; don't you be keepin' me; I'm tellin' you, as an honest man, that I'm goin'. I assure you I am—crossh my heart!"

"Let him go; what good is he?" Chichikov suggested to Nozdrev on the quiet.

"Why, that's true enough," said Nozdrev. "I have a mortal dislike of people who go all to pieces like that!" And he added, more loudly: "Well, the Devil with you; go and have a good time with your wife, you horse's twat, you!"

"No, brother, don't you go curshin' me for a horshe'sh twat," protested his brother-in-law. "I owe her my life. Really, now, she's sush a kind soul, sho darling; she'sh sho lovin' to me . . . it moves me to tearsh. She'll ask me what I shaw at the fair—I'll have to tell her everythin'. . . . Really, now, she'sh sush a darlin'."

"Well, go on home, then; tell her a pack of lying nonsense! Here's your cap."

"No, brother, you oughtn't to be shaying things like that 'bout her at all, at all; by doing that same you, one may shay, are doin' a wrong to my own sheff, she'sh sush a darlin'."

"Well, then, go to her—the sooner the better!"

"Yesh, brother, I'll go; forgive me for not being able to shtay. I'd be glad to, with all my shoul, but I can't."

His brother-in-law for a long while kept on reiterating his excuses, without noticing that he himself had long been sitting in his carriage, had long since driven out of the gates, and that for a long while only the deserted fields lay before him. It must be supposed that his wife did not hear many details about the fair from him that night.

"What trash!" Nozdrev was saying, standing before the window and watching the receding vehicle. "Look at him go! That little off-horse of his isn't bad; I've long since been wanting to get hold of it. But then there's no getting together on terms with him. A horse's twat, just a plain horse's twat!"[3]

After that they came back into the dining room. Porphyry brought in candles and Chichikov noticed in the hands of his host a pack of cards that had bobbed up from no one knew where.

"Well, what do you say, brother?" Nozdrev was saying, squeezing the sides of the deck with his fingers and buckling it a little, so that the band about it burst and flew off. "I'm starting the bank at three hundred—oh, just to pass the time away!"

But Chichikov made believe he had not even heard what the host was talking about and said, as though he had just recalled it suddenly: "Ah! Before it slips my mind, I have a certain request to make of you."

"What is it?"

"Give me your word first that you'll grant it to me."

"But what is your request?"

"Well, you just give me your word!"

"If you like——"

"Your word of honor?"

"My word of honor!"

"Here's my request: you must have, I surmise, a large number of dead serfs who haven't yet been taken off the census in the Bureau of Audits?"

"Why, so I have. What of that?"

"Transfer them to me, let them stand in my name."

"And what would you be wanting with them?"

"Why, I happen to need them."

"But whatever in the world for?"

"Why, I just happen to need them . . . for reasons of my own; in short, I need them."

"Well, now, you must have cooked up something, for sure. Own up—what is it?"

"Why, what could I have cooked up? Out of a trifle like that one could hardly cook up anything."

"But what do you need them for?"

"Oh, what an inquisitive fellow! He'd like to lay his hands on every sort of trash—and stick his nose into it as well!"

"But how is it you don't want to say anything about it?"

"Yes, but how would it profit you to know? Well, I want them just so; I've gotten a whim, sort of, into my head."

"Very well, then; until such time as you tell me I'm not going through with it."

"There, you see now; that's already actually dishonest on your part—you give your word, and then start backing out."

"Well, you may act as you wish; but I'm not doing anything until you tell me what you want them for."

"What could I possibly tell him?" Chichikov thought to himself and, after a moment's reflection, declared that he needed the dead serf souls to acquire a position in society; that he did not own any large estates and so, until such time as he did, he ought at least to be able to lay claim to some wretched souls, of any sort.

"You lie, you lie!" said Nozdrev, without letting him finish. "You lie, brother!"

Even Chichikov himself perceived that his invention was none too clever, and that his pretext was rather feeble.

"Very well, then, I'll be more straightforward with you," he said, having recovered himself, "only please don't let it out to anybody. I've gotten it into my head to marry; but you must know that my bride's father and mother are most ambitious folk. What a fix I'm in, to be sure! I'm sorry I ever became mixed up with them; they want their daughter's bridegroom to have no less than three hundred serfs, without fail, and since I have practically all of a hundred and fifty peasants lacking—"

"There, you're lying, you're lying!" Nozdrev again took to shouting.

"Well, now," said Chichikov, "this time I haven't lied even that much," and he marked off with his thumb the very least moiety from the tip of his little finger.

"I'll stake my head on it you're lying!"

"I say, though, this is insulting! What am I, after all? Really, why must I necessarily be lying?"

"Oh, come, after all, I know you; you're a great swindler, allow me to tell you that out of friendship! If I were your superior official I would hang you on the first tree I came to."

Chichikov took offense at this remark, since he always found distasteful every expression that was to any extent coarse or derogatory to his dignity. He actually did not like to tolerate familiar treatment of himself in any case whatsoever, unless, perhaps, the person extending such treatment was of far too lofty a station. And for these reasons he now became thoroughly offended.

"By God, I'd hang you," Nozdrev reiterated. "I'm telling you this frankly, not so as to offend you, but simply as a friend."

"There are limits to everything," said Chichikov, with a feeling of dignity. "If you want to show off with speeches like that you'd better go to the barracks," and immediately added: "If you don't want to make me a present of them, then you might sell them to me."

"Sell them! Why, I know you—why, you're a scoundrel—why, would you give anything like a price for them?"

"Eh, but you're a fine fellow, too! Look here! What are your souls like, made of diamonds, or what?"

"There, it's just as I thought. Why, I knew what you were like."

"Good heavens, brother, what a grasping disposition you have! What you ought to do is simply make me a present of them!"

"Well, look here, just to prove to you that I'm not some sort of a skinflint, I won't take anything for those souls. Buy the stallion off me, and I'll throw the souls in."

"Good heavens, what would I do with a stallion?" asked Chichikov, really astonished by such a proposal.

"What do you mean, what would you do with him? Why, I paid ten thousand for him, yet I'm letting you have him for four."

"Yes, but what would I be doing with a stallion? I'm not running a stud farm."

"But look here, you don't understand; why, I'll take only a measly three thousand from you, and the other thousand you can pay me later."

"Yes, but I don't need a stallion, God be with him!"

"Well, then, buy the light-chestnut mare."

"I don't need a mare either."

"For the mare, and the gray horse that I showed you, I'll take only two thousand from you."

"Yes, but I don't need any horses."

"You'll sell them; they'll give you three times as much as you paid for them at the first fair."

"Then it would be better if you were to sell them yourself, since you're so sure you can make a triple profit on them."

"I know I could, but then I want you to get some good out of it too."

Chichikov thanked him for his good intentions and refused outright both the gray horse and the light-chestnut mare.

"Well, then, buy some of the dogs. I'll sell you such a pair as will make you tingle with delight; the bitch has whiskers, so help me; their coats bristle like a badger's; the way their ribs are rounded like a barrel is something beyond the mind to grasp; their paws are just like pads, they won't leave tracks on the ground!"

"But what would I be doing with dogs? I don't hunt."

"Why, I'd like you to have dogs. Look here, now: if you don't want the dogs, then buy the hurdy-gurdy from me. A marvelous hurdy-gurdy! It cost me, as I am an honest man, a thousand and a half; I'll give it away to you for nine hundred."

"But what would I be doing with a hurdy-gurdy? For I'm no German, to be lugging it up and down all the roads, begging for coppers."

"But this isn't the sort of hurdy-gurdy the Germans carry around. It's an organ; take a special look at it, it's all made of mahogany. There, I'll show it to you once more!"

At this point Nozdrev, seizing Chichikov by the hand, began dragging him into the other room and, no matter how the latter held back, hand and foot, resisting, and protesting that he already knew what the hurdy-gurdy was like, he nevertheless had to listen once more to just how Malbrouk to the wars had gone.

"If you don't want to lay out any money for it, then I'll tell you what I'll do, you just listen: I'll give you the hurdy-gurdy, *and* all the dead souls I own, as many as there are of them, and you give me your carriage and three hundred to boot."

"There, what else! And what am I going to travel about in?"

"I'll give you another carriage. There, let's go to the wagon shed, I'll show it to you! All you'll have to do will be to give it a new coat of paint, and you'll have a marvelous carriage!"

"Eh, some fiend that won't be downed must have gotten into him!" Chichikov thought to himself, and decided, no matter what happened, to get out of acquiring any light carriages, hurdy-gurdies, and all dogs of any sort whatsoever, despite the barrel-like formation of their ribs, beyond the powers of the mind to grasp, and the padlike formation of their paws.

"Why, you get the light carriage, the hurdy-gurdy, *and* the dead souls, all in one lot!"

"Don't want them!" Chichikov refused once more.

"But just why don't you want them?"

"Because I simply don't want them—and that's all there is to it."

"Really, now, what a man you are! I can see one can't deal with you the way one usually deals with good friends and comrades.... What a fellow, really! One can see at once that you're a two-faced fellow!"

"Well, what am I, a fool, really? You just judge for yourself: why should I acquire anything I have absolutely no need of?"

"There, now, don't talk any more, if you please. I know you very well by now. What a rascally creature you are, to be sure. Well, look here: do you want to have a go at a game of banker? I'll stake all the dead ones on one card, and the hurdy-gurdy, too."

"Well, to decide it by cards means to be subjected to the unknown," Chichikov said, and at the same time eyed askance the cards in his host's hands. Both of the shuffles which Nozdrev made looked very much like false ones to Chichikov, while the very design on the back of the cards seemed quite suspicious.

"But why the unknown?" scoffed Nozdrev. "There's nothing of the unknown about it! If there be but any luck on your side, you can win a hell of a lot. There it is, what luck!" he was saying, beginning to throw out the cards, to arouse interest. "What luck! What luck! There, it just runs after you! There's that cursed nine on which I lost every stitch I had! I felt it would sell me out but, just the same, shutting my eyes, I thought to myself: 'May the Devil take you, go ahead and sell me out, and be damned to you!' "

While Nozdrev was speaking thus, Porphyry brought in another bottle. But Chichikov refused positively either to play or to drink.

"But why don't you want to play?" asked Nozdrev.

"Well, just because I don't feel so disposed. And besides, to tell you the truth, I'm not at all fond of playing."

"But why aren't you fond of it?"

Chichikov shrugged his shoulders and said: "Because I'm not."

"What a rubbishy fellow you are!"

"Well, what can I do? That's the way God made me."

"You're just a horse's twat! I was thinking up to now that

you're a decent fellow, at least to some extent, but you don't understand good treatment, nohow. There's no way of talking with you as one would with someone intimate, nohow. There's no straightforwardness at all about you, no sincerity! You're a perfect Sobakevich, that's the sort of scoundrel you are!"

"But what are you cursing me for? Am I at fault because I don't play? Sell me the souls by themselves, if you're the sort of a man who shivers over such trash."

"You'll get fiddlesticks out of me! I wanted to give them to you for nothing, I did, but now you'll never get them! If you were to give me three kingdoms for them I wouldn't give them to you. What a sharper! You're as abominable as a chimney sweep. From now on I want to have nothing whatsoever to do with you. Porphyry, you go and tell the stableman not to give any oats to his horses—let them eat hay, that's good enough for them!"

This last decision was something utterly unexpected to Chichikov.

"It would be best if you'd simply never show me your face again!" announced Nozdrev.

Despite such a falling-out, however, the host and his guest had supper together, although this time there were no wines whatsoever with fancy labels standing on the table. There was only one bottle sticking up like a sore thumb, of some Cyprus wine, which was in every way of the sort that is called red ink. After supper Nozdrev told Chichikov, leading him off to a side room where a bed had been made for him: "There's your bed! I don't want to wish you a good night, even."

Chichikov, after Nozdrev's departure, was left in a most unpleasant state of spirits. Inwardly he was vexed with himself, upbraiding himself for having gone with Nozdrev and losing his time for nothing; but still more did he upbraid himself for having broached this business to him; he had acted incautiously, like a child, like a fool, inasmuch as the business was not at all of such a nature as a Nozdrev could be trusted to know. . . . Nozdrev, as a man, was so much trash; Nozdrev was capable of telling a pack of lies, of bruiting about the Devil alone knew what—likely as not, there would be plenty of crazy rumors as a result. . . . It was bad, bad! "I'm simply a fool!" he kept saying to himself. He slept very poorly that night. Some sort of tiny, exceedingly lively insects were biting him, inflicting unbearable pain, so that he would scrape the bitten place with his whole hand, adding: "Ah, may the Devil take you, together with Nozdrev!" He awoke early in the morning. The first thing he did, after putting on a dressing gown and pulling on his boots, was to set out through the yard toward the stable, to give Seliphan orders about harnessing the light carriage immediately. As he was returning through the yard he encountered Nozdrev, who was also in a dressing gown, with a pipe clenched between his teeth.

Nozdrev greeted him friendlily and inquired how he had slept.

"So-so," Chichikov replied, quite dryly.

"As for me, brother," said Nozdrev, "I've had such vile things bothering me all night that it's a foul thing even to tell about them; and my mouth, after yesterday, feels as if a squadron had bivouacked there. Just imagine, I dreamt that I was flogged—I swear it, I swear I dreamt that. And just imagine who it was that flogged me? There, you'll never guess it, it was Second Captain of Cavalry Potseluev—he and Kuvshinikov."

"Yes," Chichikov thought to himself, "it would be a good thing if you were really to be skinned alive."

"Yes, flogged, by God! And most painfully! I awoke and, the Devil take it, something was really making me scratch—probably those damned witch-fleas. Well, you go and dress now; I'll come to see you right away. All I've got to do is to bawl out my scoundrel of a steward."

Chichikov went off to his room to wash and dress. When, after doing so, he came out into the dining room, the tea things and a bottle of rum were already standing on the table. There were traces of yesterday's dinner and supper in the room; the floor brush, apparently, had not been applied at all. Bread crumbs were all over the floor, while tobacco ashes were to be seen even on the tablecloth. The host himself, who lost no time in entering, did not have a thing on under his dressing gown, but his exposed chest sprouted a luxuriant something that looked like a beard. Chibouk in hand and sipping out of a teacup, he would have made a very picturesque subject for a painter who had no overwhelming love for slicked-down and curlicued gentlemen, like to wigmakers' signs, or for those who are closely clipped.

"Well, what do you think?" asked Nozdrev, after a short silence. "Wouldn't you like to play for those souls?"

"I've already told you, brother, that I don't play; if you'd like me to buy them I'll do so, by all means."

"I don't want to sell them—that wouldn't be the friendly thing to do. What the Devil, I'm not going to start picking up coppers off a dunghill with my teeth. A little game of banker, now, that's another matter. Let's have one little deal at least!"

"I've already told you—no."

"But would you want to swap?"

"No, I wouldn't."

"Well, look here, let's have a game of checkers: if you win, the dead souls are all yours. For I have a lot of them that ought to be stricken from the census in the Bureau of Audits. Hey, there, Porphyry, bring the checkers and the checkerboard here!"

"You're putting yourself out for nothing—I'm not going to play."

"Why, this isn't like banker; there can be no luck or trickery here—everything depends on skill. I'm even telling you beforehand that I can't play the game at all unless you give me a handicap."

"Suppose I do sit down," Chichikov thought to himself, "and play him a game of checkers. I used to play checkers not so badly, and as for tricks, it would be hard for him to try any in this game."

"So be it, then, if you like; I'll play you a game of checkers."

"The souls are staked against a hundred rubles!"

"But why? It'll be enough if they're staked against fifty."

"No, what sort of stake is fifty? Better make it a hundred, and I'll throw in a fair-to-middlin' puppy or a gold watch seal."

"Very well, if you like!" said Chichikov.

"How many checkers do you give me as a handicap?" asked Nozdrev.

"Why should I? I'm not giving you any handicap, of course."

"Allow me two moves extra, at least."

"I don't want to; I play poorly myself."

"We know all about you fellows who claim to play poorly!" said Nozdrev, advancing one of his checkers.

"It's rather a long time since I've tried my hand at checkers!" said Chichikov, moving a checker.

"We know all about you fellows who claim to play poorly!" said Nozdrev, moving a checker but at the same time moving up another one as well with the cuff of his sleeve.

"It's rather a long time since I've tried my hand—hey, there! What's going on here, brother? You move that back from there!" said Chichikov.

"Move what back?"

"Why, that checker, now," said Chichikov, and at the same moment perceived, almost under his very nose, still another checker which, so it seemed, was trying to sneak through into the king's row. Whence it had bobbed up, God alone could tell. "No," said Chichikov, getting up from the table, "it's absolutely impossible to play with you. People don't move like that, three checkers at a time!"

"But why say there are three? That was just an error. One must have been moved forward by accident; I'll move it back, if you like."

"And where did the other one bob up from?"

"What other one?"

"Why, this one, that's trying to sneak into the king's row?"

"There you go! As though you didn't remember!"

"No, brother, I kept track of all the moves and remember everything; you put it there just now. There's the right square for it!"

"What do you mean? What square?" asked Nozdrev, turning red. "Why, brother, you're making things up, as I see it!"

"No, brother, it looks as if you were the one who's making things up—but not any too successfully."

"What do you take me for, then?" asked Nozdrev. "Why, am I the sort that goes in for cheating?"

"I don't think you're anything, only from now on I'm never going to play with you."

"No, you can't get out of it," said Nozdrev, getting up pressure, "the game has been started."

"I have the right to get out of it, because you're not playing in a way that befits an honest man."

"No, you're lying, you can't say such things!"

"No, brother, you're lying yourself!"

"I wasn't cheating, and you can't back out of it; you must finish the game!"

"You'll never make me do that," said Chichikov coolly and, walking up to the board, mixed up the checkers.

Nozdrev flared up and walked up so close to Chichikov that the latter had to back away a couple of steps.

"I'll make you play. Your mixing up the checkers doesn't matter! I remember all the moves. We'll place them back the way they were."

"No, brother; it's all over and done with; I'm not going to play with you."

"So you won't play?"

"You can see for yourself that it's impossible to play with you."

"No, you come right out with it: you don't want to play?" Nozdrev was saying, walking up closer.

"No, I don't want to," said Chichikov but, just the same, brought both his hands nearer his face, against any contingency, since things were really getting hot. This precaution was quite called for, inasmuch as Nozdrev swung his arm back . . . and there was a very great possibility that one of the full and prepossessing cheeks of our hero would have been covered with an ignominy that could never be washed away; but, having fortunately warded off the blow, he seized both of Nozdrev's eager hands and held them fast.

"Porphyry! Pavlushka!" Nozdrev kept yelling in fury, striving to free himself.

Hearing this, Chichikov released Nozdrev's hands so as not to allow the domestics to become witnesses to so temptingly demoralizing a scene, and feeling at the same time that it would have been useless to hold on to Nozdrev. At this very point Porphyry entered, and with him Pavlushka, a husky lout by the looks of him, with whom it would have been entirely disadvantageous to tangle.

"So you don't want to finish the game?" asked Nozdrev. "Come right out with it!"

"There's no possibility of finishing the game," said Chichikov, and glanced out of the window. He caught sight of his carriage, which was standing all ready, while Seliphan, it seemed, was merely waiting for a wave of the hand to roll up to the front entrance; but there was no earthly possibility of getting out of the room: there were two husky fools of serfs standing in the doorway.

"So you don't want to finish the game?" Nozdrev repeated, with a face that was as blazing as if it were actually on fire.

"If you had played like an honest man . . . but now I can't."

"Ah, so you don't want to, you scoundrel! When you saw that you weren't winning, why, you couldn't play? Beat him up!" he cried out frenziedly, turning to Porphyry and Pavlushka, while he himself clutched his chibouk, with its long cherry-wood stem, as if it were a club. Chichikov turned as white as a linen sheet. He wanted to say something, but felt that his lips were merely moving without making a sound.

"Beat him up!" Nozdrev kept yelling, clutching his cherry-wood chibouk and straining forward, all ablaze and sweating, as though he were storming an impregnable fortress. "Beat him up!" He kept yelling in much the same voice which some desperate lieutenant, whose harebrained bravery has already gained such a reputation that a specific order has been issued to hold him back by his arms during the heat of battle, uses to yell "Forward, lads!" to his platoon during a great assault. But the lieutenant has already felt the martial fervor, everything has begun going round and round in his head: Suvorov, that great general, soars in a vision before him; the lieutenant strains forward to perform a great deed. "Forward, lads!" he yells, dashing ahead, without reflecting that he is jeopardizing the plan of attack already decided upon, that countless gun muzzles are thrust out of the embrasures of the fortress, the impregnable walls of which reach up beyond the clouds, that his impotent platoon will be blown up into the air like so much swan's-down, and that the fated bullet is already whizzing through the air, just about to shut off his vociferous throat. But if Nozdrev was portraying in his person the lieutenant attacking the fortress, desperate and at a loss, the fortress he was storming did not in any way resemble an impregnable one. On the contrary, the fortress was experiencing such fright that its heart was in its very heels. Already the chair, with which he had conceived the notion of defending himself, had been wrested out of his hands by the serfs; already, with his eyes shut tight, neither dead nor alive, he was preparing for a taste of his host's Circassian chibouk, and God knows what might have befallen him; but it pleased the Fates to save the ribs, shoulders, and all the well-nurtured parts of our hero. In an unexpected fashion there suddenly came, as if from the clouds, the quivering sounds of jingle bells; there came clearly the rattle of cart wheels flying up to the front entrance, and the heavy snorting and labored breathing of the heated horses of a halted troika echoed even in the very room. All involuntarily looked out of the window: some mustachioed fellow in a semimilitary frock coat was clambering out of the cart. After inquiring in the entry, he entered at precisely the moment when Chichikov, not having yet had a chance to recover from his fright, was in just about the most piteous situation in which mortal man ever found himself.

"Permit me to ask, which one of you is Nozdrev?" said

the stranger, after looking with a certain perplexity at Nozdrev, who was standing with the chibouk in his hand, and at Chichikov, who was barely beginning to get over his unenviable situation.

"Allow me first to ask whom I have the honor of talking to?" asked Nozdrev, coming nearer to him.

"I am Captain of the District Police."

"And what is it you wish?"

"I have come to inform you of the notice communicated to me, that you are subject to arrest until such time as a final decision is reached in your trial."

"What nonsense is this—what trial?"

"You were implicated in an affair involving a personal assault, with birch rods, upon one Maximov, a landowner, while you were in a state of intoxication."

"You're lying! I never even set eyes on any landowner by the name of Maximov!"

"My dear Sir! Allow me to inform you that I am an officer. You can say such things to your servant, but not to me."

At this point Chichikov, without waiting for what answer Nozdrev would make to this, grabbed his cap as fast as ever he could and, shielding himself behind the Captain of the District Police, slipped out on the front steps, got into his light carriage, and ordered Seliphan to give his horses the whip and drive them for all they were worth.

CHAPTER FIVE

Our hero, however, had had a considerable fright. Although his light carriage raced along at a breakneck speed, and Nozdrev's village had long since vanished out of view, screened by fields, hillsides and hillocks, he nevertheless kept on looking over his shoulder with fear, as though expecting that at any moment a pursuit would overtake him. He drew his breath with difficulty, and when he attempted to place his hand against his heart he felt that it was fluttering like a caged quail. "Eh, what a fine kettle of fish he cooked up! Look you, what kind of a man he is!" At this point a great number of all sorts of hard and potent wishes were dispatched in Nozdrev's direction; one even came upon words that were not at all genteel. Well, what can one do about it? A Russian fellow, and heartily vexed, at that! In addition, this was not at all anything to jest about.

"No matter what you say," said Chichikov to himself, "but if that Captain of the District Police hadn't hurried up in the very nick of time perhaps I would never have had another chance to see God's daylight again! I would have disappeared like a bubble on the water, with nary a trace, leaving no descendants and bequeathing neither property nor an honored name to my future children!" Our hero was very much concerned over his descendants.

"What a miserable squire that was!" Seliphan was thinking to himself. "Never have I seen his like. I could spit at him for that, what I mean. Wouldn't be so bad if you didn't give a man anything to eat, but as for a horse, you're bound to feed it, inasmuch as a horse loves its oats. Them's its vittles; what fine living, for instance, is to us, oats is to a horse—them's its vittles."

The horses, too, apparently entertained but a poor opinion of Nozdrev: not only were the sorrel and Assessor out of sorts, but so was the piebald himself. Even though the poorer sort of oats usually fell to his portion, and Seliphan never poured them into his manger otherwise than by saying before he did so: "Eh, you scoundrel!" yet, notwithstanding, they were oats after all, and not common hay; he chewed them with pleasure and frequently would shove his long muzzle into the mangers of his mates, to taste what sort of victuals they had, especially when Seliphan was not around the stable; but this time all they had got was hay— that wasn't so good! All of them were dissatisfied.

But shortly all these dissatisfied beings were interrupted, in the very midst of their effusions, in a sudden and altogether unexpected fashion. All, not excluding even the coachman himself, recovered themselves and came to their senses only when and as a barouche harnessed to a team of six ran full tilt on top of them, and, almost over their heads, there resounded the scream of the ladies seated in the barouche, and the recriminations and curses of the other coachman: "Ah, what a swindler! Why, I was yelling to you at the top of my voice: 'Turn to the right, you crow!' Are you drunk, or what?"

Seliphan felt that he had been negligent, but since no Russian likes to admit to another that he is ever to blame he accordingly summoned all his dignity and had an immediate comeback: "And where do you think you're goin' at a clip like that? Have you left your eyes in hock at a pothouse, or what?" Following which he began backing his carriage, in order thus to get free of the other's harness, but that was easier said than done—everything was in a tangle. The piebald sniffed inquisitively at the newly acquired friends he found on either side of him.

In the meantime the fair occupants of the barouche were looking on at all this with an expression of fright on their faces. One was an old woman; the other was a young thing of sixteen, with aureate hair quite deftly and endearingly smoothed back on her small head. The pretty little oval of her face was as rounded out as a small newly laid egg, and, like an egg, exhibited a certain translucent whiteness, as when the fresh egg, just laid, is held up against the light in the swarthy hands of the housekeeper testing it, and allows the rays of the beaming sun to pass through it; her fragile little ears were also translucent, glowing rosily from the warm light penetrating them. With all this the fright on her open, motionless lips, the tears welling up in her eyes, were, in her case, so endearing that our hero contemplated her for a few minutes without paying any attention whatsoever to the mix-up that had involved the coachmen and their horses.

"Back 'er up, why don't you, you Nizhegorod crow!" the other coachman was shouting. Seliphan drew his reins back, the other coachman did the same with his, the horses backed up a little, and then collided again, having stepped over their traces. At this conjunction of events the piebald found the newly formed acquaintance so much to his liking that he did not want, under any circumstances, to get out of the rut in which unforeseen circumstances had placed him and, having put his muzzle upon the shoulder of one of his new friends, seemed to be whispering something into the other's very ear, probably the most arrant nonsense, inasmuch as the newcomer kept incessantly twitching his ears.

The muzhiks from a village that was, fortunately, not far off, had of course managed to gather at such a hullabaloo as this. Since such a spectacle is, to the muzhik, a veritable godsend, the very same thing that his newspapers and his club are to the German, there was accordingly no end of them milling around in a short while, and only the old women and the veriest babes stayed behind in the village itself. The muzhiks unloosed the traces; a few taps on the muzzle of the piebald horse persuaded him to back away; in short, the horses were separated and parted. But whether it was due to the vexation which the newcome horses felt over being torn away from their friends, or simply because of some foolish notion they had got into their heads, the fact remained that no matter how much their coachman lashed them they would not stir and remained as if rooted to the spot. The concern of the muzhiks grew to an incredible pitch. Each one would interrupt the others to put forward his own advice.

"You go ahead, Andriushka, and lead off the off-horse that's on the right side, whilst Uncle Mityai mounts the shaft-horse! Git up there, Uncle Mityai!"

Uncle Mityai, spare and lanky, with a red beard on him, got up on the shaft-horse and, perched up there, could have doubled for a village belfry or, better still, for the long crane with which they get the bucket out of some wells. The coachman gave his horses the whip, but nothing came of it: Uncle Mityai was of no help at all, at all.

"Hold on, hold on!" shouted the muzhiks. "Let you, Uncle Mityai, git up on the off-horse, and as for the shaft-horse, let Uncle Minyai git up on him!"

Uncle Minyai, a broad-shouldered muzhik, with a beard as black as coal, and a belly that resembled the gargantuan samovar in which mulled mead is prepared for a whole shivering market place, willingly mounted the shaft-horse, which caved in almost to the ground under him.

"Now we're gettin' somewheres!" shouted the muzhiks. "Make it hot for him! Make it hot for him! Give a taste of the whip to that feller there, that light bay. What's he buckin' for, like a *coramora?*" *

But, perceiving that they were not getting anywhere, and that no amount of putting on the heat had been of any avail, Uncle Mityai and Uncle Minyai both seated themselves on the shaft-horse, while on the back of the off-horse they seated Andriushka. At last the coachman, losing patience, chased away Uncle Mityai and Uncle Minyai both; and did right well, too, inasmuch as there was such steam rising from the horses as if they had covered the distance between two stage posts without halting to breathe. He allowed them a minute or so for rest, after which they started off by themselves.

While all these horsy maneuvers were going on, Chichikov had been looking very attentively at the pretty

---

* A *coramora* is a great, long, torpid mosquito; occasionally one may chance to fly into a room and stick somewhere on a wall all by itself. You can walk up to it calmly and seize it by one of its legs, to which its only reaction will be to arch itself, or to *buck*, as the common folk put it. *Author's note.*

little unknown. He made several attempts to start a conversation with her, but somehow it did not catch on. And in due course the ladies had driven off, the pretty little head with its very fine features, as well as the slender little waist, had disappeared from view, like something akin to a vision, and again there remained only the road, the light carriage, the troika of horses familiar to the reader, Seliphan, Chichikov, and the smooth and empty expanse of the surrounding fields.

Everywhere in life, no matter where it may run its course, whether amid its harsh, raspingly poor and squalidly mildewing lowly strata, or amid its monotonously frigid and depressingly tidy upper classes—everywhere, if it be but once, man is fated to meet a phenomenon which is unlike everything that he may have chanced to meet hitherto; which, if but once, will awaken within him an emotion that is unlike all those which he is fated to experience all life long. Everywhere, running counter to all the sorrows of which our life is compact, a glittering joy will gaily flash by as, at times, a glittering equipage with gold on its gear, with its picturesque horses, and sparkling because of its gleaming plate glass, will suddenly, unexpectedly, speed by some backwood poverty-stricken hamlet that had never beheld anything but a country cart, and for a long while will the muzhiks stand there, their mouths gaping and without putting on their doffed headgear again, even though the wondrous equipage has long since whirled away and vanished out of sight. And in much the same way has this blonde suddenly appeared in our narrative, in a perfectly unexpected manner, and has disappeared in the same way. Had there happened to be at the time, instead of Chichikov, some youth of twenty—whether he were a hussar, or simply one who has just begun the course of his life—and, Lord!—what would not have awakened, what would not have stirred, what would not have found a voice within him! Long would he have stood on the same spot, bereft of all sensation, his eyes staring senselessly into the distance, grown oblivious both of the road and of all the reprimands and goings-over in store for him for having tarried, grown oblivious of self, and of his work, and of the world, and of all the things that there are in the world.

But our hero had already reached middle age and was of a circumspectly congealed character. He, too, was plunged into thought, and kept thinking on and on, but in a more sedate manner; his thoughts were not so irresponsible and, to some extent, were even very substantial. "A glorious little creature!" said he to himself, opening his snuffbox and putting a pinch up his nostrils. "But then what, chiefly, is so good about her? It is good that she has only just now, evidently, finished some boarding school or scholastic institute; that as yet there isn't anything womanish about her, as they say derogatively, i.e., precisely that which is most unpleasant about the dear creatures. She is now like a child; everything about her is simple—she will say whatever may come to her mind, will laugh outright wherever and whenever she may feel like laughing. One can fashion anything out of her; she can be a miracle, and she may turn out to be so much trash—and will! In one year they'll pump her so full of all sorts of womanishness that her own father won't recognize her. Whence will come both the stuffiness and the primness? She will take to being guided by precepts drilled into her, will take to racking her head and considering whom she may talk to, and how, and for how long she should talk, and how this one or that one should be regarded; at every moment she will be afraid of saying more than is necessary; she will become all muddled herself, and it will all wind up by her lying all her life, and the upshot will be the Devil's own mess!"

Here he ceased his mental soliloquy for some time and then added: "But it would be curious to know, of what family is she? Well, what's her father like? A rich landed proprietor of well-esteemed character, or simply a prudent fellow whose capital was acquired in serving the State? For if, let us suppose, they were to give this girl a dowry of two hundred thousand or so, she might turn out to be a most dainty tidbit. This might constitute, so to say, happiness for some decent fellow."

The two hundred thousand or so came to be delineated in his head so vividly that he began, inwardly, to be vexed with himself because during the to-do about the two vehicles he had not found out from the outrider or the coachman who and what the chance-met travelers were. In a short while, however, the appearance of Sobakevich's village distracted his thoughts and made them revert to their constant theme.

The village seemed to him quite large; two forests, one of birch, the other of pine, like two wings, the one lighter in hue, the other darker, were, respectively, on his right and left; between them one could see a wooden house with a mezzanine, red roof, and walls of dark (or, to put it better, a *wild*, natural, nondescript) gray—a house of the sort that we build for military settlements and German colonists.

One could perceive that, during its erection, the builder had had to contend incessantly with the taste of the owner. The builder was a pedant and had longed for symmetry; the owner had wanted convenience and, evidently, as a consequence of this had boarded up on one side all the windows corresponding to those on the other, and, in place of them, had bored through a single, small one, which had probably been needed for some dark storeroom. The frontal, too, had by no means come out in the center of the house, no matter how hard the architect had striven, inasmuch as the owner had ordered one of the side columns to be chucked out, and for that reason only three columns had survived, and not four, as originally intended. The courtyard was surrounded by a fence of solid and inordinately thick boards. This landed proprietor, so it seemed, took great pains to attain solidity. Full-weighted and stout timbers, destined to endure through the ages, had gone for the construction of the stables, sheds, and kitchens. The rustic huts of the muzhiks had also been wondrously made of hewn logs; there were no planed walls, no fretwork designs, or the like doodads, but everything was driven home tight and right. Even the water well was bound in such strong oakwood as is used only for building mills and ships. In a word, everything that our hero might look at was steadfast, without any sway or play, with a certain strong and unwieldy orderliness about it.

As Chichikov drove up to the front entrance he noticed two faces that had peered almost simultaneously through the window—one feminine in a house cap, and elongated like a cucumber, and a masculine one, round, broad, like those Moldavian gourds called *gorliankas* or calabashes, out of which they make, in Russia, balalaikas, two-stringed light balalaikas, the pride and joy of some frolicsome twenty-year-old country lad, a fellow who knows how to wink and is a dandy, and who not only winks at but whistles after the snowy-breasted and snowy-necked maidens who gather around to listen to his soft-stringed strumming. Having peered out, both faces hid at the same moment. A flunky in a gray jacket with a stiff blue collar came out on the steps and led Chichikov into the entry, where the host himself came out to him. Upon beholding his guest he said abruptly: "If you please!" and led him into the inner quarters.

This time, as Chichikov glanced at Sobakevich out of the corner of his eye, he looked to him like a bear, just a middlin'-sized bear. To complete the resemblance, the frock coat upon him was absolutely the color of a bear's pelt; the sleeves were long, the trousers were long, he set his feet down lumberingly, this way and that way, and was forever stepping upon the feet of others. His face was of a red-hot, fiery hue, the ruddy hue you find on a five-kopeck copper. As everyone knows, there are many such faces in this world, over the finishing of which Nature did not expend much thought or ingenuity, on which she did not use any small, delicate tools such as fine files, fine gimlets, and so forth, but simply hacked away with a full swing of the arm: one swipe of the ax, and there's the nose for you; another swipe, and there are the lips; with a great auger she gouged out the eyes and, without wasting any time on trimming and finishing, she let her handiwork out into the world, saying: "It lives!" Just such a sturdy and wondrously roughhewn countenance did Sobakevich have; he kept it down for the most part, rather than looking up; he hardly turned his neck and, because of this unwieldiness, looked but rarely at whomever he was speaking to, but always either at an angle of the stove or at the door. Chichikov glanced at him once more out of the corner of his eye, as they were passing into the dining room: a bear! A perfect bear! And, as the last, inevitable, needed touch to round out so strange an affinity, his very name was actually Michail Semënovich. . . .[4] Knowing his way of stepping on the feet of others, Chichikov placed his own very carefully and allowed him to go ahead. The host himself, apparently, felt conscious of this failing and immediately inquired: "I haven't inconvenienced you, have I?" But Chichikov thanked him, saying that no inconvenience had yet occurred.

When they entered the drawing room Sobakevich indicated an easy chair, again saying: "If you please!" Seating himself, Chichikov cast a glance over the walls and the pictures hanging on them. They were all of fine, daring fellows, those pictures; Greek military leaders, almost all of them, engraved at full length: Maurocordato, in red pantaloons and uniform coat, with spectacles on his nose; Kolokotronis, Miaules, Kanaris.[5] All these heroes had such sturdy thighs and unheard-of mustachios that they made shivers run up and down your spine. In the midst of these stalwart Greeks—there was no telling how or why he'd gotten there—was the Russian Bagration,[6] a gaunt little, thin little chap, with tiny banners and cannon below him and squeezed into the narrowest of frames. Then, next in turn, came the Greek heroine Bobelina, one of whose legs alone seemed bigger than the torso of any of those dandies who throng the drawing rooms nowadays. The host, who was himself a hale and stalwart fellow, wished, it seemed, to have his very room adorned with people who were likewise stalwart and hale. Near Bobelina, in the very window, hung a cage out of which peeked a blackbird, its dark plumes speckled with white, which bird likewise bore a very great resemblance to Sobakevich. The guest and host did not have to sit in silence for more than a couple of minutes when the drawing-room door opened and the hostess entered, a very tall lady, wearing a house cap adorned with ribbons that had been redyed at home, and with homemade dyes, at that. She entered staidly, holding her head as straight as a palm tree.

"This is my Theodulia Ivanovna," said Sobakevich.

Chichikov approached Theodulia Ivanovna to kiss her fair hand, which she all but shoved into his mouth, during which operation he had an opportunity to note that her hands had been washed in dill-pickle brine.

"Allow me to introduce you, my little pet," Sobakevich continued. "This is Pavel Ivanovich Chichikov! I had the honor of making his acquaintance at the Governor's and the Postmaster's."

Theodulia Ivanovna invited him to be seated, saying, just as her husband had done: "If you please!" and making a motion with her head like that of an actress portraying a queen. After which she seated herself on the divan, drew her merino shawl about her, and from then on did not so much as bat an eye or twitch an eyebrow.

Chichikov once more lifted up his eyes, and once more

caught sight of Kanaris with his stout thighs and the mustachios stretching away to infinity, of Bobelina, and of the blackbird in its cage.

For almost all of five minutes they all maintained silence, broken only by the pecking noise made by the blackbird's beak against the wood of its cage as it angled for grains of wheat at the bottom. Chichikov once more cast his glance over the room and all that was in it: everything was solid, unwieldy in the highest degree, and bore some sort of strange resemblance to the master of the house himself. In a corner of the drawing room stood a potbellied walnut bureau on four utterly preposterous legs, a perfect bear of a bureau! The table, the armchairs, the chairs, all had a most ponderous and disquieting quality about them; in short, every object, every chair, seemed to be saying: "I, too, am Sobakevich!" or: "I, too, look very much like Sobakevich!"

"We were recalling you at a party given by Ivan Grigoriyevich, the Chairman of the Administrative Offices," said Chichikov at last, perceiving that neither one of the others felt inclined to start a conversation. "Last Thursday, it was. We passed our time very pleasantly there."

"Yes, I wasn't at his place then," Sobakevich answered.

"And what a splendid man!"

"Whom do you mean?" asked Sobakevich, looking at an angle of the stove.

"The Chairman of the Administrative Offices."

"Well, perhaps he may have struck you that way; he may be a Mason, but just the same he's a fool whose like the world has never yet produced."

Chichikov was somewhat perplexed by this rather harsh

characterization but then, recovering, went on: "Of course, every man has his weak points; but you take the Governor, what a superb fellow!"

"The Governor is a superb fellow?"

"Yes, isn't he?"

"A brigand—the biggest one on earth!"

"What—the Governor is a brigand?" said Chichikov, and absolutely could not grasp how the Governor could have joined the ranks of the brigands. "I must confess I would never think so," he went on. "Allow me to observe, however, that his actions do not at all indicate anything of the sort; on the contrary, there is rather a great deal of gentleness about him, actually." Here he adduced, in proof, the purses embroidered by the Governor's own hands, and commented, with praise, on the kindly expression on the Governor's face.

"And his face, too, is a brigand's!" said Sobakevich. "Do but put a knife in his hands and let him loose on the highway, and he'll slit your throat—he'll slit your throat for the smallest copper! He, and the Vice-Governor with him, Gog and Magog, that's what they are!"

"No, he must be on the outs with them," Chichikov thought to himself. "There, I'll try him out with the Chief of Police—he's a friend of his, I believe." "However, as far as I am concerned," he said aloud, "I confess I find the Chief of Police to my liking most of all. What a straightforward, frank character he has; one can see something simplehearted in his very face."

"A swindler!" said Sobakevich with the utmost *sang-froid*. "He'll sell you out and he'll take you in, and dine with you right after that. I know them all, they're all swindlers, every man jack of them; the whole town is like that, one swindler mounted on a second and using a third one as a whip. Judases, all of them. There is but one—and only one—decent man; that's the Public Prosecutor, and even he, if the truth were to be told, is a swine."

After such eulogistic although somewhat brief biographies, Chichikov perceived that it wouldn't do to mention the other officials, and reminded himself that Sobakevich did not relish giving a good report of anybody.

"Well, now, pet, let's go in to dinner," said Sobakevich's spouse, turning to him.

"If you please!" said Sobakevich.

After which, approaching a table set with plates of various cold delicacies, guest and host drank a pony of vodka each, as is the proper usage; they had a snack, as all spacious Russia does throughout all its towns and villages, of all sorts of salted delicacies, and other such appetite-arousing blessed dainties, and then floated along into the dining room, the hostess, like a stately goose, hastening ahead of them. The small table was set for four places. To take the fourth place there very soon appeared a—it is hard to say positively just who she was, a lady or a miss, a relative, a chatelaine, or simply some woman living in the house—something without a house cap, about thirty, wearing a brightly colored and patterned shawl. There are faces which exist upon earth not as primary objects but as specks or spots of foreign matter upon objects. They always occupy the same seat, they all hold their heads in the same way, one is almost ready to consider them as furniture, and thinks that never, since birth, has a cross word issued from such lips as those; but if you'd happen to hear her somewhere in the maids' room, or in a pantry, you would be simply amazed!

"The cabbage soup, my pet, is very good today," said Sobakevich, having sipped the soup and dumped into his plate an enormous helping of *nurse,* a well-known Russian variation of haggis, which is served with cabbage soup and consists of a ram's stomach stuffed with buckwheat groats, brains and trotters. "You won't get to eat a pudding like that in town"—he turned to Chichikov—"They'll serve you the Devil knows what there!"

"However, the Governor doesn't keep such a bad table," remarked Chichikov.

"But do you know what all those courses are made of? You wouldn't eat them if you were to find out."

"I don't know how they're prepared, I'm in no position to judge that; but the pork chops and stewed fish were excellent."

"It just struck you that way. For I know what they buy in the market. The buying will be done by his rascal of a chef, who learned his trade from a Frenchman; he'll skin a cat, and then serve it up to you at table for rabbit."

"Faugh, what a nasty thing to say!" said Sobakevich's spouse.

"Well, isn't it so, my little pet? That's how they do things; I'm not to blame, they do everything that way. Every sort of refuse, stuff that our wench Akulka throws into the cesspool, if you'll permit me to use the word, they pop into their soup. Into the soup with it! That's the place for it!"

"You'll always come out with something of that sort at table," Sobakevich's spouse again protested.

"Well, now, my pet," Sobakevich persisted, "if I did

things like that myself it would be a different matter, but I'm telling you right to your face that I'm not going to eat any abominations. You can plaster frogs' legs even with sugar, as far as I'm concerned, and I won't take 'em into my mouth, nor will I take oysters, for the matter of that—an oyster's looks remind me too much of something else. Take some of the mutton," he went on, turning to Chichikov; "it's a whole side of mutton, with buckwheat groats. These aren't your fricassees, which are made in lordly kitchens out of mutton that's been knocking around on the market stalls for four days in a row. It's all a scheme thought up by the German and the French doctors; if I had my way, I'd string up the whole lot of them. They've thought up dieting, the hunger cure! Since theirs is a thin-boned German constitution, they imagine they'll make the thing work with the Russian stomach! No, it's all wrong, it's all pure invention, it's all—" at this point Sobakevich even shook his head angrily. "They're forever talking about enlightenment, enlightenment, but all this enlightenment is just so much . . . flapdoodle! I might even use another word, only it would be impolite at table. I don't do things that way. If it's pork I want, I order the whole swine to be served at table; if it's mutton, drag in the whole ram; if goose, the whole goose! Better for me if I eat but two courses, but eat a goodly enough portion of each, as the soul craves." Sobakevich confirmed this by action: he overturned half the side of mutton onto his plate, and ate it all up, gnawing clean and sucking dry every last bit of a bone.

"Yes," reflected Chichikov, "this fellow is no fool when it comes to his belly."

"I don't run things," Sobakevich kept on talking, wiping

his hands on his napkin, "I don't run things the way some Pliushkin does; he owns eight hundred souls, yet he lives and dines worse than my shepherd does."

"Who is this Pliushkin?" Chichikov inquired.

"A swindler," Sobakevich answered. "Such a miser as it would be hard to imagine. The convicts in stocks at the prison live better than he does; he's starved all his people to death."

"Really?" Chichikov chimed in with concern. "And you say that his people are actually dying off from hunger in great numbers?"

"They're dying off like flies."

"Dying off like flies—can such things really be! But permit me to ask, how far away from your place does he live?"

"A little over three miles from here."

"A little over three miles from here?" Chichikov exclaimed, and even felt a slight heart tremor. "But, when one drives out of your gates, would his place be to the right or to the left?"

"I wouldn't advise you even to know the way to that dog!" said Sobakevich. "There's more excuse for going to some unseemly place than to his house."

"No, I didn't ask for any particular reasons . . . but only because I am interested in knowing all sorts of places," Chichikov said in answer to this.

The side of mutton was followed by round tarts, filled with curds, each one of which was considerably bigger than the dinner plates, then a turkey as well grown as a calf, stuffed with all sorts of good things: eggs, rice, livers, and goodness knows what else that is bound to lie like a stone on one's stomach. And with that the dinner was brought to an end; but, when they got up from the table, Chichikov felt all of five-and-thirty pounds heavier.

They went off to the drawing room, where a saucer of preserves had already appeared on the table—not of pears, however, or of plums, or any known berry; however, neither the guest nor the host touched it. The hostess went out for some additional saucers. Taking advantage of her absence, Chichikov turned to Sobakevich, who, lying back in an easy chair, could only grunt occasionally after such a filling dinner and emit some indistinct sounds from his mouth, making the sign of the cross and putting his hand over it every minute or so.

"There's a certain little matter I'd like to talk over with you," Chichikov said, turning to him.

"Here are some more preserves," said the hostess, coming back with another saucerful. "Radish, cooked in honey!"

"Well, we'll tackle it later!" said Sobakevich. "You go to your room now; Pavel Ivanovich and I will shuck our coats and rest a bit."

The hostess was not slow in evincing a readiness to send for down beds and pillows, but the host said: "Never mind, we'll take a rest in the easy chairs," and the hostess went off.

Sobakevich cocked his head slightly, getting ready to listen to just what the little matter consisted of.

Chichikov began in a sort of roundabout manner, touching, in a general way, upon the whole of Russia and commenting with great praise upon its vast extent; he said that even the ancient Roman Empire had not been so great, and that foreigners were justly astonished (Sobakevich merely kept on listening, with his head cocked to one side) . . . and also that, owing to the existing circumstances in this realm, whose equal in glory was nowhere to be found, the serfs listed in the Bureau of Audits, even though they might have ended their earthly course, were nevertheless, until the submission of a new census to the Bureau of Audits, considered on the same basis as those alive, so as not to burden the Administrative Offices with a multitude of petty and useless inquiries and so as not to increase the complexity of the governmental mechanism, which, even without that, was quite complicated (Sobakevich kept on listening, with his head cocked to one side)... and also that, notwithstanding, with all the justice of this measure, it proved, on occasion, quite burdensome to many of the serfowners, obligating them to keep on paying taxes as if these souls, not actually in existence, were still living chattels, and that he, Chichikov, out of a feeling of personal regard for him, Sobakevich, was actually ready to assume, in part, this really onerous obligation. Concerning the main theme Chichikov expressed himself with the utmost caution: he by no means called the serf-souls dead, but merely not actually in existence.

Sobakevich kept on listening, just as before, with his head cocked to one side—and if but something, in the least resembling an expression, would appear on his face! It seemed as if there were no soul at all in his body, or, if it were there, it was not at all in the place it should be, but, as with Koshchei the Deathless in the fairy tale, somewhere beyond many hills and dales and sheathed in such a thick shell that everything which stirred at the bottom of his soul created absolutely no commotion on the surface.

"And so? . . ." asked Chichikov, awaiting, not without a certain trepidation, the other's reaction.

"You need dead souls?" said Sobakevich, very simply, without the least surprise, as if it were grain they were talking about.

"Yes," said Chichikov, and again softened the expression by adding: "Those that are not actually in existence."

"They can be found; why not?" said Sobakevich.

"And, should any be found, then, doubtless . . . you would be pleased to get them off your hands?"

"I'm ready to sell them, if you like," said Sobakevich, this time with his head somewhat raised, and surmising that the buyer must surely have some advantage in view here.

"The Devil take it!" Chichikov thought to himself. "This fellow is already selling them before I've let a peep out of me!" and said, aloud: "And what would the price be, for instance? Although, by the bye, this is such a thing . . . that it's even odd to talk of the price—"

"Well, not to be asking too high a price of you, a hundred rubles a head," Sobakevich told him.

"A hundred rubles a head!" Chichikov cried out, letting his jaw drop and, after looking right into the other's eyes, without knowing whether he had heard aright himself or whether Sobakevich's tongue, because of its heavy nature, had not worked right, blurting one word out instead of another.

"Why, now is that dear for you?" uttered Sobakevich, and then added: "But, in that case, what is your price?"

"My price! We are making some mistake, probably, or we do not understand each other, having forgotten what the talk is really about. For my part, placing my hand on my heart, I propose paying eight ten-kopeck pieces for each soul—that is my top-notch price!"

"So that's what you're aiming at, eight ten-kopeck pieces per head!"

"Well, now, in my judgment, I think one can't give more than that."

"But it isn't bast slippers I'm selling."

"Just the same, you must agree yourself, these, too, aren't what you might call people."

"So you think you'll find a big enough fool to sell you for a couple of ten-kopeck pieces a soul listed with the Bureau of Audits?"

"But, if you please, why do you describe them that way? For the souls of themselves have long since died; all that is left of them is but an insubstantial sound. However, in order not to go into further talk on this matter, I'll give you a ruble and a half, if you like, but I can't give you any more than that."

"You ought to be ashamed even to mention such a sum. If you want to trade, talk a real price."

"I can't, Michail Semënovich; upon my conscience, believe me, that which is impossible to do, there is no possible way of doing," Chichikov maintained, but just the same tacked on another half-ruble.

"But what are you so tight about?" asked Sobakevich. "Really, the price isn't so high! Another swindler will take you in, will sell you trash and not souls; whereas mine are all as sound as a nut, all hand-picked—if it isn't some master craftsman, then it's some other husky muzhik. Just take a close look: here's Miheiev, for example, a coachmaker! Why, he never turned out a vehicle but what it was on springs. And it wasn't the way they work it in Moscow, to last you an hour or so; what solidity he put into his work—and he'd upholster it himself, and lacquer it as well!"

Chichikov opened his mouth to remark that, after all, this Miheiev had long been not of this world; but Sobakevich had got into the vein, as they say. Whence came this gift of gab and the pace of his speech?

"And what of Stepan the Cork, the carpenter? I'll lay my head on the block if you'll find such another peasant anywhere! Why, what strength he had! If he had been serving in the Guards, God knows what rank they would have given him—seven foot one and three-quarter inches in height, he was!"

Chichikov again wanted to remark that the Cork, too, was no longer of this world; but Sobakevich, evidently, had thoroughly warmed up to the subject; his speeches poured forth in such torrents that all one could do was listen.

"Milushkin, a bricklayer! He could build you a furnace or an oven fit for any house you like. Maxim Teliatnikov, a bootmaker: he'd just run his awl through a piece of leather, and there was a pair of boots for you, and not a pair but you'd want to thank him, and it wasn't as if he ever took a single drop of spirits in his mouth. And what about Eremei Sorokoplekhin? Why, that muzhik alone was worth all of the others put together; he used to trade in Moscow, bringing me in five hundred in quitrent alone. There, that's the kind of people they are! Not the kind some Pliushkin or other would sell you."

"But, if you please," Chichikov got out at last, amazed by such a copious inundation of speeches, to which, it seemed, there was never an end, "why do you enumerate all their good points? For there's no good in them now whatsoever—they're all dead folk. All a dead body is good for is to prop up a fence with, says the proverb."

"Why, of course, they're dead," said Sobakevich, as though he had come to his senses and remembered that they were dead in reality, but then added: "However, it may also be said, what good are the people that are now numbered among the living? What sort of people are they? They're so many flies, and not people."

"Yet, just the same, they are in existence, whereas the others are but a dream."

"Well, no, they're no dream! Allow me to inform you that you'll never find such men as Miheiev was; he was such a mountain of a man that he could never get into this room; no, he was no dream! And as for those hams of shoulders he had, there was such a store of strength in them as no horse has. I'd like to know where else you'd find such a dream!"

The last words he uttered with his face already turned to the portraits of Bagration and Kolokotronis, as usually happens during a conversation when one of the speakers will suddenly, for some unknown reason, turn not to the person to whom his words are directed but to some third person who chances to come in, even a total stranger, from whom he knows he will receive neither an answer nor an opinion, nor any confirmation, but upon whom, nevertheless, he will fix his gaze as though he were calling him in as a mediator; and, somewhat abashed at first, the stranger does not know whether he ought to make any reply in a matter which he had heard nothing of, or simply stand there a while, as an appropriate observance of the civilities, and only then take his leave.

"No," said Chichikov, "more than two rubles I cannot give you."

"If you like, in order that you may not hold anything against me, or claim that I am asking too much from you and am unwilling to oblige you in any way, if you like I'll let you have them at seventy-five rubles a soul, but it must be in government notes—and really, I'm doing it only out of friendship!"

"Really, now, what is he up to?" Chichikov thought to himself. "Is he taking me for a fool, or what?" and then added, out loud: "I find it strange, really; it seems as if we were going through some sort of a theatrical performance or a comedy; I can't explain it any other way.... You are, it seems, a man who is quite intelligent, possessing knowledge and an education. Why, the matter under discussion has no more substance than a puff of air! What can such stuff be worth? Who needs it?"

"There, now, you are buying it, therefore there must be a need for it."

Whereupon Chichikov bit his lip and could not find any answer to make. He did begin talking about certain circumstances in his family and household, but Sobakevich's answer was a simple one: "There's no necessity of my knowing what your circumstances are; I don't mix into family affairs—that is your own business. You had need of souls, and so I am selling them to you, and you will regret not having purchased them."

"Two round rubles apiece," said Chichikov.

"Eh, really! 'Teach a magpie to say Joe, and it will call all men so,' as the saying goes—you've gotten that tune of two rubles into your head and simply don't want to change it. You give me a real price!"

"Well, now, the Devil with him!" Chichikov thought to himself. "I'll add on half a ruble per soul for him, the dog, by way of a tip!"—"I'll add on half a ruble apiece, if you like."

"Well, if you like, I too will give you my last word: fifty rubles a head. Really, I'm taking a loss; you can't get such good people cheaper anywhere!"

"What a kulak!" said Chichikov to himself, and then went on, aloud, with a certain vexation: "But what is all this, really? Just as if this were truly serious business! Why, I'll get them for nothing some other place. And everybody will hand them over to me right willingly, only to get rid of them as quickly as possible. Only a fool would want to hold on to them and pay taxes on them!"

"But do you know that purchases of that sort—I am telling you this just among ourselves, out of friendship— aren't always permissible, and were I, or somebody else, to divulge the matter, such a purchaser would not have any standing as far as contracts are concerned, or if he wanted to enter into any advantageous transactions?"

"Just see what he's aiming at, the scoundrel!" thought Chichikov, and at once uttered, with an air of the utmost *sang-froid:* "Just as you wish; I am not buying them for any particular need, as you think, but just so…because my own ideas so incline me. If you won't take two and a half, I'll have to bid you good-by!"

"You can't make him yield his ground, he isn't the yielding kind!" Sobakevich reflected. "Well, God be with you, give me thirty rubles a head and they're all yours!"

"No, I can see you don't want to sell. Good-by!"

"Hold on, hold on!" said Sobakevich, without letting go of Chichikov's hand and stepping on his foot, since our hero had forgotten to be cautious and, as a punishment therefor, had to draw his breath in with a hiss and to hop around on one foot.

"I beg your pardon! I think I've inconvenienced you? Sit down here, I beg of you! If you please!"

Here he plumped him into an easy chair, even with a certain dexterity, like one of those bears that have been through a trainer's hands and can not only turn cartwheels but go through sundry pantomime routines in answer to such questions as, "And now show us, Misha, how do womenfolk carry on in a steam bath?"—"And how, Misha, do little boys go about stealing peas in a truck patch?"

"Really, I am wasting my time here; I must hurry."

"Sit here for just a minute more; I'll tell you something that will please you right away." Here Sobakevich moved his seat nearer to Chichikov and said softly in his ear, as though it were a secret: "Do you want to clinch the bargain?"

"You mean at twenty-five rubles? Never, never, never! I wouldn't give in ever so little, I won't add on another kopeck."

Sobakevich fell silent. Chichikov, too, fell silent. Their silence lasted for two minutes or so. Bagration, he of the eagle nose, was looking down with exceeding attentiveness from his wall upon this trade.

"What, then, will be your last price?" asked Sobakevich.

"Two and a half."

"Really, you hold a human soul at the same value as a boiled turnip! Give me three rubles, at least."

"I can't."

"Well, there's nothing to be done with you, take them if you like. I'm taking a loss, but I guess that's just my doggy nature,* I can't help pleasuring a fellow man. And I guess we've got to put through a purchase deed, so's everything will be in order?"

"That's understood."

"Well, there you are, then; we'll have to go into town."

Thus was the deal consummated. Both decided to be in town no later than the next day to attend to the purchase deed. Chichikov asked for a list of the serfs. Sobakevich willingly agreed and, right then and there, having gone to a bureau, with his own hand began an abstract of all the dead souls involved, giving not only their names but even designating their good points.

As for Chichikov, he, for lack of anything to do, occupied himself with an inspection, since he was behind him, of Sobakevich's ample build in its entirety. As soon as he glanced at his back, as broad as the backs of those thickset Percheron-like draft horses which are bred in the Viatskaya region, and at his legs, resembling those stubby, thick cast-iron pillars which are placed along street curbs, he could not help but exclaim inwardly: "God hath surely blessed you bounteously! There, it's just as they say: you

---

*"Sobakevich" is derived from *sobaka,* a dog. *Trans.*

are not well cut but stoutly stitched! Were you born the bear you are, or were you turned into a bear by your backwoods life, by the planting of grain and the pother with the muzhiks, and is it through these you have become what is called a tightfisted man, a kulak? But no: I think you would be still the same, even if you had had a fashionable education, if they had placed you amid the social whirl and you were to live in St. Petersburg and not in the backwoods. The sole difference is that now you can put away half a side of mutton with buckwheat groats, chasing it down with a tart of curds as big as a plate, whereas in the capital you would dine on dainty cutlets of some sort with truffles. There, now you have muzhiks under your domination; you get along well with them and, of course, would take no advantage of them, inasmuch as you own them, and it would be so much worse for you if you did; but, were you living in the capital, you'd have a lot of quill-drivers under you, whom you would ride hard, having figured out that, after all, they weren't your chattel slaves; or you would be dipping your fingers in the public treasury! No, he who is tightfisted is never fated to loosen up and become openhanded! But if you make a tightfisted man unbend but a finger or two, it's so much the worse! If he skims but lightly over the surface of some science or lore he will, later on, upon attaining a more prominent place, let all those who may have really mastered some science or lore feel his heavy hand! And, to boot, he's as likely as not to say then: 'Let's show them who I am!' And he'll cook up a decree so complicated that many a man will have the Devil's own time of it. . . . Eh, if only all these kulaks were to go to—"

"The list is ready," said Sobakevich, turning around.

"Ready? Let's have it, please!"

He ran his eyes over it and was struck by its accuracy and meticulousness: not only were the trade, position, years and family status of each dead soul circumstantially written out, but there were even to be found, on the margins, special notations regarding that soul's conduct and sobriety—in a word, the list was a delight to behold.

"And now for a small deposit, if you please."

"But why do you need any deposit? You will get all the money at once in town."

"Well, you know, it's the usual thing," Sobakevich retorted.

"I don't know how I can give it to you; I did not bring any money with me. Well, yes, here are ten rubles."

"What do ten rubles mean? Let me have fifty rubles, say, at the least!"

Chichikov began making excuses that he did not have that much with him, but Sobakevich told him so affirmatively that he did have the money that Chichikov took out another note in no time at all as he said: "Here are fifteen more, if you like, a total of twenty-five. But please let me have a receipt."

"But what do you need a receipt for?"

"Well, you know, it's better to have a receipt. Who knows what any hour may bring? . . . Anything may happen."

"Very well, pass the money over."

"Why pass it over? I have it right here in my hand! You can take it the minute you've written out the receipt."

"But, if you please, how am I to write out a receipt otherwise? One must see the money first of all."

Chichikov's hands released the notes to Sobakevich, who, drawing near to the table and covering them with the fingers of his left hand, wrote out with the other on a slip of paper that he had received, in full, five-and-twenty rubles in government notes as a deposit on the sale of certain serfs. Having written out this memorandum, he looked the bills over once more.

"This note is rather old," he pronounced, scrutinizing one of them against the light; "it's a bit torn; but among friends there's no use minding such a thing."

"Kulak, kulak!" Chichikov thought to himself. "And a low-down beast, to boot."

"And would you like to have any souls of the female sex?"

"No, thank you."

"Why, I actually wouldn't take much. For friendship's sake, just a mere ruble a head."

"No, I don't need any females."

"Well, if you don't need any, then there's no use even talking about it. Every man to his taste; what's one man's meat is another man's poison, as the proverb has it."

"There's one more thing I wanted to ask of you, and that is to have this deal remain in confidence between us," Chichikov said as he was taking his leave.

"Why, that goes without saying. There's no use mixing any third party into this; that which takes place among intimate friends in all sincerity must remain a part of their mutual friendship. Good-by! Thanks for paying me a visit; I ask you not to forget me in the future as well—if you ever have an hour or so to spare, drive up for dinner and to spend some time. Perhaps there may be another occasion when we can be of some service to each other."

"You've got another guess coming!" Chichikov was thinking as he took his seat in the carriage. "Not after skinning me two and a half rubles apiece for dead souls, you God-damned kulak!"

He was dissatisfied with the way Sobakevich had acted. After all, no matter what you say, he knew the man; they had met each other at the Governor's and at the house of the Chief of Police, and yet he had acted like an utter stranger, had taken money for actual trash! When the carriage had rolled out of the courtyard he looked back and saw that Sobakevich was still standing on the front steps and, it seemed, was keenly watching him, wishing to know in which direction his guest would drive.

"The scoundrel! He's still standing there!" Chichikov got out through clenched teeth, and ordered Seliphan, after turning toward the huts in the village, to drive off in such a way that the vehicle might not be seen from the proprietor's courtyard. He wanted to drop in on Pliushkin whose people, according to what Sobakevich had said, were dying off like flies; but he did not want Sobakevich to know about this contemplated visit. When the carriage was already at the end of the village, he called over to him the first muzhik he saw who, having picked up somewhere along the road an exceedingly thick log, was lugging it along on his shoulder to his hut, like some indefatigable ant.

"Hey, there, you with the beard! And how does one get to Pliushkin's place, but so's not to drive past the master's house?"

The muzhik, apparently, was in a quandary over this question.

"Well, don't you know?"

"No, master, I don't."

"Oh, you! And yet your hair is streaked with gray! Don't you know Pliushkin the miser, the fellow who feeds his people so poorly?"

"Ah, the patched—! The patched—!" the muzhik cried out. There was a tacked on substantive to the word *patched*, a very apt one, but not used in polite conversation, and for that reason we will let it pass. However, it may be surmised that the expression came very close to the mark, inasmuch as Chichikov, even though the muzhik had long since dropped out of view, was nevertheless still smiling as he sat in his carriage. The Russian people have a puissant way of expressing themselves! And if they bestow an apt word upon any man, it will follow him into his lineage and into his posterity; he will drag it along with him wherever he serves, and into his retirement, and to St. Petersburg, and to the ends of the earth. And no matter how cunningly you contrive thereafter and glorify and ennoble your nickname, even though you set the scribbling small fry to deriving it, for hire, from some ancient lordly line, nothing will avail you: the nickname will, of its own self, caw with all its corvine throat and will proclaim clearly what nest the bird has flown out of. That which is aptly uttered is tantamount to that which is written: there's no rooting it out, though you were to use an ax. And how very apt, of a certainty, is that which has come out of the very core of Russia, where there is no German, nor French, nor Finnish, nor any other sort of tribe, but the purest virgin gold, the living and lively Russian wit, that is never at a loss for a word, that doesn't brood over it, like a setting hen, but comes spang out with it, like a passport to be carried through all eternity, and there's no use your adding on later what sort of nose or lips you have: you are drawn, at a stroke, from head to foot!

Even as an incomputable host of churches, of monasteries, with cupolas, bulbous domes, and crosses, is scattered all over holy and devout Russia, so does an incomputable multitude of tribes, generations, peoples, swarm, flaunt their motley and scurry across the face of the earth. And every folk that bears within itself the pledge of mighty forces, that is endowed with the creative aptitudes of the soul, with a vivid individuality of its own and with other gifts of God, each such folk has become singularly distinguished by some word all its own, through which, expressing any subject whatsoever, it reflects in that expression a part of its own character. With a profound knowledge of the heart and a wise grasp of life will the word of the Britisher echo; like an airy dandy will the impermanent word of the Frenchman flash and then burst into smithereens; finically, intricately, will the German contrive his intellectually gaunt word, which is not within the easy reach of everybody. But there is never a word which can be so sweeping, so boisterous, which would burst out so, from out of the very heart, which would seethe so and quiver and pulse so much like a living thing, as an aptly uttered Russian word!

CHAPTER SIX

In former days, long ago, during the years of my youth, during the years of my childhood, now as irretrievably fled as a gleam of light, it was a gladsome thing for me to be driving up for the first time to some unfamiliar place; it was all one whether it were some hamlet, some poor, wretched little town (yet the chief one of its district), or some settlement, or some borough—the curious eye of the child would discover a great deal that was curious about the place. Every structure, everything, as long as it bore upon it the impress of some noticeable peculiarity, everything would bring me to a stop and amaze me. Whether it were a stone government building of the familiar style of architecture, with half its windows false ones, sticking up all by its lonesome amid a cluster of the one-story little houses of hewed timber inhabited by the local burghers, or a well-rounded cupola, covered all over with white sheet iron, rearing over a new church whitewashed so that it was as white as snow, or a market place, or some dandy of the district whom one chanced upon in a town—nothing evaded the fresh, fine observation and, with nose thrust out of the traveling cart, I would stare at some frock coat, of a cut hitherto never seen, and at wooden bins full of nails, full of sulphur that showed yellowly even from afar, full of raisins and soap, all these to be glimpsed through the doors of a greengrocer's, together with jars of stale candies brought all the way from Moscow. I stared, as well, at an infantry officer walking on one side of the street, blown thither by a chance wind from God knows what province, to endure the ennui of the district town, and at a merchant in a Siberian greatcoat, who flashed by in a racing sulky—and in my thoughts I would whirl off after these people, into their meagre way of life. A petty clerk of the district administration might happen to pass by me, and I would already be in deep thought: whither was he bound, to an evening at the home of some brother quill-driver, or straight for home, in order, after having sat on his front porch for half an hour or so, before the dusk came down for good and all, to sit down to an early supper with his mother, his wife, his wife's sister, and his whole household; and what would the talk be about around the time when a serving wench with many beads encircling her neck, or a boy in a quilted short jacket, would bring in (this would be after the soup had been served) a tallow candle in an ancient candlestick that had seen endless service in the house?

As I drove up to the village of some landed proprietor or other I would eye curiously the tall, narrow wooden belfry, or the old, sprawling, weather-beaten, wooden church itself. In the distance I could catch enticing glimpses, through the leafage of the trees, of the red roof and white chimneys of the proprietor's house, and I waited impatiently until the gardens that screened it would part to either side and it would appear in all its entirety, with all its exterior, which at that time (alas!) did not appear at all vulgar, and by that exterior I tried to guess just who and what the landed proprietor himself was—was he stout, and did he have sons, or all of a half-dozen daughters, with sonorous maidenly laughter, forever playing games, and with the youngest little sister, as always, the greatest beauty of them all, and were their eyes dark, and whether the proprietor himself was a jolly fellow or as dour as September in its last days, forever consulting his calendar and discoursing on rye and wheat, which were such boresome topics for youthful people.

Now I drive up apathetically to every unfamiliar village and look apathetically at its vulgar appearance; to my time-chilled gaze things seem bleak, and I am not amused, and that which in former years would have aroused an animated expression, laughter, and unceasing speeches, glides past me now and my expressionless lips preserve an impassive silence. Oh, my youth! Oh, my fresh vigor!

While Chichikov was mulling over and inwardly chuckling at the nickname which the muzhiks had bestowed upon Pliushkin, he had not noticed how he had driven into the centre of a far-spreading settlement, with a multitude of huts and lanes. In a short while, however, a most jarring jolt, brought about by a corduroy roadway, a roadway before which the cobbled one in town was a mere nothing, let him perceive where he was. The logs of this roadway now rose, now fell, like the keys of a pianoforte, and the incautious rider acquired either a lump on the back of his neck, or a livid bruise on his forehead, or might even chance to nip, most painfully, the tip of his tongue between his teeth. He noticed some sort of especial tumble-down air over all the structures in the village; the logs of the huts were dark of hue and old; many of the roofs had gaps through which one could see the sky as through a sieve; on some only the weather vane, in the form of a little horse, remained up above—that, and the transverse poles which looked like ribs. Apparently the owners themselves had carried off the shingles and deal of the roofs, reasoning, and quite justly so, that the huts afforded no shelter from the rain, while in fine weather it's dry and there's no sense in coddling one-self indoors when one can find room to sprawl out both at the pothouse and on the highroad—in short, wherever you list. The windows in the small huts were without panes; some were stuffed up with rags or a sheepskin jacket; the tiny railed balconies under the eaves which, for some un-known reason, are tacked onto some Russian huts, had be-come askew and weather-beaten, yet without acquiring any picturesqueness thereby. Behind the huts, in many places, were rows of enormous stacks of grain which had been stagnating there, as was very evident, for a long time; in hue they resembled old, badly baked brick; all sorts of weeds were growing on top of them, and here, and there even a shrub would be clinging to one of the sides. The grain evidently belonged to the master. Out from behind the stacks of grain and the tumble-down roofs reared up and momentarily appeared and disappeared in the clear air, now on the right, now on the left, depending on the turns the carriage made, two village churches that were side by side; a deserted one of wood, and one of stone, with yellowish walls; it was all in stains and blotches and with cracks everywhere.

Parts of the proprietor's house began to emerge and, fi-nally, it came into full view at the spot where the chain of huts ended and was succeeded by a truck garden or cab-bage patch which had been allowed to turn into a waste-land, with a low picket fence, broken in some places, thrown about it. Like some decrepit invalid did this strange castle appear—long, inordinately long. In places it was of only one story, in others of two stories; on its dark-hued roof, which did not everywhere afford dependable protection to the house in its old age, two belvederes were sticking up, facing each other; both of them were rickety by now, devoid of the paint that had coated them at one time. The walls of the house showed cracks here and there that exposed the naked plastering and lath and, as one could see, had endured a great deal from inclement weather, rains, whirlwinds and autumnal changes. Of the windows only two were in use; the others were shuttered or simply boarded over. These two windows, for their part, were also purblind; on one of them, showing darkly, had been pasted a triangle of dark-blue paper, such as comes wrapped around loaves of sugar.

The old vast garden, stretching away behind the house, extending beyond the settlement and then losing itself in an open field, a garden gone wild, overgrown and stifled with weeds, was the only thing that lent a fresh air to the widely scattered settlement and the only thing that was fully picturesque in its pictorial desolation. The joined summits of trees that had attained their full growth in freedom lay in green clouds and irregular cupolas of trembling foliage against the sky line. The white, colossal trunk of a birch that had been deprived of its crest by some tempest or thunderstorm rose up out of this green thick tangle and, high in the air, looked like a round, regular column of dazzling marble; the oblique, sharply pointed fracture in which it terminated in lieu of a capital showed darkly against its snowy whiteness, like a cap or some black-plumed bird. The hopvines that stifled the elder, rowan and hazel bushes below, and then ran all over the tops of the paling, at last darted halfway up the broken birch and entwined it. After reaching its middle, the vine hung down from there and was already beginning to catch at the tips of other trees, or else dangled in the air, its slender, clinging tendrils coiled into rings and lightly swaying in the breeze. In places the green, sunlit thickets parted and revealed some depression in their midst, sunless and gaping like a dark maw; it would be all enveloped in shadow and one could barely, barely glimpse in its dark depths a white narrow path running through it, fallen railings, a rickety arbor, the hollow decayed trunk of a willow, a hoary Siberian pea-tree that stuck out from behind the willow its thick, bristling tangle of twigs and leaves, dried and dead because of the fearful underwoods and, finally, a new maple branch, extending from one side its green paws of leaves. Getting under one of these leaves, God alone knows how, the sun would suddenly transform it into a thing of transparency and fire that shone wondrously amid this dense darkness. Off to one side, at the very edge of the garden, a few tall aspens, rising above their fellows, lifted high into the air the enormous raven nests upon their quivering summits. Some of these aspens had branches broken but not completely severed, which dangled, their leaves, all withered. In short, everything was as beautiful as neither Nature alone nor art alone can conceive, but only when they come together, when over the labor of man, often heaped up without any sense, Nature will run her conclusive burin, will lighten the heavy masses, will do away with the coarsely palpable regularity and the beggar's rents, through which the unconcealed, naked plan peers out, and will bestow a wondrous warmth on everything that had been created amid the frigidity of a measured purity and tidiness.

After making a turn or two on the road, our hero found himself at last before the very house, which now seemed more woebegone than ever. Green mold had already covered the timeworn wood of the enclosure and the gate. A throng of buildings—quarters for the domestic serfs, granaries, storehouses, all almost visibly moldering away— filled the whole courtyard; near them, to right and left, one could see gates leading into other yards. Everything testified that once upon a time husbandry had been carried on on a large scale here; now everything here bore a dismal look. One could not notice anything that might animate the picture, neither a door opening, nor people coming out of anywhere, nor any of the living fuss and bustle which enliven a household. The main gate alone was open, and that one only because a muzhik had driven in with a laden, matting-covered cart, and seemed to have come on the scene for the sole purpose of animating this extinct place; another time this gate, too, would have been locked tight, inasmuch as it had a colossus of a padlock hanging on an iron ring. Near one of the structures Chichikov soon noticed some sort of figure that began bickering with the muzhik who had driven in the cart. For a long while Chichikov could not make out the sex of this figure, whether it were a peasant woman or a muzhik. The clothing upon it was utterly indeterminate, resembling very much a woman's gown; on its head was a nightcap, such as village serving women wear about the house; the voice alone sounded to Chichikov somewhat too hoarse for a woman's.

"Oh, it's a peasant woman!" he thought to himself, and added on the spot: "Oh, no!... Oh, of course it's a woman!" he decided at last, after a closer scrutiny. A visitor, it seemed, was a *rara avis* for her, inasmuch as she looked closely not only at him but at Seliphan as well, and the horses, too, beginning with their tails and ending with their very noses. By the keys that were dangling from her waist and from the fact that she was cursing out the muzhik in rather abusive terms, Chichikov concluded that this must surely be the housekeeper.

"I say, mother," he began, getting out of the carriage, "is your master—"

"Not to home," the housekeeper cut him short, without waiting for him to finish the question and then, after the lapse of a minute, added: "And what was it you wanted?"

"I have business with him."

"Go in the house!" said the housekeeper, turning around and showing him her back, soiled with flour and flaunting a great rent toward the bottom.

Chichikov stepped into a dark, wide entry, out of which cold blew upon him as from a cellar. From the entry he found his way into another room that was likewise dark, very, very meagrely lit by a light that came through a broad crack beneath a door. Opening this door he at last found himself in the light and was struck by the disorder that appeared before his eyes. It seemed as if a general house-cleaning were going on and all the furniture had been piled up here for the time being. There was even a broken chair standing on one of the tables and, side by side with it, a clock whose pendulum had stopped and to which a spider had already cunningly attached its web. Here, too, with one of its sides leaning against the wall, stood a dresser with antiquated silver, small carafes, and Chinese porcelain. The top of a bureau, with a marquetry of mother-of-pearl mosaic, which had already fallen out in places and left behind it only yellowish little grooves and depressions filled with crusted glue, was a great and bewildering omnium-gatherum: a mound of scraps of paper, closely covered with writing, pressed down with a paperweight of marble turned green and having an egg-shaped little knob; some sort of ancient tome in a leather binding and with red edges; a lemon, so mummified that it was no bigger than a walnut; a broken-off chair arm; a wineglass with some kind of liquid and three dead flies, covered over with a letter; a bit of sealing wax; a bit of rag picked up somewhere; two quills, stained with ink, and as emaciated as if they had consumption; a quill toothpick, perfectly yellowed, which its owner had probably been picking his teeth with even before Moscow's invasion by the French.

Hung about the walls, quite closely and without much discrimination, were several pictures. One was an oblong yellowed engraving of some military engagement or other, with enormous drums, soldiers in cocked hats yelling fit to split their throats, and drowning steeds; it was unglazed, set in a frame of mahogany with very thin strips of bronze and with whorls, also of bronze, at the corners. Alongside of the other pictures was an enormous, time-blackened one that took up half a wall by itself, done in oils and depicting flowers, fruits, a cut watermelon, a boar's head, and a wild duck hanging head downward. Suspended from the middle of the ceiling was a lustre in a canvas bag, which because of its accumulated dust had taken on the appearance of a cocoon, with the silkworm still inside. In one corner of the room had been piled up a heap of those things which were of a coarser nature and unworthy of knocking about on the tables. Precisely what the heap consisted of it would have been difficult to determine, since the dust upon it was so copious that the hands of whosoever touched it took on a gloved look. More noticeable than the other things were two that stuck out of the pile: a piece broken off a wooden shovel and an old boot sole. One could by no means have told that a living creature inhabited this room had not an old, worn nightcap, lying on one of the tables, proclaimed the fact.

As Chichikov was examining the whole queer setting of the room, a side door opened and the same housekeeper whom he had encountered out in the yard entered. But now he perceived that this was a chatelain rather than a chatelaine; a chatelaine, at least, has no beard to shave, whereas this fellow on the contrary had one and did shave it, although, it seemed, he did so rarely enough, since all his chin and his jowls resembled a wire-bristled currycomb. Chichikov, assuming a questioning expression, waited impatiently for what this chatelain might want to tell him. The chatelain, for his part, waited for what Chichikov at last, astonished by such a strange misunderstanding, decided to ask: "Well, what about your master? Is he at home, or what?"

"The master is here," said the chatelain.

"But where?" Chichikov persisted.

"What's the matter with you, father, are you blind or what?" asked the chatelain. "Oh, you! Why, I am the master!"

At this point our hero involuntarily took a step backward and looked at the other intently. It had been his lot to see not a few of all kinds of people, even such folks as the reader and I may never have a chance to see; but such a specimen as this he had never yet beheld. His face did not present anything peculiar; it was almost the same as that of many gaunt old men, save that his chin alone jutted out far too much, so that he had to cover it with his handkerchief every time he spat, to avoid slavering it; the fire in his little eyes had not died out and they darted about under his high, bushy eyebrows very much as mice do when, thrusting out of their dark holes their sharp little snouts, their ears perked and their whiskers twitching, they are spying out whether the cat is lurking about in ambush somewhere or whether some mischievous boy is about, and sniff the very air with suspicion.

Far more remarkable was his attire. Through no means and efforts could one ferret out what his dressing gown had been concocted from; the sleeves and upper portions had become greasy and shiny to such a degree that they resembled the sort of Russia leather which is used for boots; dangling in the back were four flaps instead of two, out of which the cotton-wool quilting was actually crawling in tufts! About his neck, too, he had tied a something that one could not make out; it might have been a stocking, or a bandage, or an abdominal supporter, but nothing that one could possibly consider a cravat. In a word, had Chichikov met him thus accoutred at a church door he would most probably have slipped him a small copper coin, inasmuch as it must be said to our hero's credit that his heart was a compassionate one and he could never hold himself back from giving a small copper coin to a poor man.

But this was no beggar standing before him; standing before him was a landed proprietor. This landed proprietor owned a thousand serf souls and more, and there would be no use in trying to find another who had so much wheat, in grain, flour, or simply in stocks, or one whose storerooms, warehouses, and drying sheds were cluttered with such a world of linens, cloths, sheepskins (both dressed and raw), dried fish of all sorts, and all kinds of vegetables and salted meat. Had anyone peeped into his work yard, where there was a reserve laid by of every sort of wood and wooden utensils, never used, it would have seemed to him that he must somehow have strayed into the famous Chip Fair in Moscow, whither the wide-awake matriarchs resort daily, with their cooks behind them, to put in supplies for their households, and where every sort of wood rises in mountains of white: nailed, turned, joined, to say nothing of wickerwork; there are barrels here, and chopping bowls, and tubs, and water casks, and noggins, with spouts and without, and dippers, and bast baskets, and slop pails, to keep mops and suchlike in, and hampers of thin bent aspen wood, and cylindrical boxes of woven birch bark, and a great deal of all that goes to supply the needs of rich Russia and poor. What need, it seemed, had Pliushkin of such a mountain of these wares? He would never have been able to use them up in his whole lifetime even if he owned two estates instead of only one, but even this accumulation seemed small to him. Not satisfied with this, he would also patrol the lanes and byways of his village every day, peering under little bridges, under planks, and in every nook and cranny, and everything that he came upon—an old sole, a countrywife's rag, a rusty nail, a clay shard—everything would be dragged off to his place and piled on that heap which Chichikov had noticed in a corner of the room.

"There, the fisherman is setting out for his catch!" the muzhiks would say when they caught sight of him setting out to try his luck. And truly, there was no need of sweeping the street after he had passed by; if a cavalry officer riding by happened to lose a spur, that spur was on the instant on its way to the pile we know of; if a peasant woman, having grown absent-minded somehow at the water well, would forget her bucket there, he would lug the bucket off, too. However, if some muzhik, having seen him, would catch him red-handed on the spot, he would not argue and would give up the purloined article; but if ever it landed on that pile, then it was all over and done with: he called God to witness that he had bought the article at such-and-such a time from so-and-so. Or it had come down to him from his grandfather. In his room he would pick up from the floor whatever met his eye—a bit of sealing wax, a scrap of paper, a feather—and all this he would lay on the table or on a window sill.

And yet there had been a time when he had been but a thrifty householder! He had been married and had a family, and one or another of his neighbors would drop in on him for dinner, to listen to him and learn husbandry and a wise thriftiness. All things went yarely and were performed at a smooth, even pace: the mills, the fulleries turned; the cloth manufactories, the carpenters' benches, the looms were all busy; the keen eye of the master penetrated everywhere and into everything and, like the toil-loving spider, he ran bustlingly yet smartly from one end of his husbandly web to the other. His feathers did not reflect any emotions that were too strong, but one could see intelligence in his eyes; with experience and a knowledge of the world was his speech imbued, and it was a pleasure for his guest to listen to him; the affable and talkative mistress of the house was famed for her hospitality; two pretty daughters would come out to meet you, both with flaxen-fair curls and as fresh as roses; the son would come running out, a sprightly little urchin, and would kiss everyone, paying but little attention to whether the guest liked it or not. All the windows in the house were open; the attics had been taken for his own by the tutor, a Frenchman, who was exemplarily clean-shaven and a great hand with a hunting gun; he would often bring for dinner some black grouse or wild ducks, while at times there would be only sparrow eggs, which he would order to be made into an omelet, inasmuch as there was not another soul in the house that would eat them. There was also a fair compatriot of his living in the attics, a preceptress for the two girls. The master of the house himself would come to dinner in a frock coat, somewhat worn, it is true, yet neat, just the same—the elbows were in good order and there was never a patch showing anywhere.

But the good lady of the house died; some of the keys and, together with them, some of the petty cares, passed on to the master. Pliushkin became more restless, and, like all widowers, more suspicious and more miserly. He could not rely in everything upon Alexandra Stepanovna, his elder daughter, and he was right in this, inasmuch as Alexandra Stepanovna shortly ran off with a second captain of cavalry attached to God knows what regiment, and married him somewhere in a hurry, in some village church, knowing that her father had no great love for military officers, because of an odd prejudice that all military men, now, were inveterate gamblers and profligate scalawags. The father sent a curse after her by way of a godspeed, but did not bother with a pursuit. The house became still emptier. The miserliness of the master began to evince itself more markedly; the gray that gleamed in his coarse hair, a faithful mate of miserliness, helped it to develop still more. The French tutor was dismissed, inasmuch as the time had come for the son to enter the military service. *Madame la gouvernante* was sent packing, inasmuch as it had turned out that she had not been entirely blameless in the abduction of Alexandra Stepanovna. The son, having been sent to the capital city of the province in order to find some berth in the administration which in his father's opinion would benefit him, joined a regiment instead and informed his father only after doing so, when he wrote asking him for money to outfit himself; quite naturally he received in answer to this that which is called among the common folk a fig. Finally his last daughter, who had stayed on in the house with him, died, and the old man was left sole watchman, guardian, and possessor of his riches.

His lonely life afforded rich fare to his miserliness, which, as everybody knows, has a wolfish appetite and which, the more it devours, the more insatiable it becomes; the human emotions which, even as it was, were none too deep within him, shoaled more with every minute, and every day this decrepit ruin would suffer some loss. And it so fell out, at such a moment, as though on purpose to confirm his opinion of military men, that his son lost heavily at cards; he sent him a father's heartfelt curse and thenceforth never evinced any interest to learn whether his son was still in this world or not. With every year more and more windows were boarded up in the house until at last but two remained unobstructed, of which one, as the reader has already seen, had been pasted over with paper. With every year the important aspects of his estate disappeared more and more from his view, while his petty outlook was turned upon scraps of paper and stray feathers, which he accumulated in his room. He grew more and more inaccessible to the commission merchants who came around to buy the produce of his estate—the commission men used to dicker with him, and dicker some more, and finally gave him up for good, saying this was a fiend and not a man. His hay and wheat rotted; the grain stacks and the hayricks turned into downright manure—you could just go ahead and grow cabbages on them; the flour in his cellars had turned into stone and you had to take an ax to it; it was a fearsome thing to touch his clothes, his linens, his homespuns—they turned to dust under your fingers. He was already beginning to forget how much he had of this or that, and remembered only in what spot the little carafe stood that held the heeltaps of some cordial, on which carafe he had put a secret mark, so that no one might thievishly swig a drink, and he likewise remembered where the old quill ought to be and where that stub of sealing wax was. And yet, in his domestic economy, the revenues and perquisites accumulated as hitherto: each muzhik was bound to bring in the same quitrent, every peasant woman had to bring in the same allotment of nuts, each spinster had to work just as many linen looms. All that the estate produced was dumped into the storerooms and all turned to rot and rents, and he himself had turned, at last, into a rent on the cloak of humanity.

Alexandra Stepanovna happened to visit him twice, somehow; the first time with her little son, trying to see if she mightn't get something out of him—evidently the nomadic life with her second captain of cavalry was not as enticing as it had seemed before marriage. Pliushkin forgave her, it must be said, and even allowed his grandson to play awhile with some button lying on one of the tables, but not a copper of money did he part with. The second time Alexandra Stepanovna arrived with two little ones and brought him an Easter cake for his tea and a new dressing gown, inasmuch as father had a dressing gown which it was not only a pity but an actual disgrace to look at. Pliushkin petted both his grandchildren a little and, having seated one of them on his right knee and the other on his left, gave them an absolutely perfect hossy-ride; the Easter cake and the dressing gown he accepted but gave his daughter absolutely nothing, and Alexandra Stepanovna went back even more empty-handed than she had come.

And so that's the kind of landed proprietor who was standing before Chichikov! It must be said that one encounters such a phenomenon but rarely in Russia, where all things love to open up rather than to shrink into a ball like a hedgehog, and it is all the more striking when there turns up in the immediate vicinity of such a phenomenon some landowner roistering with all the expansiveness of

Russian derring-do and seigniorage, burning his candle, as they say, at both ends. The unfamiliar wayfarer will stop in astonishment at the sight of his dwelling, wondering what prince of the blood had suddenly turned up amid the petty, drab landed proprietors; like palaces do his houses of white stone look with their innumerable multitude of chimneys, belvederes, weathercocks, surrounded with a drove of built-on wings and all sorts of apartments for the accommodation of any and all guests who might come. What won't you find on his place? Theatricals; balls; all night will his garden glow decorated with Chinese lanterns and lampions, and be pealing with the thunder of music. Half the province is attired in its best and gaily strolling under his trees, and no one will perceive anything wild or sinister amid this forced illumination when out of the woody density some branch, lit up by the artificial light yet deprived of its vivid greenery, leaps forth theatrically, while because of this light the night sky appears still darker, still more austere and twenty times more awesome, and the trees, receding still further into the impenetrable darkness, their leaves quivering on high, make their austere summits protest indignantly at this tinselly brilliance below which lights up their roots.

Pliushkin had been standing thus for several minutes by now, without uttering a word, while Chichikov still could not start a conversation, being distracted both by the appearance of his host and by everything in his room. For a long time he could not hit upon the words in which to explain the reason for his coming. He was just about to express himself in some such high-flown vein as that, having heard such a great deal about Pliushkin's virtue and the rare qualities of his soul, he had deemed it his duty to pay him his due tribute of respect in person; but he brought himself up short and sensed that this was a bit too thick. Casting another look out of the corner of his eye at all the things in the room, he sensed that for such words as "virtue" and "rare qualities of the soul" one might well substitute the words *economy* and *orderliness,* and for that reason, having reworked his speech accordingly, he said that having heard of his economy and his rare skill in estate management, he had deemed it his duty to make his acquaintance and to pay him his respects in person. Of course, he might have given another and a sounder reason, but at the time nothing else popped into his head.

In answer to this Pliushkin mumbled something or other through tightened lips, inasmuch as he had no teeth; precisely what it was is not certain, but probably the sense was: "Eh, may the Devil take you, respects and all!" But since hospitality is so prevalent among us that not even a miser may transgress its laws, he at once added, somewhat more distinctly: "I beg of you to be seated!"

"It's rather a long while since I've seen any callers," he went on, "and, I admit, I see but little good in 'em. They've started a most indecent custom of gadding about from house to house and yet it means a detriment to one's household . . . and besides, you've got to give their horses hay! I've long since had my dinner, then, too, my kitchen is low-ceiled, as abominable a kitchen as you ever saw, and the chimney, now, has fallen all to ruin; if you light the stove you'll put the whole place on fire, like as not—"

"So that's how the wind blows!" Chichikov reflected inwardly. "It's a good thing, then, that I managed to stay my hunger with a tart of curds and a slice of the side of mutton at Sobakevich's."

"And what a vile come-uppance, there isn't as much as a wisp of hay on the whole place!" Pliushkin continued. "And, really, how is one to store it up? There's so little land; the muzhik is lazy, not overfond of work; all he thinks of is how he might sneak off to the pothouse . . . like as not, one may have to go out into the world and beg in one's old age!"

"However, I've been told," Chichikov put in discreetly, "that you have over a thousand souls."

"And who was after telling you that? Why, father o' mine, you should have spit in the eye of whoever told you that! He must have been a great wag; evidently he wanted to have a bit of fun at your expense. There, they're blabbing about a thousand souls, but you just go and count 'em, and you won't count up anything at all! The last three years the accursed fever has carried off no end of my muzhiks."

"You don't say! And has it actually carried off many?" Chichikov exclaimed with concern.

"Yes, a lot of them have been carried off."

"Yes, but permit me to ask, what was the exact number?"

"Eighty head."

"No!"

"I'm not going to lie about it, father o' mine."

"Allow me to ask you something else—you reckon these souls from the day when you submitted the last census to the Bureau of Audits?"

"I'd thank God if that were the case," said Pliushkin, "but the trouble is that they would add up to a hundred and twenty since that time."

"Really? All of a hundred and twenty?" Chichikov exclaimed, and even let his jaw drop a little from astonishment.

"I'm too old, father o' mine, to go in for lying now; I'm going on my seventh decade!" said Pliushkin. He had, apparently, taken umbrage at such an almost joyous exclamation. Chichikov perceived that such a lack of concern for another's woe was really unseemly, and for that reason immediately heaved a sigh and said that he commiserated with him.

"Yes, but commiseration isn't anything you can put in your pocket," Pliushkin remarked. "There's a certain captain, for instance, living near me; the Devil knows where he has bobbed up from—claims he's a relative of mine. 'Dear Uncle, dear Uncle!'—and he kisses my hand. Well, when he starts in commiseratin', he'll set up such a howl that you'd better watch out for your ears. His face is all ruddy—he must be hanging on to strong brandy for dear life, I guess. Probably squandered every copper he had at the time he was serving as an officer, or some play-acting jade wheedled everything out of him, so now he's taken to commiseratin'!"

Chichikov made an attempt to explain that his commiseration was not at all of the same sort as the captain's, and that he was ready to prove this not in empty words but in deeds and, without putting the matter off any further, without any beating about the bush, announced right then and there his readiness to assume the obligation of paying taxes on all those serfs who had died through such unfortunate causes. This proposal, it seemed, utterly amazed Pliushkin. For a long while he stared at his guest with his eyes starting out of his head and finally asked: "But I say, father o' mine, were you ever in the military service, by any chance?"

"No," Chichikov answered him, rather slyly, "I was in the Civil Service."

"Civil Service?" Pliushkin repeated and fell to munching his lips, as though he were eating something. "But how can you do such a thing as that? Why, it would mean a loss to you, wouldn't it?"

"To afford you pleasure I am ready even to face a loss."

"Ah, father o' mine! Ah, my benefactor!" Pliushkin cried out, not noticing in his joy that the snuff had slipped out of his nose quite unpicturesquely, looking like coffee grounds, and that the skirts of his dressing gown, opening, had revealed his underlinen, which was not a quite seemly object to contemplate. "There, how you have comforted an old man! Ah, my Lord! Ah, all ye saints!" After which Pliushkin could not utter another word. But hardly a minute has passed when this joy, which had so momentarily appeared upon his wooden features, passed just as momentarily, just as if it had never been, and his face assumed anew an expression of worry. He even mopped his face with his handkerchief and, having rolled it up into a wad, began passing it over his upper lip.

"But just how, if you will be kind enough to tell me, since I don't want to anger you—how are you undertaking to pay taxes on them? Will you pay them every year, and will you pay the money out to me or to the Treasury?"

"Why, here's how we'll work it: we'll put through a purchase deed for them, just as though they were still living and as though you had sold them to me."

"Yes, a purchase deed—" said Pliushkin, falling into

deep thought and beginning to chew his lips again, as if he were munching something. "That there purchase deed now, it all means expenses. The clerks are so conscience-less! In former days you could get away with giving them half a ruble in coppers, and a bag of flour, maybe, but nowadays you've got to send 'em a whole wagonload of all sorts of grits, and then add on a red ten-ruble note, that's how avaricious they are! I don't know why no one else ever gives a thought to this. There, if but someone would say a word or two to such a fellow that would be the salvation of his soul! Why, you can move anyone you like with a good word. No matter what anyone may say, there's no one can withstand a soul-saving word!"

"Well, you would withstand it, I think!" Chichikov thought to himself and at once declared that, out of personal regard for Pliushkin, he was willing to take upon himself even the expenses connected with the purchase deed.

On hearing that Chichikov was assuming even these expenses Pliushkin concluded that his guest must be an utter simpleton and had merely pretended when claiming that he had been in the Civil Service but, of a certainty, must have served as an officer and dangled after play actresses. With all that, however, he could not conceal his joy and wished all sorts of pleasant things not only to Chichikov but even to his little ones, without having asked whether he had any or not. Walking up to the window, he rapped his fingers against the glass and called out: "Hey, Proshka!"

A minute later they heard someone hurrying into the entry at a run and fussing there a long while with much clatter of boots; at last the door opened and Proshka came in—a lad of thirteen, in boots so large that at every step he took he all but stepped out of them. The why and wherefore of Proshka having such large boots can be learned without much delay: Pliushkin had for all his domestics, no matter how many of them might be in the house, but the one pair of boots, which always had to be left standing in the entry. Everyone who was summoned to the master's chambers usually had to prance barefoot through the entire yard, but upon coming into the entry had to put on these boots and appear in the room only when thus shod. On coming out of the room he had to leave the boots in the entry again and set out anew on his own soles. Had anyone glanced out of the little window at the time of autumn, and especially when slight hoarfrosts set in of mornings, he would have seen all the domestics going through such leaps as even the sprightliest of male ballet dancers could hardly succeed in performing.

"There, have a look, father 'o mine, what a phiz!" said Pliushkin to Chichikov, pointing a finger at Proshka's face. "Why, he's as stupid as a block of wood, but you just try to leave anything lying around—he'll steal it in a moment! There, what did you come for, you fool? Tell me, what for?" Here he fell into silence for a short while, to which Proshka responded with a like silence. "Get a samovar going, do you hear? And here, take this key, give it to Mavra and let her go to the storeroom; there, on a shelf, is a rusked Easter cake that Alexandra Stepanovna brought me—let it be served with the tea! Hold on, where are you off to? You great big fool! Eh, you, what a great big fool you are! Has the fiend got you by the legs, or what, that you're itching to be off? You listen to all I've got to tell you first. The rusk may have gotten moldy on top, I guess, so let her scrape it off with a knife, but don't let her throw the crumbs away—let her bring them over to the henhouse for feed. And look you, now, don't you be going into the storeroom, brother, or else I'll treat you to—you know what? A bundle of birch twigs, just to let you know what they taste like, now! There, you've got a glorious appetite as it is, but that will whet it still more! There, you just try to set foot in the storeroom, for I'll be watching you from the window all the time! You can't trust them in a single thing," he resumed, turning to Chichikov after Proshka, boots and all, had cleared out of the room.

After that he began casting suspicious glances at Chichikov as well. The various aspects of such an unusual magnanimity began to seem improbable to him, and he thought to himself: "Why, the Devil knows him, perhaps he is merely a common blowhard, like all those profligate scalawags; he'll go on lying and lying, just for the sake of talking and getting his fill of tea, and then go off in his fine carriage!" And therefore, out of precaution, and at the same time wishing to test him out to some extent, he said it might not be a bad idea to make out the purchase deed as speedily as possible, since the life of man is so uncertain—today he lives, but as for the morrow, God alone knows.

Chichikov evinced a readiness to make out the purchase deed that very instant; all he asked for was a list of the dead serfs.

This pacified Pliushkin. One could see that now he was contemplating some action, and sure enough, taking his keys he walked up to the dresser and, having opened the door, rummaged for a long time among the tumblers and cups therein and at last declared: "There, I can't find it, and yet I had a glorious cordial, if only it hasn't been drunk up—my people are such thieves! But wait, isn't this it?" Chichikov beheld a small carafe in his hands, which was all covered with dust, as if with a jersey. "Goes back to my late wife; she made it herself," Pliushkin went on. "My scoundrelly housekeeper had overlooked it altogether and didn't even cork it up, the creature! Little bugs and all sorts of trash managed to get in it, but I got all the rubbish out and now it's as clear as can be—let me pour a little glass out for you."

But Chichikov did his best to decline such a fine cordial, saying that he had already dined and wined.

"You have already dined and wined!" Pliushkin exclaimed. "Why, of course, one can always tell a man who moves in good society no matter where he is—he doesn't eat, yet he's full; but when it's some petty thief or other, it doesn't make any difference how much you feed him. . . . That captain will come, for instance: 'Uncle dear,' says he, 'let me have something to eat!' And I'm as much of an uncle to him as he is a grandfather to me. Probably he must go without anything at all to eat at home, and so he's traipsing around! Oh, yes, you need a list of all these drones? By all means! I wrote all their names out on a separate piece of paper, to the best of my knowledge, so's to cross them out, first thing, when submitting a new census."

Pliushkin put on spectacles and fell to rummaging among his papers. As he untied all sorts of packets he regaled his guest with such dust that the latter had to sneeze. At last the old man drew out a bit of paper, entirely crisscrossed with writing. The names of the peasants were as closely clustered on it as midges. There were all sorts of names on it: Paramons, and Pimens, and Panteleimons, and there even popped up a certain Grigoriy Doezhaine-doyedesh (Try-to-get-there-but-you-won't); there were actually more than a hundred and twenty of them. Chichikov smiled upon seeing such a host. Having put the list away in his pocket, he remarked to Pliushkin that, to execute the purchase deed, his host would have to go into town.

"Into town? But how can I? And how can I ever leave the house? For not a one of my people but is a thief or a swindler; they'll strip me so in one day that there won't be a nail left to hang my overcoat on."

"Haven't you some friend in town, then?"

"There, now, what friend? All my friends have died off, or have dropped their friendship. . . . Ah, father o' mine, how can a man fail to have some friend! Of course I have!" he cried out. "Why, I know none other than the Chairman of the Administrative Offices himself; in the old days he even used to come out to see me. How can I help but know him? We used to eat out of the same trough, we used to climb fences together! What else should we be but friends? And what a friend! Should I write to him, then, perhaps?"

"Why, by all means write to him!"

"Surely, and what a friend, at that! We were school-mates."

And suddenly some warm ray glided over those wooden features; there appeared an expression of—no, not of emotion, but of a reflection of emotion: a phenomenon like that of the unexpected emergence upon the surface of the waters of a drowning man, which evokes a joyous shout from the crowd thronging the bank; but his brothers and sisters have rejoiced in vain, and in vain do they cast from the bank a rope and wait whether there will not appear anew the drowning man's back, or his arms wearied with the struggle—he has come up for the last time. All is over, and even more fearsome and desolate does the stilled surface of the unresponsive element become thereafter. And so it was with Pliushkin's face: immediately following the emotion that had glided over it, it became still more impassive and still more common.

"I had a sheet of blank paper lying on the table," said he, "but I don't know where it has ever gone to; my people are all such a worthless lot!" Here he began looking for it on the table and under it; he groped all over and at last set up a shout: "Mavra! Hey, there Mavra!" A woman appeared in answer to the call, carrying a plate with the rusked Easter cake which the reader is already familiar with. Whereupon the following dialogue took place between them:

"Wherever did you hide that paper, you she-robber?"

"Honest to God, Master, I ain't laid eyes on any paper, save for a small scrap that you used to cover your wineglass with."

"There, I can see by your eyes that you sneaked off with it."

"And what for would I be sneaking off with it? Why, I have no use for it at all: I don't know how to read or write."

"You lie; you carried it off to that little sexton; he's forever scribbling away, and so you carried it off to him."

"Why, that sexton, should he want to, can get his own paper. He never laid eyes on your scrap of paper."

"You just wait; on the dread Day of Judgment the devils

will make it hot for you with their iron pitchforks. You'll see how hot they'll make it for you!"

"But why should they be making it hot for me, when I never laid a finger on that paper? If it were some other womanish frailty, well and good, but thieving is something no one has ever yet reproached me with."

"Oh, but will the devils make it hot for you! 'There,' they'll be saying, 'take that, you conniver, for the way you fooled your master!' and they'll make it hot for you with their red-hot pitchforks, that they will!"

"And I'll say: 'You got no call to do it! As God is my witness, you got no call to do it, I didn't take it—' why, it's lying right there on the table! You're always after reproaching a body, for nothing at all!"

And, true enough, Pliushkin caught sight of the paper; pausing for a moment, he munched his lips and said: "There, why did you fly off the handle like that? What a touchy creature! You tell her but one word, and she'll come back at you with ten. Go on, now, bring me something so's I can seal a letter. Wait, hold on! You'll grab a tallow candle; tallow is too good, it will burn up and there's nothing left, just so much loss; guess you'd better bring me a bit of kindling wood!"

Mavra went off, while Pliushkin, seating himself in an easy chair and picking up a quill, for a long while kept on turning the paper this way and that, figuring if there weren't some possibility or other of tearing even one-eighth off it, but finally became convinced that there was no possible way of accomplishing this, whereupon he thrust the quill into the inkpot that held some sort of fluid with scum on top and a multitude of flies at the bottom, and fell to writing, forming letters that looked like musical notes, at every moment curbing the impetuosity of his hand to keep it from racing all over the paper and instead meanly adding crabbed line to crabbed line as he reflected, not without regret, that there would still be a great deal of white space left.

And is it to such insignificance, such pettiness, such vileness that a man could sink? Could a man change to such an extent? And does all this have any verisimilitude? All this has verisimilitude, all this can befall a man. The fiery youth of the present would recoil in horror were you to show him a portrait of himself in his old age. Take along with you, then, on setting out upon your way, as you emerge from the gentle years of youth into stern, coarsening manhood, take along with you all the humane impulses, abandon them not on the way; you will never retrieve them after! Sinister, fearsome is the old age that will come upon you farther along the way, and it never releases aught nor ever aught returns! The grave is more merciful than it; upon the grave will be inscribed: "Here Lies a Man," but naught will you read upon the frigid, insensate features of inhuman old age.

"But do you know some friend of yours, perhaps," asked Pliushkin, folding the letter, "who might have need of runaway souls?"

"Why, have you any runaways too?" Chichikov asked quickly, immediately on the *qui vive*.

"That's just it, I do have. My son-in-law made inquiries; he says that apparently there's never a trace left of them by now; but then, he's a military man, all he can do right is clink his spurs. Whereas if one were to try the courts—"

"And how many might you have of them?"

"Well, they may add up to as many as seventy."

"No?"

"But, it's so, by God! Why, not a year passes but what some of them run off from me. My people are no end gluttonous; out of sheer idleness they've gotten into the habit of stuffing their guts, whereas I haven't a thing to eat even myself.... Yes, and I would take anything you'd give me for them. So you just advise your friend, now, if he should recapture but half a score souls he would already have a goodly sum. For, after all, a serf soul registered with the Bureau of Audits is worth five hundred rubles or so."

"No, we won't let any friend have even a sniff of this," said Chichikov to himself, and then explained that one could never find such a friend as that, inasmuch as the mere outlay involved would cost more than any serf was worth, for once you tangled with the law and lawyers you would have to cut off the skirts of your own coat to get out of their clutches as fast and as far as possible; but if he, Pliushkin, was so hard pressed, then he, Chichikov, being moved by sympathy, was ready to give him ... but it was such a trifle that it was not worth while even talking about it.

"But how much would you give?" asked Pliushkin, and became the utter Harpagon; his hands began to quiver like quicksilver.

"I would give you five-and-twenty kopecks per soul!"

"And what would your terms be—spot cash?"

"Yes, you would get the money at once."

"Only, father o' mine, for the sake of my poverty, you ought to make it forty kopecks each, really."

"My most esteemed friend!" said Chichikov. "By right it should be not only forty kopecks a soul; I would, if I could, pay you five hundred rubles apiece! I would pay it with pleasure, inasmuch as I behold before me a venerable, kindly old man who is enduring hardship because of his own kindheartedness—"

"Ah, by God, that is so! By God, that's the truth!" said Pliushkin, hanging his head down and shaking it contritely. "It all comes of being so kindhearted."

"There, you see, it didn't take me long to grasp your character. And so, why shouldn't I give you five hundred rubles per soul? But . . . I haven't the wherewithal! I am ready, if you like, to add another five-kopeck piece, so that every soul will stand me thirty kopecks."

"Well, father o' mine, it's all up to you, but you might tack on just two kopecks apiece to that."

"I will tack on just two kopecks apiece, if you like. How many of these runaways have you? You said seventy, I think?"

"No, they'll come to seventy-eight."

"Seventy-eight, seventy-eight, at thirty-two kopecks per soul, that'll come to—" At this point our hero paused for thought, but only for a second, no more, and promptly announced: "That'll come to twenty-four rubles and ninety-six kopecks!" He was strong in arithmetic. Right then and there he made Pliushkin write out a receipt and handed the money over to him, which the latter cupped in both his hands and carried over to the bureau as though he were carrying something fluid, fearing at every moment to let it slop over. On reaching the bureau he examined the money once more and tucked it away, also with the utmost care, in one of the drawers, where in all probability it was destined to remain buried until such time as Father Karp and Father Polikarp, the two priests of his village, would bury him himself, to the indescribable joy of his son-in-law and his daughter, and perhaps even that of the captain who had enrolled himself among Pliushkin's kin. Having hidden the money, Pliushkin sat down in an easy chair and apparently could find no other subject for conversation.

"Well, now, are you already preparing to leave?" he asked, noticing a slight movement on the part of Chichikov, who had only wanted to get a handkerchief out of his pocket. This question reminded him that there really was no use in tarrying any longer. "Yes, it's time for me to be going!" he announced, picking up his hat.

"And what about a cup of tea?"

"No, I'd better have a cup of tea with you some other time."

"But, I say! Why, I've ordered a samovar. I'm no great lover of tea, I must tell you, it's an expensive beverage, and besides that the price of sugar has gone up unmercifully. Proshka! We don't need the samovar! You bring that dried Easter cake back to Mavra, you hear? Let her put it back in the same place it was—or no, let's have it here, I'll carry it back myself. Good-by, father o' mine! And may God bless you! As for the letter, you hand it over to the Chairman of the Administrative Offices. Yes! Let him read it; he's an old friend of mine. Of course! We used to eat out of the same trough—"

After which this strange phenomenon, this shriveled little dotard, escorted him out of the courtyard, ordering the gates to be locked immediately thereafter; then he made the rounds of his storerooms, to make sure that all the watchmen were at their posts—they were stationed at every corner and had to pound small scoops against empty little casks that did duty for the traditional sheets of iron; then he looked in at the kitchen where, under pretext of seeing whether his people were getting good fare, he filled himself with plenty of cabbage soup and buckwheat groats and, having scolded every last one of his domestics for their thievish and loose ways, returned to his own room. Left to himself, he even thought of how he might show his gratitude to his recent caller for such a really unparalleled magnanimity. "I'll make him a present," he reflected to himself, "of my pocketwatch; after all it's a good watch, of silver, and not just ordinary pinchbeck or bronze; it's a trifle out of order, true enough, but then he can get it repaired himself; he's still a young man, so he has to have a watch to make his fiancée like him. Or no," he added after some meditation. "I'd better leave it to him after my death, in my will, to remember me by."

But our hero, even without the watch, was in most cheerful spirits. Such an unexpected acquisition was a veritable gift. Really, no matter what you might say, there were not only the dead souls alone, but runaway souls as well— two hundred creatures and a bit over, in all! Of course, even as he had been driving up to Pliushkin's village he had a premonition that he would gain something or other, but that it would be such a windfall he had never anticipated. All the way back he was unusually jolly; he whistled in a low key; he made music with his lips, putting a fist to his lips as if he were playing on a trumpet, and finally struck up some song or other, a thing so unusual that Seliphan himself listened, listened and then, with a slight shake of his head, said: "Just you listen how the master's singing!"

It was already dusk when they drove up to town. Light and shadow had become thoroughly intermingled and, it seemed, all objects had also become intermingled among themselves. The striped tollgate had taken on some indeterminate hue; the mustachios of the soldier on sentry duty seemed to be up on his forehead and considerably above his eyes, and as for his nose, why, he seemed to have none at all. The thunderous rattling of the carriage and its leaps into the air made the occupant notice that it had reached a paved way. The street lamps had not been lit yet; only here and there were lights beginning to appear in the windows of the houses, while in the lanes and the blind alleys scenes and conversations were taking place inseparable from this time of day in all towns where there are many soldiers, cabbies, workmen, and beings of a peculiar species who look like ladies, wearing red shawls and shoes without stockings and who dart like bats over the street crossings at nightfall. Chichikov did not notice them, nor did he notice even the exceedingly slim petty officials with slender canes who, probably after taking a stroll beyond the town, were now returning to their homes. At rare intervals there would come floating to Chichikov's ears such exclamations, apparently feminine, as "You lie, you drunkard, I never let him take no such liberties as that with me!" or: "Don't you be fighting, you ignoramus, but come along to the station house and I'll show you what's what!" In brief, such words as will suddenly scald, like so much boiling water, some youth of twenty as, lost in reveries, he is on his way home from the theatre, his head filled with visions of a Spanish street, night, a wondrous feminine image with a guitar and ringlets. What doesn't he have in that head of his and what dreams don't come to him? He is soaring in the clouds, and he may just have dropped in on Schiller for a chat, when suddenly, like thunder, the fatal words peal out over his head, and he perceives that he has come back to earth once more, and not only to earth, but actually to Hay Market, and right by a pothouse, at that; and once more life has taken to strutting its stuff before him in its workaday fashion.

Finally the carriage, after a considerable bounce, plunged, as if it were sinking into a pit, into the gates of his inn, where Chichikov was met by his servant Petrushka, who held the skirts of his frock coat with one hand (inasmuch as he did not like having them come apart) and with the other helped his master to climb out of the carriage.

The tavern servant, too, came running out with a candle and the inevitable napkin over his shoulder. Whether Petrushka was gladdened by the arrival of his master no one knows; but at any rate he exchanged winks with Seliphan, and his usual sullen air seemed on this occasion to clear up to some extent.

"You've been pleased to take a long holiday," said the inn waiter, lighting the stairs.

"Yes," said Chichikov, when he had ascended them. "Well, and what's new with you?"

"Everything's well, glory be to God," said the server, scraping. "Yesterday we had some lieutenant or other arrive; he's taken Room Sixteen."

"A lieutenant?"

"Don't know who he is; from Riazan; got bay horses."

"Fine, fine; keep on being a good boy," said Chichikov, and entered his room. As he was passing through the entry he turned up his nose and said to Petrushka: "You might open the windows, at least!"

"Why, I did have them open," said Petrushka, but he was lying. However, his master himself knew that he was lying, but he no longer wanted to argue the matter any further. After the trip he had made he was feeling great fatigue. Having eaten the lightest of suppers, consisting only of a suckling pig, he immediately undressed and, climbing in under his blanket, fell into fast, sound slumber, fell into that marvelous slumber which is known only to those fortunate beings who are bothered neither by hemorrhoids, nor fleas, nor overdeveloped mental faculties.

CHAPTER SEVEN

Fortunate is the wayfarer who, after a long, tedious journey with its cold spells, slush, mire, stage-post superintendents grumbling from lack of sleep, the jingle-jangling of bells, carriage repairs, heated arguments, stagecoach drivers, blacksmiths, and all sorts of scoundrels whom one meets on the road, beholds at last a familiar roof and the little lights that seem rushing forward to meet him. And he will anticipate in his mind's eye the familiar rooms, the joyous shouts of his people running out to meet him, the noise and romping of children, and soothing, low-voiced converse, constantly interrupted by flaming kisses, which have the power to eradicate from memory all that had been dis-

agreeable. Happy is the family man that hath such a retreat—but woe to the bachelor!

Happy is the writer who, after passing by characters that
are tedious, repulsive, overwhelming in their sad actuality,
is nearing characters that manifest the high dignity of man;
happy the writer who has picked out only the few exceptions from the great slough of images swirling about him
day after day, the writer who has not changed even once the
lofty strain of his lyre, has never descended from his aerie
to his poor, insignificant brethren, and who, without touching the earth, has devoted himself wholly to his images and
forms, far removed from that earth and enlarged to heroic
size. Doubly to be envied is his resplendent lot: he dwells
amid these images and forms as if in the midst of his own
family; and, in the meantime, his fame is trumpeted far and
wide—and loudly. He has beclouded men's eyes with incense smoke that transports their senses; he has flattered
them wondrously, concealing the seamy side of life and
presenting to them Man, the Glory of Creation. All and
sundry, with much clapping of hands, hasten after him
and run headlong at the tail of his triumphal chariot. A
great universal poet do they style him, soaring high above
all the other geniuses of the world, even as an eagle soars
above other high-flying birds. At the very mention of his
name young ardent hearts will be overcome with awe and
trembling; responsive tears will glisten in all eyes.... There
is none that is his equal in power—he is God!

Not such, however, is the lot, and different is the fate, of
the writer who has dared to bring out all the things that are
before man's eyes at every minute, yet which his unheed-

ing eyes see not—all that fearsome, overwhelming slimy morass of minutiae that have bogged down our life, all that lurks deep within the cold, broken, workaday characters with which our earthly path, at times woeful and dreary, is beset. Different is the fate of the writer who has dared, as if with the puissance of an implacable burin, to bring out all these things in bold and vivid relief before the eyes of all men! It will not be given to him to reap the plaudits of the populace, not his will it be to behold responsive tears and the wholehearted rapture of the souls he has stirred; not to him will come, fluttering as if on wings, the maid of sixteen with her head all in a whirl and moved by a hero-worshiping infatuation; not for him will it be to forget himself in the sweet fascination of the strains he himself has uttered; not for him, finally, is it to avoid the judgment of his times, which will style as insignificant and base the creations he has cherished; that judgment will consign him to an ignoble place in the ranks of those writers who have insulted humanity; it will ascribe to him the qualities of the chief characters he himself has depicted; it will strip him of heart, and soul, and the divine flame of talent. For the judgment of the writer's own times does not recognize that equally marvelous are the lenses that are used for contemplating suns and those for revealing to us the motions of insects imperceptible to the naked eye; for the judgment of his times does not recognize that a great deal of spiritual depth is required to throw light upon a picture taken from a despised stratum of life, and to elevate it into a pearl of creative art; the judgment of his times does not recognize that lofty, rapturous laughter is worthy of taking its place side by side with a lofty, lyrical strain, and that there is a very abyss between that laughter and the tortured posturings of a show-booth scaramouch! The judgment of his times does not recognize him and will turn everything into a reproach and an obloquy for the unrecognized writer: without discrimination, without response, without concern, he will be left behind in the middle of the road, like some traveler without kith or kin. Harsh is his course in life, and bitterly will he feel his loneliness.

But for a long while yet am I destined by some wondrous power to go hand-in-hand with my strange heroes, to contemplate life in its entirety, life rushing past in all its enormity, amid laughter perceptible to the world and through tears that are unperceived by and unknown to it! And still distant is that time when awesome inspiration will break forth like a storm and well up like a fountain in another head that is clothed in sacred horror and refulgence, and when men will sense, in abashed trepidation, the majestic thunder of other eloquent words. . . .

Let us be getting on—on! Away with the frown that has overcast the brow and with the countenance of austere gloom! Let us plunge suddenly and head first into life, with all its soundless blather and jingle bells, and see what Chichikov is up to.

Chichikov awoke, stretched his arms and legs, and felt that he had had a good sleep. After lying for two minutes or so on his back, he snapped his fingers and recalled, with a face which lighted up, that he now had just a little short of four hundred souls. Right then and there he leapt out of bed, without even first taking a look in the mirror at his face, which he was sincerely fond of and in which he found the chin, apparently, the most attractive of all, inasmuch as he used to boast about it quite often before one or another of his friends, especially if he happened to be shaving at the time of the call. "There, take a look," he would usually say, rubbing his hand over it, "what a chin I have, it's perfectly round!" But this time he did not take a look either at his chin or at his face, but simply, just as he was, put on a pair of morocco boots with fancy appliqués of variegated colors (such boots as the town of Torzhok carries on a brisk trade in, owing to the easygoing ways and ease-loving inclinations of the Russian's nature), and clad only in an abbreviated undershirt, which made him look like a Scotsman, forgetting all about his dignity and his discreet middle age, he covered the room in two leaps, each time slapping his behind quite deftly with his heels. Then, on the instant, he got down to business; as he stood before his casket he rubbed his hands with the same pleasant anticipation as that with which an incorruptible judge of a rural police court, bound for some investigation, rubs his on approaching a table set with all sorts of cold delicacies; save for this, Chichikov did not lose any time in taking certain papers out of it. He wanted to conclude everything as speedily as possible, without letting any grass grow under his feet. He had decided to formulate the title deeds himself, both original and duplicate, so as to avoid paying anything to the pettifogging quill drivers. He knew the correct form perfectly; combining the work with his morning tea (with sweet pretzels and rich cream) which the tavern waiter brought in, placing it deftly, with much clattering of the teathings, almost under his very nose, he speedily wrote out in majuscules: *In the Year One Thousand Eight Hundred and*—; then, immediately following, in minuscules: *So-and-*

so, a Landed Proprietor, and everything else that was required.

In two hours all was in readiness. When, having finished, he glanced at these papers, at these fantastic souls, at these muzhiks who, verily, had been muzhiks once upon a time, had worked, had plowed, liquored, driven horses, and fooled their masters or, it may be, had been simply good muzhiks, some strange feeling that he himself could not comprehend immediately took possession of him. Every one of these memoranda seemed to have some sort of character of its own, and because of this it seemed as if the muzhiks themselves took on their own characters. The muzhiks belonging to Korobochka had, almost to a man, supplemental qualifications and nicknames. Pliushkin's memorandum was distinguished by its conciseness of phrase: frequently only the first syllables of his dead serfs' first names and patronymics would be written down, followed by two dots. Sobakevich's list struck one by its unusual fullness and particularization: not one of the muzhik's qualities had been passed over; of one it was said: *A good Joiner;* another had a notation opposite his name: *Knows his Work and doesn't touch Spirits.* Just as circumstantially had Sobakevich supplied not only the names of the dead soul's father and mother, but also stated what the behavior of both had been; only one, a certain Phedotov, had written opposite his name: *Father Unknown, but born of Capitolina, a House Wench; nevertheless is of Good Character and no Thief.*

All these details imparted a certain air of freshness: it seemed as if these muzhiks had been alive only yesterday. As he gazed long at the names, Chichikov fell into a touched mood and, with a sigh, he uttered: "Good heavens, how many of you are hen-tracked in here! What, my hearties, were you doing in your time? How did you scrabble along?"

And his eyes stopped involuntarily at one of the names. It was one already familiar to the reader, that of Petr Saveliev, or No-Respect-for-the-Pig-Trough, who had at one time belonged to Korobochka, the landed proprietress. Again Chichikov could not restrain himself from saying: "Eh, what a long fellow you are—you've raced off over a whole line! Were you a master craftsman, or just a muzhik, and what sort of death were you carried off by? Was it in some pothouse, now, or were you run over by a lumbering cart as you lay sleeping off your drink in the middle of the road?

"Stepan the Cork—*Carpenter, of Exemplary Sobriety*. Ah, there he is, Stepan the Cork, there's the mighty giant who was fit to be in the Guards! Guess he covered all the provinces on foot with his ax stuck in his belt and his boots slung over his shoulders; he'd eat a copper's worth of bread and two of dried fish, yet in his purse, like as not, he'd lug home a hundred solid silver rubles every time, and maybe even sew a government note in his linen breeches or put it in the toe of his boot. Where did death overtake you? Did you, for the sake of bigger earnings, clamber up on a scaffold under the very cupola of a church, and maybe even pull yourself up on the cross itself, and, slipping off the plank up there, smash against the ground, with only some Uncle Mihei who happened to be standing near you to say, as he scratched the nape of his neck: 'Eh, Vanya, but you had to go and do it!' while he himself, with a rope tied around him, climbed up to take your place?

"Maxim Teliatnikov—*Cobbler*. Ha, a cobbler! 'Drunk as a cobbler,' the saying goes. I know you, I know you, dear man; if you like, I'll tell you your whole life's history. You learned your trade from a German, who fed all of you apprentices together, beat you over the back with a strap for slovenliness, and wouldn't let you out into the streets to skylark and carry on, and you turned out to be a miracle and not just a cobbler; and the German master could not sing your praises enough when he talked about you with his *frau* or a *kamerad*. And what happened after your apprenticeship was over? 'Why, now I'll start a little place of my own,' you said, 'but I won't do it the way a German does, who shivers over every copper; me, I'm goin' to get rich quick.' And so, having paid a considerable quitrent to your master, you set up a little shop, after getting a heap of orders, and got down to work. You'd gotten yourself some rotten leather somewhere, at one-third the regular price, and, sure enough, you made yourself a double profit on every pair of boots you turned out; but within a fortnight the boots you'd made were all cracked and split, and you were cursed out in the vilest way. And so that little shop of yours became deserted, and you started in taking a drop now and then and traipsing around the streets, saying all the time: 'No, but things are bad in this world! There's no such thing as making a living for a born Russian; them furriners won't never let you!'

"And what muzhik is this? Elizavet' the Sparrow! Hell and damnation and the bottomless pit—a wench! How did she ever get shuffled in here? That Sobakevich is a scoundrel; even in a thing like this he had to take me in!"

Chichikov was right; this was a wench, sure enough. How she had ever got in there no one could tell; but so artfully had her name been written out that from a distance one might have taken her for a muzhik, and even her name had been spelled in such a way that, at a careless glance, it might pass for a masculine one. However, Chichikov did not take this into consideration and crossed her off his list right then and there.

"Grigoriy Try-to-get-there-but-you-won't! What sort of a man were you? Did you go in for hauling and, having gotten yourself a troika and cart covered with matting, renounced forever your home, your native lair, and started transporting merchants to the fairs? Was it on the road that you surrendered your soul to God, or did your own friends do away with you over some stout and red-cheeked soldier's wife? Or did some vagabond lurking in a forest get a hankering for your strapped mittens and your troika of squat but sturdy ponies? Or did you yourself, perhaps, as you lay in your broad bunk near the ceiling, get to thinking, and to thinking, and then, for no reason on earth, after first turning in at a pothouse, dive right into a hole in the ice and vanish out of sight and mind? Eh, what a folk the Russians be! It doesn't like dying a natural death.

"And what about you, my darlings?" he went on, shifting his eyes to the scrap of paper whereon the runaway souls of Pliushkin were listed. "Even though you be among the living, yet of what good are you? You might just as well be dead, for all the use you are. And wherever are your spry legs carrying you to now? Did you run off because you had a bad time of it at Pliushkin's, or are you roaming the woods and stripping travelers as the spirit moves you? Are you doing time in prisons, or have you attached yourselves to other masters and are again tilling the soil? Eremei Kariakin; Nikita Volokita (Ladies' Man), and his son, Anton Volokita. One can see by their very nicknames that these fellows knew how to get around.

"Popov, a domestic . . . probably had book learning—he wouldn't take a knife to anyone, I guess, but became a thoroughgoing thief after some refined, genteel fashion. But there, the Captain of the Rural Police must have nabbed you by now, and you with never a passport (though you call it *pash*port) on you. You stand there alertly enough during the confrontation. 'Whom do you belong to?' says the Captain of the Rural Police, putting in, on this most probable occasion, a pretty strong word or two for your benefit. 'I belong to such-and-such a landed proprietor,' you answer, right smart. 'What are you doing here, then?' says the Captain of the Rural Police. 'He's given me leave, so's I can earn my quitrent,' you answer, with never a hitch. 'Where's your passport?' 'With the master that hired me, Pimenov, a burgher.' 'Call Pimenov! Are you Pimenov?' 'I am that.' 'Did he give you his passport?' 'No, he didn't give me no passport at all, at all.' 'What are you lying for?' says the Captain of the Rural Police, with the addition of a pretty strong word or two. 'That's right,' you answer smartly. 'I didn't give it to him, 'cause I got into the house late, but instead I handed it over for safekeeping to Antip Prohorov, the bell ringer.' 'Call the bell ringer! Did he give you his passport?' 'No, I never got no passport off him.' 'Well, what are you lying for again?' says the Captain of the Rural Police, driving the speech home with a rather strong word or two. 'Where is your passport, then?' 'I did have it,' says you, quick as a wink, 'but I must have dropped it on the road somehow, it looks like.' 'And what about that there soldier's

overcoat?' says the Captain of the Rural Police, again nailing you with an additional strong word or two. 'What did
you go and swipe that for? And also that chest full of copper coins from the priest?' 'By no manner of means, I
didn't,' says you, without as much as shifting a foot. 'I've
never yet been caught in a stealing matter.' 'But how come
they found the soldier's overcoat in your possession?' 'I
wouldn't be knowing—probably somebody else brought it
in and put it down near me.' 'Ah, you low-down beast, you
low-down beast, you!' says the Captain of the Rural Police,
shaking his head and putting his arms akimbo. 'Why, clap
him in leg irons and take him to prison!' 'By all means! I'll
go with pleasure,' you answer. And so, taking a snuffbox out
of your pocket, you friendlily treat to a pinch each of the
two invalided soldiers of some sort who are putting the leg
irons on you, and ask them whether they've been in retirement long and what war they'd been in. And now you're living your life in prison, whilst your trial is going on in court.
And the court hands down its written verdict: you're to be
transferred from the prison at Czarevo-Kokshaisk to the
prison at such-and-such a town; and the court there hands
down another written verdict: you're to be transferred to
Vesiegonsk, or something like that; and so you move from
prison to prison, and you say, as you look your new
dwelling place over: 'No; the prison at Vesiegonsk, now, is
cleaner nor this; there you could even play at ninepins,
there's so much room there; and besides, it's more sociable
there, sort of.'

"Habakkuk Phyrov! What are you up to, brother? Where
are you, what regions are you knocking about in? Has fate
carried you off to the Volga, and have you fallen in love

with a free life, having joined the brotherhood of barge haulers? . . ."

At this point Chichikov paused and fell into a slight reverie. What was it about? Was it about the fate of Habakkuk Phyrov, or had he gone into a reverie just so, as every Russian does, no matter what his years, rank, and estate, when he thinks of the riotousness of a free and reckless life? And truly, where was Phyrov now? Why, he was having himself a noisy and merry time on the grain wharf, having come to terms with the grain traders. With flowers and ribbons on their hats the whole band of haulers is making merry, saying good-by to their mistresses and wives; tall, well built, in necklaces and ribbons, they dance in a ring and sing songs; the whole square is seething, and in the meantime, amid shouts, curses, and urgings, the stevedores hook on their backs loads of more than three hundred pounds, noisily pouring wheat and peas into the holds of the deep vessels and piling up bags of oats and groats, and farther on one can see all over the square heaps of bags, piled up into pyramids like cannon shot, and enormous does all this arsenal of grain seem until it shall have been all repiled within the deep river barges, and the endless fleet will start down the river with the spring ice, in single file, like a flight of wild geese. That is when you'll have your fill of work, you barge haulers! And unitedly, as before you had made merry and had played like so many friends, you will buckle down to toil and sweat, hauling the towrope to the strain of a song as endless as all Russia!

"Oho, ho! It's twelve o'clock!" said Chichikov at last, after glancing at his watch. "What have I been fussing around like that for? And it wouldn't be so bad if I'd been doing something useful, but this is just nothing at all; first of all I started spouting bosh, and then I went off into a reverie. What a fool I am, really!"

Having said which, he shaved, changed his Scotch costume for a European one, pulling his plump belly in by another notch in his belt, sprayed himself with Eau de Cologne, picked up his warm cap and put the papers under his arm, and was off to the Administrative Offices to execute the purchase deeds. He was hurrying not because he was afraid of being late; he was not afraid of that, inasmuch as the Chairman was a friend of his and could prolong or abridge an interview at his desire, much like ancient Zeus of Homer, who prolonged the days or sent quick-passing nights whenever the need arose either to bring to a close a martial contest between the heroes he liked, or to permit them to fight to a finish. Rather, Chichikov himself felt within him a desire to bring the matter to an end as soon as possible; until such time as it was ended, everything seemed to him to be in an uneasy and awkward state; despite everything the thought would occur to him that the souls were not quite the real thing and that in such cases it is always necessary and best to shed the onus from one's shoulders as quickly as possible.

He had hardly come out into the street, mulling over all this and at the same time feeling the weight of his brown cloth coat, lined with selected bearskins, which he was wearing thrown over his shoulders, not at all because it was cold but in order to inspire awe in pettifogging small fry, when at the very turn into a bylane he ran into another gentleman, also wearing a brown cloth lined with selected

bearskins and in a warm cap with ear flaps; he had on fine
kid gloves and there was a smile on his lips. The smile
spread more and more; his face lighted up, and he called
out: "Pavel Ivanovich!" It was Manilov. They immediately
clasped each other in an embrace and for five minutes or so
remained in that position right out in the street. The kisses
each bestowed on the other were so hard that both of them
felt their front teeth aching almost throughout the rest of
that day. Only Manilov's nose and lips remained on his face
for joy; his eyes had vanished utterly. For a quarter of an
hour did he hang on with both his hands to Chichikov's
hand and made it fearfully hot and uncomfortable. In most
refined and pleasant terms he told how he had flown to
town, as if on wings, to clasp Pavel Ivanovich to his bosom;
his speech was concluded with such a compliment as might
perhaps be appropriate only to some gentle maiden with
whom one is about to dance. Chichikov opened his mouth,
not knowing yet himself how to thank the other, when
Manilov suddenly took out from under his fur-lined coat a
paper rolled up into a tube and tied with a narrow little
pink ribbon.

"What's this?"

"The little muzhiks."

"Ah!" Chichikov unrolled it right then and there, ran his
eyes over it, and wondered at the neatness and beauty of
the handwriting. "That's splendidly written," said he; "it
won't be necessary to rewrite it even. There's even a border
around it! Whoever made that border so artfully?"

"Why, you mustn't even ask," Manilov told him.

"You?"

"My wife."

"Ah, my God! Really, I feel conscience-stricken over having put you to so much trouble."

"There's no such thing as trouble where Pavel Ivanovich is concerned."

Chichikov bowed in acknowledgment. Learning that he was going to the Administrative Offices to execute the title deeds, Manilov expressed a willingness to accompany him thither. The friends linked arms and started off together. At every slight rise in the ground, or a hummock, or a step, Manilov would support Chichikov and almost give him a hand up, adding with a pleasant smile that under no circumstances would he permit Pavel Ivanovich to stub his little feet. Chichikov felt compunctions, not knowing how to thank him, inasmuch as he sensed that he was somewhat heavy on the hoof. Rendering each other such mutual services they managed at last to reach on foot the square where the Administrative Offices were located, a great three-story building of stone, all as white as chalk, probably to convey an idea of the purity of soul of the functionaries who had their offices within. The other structures on the square were hardly in keeping with the grandeur of the stone building. These other structures were: a sentry box, near which a soldier with a gun was standing; two or three cabstands and, to conclude the list, long board fences with the familiar fenciana and art work, sketchily executed in charcoal and chalk. There was nothing else to be found upon this barren (or, as it would be described by our writing brethren, beautiful) square. Several heads of the incorruptible priests of Themis popped out of the windows on the second and third floors and hid themselves the same minute: probably a superior was entering the room at that moment.

The friends did not walk but rather dashed up the stairs, since Chichikov, trying to avoid being supported under the arm by Manilov, had quickened his step, whereupon Manilov, for his part, flew forward, striving not to allow Chichikov to become fatigued, and for that reason both were puffing quite hard as they stepped into the dark corridor. Neither in the corridors nor in the chambers were their eyes overwhelmed with cleanliness. At that time cleanliness was still not considered a matter to be greatly concerned about, and that which was dirty just remained dirty, without acquiring any attractiveness thereby. Themis in all her simplicity, just as she is, was receiving her guests in negligée and dressing gown. The chancellery chambers through which our heroes passed truly merit description, but the author cherishes a strong timidity in so far as all administrative places are concerned. Even when he has had occasion to traverse such of these chambers as had a resplendent and ennobled air about them, with waxed floors and highly polished tables, he has tried to dash through them as quickly as possible, with his eyes meekly lowered and directed at the ground, and for that reason he is utterly ignorant of how well and flourishingly everything is going on there.

Our heroes saw a great deal of paper, both for rough drafts and of the finest white for final copies; they saw heads bent over their work, and broad napes of necks, and many frock coats, and dress coats of a provincial cut, or simply some sort of short jacket of light gray, which stood out quite sharply, which jacket, with its head twisted almost entirely to one side and all but resting on the very paper, was nimbly and with a full sweep writing out some protocol or other concerning a land-grab, or the inventory of an estate appropriated by some peaceful landed proprietor or other who was tranquilly finishing out his days while the suit was going on, and who had lived long enough to beget him not only children but grandchildren under the benign shelter of this suit. And one could hear, in snatches, brief remarks, uttered in a whisky tenor: "Lend me, Theodossei Theodossievich, the file on Number Three Hundred and Sixty-Eight!" "You always manage to carry off the stopper of the office ink bottle somewhere!" At times a voice, more majestic and beyond a doubt belonging to one of the higher officials, would ring out imperiously: "There, transcribe that! And if you don't, I'll have them take the boots off you and keep you here for six days without food or drink." Great was the scratching of quills, and the sound thereof was as if several carts laden with brushwood were driving through a forest carpeted with dead leaves a yard deep.

Chichikov and Manilov approached the first desk, seated at which were two clerks who were still young in years, and inquired:

"Where are the purchase deeds attended to, if you gentlemen please?"

"But just what is it you want?" both clerks asked, turning around.

"Why, I have to submit an application," said Chichikov.

"But just what was it you bought?"

"I would first like to know where the desk for making out purchase deeds is; is this it, or is it elsewhere?"

"Yes, but tell us first what you bought and what you paid,

and then we'll be able to tell you where to go; as it is, we don't know where to send you."

Chichikov perceived at once that these clerks were simply inquisitive, after the manner of all young clerks, and wanted to lend greater weight and importance to themselves and their duties.

"Look here, my dear Sirs," said he, "I know very well that all matters relating to purchase deeds, no matter what the amount involved is, are attended to in one place, and therefore I am asking you to show me the desk; but if you don't happen to know what is going on around you, why, we'll ask some of the others."

To this the clerks made no answer, save that one of them merely jabbed his finger in the direction of a corner of the room, where an old codger was seated at a desk and shuffling some papers. Chichikov and Manilov threaded their way between the desks toward him. The codger was attending to his work very closely.

"May I ask," Chichikov began, with a bow, "whether this is the desk for purchase deeds?"

The codger raised his eyes and said, articulating almost every syllable: "The purchase deeds are not handled here."

"Where then?"

"You want the Division of Purchase Deeds."

"And where is the Division of Purchase Deeds?"

"That's under Ivan Antonovich."

"And where is Ivan Antonovich?"

The codger jabbed his finger in the direction of another corner of the room. Chichikov and Manilov marched off to see Ivan Antonovich. Ivan Antonovich had already sneaked a glance at them and looked them over out of the corner of

his eye, but the same moment had plunged still more assiduously into his writing.

"If I may ask," Chichikov said, with a bow, "is this the
desk for purchase deeds?"

Ivan Antonovich acted as if he had not even heard them
and became perfectly absorbed in his papers, without making any response. One could see right off that here was a
man who had already attained years of discretion, that this
was no young chatterbox and flibbertigibbet. Ivan
Antonovich, it seemed, had already put far more than forty
years behind him; his hair was black, thick; the whole middle of his face jutted forward and ran mostly to nose; in
short, it was the sort of face that, in common usage, is called
a mug.

"If I may ask, is this the Division of Purchase Deeds?"
Chichikov repeated.

"It is," said Ivan Antonovich, turning his mug around
and then again applying himself to his writing.

"Well, my business is this: I have bought up from various
owners of this district serfs whom I want to transfer elsewhere. Each purchase deed is made out—all that remains
is to execute it."

"And are the sellers present in person?"

"Some are here; from others I have letters of authorization."

"And have you brought the application with you?"

"I've brought that as well. I'd like ... I'm in a hurry ... so
could this matter be concluded today, if you like?"

"What! Today? Today is out of the question," said Ivan
Antonovich. "It is necessary to make further inquiries,
whether there are any liens and the like."

"However, if it comes to that, in order to expedite matters, well, Ivan Grigoriyevich, your Chairman, is a great friend of mine—"

"But then, Ivan Grigoriyevich isn't the only one here; there are others, too," Ivan Antonovich remarked sternly.

Chichikov grasped the hint the other had thrown out and said: "The others won't suffer; I was in the service myself; I know what it's all about—"

"Go to Ivan Grigoriyevich," said Ivan Antonovich in a somewhat kindlier tone. "Let him issue the order through the proper channels, and the matter won't suffer when our turn comes."

Chichikov, taking out a bank note, laid it down in front of Ivan Antonovich, which the latter failed utterly to notice and instantly covered with a ledger. Chichikov was about to draw his attention to it, but Ivan Antonovich intimated with a motion of his head that there was no need of pointing it out.

"This fellow here will bring you to the Chairman's office," said Ivan Antonovich with a nod of his head, and one of the ministrants near by, who had sacrificed at the altar of Themis so arduously that both his sleeves had burst at the elbows and had long since been obtruding their lining, for which zeal he had even attained in his time to the first rung in the ladder of ranks, that of Collegiate Registrar, served our friends even as Virgil on a time had served Dante, and guided them to the Presence, in whose office there was but one capacious armchair wherein, behind a desk with two thick tomes and a trihedral column that was surmounted by the imperial coat of arms and a decree of Peter the First on each flank, sat the Chairman himself, solitary as the sun.

Before the portals of this place the new Virgil experienced such reverent awe that he by no means dared to set his foot over the threshold and turned about, showing a back that was as frayed as an old straw matting with here and there a bit of down sticking to it.

As they entered this official chamber they perceived that the Chairman was not alone; near him sat Sobakevich, who had been entirely screened by the trihedral symbol of authority. The arrival of the newcomers evoked an exclamation; the administrative throne was shoved back noisily. Sobakevich also rose up from his chair and became visible on every side, long sleeves and all. The Chairman took Chichikov into his embraces and the chamber resounded with kisses; they inquired about each other's health, whereupon it turned out that each had a pain in the small of his back, which was at once explained by their sedentary mode of life. The Chairman, apparently, had already been informed by Sobakevich about Chichikov's purchase, inasmuch as he took to congratulating him, which at first embarrassed our hero somewhat, especially when he perceived that both Sobakevich and Manilov, the two sellers, with each of whom he had put the deal through privately, were now standing together and face to face. However, he thanked the Chairman and, immediately turning to Sobakevich, asked:

"And how is your health?"

"Thank God, I have nothing to complain of," said Sobakevich. And, true enough, there was nothing to complain of: sooner would iron catch a cold and start coughing than this wondrously fashioned landed proprietor.

"Why, you were always famed for your health," said the Chairman, "and your late father, too, was a strong man."

"Why, he used to go after bears singlehanded."

"It seems to me, however," said the Chairman, "that you, too, could knock a bear over if you felt like tackling one."

"No, I couldn't," said Sobakevich; "my late father was stronger than I." And, after heaving a sigh, he went on: "No, people aren't what they used to be; you take even my life, now, what sort of a life is it? Just puttering along—"

"Well, in just what way is your life so unattractive?" inquired the Chairman.

"It isn't right, it isn't right!" said Sobakevich, with a shake of his head. "Just judge for yourself, Ivan Grigoriyevich: here I'm going on my fifth decade and I haven't been sick even once—haven't had as much as a sore throat, never even as much as a boil or carbuncle. . . . No, that doesn't bode any good! Some time or other I'll have to pay for it." And at this point Sobakevich was plunged into melancholy.

"Eh, what a man!" both Chichikov and the Chairman thought at the same moment. "Just think what a thing he has picked to complain about!"

"I have a little note for you," said Chichikov, taking Pliushkin's letter out of his pocket.

"From whom?" asked the Chairman and, after breaking the seal, exclaimed: "Ah, from Pliushkin! So he's still vegetating in this world. . . . What a fate! Why, he was the most intelligent, the richest of men! But now—"

"A dog," said Sobakevich. "A swindler. He has starved all his people to death."

"By all means, by all means," said the Chairman to

Chichikov, after reading the letter, "I am ready to act as his agent. When do you wish to execute the purchase deeds, now or later on?"

"Now," said Chichikov. "I would even ask you, if it's at all possible, to put the matter through today, inasmuch as I would like to leave town tomorrow. I have brought both the purchase deeds and the application."

"That's all very well, but, whether you like it or not, we shan't let you go so soon. The purchase deeds will be ready today but, just the same, you'll have to tarry with us for a while. There, I'm going to issue the instructions right now," said he and opened a door that led into the general chancellery, all filled with clerks who had made themselves like so many toil-loving bees clustering upon their honeycombs (if one can but compare chancellery papers to honeycombs). "Is Ivan Antonovich here?" he called out.

"He's here!" a voice answered from the room.

"Send him in to me!"

Ivan Antonovich, he of the mug, with whom the reader is already acquainted, appeared in the Chairman's office and made a deferential bow.

"Here, Ivan Antonovich, take all these purchase deeds; they belong to this gentleman—"

"And don't forget, Ivan Grigoriyevich," Sobakevich chimed in, "that you'll need witnesses, at least two for each party to the contract. Send to the Public Prosecutor's right now; he is a man of leisure and most probably is sitting home this very minute. Zolotukha, that shyster and the foremost bribetaker in the world, does all his work for him. The Inspector of the Board of Health, now, he's a man of leisure too, and is most probably at home as well, if he hasn't traipsed off to play cards somewheres; and there are many others, besides, who are still nearer at hand: Truhachevsky, Begushkin—they're all useless and merely cumber the earth."

"Just so, just so!" said the Chairman, and immediately sent one of the chancellery clerks after all these gentlemen.

"I would also ask you," said Chichikov, "to call in the agent of a certain landed proprietress with whom I have also made a deal. He is the son of Father Cyril, the Dean; this chap is one of the clerks right here."

"Of course, we'll call him in too!" said the Chairman. "We'll attend to everything. And as for the clerks, don't give any of them anything—I beg of you, don't! Friends of mine must not pay." Having said this, he issued some order to Ivan Antonovich on the spot, which order evidently did not prove to his liking. The purchase deeds had apparently produced a good effect on the Chairman, especially when he saw that the purchases amounted to almost a hundred thousand rubles in all. For several moments he gazed into Chichikov's eyes with an expression of great pleasure, and finally said: "So that's how things are! That's the way, Pavel Ivanovich! So you have made acquisitions!"

"I have," Chichikov answered him.

"A good thing! Really, a good thing!"

"Yes, I can see myself that I could not have done better. No matter how things are, man's goal is still indeterminate as long as he has not planted his foot upon some solid foundation instead of some freethinking chimera of youth." At this point, quite fittingly, he chided all young people for their liberalism, and justly so. Yet, remarkably enough, there was a certain lack of assurance in his words, as though he had at the same time said to himself: "Eh, brother, but you're lying, and mighty hard, at that!" He even avoided looking up at Sobakevich and Manilov, out of fear of detecting something on their faces. But his fears were groundless: Sobakevich's face did not so much as twitch, and as for Manilov, he, as though bewitched by an apt phrase, was so pleased that he merely kept tossing his head approvingly from time to time, having plunged into that state in which a lover of music finds himself when some cantatrice has outdone the violin itself and has squeaked out so fine and high a note as is beyond the power of even a bird's throat.

"Yes, but why don't you tell Ivan Grigoriyevich," Sobakevich commented, "just what, precisely, you have acquired? And you, Ivan Grigoriyevich, why don't you ask what acquisition he has made? For what folk he has bought! Pure gold! Why, I sold him even Miheiev, the coachmaker."

"No, not really—you sold him even Miheiev?" the Chairman expressed his amazement. "I know this coachmaker Miheiev, a splendid master craftsman; he rebuilt my droshky for me. But, if I may ask, how is it possible? Why, you told me at one time that he had died—"

"Who, Miheiev dead?" Sobakevich said, not in the least at a loss. "It's his brother who died; but Miheiev himself is as alive as can be and has become healthier than ever. Just a few days ago he constructed such a light carriage that a better couldn't be built even in Moscow. Really and truly, he ought to be turning out work solely for the Emperor."

"Yes, Miheiev is a splendid master craftsman," said the

Chairman, "and I actually wonder how you were able to bear parting with him."

"As if it were a case of Miheiev alone! But what about Stepan the Cork, my carpenter, and Milushkin, my brick-layer, and Teliatnikov, Maxim, my bootmaker? For they all went; I sold all of them!" And when the Chairman asked just why they had all been sold down the river, since they were people indispensable in a household and all masters of their crafts, Sobakevich made answer, with a hopeless wave of his hand: "Why, I simply must have had a fit of foolishness. 'Let's sell 'em,' I said, and sell 'em I did, foolish-like!" After this he hung his head down, as though he him-self repented this transaction, and added: "There, even though you see a gray-haired man before you, yet to this day he hasn't gotten any sense into his head."

"But allow me to ask, Pavel Ivanovich," said the Chair-man, "how is it you're buying peasants without any land? Or are you buying them for resettlement?"

"Yes, for resettlement."

"Well, if it's for resettlement, that's another matter; and whereabouts will you resettle them?"

"Whereabouts? . . . In the province of Kherson."

"Oh, there are fine lands there," said the Chairman and commented most approvingly on the way things grew in that region.

"And have you sufficient land?"

"As much as will suffice for the peasants I bought."

"Have you a river there, or a pond?"

"A river. However, there's a pond there as well." As he said this, Chichikov by an ill chance looked at Sobakevich, and although Sobakevich was as imperturbable as ever, yet it seemed to Chichikov as if the landowner had written on his face: 'Ouch, but you're lying! I doubt if there's any river and pond—or any land, for the matter of that!'

While these conversations were going on, the witnesses began to appear, one by one. The reader is acquainted with them: the blinking Public Prosecutor, the Inspector of the Board of Health, Truhachevsky, Begushkin, and the others who, according to the words of Sobakevich, were all useless and merely cumbered the earth. Many of them were utter strangers to Chichikov; to make up the necessary number of witnesses, some of the clerks were recruited on the spot. They also brought along not only the son of Father Cyril, the Dean, but even the Dean himself. Each one of the witnesses affixed his signature, with all his attributes and ranks, some in a backhanded scrawl, some in slanting pothooks, some almost upside down, putting down such characters as were even not to be found in the Russian alphabet. Ivan Antonovich, whom we already know, had managed his end quite deftly and quickly; the purchase deeds were recorded, marked, entered in the proper ledger and wherever else was necessary, the tax of one-half of one per cent and the charge for the notices in the *Moscow News* were already manipulated, and Chichikov somehow had to pay but a mere moiety. The Chairman even issued an order that only half the revenue tax be taken from him, while the other half, in some unknown manner, was transferred to the account of some other applicant.

"And so," said the Chairman, when everything had been concluded, "all that is left now is to wet the bargain."

"I'm ready," said Chichikov. "It all depends on you to name the time. It would be a sin on my part to refuse to open two or three bottles of the bubbly stuff for such a pleasant gathering."

"No, you haven't understood me aright; it's we ourselves who will stand the bubbly stuff for you," said the Chairman. "That is our obligation, our duty. You're our guest; it is up to us to treat you. Do you know what, gentlemen? For the time being, here's what we'll do: let all of us, just as we are, start out for the house of the Chief of Police; he is our miracle worker; he has but to wink as he passes by Fish Row or a wine cellar, and then, don't you know, what a snack we'll have! And, to celebrate this occasion, we'll have a little game of whist as well."

No one could turn down a proposition like that. The witnesses, at the mere mention of Fish Row, felt their mouths watering; all immediately picked up their caps and hats and the session was over. As they were passing through the chancellery, Ivan Antonovich, he of the mug, said on the quiet to Chichikov, after making him a respectful bow: "You've bought up serfs for all of a hundred thousand, yet all you've given me for my work is a single whitey for twenty-five rubles."

"But then, what sort of serfs are they?" Chichikov answered him, also in a whisper. "The most worthless and insignificant sort, and not worth even half that." Ivan Antonovich perceived that this client was of a firm character and would not shell out any more.

"And what did you pay Pliushkin for each soul?" Sobakevich whispered in Chichikov's other ear.

"And why did you tack the Sparrow onto the list?" Chichikov asked him by way of a reply to this.

"What Sparrow?" asked Sobakevich.

"Why, the countrywife, Elizaveta Sparrow, and you even wrote her first name out with a masculine ending."

"No, I never tacked on any Sparrow," said Sobakevich, but walked away to join the others.

They all made their way in a friendly throng to the house of the Chief of Police. The Chief of Police, sure enough, turned out to be a miracle worker. No sooner had he heard just what was up than he had summoned a roundsman, a spry lad in patent-leather top boots and, apparently, had whispered but a couple of words in his ear and merely added, aloud: "Do you get it?" and, lo and behold—in a room adjoining the one where the guests were ardently at whist there had already appeared a table and, on that table, salted sturgeon (the great white kind), salted sturgeon (the ordinary kind), smoked and salted salmon, caviar (both pressed and freshly salted), herrings, still a third species of sturgeon (the stellated), cheeses, smoked tongues and dried-and-salted sturgeon fillets—all this a tribute from Fish Row. Then there appeared additional contributions from the master himself, the products of his kitchen: a fish-head pie, into which had gone the cartilage and head trimmings of a three-hundred-and-twenty-five-pound sturgeon; another pie with pepper mushrooms; fritters: dumplings fried in butter and dumplings boiled.

The Chief was, in a sort of way, the father and benefactor of the town. He was in the midst of the citizens altogether as if in the bosom of his own family, and as for the shops and the market place, he dropped in on them as if into his own pantry. In general, he had found his proper niche, as they say, and had mastered his job to perfection. It was even hard to decide whether he had been made for the job or the job for him. So cleverly did he handle it that he made twice as much of a good thing out of it as his predecessors had done, and yet at the same time he had earned the love of the whole town. The merchants, first of all, loved him very much precisely because there was nothing stuck up about him; he stood godfather to their children, he was on hail-fellow-well-met terms with them and although at times he did take a powerful chunk out of their hides, yet he did it somehow with exceeding adroitness. He'd even pat you on the back, and laugh right hearty and treat you to a cup of tea; why, he'd give you his promise to drop in for a game of checkers, and would ask you how everything was going with you, how business was, and this and that; if he learned that one of your little ones happened to fall ill, he'd actually advise you what medicine to use. In a word, he was one fine fellow! He might be driving along in his droshky, watching that order was being maintained, yet he'd find time to say a word to this one or that: "Well, what's what, Miheich! I ought to finish that game with you sometime!" "Yes, Alexei Ivanovich," the merchant would answer, doffing his hat, "you really ought to." "Well, Iliya Paramonich, you drop in on me, brother, and take a look at my trotter; I'll race him against yours—you harness yours to a sulky, too, and we'll have a go at it." This merchant, who was insane on the subject of his trotting horse, would smile heartily in answer and, stroking his beard, would say: "Yes, we'll have a go at it, Alexei Ivanovich!"

Even all the hucksters, who usually at such a time doffed their headgear, would look at one another with pleasant expressions, as much as to say: "Fine man, this Alexei Ivanovich!" In short, he had contrived to acquire a thorough folksy popularity, and the general opinion of the merchants was that this Alexei Ivanovich, now, even though he'll take something, will, on the other hand, never go back on you, nohow.

Perceiving that the snack was ready, the Chief of Police proposed to his guests that they conclude their whist after having a bite, and they all trooped into the room, the aromas from which had long since been pleasantly titillating the nostrils of the guests and into which Sobakevich had long been peeping, having marked from afar a sturgeon placed to one side, on a special platter. The guests, having each drained a glass of vodka of a dark, olivine hue—such a hue as is to be found only on certain translucent stones from Siberia, which in Russia are graven into seals—armed themselves with forks and attacked the table from all sides, each one, as they say, revealing his nature and his leanings, this one pressing hard on the caviar, that one assaulting the smoked salmon, still another tackling the cheese. Sobakevich, paying no attention to all these trifles, settled down to work on the sturgeon he had had his eye on and, while the others were drinking, chatting, and eating, he, in just a little more than a quarter of an hour, polished it all off, so that when the Chief of Police did recall it, saying: "And how will this work of nature strike you, gentlemen?" and had walked up to it with the others, fork in hand, he saw that there was but an inedible tail left of this work of nature. As for Sobakevich, he bristled up as if this hadn't been his work at all, and, having withdrawn as far as possible from the others, was prodding his fork into a plate of some sort of small, dried fish. Having put away the exceptional sturgeon, Sobakevich settled down in an easy chair and no longer ate or drank another thing, but merely puckered and blinked his eyes.

The Chief of Police evidently was not fond of sparing liquors—there was no counting the toasts. The first toast was drunk, as our readers may even have surmised for themselves, to the health of the newly baked landowner of Kherson; then came one to the well-being of his serfs and their happy resettlement, then another to the health of his future wife (naturally a great beauty), which evoked a pleasant smile from the lips of our hero. They beset him on all sides and fell to imploring him most convincingly to stay on in their town for at least two more weeks: "No, Pavel Ivanovich! Say whatever you like, but it's just as if you were merely chilling the house, setting your foot on the threshold and then backing out! No, you really must spend some time with us! There, we'll marry you off. Isn't that so, Ivan Grigoriyevich—we'll marry him off?"

"We will, we will!" the Chairman chimed in. "You can resist hand and foot, but it won't do you any good! We'll marry you off just the same. No, father o' mine, since you've fallen into our clutches, you mustn't complain! We don't like to fool around."

"Well, now, what's the use of resisting hand and foot?" said Chichikov. "After all, a marriage isn't just one of those things . . . as long as a bride can be found—"

"Oh, there will be a bride! How else? There will be everything, everything you wish!"

"Well, in that case—"

"Bravo! He's staying on!" they all set up a shout. *"Viva!* Hurrah for Pavel Ivanovich—hurrah!"* And they all drew near him, glass in hand, to clink his. Chichikov dutifully clinked glasses with all of them. "No, no, let's clink glasses some more," said those who felt especially lively, and they clinked glasses with him anew, and for a third time as well did they all clink glasses. In a short while they all grew extraordinarily jolly. The Chairman (you couldn't find a more charming man, once he became thoroughly jolly) embraced Chichikov several times, uttering in heartfelt effusiveness: "My soul! My little darling, you!" and even, snapping his fingers, went into a dance around him, singing as he did so the well-known song: "Ah, you Kamarinsky muzhik, you so-and-so and this-and-that!"

After the champagne they uncorked some Hungarian wine, which added still more spirit and gaiety to the gathering. They had forgotten all about whist; they disputed and shouted and spoke of everything on earth, of politics and even of military matters; they propounded free and daring ideas for which, at another time, they themselves would have given their children a sound whipping. Right then and there they resolved a multitude of the most difficult problems. Never had Chichikov felt himself in so jolly a mood; by this time he imagined he really was a landowner of Kherson; he spoke of sundry improvements, of the scientific rotation of crops, of the happiness and bliss of twin souls, and began reciting to Sobakevich Werther's versified epistle to Charlotte, in answer to which Sobakevich only batted his eyes as he sat in his easy chair, inasmuch as after the sturgeon he felt a great inclination to slumber. Chichikov surmised even himself that he was becoming too expansive, asked for a carriage and gladly availed himself of the Public Prosecutor's droshky. The Public Prosecutor's coachman, as it turned out on the way, was an experienced lad, inasmuch as he directed the reins with only one hand while with the other, placing it behind him, he kept the gentleman upright. In such fashion did the Public Prosecutor's droshky get him at last to his inn, where for a long while yet all sorts of nonsense kept coming to the tip of his tongue: about a flaxen-fair bride with rosy-red cheeks—and a little dimple on the right one; about villages in Kherson; about lots of capital. Seliphan was even given certain husbandly instructions about getting all the newly resettled serfs together, so as to call a muster of them. Seliphan listened in silence for a very long while and then went out of the room, after saying to Petrushka: "Go and undress the master!"

Petrushka began taking the boots off Chichikov and almost dragged his master to the floor together with them. But at last the boots were taken off, the master properly undressed and, after tossing a few times in bed, which creaked unmercifully, he fell asleep, to all intents and purposes a downright landowner of Kherson. And Petrushka in the meantime took out into the corridor his master's trousers and the frock coat of scintillating bilberry red, which, after spreading it on a hanger, he began cleaning with a beater and a brush, filling the whole corridor with dust.

As he was about to remove the garment he happened to look down from the gallery and caught sight of Seliphan in the courtyard, returning from the stable. Their eyes met and intuitively they understood each other: the master is asleep!—they would be able to drop in at a place or two. Right away, having carried the frock coat and trousers inside the room, Petrushka went down and the two walked off together, without saying a word to each other about their destination and chaffing each other on their way about something utterly irrelevant. Their jaunt was not a protracted one—to be precise, they crossed over to the other side of the street, to a house that was opposite the inn, and entered a low little glass door, all covered with soot, which led into something that was practically a basement, where there was already a number of all sorts of folk seated at wooden tables: those who were clean-shaven and those who were bearded, those who wore unlined sheepskin jackets and those who wore little more than a shirt, while here and there was a fellow in a frieze overcoat. What Petrushka and Seliphan did there God alone knows; but they came out an hour later, arm in arm, preserving a perfect silence, paying a great deal of attention to each other and mutually watchful of bumping into any sharp corners. Arm in arm, without letting go of each other, they took all of a quarter of an hour to climb the staircase until finally they got the better of it and reached the top. Petrushka stopped for a minute before his low cot, considering how he might lie down most conveniently and wound up lying right across it, so that his feet were propped against the floor. Seliphan, too, lay down on the same cot, pillowing his head on Petrushka's belly and forgetting entirely that this was not at all the place where he was supposed to sleep, which was in the domestics' quarters, perhaps, if not in the stable, next to the horses. Both fell asleep the same minute, raising snores of unheard-of intensity, to which their master in the other room responded with a high-pitched nasal wheezing.

Soon after the arrival of the two everything quieted down, and the inn was enveloped in profound sleep, save that in a single little window there was still a light to be seen, where some lieutenant, the one who had come from Riazan, lived. Evidently he had a great weakness for boots, inasmuch as he had already bought himself four pair and was now incessantly trying on a fifth. Several times he approached the bed in order to throw them off and lie down, but somehow could not bring himself to do so; the boots really were well made, and for a long while yet did he keep on lifting now this foot and now the other and inspecting the deftly and wondrously turned heel of each boot.

CHAPTER EIGHT

Chichikov's purchases became the subject of much talk. Surmises, opinions, and discussions as to whether it was profitable to buy peasants for resettlement now absorbed the whole town. Many of the disputants evinced a thorough knowledge of the subject.

"Of course," some maintained, "that is very true; there's no arguing against it—lands in the southern provinces are undeniably good and fertile; but how will things be for Chichikov's serfs without any water? There's no river there at all."—"The lack of water wouldn't matter; it wouldn't matter in the least, Stepan Dmitrievich, if it weren't that resettlement is an unreliable thing all around. Everybody knows what the muzhik is: he'll be on new land, and he'll have to work that land with nary a thing—he won't have a hut nor a yard. Well, he'll run off as sure as two times two, he'll make himself that scarce you'll find nor hide nor hair of him."—"No, hold on, hold on, Alexei Ivanovich, I don't agree with what you're saying, that Chichikov's muzhiks will run off. The Russian can adapt himself to everything and become used to every climate. You can send him even to Kamchatka, the only thing you'll have to supply him with will be mittens; then he'll slap his hands together, take an ax in them, and be off to chop down timber for a new hut."—"But, Ivan Grigoriyevich, you've left out one important factor: you haven't yet asked what sort of muzhik Chichikov owns. Have you forgotten that no landowner will sell a good serf? I am ready to lay my head on the block if the kind of muzhik Chichikov owns isn't a thief and the most abandoned of drunkards, an idle vagabond and of violent conduct."—"Just so, just so; I agree with that; it's true no one will sell good serfs, and that Chichikov's serfs are drunkards; but it must be taken into consideration that that is precisely what the moral consists of: they are good-for-nothings now but, having resettled in a new land, they may become excellent and submissive people in no time at all. There have already been not a few such examples, not only in daily life but throughout history as well."

"Never, never!" maintained the manager of the government factories. "Believe me, such a thing can never be, since Chichikov's peasants will have two powerful enemies to contend against. Their first enemy is the proximity of the provinces in Little Russia where, as you know, spirits are freely sold. I assure you that within two weeks they will drink themselves into the blind staggers. The other enemy is none other than wanderlust, which will be inevitably acquired by the peasants during the process of their resettlement. If these are to be guarded against it will be necessary for Chichikov to keep them perpetually under his very eyes and he'll have to rule them with a hand of iron and bear down on them hard for every offense, no matter how trifling, and he won't be able to rely upon anybody else to do it for him, either, but, should the occasion call for it, he must be able himself, with his own two fists, to knock the muzhik's teeth out or plant a good, solid clout on the back of his neck, or both."—"But why should Chichikov be bothered himself and have to clout the backs of their necks? He can find an overseer, can't he?"—"Oh, sure, you'll find an overseer! They're all cheating rogues!"— "They're cheating rogues because the masters don't attend to their business!"—"That's the truth!" many chimed in. "If the master himself knows anything at all about what's what when it comes to running an estate, and if he's any kind of a judge of character, he'll always have a good overseer."

But the factory manager said that you couldn't find a good overseer for less than five thousand. The Chairman, however, said that you could dig one up for even three thousand. Whereupon the factory manager said: "Where will you dig him up, then? In your nose, maybe?"—"No," said the Chairman, "not in my nose but in this very district—Petr Petrovich Samoilov, to be precise—there's the overseer you need for Chichikov's muzhiks!"

Many felt strongly about Chichikov's situation, and the difficulty of resettling such an enormous number of peasants frightened them exceedingly: they even began to be greatly apprehensive lest an actual uprising occur among such unruly folk as Chichikov's peasants. In answer to this the Chief of Police assured them that there was no need to apprehend an uprising; that for the averting thereof there existed the power of the Captain of the Rural Police; that, if, instead of coming himself, the Captain of the Rural Police were to send merely his uniform cap, that cap alone would drive the peasants to the very place of their resettlement. Many offered their opinions on how to root out the spirit of revolt that had swept like a storm over these peasants of Chichikov's. These opinions were of every sort; there were such as reeked far too much of military harshness, and of a severity that was all but excessive; there were, however, such opinions as were inspired with gentleness. The Postmaster remarked that a sacred obligation lay ahead of Chichikov, that he could become a father, in a sort of way, to his peasants; as he expressed it, Chichikov might even bring about benevolent enlightenment and, in connection with this, he commented with praise on the Lancasterian method of mutual education.[7]

In such fashion did the good people of the town dispute and talk, and many, moved by sympathy, imparted to Chichikov certain of these counsels personally, even proposing a convoy for the safe transportation of the peasants to their new locality. For these counsels Chichikov thanked them, saying that should the need arise he would not fail to avail himself of them; but as for the convoy, he turned it down in positive terms, saying that it was absolutely unnecessary, inasmuch as the peasants he had bought up were extraordinarily docile in character, since they themselves voluntarily favored the resettlement, and that there couldn't possibly be any uprising among them.

All this talk and discussion, however, brought about the most beneficent consequences, such as Chichikov could hardly have expected—to wit, rumors spread that he was no more and no less than a millionaire. The citizens of this town had, even without this, as we have already seen in the first chapter, come to love Chichikov with all their hearts, and now, after such rumors, they came to love him with their hearts and souls both. However, if the truth were to be told, they were all kindhearted folk; they lived in concord among themselves, treating one another like perfect friends, and their conversations bore the impress of a certain peculiar simpleheartedness and intimacy: "My dear friend Iliya Iliich!"; "I say, brother Antipator Zakharievich!"; "You've gotten all balled up in your lies, Ivan Grigoriyevich, my little darling!" In the case of the Postmaster, whose name was Ivan Andreievich, they always tacked on the tag: *"Sprechen Sie Deutsch?"*—thus: *"Sprechen Sie Deutsch,* Ivan Andreich?"* In short, everything was very much on an it's-all-one-big-family footing. Many of them were not without culture: the Chairman of the Administrative Offices knew the *Liudmilla* of Zhukovsky by heart, which poem was at that time a novelty hot out of the oven, and recited many passages in a masterly fashion, especially: "Sleeps the pine grove; the dale slumbers," and when he came to "Hush!" he would pronounce it in such a way that one really seemed to see the dale slumbering; for the sake of greater verisimilitude he would at this point even half-shut his eyes. The Postmaster went in more for philosophy and read quite diligently, even burning the midnight oil,

---

*A very innocuous bit of paronomasia or echolalia on *Deutsch* and the suitably modified *ich* ending of the Postmaster's patronymic. *Trans.*

such things as Young's *Night Thoughts* and Eckartshausen's *Key to the Mysteries of Nature,* from both of which he copied quite lengthy excerpts, but of just what nature these excerpts were no one knew. However, he was a wit, colorful in his choice of words, and fond, as he himself put it, of "garnishing" his speech. And the way he garnished his speech was through a multiplicity of sundry tag ends and oddments of phrases, such as "My dear sir; some sort of a chap; you know; you understand; you can just imagine; relatively speaking, so to say; in a sort of a way," and other such verbal small change, which he poured out by the bagful; he also garnished his speech, quite successfully, by blinking one eye, or puckering it up, all of which added quite a caustic air to many of his satirical innuendoes.

The others also were more or less enlightened folk; this one would read Karamzin the historiographer, that one the *Moscow News*—while a third one might read nothing whatsoever. One might be what is called a "hangman's blindfold"—that is, a man who has to be kicked in the behind to arouse him to anything; another simply a solitary sluggard who, as they say, lies abed all his life long, whom it would be even no use to arouse, he'd simply roll over on the other side. All the men were of the sort upon whom their wives, during the tender talks that take place in privacy, bestow pet names, such as Dumpling, Chubby, Tummy, Blackie, Kiki, Zuzu, and the like. But, in general, they were a kindly folk and full of hospitality, and a man who had partaken of their bread and salt or had sat through an evening of whist with them already became something near and dear to them; all the more so a Chichikov, with his enchanting qualities and ways, who really knew the great secret of making oneself liked. They fell in love with him to such an extent that he could not see any means of escaping from the town; he never heard anything but: "There, one short week more, stay with us for just one short week more, Pavel Ivanovich!" In short, they simply dandled him like a baby, to use the common phrase.

But incomparably more remarkable was the impression (truly a matter to marvel at!) which Chichikov made on the ladies. In order to explain this, to however slight an extent, it would be necessary to say a great deal about the ladies themselves, about their society, to describe in living pigments, as the phrase goes, their spiritual qualities; but all that is a very difficult thing for the author. On the one hand he is held back by his boundless respect for the helpmeets of the dignitaries, while on the other hand ... on the other hand it is simply a difficult thing to do. The ladies in the town of N—— were ... no, I simply can't do it, I really do feel a certain timidity. The most remarkable thing about the ladies of the town of N—— was ... Why, it's actually odd, the quill absolutely refuses to move, just as if it were loaded with lead, or something. So be it, then: the description of their characters will evidently have to be left to him whose pigments are more vivid—and who has a greater variety of them on his palette; as for us, we'll simply have to say a word or two, perhaps, about their appearance, and about that which is rather superficial.

The ladies of the town of N—— were what is called presentable, and in this respect they might be boldly held up as an example to all others. When it came to such things as deportment, keeping up the tone, observing etiquette, as well as a multitude of the most refined properties and, in particular, following the mode down to its very least trifles—why, in such things they were far ahead of the ladies of even St. Petersburg and Moscow. They dressed with great taste, and drove about town in their carriages, even as the latest fashion decreed, a footman swaying behind, and the livery on him all gold galloons. The visiting card, even if one were forced to improvise one out of a deuce of clubs or an ace of diamonds, was nevertheless a very sacred thing. Because of just such a thing two of the ladies, not only great friends but actually relatives, broke off their friendship for good and all; to be precise, one of them had been negligent about returning a call. And no matter how hard their husbands and male kindred strove afterward to reconcile them, it was no go; it turned out that one can accomplish all things in this world, save one alone: the reconciliation of two ladies who have fallen out over a neglected return call. And so both ladies remained "mutually disinclined," to use an expression current in the *grand monde* of the town.

The matter of precedence at social functions also brought about a great many quite stirring scenes, which at times inspired the husbands with perfectly chivalric and magnanimous notions of knight-errantry. No duels, of course, took place among them, inasmuch as all of them were Civil Service officials, but to make up for that each would try to pull some dirty trick on the other wherever and whenever possible, which, as everybody knows, can on occasion inflict greater damage than any duel.

When it came to morals the ladies of the town of N—— were strict, filled with noble indignation against vice in any form and temptations of every sort, punishing frailties without any mercy. But if what is known as *a thing or two* did occur among them it occurred in secret, so that there was no hint whatsoever given of what was going on; propriety was entirely preserved, and the husband himself had been so well trained that, even if he did happen to catch a glimpse of *a thing or two,* or heard thereof, he would answer succinctly and sensibly with the proverb: *Mind your own p's and q's—let folks do whatever they choose.* It must also be said that the ladies of the town of N—— were distinguished, like many ladies in St. Petersburg, by an unusual fastidiousness and decorum in their choice of words and expressions. Never did they say: "I blew my nose; I sweated; I spat": instead they said: "I relieved my nose; I had to use my handkerchief." One could not, under any circumstances, say: "This glass (or this plate) stinks," and one could not even say anything that would give a hint of this, but instead of that they would say: "This glass is misbehaving," or something else of that nature. In order to ennoble the Russian language still more, almost half the words therein were utterly rejected in conversation, and for that reason they frequently had to resort to the French language; also, to make up for their nicety in Russian, things were altogether different when it came to French—words far coarser than any of the examples given above were perfectly *propre* therein. And there you have whatever can be said (speaking quite superficially, of course) about the ladies of the town of N——. But if one were to look below the surface then, naturally, many other things would be revealed; however, it is quite dangerous to look below the surface of feminine hearts. And so, limiting ourselves to superficiality in this case, let us be getting on.

Up to now all the ladies had somehow discussed Chichikov but little, giving him his full due, however, for having such agreeable social graces. But from the time that rumors began to spread about his millionairehood they began finding many other good points about him. However, the ladies were not at all avaricious schemers; the fault of the whole thing lay in the very word *millionaire*—not in the millionaire himself but precisely in the very word, inasmuch as the very sound of the word contains, outside of any vision of moneybags, a something that has an effect not only on men who are scoundrels or are wishy-washy, but on men who are fine by nature; in a word, it had an effect on everybody. The millionaire has one great advantage, in that he can witness meanness that is utterly disinterested, meanness not based upon any ulterior motives whatsoever; many know very well that they won't get a thing out of him and that they aren't entitled to anything, yet they'll never fail at least to catch his eye, or to laugh ingratiatingly, or to doff their hats, or to wangle an invitation to the dinner to which, as they have learned, the millionaire had been invited. It can't be said that this tender predisposition to meanness had been experienced by the ladies; however, in many of the drawing rooms they began saying that while Chichikov was not, of course, the handsomest of men, he was, just the same, all that a man should be, that were he but a little fatter (or stouter, rather) it would be a pity. In connection with this something would be said, even quite offensively, somehow, concerning the man who was decidedly thin, that he was something in the nature of a toothpick rather than a man. Many and sundry additional touches appeared in the attire of the ladies. There was a great stir in Drapers' Row, almost a crush. There was something very like a parade of carriages, so many of them had gathered there. The merchants were amazed on seeing several bolts of goods they had brought home from the fair, and which had been left on their hands because the price had seemed high, now suddenly become all the go and being snatched out of their hands. During mass one of the ladies was seen with such a rouleau or hoop at the bottom of her dress that made it spread out over half the church, so that the usher, who was near by, had to issue orders for the commoner folk to move back—nearer to the porch, that is—lest Her Highness' raiment get rumpled somehow.

And as for Chichikov himself, he could not but notice, if only in part, such unusual attentiveness. As everybody knows, a feminine opinion approving a man's looks will buck him up considerably. This induces such a radiant mood that he actually becomes an Adonis. In a certain species of wild duck, for instance, the drake's plumage will, at the mating season, burst into such vivid hues as it never had before. Chichikov's mien became even more agreeable than hitherto, his motions and gestures more unconstrained, and his very collars were snowier, somehow, and hugged his jowls more caressingly. He sported a new watch chain. He became alluring.

On one occasion when he came home he found a letter on his table. Whence it had come and who had brought it he could not find out; the tavern waiter remarked that someone had brought it but had not wanted to say whom it was from. The letter began in very positive terms, precisely as follows: "No, I really must write you!" After that it went on to say that there is such a thing as a secret affinity between souls; this verity was clinched with a number of full stops that took up almost half a line. Then followed a few thoughts, quite remarkable for their incontrovertibility, so that we deem it almost indispensable to make an abstract of them: "What is our life? A vale of sorrows. What is the world? An insensate human herd." Next the fair writer mentioned that she was bedewing with tears certain lines written by her angelic mother—five-and-twenty years had gone since she had passed from this world; she called on Chichikov to come out into the wilderness, to leave forever the city, where people in stifling enclosures cannot breathe the free air; the end of the letter even echoed downright despair and concluded with the following lines:

> *Two turtledoves will show thee*
> *Where my cold corpse lies;*
> *Their lovelorn cooing tells thee:*
> *She died amid tears and sighs.*

There wasn't much metre, especially in the last line; this, however, mattered but little—the letter was written in the spirit of that time. Nor was there a signature of any sort, either first name or last—not even a date line. The postscript merely added that his own heart ought to surmise who had written these lines, and that at the Governor's ball, which was set for the morrow, the writer herself would be present.

This piqued his interest very much. There was so much about the anonymity of the letter that was enticing and excited the curiosity, that he read it through a second time, and a third, and said, at last: "Well, now, it would be curious to know just who wrote that!" In brief, the matter evidently became serious, for he kept mulling over it for more than an hour. At last, he threw up his hands and, cocking his head, declared: "The letter is surely written in a very, very flowery way!" After which, it need hardly be said, the letter was folded and tucked away in the casket, next to some theatrical handbill or other and an engraved wedding invitation which had been preserved for seven years in the same position and the same spot.

A little later, sure enough, an invitation to the Governor's ball was brought to him, balls being quite the usual thing in provincial capitals; where the Governor is, there is bound to be a ball, otherwise the proper affection and respect on the part of the gentry would never be forthcoming.

Everything immaterial was dropped and put aside that very minute, and everything was directed toward preparations for the ball, inasmuch as there truly were many exciting and stirring reasons for attending it. But then, it is probable that so much time and energy was never expended on dressing since the very creation of the world. A whole hour was consecrated to the mere contemplation of his face in the mirror. He tried to impart to it any number of varying expressions; now an important and a dignified one, now a deferential one, yet not devoid of a certain slight smile, then simply a deferential one, without the smile. Several bows were dealt out in front of the mirror, accompanied by indistinct sounds bearing some resemblance to French, although Chichikov was utterly ignorant of that language. He even surprised himself with a host of pleasing mannerisms: he twitched his eyebrow as if winking, and moved his lips, and did something or other even with his tongue; in a word, what doesn't one do when left all to oneself, assured that nobody is peeping at one through a crack in the door and feeling, on top of that, that one is not at all hard to look at? Finally he chucked himself under the chin, ever so slightly, saying: "Eh, you little good-looker, you!" and began dressing. A most contented mood never deserted him all the time he was dressing; as he put on his suspenders or tied his cravat he scraped and bowed with an especial adroitness and, although he had never danced, he performed a caper. This caper had a slight and harmless sequel: the bureau shook and a clothesbrush fell off the table.

"Say what you will, but balls are a fine thing!" Chichikov mused. "It may be freezing, and the crops may have been poor, or there may be something else for you to fret about, but when people come together they forget all their troubles. There's something to amuse everybody—dancing for the young people, cards for those who've reached years of discretion. One can look on while others dance, and have one's fill of whist; and just the society, the throng around you, means a great deal. All is gaiety, all is bright. And then there's the supper—the Governor's chef is famous. There'll be hazel grouse with mayonnaise. Maybe, also, a cold fresh sturgeon or two, with truffles, capers, herbs, and so on; then we'll give the fish some chilled bubbly stuff to swim in! Devil take it, what a lot of all sorts of things there is in this world! I love pleasant, harmless sociability!"

His arrival at the ball created an extraordinary sensation. Everyone there, without an exception, turned to greet him, even if he were holding cards, or was at the most interesting point of the conversation, just after saying:

"... while the lower district court maintains, in rejoinder to this—" But just what the lower district court maintained was at once brushed aside by the speaker as he hastened to greet our hero. "Pavel Ivanovich!"—"My most esteemed Pavel Ivanovich!"—"Pavel Ivanovich, my soul!"—"So here you are, Pavel Ivanovich!"—"Yes, here he is, our Pavel Ivanovich!"—"Let me clasp you to my bosom, Pavel Ivanovich!"—"Let's have him here; come, I'm going to kiss my Pavel Ivanovich real hard!"

Chichikov felt himself in several embraces at the same time. He had not succeeded in freeing himself entirely from the embraces of the Chairman of the Administrative Offices when he found himself in those of the Chief of Police; the Chief of Police passed him on to the Inspector of the Board of Health; the Inspector of the Board of Health to the tax farmer; the tax farmer to the Town Architect.... The Governor, who at the time of Chichikov's entrance had been standing near the ladies, holding a snap-cracker motto in one hand and a small, fluffy white lap-dog in the other, upon catching sight of Chichikov threw both motto and lap-dog to the floor, so that the poor creature whimpered. In a word, Chichikov spread extraordinary rejoicing and gaiety on all sides of him. There wasn't a face that did not express pleasure or, at least, a reflection of the general pleasure. Thus do the faces of all the bureaucrats light up when some high official arrives for an inspection of the departments entrusted to them, after their first fright has subsided and they perceive that not a few things are to the liking of the great man; he himself has at last condescended to jest a little—that is, to drop a few words with a pleasant smile—whereupon those bureaucrats who are around him, and somewhat nearer him in rank, laugh in response to his sally twice as hard as need be; those who, truth to tell, had heard but poorly the words he has let drop, make up for that by laughing with all their heart; and, finally, some policeman or other, stationed far-off near the door, at the very exit, who has never laughed in all his born days and who just before had shaken his fist at the people outside—why, even he, in accordance with the immutable laws of reflection, expresses on his face some sort of smile, although this smile rather resembles the grimace of someone getting set to sneeze after a pinch of rappee.

Our hero responded to all and sundry and felt somehow extraordinarily adroit; he bowed right and left, bending somewhat to one side, as was his wont, but perfectly at his ease, so that he bewitched everybody. The ladies encircled him on the spot, forming a glittering garland about him and wafting whole clouds of fragrant odors; one breathed of roses, another spread an aura of spring and violets, a third was permeated through and through with mignonette—Chichikov could but lift up his nose and breathe in the fragrances.

There was no end of tastefulness about their attire: the muslins, satins, and tulles were of such fashionable pastel shades that one could not even give their names, to such a degree had the refinement of taste attained! Bows of ribbon and flower corsages fluttered here and there over their gowns, in a most picturesque irregularity, although a clever head and clever hands must have expended considerable thought and toil upon that same irregularity. Or one would come upon a gossamer headdress that perched only on the shell-pink ears and seemed to be saying: "Watch out—I'm going to fly away! The only pity is that I won't lift with me the beauty wearing me!" Their waists were tightly laced and their forms most sturdily shapely and pleasing to the eye (it must be noted that the ladies of the town of N——ran, on the whole, to plumpness, but they laced themselves in so artfully and had such pleasant ways about them that the plumpness was not in any way noticeable). They had premeditated and foreseen everything with unusual thoroughness; the neck, the shoulders were exposed precisely as much as need be and by no means one jot further; each one had revealed her possessions only to that degree which her inner convictions made her feel would just about suffice to seal a man's doom, while the rest was tucked away with unusual taste: either there was some sort of ethereal neckpiece, of some material as insubstantial as cotton-candy; or else small, crenelated ramparts of the finest cambric, known under the name of *modesties,* emerged from the dress. These *modesties* concealed, fore and aft, that which no longer could seal a man's doom, and yet at the same time compelled him to suspect that this was precisely where his doom lurked.

Their long gloves were put on not all the way up but with *malice prepense* left bare the seductive parts of their arms above the elbows; many of these arms were of enviable freshness and plumpness; in some cases the kid gloves had actually burst from having been pulled up a little too far. In short, everything seemed to bear the inscription: "No, this is no province; this is a metropolis; this is Paris itself!" Only here and there some such mobcap as the world had never yet beheld would suddenly emerge, or even some weird feather, almost a peacock's, running counter to all modes, in keeping with the wearer's own taste. However, such things are inevitable; such is the nature of a provincial capital: somewhere it is bound to show its true nature.

"However, which one of them wrote that letter?" Chichikov wondered as he stood before them, and had even craned forward for a better look when a whole procession of elbows, cuffs, sleeves, ends of ribbons, perfumed chemisettes, and dresses scraped his very nose. The gallopage was going full blast; the Postmaster's good lady, the Captain of the Rural Police, a lady with a blue feather, a lady with a white feather, a Georgian prince by the name of Chipkhaihilidzev, a bureaucrat from St. Petersburg, a bureaucrat from Moscow, a French gentleman called Coucou, a Perhunovsky, a Berebendovsky—they were up and away, all swirling and whirling.

"There she goes! The province is off on the light fantastic!" Chichikov murmured, staggering back and, as soon as the ladies had found their seats, his eyes began their search anew, to see if by some expression of face or eyes he might not discern the fair creature who had composed the letter; but no such expression either of face or feature availed, and he could not discern her. Yet one could note everywhere something that was just the least bit revealing, something so imperceptibly exquisite—ooh, how exquisite!... "No," said Chichikov to himself, "women are such a thing that—" at this point he actually had to make a hopeless gesture with his hand—"there's really no use even talking! There, you just go ahead and try to describe or convey all that flits over their faces, all those slight emanations, hints . . . why, you simply won't be able to convey a thing. Their eyes alone are such a realm that, once a man has ventured therein, that's the last you've seen of him! For you'll never drag him out of there, not with an iron hook or anything else. There, for instance, try to tell merely about the light in those eyes, melting, velvety, honeyed—God alone knows what other kind of light there may not be!—both harsh and soft, or even altogether languishing, as some put it, full of voluptuousness—or without any voluptuousness but still worse than if it were full of it; that light will catch at your heart and, as if it were a violin bow, will start playing upon every fiber of your soul. No, one simply cannot find the right words to describe them—women are the fancy-goods half of humankind, and that's all there is to it!"

My fault! It seems that a phrase overheard in the street has escaped the lips of my hero. What is one to do, then? Such is the situation of the writer in Russia! However, if a word off the street has crept into a book, it isn't the writer who is at fault but the readers; and, first and foremost, the readers of the higher social strata: they are in the van of those from whom one will not hear a single decent Russian word, but when it comes to words in French, German, and English they will, likely as not, dish them out to you in such quantity that you will actually get fed up with them, and they will dish them out without spilling a drop of all the possible pronunciations: French they'll snaffle through their noses and with a lisp; English they'll chirp as well as any bird could, even to the extent of making their physiognomies birdlike, and will even mock him who is unable to assume a birdlike physiognomy; while German they'll grunt as gruffly as any boar. And the only thing they won't dish out to you is any good, plain Russian thing—save that, out of patriotism, they may build a log cabin in the Russian style for a summerhouse. That's the sort readers of the higher social strata are, while all the others who try to number themselves among them simply follow suit! And yet, at the same time, how very pernickety they are! They want, without fail, everything to be written in the most austere language, refined and genteel; in a word, they want the Russian language to descend, suddenly and of itself, out of the clouds, all properly finished off, and to have it perch right upon their tongues, with nothing more for them to do than merely to open their mouths wide and thrust their tongues out. Of course, the feminine half of humankind is whimsical; but it must be confessed that worthy readers can be still more whimsical on occasion.

As for Chichikov, he in the meantime was getting utterly bewildered as to which of the ladies was the one who had composed the letter to him. When he tried to fix his gaze more intently on this one or that one, he perceived that the ladies, for their part, were also evincing something that inspired the soul of a poor mortal both with hope and sweet torments, so that at last he was forced to say: "No, there's no possible way of guessing who she is!"

This, however, did not in any way diminish the jolly mood he was in. Unconstrainedly and adroitly he exchanged pleasantries with some of the ladies, approaching now one, now another with brisk, small steps or, as they say, he minced along, as little aged beaux do upon built-up heels (they call such old gallants *little mouse stallions*), prancing around the ladies quite spryly. At every few steps, mincing along rather deftly and turning right and left, he would suddenly throw in a punctuating scrape of his small foot, by way of a curlicue, as it were, or something like a comma. The ladies were very much pleased with him and not only found a heap of amiable and pleasant things about him, but even began to discern a majestic expression on his face, something actually Mars-like and military, which, as everyone knows, the women find very pleasing. They were even beginning to squabble over him a little: having noticed that he usually took his stand near the door, some of the ladies vied with one another and hastened to take a seat as near as possible to the door, and if one of them had the good fortune to get ahead of the others in this an unpleasant scene would almost take place, and to many of them who had wished to do the very same thing such brazenness appeared much too revolting.

Chichikov became so engrossed in conversations with the ladies, or, to put it better, the ladies engrossed him so and put his head in such a whirl with their conversations, which they peppered with such a lot of the most intricate and refined allegories—all of which had to be resolved, the effort of which caused his forehead to become actually beaded with sweat—that he had forgotten to fulfill an obligation of good manners: that of approaching his hostess first of all. He bethought himself of this remissness only when he heard the voice of the good lady herself, who had been standing before him for several minutes by now. The Governor's lady uttered in a somewhat kindly and arch voice, with an agreeable toss of her head: "Ah, Pavel Ivanovich, so that's how you are!" I cannot convey the precise words of the Governor's lady, but something full of great amiability was said, in that spirit in which the ladies and gallants make themselves understood in the novels of our worldly writers (who are great hands at and fond of describing salons and of boasting of their knowledge of the highest *ton*), in some such vein as: "Can it be possible that others have taken such possession of your heart that there is no longer any room therein—nay, not the tiniest nook!— for those whom you have so compassionlessly forgotten?" Our hero instantly turned to the Governor's lady and was all set to deliver his answer to her—an answer probably in no way inferior to those which are delivered in the fashionable novels by the Zvonskys, Linskys, Lidins, Gremins, and all sorts of adroit military men—when, chancing to raise his eyes, he was suddenly rooted to the spot as if thunderstruck.

It was not only the Governor's lady who was standing before him; she was holding by the hand a young girl of sixteen, a dewy little blonde, with fine and regular features, with a sharp little chin, her whole face a bewitchingly rounded-out oval, such as an artist would have taken for his Madonna and which one but rarely comes upon in Russia, where all things like to evince themselves on a sweeping scale—all things, with never an exception: the mountains, and the forests, and the steppes, and faces, and lips, and feet. It was the very same blonde whom he had met on the road while traveling from Nozdrev's, when through the stupidity of the coachmen or the horses their vehicles had so oddly collided, their harness tangling together, and Uncle Mityai together with Uncle Minyai had undertaken the task of disentangling them. Chichikov became so confused that he was unable to bring out a single sensible word and mumbled the Devil knows what, but something which neither a Gremin nor a Zvonsky nor a Lidin would ever have uttered under any circumstances.

"You haven't been introduced to my daughter yet, have you?" said the Governor's lady. "She is just out of boarding school."

He answered that he already had had the good fortune to encounter her by chance; he made an attempt to add something else, but that something else did not turn out well. The Governor's lady, after a few more words, at last went off with her daughter to the other end of the room to the other guests, but Chichikov still did not stir from the spot, like a man who has gaily sallied out of doors for a stroll, his eyes disposed to take in all the sights, and then suddenly comes to a dead stop, remembering that he has forgotten something, and when that happens you won't find anything sillier than this individual: in an instant the carefree expression deserts his face; he strives to recall just what it is he has forgotten: was it a handkerchief, by any chance? But the handkerchief is right in his pocket. Was it money, perhaps? But the money, too, is right in his pocket; he has everything with him, and yet at the same time some unseen demon is whispering into his ears that he has forgotten *something*. And by this time he is staring absent-mindedly and in a muddled way at the throng moving past him, at the vehicles dashing by, at the shakos and guns of a regiment on the march, or even at some sign, yet without really seeing a thing. And so it was with Chichikov: he suddenly became aloof from everything that was going on about him. At this point a multitude of hints and questions permeated with finesse and politesse was directed at him from fragrant feminine lips: "Is it permitted for us poor dwellers upon this earth to make so bold as to inquire what the subject of your reveries is?"— "Where are located those happy regions where your thought is soaring?"—"May one know the name of her who has plunged you into this sweet vale of pensiveness?"

But his response to all this was utter inattentiveness and the pleasant phrases were entirely lost on him. He was actually uncivil to such an extent that in a short while he left them and went over to the other side of the room, wishing to spy out where the Governor's lady had gone with her daughter. But the ladies apparently did not feel like giving him up so quickly as all that: each one had inwardly resolved to resort to all those weapons so dangerous for our hearts and to utilize all that was best and most effective in her armamentarium. It must be remarked that certain ladies—I am saying certain ladies, which is not the same as saying all ladies—have a little weakness: if they should happen to notice some especially fine point about themselves, be it the brow, or the mouth, or the hands, why, they already think that the best feature will be the first thing to strike the eyes of all beholders, and that all these beholders will instantly break into unanimous speech: "Look, look what a splendidly beautiful Greek nose she has!" or: "What a regular, enchanting brow!" As for her who has fine shoulders, she feels certain beforehand that all the young men will go off into utter raptures and will be unable to stop repeating every time she passes by: "Ah, what marvelous shoulders on that one!" but that they won't as much as glance at her face, or nose, or forehead—and, even if they should glance at them, these other beauties would be regarded as merely extraneous. That's how certain ladies think. Each lady took an inner vow to be as enchanting as possible during the dances and to display in all its splendor the surpassing excellence of whatever was most surpassingly excellent about her. The Postmaster's good lady, as she waltzed, let her head loll to one side in so languishing a way that one really sensed something not of this mundane sphere about her. One most amiable lady who had come here not at all for the dancing, because of a slight *incommodité*, as she put it, which had befallen her in the form of a pea-like growth on her right foot, and who in consequence thereof had actually been compelled to wear plush booties—why, even she, in spite of everything, had not been able to hold out and had danced a few turns in her plush booties, for the specific purpose of not letting the Postmaster's good lady really get too many high and mighty notions into her head.

All these maneuvers, however, failed utterly in making any impression on Chichikov. He did not so much as look at the figures the ladies performed as they danced but kept ceaselessly rising on tiptoes to see if he could discover where the engrossing blonde had gone to; he bent his knees a little, too, keeping a sharp lookout between the shoulders and backs of the dancers; finally his search was successful and he caught sight of her sitting with her mother, over whose head some sort of plumed oriental turban was majestically swaying. Apparently Chichikov wanted to take them by frontal attack. Whether it was the mood of spring which affected him, or whether something else was egging him on, the fact remains that he resolutely pressed forward, disregarding everything. The tax farmer received such a shove from him that he staggered and barely managed to balance himself upright on one foot. Had he not succeeded in doing so he would have bowled over a whole row of others in his wake. The Postmaster also had to back away and regarded Chichikov in amazement not unmixed with fine irony. Chichikov, however, was utterly unheeding; he had eyes only for the blonde in the distance, who was pulling on a long glove and, beyond a doubt, was all consumed by the desire to be off and flying over the parquet floor. For in the meantime there, over to one side, four couples were going through a mazurka, their heels splintering the parquet, while an army officer (a second captain, to be precise) putting not only body and soul but arms and legs into his work, was performing such steps as no one had ever chanced to perform even in a dream. Chichikov darted past the mazurka, almost at the very heels of the dancers, and headed straight for the spot where the Governor's lady and her daughter were seated. He approached them, however, with the utmost timidity; he no longer minced along spryly and gallantly; he had become a trifle halting, actually, and a certain awkwardness manifested itself in all his movements.

One cannot say with certainty whether the emotion of love had really awakened in our hero; it is even to be doubted if gentlemen of this sort—that is to say, those who aren't what you might call stout, yet who at the same time aren't exactly thin, either—are capable of falling in love; but with all that there was something so strange here, something of such a nature as even he could not explain to himself: it appeared to him, as he himself confessed subsequently, that the entire ball, with all its chatter and hubbub, had for a few minutes moved somewhere far off into the distance, as it were; the violins and horns were scraping and caterwauling somewhere far beyond hill and dale, and everything had become misted over with a haze which resembled a hastily daubed-over background on a painting. And out of this murky, roughly sketched-in background only the fine features of the seductive blonde emerged clearly and definitely: the rounded-out oval of her little face; her waist, ever, ever so slender, such as the boarding-school miss has the first few months after graduation; her white, almost simple little dress, lightly and deftly and clingingly draping her youthful, graceful small limbs, defining all their pure lines. She seemed to resemble some toy finely and cleanly carved out of ivory; she alone emerged white, translucent, and radiant from out the turbid and opaque throng.

Evidently that is how things are in this world; evidently even the Chichikovs, for a few moments in their life, turn into poets—however, the word *poet* might be too extravagant in this instance. At any rate, he felt something altogether like a young man, just a hair's breadth short of a hussar, in fact. Seeing a vacant chair near the two ladies he instantly availed himself of it. The conversation did not catch on at first, but later it went well; he even began to feel a bit cocky, but . . . at this point, to our utmost distress, it must be observed that men of dignity and occupying important posts are rather on the ponderous side when it comes to making conversation with ladies; it is Messieurs the lieutenants who are master hands at this sort of thing, but by no means anybody above the rank of captain. How they do it, God alone knows; it would seem that they aren't saying anything so very ingenious, and yet the young girl they are saying it to will simply rock in her seat from laughter; as for a state councilor, he'll say God knows what:

either he'll start a conversation about how vast a realm Russia is, or will turn a compliment which, even though it may have been conceived not without wit, will nevertheless reek horribly of printer's ink; on the other hand, if he should somehow happen to say something funny, he will laugh at it himself immeasurably more than will the fair creature listening to him. We are making this observation here so that the readers may perceive why the blonde began to yawn while our hero was telling his stories. Our hero, however, did not notice this at all, relating a multitude of pleasant things, which he already had had occasion to deliver on similar occasions in various places, to wit: in the province of Simbirsk, at the house of Sophron Ivanovich Bezpechnyi, there being present at the time his daughter, Adelaïda Sophronovna with three of her sisters-in-law, Maria Gavrilovna, Alexandra Gavrilovna, and Adelgeída Gavrilovna; at the house of Fedor Fedorovich Perekroyev, in the province of Ryazan; at the house of Frol Vasilievich Pobedonosnov, in Penzenskaya province, and at the house of his brother Petr Vasilievich, there being present at the time his sister-in-law Katherina Michailovna and her second cousins Rosa Fedorovna and Emilia Fedorovna; in the province of Viatka, at the house of Petr Varsonophievich, there being present his daughter-in-law's sister Pelagea Egorovna with her niece Sophia Rostislavna and two stepsisters, Sophia Alexandrovna and Maclatura Alexandrovna.

All the ladies found such conduct on the part of Chichikov not at all to their liking. One of them purposely passed by him, in order to let him see this, and even brushed against the blonde rather carelessly with the rouleau of her dress, while she managed the scarf that was fluttering about her shoulders in such a way that its tip flipped into the girl's very face; at the same time a rather pointed and malicious remark issued, together with the fragrance of violets, from the lips of a lady behind him. Whether he really had not heard it, or merely made believe he had not heard it, doesn't matter; this failure to hear it was still a bad thing, inasmuch as one should trust the opinion of ladies. He did repent this failure, but only later on, and consequently too late.

Indignation, in all respects justifiable, was evinced on many faces. No matter how great Chichikov's weight was in society, and even though he was a millionaire and there was an expression on his face not only of majesty but actually of something Mars-like and warriorly, there are nevertheless things which the ladies will not forgive anybody, no matter who he may be, and in that case you can simply write him off as a total loss! There are occasions when a woman, no matter how weak and impotent in character she may be in comparison with a man, will yet suddenly become not only harder than any man, but even harder than anything and everything on earth. The neglect shown by Chichikov, though it was almost unintentional, actually brought about among the ladies that accord which had been on the verge of collapse at the time they had been vying for a seat nearest him. They discovered trenchant innuendoes in certain ordinary words he had dropped briefly and utterly at random. To round out the sum of his misfortunes, some one among the younger men had improvised on the spot certain satirical verses on the dancing elite, without which verses, as everybody knows, virtually no provincial dance would be complete. These verses were immediately ascribed to Chichikov. Indignation grew, and in different corners the ladies actually fell to discussing him in a most inauspicious manner; as for the poor boarding-school miss, she was utterly annihilated; her doom was signed and sealed.

And in the meantime an unpleasant surprise, as nasty as nasty could be, was preparing for our hero; at the very time that the little blonde was yawning, the while he was relating to her certain minor incidents which had befallen him at sundry times, and had even just touched upon the Greek philosopher Diogenes—at that very time, coming out of the farthest room, Nozdrev appeared. Whether he had torn himself away from the buffet, or whether he had emerged from the small green drawing room, where a game more ardent than ordinary whist was going on, and whether he had emerged of his own free will or had been bounced out, the fact remains that appear he did: jolly, jubilant, clutching the arm of the Public Prosecutor, whom he had probably been dragging along for some time by now, inasmuch as the poor Public Prosecutor was turning his bushy eyebrows every which way, as if he were cudgeling his brains for a way to get out of this personally conducted tour. And, really, it was unbearable. Nozdrev, having sipped courage from two cups of tea (not without rum, of course), was lying unmercifully. Catching sight of him from afar, Chichikov decided to make an actual sacrifice—that is, to leave his enviable position and, in so far as it was possible, to beat a hasty retreat; this encounter boded him no good. But, as sheer hard luck would have it, the Governor bobbed up, manifesting extraordinary joy at having found Pavel

Ivanovich; he detained him and begged him to act as judge in his dispute with two ladies as to whether the love of woman were a lasting thing or no. And meanwhile Nozdrev had caught sight of Chichikov and was heading straight toward him.

"Ah, the landowner of Kherson, the landowner of Kherson!" he kept shouting, walking up to him and emitting peal upon peal of laughter that made his cheeks, as fresh and dewy as a spring rose, quiver. "Well? Have you done a great deal of trading in dead souls? For you don't know, Your Excellency," he bawled right then and there, turning to the Governor, "that he trades in dead souls! By God, he does! I say, Chichikov! Why, you're such a fellow—I tell you this in friendship, for all of us here are your friends—there, His Excellency is here too—why, I would string you up, I would, by God!"

Chichikov was utterly stunned.

"Would you believe it, Your Excellency," Nozdrev went on, "when he said to me: 'Sell me some dead souls,' I simply split my sides laughing. I come here, and they tell me that he has bought three millions' worth of serfs for resettlement. What serfs—what resettlement! Why, he was bargaining for dead souls with me! I say, Chichikov, why, you're a beast—by God, but you are! There, even His Excellency right here . . . or you, Prosecutor: isn't that the truth?"

But the Public Prosecutor, and Chichikov, and the Governor himself were thrown into such confusion that they could not think of any answer whatsoever; yet in the meantime Nozdrev, without paying the least heed to anything, was grinding out his half-inebriate, half-sober speech:

"Why, you, brother, you ... you ... I won't go away from you until I learn why you were buying up dead souls. I say, Chichikov, why, you really ought to be ashamed; you haven't a better friend than I, you know that yourself. . . . There, even His Excellency right here ... or you, Prosecutor: isn't that the truth? You'd hardly believe, Your Excellency, how attached we are to each other; that is, if you were simply to say ... there, I'm standing right here, and you were to say: 'Nozdrev, tell me, upon your conscience, whom do you hold dearer, your own father or Chichikov?' I'd say: 'Chichikov!' By God, I would! ... Here, my soul, let me plant *un baiser* on your cheek. Really, Your Excellency, you must permit me to give him a kiss. Yes, Chichikov, don't you be resisting now, let me plant one teeny-weeny *baiser* on your snow-white cheek!"

Nozdrev was shoved back so hard with his *baisers* that he was sent flying and all but fell to the floor. Everybody drew away from him and no one listened to him any more. But just the same what he had said about the buying up of dead souls had been uttered at the top of his voice and had been accompanied with such loud laughter that it had attracted the attention even of those who had been in the farthest corners of the room. This bit of news appeared so strange that all those present stopped still, with a certain wooden, foolishly questioning look. Chichikov noted that many of the ladies exchanged winks among themselves with malevolent, caustic smiles, and in the expression of certain faces there appeared a something so equivocal that it increased his confusion still more. That Nozdrev was an arrant liar everybody knew, and it was not at all a rare thing to hear him spout downright nonsense; but mortal man ... really, it is hard to comprehend how mortal man is fashioned: no matter how a bit of news may start on its course, just as long as it be news he will inevitably impart it to some other mortal man, even though it be for no other purpose than to say: "Just see what a lie they've spread around!" And the other mortal man will with pleasure incline his ear, although he will say in his turn: "Yes, that's a downright vulgar lie, unworthy of any attention whatsoever!" And right after that he will not waste an instant setting out in search of a third mortal man, so that he may, after having retailed the story to him, exclaim in chorus with the latter in noble indignation: "What a vulgar lie!" And this story will inevitably make the rounds of the whole town, and all the mortal men, no matter how many of them there may be, will inevitably have their bellyful of talk, and then will admit that the matter doesn't deserve any attention and isn't even worth talking about.

This incident, apparently so nonsensical, perceptibly upset our hero. No matter how foolish the words of the fool, yet at times they will suffice to throw a wise man into confusion. Chichikov began to feel ill at ease and out of sorts, every whit as if he had set a beautifully polished boot into a filthy, stinking puddle; in a word, things were bad, downright bad! He tried not to think of it; he tried to distract himself, to find some amusement, to sit down to whist, but everything went as badly as a crooked wheel: twice he played out of turn and forgetting that it was not up to him to cover the third card, swung back his arm and idiotically covered his own card. The Chairman of the Administrative Offices could not, no matter how he tried, understand how Pavel Ivanovich, who had such a good—and, one might even say such a fine—grasp of the game could make mistakes like that, and even got the best of Pavel Ivanovich's king of spades, in which, according to the latter's own expression, he had placed his trust as in God. Of course the Postmaster and the Chairman of the Administrative Offices, and even the Chief of Police himself, kept twitting our hero in time-honored fashion: Was he in love, perhaps, and we know, now, that Pavel Ivanovich's little heart has been smitten; we know, as well, who loosed the arrow that wounded it.... But all this did not console him in the least, no matter how hard he tried to smile and to return their banter.

At supper, too, he found it impossible to relax, despite the fact that the gathering at the table was a pleasant one and that Nozdrev had long since been led out, inasmuch as the ladies themselves had at last remarked that his conduct was becoming far too *scandaleuse.* At the very height of the cotillion he had plumped down on the floor and begun grabbing the dancers by their skirts and coat flaps, which, to use an expression of the ladies, was already beyond anything, really. The supper was a very jolly one; all the faces, glimpsed between triple candelabra, flowers, bottles, and *bonbonnières,* were glowing with the most unconstrained pleasure. Army officers, ladies, frock-coated gentlemen— all became amiable, even to the point of being cloying. The gentlemen leapt up from their seats and ran to relieve the waiters of their platters, so as to offer them, with extraordinary adroitness, to the ladies. One colonel offered a sauceboat at the end of his unsheathed sword to a lady. Men who had attained the decorous age, among whom Chichikov was seated, were carrying on loud discussions, driving home the point of their weighty words with gobs of fish or veal ruthlessly smothered in mustard, and their discussions dealt with the very subjects in which he always took part; but he looked like a man fatigued or broken up by a prolonged trip, who can't get a thing into his head and who finds it beyond his strength to grasp any matter. He did not even wait for the supper to be over, and went home incomparably earlier than he usually did.

There, in that small room which is so familiar to the reader, with the door to the adjoining room blocked off by a bureau, and with the cockroaches occasionally peeping out of their corners, the state of his thoughts and spirit was just as uneasy as that misnamed easy chair in which he was sitting. His heart was troubled, confused; some oppressive void persisted therein.

"May the Devil take all of you who invented these balls!" he soliloquized, heartily vexed. "There, what are they rejoicing over, like a pack of fools? There are poor crops throughout the province; prices are sky-high; and so they go in for balls! They'll get together for three hours, and there will be enough gossip for three years thereafter. . . . You might think man was an intelligent animal, yet look at how he spends his time! Balls! What a thing to astonish one with, dolling themselves up in womanish rags! What a rare sight, one of them swathing herself in a thousand rubles' worth of trumpery! And all this is at the expense of the serfs' quitrents or, which is still worse, at the expense of our brother's conscience. For everyone knows why you take a bribe and perjure your soul, so as to get enough for your wife's fancy shawl or all sorts of crinolines, or whatever they call 'em, may they all fall in the bottomless pit! And what is it all about? So that some gossiping Sidorovna, who goes about in a quilted blouse, might not say that the Postmaster's wife had a better gown on her than your wife, and over that dressmaker's word bang! goes a thousand rubles. 'A ball! A ball! What fun!' They shout. A ball is just so much rubbishy foolishness. It isn't in the Russian spirit, nor after the Russian nature. The Devil alone knows what it is; a full-grown man, of full age, will suddenly jump out in the middle of the floor, dressed all in black, all plucked and slicked up, his clothes so tight-fitting on him that they make him look like an imp, and starts off dancing and prancing. One of these fellows, even while he is paired off for the dance, will be talking some important matter over with another man, yet at the same time his legs will be cutting capers like a young goat's, now to the right, now to the left . . . as if there were fleas biting him! All this out of aping, all this out of aping! Since the Frenchman at forty is as much of an infant as he was at fifteen, let us even do the same thing! No, really . . . after every ball one feels just as if one had committed some sin; one doesn't want even to remind oneself of it. There's simply nothing at all inside your head, as after a conversation with a man from high society: he'll give you a heap of talk about all sorts of things, he'll touch on all things lightly, he'll tell you everything he has gotten a smattering of out of books—a motley, pretty stream of talk—but you just go and try to carry anything of it away in your head and you'll see later on that a talk with even an ordinary shopkeeper, who knows nothing but his own business, yet knows it soundly and through experience, is better than all these baby-rattles. There, what can you squeeze out of it, out of this ball? There, what if we were to suppose that some writer or other had gotten it into his head to describe all this scene, as it is? Why, even there, even in a book, it would turn out just as senseless as it is in nature. What is that scene? Is it moral or immoral? Why, only the Devil knows just what it is! You spit in disgust and then slam the book shut."

Thus did Chichikov inveigh against balls in general; but apparently there was still another cause for indignation mixed in here. His chief vexation was not against the ball, but because he had chanced to come a cropper, because he had suddenly appeared before the eyes of all in God knows what guise, because he had played some sort of bizarre, equivocal role. Of course, after looking at it with the eye of a prudent, sensible man, he saw that all this was so much bosh, that a foolish word didn't mean a thing, especially now, when the main business had already been fully put through—and put over. But man is a strange creature: Chichikov was powerfully aggrieved by the attitude of dislike on the part of those very people for whom he had no respect and of whom he spoke so harshly, condemning their worldly vanity and their gay raiment. This matter was all the more vexatious to him because, having analyzed it clearly, he perceived that he himself had been in part the cause of it. He did not, however, get angry at himself, and, of course, was right in this. We all of us have a slight weakness of going a little easy on ourselves; we will rather try to seek out some fellow man on whom we may vent our chagrin—a servant, for instance, or some petty clerk, some underling of ours who turns up at the opportune moment, one's wife or, finally, a chair, which will be thrown the Devil knows how far, against the very door, so that its back and one of its arms will fly off—there, take that, and know what it means to arouse our wrath!

And so Chichikov, too, speedily found a fellow man who had to shoulder all that chagrin could inspire our hero with. This fellow man was none other than Nozdrev, and it need hardly be said that he was so well basted on all sides and quarters as only a knave of a village elder or a stage-coach driver is basted by some experienced army captain who has been around, or occasionally even by a general who, in addition to many expressions which have become classics, will add a great many as yet unknown, the invention of which appertains to him alone. Nozdrev's entire family tree was splintered into kindling, and many members of Nozdrev's family in the ascendant line had to suffer grievously.

But while Chichikov was sitting in his uneasy easy chair, troubled by his thoughts and sleeplessness, heartily reviling Nozdrev and all his kith and kin, and before him warmly glowed a tallow candle, the wick of which had long since become covered with candle snuff as if with a black cowl and was threatening to go out at any moment, and sightless black night was peering in at the windows, just about to turn bluish because of the approaching dawn, and roosters, afar off, were exchanging their clarion calls, and throughout the town, all sunk in slumber, there may not have been a soul out on the streets save for some frieze overcoat tipsily weaving along somewhere, some poor wretch, his class and rank unknown, and himself knowing only (alas!) the path, all too deeply beaten and much trodden by the unruly, loose, hard-drinking Russian folk—at this time, in another quarter of the town, an event was taking place which was about to augment the unpleasantness of our hero's position. To be precise, through the remote streets and by-lanes of the town a quite odd vehicle, which made one wonder what name one could give it, was jarringly lumbering along. It resembled neither a tarantass, nor a calash, nor a light covered carriage, but rather a round-cheeked, bulging watermelon placed on wheels. The cheeks of this watermelon—i.e., its small doors— which still bore traces of yellow paint, closed but poorly, owing to the sad state of the handles and catches, which were haphazardly tied together with bits of rope. The watermelon was filled to bursting with calico pillows shaped like tobacco pouches, like bolsters, or simply like pillows; it was stuffed with bags of bread loaves (plain and braided), rusks, biscuits, and pretzels of biscuit dough. There was even a chicken pie, and another of salted beef, both peeping coyly out of one of the bags. The footboard behind was occupied by a person of flunky extraction, in a short jacket of homespun striped ticking, his chin unshaven and his head slightly grizzled—a person usually described as a *lad*. The noise and whining from the iron clamps and rusty bolts awakened, at the other end of the town, a sentry in his box, who, picking up his halberd, set up a shout with all his might, though still half asleep: "Who goes there?" But, perceiving that no one was going there and that there was only a clatter of wheels in the distance, he contented himself with catching some beastie or other on his coat collar and, walking up to a street lamp, executing it summarily on his thumbnail, after which, putting his halberd away in a corner, he again fell asleep, acording to all the canons of his order of knighthood.

The horses were forever stumbling to their foreknees, inasmuch as they were not shod and, in addition to that, had but little acquaintance with the restful paved road of the town. This antediluvian shandrydan, having made several turns from one street to another, finally turned into a dark by-lane near the small parish church of Nikola-Out-in-the-Sticks, and stopped before the house of the Dean's wife. A wench, with a kerchief on her head and dressed in a warm sleeveless jacket, crawled out of the vehicle and began pounding with her fists on the gate as hard as any man could have done (the lad in the short jacket of striped ticking was only later on dragged off his perch by his feet, inasmuch as he was sleeping the sleep of the dead). Dogs started barking and the gates, gaping open at last, swallowed, though with difficulty, this cumbersome conveyance. It drove into a crowded yard, cluttered with firewood, henhouses, and all sorts of flimsy coops and hutches; a gentlewoman crawled out of the vehicle, this gentlewoman being none other than Korobochka the landowner, relict of a collegiate secretary. Soon after our hero's departure the little crone had been overcome by such uneasiness about a possible swindle on his part that, after lying awake for three nights in a row, she had decided to go into town—despite the fact that her horses were not shod—and there learn for sure what dead souls were fetching and whether she hadn't—God forbid!—missed a trick in selling them for what may have been next to nothing. What effect this arrival brought about the reader may learn from a certain conversation which took place between two ladies. This conversation . . . but better let this conversation come in the next chapter.

CHAPTER NINE

In the morning, even before the time which is in the town of N—— set aside for paying calls, out of the doors of a wooden house painted orange, with a mezzanine and blue pillars, a lady in an elegant checkered cloak fluttered out, escorted by a footman in a great coat with a series of collars and with a gold galloon on his round, sleek hat. The lady instantly, with inordinate haste, fluttered up the let down steps into a barouche standing near the entrance. The footman at once slammed the carriage door shut after his mistress, folded up the steps and, grabbing hold of the straps behind the barouche, shouted to the coachman: "Let 'er go!" The lady was the bearer of a bit of news she had just heard and felt an insuperable urge to impart it to somebody as quickly as possible. She looked out of the carriage window every minute and saw, to her unutterable vexation, that half her journey lay still ahead of her. Each house front seemed to her wider than usual; the white stone poorhouse with its small narrow windows stretched out for an insufferably long time, so that she could not restrain herself from saying at last: "What a confounded building—there's never an end to it!" The coachman had already received his commands twice: "Faster, faster, Andriushka! You're driving unbearably slowly today!"

Finally the destination was reached. The barouche came to a stop before a house that was also of wood, one-storied, of a dark-gray hue, with small white bas-reliefs above the windows and a high wooden trellis right in front of them, and a cramped little garden in front, behind the palisade of which the puny little trees had whitened from the town dust which never departed from them. Through the windows one could glimpse flowerpots, a parrot swaying in its cage, hanging onto a ring with its beak, and two lap-dogs snoozing in the sun.

In this house lived the closest and truest feminine friend of the lady who had just arrived. The author is very hard put to it to name both ladies in such a way as not to make them angry at him, as they used to be angry in the old days. To give them fictitious names is fraught with danger. No matter what name you think up, it will inevitably be found in some corner or other of our realm, for all it is so vast; someone is bound to bear it, and will inevitably become incensed not only to the extent of wishing to beat me within an inch of my life, but actually to death; she'll take to saying that the author had purposely made a secret trip to the town to find out everything and will tell you just what sort of creature the author himself is, and what sort of wretched little sheepskin jacket he walks around in, and which Agraphena Ivanovna he calls on, and what dishes he is fond of. But if one were to mention ranks—God save us, that would be still more dangerous! Nowadays all our ranks and classes are in so touchy a mood that anything and everything which may be between the covers of a printed book already has the appearance of personal remarks for them—such, evidently, is the spirit in the air. It suffices merely to say that there is a stupid man in a certain town, and that is already a personal reflection: a gentleman of respectable appearance will suddenly pounce upon you and set up a shout: "Why, I, too, am a man, ergo, I, too, am stupid!"—in a word, he'll surmise in the wink of an eye just what you're up to.

And therefore, for the avoidance of all this, let us call the lady whom the guest had come to see what she was almost unanimously called in the town of N——: a lady agreeable in all respects. This appellation she had acquired quite legitimately, inasmuch as she truly enough had not spared any pains to make herself amiable to the utmost degree even though, of course, there could be glimpsed through her amiability a—ooh, ever so brisk!—liveliness of a feminine nature; and even though, on occasion, pins and nee dles ooh, ever so piercing!—would be poking through some pleasant word of hers. And may God avert that which seethed within her heart against her who had in some way and through some means wormed her way through into the front ranks. But all this was clothed in the most refined social grace, such as is to be found only in a provincial capital. She performed every move with taste, was even fond of verse, even knew how to keep her head in a dreamy pose at times, and everybody concurred that she was, really, a lady who was agreeable in all respects.

As for the other lady—that is, the one who has just arrived—her character did not have so many facets, and for that reason we will call her a lady who was simply agreeable.

The arrival of the guest had awakened the lap-dogs snoozing in the sun: the shaggy Adele, who was forever tangling up in her long wool, and the darling little hound Potpourri, who had such darling, slender little legs. Both the one and the other, barking, their tails curled into rings, dashed into the foyer, where the guest was divesting herself of her cloak, revealing at last a dress of modish color and design, with long streamers at the neck; jasmine was wafted all over the room. Barely had the lady who was agreeable in all respects learned of the arrival of the lady who was simply agreeable when she had already run into the foyer. The ladies seized each other's hands, kissed and screamed, as boarding-school misses scream at a reunion shortly after graduation, before their mammas have yet had a chance to explain to them that the father of one of them is poorer and of lower rank than the father of the other. The kiss was consummated sonorously, inasmuch as the lap-dogs had begun barking a new, for which they were flicked with a handkerchief, and both ladies went into the drawing room—blue, naturally, with a divan, an oval table, and even small screens, with ivy twining over them; after them ran the shaggy Adele, growling, and tall Potpourri, on his darling, slender little legs.

"Here, here, in this cozy nook," the hostess was saying, seating her guest in a corner of the divan. "There, that's it—that's it! There's a cushion for you, too!" Having said which she thrust a cushion behind her guest's back, which cushion had a knight embroidered in wool upon it, in that invariable fashion in which all knights are embroidered on canvas: the nose had come out as a ladder and the lips as a quadrangle. "But how happy I am that it's you! . . . I hear somebody driving up, and I think to myself, who could it be as early as this? Parasha says: 'It's the Vice-Governor's lady,' and I say: 'There, that fool has come to bore me again!' and was on the very verge of saying that I was not at home—"

The guest was just about to get down to business and impart her news, but an exclamation emitted at this point by the lady who was agreeable in all respects suddenly gave a different turn to the conversation.

"What a cheerful little print!" exclaimed the lady who was agreeable in all respects, gazing at the dress of the lady who was simply agreeable.

"Yes, it is very cheerful. Praskovia Fedorovna, however, thinks that it would be better if the checks were somewhat smaller, and if the polka dots were not brown but blue. I sent some material to my sister—it's so bewitching that one simply can't express it in words. Just imagine: teeny-weeny stripes, so-o-o narrow, as narrow as human imagination can picture; the background is blue, and running across the stripe is a design of tiny eyes and tiny paws, tiny eyes and tiny paws, all over. . . . In a word, it's beyond all compare! One can say positively that there's never been anything like it in all the world!"

"My dear, but that's so loud!"

"Ah, no! It isn't loud at all!"

"Ah, but it is!"

It must be remarked that the lady who was agreeable in all respects was very much of a materialist, inclined to negation and skepticism, and that she flatly rejected quite a few things in life.

At this point the lady who was simply agreeable explained that it was not at all loud, and then cried out: "Yes, allow me to congratulate you—flounces are no longer being worn."

"What—they aren't?"

"Little scallops will be worn instead."

"Ah, that isn't pretty! Little scallops, indeed!"

"Little scallops—little scallops are all the go; a pelerine

all of little scallops; little scallops on the sleeves; epaulets of little scallops; little scallops below, little scallops everywhere!"

"It isn't pretty, Sophia Ivanovna, not if the whole thing is in little scallops."

"It's darling, Anna Grigoriyevna, you'd hardly believe how darling it is: you sew them in two ruchings, with wide armholes, and then, on top. . . . But now, here's something that will simply amaze you; here's where you'll say that . . . there, you'll be amazed: just imagine, they've started making the bodices still longer, with a sort of little peak in front, and the front whalebone going entirely out of bounds; the skirt is gathered all around, the way they used to have their farthingales in the old days—they even pad the back a little with cotton wool, actually, so as to make one a perfect *belle femme.*"

"Well, now, this is really . . . I must confess!" said the lady who was agreeable in all respects, tossing her head with a feeling of dignity.

"Just so, it really is, I must confess too!" answered the lady who was simply agreeable.

"You may do whatever you wish, but I'm not going to imitate this style for anything."

"Nor I. . . . Really, when one imagines to what lengths fashion will go at times . . . it's beyond anything! I wheedled a pattern out of my sister, just for the fun of the thing; my Melania has started in to sew it."

"Why, have you really got a pattern?" cried out the lady who was agreeable in all respects, not without a perceptible flutter of her heart.

"But of course; my sister brought it with her."

"Let me have it, my soul, for the sake of all that's holy!"

"Ah, I have already given my word to Praskovia Fedorovna. After her, perhaps."

"But who's going to wear anything after Praskovia Fedorovna? It would be far too strange on your part if you were to give preference to strangers above your close friends."

"Yes, but she's also a grandaunt of mine."

"God knows what sort of an aunt she is to you, on your husband's side. . . . No, Sophia Ivanovna, I won't even listen to anything; it looks as if you actually wanted to insult me. Evidently you have already tired of me, evidently you want to break off all your friendship with me."

Poor Sophia Ivanovna did not know what to do. She herself felt in what a terrific cross fire she had placed herself. There, she had to go and brag! She was ready to stick her silly tongue as full of pins as a pincushion for this.

"Well, and what about our seductive Adonis?" the lady who was agreeable in all respects was asking in the meantime.

"Ah, my God! Why am I sitting here like this? That's a fine thing! Why, Anna Grigoriyevna, do you know the reason for my coming to you?" At this point the visitor's breath failed her; the words were ready to start winging like hawks out of her mouth, one after another, and one had to be inhuman to the same degree as her bosom friend to venture upon stopping her.

"No matter how you may sing his praises and exalt him," that friend was saying with animation, "I'll nevertheless tell you outright, and I'll even tell him so to his very face, that he is a worthless man—worthless, worthless, worthless!"

"Yes, but do listen to what I'm going to tell you—"

"They have spread it about that he is a fine man, but he isn't fine at all, he isn't, not at all; and his nose . . . is a most odious nose."

"But allow me, do but allow me just to tell you . . . Anna Grigoriyevna, my dearest darling, do allow me to tell you! Why, this is a whole story, do you understand? *Ce qu'on appelle histoire!** the caller was saying, with an expression verging on despair and in an utterly imploring voice. It might not be amiss to remark that very many foreign words were interspersed in the speech of both ladies and at times there would be entire long phrases in French. But no matter how imbued with reverent awe the author is toward those salutary benefits which the French tongue confers upon Russia, no matter how imbued he is therewith for the praiseworthy custom of our higher society in expressing itself in that language at all the hours of the day and night (of course out of a profound feeling of love for their native land), yet with all that he simply cannot bring himself to introduce a phrase from any alien tongue into this Russian epic of his. And so, let us go on without any foreign phrases.

"But what's the story?"

"Ah, Anna Grigoriyevna, my life! If you could but fancy the situation in which I found myself! Just imagine: the Dean's wife comes to me—the Dean's wife, you know, the wife of Father Cyril—and what do you think? Our visitor, now, in whose mouth butter wouldn't melt, what sort of a fellow do you think he is?"

---

*"It's a story that one can call a story!" *Trans.*

"What, can it be possible that he's been dangling after the Dean's wife too?"

"Ah, Anna Grigoriyevna, if it had been only a matter of dangling it would be nothing. Do but listen to what the Dean's wife told me. A certain landowner, she says, by the name of Korobochka, arrived at her house, frightened out of her wits and as pale as death, and she has a story to tell— and what a story! Do but listen, it's for all the world like a storybook: suddenly, in the dead of night, a most dreadful knocking resounds at her gates, such knocking as you can't imagine, and there are shouts: 'Open up, open up, or we'll break down the gate! . . .' How does that strike you? What sort of a seductive Adonis is he, after that?"

"But what about Korobochka? Why, is she young and good-looking?"

"Not in the least; she's an old woman."

"Ah, how charming! So he's going after an old woman now? Well, after this, the taste of our ladies must be a fine one; they surely have found somebody worth falling in love with!"

"But it isn't that, Anna Grigoriyevna, it isn't at all the way you suppose. You just imagine this: a man armed from head to foot appears on the scene, on the style of Rinaldo Rinaldini, and demands: 'Sell me,' he says, 'all the souls who have died!' Korobochka answers him, reasonably enough, telling him: 'I can't sell them to you, because they are dead.'—'No,' says he, 'they are not dead. It's up to me to decide,' he says, 'if they are dead or not; they are not dead, they aren't!' he yells. 'They aren't!' In a word, he created a terribly *scandaleuse* commotion: the whole village came on the run, children bawling, everybody shouting, nobody can understand anybody else—well, it was simply *horreur, horreur, horreur!* . . . But you can't even imagine, Anna Grigoriyevna, how upset I became when I heard all this. 'My mistress, darling,' Mashka says to me, 'do take a look in the mirror, you're all pale!'— 'I've no time for mirrors now,' I tell her, 'I must dash over to Anna Grigoriyevna and tell her everything!' That same moment I give orders to have the barouche harnessed; Andriushka, my coachman, asks me where he is to drive to, but I can't utter even a word; I stare him right in the eyes, like a fool. I think he must have thought me mad. Ah, Anna Grigoriyevna, if you could but picture to yourself how upset I got over all this!"

"This is quite bizarre, though," said the lady who was agreeable in all respects. "What in the world could these dead souls signify? I understand precisely nothing of all this, I must confess. There, it's the second time that I'm hearing about these same dead souls, and on top of that my husband tells me that Nozdrev is lying: surely, then, there is bound to be something in it, after all."

"But do picture to yourself, Anna Grigoriyevna, the situation I was in when I heard that. 'And now,' says Korobochka, 'I don't know,' she says, 'what I am to do. He forced me,' says she, 'to sign a forged paper of some sort and threw down fifteen rubles in government notes. I,' she says, 'am an inexperienced, helpless widow woman, I don't know a thing. . . .' So that's the kind of things that go on around us! But if you could only picture to yourself, if even just a little, how thoroughly upset I was!"

"Well, just as you will, but this isn't at all a matter of

dead souls; there's something else going on, hidden behind all this."

"I, too, have been thinking the same thing, I must confess," said the lady who was simply agreeable, not without surprise, and instantly felt a strong urge to learn just what that hidden something going on behind all this might be. She even said, slowly: "And what do you suppose is going on?"

"Well, what do you think?"

"What do I think? I am, I confess, totally at a loss."

"Well, just the same, I'd like to know what your ideas are about this?"

But the lady who was simply agreeable could not find anything to say at this point. All she knew was how to get upset, but the ability of forming some sagacious supposition was utterly lacking in her, and hence, more so than any other woman, she had need of tender friendship and of counsel.

"Very well, then, listen to what sort of thing these dead souls are," said the lady who was agreeable in all respects, and at these words her visitor became all attention: her little ears perked up of themselves, she sat up very straight, so precariously perched on the divan that one wondered how she retained her seat and, despite the fact that she ran somewhat to embonpoint, suddenly grew slimmer, and as light as swan's-down, apt to go sailing through the air at the least puff. Thus a Russian squire, a great lover of dogs and a very Nimrod, on approaching a forest out of which a hare tracked down by beaters is about to emerge, becomes all transformed, with his mount and long whip, within one congealed moment, into gunpowder ready to be touched off at any instant. He is all eyes, piercing the murky air, and will infallibly overtake the beast, will infallibly finish it off, being irresistible, no matter how the whole snowy steppe may rise up and storm against him, hurling silvery star-shaped snowflakes against his lips, his mustache, his eyes, his eyebrows, and his beaver cap.

"The dead souls are—" began the lady who was agreeable in all respects.

"What are they, what are they?" her guest caught her up, all aquiver.

"—dead souls!"

"Ah, do tell me, for God's sake!"

"All this is simply an invention that serves as a blind; but the real thing is this: he wants to carry off the Governor's daughter."

This conclusion was truly unexpected and an unusual one in every way. The lady who was simply agreeable, upon hearing this, just turned to stone where she sat; she grew paler and paler, as pale as death, and this time became upset in earnest.

"Ah, my God!" she cried out, wringing her hands. "Well, that's something I could never have supposed!"

"But I, I confess, as soon as you opened your mouth, had already surmised what was what," answered the lady who was agreeable in all respects.

"But, after this, Anna Grigoriyevna, what do they teach these hussies in boarding schools! There's innocence for you!"

"What innocence! I heard her saying such things as,

I must confess, I would never have the courage to repeat."

"Do you know, Anna Grigoriyevna, why, it simply rends one's heart when one sees what limits immorality has reached at last!"

"And yet the men lose their heads over her. But if you were to ask me, I must confess I can't see a thing in her. . . . She's insufferably affected."

"Ah, Anna Grigoriyevna, my soul! She's a stone image— if only there were some kind of expression on that face of hers."

"Oh, and *how* affected! Oh, how affected! God, how affected! Who taught her all that I don't know, I'm sure, but never yet have I seen a creature with so much namby-pambiness about her."

"Why, dearest darling! She's a stone image, and pale as death."

"Ah, don't say that, Sophia Ivanovna: she rouges unmercifully."

"Ah, what are you saying, Anna Grigoriyevna. She is chalk, chalk, simply chalk!"

"Darling, I was sitting right next to her, I ought to know: she had rouge on her a finger thick and peeling off in chunks, like plaster. Her mother taught her; she's a coquette herself, and the daughter will yet surpass her dear mother."

"Oh, no, if you please, oh, no; you can ask me to take any oath you like on it; I am ready, right here and now, to lose my children, my husband, all our estate, if she has even one tiny drop, even one little particle, even a shadow of red in her cheeks!"

"Ah, what are you saying, Sophia Ivanovna!" said the lady who was agreeable in all respects, and wrung her hands.

"Ah, really, Anna Grigoriyevna, how can you be like that! I am really amazed at you!" said the simply agreeable lady and wrung her hands in turn.

Still, let it not strike the reader as strange that both ladies could not come to an agreement as to what they had seen at almost one and the same time. There really are in this world many things which do have that very peculiarity: if one lady will take a look at them, they will turn out to be perfectly white, whereas if another lady takes a look at them they will turn out to be red, red as bilberries.

"Well, here's one more proof for you that she's pale," the lady who was simply agreeable went on. "I remember, as if it were right now, that I was sitting next to Manilov, and I said to him: 'Look, how pale she is!' Really, one must be as addlepated as our men are to go into raptures over her. And as for our seductive Adonis . . . ah, how repulsive he seemed to me! You can't picture, Anna Grigoriyevna, how very, very repulsive he seemed to me."

"And yet, just the same, there were certain ladies who were not at all indifferent toward him."

"I, Anna Grigoriyevna? There, now, you can never say that, never, never!"

"Why, I'm not talking about you. As though there were nobody else in the world outside of yourself!"

"Never, never, Anna Grigoriyevna! Permit me to tell you that I know myself very well; but as for certain other ladies, perhaps, who assume the role of being unattainable—"

"Really, you must excuse me, Sophia Ivanovna! You

must really permit me to tell you that I have never yet indulged in such *scandaleuse* goings on. In the case of anybody else, perhaps, but never in mine—you must really allow me to point this out to you."

"But just why have you taken offense? For there were also other ladies present there who had been the first to grab that chair near the door so as to sit closer to him."

Well, now, after such words as these, uttered by the lady who was simply agreeable, a storm was inevitably bound to break; but, most amazingly, both ladies suddenly quieted down, and nothing whatsoever ensued. The lady who was agreeable in all respects recalled that the pattern for the latest thing in dresses was still not in her hands, while the lady who was simply agreeable surmised that she had not yet contrived to extract any details as to the discovery made by her friend, and therefore peace followed very shortly. However, it could not be said of both these ladies that a necessity for saying mean things was a part of their natures, and in general there was nothing of the malicious about their characters; but, just so, without their sensing it, a slight desire to be catty to each other would be gendered of itself in their conversation; one of them, for the sake of a little gratification, would, when the occasion arose, slip in a lively word or so: "There, now, that for you! There, have a taste of that!" Of various kinds are the urgings of the heart in mankind—and womankind.

"However, there is one thing that I can't understand," said the lady who was simply agreeable. "How could Chichikov, being merely a traveler passing through, ever find the hardihood for such an escapade? It's impossible that there should be no accomplices involved here."

"And do you think there aren't any?"

"And who do you suppose could be helping them?"

"Well, why not Nozdrev himself?"

"Can it possibly be Nozdrev?"

"Who else, then? Why, that would be his very dish. You know, he wanted to sell his own father or, better still, to lose him at cards."

"Ah, my God, what interesting things I am learning from you! I could never, in any circumstances, have supposed that Nozdrev, too, is mixed up in this affair!"

"Well, I always did suppose that."

"When one comes to think of it, really, what things don't go on in this world! There, now, could one have supposed, at the time when Chichikov—do you remember?—had just arrived in our town, that he would create such a strange stir in the world? Ah, Anna Grigoriyevna, if you but knew how all upset I was! If it were not for your affability and friendship . . . there, really, I was already on the very verge of passing out. . . . Where was I to go? My Mashka sees that I am as pale as death. 'Mistress, dearest darling,' she says to me, 'you are as pale as death!'—'Mashka,' I tell her, 'I have no time for that now!' So that's how things are! And so Nozdrev is in this too! Well, I never!"

The lady who was simply agreeable wanted very much to worm out further details as to the elopement—that is, what night and hour it was set for, and so on; what she wanted, however, was far too much. The lady who was agreeable in all respects reacted firmly by claiming to know nothing. She did not know how to lie; to assume something or other was another matter, but even that held good only in a case where the assumption was based upon an inner conviction. Once an inner conviction was felt, she could stand up for herself; and were some expert advocate, celebrated for his gift of overcoming the opinions of others, to attempt a contest in such a case, he would have perceived the full significance of an inner conviction.

There is nothing unusual about the fact that both ladies became at last utterly convinced of that which hitherto they had merely assumed and known to be a mere assumption. Our fraternity—we intelligent people, as we style ourselves—acts in almost the same way, and our learned ratiocinations serve as a proof of this. At first the savant, when it comes to such things, will steal up on them as a most arrant knave, cringing and wheedling: he'll start off timidly, moderately; he'll start off by posing a most modest query: Is this not derived from that? Is it not from this locality that such-and-such a country has received its name? Or: Does not this document appertain to another, later period? Or: Do we not have to understand, under the name of this nation, that other nation? Without losing any time, he will cite this ancient writer and that, and no sooner does he perceive some hint or other of what he's after, or simply what seems a hint to him, than he already puts on speed and takes heart, talks with the ancient writers without standing on ceremony, puts questions to them, and even answers for them himself, forgetting altogether that he had started off with a timid assumption. It already seems to him that he perceives the point, that it is clearly evident, and his ratiocination concludes with the words: And it was thus that this event came about! It is such-and-such a nation that we must understand under the name of that other! And so it is from this point of view that we must regard the subject.

Then he proclaims it for all the world to hear, ex cathedra, and the newly discovered truth is off on its jaunty travels through the world, gathering unto itself followers and devotees.

Just as both ladies had so successfully and wittily resolved such a tangled situation, the Public Prosecutor, with his perpetually frozen physiognomy, his bushy brows and blinking eye, entered the drawing room. The ladies, breaking in on each other, began imparting all these events to him; they told him about the purchase of dead souls, about the contemplated carrying-off of the Governor's daughter, and got him to the point where he absolutely did not know what was what, so that, no matter how long he continued standing on the same spot, batting his left eye and flicking his beard with his handkerchief, brushing the snuff off it, he still could make neither head nor tail of anything. In the end both ladies left him standing there and each went her way to stir up the town.

This enterprise they contrived to carry out in just a trifle over half an hour. The town was positively stirred up; everything was in a ferment; and if there were but anybody that could make out anything! The ladies were so successful in beclouding the eyes of everybody that all, and especially the officials and clerks, were left stunned for some time. During the first moment their state was like that of a schoolboy up whose nose, while he is asleep, his mates, who have risen before him, have thrust a *hussar*—a small twist of paper filled with snuff. Having in his half-sleep drawn in all that snuff with all the heartiness of a sleeper, he awakens, jumps up, stares about him like a fool, his eyes popping in all directions, and cannot grasp where he is or what has happened to him, and only after a time does he make out the walls lit by the indirect rays of the rising sun, the laughter of his mates, who have hidden themselves in corners, and the arrival of morning as it peeps in through the window, to the accompaniment of the awakened forest, resounding with thousands of bird voices, and a glimpse of a shining river, disappearing here and there in glittering eddies between slender reeds and with clusters of naked urchins everywhere, egging on one another to dive in—and only after he has taken all this in does the victim become aware that there's a *hussar* stuck up his nose. This, to perfection, was the state during the first moment of the inhabitants and officials of the town. Each one would come to a dead stop, like a ram, with his eyes bulging. The dead souls, the Governor's daughter, and Chichikov became churned and confounded in their heads in an extraordinarily odd fashion; and only later on, after the first stupefaction, they began, but only apparently, to distinguish each factor and to separate it from the others, began to demand an explanation and to become angry on seeing that the matter would in no wise explain itself.

"After all, what sort of a come-uppance is this, really? What sort of a come-uppance are these dead souls? There's no logic to dead souls; how, then, can one buy up dead souls? Where would you ever dig up a fool big enough to buy them? And what sort of fairy gold would he use to buy them with? And to what end, for what business, could one utilize these dead souls? And how on earth has the Governor's daughter gotten mixed up in this? If he really did want to carry her off, then why did he have to buy up dead souls for that? And if he really wanted to buy up dead souls, then for what would he want to be carrying off the Governor's daughter? Was he after making her a present of these dead souls, or what? And really, when you came down to it, what sort of poppycock had they spread through the town? What in the world are things coming to when, before you can as much as turn around, they've already up and spread a story like that? And if only there were the least sense to it. . . . However, spread it they did, therefore there must have been *some* reason to it. . . . But what reason can there be to dead souls? Why, there just isn't any! All this is simply the Devil riding on a fiddlestick, so much moonshine, stuff and nonsense, pigeon milk and horse feathers! This is, simply—oh, may the Devil take it all! . . ."

In a word, rumors upon rumors flew on their merry way and the whole town began talking of dead souls and the Governor's daughter, of Chichikov and the dead souls, of the Governor's daughter and Chichikov, and the whole jolly mess stirred and rose. The whole town, which up to now seemed to be dozing, swirled up like a whirlwind. All the lie-abeds and sit-by-the-fires who had been lolling and vegetating at home in their dressing gowns for years, placing the blame for their indolence either upon the bungling bootmaker who had made their boots too tight, or on their worthless tailor, or on their drunkard of a coachman, now came crawling out of their holes; all those who had long since terminated all their friendships and who, as the expression goes, knew only those two worthy landowners, Zavalishin and Polezhaev (famous terms, these, derived from the infinitives *to hit the hay* and *to lie down for forty winks,* which have great currency among us in Russia, on an equal footing with the phrase "to drop in on Sopikov and

Hrapovitsky" [Wheezer and Snoreaway], designating any and every manner of sleeping like the dead, on one's side, flat on one's back, and in all other positions, to the accompaniment of window-shattering snores, nose-flute solos, and other such obbligatos); all those whom you could never entice out of their houses even with an invitation to partake of a fish chowder costing five hundred rubles, cooked with sturgeons five feet long and served with all sorts of pastries that would melt in your mouth—well, even all these came crawling out of their holes. In short, it turned out that the town was bustling enough and great enough and as well populated as need be.

Some Sysoi Paphnutievich or other and a certain Macdonald Carlovich, both of whom no one had even heard of before, bobbed up on the scene; some sort of individual, as lanky as lanky could be, one of whose hands had been shot through, of a stature so tall that its like had never been seen, became a fixture in the drawing rooms. The streets were thronged with ordinary covered droshkies, with unbelievable droshkies of another sort, wide and of infinite seating capacity, with arks that clattered along and arks whose wheels squealed and whined—and the fat was in the fire. Some other time and under different circumstances such rumors might have attracted no attention at all to themselves, but it was a long time that the town of N—— had been getting no news whatsoever. There had not been, for the space of three months, anything occurring, even anything of that which, in our capitals, is call *commérages,* or comethers, which, as everybody knows, are the same thing to a town as the timely arrival of a food-supply transport is to an army.

Amid all this town tittle-tattle there suddenly turned out to be two diametrically opposed schools of thought, and two diametrically opposed parties were suddenly formed: the masculine and the feminine. The masculine party, being the most addlepated, turned its attention upon the dead souls. The feminine party busied itself exclusively with the carrying off of the Governor's daughter. In this party, it must be remarked to the credit of the ladies, there was incomparably more orderliness and circumspection. Such evidently is their very function, to be good mistresses of households and good organizers. In a very short while everything with them took on an animated, definite air, assuming clear and self-evident forms; everything became explained, clarified; in short, the result was a finished little masterpiece in oils. It turned out that Chichikov had already been enamored for a long time, and the pair had been meeting each other in a garden by moonlight; that the Governor would long since have given him his daughter, inasmuch as Chichikov was simply made of money, had it not been for Chichikov's wife, whom he had abandoned (whence they had learned that Chichikov was married, no one could tell), and that the wife, who was suffering because she was hopelessly in love with him, had written a most touching letter to the Governor, and that Chichikov, perceiving that the blonde's father and mother would never give their consent, had decided upon an abduction.

In other houses this story was told somewhat differently: Chichikov didn't have any wife at all, at all, but that he, as a man of finesse and one who always preferred to play a sure thing, had, in order to get the daughter's hand, begun matters with the mother, and had a secret affair of the heart with her, and that later on he had made a declaration concerning the daughter's hand, but that the mother, having become frightened lest such a sacrilege take place, and her soul experiencing the pangs of conscience, had rejected him flatly—and that was why Chichikov had decided upon an abduction. To all this there were joined many explanations and emendations, in keeping with the pace at which the rumors finally penetrated into the most godforsaken blind alleys. For in Russia the lower social strata are very fond of chewing over bits of gossip about the upper strata, and therefore they started talking about this affair even in those humble houses where the people had never even set their eyes on or heard tell of Chichikov, launching addenda and even greater elucidations in their turn.

The subject was becoming more entertaining with every minute; it took on with every day more definitive forms and at last, just as it was, in all its definitiveness, was brought to the very ears of the Governor's lady herself. The Governor's lady, as the mother of a family, as the first lady in town, finally as a lady who had not suspected anything of the sort, was absolutely insulted by such stories and was thrown into indignation, a just one in all respects. The poor little blonde went through the most unpleasant tête-à-tête that had ever befallen a girl of sixteen. Whole torrents of interrogations, inquisitions, reprimands, threats, reproaches and exhortations were loosed, so that the girl threw herself down in tears, sobbed, and could not understand a single word; the doorman was given the strictest orders not to admit Chichikov at any time or under any pretext.

Having accomplished their work as far as the Governor's lady was concerned, the ladies exerted themselves to press the masculine party hard, trying to incline the weaklings to their side and asserting that the dead souls were all a fiction and that that fiction had been used merely to divert all suspicion and the more successfully to carry out the abduction. Many of the men actually deserted and went over to the feminine party, despite the fact that they were subjected to powerful recriminations from their very fellows, who cursed them out as old women and weak sisters, names which are, as everyone knows, most derogatory to the masculine sex.

But, no matter how the men armed themselves and resisted, in their party there was no such discipline as in the feminine. Everything with them was somehow coarse, unfinished, clumsy, unfit, ill-made, no good at all; their heads were filled with commotions, hurly-burly, muddlement, slovenliness of thought—in a word, everything manifested the nature of the male, which is vacuous in all things, a nature that is coarse, ponderous, incapable either of running a household or of heartfelt convictions, of little faith, lazy, filled with incessant doubts and perpetual apprehension. The men maintained that all this was so much bosh, that such a business as the abduction of a Governor's daughter was work cut out more for hussars than for civilians, that Chichikov wouldn't do a thing like that, that the women were lying, that a woman was like a sack—she'll take in anything, carry it along, and then pour it out of her mouth; that the main thing to pay attention to was the dead souls; however, the Devil alone knew what they signified, but just the same there was something quite nasty, quite bad about them. Why it seemed to the men that there was something nasty and bad about these souls we shall learn immediately. A new Governor General had been appointed for the province, an event which, as everybody knows, puts officialdom in a state of alarm: there would be a succession of shake-ups, dressings down, rakings over the coals, and all sorts of suchlike fare with which a superior in Civil Service regales his subordinates. "Well, now," the officials pondered, "what if he were merely to find out that silly rumors like that were going round in this town? Why, for that one thing alone he's likely to boil over, and it won't be a matter of saving your skin then, but your very life!" The Inspector of the Board of Health suddenly paled, seeing in his imagination God knows what: whether the phrase *dead souls* did not signify those patients who had died in considerable numbers in the infirmaries and similar institutions from an epidemic fever against which no adequate measures had been taken, and whether Chichikov were not an official sent from the chancellery of the Governor General to conduct an undercover investigation.

He imparted these notions to the Chairman of the Administrative Offices. The Chairman of the Administrative Offices pooh-poohed the idea, and then turned pale, putting to himself the question: But what if the souls bought up by Chichikov were really dead? And yet he had permitted a purchase deed to be executed, and not only that but he himself had played the rôle of Pliushkin's agent, and were this to come to the knowledge of the Governor General, what would happen then?

He did nothing more about this, outside of mentioning it to this one and that one, and suddenly this one and that one turned pale: fear is more catching than the plague and is communicated in an instant. All suddenly sought out in themselves such sins as they had not even committed. The phrase *dead souls* had such an ominously ambiguous ring about it that people began suspecting whether there might not be lurking therein some hint as to certain bodies that had to be buried in a hurry in consequence of two events that had happened not so long before. The first event had to do with certain merchants of Solvychegodsk who had come to town to attend a fair and who, after their trading, had tendered a small spree to their friends, certain merchants of Ustsysolsk, a little spree with a Russian sweep, but with a few German trimmings: orgeats, claret punches, balsams, and the like. The little spree had wound up, as is usually the way, with a free-for-all. The men of Solvychegodsk had done in those of Ustsysolsk, even though they had received plenty from them in the way of broken ribs, wallops in the giblets, and biffs on the button, testifying to the inordinate size of the fists the late lamented had been endowed with. One of the victors even had had his air pump, to use an expression of the fighters, broken off—that is, his whole nose had been beaten to such a pulp that there wasn't even half a finger's length of it left on his face. The merchants pleaded guilty in the affair, giving as an explanation that they had been having a bit of fun. There were rumors current that in pleading guilty each of the defendants had apparently put in an additional plea of four government notes; however, the matter is too obscure; from the interrogations and investigations undertaken it turned out that the Ustsysolsk lads had died of charcoal fumes engendered by a faulty heating system, and hence they were so buried, as victims of suffocation by carbonic gas.

The other occurrence, which had happened not so long ago, was as follows: the government serfs from the hamlet of Vshivaya Spess (Lousy Pride), having joined forces with the same category of serfs from the hamlet of Borovka, named after a species of edible mushroom, and also called Zadirailovo (or Quarrelsome), had, it would seem, wiped the Rural Police off the face of the earth, in the person of its Assessor, some Drobyazhkin or other; apparently the Rural Police—that is, Drobyazhkin the Assessor—had got into the habit of coming to their village far too often (which, in certain cases, is as bad as any epidemic fever), the reason therefor being that the Rural Police, having a certain weakness in matters of the heart, had been eying the wives and wenches of the village. However, the facts are not known definitely, although in their testimony the peasants expressed themselves forthrightly that the Rural Police, now, was as lickerish as a tomcat, and that they'd given him warning more nor once, and at one time had even driven him mother-naked out of one of the huts into which he'd made his way. Of course the Rural Police deserved punishment for his frailties of the heart, but at the same time the peasants of Lousy Pride, as well as those of the hamlet of Quarrelsome, could not be acquitted, either, for having taken the law into their own hands, provided they had really taken an active part in the slaying. But the affair was an obscure one; the Rural Police had been found out on a highroad; the uniform or jacket on the Rural Police was worse than any rag and as for his physiognomy, why, you couldn't even make out it had ever been a face, let alone identify it. The trial dragged along from court to court and finally reached a superior one, where it was first deliberated *in camera* to the following effect: Whereas it was not known precisely which of the peasants had participated in the crime, and yet there had been a host of them; and whereas this Drobyazhkin, he was a dead duck, and therefore there would be but little good to him even if he were to win the trial, whereas the muzhiks were still alive and kicking, ergo, a decision in their favor was quite important to them; therefore, and pursuant thereto, the decision was as follows: The Assessor Drobyazhkin had himself been the cause of the rumpus, inflicting injustice and oppressions upon the peasants of Lousy Pride, as well as those of the hamlet of Quarrelsome; and insofar as his death was concerned, it had occurred while he was on his way home in a sleigh, from a stroke of apoplexy. The matter, it would seem, had been disposed of, neatly and sweetly; but the bureaucrats, for some unknown reason, began to think that probably it was these dead souls that the present fuss was all about.

And things so fell out that, as if on purpose, at a time when Messieurs the bureaucrats were in a difficult enough position without this, two documents reached the Governor simultaneously. The contents of one informed him that, according to data and information received, there was in their province an utterer of counterfeit government notes, concealing himself under various aliases, and that the strictest search for him was to be instituted at once. The contents of the other document consisted of a communication from the Governor of an adjacent province concerning a brigand who had fled from the long arm of the law, and that if any suspicious person who could not produce any credentials or passports should turn up in their province, he was to be immediately apprehended.

These two documents simply stunned everybody. Previous conclusions and surmises were all knocked galley-west. Of course, one could not by any means suppose that this had anything to do with Chichikov; nevertheless, when each one had mulled the matter over for himself, when they all recalled that they still did not know just who Chichikov really was, that he himself had given but a vague report as to his person (true enough, he had said that he had suffered for the truth during his service, but then all this was somehow vague); when, recalling all this, they also recalled that he himself had spoken of apparently having a great number of enemies who had even made attempts on his life—when they had reasoned all this out and recalled everything, they pondered still more deeply: consequently, his life must be in danger; consequently, he was being pursued; consequently, he must have been up to something or other, after all. . . . But just who was he in reality?

Of course it was unthinkable that he was capable of uttering counterfeit notes, and all the more unthinkable that he could be a brigand—his very appearance inspired confidence and respect—but with all that, who could he really be, after all? And so Messieurs the bureaucrats now put to themselves a question which they should have put in the very beginning, in the first chapter of our epic, that is.

They pondered and pondered and at last came to the decision to make thorough inquiries among those whom Chichikov had traded with and bought these enigmatic dead from, in order to learn, at least, what each transaction had consisted of, and what, precisely, was the meaning of these dead souls, and whether he had not explained to somebody, even though perhaps by mere chance, even though in some indirect, incidental way, his real intentions, and whether he had not told somebody just who he was in reality.

To the Public Prosecutor fell the lot of having a talk with Sobakevich, while the Chairman of the Administrative Offices volunteered to go to Korobochka. And let us, too, set out after them, and learn just what it was they found out.

CHAPTER TEN

Sobakevich had taken up his quarters with his spouse in a house somewhat remote from the more bustling sections of the town. The house he had chosen was of exceedingly solid construction; the ceiling was not likely to collapse and one could live there in safety and security. The owner of the house, a merchant by the name of Kolotyrkin, was also a solid fellow. Only Sobakevich's wife was with him, but not his children. He was already beginning to weary of the town and by now was thinking of leaving it, staying on only to collect the ground rent for some land that three burghers in the town had leased for growing turnips, and the completion of some modish capote quilted with cotton wool which his spouse had got it into her head to order from a tailor in town. As he sat in his easy chair he was about to launch into a diatribe against both the prevalent knavery and the whims of fashion, without looking at his wife, however, but at an angle of the stove. It was at this point that the Public Prosecutor entered. Sobakevich said: "Please be seated," and, after rising a little in his easy chair, sat down again.

The Public Prosecutor approached to kiss Theodulia Ivanovna's little hand and then also took a chair. Theodulia Ivanovna, after duly receiving the kiss upon her hand, took a chair in her turn. All three chairs were enameled with green paint and had little jugs painted at the corners.

"I have called to discuss a certain matter with you," said the Public Prosecutor.

"Go to your room, my pet! The dressmaker is probably waiting for you there." Theodulia went to her room.

"Permit me to ask," the Public Prosecutor began, "just what kind of serfs did you sell to Pavel Ivanovich Chichikov?"

"What do you mean, what kind?" Sobakevich countered. "That's what the purchase deed is for, it specifies what kind; the coachmaker alone was—"

"However, throughout the town," the Public Prosecutor put in, "throughout the town there are rumors afloat that—"

"There is an awful lot of fools in town, that's why there is a lot of awful rumors," Sobakevich told him imperturbably.

"However, Michail Semënych, the rumors are of such a nature that they make one's head go round and round: that the souls aren't souls; that they were bought not at all for the purpose of resettlement; and that Chichikov himself is a man of mystery. Such suspicions have turned up . . . such tittle-tattle has been spread through the town—"

"But let me ask you this: are you an old woman, or what?" asked Sobakevich.

This question abashed the Public Prosecutor. He had never yet happened to ask himself whether he was an old woman or whether he was something else.

"You really ought to be ashamed even to come to me with such inquiries as that," Sobakevich went on.

The Public Prosecutor began to excuse himself.

"You ought to go to some of those housewives who sit around evenings spinning and knitting and chinning about witches. If God has not given you horse sense enough to start a conversation about something more intelligent than that, you might go and play at knucklebones with little brats. Really, now, why have you come to mix up an honest man? What do you think I am, a laughingstock for you, or what? You don't attend to your work the way you should, you don't exert yourself to serve your country and to benefit your fellow men, unless they happen to be your fellow grafters; you never think of such things but only of how you can isolate yourself from other people as much as possible. Whichever way the fools may prod you, that's the way you'll plod along. And so you will disappear, having lived entirely in vain, and there won't be a single good thing left to remember you by."

The Public Prosecutor was at an utter loss for an answer to such an unexpected admonitory lecture. Pulverized, annihilated, he got away from Sobakevich, while Sobakevich called after him: "Git going, you dog!"

"How is it the Prosecutor left you so soon?" asked Theodulia, entering at this point.

"He felt the pangs of his conscience, so he up and left," Sobakevich told her. "There, my pet, you have an example before your very eyes. What an elderly man, with his head already gray, and yet I know that he is dangling after other men's wives to this very day. That's a way they all have— they're all dogs. And as if it weren't enough that they cumber the earth in vain, they'll also do such things as the whole kit and caboodle of them ought to be put into the same sack for and thrown into the river. The whole town is nothing but a robbers' den. There's no use in our staying on here any longer; let's leave!"

His spouse made an attempt to make him see that the capote wasn't ready yet, and that, for the holidays, she had to buy some ribbons or other for her caps, but Sobakevich told her: "All those things are just fashionable notions, my pet; they won't bring you to any good."

He ordered everything to be prepared for the trip; he himself, accompanied by a patrolman, went to the three burghers and got out of them the ground rent for the turnip patch; then he dropped in at the dressmaker's and took the capote in its unfinished state, just as it was in work, with the needle and thread stuck in it, so that it might be finished in his village, and drove out of the town, constantly repeating that it was dangerous even to visit this town, inasmuch as it consisted of nothing but one swindler on top of another and that one could easily, together with them, be swallowed up in all sorts of vices.

The Public Prosecutor, in the meantime, was so nonplussed by his reception at Sobakevich's hands that he was perplexed how he might even tell about it to the Chairman of the Administrative Offices.[A]*

However, the Chairman of the Administrative Offices had also accomplished but little in finding any explanations for the Chichikov enigma. To begin with, having set out in his droshky, he at last found himself in so narrow and be-mired a by-lane that during his entire ride through it the right wheel was higher than the left or the left was higher than the right. Because of this jouncing he had struck him-self quite hard with his cane, first on the chin, then on the nape of his neck . . . and, to finish everything off, had splat-tered himself all over with mire. He drove into the court-yard of the Dean's house amid the champing of horses, sounds of churning mud, and the grunting of swine. Leav-ing the droshky and picking his way through all sorts of hutches and coops, he reached the house and at last got into the entry. Here, first of all, he asked for a towel and wiped his face. Korobochka met him in much the same way she had met Chichikov, with the same melancholy air. She had some rag or other wound around her neck, something in the nature of flannel. There was an incomputable host of flies in the room, and some dish of something extremely repulsive prepared especially for their benefit, to which mess, however, they seemed utterly accustomed by now.

Korobochka asked him to be seated.

The Chairman began by saying that he had known her late husband once upon a time, then suddenly shifted the

---

*See Addenda and Variants, pp. 655–669. *Trans.*

conversation by asking: "Tell me, please, if it isn't true that a certain person arrived at your house late one night and threatened to kill you if you did not give up certain souls to him? And couldn't you explain to us what his intention was in acquiring them?"

"Oh, can't I, now? You just put yourself in my place—fifteen rubles he gave me, in paper money! For really, I don't know anything; I'm a widow woman, I'm an inexperienced person; it's no hard thing to take me in when it comes to business, in which, I must confess and tell you, father o' mine, I don't know a thing. When it comes to hemp, now, I know the prices; I also sold some lard on the third of—"

"But do tell me first, as circumstantially as you can, just what happened. Did he have any pistols with him?"

"No, father o' mine, when it comes to pistols, God save and preserve us, I didn't see any. But mine is a widow's lot, you can't expect me to know what dead souls are fetching right now. Don't you fail me, now, father o' mine; enlighten me, at least, so's I might know the real price."

"What price? What price are you talking about, mother? What price, now?"

"Why, what price does a dead soul fetch now?"

"Well, either she's a born fool or she's gone batty," the Chairman reflected, staring into her eyes.

"What's fifteen rubles? For I don't know: maybe they're worth fifty rubles or even more."

"Suppose you show me the notes," said the Chairman, and looked at them against the light to see if they were counterfeit or not. But the notes were all that notes should be.

"Now do tell me how he happened to buy anything from

you. Just what was it he bought? I can't get a thing into my head ... can't grasp anything—"

"Yes, he bought from me," said Korobochka. "But I say, now, father o' mine, how is it you won't tell me how much a dead soul fetches, so's I might know the going price on dead souls?"

"But, good heavens, what are you saying? Who ever heard of dead souls being sold?"

"But how is it you won't tell me the price?"

"What price are you talking about? Did he threaten you in any way at the time—did he want to seduce you?"

"No, father o' mine; but really, now, you are so. . . . Now I can see that you, too, are a commission merchant." And she peered suspiciously into his eyes.

"But, mother, I am the Chairman of the Administrative Offices here—"

"No, father o' mine, say what you like, but you're really, now. . . . You're also after doing the same ... you want to take me in yourself. But just what good will that do you? Why, it's so much worse for you. I would have sold you feathers, too; I'll have feathers around Christmas—"

"I'm telling you, mother, that I am the Chairman of the Administrative Offices. What do I need your feathers for? I don't buy up anything."

"Why, now, trading is an honest business," Korobochka kept right on. "Today I sell to you, tomorrow you sell to me. Well, now, if we'll start in taking each other in that way, where is there any justice on earth, in that case? Why, it's a sin before God."

"Mother, I'm not a commission merchant but a Chairman!"

"Well, God knows who you are. Maybe you even are a Chairman—after all, I don't know. How should I? I'm only a poor widow woman. But why are you questioning me like that? No, father o' mine, I see that you yourself ... now ... are after buying them!"

"Mother, I would advise you to see about your health," said the Chairman, growing angry. "You've got something missing here," he said, tapping his finger on his forehead, and left Korobochka.

Korobochka remained steadfast in her opinion that he was a commission merchant, and merely wondered how mean folks had become in this world, and how hard things were for a poor widow woman.[B]

The Chairman of the Administrative Offices broke a wheel of his droshky and was spattered from head to foot with stinking mud. That was all he had got out of his unsuccessful expedition, including, of course, the smashing blow on the chin from his cane. As he was driving up to his house he encountered the Public Prosecutor, who was also riding in a droshky, out of sorts and with his head cast down.

"Well, what did you find out from Sobakevich?"

The Public Prosecutor hung his head still lower. "Never in all my life," said he, "have I had such a raking over the coals."

"Why, what happened?"

"He spat all over me," said the Public Prosecutor with an aggrieved air.

"How was that?"

"It seems that I'm of no use in my work at all: I've never handed in a single adverse report on my co-workers. In other places not a week passes by but that the Public Prosecutor hands in an adverse report; I've always put *Approved* on every service record; even at times when one should really have sent in an adverse report I didn't keep any paper back."

The Public Prosecutor was really crushed.

"But just what has he got to say about Chichikov?" the Chairman persisted.

"What has he got to say? He called all of us old women, cursed us all for a pack of fools."

The Chairman of the Administrative Offices became pensive. At this point a third droshky came driving along, with the Vice-Governor therein. "Gentlemen," he said, "I have to inform you that we must be on the lookout. They're saying that a Governor General is really being appointed for our province."

Both the Chairman and the Public Prosecutor let their jaws drop.

"There, he'll come just in time for the feast! What a fine kettle of fish—the Devil alone can find the taste in it! He'll see what a confounded muddle the town is in!" the Chairman of the Administrative Offices thought to himself.

"One damned thing after another!" thought the aggrieved Public Prosecutor.

"Do you know anything about who has been appointed—what his temperament is, what sort of a man he is?" asked the Chairman.

"No one knows anything yet," answered the Vice-Governor.

Just then the Postmaster drove up, also in a droshky.

"Gentlemen, I can congratulate you on your Governor General!"

"We've heard that already, but nothing is known for a fact yet."

"Why, it's even known who he is," said the Postmaster. "It's Count Odnozorovsky-Chementinsky."

"Well, what do they say about him?"

"The strictest of men, my dear Sir," said the Postmaster. "Most far sighted, and of the shortest temper. He was formerly in some sort of a, now, you understand, important branch of the government. They got into certain sinful ways there. He gave them all a good dressing down; he pulverized 'em so fine, you understand, that there wasn't even enough left of 'em to sweep up."

"Why, there's no need at all of any strict measures in this town."

"He is a treasure house of information, my dear Sir; a man on a colossal scale, you understand?" the Postmaster went on. "There was one occasion when . . . However," he remarked, "we are talking out in the street, in front of our coachmen. Let's better get indoors."

They all realized where they were. For in the meantime spectators had gathered in the street, gawking with gaping mouths at the four men in four droshkies carrying on a conversation among themselves. The coachmen shouted at their horses and the four droshkies trailed along to the house of the Chairman of the Administrative Offices.

"The Devil sure has brought this Chichikov at the right time," thought the Chairman, taking off his mud-spattered fur coat in the anteroom.

318 · *Nikolai Gogol*

"My head is going round and round," said the Public Prosecutor, taking off his fur coat.

"I still can't make this business out, for the life of me," said the Vice-Governor, slipping out of his fur coat.

The Postmaster didn't say a word; he simply threw off his fur coat.

They all entered a room wherein all sorts of cold snacks suddenly appeared. The provincial powers that be can't do without cold snacks, and if, in any province, two officials happen to get together, the third boon companion to appear (of itself) will be a table set with cold snacks.

The Chairman of the Administrative Offices walked up to the table and poured out some of the bitterest wormwood vodka for himself, saying as he did so: "If you were to kill me, I don't know just who this fellow Chichikov is."

"And that goes for me, too," said the Public Prosecutor, "only more so. Such a mixed-up affair I have never yet come across, even in official papers, and I haven't the heart to tackle it—"

"And yet, what worldly polish . . . the man has," said the Postmaster, concocting a mixture of different vodkas for himself, beginning with a dark and finishing with a roseate one. "He's evidently been to Paris. I think he must have had a diplomatic post, or practically that."

"Well, gentlemen!" said the Chief of Police, the well-known benefactor of the town, the favorite of the merchants and a miracle worker when it came to giving a feast, as he entered at this point. "Gentlemen! I haven't been able to find out a thing about Chichikov. I didn't have a chance to rummage through his personal papers; he never leaves his room; he has come down with something. I pumped his people: Petrushka, his flunky, and Seliphan, his coachman. The first wasn't any too sober, but then he's always been that way." Here the Chief of Police walked up to the drinks and made himself a concoction of three different vodkas. "Petrushka says that his master is like any master; that Chichikov has associated with apparently the better sort of people, with Perekroev, for instance. He mentioned a lot of landowners—collegiate and state councilors, all of them. 'Not at all a foolish man,' Seliphan the coachman says of him; Chichikov was respected by everybody because he'd done his duty well in the Civil Service. He has worked in the Customs, and was connected with certain construction works for the government, but just which ones Seliphan couldn't say. 'There's three horses; one was bought,' he says, 'three years back; the gray horse,' says he, 'was swapped for another gray; the third was bought. . . .' As for Chichikov himself, his name really is Pavel Ivanovich, and he actually is a collegiate councilor." [C]

All the officials grew thoughtful.

"A decent man, and a collegiate councilor," reflected the Public Prosecutor, "and yet he decides on such an affair as carrying off the Governor's daughter, and gets such mad notions into his head as buying up dead souls and frightening aged ladies late at night—which may be becoming to some junker in the hussars, but never to a collegiate councilor."

"If he be a collegiate councilor, how can he embark on such a criminal offense as counterfeiting government notes!" reflected the Vice-Governor, who was a collegiate councilor himself, loved to play the flute, and had a soul inclined to the fine arts rather than to crime.

"Like it or not, gentlemen, this business must be wound up, one way or another. The Governor General will arrive and see that simply the Devil alone knows what is going on among us," said the Chief of Police.

"Well, what action are you thinking of taking?"

"I think one must act decisively," the Chief of Police answered.

"But decisively in just what way?"

"By detaining him as a suspicious person."

"And what if he detains *us* as suspicious persons?"

"How can that be?"

"Well, and what if he turns out to be an undercover man? Well, and what if he has secret instructions? Dead souls! Hmm! Buying them up, apparently, but supposing it's really an investigation of all those deaths certified under *cause unknown?*"

These words plunged everybody into deep thought. But the Public Prosecutor was staggered by them. The Chairman too, after uttering them, became thoughtful. Odd, that the arrivals of Chichikov and the Governor General should coincide thus. . . .

"Well, now how are we to act, gentlemen?" asked the Chief of Police, the town's philanthropist and the merchants' benefactor, and, after mixing himself a drink of a sweet vodka and a bitter he tossed it off, chasing it down with a cold delicacy.

A flunky brought in a bottle of Madeira and fresh glasses.

"Really, now, I don't know what action to take," said the Chairman of the Administrative Offices.

"Gentlemen," said the Postmaster, after draining a glass

of Madeira and shoving into his mouth some Edam cheese together with dried sturgeon steak and butter, "I am of the opinion that this matter must be rather thoroughly gone into, that it must be considered rather thoroughly, and considered *in camera*, by all of us together, together assembled, in common, the way they do things in the British Parliament, you understand, so that every avenue may be explored definitely, following every twist and turn, you understand."

"Well, why not? We'll assemble," said the Chief of Police.

"Yes," said the Chairman of the Administrative Offices, "let us assemble and decide in a body just what Chichikov is."

"That's the most sensible thing of all, to decide just what this Chichikov is."

Having said which they felt a simultaneous urge to partake of champagne, and then went their various ways, satisfied that this proposed committee would arrive at an explanation of everything and would show, clearly and definitely, just what Chichikov was.

CHAPTER ELEVEN

Having gathered at the house of the Chief of Police, the father and benefactor of the town whom the reader is already acquainted with, the officials had an opportunity of remarking to one another that they had actually lost weight because of all these worries and alarums. And truly, the appointment of a new Governor General, as well as the recent receipt of those documents the contents of which were of so serious a character and all those rumors the nature of which God alone knew, had all left perceptible traces upon their countenances, while their frock coats had become perceptibly roomier. Everything had been thrown somewhat out of kilter. The Chairman of the Administrative Offices had lost weight, and the Public Prosecutor had lost weight, and the Inspector of the Board of Health had lost weight, and a certain Semën Ivanovich, who was never called by his last name and who wore upon his right index finger a ring which he always permitted the ladies to examine—well, even he had lost weight. Of course, as is generally the case, there were to be found some courageous spirits who had not lost their presence of mind, but they were far from many—as a matter of fact there was only one: the Postmaster. He alone did not change; his character remained as imperturbable and serene as ever. Whenever such occasions as the present arose it was his wont to remark: "We know all about you Governors General! There will be three or four of you replacing one another; but it's thirty years by now, my dear Sir, that I'm doing business at the same old stand." To which the other officials would usually remark: "It's all very well for you to talk, *Sprechen Sie Deutsch,* Ivan Andreich. Your work has to do with the mail, receiving it and dispatching it. All the monkey business you can do is to close the post office an hour earlier, maybe, or accept a little something from a belated merchant for getting a letter outside of regular hours, or you may forward a parcel or two that shouldn't be forwarded. In a case like that, naturally, any man would be a saint. But suppose the Devil took to turning up at your elbow day after day, so that, even though you didn't want to take anything, he persists in thrusting temptation upon you. You, of course, haven't much to worry you, all you've got is one little son; but in my case, brother, my Praskovia Fedorovna has been endowed by God with such a blessed fertility that not a year passes without her bringing forth either a Praskushka or a Petrushka. In a case like that, brother, you'd strike up a different tune."

Thus did the officials discourse; but whether it's really possible to withstand the Devil or not is not an author's business to judge. In the council now convened there was very noticeable an absence of that indispensable something which among the common folk is called horse sense. In general we Russians have not, somehow, been created for representative bodies. In all our assemblies, beginning with the village meeting of the peasants and going all the way up to all possible sorts of learned committees and the like, a most impressive confusion will prevail if they lack a single leader who directs everything. It is difficult to say why this is so; evidently it must be so because we are that sort of folk. Only those conferences succeed which are undertaken with the ultimate goal of having a good time or a banquet, such organizations as clubs and all kinds of pleasure gardens, patterned after the German style. But as for willingness, it's on tap at a moment's notice and for any purpose you wish. We will, at the drop of a hat and with all the consistency of a weather vane, launch societies for philanthropic purposes, for the encouragement of this and that, and for heaven alone knows what else. The purpose will, every time, be splendid and beautiful, but with all that nothing will come of it. Perhaps this is due to the fact that we become quickly satisfied at the very beginning, and consider that everything has already been accomplished. For instance, having got up some society for the benefit of the poor and duly contributed considerable sums, we will immediately, to mark the occasion of so praiseworthy a deed, launch a banquet for all the leading dignitaries of the town, which banquet, in the nature of things, will eat up half the sums received; with the remaining funds magnificent quarters will be promptly rented for the committee, complete with the latest heating arrangements and all sorts of attendants. And, in the upshot, there remains for the poor all of five rubles and a half, but even then the members of the committee are not in full accord as to the disposition of this sum, and each one proposes as the recipient some worthy person who had been godmother to his child.

However, the conference now convened was of an entirely different kind—it had been called out of sheer necessity. It wasn't with any poor folk or outsiders that it had to deal; it had to deal with matters that affected each one of the officials personally. It had to deal with a peril that threatened all of them alike; therefore, willy-nilly, the conference had to attain as much unanimity and camaraderie as possible. But, for all that, the result was the deuce knows what. To say nothing of the differences of opinion natural to all councils, a hesitancy that was downright incomprehensible was revealed about the view of those gathered here. One would say that Chichikov was a counterfeiter and utterer of government notes, and then would himself add: "And maybe he isn't, at that." Another maintained that our hero was an official from the chancellery of the Governor General, and then immediately tacked on: "And yet, the Devil knows what he is; you can't read anything on his forehead." Against the conjecture whether he mightn't be a brigand in disguise all rose up in arms; they found that, outside of his appearance, which attested to his good intentions per se, there was nothing in his conversation that in any way betokened a man of violent deeds.

Suddenly the Postmaster, who for several minutes had been in some sort of reverie, moved by some inspiration or by something else, cried out unexpectedly: "Do you know, gentlemen, who this Chichikov is?"

The voice in which he uttered this was imbued with something so staggering that it compelled all of them to cry out at the same time: "No, who is he?"

"This, gentlemen, and my dear Sir, is none other than Captain Kopeikin!"

And when all of them asked, as if with one voice: "And just who might this Captain Kopeikin be?" the Postmaster said: "So you don't know who Captain Kopeikin is?"

They all answered that they didn't know in the least who Captain Kopeikin was.

"Captain Kopeikin," the Postmaster began, opening his snuffbox only halfway, out of apprehension that someone of those near him might dip his fingers therein, in the cleanliness of which fingers he had but little faith, and was even wont to add: "We know all about it, father o' mine; who knows where you've had your fingers, and yet snuff is a thing that calls for cleanliness"— "Captain Kopeikin," he repeated, but only after he had taken a pinch up his nostrils, "but then, really, if one were to tell you his story, it would turn out to be a most entertaining thing, even for some writer or other—a whole epic, in a sort of way."

All those present evinced a desire to learn this story or, as the Postmaster had put it, this most entertaining thing, even for some writer or other—a whole epic, in a sort of a way, and he began:

The Tale of Captain Kopeikin

After the campaign of eighteen-twelve my dear Sir— (thus did the Postmaster begin, despite the fact that the room held not one sir but all of six sirs)—after the campaign of eighteen-twelve a certain Captain Kopeikin was sent back from the front together with other casualties. Whether it was at Krasnyi or at Leipzig, the fact remains that he had, if you can fancy such a thing, an arm and a leg blown off. Well, at that time none of these special provisions concerning the wounded had been made yet, you know, none whatsoever; any sort of a fund for invalided soldiers, as you may imagine, was formed, in a sort of a way, only considerably later. Captain Kopeikin saw that he'd have to get some work, but the deuce of it was that the one arm he had left was, you understand, his left. He did pay a visit home, to see his father; well, his father told him: "I haven't the means to feed you; I"—just imagine such a thing—"I can barely win bread for myself." And so my Captain Kopeikin decided to set out, my dear Sir, to St. Petersburg, to petition the Sovereign as to whether there mightn't be some monarchal dispensation for the relief of such cases as his: "This is the way of things, and this and that, and I have, in a manner of speaking, laid down my life, have shed my blood. . . ."

Well, whichever way he did it, don't you know, whether through hitching rides on supply carts or on government army transports, the fact remains, my dear Sir, that in one way or another make his way to St. Petersburg he did. Well, you can just picture the thing for yourself: a fellow like that, a Captain Kopeikin of some sort, now, and suddenly he finds himself plumped down in a capital the like of which, so to say, isn't to be found anywhere in the world! All of a sudden the world, relatively speaking, unrolls before him, a veritable arena of life, as it were, such a Scheherazade fairyland, you understand. All of a sudden something like Nevsky Prospect spreads out before him, if you will picture it to yourself or, you know, some Gorohovaya, the Devil take it, or some Liteinaya. Over here some spire or other soars in the air; over there are bridges suspended in some sort of a devilish way, without any visible contact with the earth, as it were—in a word, my dear Sir, the hanging gardens of Semiramis, and that's all there is to it!

He did make a brash attempt to find rooms for himself, only everything was so dear and imposing: window curtains, and window blinds, all such devilishly expensive stuff, you understand; the rugs, my dear Sir, were Persia itself, sort of . . . in a word, relatively speaking, as it were, you trod untold wealth underfoot at every step you took. You just walked along the streets, surely a simple enough thing, now, and yet, you know, your nose could sniff thousands upon thousands in the very air; and yet my Captain Kopeikin's entire First National Bank, you understand, consisted of some ten blues, of V's, and a trifle in silver. Well, you can hardly buy a country seat with that, not really, you can't—that is to say, you *can* buy a country seat with it, provided you add forty thousand to it; but when it comes to a matter of forty thousand you have to float a loan with the king of France, naturally. Well, somehow or other he found a snug nook in a low tavern run by a Finn, for a ruble a day, the dinner consisting of cabbage soup and a bit of chopped beef. So he saw that there was no manner of use in holing in for a long stay.

He asked this one and that where he was to go and whom he was to see. They told him that there was a sort of a high commission, a department of the government, kind of, set up for such cases as his, headed by So-and-so as General in Chief. As for the Emperor, you must know that at that time His Majesty wasn't in the capital, as you may well imagine, he hadn't come back from Paris yet; everybody who was anybody was still abroad.

And so my Kopeikin, getting up very early, scraped the stubble off his face with his left hand, somehow, for even paying a barber would, in a way, have put a dent in his funds; pulled on his wretched little uniform and stumped off on his peg leg, if you can fancy such a thing, to see none other than the grandee who headed the commission. He asked people where the official lived. "There," they told him, pointing out a house on the Palace Quay. Just a wretched tumble-down shack, it was, you understand, with nothing but marble for the walls and mere parquetry for the floors, with plate-glass windows ten and a half foot high, so that, if you can picture such a thing to yourself, it seemed as if you could reach out with your hand from the sidewalk and touch the vases and things on the inside. The least little metal doorknob, you understand, was such a work of art that before you dared as much as lay your hand on it you'd have to dash over to some shop first for a copper's worth of soap and put in an hour or two, so to say, scrubbing your hands, and only after that possibly get up courage enough to desecrate that doorknob by grabbing hold of it. In short, everything was so highly waxed and polished that, in a way, it was enough to turn your head. Why, the very doorman out on the front steps looked nothing short of a generalissimo, if you follow me, with his gilt mace and a physiognomy on him like a count's—like some sort of a well-fed, fat pug dog, you know, cambric ruffs on him, and no end of swank.

My Kopeikin managed to drag himself up the marble steps on his wooden peg leg, as best as he could, and got into the reception room, where he made himself as small as possible in a corner, so as not to jostle with his elbow something or other that, as you can well imagine might be as priceless as an America or an India—some gilded porcelain vase, or something like that, if you follow me. Well, it goes without saying that he had his fill of cooling his heels standing there, inasmuch as he had come at a time when the General had, in a way, hardly risen from his bed, and his valet was bringing him some sort of a silver basin for his sundry, you understand, ablutions. My Kopeikin hangs around for four hours until an adjutant or some other official comes out and announces: "The General," he says, "will be coming out here right away." Well, by now the people in the reception room are as thick as peas. And all the folks there aren't just such country bumpkins like us, officials of the fourth and fifth grades, but colonels at the least, mind you; the room is simply chock-full of all sorts of epaulets and shoulder knots and gold braid and macaronic stuff—in a word, the cream of the cream. Suddenly a barely perceptible stir runs through the room, like some ethereal zephyr springing up, you understand; there's a bit of shushing here and there and at last the stillness becomes unbearable. The grandee enters . . . well, you can imagine what's what for yourself. A statesman, actually! About his face, his person, his bearing there was, so to say . . . well, now, a certain air in keeping with his lofty calling, you understand, and with his high rank, that's the sort of air he had, I mean. Every soul in the room drew itself up at attention, expectant, quivering, awaiting, sort of, the decision of its fate.

This grandee, or Prime Minister, or whatever, walks up now to one, now to another: "What is the purpose of your call? And yours? What is it you wish? What is your business here?" At last, my dear Sir, he comes up to Kopeikin. Kopeikin screws up his courage. "This is the way of things, Your Excellency," he says, "and this and that, and I shed my blood; I have lost, in a sort of a way, an arm and a leg; I am so incapacitated that I cannot work; I make so bold as to ask if there might not be some monarchal dispensation, some assistance, certain arrangements, of one sort or another concerning, relatively speaking, as it were, some remuneration, or pension, or what have you, you understand?"

The Prime Minister sees that the man standing before him has a wooden peg leg, and that the right sleeve of his uniform is pinned onto his breast.

"Very well," says he, "see me about it in a few days."

My Kopeikin walks out of there almost in a transport because, for one thing, he had actually been deemed worthy of an audience, so to say, with a grandee of the very first rank and, for another, because now at last the matter of his pension would, as it were, be settled. In such high spirits as you can well imagine he hops along the sidewalk; drops in at the Palkinsky tavern for a glass of vodka; has his dinner, my dear Sir, at the London, ordering a chop with capers and a pullet with all sorts of fixin's, and calling for a bottle of wine; in the evening he takes in a show—in a word, you understand, he had a bit of a fling. As he hops along the sidewalk he sees some graceful Englishwoman passing by, like some sort of a swan, as you can picture it all for yourself. My Kopeikin—his blood, now, begins coursing faster through his veins, you know—at first started running after her on his wooden peg leg, tap-tap, hot on her trail. "But no," he reflected, "let that sort of thing go for the time being! Later, perhaps, when I get my pension, but now I have spent too much, somehow."

Well, my dear Sir, three or four days later he shows up again at the Prime Minister's and waits until he comes out. "I have come," he says, after due preliminaries, "to find out Your High Excellency's decision in my case, seeing as how, because of the ill-health and wounds I have sustained" and the like of that, you understand, all in the proper style.

The grandee—just imagine!—recognized him right away.

"Ah," he says, "very good! But at present I can't tell you anything more than that you will have to wait for the arrival of the Emperor, when, without a doubt, arrangements will be made concerning disabled veterans, but without the monarch's will in the matter, so to say, there is nothing I can do." A bow, you understand, and good-by. Kopeikin, as you can imagine, walked out of there in a most unsettled state. Here he'd been already thinking that, no later than on the morrow, they would hand the money over to him: "There, dearest fellow, go ahead, drink and be merry," but instead of that he's ordered to wait, and yet there's no definite time set.

So he clumps down those stairs as sore as a boiled owl, or like a poodle over whom a cook has thrown a pail of water, with his tail betwixt his legs and his ears drooping. "Oh, no!" he thinks to himself. "I'll go to him again, will explain to him that I'm down to my last crust; if you don't help me now, I'll have to die, in a sort of a way, from hunger."

In short, my dear Sir, he goes to the Palace Quay. "You can't go in," they tell him, "the General isn't receiving today; come tomorrow." The next day the same thing happens—the doorman doesn't even want to look at him. And yet, at the same time, out of those blue V's of his he has but one left in his pocket. Before this he used to eat cabbage soup, at least, and a bit of beef, but now he'll drop in at a grocer's and get him something like a herring, or a dill pickle, and two coppers' worth of bread; in short, the poor fellow is starving, and yet at the same time he has an appetite that is simply wolfish. He'd be walking past some restaurant where the chef—just imagine!—is a foreigner, a Frenchman, you know, with a frank, open countenance, the linen on him of the finest Holland stuff, and an apron the whiteness of which equals, in a kind of a way, the whiteness of snowy expanses, and this chef is working away at an omelet with *fines herbes,* or cutlets with truffles—in a word, some superduper delicacy or other of such a tantalizing nature that you'd start eating your own self out of sheer appetite. Or he might happen to be going past the shops on Miliutinskaya; there, peeping out of the windows, in a manner of speaking, he would behold such stunning smoked salmon, and little cherries at five rubles each cherry, and a colossus of a watermelon as big as your stagecoach, leaning right out of the window, so to speak, on the lookout for a fool big enough to pay a hundred rubles for it. In short, there is temptation at every step, making his mouth water, relatively speaking, as it were, yet all he keeps on hearing is the eternal "Tomorrow!"

Picture to yourself, then, what his situation was: here, on one hand, so to say, are the smoked salmon and the gigantic watermelon, while on the other he is offered the unvarying bitter fare called *tomorrow.* Finally the poor fellow lost, in a way, all patience; he decided, at any cost, to get through to the Prime Minister, to storm the fortress, if you follow me. He hung around the front entrance, on the chance of some other caller going in, and then, with some general or other, you understand, he slipped through into the reception room, wooden peg leg and all. The grandee comes out, as usual: "What is the purpose of your call? What is the purpose of your call? Ah," says he, catching a sight of Kopeikin, "I've already informed you that you must await a decision."—"For Heaven's sake, Your High Excellency, I haven't, so to say, a crust to eat—"—"Well, what's to be done? I can't do a thing for you; try to help yourself in the meantime; seek out your own means of subsistence."—"But, Your High Excellency, you can judge for yourself, in a sort of a way, what means of subsistence I can find when I lack an arm and a leg."—"But," says the dignitary, "you must agree, in a sort of a way, that I cannot support you at my own expense; I have many disabled veterans, they all have the same rights. . . . Gird yourself with patience. When the Sovereign arrives, I give you my word of honor that the imperial graciousness will not overlook you."—"But, Your High Excellency, I cannot wait!" says Kopeikin, and says it, in a certain respect, rudely. The grandee, you understand, had become actually irked by this time. And really, now, here, on all sides of him, were generals awaiting his decisions, his orders; the affairs are, so to say, important, having to do with the State, demanding the most urgent execution—the loss of a minute may be of importance—and here you have a devil at your elbow you can't shake off, pestering you. "Excuse me," says the grandee, "I have no time now—matters more important than yours are awaiting me," reminding him in a way that was delicate, kind of, that it was time for him to go at last. But my Kopeikin—hunger was spurring him on, you know—he says:

"Do what you will, Your High Excellency, I am not stirring from the spot until you issue instructions as to my pension."

Well, now, you can just imagine: answering like that a grandee who has but to give the word and you go flying head over heels, so far that the Devil himself will never find you. . . . Right here among us, if some clerk just a grade below ours were to say something like that to one of us, why, it would be considered rudeness. But there, what a contrast, just think of the contrast: a General in Chief and some sort of a Captain Kopeikin! Ninety rubles and a zero! The General, you understand, didn't do a thing but just give him a look, no more, but his look was as good as a firearm: you had no heart left, for it went down into your boots. But my Kopeikin, if you can imagine such a thing, doesn't budge from the spot; he stands as if he were rooted there.

"Well, what are your intentions?" says the General, and then decides to let him have it good and hard, as they say. However, to tell the truth, he treated him rather mercifully; another might have scared Kopeikin so that everything would have swirled arsi-versy before his eyes for three days thereafter, but he merely said: "Very well; if you find the cost of living too high here, and can't bide quietly in the capital until such time as your future is decided upon, I shall send you out of here at the government's expense. Call the state courier here! Have this man sent back to his original place of residence under convoy!"

Well, the state courier was already standing there, you understand, such a mountain of a man, all of eight feet tall, and a hand on him, you can just imagine, that has been fashioned by Nature itself to handle stagecoach drivers— in short, as husky as they come. . . . And so they dump Kopeikin, that poor servant of God, into a small cart, and the state courier is off with him. "Well," thinks Kopeikin, "at least I won't have to pay my traveling expenses; thanks for that, at least." He's riding along with the state courier, and as he rides along with him he discourses to himself, in a manner of speaking. "It's all very well," he says to himself, "for the grand man to be saying that I ought to find my own means of subsistence and that I ought to help myself. Very well, then," says he, "I," he says, "will find the means, all right!"

Well, now, as to how he was brought back, and what place he was brought back to, nothing is known about all that. And so, you understand, even all rumors about Captain Kopeikin were plunged into the river of oblivion, into some Lethe or other, as the poets call it. But if you will permit me, gentlemen, that's precisely where the thread that knots the plot of this romantic story begins. And so, where Kopeikin went to is not known; but, just imagine, not more than two months had passed when there appeared in the forests of Ryazan a band of brigands, and the chief of this band was, my dear Sir, none other than our Captain Kopeikin.

He had collected, as it were, a whole mob from amongst all sorts of deserting soldiers. This took place, as you can well imagine, immediately after the war; everybody had gotten used to a loose way of living; a man's life wasn't valued at much more than a copper; everything was in such a state of rack and ruin that even the grass refused to grow; in short, my dear Sir, he had what simply amounted to an army. There was no passing through the highways because of him, but all his attention was devoted to government property, so to say. If it were just a traveler going about on his own business, well, they would just ask him what his business was and then let him go on his way. But, when it came to a government supply transport, either of provender or money—in a word, anything and everything that could be described as government property—there would be no such thing as its getting by.

Well, as you can imagine, the government's pocket, so to

put it, was being depleted horribly. If he happened to hear that some village was due to pay its taxes, he'd be right on the spot. He'd immediately demand that the village elder be brought before him. "Come on, brother, let's have all those imposts and taxes." Well, the old muzhik sees a devil like that before him, with only one leg, and the collar of his uniform of a cloth as red as the plumage of the firebird in the fairy tale; he scents, the Devil take it, that he'll get plenty if he refuses. "Here, father o' mine," he says, "take it all, only let me be." And to himself he thinks: "Must be some Captain of the Rural Police, for sure, or mebbe someone still worse." But the Captain, my dear Sir, never took the money save in a proper manner, as it were; he'd write out a receipt for those peasants on the spot so as, in a sort of a way, to make things easy for them: that the money had been received, for a fact, and that the taxes were all paid in full, and that they had been collected by such-and-such a Captain Kopeikin; he'd even top the whole thing off by af fixing his seal thereto.

In short, my dear Sir, there he was, robbing away, and that's all there was to it. Several times troops were sent out to capture him, but my Captain Kopeikin didn't give as much as a hoot for that. He had such a fine collection of cutthroats around him, you understand. . . . But at last, maybe because he got scary, seeing that the mess he had started, so to say, was no longer a joking matter and that measures for his apprehension were becoming intensified with every minute, and seeing also that he'd gotten quite a bit of money together by now—well, my dear Sir, he ups and makes his way out of Russia and, once out of Russia, my dear Sir, he heads for the United States of America.

And from there, my dear Sir, he writes a letter to the Sovereign, as eloquent a letter as you can possibly imagine. All those Platos and Demostheneses of antiquity, of one sort or another, they were all, one may say, so much trash, so many pettifoggers, if one compared their eloquence with that of Kopeikin's letter. "Don't you be thinking, my Sovereign," he wrote, "that I am this way or that way. . . ." What a world of well-rounded periods he let loose! "Necessity," he says, "was the cause of my actions; I shed my blood; I did not, by any manner of means, spare my life; and I have not, so to say, a crust of bread to subsist on now. Do not punish," he says, "my fellows and comrades, because they are innocent, since they were drawn in, properly speaking, as it were, by me, but rather manifest your monarchal graciousness, so that in the future, should there be any disabled veterans, as it were, they may, for example, have some provision, of one sort or another, made for them, as you may imagine. . . ." In a word, it was extraordinarily eloquent, that letter.

Well, the Sovereign was touched, you understand. Really, his monarchal heart was profoundly stirred; although this Kopeikin was, sure enough, a criminal and deserved, in a sort of a way, capital punishment, yet seeing that such an oversight as the neglect of the disabled could come about, so to say, in a perfectly unintentional manner—although, however, it was impossible at that troublous time to arrange everything right off, for God alone, one may say, is never remiss or in error—in short, my dear Sir, the Sovereign was pleased in this instance to manifest an unexampled magnanimity: he ordered the prosecution of the captured bandits to be stopped and at the same time issued the strictest decree that a committee be formed for the sole purpose of attending to the improvement of the lot of those who had been, so to say, wounded or disabled in war. And there, my dear Sir, you have the reason, so to say, because of which a basis was laid for funds to take care of invalided soldiers, which funds, one may say, now provide perfectly for all wounded soldiers, to such an extent that, truly, no similar solicitude for their care can be found either in England or among any of the other enlightened nations.[D]

—

"And that, my dear Sir, is who this Captain Kopeikin was," the Postmaster concluded his tale. "Now my present supposition is this: he has, beyond a doubt, gone through all his money in the United States, and so he has come back to us, to try once more whether he can't, in a sort of a way, so to say, carry out a new scheme—"

"But hold on, Ivan Andreievich," said the Chief of Police, suddenly breaking in on the Postmaster "why, you yourself said that Captain Kopeikin lacked an arm and a leg, whereas Chichikov—"

At this point the Postmaster cried out and slapped his forehead with all his might, calling himself publicly, before all of them, a calf's head. He could not understand how such a circumstance had not occurred to him at the very beginning of his story and confessed that the proverb about the Russian being strong when it came to hindsight was most just. However, only a minute later he was already trying to be foxy and to squirm out of the situation, saying that, after all, mechanical ingenuity had reached a very high point of perfection in England, that one could see by the papers where someone had invented wooden legs so ingeniously made that at the mere touch of an imperceptible spring they could carry a man off to God knows what regions, so that thereafter there was no such thing as finding him.

However, they all expressed extreme doubts as to whether Chichikov was Captain Kopeikin, and found that the Postmaster had gone too far afield. Still, when it came to their turn, they kept their end up and, prompted by the ingenious surmise of the Postmaster, wandered off almost as far if not further. Out of a great number of suppositions, shrewd in their own way, one in particular emerged at last (one feels oddly even mentioning it): whether Chichikov were not Napoleon in disguise; the Britishers, now, had long been envious because, forsooth, Russia was so great and vast; why, on several occasions caricatures had been actually issued depicting Ivan Ivanovich Ivanov talking with John Bull; John Bull stands there with a dog held on a rope behind him, which dog was supposed to represent Napoleon. "Look here, now," says John Bull, "if anything doesn't go just right, I'll let the dog loose on you right off." And so now, maybe, they'd actually let Boney out from the isle of St. Helena, and so there he was now, sneaking into Russia rigged out as Chichikov, but, when you got right down to it, he wasn't Chichikov at all, at all.

Of course, when it came actually to believing this, the bureaucrats did not believe, yet just the same they fell into deep thought and, as each one scrutinized this business to himself, they found that Chichikov's face, were he to turn and stand sideways, did bear a most striking resemblance to a portrait of Napoleon. The Chief of Police, who had served in the campaign of 1812 and had seen Napoleon with his own eyes, also could not but own that the Little Corporal couldn't possibly be of a greater height than Chichikov, and that in bodily build also Napoleon wasn't what you would call any too stout, even though you couldn't say he was any too slim, either.

Perhaps there are some readers who will call all this improbable; the author, too, just for the sake of pleasing them, is ready to call all this improbable; but, as ill-luck would have it, everything took place precisely as it is told here and, what is still more amazing, the town was not in some backwoods hut, on the contrary, not far from both our capitals. However, it must be remembered that all this took place only shortly after the glorious expulsion of the French. At that time all our landowners, officials, merchants, hucksters, and all our literate folk as well as the illiterate, had become—at least for all of eight years—inveterate politicians. The *Moscow News* and the *Son of the Fatherland* were read through implacably and reached the last reader in shreds and tatters that were of no use whatsoever for any practical purposes. Instead of such questions as "What price did you get for a measure of oats, father o' mine?"—"Did you take advantage of the first snow we had yesterday?" people would ask: "And what do they say in the papers?"—"Have they let Napoleon slip away from that island again, by any chance?"

The merchants were very much afraid of this contingency, inasmuch as they had utter faith in the prediction of a certain prophet who had been sitting in jail for three years by now. This prophet had come no one knew whence, in bast sandals and an undressed sheepskin that reeked to high heaven of spoilt fish, and had proclaimed that

Napoleon was Antichrist and was being kept on a chain of stone behind six walls and beyond seven seas, but that later on he would rend his chain and gain possession of all the world. The prophet, as a reward for his prediction, landed in jail, which was just as it should have been; nevertheless, he had done his work and had thrown the merchants into utter confusion. For a long while thereafter, even during their most profitable deals, the merchants, on setting out for the tavern to wet the bargains with tea, would talk a bit about the Antichrist. Many of the officials, and the gentry and nobility, also involuntarily thought of this from time to time and, infected by the mysticism which, as everybody knows, was all the go at the time, saw some sort of peculiar significance in every letter that went to form the name Napoleon; many even discovered apocalyptic numbers in the name.

And so there is nothing to wonder at if the bureaucrats involuntarily fell into deep thought at this point. In a short while, however, they came to, remarking that their imagination was far too frisky this time and that all this wasn't the right thing. They pondered and they pondered, they deliberated and they deliberated, and the upshot was that they decided that it might not be a bad idea to question Nozdrev rather thoroughly again. Since he had been the first to put out the story about the dead souls and was apparently on very close terms with Chichikov, and was consequently bound to know, beyond a doubt, a thing or two about the circumstances of the latter's life, they ought to have another go at it and see what Nozdrev had to say.

Strange people, these Messieurs the bureaucrats—and, with them, all the other ranks as well. For they knew very well that Nozdrev was a liar, that one couldn't believe him—not in a single word he uttered, not in the least trifle—and yet, just the same, they had recourse to him. There, go and cope with man! Man does not believe in God, but he does believe that if the bridge of his nose itches he in inevitably slated to die soon; he will pass over the creation of a poet, a creation as clear as the day, all permeated with the accord and lofty wisdom of simplicity, but will eagerly pounce upon a work wherein some successful charlatan talks a lot of rot, tells a pack of lies, distorts nature and turns it inside out, and this will prove to his liking, and he will set up a shout: "Here it is, here is a genuine knowledge of the secrets of the heart!" All his life he doesn't value doctors at more than a bent pin, but in the upshot turns to some old conjure woman who heals through whispered spells and gobbets of spit, or better still, he will devise for himself some decoction or other out of goodness knows what rubbish which, God knows why, he will consider the sovereign cure for what ails him.

Of course one may partly excuse Messieurs the bureaucrats because of the actually embarrassing fix they were in. The drowning man, so they say, will clutch at the least straw, for he hasn't sense enough at the moment to reflect that only a fly, perhaps, might be able to ride it out atop a straw, whereas he weighs somewhere around a hundred and fifty pounds, if not all of a hundred and eighty; but this consideration doesn't enter his head at the moment and he clutches at the straw. And so did our gentlemen clutch, at last, even at a Nozdrev. The Chief of Police that very instant dashed off a brief note to him, inviting him for that evening, and a roundsman in top boots, with an attractive glow on his cheeks, ran off with it immediately, holding onto his saber and going lickety-split to Nozdrev's lodgings.

Nozdrev was taken up with very important business. For four days by now he had not left his room, would not admit anyone, and received his meals through the transom; in fact, he had actually grown gaunt and his face had turned a greenish hue. The business demanded the utmost application: it consisted of matching, out of several gross of playing cards, a single deck, but that one was to have the most recognizable features, so that one might pin one's faith on it as on a most tried and true friend. There remained enough work for another fortnight at least. During all this time Porphyry had to scrub the mastiff pup's belly button with a special brush and wash him with soap three times a day (it had turned out to be no pug dog, after all). Nozdrev was very much angered because his seclusion had been broken in on. First of all he sent the roundsman to the Devil, but when he read in the note that there might be a chance of winnings, because they were expecting a certain novice to attend that evening, he softened at once, hastily turned the key in the lock of the room, dressed himself any old way, and was off to attend the evening party.

The statements, attestations, and suppositions of Nozdrev offered such a sharp contrast to those of the bureaucratic gentlemen that even their latest surmises were knocked into a cocked hat. Nozdrev was positively a man for whom there were absolutely no such things as doubts, and one could note just as much positiveness and assurance about his suppositions as one could note of faltering and timidity about theirs. He answered all their points without as much as a stammer; he declared that Chichikov had bought up several thousands' worth of dead souls from him, and that for his part he had sold those souls to him because he hadn't seen any reason for not doing so. To the double-barreled question: Was not Chichikov a spy, and was he not trying to unearth something? Nozdrev answered: Yes, he was; that even at school, where Nozdrev had been in the same class with him, Chichikov had been called a stool pigeon, and that because of this propensity his schoolmates, Nozdrev having been of the number, had given him a bit of a going over, so that afterward it had been necessary to apply no less than two hundred and forty leeches to his, Chichikov's, temples alone—that is he, Nozdrev, had meant to say forty leeches; the two hundred had popped out somehow of itself. To the question: Was not Chichikov an utterer of counterfeit bank notes? Nozdrev answered: Yes, Chichikov certainly was and, since the opportunity offered, told an incident illustrating his extraordinary ingenuity. The authorities having learned that there were counterfeit government notes amounting to two million rubles in the house of the aforesaid Chichikov, had sealed every door and window in the place and had placed guards, but the said Chichikov had exchanged all these notes in the space of a single night, so that the next day, when the seals were removed, the authorities perceived that all the notes were genuine.

To the question, also double-barreled: Was it not a fact that the said Chichikov had intended to carry off, or abduct, or elope with the Governor's daughter, and was it not a fact that he, Nozdrev, had himself volunteered to help and participate in this affair? Nozdrev answered: Yes, he did help, and that had it not been for him, Nozdrev, nothing at all would have happened. At this point he did bring himself up short, perceiving that he had lied absolutely without any need and might bring trouble down upon his own head, but by then it was utterly beyond his power to curb his tongue. However, it also would have been a difficult matter to do so because such very interesting particulars turned up all by themselves that there was no possible way of turning them down. He even gave the name of the village where the parish church was wherein the eloping couple proposed to get married, the village of Truhmachevka, to be precise; the priest was Father Sidor; seventy-five rubles was to be his fee for performing the ceremony, and he would never have consented to perform it for even that if he, Nozdrev, had not threatened to lodge information against him for having married Michaila, a flour dealer, to a woman who had been godmother to the same child he had acted as godfather for;* Nozdrev had even given up his own barouche to Chichikov and his bride and had made arrangements to have relays of fresh horses ready for them at all the stagecoach posts. The details had reached such a stage that he was already beginning to reel off the first names of all the stagecoach drivers involved.

The officials tried him out, gingerly, about their Napoleonic theories, but immediately had cause to regret the attempt themselves, because Nozdrev without an instant's hesitation went off into such a blue streak of drivel that it bore no resemblance either to truth or to anything

---

*Such marriages are forbidden by the Greek Orthodox Church. *Trans.*

else on earth, so that the officials, after heaving a sigh, all walked away. The Chief of Police alone kept on listening to him for a long while yet, thinking that perhaps eventually there might at least be a crumb or two of sense, but finally he, too, made a hopeless gesture, saying: "The Devil alone knows what all this is!" And they all concurred that *no matter how hard you try and pull, you'll never get any milk out of a bull.* And so the officials were left in a worse fix than they had been in before, and the whole business wound up with the conclusion that there was no way of their learning just what Chichikov was. And therein was clearly evinced what kind of creature man is: he is wise, he is clever and sensible in all things that pertain to others but not to his own self. What circumspect, firm counsel he will supply you with on the difficult occasions of life! "What a wideawake head he's got on his shoulders!" shouts the mob. "What a steadfast character!" But let some calamity come swooping down upon this wideawake head, and should it befall him to be placed himself in the difficult occasions of life, why, where in the world has his character gone to? The steadfast man of action is totally at a loss and has turned out to be a pitiful little poltroon, an insignificant, puny babe, or simply, as a Nozdrev puts it, a horse's twat.

All these bits of talk, all these opinions and rumors had for some reason affected the Public Prosecutor most of all. They affected him to such an extent that, upon getting home, he took to brooding and brooding and suddenly, without rhyme or reason, he up and died. Whether it was a stroke of paralysis that carried him off or something else, the fact remains that, just as he was sitting there, he went bang! off his chair, flat on his back. Those around him cried out, as is usually the way, while they wrung their hands: "Ah, my God!" and sent for a doctor to let his blood, yet perceived that the Public Prosecutor was already but a body bereft of its soul. Only then did they find out, with regret, that the Public Prosecutor had had a soul, although out of modesty he had never flaunted it. And in the meantime the manifestation of death was just as awe-inspiring in the case of a little man as in that of a great one: he who but a little while ago had been walking about, had been in motion, had been playing whist, signing sundry papers, and who had been seen so often among the other officials with his bushy eyebrows and his left eye always blinking, was now laid out on a table, that eye not blinking at all now, yet with one of his eyebrows still elevated with a certain questioning air. What the late lamented was asking about, why he had died or why he had lived, that God alone knows.

"But come, now, all this is absurd! This is utterly preposterous! It's impossible that these officials should frighten themselves so, should create such a pother over a rigmarole like that, should go so far astray from the truth, when even the veriest babe can see what the whole business is about!" That is what many readers will say, and they will accuse the author of writing absurdities, or will call the poor officials fools, inasmuch as man is openhanded with the word *fool* and is ready to deal it out twenty times a day to his fellow man. It suffices to have but one foolish point in one's makeup to be recognized as a fool, despite the other nine good points. It's easy enough for the readers to sit in judgment within their tranquil and lofty retreats, whence they have the whole horizon unobscured before them and can see all that is going on below where a man can see only the object which is near at hand. Even in the universal chronicle of mankind there are many unbroken centuries which one would, it seems, like to delete and do away with as unnecessary. Many delusions have overtaken this world, which delusions even a child, apparently, would not be subject to now. What crooked, godforsaken, narrow, impassable bypaths that have diverted it far from the goal has not mankind chosen in its strivings to attain the eternal truth, when spreading right before it was an open way, like to a path that leads to a great fane, meant for a king's mansions! Than all other ways is it broader and more splendid, lit up by the sun and illumined all night by lights, yet it is past it, in a profound darkness, that men have streamed. And how oft, already guided by reason that had come down from heaven, have they not contrived, even then, to backslide and to stray off, how oft have they not contrived, even in broad daylight, to come upon impassable wildernesses, how oft have they not contrived to becloud one another's eyes anew with impenetrable fog and, pursuing will-o'-the-wisps, have contrived in the very end to make their way to the very brink of an abyss, only to ask one another: Where is the way out? Where is the path? The present generation sees everything clearly now; it wonders at the delusions and laughs at the lack of comprehension of its ancestors, not perceiving that this chronicle is written over with heavenly fire, that every letter therein is calling out to it, that from every direction a piercing forefinger is pointed at it—at it and none other than it, the present generation. But the present generation laughs and, self-reliantly, proudly launches a new succession of delusions, over which its descendants will laugh in their turn, even as the present generation is laughing now.

Chichikov was utterly unaware of what was going on. As ill-luck would have it, he had contracted a slight cold at this time, and had a gumboil and a slight inflammation of the throat, in the distribution of which favors the climate of many of our provincial capitals is exceedingly generous. Lest his life, God forbid, be cut short somehow without his leaving any posterity, he decided that he had better keep to his room for three days or so. During those days he ceaselessly gargled his throat with milk and figs, the latter of which he would eat, and bound a little pad filled with camomile and camphor to his cheek. Wishing to occupy his time somehow, he had made several new and detailed lists of all the serfs he had bought, had even read an odd volume of the *Duchesse de la Vallière*, which he had dug up in his small trunk, had looked through all the various objects and little notes contained in his traveling casket, reading this one and that over for a second time, and all this had become very much of a bore to him.

He absolutely could not understand what the meaning might be of the way he was being neglected; not a single one of the town's officials had come to see him even once to find out about the state of his health, whereas only recently droshkies were forever stopping before his inn, now the Postmaster's, now the Public Prosecutor's, now that of the Chairman of the Administrative Offices. He merely kept shrugging as he paced his room. At last he felt better and rejoiced God knows how when he saw he would have a chance to go out into the fresh air. Without putting things off, he immediately tackled dressing; pouring some hot water into a tumbler, he opened his casket, took out his shaving things and proceeded to shave. And it was high time he did so, because, after running his hand over the stubble and glancing into the mirror, he himself had to admit: "Eh, what a forest you've grown!" And true enough, although it may not have been a forest exactly, a rather dark crop had sprouted all over his cheeks and chin.

Having shaved, he began dressing quickly and briskly, so that he almost bounded out of his trousers even as he was putting them on. Finally he was all dressed and, spraying himself with Eau de Cologne and muffling up as warmly as possible, went out into the street, with his cheek still tied up as a precaution. His exit, just like that of every man after recovery from illness, was almost festal. Everything he ran across had taken on a laughing air—the houses, the muzhiks passing by; however, some of the latter looked rather serious, and one or two had already managed to clout a brother muzhik on the ear.

Chichikov intended to call on the Governor first of all. On his way all sorts of ideas popped into his head; the little blonde was continually on his mind; his imagination had even grown somewhat prankish, and he had even begun to laugh and poke fun at himself. It was in such a mood that he found himself before the entrance to the Governor's house. He was just about to throw off his overcoat in the foyer when the doorman stunned him with the utterly unexpected words: "I have orders not to admit you."

"What! What are you saying? Evidently you haven't recognized me. Take a good look at my face!" Chichikov told him.

"How could I fail to recognize you! Why, this isn't the first time I see you," said the doorman. "But it's just you alone that I have been told not to admit—all the others can be received."

"There's a surprise! But why? For what reason?"

"Them's the orders, so it seems that's the way things have to be," said the doorman and added the word *Yes,* after which he took his stand before Chichikov in a free and easy manner, without bothering about that genial air with which formerly he would hasten to help him off with his overcoat. He seemed to be thinking, as he eyed him: "Eh, now, since the masters are chasing you off their front steps you must be just nothing at all, just some sort of common trash, I guess!"

"Can't understand it!" said Chichikov to himself and at once set out for the house of the Chairman of the Administrative Offices. But the Chairman of the Administrative Offices was thrown into such confusion on seeing him that he could not say two words in a row that made any sense and talked such a heap of rubbish that actually both of them felt ashamed. On leaving him Chichikov simply could not make out a thing, no matter how hard he tried, as he walked along, to penetrate what the Chairman had said and what his words could possibly have referred to. Then he dropped in on the others: the Chief of Police, the Vice-Governor, the Postmaster; but either they did not receive him or, if they did, it was in most peculiar fashion—their conversation was so constrained and incoherent, they were so utterly at a loss, and the upshot was such a preposterous muddle, that he entertained doubts as to their mental soundness. He tried to see some of the others to find out, at least, the cause of all this, and did not succeed in gaining even an inkling thereof.

As though he were half asleep he wandered aimlessly through the town, unable to decide whether he had gone out of his mind, whether the officials had lost their heads, whether all this was going on in a nightmare, or whether a mad mess that was worse than any nightmare was coming to a boil in reality. It was already late, almost at dusk, when he came back to the room from which he had set forth in such high spirits. Out of sheer boredom he ordered tea. In a thoughtful mood and in some irrational brooding on the strangeness of his position he was beginning to pour out the tea when the door opened and Nozdrev appeared in an utterly unexpected fashion.

"There, doesn't the proverb say, 'seven miles is not too much out of one's way to see a friend'!" he said, taking off his cap. "I was passing by and I see a light in your window. 'I guess,' I says, 'I'll drop in on him! Probably he isn't sleeping yet.' Ah, you've got tea on the table, that's good; I'll drink a cup with pleasure—today, at dinner, I stuffed myself with all sorts of trash; I feel my stomach starting in to fuss. Tell your man to fill my pipe. Where's your own?"

"Why, I don't smoke a pipe," said Chichikov dryly.

"Bosh; as though I didn't know you were an inveterate smoker. Hey, there! What do you call your man? Hey, there, Vahramei, listen!"

"Not Vahramei but Petrushka."

"But how is that? Why, you used to have a Vahramei."

"I never had any Vahramei."

"Yes, that's right; it's Derebin who has a Vahramei. Imagine what luck this Derebin has: his aunt has quarreled with her son because he married a serf, and now she has willed all her estate to Derebin. 'There,' I thinks to myself, 'if only one were to have an aunt like that for one's future needs!' But I say, brother, why have you withdrawn yourself like that from everybody, why don't you go anywhere? Of course I know that you are at times taken up with scientific studies, that you are fond of reading." (Just why Nozdrev had concluded that our hero was taken up with scientific matters and was fond of reading, we must confess we cannot tell, and Chichikov would be still less likely to.) "Ah, brother Chichikov! If you had but seen . . . there, now, really, you would have found food for your satirical mind!" (Just how Chichikov had come to have a satirical mind is likewise unknown.) "Just imagine, we were playing cards at the house of Lihachev the merchant, and what an amusing time we had! Perependev was with me. 'There,' he says, 'if only Chichikov were here, why, this would be just the thing for him!' " (And yet Chichikov had never in all his born days known any Perependev.) "But own up, now, brother—why, you acted most abominably toward me that time, you remember, when we were playing checkers! For I had won. . . . Yes, brother, you simply diddled me that time. But then, may the Devil take me, I simply can't bear a grudge. Just the other day, at the house of the Chairman of the Administrative Offices . . . ah, yes! I must really tell you that the whole town has turned against you. They think that you are turning out counterfeit bank notes; they started pestering me, but I stood up for you as firm as a rock; I told them a great deal about you, that I had gone to school with you and had known your father. Well, there's no use talking, I spun them a fine yarn."

"I am turning out counterfeit notes?" Chichikov cried out, jumping up from his chair.

"But why, after all, did you throw such a scare into them?" Nozdrev went right on. "The Devil alone knows what they're up to; they're scared out of their wits; they've rigged you out as a brigand and as a secret agent. . . . As for the Public Prosecutor, he cashed in out of fright—his funeral is tomorrow. Aren't you going to attend it? They're all afraid of the new Governor General, to tell the truth, afraid that there might be some fuss on account of you. But my opinion of the Governor General is that if he should start walking around with his nose stuck up in the air and take to acting big, he won't be able to do a single thing with the gentry. The gentry demand cordiality, isn't that so? Of course, one can bury oneself in one's study and never give a ball, but what will he accomplish by doing that? Why, you can't gain anything that way. But, just the same, Chichikov, that's a risky business you've embarked on—"

"What risky business?" Chichikov asked cagily.

"Why, that of carrying off the Governor's daughter. I expected that, I confess I did, by God! Right off, the minute I saw the two of you together at the ball. 'Well, now,' I thinks to myself, 'Chichikov surely isn't just wasting his time—'

"However, it's a pity you made such a choice; I can't discover anything so fine about her. But there is one woman, a relative of Bikussov's, his sister's daughter—well, there's a girl! The finest piece of goods!"

"Why, what are you saying? What are you raving about? What's all this about carrying off the Governor's daughter? What are you saying?" Chichikov was asking, his eyes starting out of his head.

"Come, that'll do, brother; what a secretive fellow! I came to you, I confess, for that very purpose. I'm ready to help you, if you like. So be it: I'll hold the crown over you at the wedding ceremony; I'll supply the barouche and provide the relays of horses, with but one condition: you must let me have a loan of three thousand. I need them, brother, as if I had a knife at my throat!"

All the time that Nozdrev was chattering away Chichikov had kept rubbing his eyes, wishing to make sure whether he were hearing all this in a dream or in reality. Turning out counterfeit notes—abduction of the Governor's daughter—the death of the Public Prosecutor, of which he was apparently the cause—arrival of the Governor General—all these statements had thrown him into a considerable fright. "Well, if things have come to such a pass," he thought to himself, "then there's no use hanging around here; I'll have to make tracks out of here fast as I can."

He tried to get rid of Nozdrev as quickly as possible, then immediately called Seliphan and ordered him to be ready at dawn, so that they might leave the town no later than six o'clock in the morning, without fail; he gave orders to have everything in the carriage looked over, to grease the wheels, and so on and so on. Seliphan said: "Right you are, Pavel Ivanovich," but nevertheless lingered in the doorway for some time, without stirring from the spot. The master also issued immediate orders to Petrushka to drag the small trunk out from under the bed (it had gathered quite a coat of dust by now) and, with his assistance, began packing away, without being too particular, socks, linen (putting the clean and the soiled together), boot trees, a calendar....

All this was put away just as it came to hand: he wanted to have everything ready that evening without fail, so that there might not be any delay on the morrow.

Seliphan, after lingering in the doorway for a couple of minutes, finally walked very slowly out of the room. Slowly, as slowly as one can possibly imagine, did he go down the stairs, leaving the imprint of his wet boots on the worn steps, and for a long while did he keep scratching away at the nape of his neck. What did this scratching signify? And what was its general portent? Was it vexation that now the meeting set for tomorrow with some brother muzhik, in an unprepossessing broad-belted sheepskin jacket, would not come off in some pothouse licensed by the Czar? Or had he already started an affair in this new place with someone who had pierced him to the very heart, and now he would have to leave off standing of evenings near the gates, leave off a politic holding of white hands at that hour when, as soon as the town had pulled the cowl of dusk over it, some husky lad in a red blouse strums his balalaika before all the house help, and working folk of all callings chat quietly among themselves after the toil of the day? Or, simply, did it portend that it was a pity to leave a place that had already been warmed in the domestics' quarters, under a sheepskin, near the oven, and cabbage soup served with a soft, city-made meat pie, only to go off anew out in the rain and the mire and all sorts of inclement weather that overtakes one out on the road? God knows— one cannot guess with certainty. Many and sundry are the things portended when the Russian folk scratch the napes of their necks.

CHAPTER TWELVE

However, nothing came out the way Chichikov had intended. To begin with, he awoke considerably later than he had thought he would—that was the first upset. Upon getting up he immediately sent Petrushka to find out if the carriage was harnessed and whether everything was in readiness, but the report came back that it was not harnessed yet and that nothing was in readiness—this was the second upset. He became very angry and even got set to give something in the nature of a drubbing to our friend Seliphan and was merely waiting with impatience to hear what explanation the other would offer as an excuse. In a short while Seliphan appeared in the doorway and his master had the pleasure of hearing those very same speeches which one usually hears from a servant on the occasions when one must make haste in departure.

"Yes, but, Pavel Ivanovich, the horses have to be shod."

"Oh, you swine! You blockhead! How is it you didn't say something about it before? Wasn't there time enough, perhaps?"

"Why, yes, there was time enough. . . . But then, there's that wheel, too, Pavel Ivanovich; the iron rim will have to be changed entirely, seeing as how the road is now full of holes, there's been such hard rains all over. . . . Also, if you'll allow me to tell you, the front of the carriage has been jarred all loose, so that, like as not, it may not make two stages!"

"You scoundrel!" Chichikov cried out, wringing his hands, and walked up so close to him that Seliphan, out of fear of receiving a free gift from him, backed away and side-stepped. "Do you want to be the death of me, eh? Are you after slitting my throat? Have you set your mind on slitting my throat on the highway, you robber, you damned swine, you sea monster, you! Eh? Eh? We've been stopping at this one spot for three weeks now, haven't we, eh? If you'd only given me an inkling, you shiftless lout—but no, now, at the eleventh hour, you let me have it all at once! When everything is all set to get in the carriage and be off, eh? So that's the very time you have to go and play me a dirty trick like that, eh? Eh? For you knew all this before, didn't you? For you did know it, eh? Eh? Answer me! You did know? Eh?"

"Yes, I did know," answered Seliphan, casting down his head.

"Well, why didn't you tell me, then, eh?"

To this query Seliphan made no answer but, with his head cast down, seemed to be saying to himself: "Look you, how oddly things have fallen out; for I did know, but didn't say anything!"

"And now get along with you; fetch blacksmiths, and have everything done inside of two hours. Do you hear? In two hours, without fail, but if it isn't ready then I'll ... I'll ... bend you into a horseshoe and tie you into a knot!" Our hero was very, very angry.

Seliphan was turning toward the door to go and carry out his orders, but stopped and said: "And another thing, Sir, the piebald ought to be sold, really; he's—he's altogether a low-down creature, Pavel Ivanovich; what a horse he is—may God save us from such another; he's just a hindrance."

"That's right! There, I'll go a-running to the horse market this very minute to sell him!"

"Honest to God, Pavel Ivanovich, it's only that he's good to look at, but when you come right down to it he's the orneriest brute there is; you won't find a horse like that nowhere—"

"You fool! When I want to sell him I'll sell him. You have to start lecturing on top of everything else! There, I'm going to see: if you don't bring me the blacksmiths right away, and if everything isn't in readiness inside of two hours, I'll give you such a drubbing that . . . you won't be able to tell your own face in the mirror! Git! Go on!"

Seliphan got.

Chichikov became thoroughly upset and threw to the floor the sword which accompanied him on all his travels, to inspire appropriate awe whenever necessary. For more than a quarter of an hour did he fuss and bother with the blacksmiths until he came to terms with them, inasmuch as the blacksmiths were, as usual, out-and-out knaves and, having surmised that the work was urgently needed, had jacked up their price exactly sixfold. No matter how heated he became, calling them swindlers, robbers, highwaymen, even hinting at what would happen to them on the dread Day of Judgment, he did not penetrate their hides at all; they ran utterly true to form: not only did they not abate their price, they even fussed around with their work not for two hours but for all of five and a half. During this time Chichikov had the pleasure of experiencing those delectable moments which every traveler is familiar with, when everything has been packed away in the trunk and there is nothing in the room except bits of string, scraps of paper, and all sorts of trash littering the floor; when a man belongs neither to the road nor to any settled place, as he watches through the window the passers-by shuffling along and discussing their picayune affairs, as they lift up their eyes with some sort of silly curiosity to look up at him, then go on their way again, which irritates still more the bad temper of the traveler who isn't traveling. Everything around him, everything that meets his eye— the wretched little shop opposite his windows, and the head of an old woman who lives in the house across the way, as she walks up to her window with its short curtains—everything is repulsive to him, yet go away from the window he will not. He stands there, now oblivious, now turning anew a sort of dulled attentiveness upon everything before him, whether it is stirring or not, and out of vexation he will swat some poor fly that persists in buzzing and beating against the window-pane even as he is swatting it.

But there is an end to all things, and the longed-for moment arrived. Everything was in readiness; the front of the carriage had been properly repaired; a new iron rim had been put on the wheel, the horses were brought from their watering, and the brigand blacksmiths went off, after having counted over their silver rubles and having wished Chichikov godspeed. Finally the carriage itself was harnessed, and two hot twisted loaves, just purchased, were placed therein, and Seliphan had already thrust a thing or two for himself in the boot under his seat and, while the tavern server in his invariable jacket of linsey-woolsey stood by and waved his cap in farewell, and while sundry other flunkies and coachmen, from the tavern as well as outsiders, gathered to gape at someone else's master departing, and amid all the other circumstances usually attendant upon a departure, our hero at last seated himself in the vehicle, and the light carriage, of the sort that bachelors ride in, which had for so long been stalled in the town, and which the reader may have become so fed up with by now, at last rolled out of the gates of the inn.

"Glory be to God!" Chichikov reflected, and crossed himself.

Seliphan lashed out with his whip; Petrushka, who had been hanging on a footrest for some time, got up on the seat beside him, and our hero, seating himself more comfortably upon a small Georgian rug, put a leather cushion back of him, incidentally crushing the two hot loaves, and the vehicle was once more bouncing and swaying along, thanks to the pavement, which, as we know, had a resilient force. With some sort of undefined emotion did he look upon the houses, the walls, the fences and the streets, all of which also seemed to be bouncing and swaying as they slowly fell behind, and God knows if he were ever fated to see all these things again in his whole lifetime.

At a turn into one of the streets the carriage had to stop, inasmuch as an endless funeral procession was passing down its whole length. Chichikov, leaning out, bade Petrushka ask whose funeral it was and learned it was the Public Prosecutor's. Filled with unpleasant sensations, he immediately hid himself in a corner, pulling the leather apron over himself and drawing the curtains to. At this point, while the vehicle was thus halted, Seliphan and

Petrushka, with their hats piously doffed, were observing who was present, how everything was going, who was riding and who was driving, what they were riding or driving, reckoning up the number of all the folk there, both afoot and riding, while their master, having enjoined them not to recognize and not to return the salutes of any of their acquaintances among the coachmen and footmen, also began diffidently observing things through the little glass panes in the leather curtains. The coffin was followed by all the officials, on foot and bareheaded. Chichikov became apprehensive lest they recognize his carriage, but the officials had other things on their minds. They had not even gone in for the varied workaday small talk, such as those escorting a dead man usually carry on among themselves. All their thoughts at this juncture were concentrated on themselves: they were thinking of what the new Governor General would be like now, how he would set about his work, and what reception they would get at his hands.

Behind the officials came the carriages, driven at a walk, out of which the ladies, in mourning caps, were peeping. By the movements of their lips and hands one could see that they were taken up with animated talk; it may even be that they, too, were talking about the coming of the new Governor General, and speculating as to what balls he would give, and were taken up with their eternal little scallops and their darling appliqués. Finally, behind the carriages, followed several empty droshkies, stretched out in single file; at last there was nothing more, and our hero could drive on. Drawing back the leather curtains, he heaved a sigh and uttered: "There, the Public Prosecutor lived on and on, and then he up and died! And now they

will print in the papers that a respected citizen, a rare father, an exemplary spouse, has departed this life to the
great sorrow of his subordinates and of all mankind, and
what sort of stuff won't they write! They will add, likely as
not, that he was followed to his grave by the lamentations
of widows and orphans, and yet, if one were to go into this
matter rather thoroughly, why, on investigation it would
turn out that all there really was to you was your bushy eyebrows." Here he ordered Seliphan to drive on faster and in
the meantime thought to himself: "That's a good thing,
though, meeting this funeral; they say meeting a dead man
is an omen of good luck."

The light carriage had meanwhile turned into more deserted streets; soon there were only long wooden fences
stretching along, heralding the end of the town. And now
the cobbled roadway had come to an end, then the tollgate
was passed and the city was behind him, and then there was
nothing more, and he was again off on his travels. And
again on both sides of the highway began a new succession
of mile after mile, with post-station superintendents, and
water wells, and strings of wagons, and drab villages, with
samovars, countrywives, and the spry, bearded innkeeper
running out of his stable yard with a measure of oats in his
hands; a wayfarer in bast slippers all worn through, plod-
ding along to cover a distance of more than five hundred
miles; wretched little towns, jerry-built, with miserable little shops, flour barrels, bast slippers, twisted loaves, and
other such small wares; striped tollgates; bridges under repair, fields so vast that the eye could not encompass them
on this side of the road and the other, antediluvian traveling coaches of the landed gentry, a soldier on horseback,

carrying a green box with leaden grapeshot and labeled Such-and-such an Artillery Battery; strips of green, yellow, and freshly furrowed black, flashing by on the steppes; a plaintive, long-drawn-out song afar off; crests of pines swathed in mist; the pealing of church bells, becoming lost in the distance; crows as thick as flies, and a horizon with never an end to it. . . .

Russia! Russia! I behold thee—from my alien, beautiful, far-off place do I behold thee. Everything about thee is poor, scattered, bleak; thou wilt not gladden, wilt not affright my eyes with arrogant wonders of nature, crowned by arrogant wonders of art, cities with many-windowed, towering palaces that have become parts of the crags they are perched on, picturesque trees and ivies that have become part of the houses, situated amid the roar and eternal spray of waterfalls; I will not have to crane my head to gaze at rocky masses piled up, without end, on the height above; there will be no flash of sunlight coming through dark arches thrown up on one another, covered with grapevines, ivies and wild roses without number—there will be no flash through them of the eternal lines of gleaming mountains in the distance, soaring up into argent, radiant skies. All is exposed, desolate, and flat about thee; like specks, like dots are thy low-lying towns scattered imperceptibly over thy plains; there is nothing to entice, nothing to enchant the eye. But just what is the incomprehensible, mysterious power that draws one to thee? Why does one hear, resounding incessantly in one's ears, thy plaintive song, floating over all thy length and breadth, from sea to sea? What is there in it, in this song of thine? What is it about that song which calls one, and sobs, and clutches at one's very heart? What sounds are these that poignantly caress my soul and strive to win their way within it, and twine about my heart? Russia! What wouldst thou of me, then? What incomprehensible bond is there between us? Wherefore dost thou gaze at me thus, and wherefore has all that is in thee and of thee turned its eyes, filled with such expectancy, upon me? . . . Yet still, filled with perplexity, I continue standing motionless, though an ominous cloud, heavy with coming rains, has cast its shadow over my head, and thought has grown benumbed before thy vast expanse. What does that unencompassable expanse portend? Is it not here, within thee and of thee, that there is to be born a boundless idea, when thou thyself art without mete or end? Where else if not here is a titan to arise, where there is space for him to open as a flower opens, and to stretch his legs? And thy mighty expanse awesomely envelops me, with fearful might finding reflection in my very heart of hearts; through thy preternatural sway have my eyes come to see the light. . . . Ah, what a refulgent, wondrous horizon that the world knows naught of! Russia! . . .

"Whoa, whoa, you fool!" Chichikov yelled at Seliphan.

"I'll give you a taste of my cutlass!" yelled a state courier with mustachios a yard long, swooping down on them at a gallop. "Can't you see—may the Foul One flay your soul—that this is an official vehicle?"

And, like an apparition, the troika vanished amid thunder and dust.

How much of the strange, and of the alluring, and of that which carries you away, and of the wonderful there is in the words *the road!* And how wondrous it is itself, this road! A radiant day, autumn leaves, chill air. . . . Muffle yourself closer in your traveling cloak, pull your cap down over your ears and let us settle down more closely and snugly in the corner of the carriage! For the last time has a passing shiver run through all your limbs, and has already been replaced by a pleasant warmth. The horses race on and on. . . . How temptingly drowsiness steals up on you and your eyes close, and by now it is through your sleep that you hear "Not the White Snows," and the snorting of the horses, and the rumble of the wheels, and you are already snoring, wedging your neighbor into the very corner. You awake: five stages have already sped by and been left behind; the moon is out; you don't know what town it is— there are churches with ancient, wooden cupolas, and sharp-pointed spires dark against the sky; there are dark houses of timber and white ones of stone; the moonlight falls in patches on this spot and that, as though kerchiefs of white linen were spread over the walls, over the paved way, over the streets; shadows as black as charcoal cut across them at a slant; the wooden roofs, under the oblique light of the moon, gleam like flashing metal; and there is never a soul abroad anywhere: everything slumbers. Save that, all by its lone, a little light may be glimmering in some little window somewhere: is it some burgher of this town cobbling his pair of boots, some baker bustling about his broken-down oven? How do they concern us? But the night! . . . Heavenly powers! What a night is being consummated up in the heavens' heights! And the air, and the sky, distant, lofty, so unencompassably, harmoniously and radiantly spreading there, in its inaccessible profundity! . . . However, the cold breath of night is blowing freshly into your very eyes and lulling you to sleep, and you are already slumbering, and sink into forgetfulness, and snore away, while your poor neighbor, wedged into the corner, angrily turns over on his other side, feeling your weight upon him.

You awaken—and again fields and steppes are before you; nothing to be seen anywhere: wasteland everywhere, everything is out in the open. A milestone with a figure on it flits into sight; morning is beginning; there is a pale golden streak against the chill skyey rim, now turned white; fresher and sharper becomes the wind—muffle yourself closer in your warm traveling cloak! . . . What a glorious cold! What wonderful sleep, enveloping you anew! A jolt—and you are again awakened. The sun is high in the heavens.

"Easy, there, easy, now!" you hear a voice urging; the vehicle goes down a steep declivity; there is a broad dam below, and a broad, clear pond gleaming in the sun like the bottom of a copper vessel; there is a village, its huts scattered over the slope of a hill; the cross of the village church glitters like a star off to one side; the muzhiks are chattering, and a ravenous, clamoring hunger assails you. God! How good thou art for one at times, thou long, long road! How oft, like one perishing and drowning, have I clutched at thee, and every time thou hast magnanimously delivered me and saved me! And how many wonderful projects, poetic reveries, hast thou brought forth, how many impressions have I not experienced on the road!

Why, even our friend Chichikov felt himself under the spell of reveries that were not altogether prosaic. Let us see, then, just what it was he felt. At first he had felt nothing and had merely kept looking over his shoulder from time to time, wishing to make sure that he had really left the town behind him; but when he perceived that the town had long since disappeared, that one could no longer see any blacksmith shops, or mills, or any of that which is to be found on the outskirts of a town, and that even the white spires of its stone churches had long since sunk into the ground, he turned his full attention exclusively to the road, looking merely to his right and left, and it was as if the town of N—— had never existed in his memory, as though he had passed through it long ago, in his childhood. Finally the road as well ceased to entertain him; his eyes began to close a little and his head to incline toward the cushion. The author confesses that he is actually very glad of this, since it will afford him an opportunity of saying something about his hero, inasmuch as up to now, as the reader has seen, the author has been incessantly hindered now by Nozdrev, now by balls, then by ladies, then by the tittle-tattle of the town, then, finally, by thousands of those trifles which seem trifles only when they are put into a book but which, while they are in circulation in the world, are held to be quite important matters. But now let us put absolutely everything to one side and get right down to business.

It is very much to be doubted if the hero we have chosen has proven to the liking of the readers. He won't be to the liking of the ladies, that we can state positively, inasmuch as the ladies demand that the hero be utter perfection and if there be any spiritual or bodily blemish in him, no matter how slight, why, it's just too bad! No matter how deeply the author peer into his soul, though he reflect his image clearer than a mirror, they won't have him at any price. The very corpulence and middle age of Chichikov will be much to his detriment, for corpulence is under no circumstances forgivable in a hero, and quite a great number of ladies will turn away and say: "Faugh! What a repulsive fellow!" Alas! The author is fully aware of all this, yet for all that he cannot take a virtuous man as a hero. But ... it may befall that in this very narrative other chords, as yet unstruck, will be heard, that the incalculable riches of the Russian spirit will be set forth, that someone worthy to be called a man, endowed with divine attributes of valor and virtue, or a wonderful Russian maiden, such as is not to be found anywhere else in the world, with all the wondrous beauty of a woman's soul, all compact of magnanimous striving and self-denial, may yet traverse our pages. And lifeless will seem beside them all the virtuous people of other tribes, even as a book is lifeless before the living word! Russian emotions will spring into life ... and the readers will perceive how deeply has been implanted in the Slavic nature that which has but skimmed the surface of the nature of other peoples. ...

But why and wherefore speak of that which lies ahead? It is unseemly in the author, who has long since been a man, schooled by a rigorous inner life and the invigorating sobriety of solitude, to forget himself like a mere callow youth. There is a turn, and a place, and a time for everything! But, just the same, we have not taken a man of virtue for our hero, after all. And one may even explain why he wasn't taken. Because it is high time to give a rest to the poor man of virtue; because the phrase "man of virtue" is formed all too glibly and idly by all lips; because the man of virtue has been turned into a hack and there isn't a writer who doesn't ride him hard, urging him on with a whip or whatever else comes to his hand; because they have overworked the man of virtue to such an extent that now there isn't even a shadow of virtue about him, and there is nothing but skin and bones left of him instead of flesh and blood; because it is only through hypocrisy that they trot out the man of virtue; because the man of virtue isn't held in much esteem. No, it's high time, at last, to put an actual scoundrel in harness! And so let us harness a scoundrel.

Obscure and humble is the origin of our hero. His parents were of the nobility, but whether hereditary or from a new-baked lot, God knows. He did not resemble them in face; at any rate, a female relative who was present at his birth, a short little, squat little bit of a woman, one of those who are usually called peewees, cried out, as she took the child in her arms: "He didn't come out at all the way I thought he would! He ought to have taken after his grandmother on his mother's side, which would of course have been best of all, but instead of that he was born simply to bear out the saying: *neither like his mother nor like his dad, but like some unknown, passing lad.*" Life, in the beginning, looked at him somehow sourly and dourly, as if through some turbid little window drifted over with snow; not a friend did he have in his childhood, not a playmate! A tiny chamber, with tiny windows that were never opened, winter or summer; his father an ailing man, in a long frock coat lined with the skins of stillborn lambs, and knitted scuffs on his bare feet, gasping incessantly as he wandered through the room and spitting into a sand-filled cuspidor that stood in a corner; Pavlusha everlastingly sitting on a bench with a quill in his hand, ink on his fingers and even on his lips, the everlasting copybook maxims before his eyes: *Tell No Lies, Obey*

Your Elders, and *Cherish Virtue Within Your Heart;* the eternal scraping and flip-flapping of the scuffs through the room; the voice, familiar yet always stern: "Up to your fool tricks again?" resounding at the moment when the child, bored with the monotonousness of his task, would add some curlicue or a little tail to a letter, and everlastingly the familiar, always unpleasant feeling when, immediately following these words, the tip of his ear would be most painfully tweaked by the nails of the long fingers reaching out from behind him: there you have the poverty-stricken picture of his early childhood, of which he had barely retained a pallid memory.

But in life everything changes quickly and briskly and one day, with the first spring sun and the spring freshets, the father took his son in a miserable little cart, drawn by a little brown skewbald nag, the kind that is known among horse traders as crowbait; the coachman who drove it was a small hunchback, the progenitor of the only family of serfs owned by Chichikov's father and filling almost all the domestic posts in the household. With that crowbait they plodded along for a day and a half and a bit more; on the road they stopped over for a night, made their way across a river, had snacks of cold meat pie and fried mutton, and only on the morning of the third day did they make their way into town. The town streets dazzled the boy's eyes with their unexpected splendor, making him gape in openmouthed wonder for several minutes. Then the crowbait and the cart went kerplunk into a loblolly forming the beginning of a narrow by-lane that ran downhill and was practically a pond of mud nearly all its length; for a long while did the poor beast toil with all its poor might, churn-

ing the mud with its legs and urged on by the hunchback
and the master himself, and finally dragged them into a tiny
courtyard, standing on the slope of a hill, with two apple
trees in blossom before the little old house and a bit of garden behind it, a ground-hugging, tiny garden, consisting
only of mountain ash and alder bushes and hiding in its
depth a small wooden arbor, roofed with laths and with a
narrow little window with an opalescent pane.

In this house lived a relative of theirs, a decrepit little
crone, who still went every morning to market and afterward dried her stockings while sitting at a samovar. She
patted the boy's cheek and admired his chubbiness. He was
to stay with her and attend classes daily in the school in
town. His father, after staying the night, rode away the very
next day. At the parting no tears were shed by the paternal
eyes; all he gave the boy was half a ruble in coppers, for
pocket money and dainties and, what is far more important,
sage admonishment: "Mind now, Pavlusha; study, don't
play the fool, and don't be a worthless scamp; above all,
please your teachers and superiors. If you will please your
particular superior, then, even though you may not be so
successful in learning, and God may have given you no talent, you will nevertheless get along and come out ahead of
all the others. Don't be too friendly with your schoolmates,
you won't learn much good from them; but, if you must
make friends, let it be with those who are better off than the
rest, so that if the occasion arises they may be of use to you.
Don't treat and pamper anybody, but rather manage things
so that you'll be the one treated and, most of all, take care
of each copper and save it: money is the most reliable thing
in this world. Your comrade or your friend will fool you

and, when it comes to trouble, will be the first to betray you, but the copper will never betray you, no matter what trouble you may get into. You can do everything and overcome everything in this world with a copper."

Having delivered himself of this admonition, the father parted with his son and once more plodded off for home on his crowbait, and from then on Pavel never saw him again; but his words and admonitions took deep root within his soul.

Pavlusha began going to school the very next day. He did not evince any special aptitude for any particular branch of learning, and was distinguished only for diligence and neatness; but on the other hand he did evince great intelligence in another direction—the practical. He had suddenly surmised and grasped what was what, and managed things in his relations with his schoolmates in such a way that they treated him, whereas he not only never treated them but even at times, having hoarded what he had received, would subsequently sell it to the very ones who had treated him to it. Even as a child he already knew how to deny himself in everything. Out of the half-ruble given him by his father he did not expend a kopeck; on the contrary, that very same year he made an increment thereto, demonstrating an almost extraordinary resourcefulness: he modeled a bullfinch out of wax, colored it, and sold it very profitably. Then, for a certain period, he embarked on other speculations. For instance, having bought food of one sort or another in the market, he would pick a seat during classes near those boys who were better off financially and, as soon as he noticed that one of his schoolmates was becoming queasy—a sure sign of approaching hunger—he would thrust out from under his bench, as though by chance, the end of a pasty or a roll and, having aroused the other's appetite, would demand sums commensurate therewith. He spent two months fussing unremittingly in his room over a mouse, which he had imprisoned in a small wooden cage and, at last, attained his end: the mouse would, at command, stand up on its hind legs, or lie down and get up; then he sold it, also very profitably. When he had accumulated coins amounting to five rubles, he sewed up the little bag and began saving coins in another one.

In his relations with the officials of the school he conducted himself even more cleverly. Nobody could keep his seat on the bench as meekly as he. It must be noted that his teacher was a great lover of quiet and good conduct and could not bear clever and sharp-witted boys: it seemed to him that they must infallibly be laughing at him. It was sufficient for such a lad merely to stir in his seat or somehow, by mischance, to twitch his eyebrow, to fall a victim to his wrath He would persecute and punish such a boy implacably. "Brother, I'll drive the insolence and insubordination out of you!" he would say. "I know you through and through, better than you know yourself. There, you'll stand on your knees plenty for me! You'll go without plenty of lunches!" And the poor urchin, without himself knowing why, had to scrape his knees raw on the floor and had to go without lunch for days at a time. "Aptitudes and talents are all bosh," this teacher used to say. "All I look for is conduct. I'll give good marks in all subjects to the boy who doesn't know his *a* from a hole in the wall, as long as he conducts himself meritoriously; but as for the lad in whom I see an evil spirit and a mocking air, I'll give him a zero, even though he could give pointers to Solon!" Thus spoke this teacher, who hated Krylov with a mortal hate because the fabulist had said: "For my part go ahead and sing, if to your work but skill you bring," and was forever telling, with an actual delight in his face and eyes, how in the school where he had previously taught everything was so quiet that one could hear a pin drop, how not a single one of the pupils there coughed or blew his nose in class even once all the year round, and how, until the final dismissal bell, one could not hear whether there was a living soul in the room.

Chichikov instantly perceived the spirit of this school-master and what a pupil's conduct was expected to consist of. He did not bat an eye or twitch an eyebrow during the whole session, no matter how hard his schoolmates pinched him from behind; as soon as the bell sounded he would make a headlong dash and fetch the teacher's three-cornered cap (that's what this teacher actually wore, a three-cornered cap); having handed him the three-cornered cap, he would be the first to walk out of the class and would try to come within the teacher's ken at least three times as the latter walked along, incessantly taking his cap off to the schoolmaster. This strategy was crowned with utter success. During his entire stay in the school his standing was excellent and upon graduation he received a full certificate of merit in all subjects, a diploma, and a book with an inscription in gold: *For Exemplary Diligence and Excellency of Conduct.*

By the time he left school he was already a youth of rather engaging appearance, with a chin that called for the

razor. At this time his father died. Chichikov's inheritance
turned out to consist of four irretrievably worn jerseys, two
old frock coats lined with skins of stillborn lambs, and an
insignificant sum of money. His father evidently had
known only how to advise saving coppers but had not saved
many of them himself. Chichikov immediately sold the
run-down little homestead and its trifle of land for a thousand rubles, and as for his family of serfs, he moved them
into town, proposing to settle there permanently and enter
the Civil Service. It was around this time that the poor
teacher who had been such a lover of meritorious conduct
and quiet was dismissed, for stupidity or some other failing.
Out of grief the teacher took to drink; finally he didn't have
anything for drink even; without a crust of bread and without help, he was perishing somewhere in town in an un-
heated, forgotten little hole in the wall. His former pupils,
the clever and witty fellows in whom he had been forever
imagining disobedience and insolent behavior, upon learning of his pitiful plight immediately took up a collection
for him, even selling many things they needed. Pavlusha
Chichikov alone talked himself out of contributing by de-
claring he had nothing to give, and merely gave a five-
kopeck or some other small silver coin, which his
schoolmates threw right back at him, saying: "Oh, you
tightwad!" The poor schoolmaster buried his face in his
hands when he learned about this action on the part of his
former pupils: tears, like those of a helpless child, gushed
from his dimming eyes. "On my deathbed has the Lord
caused me to weep," he uttered in a faint voice, and sighed
heavily when he heard about Chichikov, adding thereafter:

"Eh, Pavlusha! So that's how a man can change! Why, how well behaved he was! Nothing unruly about him, smooth as silk he was! He has taken me in, taken me in no end. . . ."

It cannot be said, however, that the nature of our hero was really so harsh and callous and that his feelings were so dulled that he knew neither pity nor compassion. He felt both the one and the other; he was even willing to help, but only if that help did not call for a great sum, only if it did not involve his having to touch that money which he had definitely proposed to leave untouched. In short, his father's admonition, "Take care of each copper and save it," had had its beneficial effect. But essentially he did not have any attachment for money *qua* money; meanness and miserliness had not taken possession of him. No, it was not these that motivated him; he envisaged ahead of him a life of all ease, with all manner of good things: carriages, an excellently built house, delectable dinners—these were the things that incessantly swarmed through his head. It was in order that he might ultimately and inevitably partake of all this later on, in due course of time, that every copper was saved, was stingily denied for the time being both to himself and to others. When some Croesus whirled past him in a light handsome droshky, drawn by thoroughbreds in rich harness, he would stop as if he were rooted to the spot and then, upon coming to as if after a long sleep, would say: "And yet that fellow was nothing but an office clerk, and used to have his hair cut badger style!" And everything that had an aura of riches and well-being made an impression upon him which he himself could not analyze.

Upon getting out of school he did not want to take any time out, so strong was his desire to get down to business and to obtain a post as quickly as possibly. However, despite the certificates *cum laude* he had received, it was only with great difficulty that he got into the Treasury Department—even in the remotest backwoods one needs influence! The place that fell to his lot was an insignificant one, the salary some thirty or forty rubles a year. But he resolved to buckle down fervidly to his work, to conquer and overcome all things. And he most certainly evinced unheard-of self-sacrifice, patience, and self-denial even in necessities. From early morn till late at night, with neither his spiritual nor his bodily forces flagging, he wrote on and on, plunged up to his ears in the chancellery papers; he did not go home but slept in the chancellery chambers upon the desks, dining at times with the chancellery watchmen, yet with all that was able to preserve his neatness, to dress decently, to impart a pleasing expression to his face and even a something that was genteel to his every movement. It must be said that the clerks in the Treasury were especially distinguished for their unprepossessing and unsightly appearance. Some had faces for all the world like badly baked bread: one cheek would be all puffed out to one side, the chin skewed off to the other, the upper lip blown up into a big blister, which, to top it all off, had burst; in short, it wasn't at all a pretty face to look at. They spoke, all of them, somehow dourly, in such a voice as if they were getting all set to slap somebody down; they offered frequent libations to Bacchus, thus demonstrating that there were still many vestiges of paganism in the Slavic nature; on occasion they even came to the office full to the gills, as they say, because of which the office was not any too fine a place and the air was not at all aromatic.

Among such clerks Chichikov could not but be noticed and marked out, offering as he did a perfect contrast not only by the prepossessing appearance of his face but, as well, by the cordiality in his voice and his total abstinence from the use of strong spirits.

Yet with all that his path was a hard and thorny one. It fell to his lot to have as his immediate superior a Registrar who had already grown old in the service, who was the personification of indescribably stony insensibility and imperturbability, unapproachable, everlastingly the same; a man who had never in his life shown a smile on his face, who had not even once greeted anybody with so much as an inquiry about his health. Nobody had ever seen him, even once, being anything else but what he always was—not even in the street, not even at home. If he had even once evinced any concern for anything, if he had even once got drunk and in his drunkenness broken into laughter, if he had even once given himself up to wild merrymaking, such as a brigand gives himself up to in a moment of drunkenness! But there was not as much as a shadow of anything even as human as that about him. There was just nothing at all in him, either of wickedness or of goodness, and there was a manifestation of something frightful in this absence of everything. His face, as hard as marble, without any sharp irregularity, did not hint at any resemblance to any other face; his features were in severe proportionality to one another. Only the numerous pockmarks and bumps thickly strewn over them made his face one of the number of those upon which, as the folk expression has it, the Devil comes of nights to grind peas.

It looked as if it were beyond any human powers to get

at this man and win his good graces, but Chichikov made the attempt. As a beginning he started catering to him in all sorts of imperceptible trifles: he examined closely the way he cut his quills and, having prepared several modeled after his, put them close to the Registrar's hand every time he needed a quill; he blew and brushed grains of blotting sand and snuff off the Registrar's desk; he dug up a new rag to clean the Registrar's inkpot with; he would find the Registrar's cap for him, wherever he may have put it (and a most abominable cap it was, at that—just about the most abominable the world had ever seen), and would always lay it near the Registrar just a minute before the office closed; he brushed off the Registrar's back if the latter happened to soil it with whitewash off the wall.

But all this remained absolutely without any notice, just as though nothing whatsoever had been done. Finally he got wind of the Registrar's family life; he learned that the Registrar had a mature daughter, with a face that also looked as if peas were ground on it of nights. It occurred to him to attack the fortress from this side. He found out what church she attended of Sundays and each time took his stand across the aisle from her, neatly dressed, with his shirt bosom stiffly starched. And the ruse met with success: the dour Registrar was swayed and invited him to tea! And before the clerks in the chancellery had a chance to look around, matters were so arranged that Chichikov moved into the Registrar's house, became a useful and indispensable person there, doing the buying of the flour and sugar for the household, treating the daughter as a fiancée, calling the Registrar his papa dear and kissing his hand. Everybody in the Treasury assumed that by the end of February, before Lent, the wedding would take place. The dour Registrar even began working on the higher-ups for a better place for Chichikov, and after a while Chichikov was himself filling a Registrar's post that had just become vacant. This, apparently, was precisely what the chief purpose of his ties with the old Registrar had been, because right then and there he secretly sent his trunk back home, and the next day found him in another lodging. He stopped calling the old Registrar papa dear and no longer kissed his hand; and as for the wedding, matters there somehow got lost in the shuffle, as though nothing at all had ever happened. Just the same, whenever he encountered the old Registrar, he would cordially shake his hand and invite him to tea, so that the old man, despite his eternal stoniness and hard indifference, would shake his head every time and mutter under his breath: "He took me in, he took me in, limb of Satan that he is!"

This was the most difficult threshold he had to cross, and he had crossed it. From then on things went more smoothly and successfully. He became a man of mark. He turned out to be possessed of everything necessary to get on in this world: affability in social intercourse and actions, as well as shrewdness and energy in business matters. With these for equipment he got himself in a short while what is called a soft thing and worked it to excellent advantage. The reader must be informed that just about that time the severest persecutions were launched against bribery of any sort. Chichikov was not a bit scared over these persecutions and at once turned them to his own advantage, thus demonstrating a downright Russian ingenuity which appears only during times of great stress. Here is how matters were arranged: as soon as a client came and shoved his hand into his pocket to pull out therefrom the well-known letters of recommendation (as we in Russia put it), bearing the signature of none other than the Minister of Finance—[8] "No, no!" Chichikov would say with a smile, restraining the client's hand. "Do you think I would ever . . . no, no! This is our obligation, we are in duty bound to perform this service without any extra recompense whatever! As far as all this is concerned, you may rest assured: everything will be completed by tomorrow. Please let me know where you are staying; you don't even have to bother about this, everything will be delivered to your place of residence." The client, enchanted, goes home practically in raptures as he reflects: "There, at last, is a man—we ought to have more like him! He is simply a jewel beyond all price!" But the client waits a day, then another; nobody brings any papers to his place of residence, and the same holds true of the third day. He hies him to the chancellery: the papers having to do with his case haven't even been touched—whereupon he turns to the jewel beyond all price.

"Ah, you will have to forgive us!" says Chichikov, with the utmost deference, clasping both of the client's hands. "We were simply swamped with work; no later than tomorrow, however, all your papers will be done—tomorrow, without fail! Really, I feel conscience-stricken!" And all this is accompanied by enchanting gestures; if at that moment the client's coat happened to fly open Chichikov's hand would try to correct the matter and hold the coat in place for him. But neither on the morrow, nor on the day after, nor on the third day, do the papers show up at the client's place of residence. The client begins getting the idea.

"Come, now, what's up?" he asks those in the know, and is told: "You'll have to shell out something to the clerks who prepare the papers."—"Well, why not? I am ready to hand out a quarter of a ruble or even two quarters."—"No, not twenty-five kopecks, but a twenty-five ruble whitey[9] to each one involved."—"Twenty-five rubles to each of those quill-drivers?" the client yelps. "But what are you getting so het up about?" they ask him. "Things will work out your way, after all; the quill-drivers won't get more than a quarter of a ruble each, while the rest will go to the higher-ups." The client, who has been so slow to catch on, smites his forehead and curses, for all he's worth, the new order of things, the persecutions launched against bribetaking, and the polite, refined ways of the officials. "Formerly one at least used to know what to do: you brought an offering of a red ten-ruble note and the thing was in the bag. But now you have to shell out a twenty-five ruble whitey to each one involved, and on top of that have to waste a week fussing and bothering before you as much as catch on to what's what. May the Devil take all this disinterestedness and official gentility!"

The client is, of course, right; but then there are no bribetakers now; now all Directors are the most honest and noblest of men; it's only the secretaries and the quill-driving small fry who are hornswoggling rogues.

In a short while a vaster field opened up before Chichikov: a commission was formed for the construction of some government edifice or other, quite an important one. He, too, found a snug berth thereon and turned out to be one of its most active members. The Commission got down to business without any delay. For six years did this

Commission fossick about the building, but either the climate or something hindered, or there was something peculiar in the very nature of the building materials, for the government building simply wouldn't rise above the foundation, nohow. And yet at the same time, on the outskirts of the town, each one of the members of this Commission turned out to have his own handsome house of civic architecture—evidently the nature of the ground was somewhat more favorable there. The members of the Commission were beginning to prosper and went in for raising families. Only at that point, and only then, did Chichikov begin to extricate himself little by little from under the stringent, self-imposed laws of abstinence and from inexorable self-denial. Only at this point was his protracted fast mitigated at last, and it turned out that he had always been not averse to sundry delights which he had been able to abstain from in the years of ardent youth, when no man is perfect master of himself. Certain extravagances made their appearance: he got himself a rather good chef, went in for shirts of the finest Holland linen. By this time he was buying such suitings as nobody else in all the province wore, and it was at this period that he became quite partial to brown tones and scintillating reddish shades. By now he had acquired an excellent pair of horses and would himself take one of the reins, making the off-horse prance and caracole; by this time he had got into the way of rubbing himself down with a sponge soaked in water mixed with Eau de Cologne; he was already buying a certain soap, far from cheap, to impart a satiny smoothness to his skin; by this time—

But suddenly, to replace the stuffed shirt hitherto in power, a new chief executive was sent; a military man, stern, a foe to all bribetakers and of all that is called wrong-doing. The very next day he threw a scare into every last one of those under him; he demanded accounts, perceived discrepancies therein, coming upon shortages at every step; it did not take him more than a minute to notice the houses of handsome civic architecture—and the shake-up was on. Officials were removed from their posts; the houses of civic architecture went to the Treasury and were turned into various charitable institutions and schools for soldiers' sons born in military cantonments; the well-feathered nests were scattered to the four winds, and Chichikov's even more so than any of the others. His face, despite its amiability, suddenly proved not to the liking of the chief—just why, God alone knows: at times there just aren't any reasons for such things—and he conceived a mortal hatred for Chichikov. And the implacable new chief was a mighty terror unto them all. But since he was, after all, a military man, and consequently not wise to all the refinements of civilian chicanery, it followed that after some time, thanks to their appearance of righteousness and their ability to simulate and assimilate, other officials wormed themselves into his good graces, and the General in a short while found himself in the hands of still greater hornswogglers, whom he did not at all consider to be such; he was actually satis-fied because he had, at last, chosen the proper men and boasted in all seriousness of his exceptional ability to dis-cern capable people. It did not take at all long for the offi-cials to catch on to his temperament and character. All who were under his supervision became, with never an excep-tion, awesome persecutors of wrongdoing; everywhere, in all matters, did they pursue it, even as a fisherman with a harpoon pursues some fleshy white sturgeon, and pursued it with such success that in a short while each one of them turned out to have a nest egg of a few thousand.

It was at this time that many of the former officials turned to the path of righteousness and were taken back into service. But Chichikov no longer could, in any way, worm his way in, no matter how the General's head secretary, who had attained utter mastery in leading the General by the nose, exerted himself and stood up for him, urged on by certain notes signed by none other than the Minister of Finance himself; in this matter he could accomplish absolutely nothing. The General, true enough, was the sort of man who could be led about by his nose (without his knowing he was thus led, however) but, to make up for that, once he got any notion into his head it was fixed there once and for all, like a nail driven dead home, and there was no such thing as prying it out.

All that the clever secretary was able to accomplish was to do away with the blot upon Chichikov's service record, and he could move his chief to agree to this in no other way than through appealing to his compassion, depicting for him in lively colors the touching plight of Chichikov's unhappy family, which, fortunately, Chichikov did not have.

"Oh, well!" said Chichikov. "I got a bite and started pulling in the line, but the fish got off the hook, and don't ask me how! No use crying over spilt milk; I'll have to buckle down to work." And so he resolved to begin his career anew; to gird himself anew with patience, to limit himself anew in all things, no matter how freely and luxuriantly he had let himself blossom out before. It was necessary to shift to another town, and there begin all over again making a name for himself. Somehow nothing would catch on. He had to change two or three posts in the very shortest space of time. These posts, in some way, were mean, degrading. The reader must be told that Chichikov was the most fastidious man that had ever existed on this earth. Even though in the beginning he had had to elbow his way through a mean social stratum, yet in his soul he had always clung to cleanliness, he liked chancelleries that had desks of lacquered wood and where everything was on a genteel footing. Never did he permit himself to utter an unseemly word and always took offense if in the words of others he felt an absence of proper respect for rank or calling. The reader, I think, will be pleased to learn that he changed his linen every two days; while in the summertime, when it was very hot, he would change it even every day; any odor that was in the least unpleasant was actually offensive to him. That was why, every time Petrushka came to undress him and take off his boots, he would put a clove up his nose, and in many instances his nerves were as sensitive as a young girl's, and therefore it was a hard thing for him to find himself anew in those ranks where all reeked of rotgut and indecorum.

No matter how he called upon his spirits for fortitude, he nevertheless lost weight and his face actually took on a greenish hue during these tribulations. On more than one occasion hitherto he had begun to put on weight and to take on those rounded and decorous contours which the reader has seen when he first made his acquaintance, and, time and again, as he contemplated himself in the mirror, he would ponder on many pleasant things—a little woman, a nursery—and a smile would follow such thoughts; but now, whenever he would by some chance catch a glimpse of himself in a mirror, he could not but cry out: "Most Holy Mother of God! Why, how repulsive I have become!" And after that for a long while he would avoid looking into any mirror.

But our hero endured everything, endured it with fortitude; patiently did he endure it, and, at last, changed over to a position in the Customs. It must be said that this branch of the Civil Service had long been the secret object of his designs. He had noticed what elegant little foreign thingumbobs the Customs clerks acquired, what porcelains and cambrics they sent on to their sisters and their cousins and their aunts. More than once had he said with a sigh: "There's what one ought to get into: not only is the frontier right near by but the people are enlightened as well, and what a supply of shirts of fine Holland linen one could put by!" It must be added that, besides this, he was thinking of a particular kind of French soap which imparted an unusual whiteness to the skin and a freshness to the cheeks; God knows just what it was called, exactly, but, according to his suppositions, it would infallibly be found at the frontier. And so he had long been longing to get into the Customs, but had been held back by sundry current benefits accruing from the Building Commission, and he had reasoned, justly enough, that the Customs was, after all, no more than the proverbial two birds in the bush whereas the Building Commission was an actual bird in the hand. But now he decided, come what may, to gain his way into the Customs—and gain his way he did.

He tackled his work with unusual zeal. It seemed as if fate itself had cut him out for a Customs clerk. Such smartness, penetration, and perspicacity had not only never been seen but had never even been heard of. Within three or four weeks he had acquired such a grasp of the work that he knew absolutely everything: he did not even weigh or measure anything, but found out from the bill of lading how many yards of woolen or other cloth there were in each bolt; by merely hefting a parcel he could tell you rightly how many pounds it weighed. And when it came to searches, there, as even his co-workers expressed it, his scent was simply as keen as a hound's: one could not but be amazed at seeing that he had patience enough to tap and finger every tiny button, yet all this was carried through with a lethal *sang-froid* that was incredibly polite. And while those who were submitting to the search were going mad, beside themselves from rage and feeling an evil impulse to slap him all over his pleasant countenance he, without changing either his expression or his polite behavior, would merely add: "May I trouble you to stand up a little, if you'll be so kind?" or: "Won't you please step into the next room, Madam? The wife of one of our clerks will interview you there," or: "Permit me, I'll have to make a small rip in the lining of your overcoat with my penknife." And, as he said this, he would begin pulling shawls and kerchiefs out of there as coolly as if he were pulling them out of his own trunk. The only explanation even his superiors could offer was that he was a fiend and not a human being: he searched out contraband in wheels, in shafts, in horses' ears, and in who knows what other places, where no author on earth would so much as think of venturing into, and where only Customs inspectors are allowed actually to venture, so that the poor traveler, after crossing the frontier, still could not come to for several minutes and, as he mopped the sweat that had broken out in beads all over him, could but keep on making the sign of the cross over himself and muttering: "Well, well!" The poor traveler was in quite the same fix as the schoolboy who runs out of the principal's private study, whither the principal had summoned him to admonish him a little, but instead of that had given him a totally unexpected birching.

In a short while he made life utterly miserable for all contrabandists. He was the terror and despair of all Polish-Jewish smugglers. His honesty and incorruptibility were insuperable—almost unnatural. He even passed up the opportunity of accumulating a tidy sum from the various goods that were confiscated and the sundry trifling objects that were impounded, but never turned over to the government, to avoid extra clerical work. Such zealously disinterested service could not but become the subject of general wonder and, at last, come to the notice of his superiors. He was promoted to a higher rank and given an increase in pay, following which he submitted a project for catching all the smugglers, asking only for means to carry out the project himself. He was immediately entrusted with a command of men and unlimited authority to conduct searches of any and every nature. And that was just about all he had been after.

About this time a powerful smuggling syndicate had been formed along well-planned, thoroughly organized lines; the audacious enterprise promised to yield millions in profits. He had long since had information concerning it and had even turned down the emissaries who had been sent to bribe him, saying dryly: "Not yet." But the moment he had everything placed at his disposal, he let the syndicate know, saying: "Now is the time."

His reckoning was all too correct. He could now receive in a single year that which he might not have won in twenty years of the most zealous service. Hitherto he had not wanted to enter into any relations with the smugglers, inasmuch as he had been no more than a common pawn, ergo, he would not have received much, but now . . . now it was another matter: he could put whatever terms he liked to them. So that the business might be carried on without the least hindrance he won over another official, a fellow worker who was unable to withstand temptation despite the fact that his hair was already gray. The terms were agreed upon and the syndicate went to work. The work began brilliantly. The reader must have heard, beyond a doubt, the oft-repeated story about the ingenious journey performed by some Spanish rams which, after crossing the frontier in double coats of wool, had carried through thereunder a million's worth of Brabant lace. This incident took place precisely at the time when Chichikov was serving in the Customs. Had not he himself taken part in this enterprise no free traders in the world, no matter how ingenious, could have brought such an enterprise to a successful conclusion. After those rams had crossed the frontier three or four times the two officials found that each one had a capital of four hundred thousand rubles. Chichikov, they say, had actually amassed more than five hundred thousand, since he was smarter than the other. God knows to what an enormous figure the goodly sums would have grown, if it were not that some black cat ran across their path. The Devil made both officials lose their wits: to put it simply, they waxed too fat and kicked their heels, and had a falling out over nothing at all.

Somehow, during a heated conversation, and perhaps even in his cups, Chichikov called the other official a priest's son, while the other, who actually was a priest's son, became for some reason sorely offended and answered Chichikov right then and there, forcefully and with unusual sharpness, in precisely the following terms: "No, you lie—I'm a State Councilor, and no priest's son; but as for you, why *you* are a priest's son for sure!" And immediately thereafter he added, just to pique and vex the other more: "So there, that's just what you are, now!" Although he thus won a crushing, all-round victory, having turned upon him the very name Chichikov had bestowed upon him, and although the expression "So there, that's just what you are, now!" might have been considered a strong one, yet not content with this he also lodged secret information against him. However, they do say that even without this there had been a quarrel between them over some female, as fresh and firm as a juicy turnip, to use an expression of the clerks in the Customs; it was also said that certain bravoes had been hired to waylay our hero some eventide in a dark bylane and beat the daylight out of him, but that both officials were made fools of and that the female gave herself to a certain second captain by the name of Shamsharev.

Just how it all really happened, God alone knows; it would be better for the reader, if he is willing enough, to finish that story for himself. The main thing is that their connections with the smugglers, hitherto covert, now became overt. Even though the State Councilor was ruined himself, he had also cooked his co-worker's goose for him.

Both officials were arrested, all their worldly goods were inventoried, impounded, and confiscated, and all this broke suddenly, like a thunderbolt, over their heads. They came to, as if out of a daze, and saw with horror what they had done. The State Councilor could not stand up against his fate and perished in some backwoods or other, but the Collegiate Councilor did stand up. He had been able to secrete a part of his funds, no matter how keen the scent of the higher-ups who had trooped together for the investigation; he brought into play all the fine dodges of a mind by now all too experienced and knowing people all too well: on one he would work through the charm of his manners, on another through a touching speech, on a third through the use of the insidious incense of flattery, which in any case could do no harm in the matter; on a fourth he would use a little palm oil; in short, he worked the business all around in such a way that at last he was dismissed with less ignominy than his co-worker, and got away without having to go through a trial on a criminal charge. But he had neither any great capital remaining, nor any of the sundry little thingumbobs from abroad; nothing remained to him: other willing hands had been found to grab everything that had been his. All that he had retained was some ten measly thousand, squirreled away for a rainy day, and two dozen Holland shirts, and a small light carriage, such as bachelors like to drive about in, and two serfs: Seliphan the coachman and Petrushka the flunky; and, also, the clerks in the Customs House, moved by the goodness of their hearts, had left him five or six cakes of the soap for preserving the freshness of his cheeks. And that was all.

And so, such was the situation in which our hero found

himself anew! Such was the mountain of woes that crashed upon his head! That was what he called suffering for the truth while serving his country. At this point it might be concluded that after such tempests, tribulations, after such slings and arrows of outrageous fortune and the grievousness of life, he would retire with his remaining measly ten thousand, which he had won with his heart's blood, into the peaceful backwoods of some small district town and there vegetate forever in a chintz dressing gown, by the window of a squat little house, settling, of Sundays, the fights that sprang up under his windows among the muzhiks, or, for exercise and fresh air, taking a walk to his henhouse to feel with his own hands whether the hen intended for the soup was plump enough, and he would thus pass his quiescent yet, after a fashion, not entirely useless old age.

But things did not work out that way. One must render full justice to the insuperable strength of his character. After all that which would have sufficed if not to kill, then at least to chill and tame any man forever, his incomprehensible passion had not become extinguished within him. He was filled with grief, with vexation, he murmured against the whole world, he was furious against the injustice of fate and indignant at the justice of men, and yet, despite everything, could not abstain from making new attempts. In short, he evinced a patience before which the wooden patience of the German is as nothing, since in the case of the latter it is due to nothing but the slow, sluggish circulation of his Teutonic blood. Chichikov's blood, on the contrary, surged mightily, and there was needed a great deal of rationalizing will to hold in check all that was fain to leap forth and have an untrammeled fling. He reasoned, and in his reasoning one could perceive a certain aspect of justice: "But why should it be I? Why has calamity crashed down upon me? Who is the man, working for the government, who isn't wide awake to the main chance? They all stuff their little tin boxes. I have never brought misfortune upon anybody; I have never robbed the widow and the orphan, have never ruined any man and sent him out into the world to beg; I have merely helped myself from the surpluses. I took mine where anybody would have taken his; if I hadn't helped myself, others would have helped themselves. Why, then, should the others prosper and wax fat and why must I perish like a miserable crushed worm? And what am I now? What am I good for? With what eyes can I now look into the eyes of any respectable father of a family? How can I help but feel the pangs of conscience, knowing as I do that I am cumbering the earth in vain? And what will my children say to me later on? 'There,' they'll say, 'our father was a low-down animal, he didn't leave us any estate whatsoever.' "

As we already know, Chichikov was mightily solicitous about his descendants. What a touching subject! Here and there, perchance, one could come upon a man who perhaps would not plunge his arm quite so far into the grab bag were it not for the question which, no one knows why, bobs up of itself: "But what will my children say?" And so the future founder of a line, like a cautious tomcat, looking out of the corner of only one of his eyes to see if the master isn't watching from somewhere, hastily grabs at anything that is nearest him, whether it happens to be a piece of soap, or tallow candles, or lard, or a canary—in a word, whatever he can put his paws on; he won't let anything get by him. Thus did our hero complain and weep, yet at the same time enterprise did not die out in his head; everything there somehow longed constantly to be a-building and merely waited for a plan.

Anew he withdrew into himself, like a hedgehog; anew he undertook to lead a hard life; anew he limited himself in all things; anew, from cleanliness and a decent position in society, he descended into muck and a lowly life. And, while waiting for something better to turn up, he was actually forced to follow the calling of a legal agent, a calling whose followers have not yet won a status among us, being jostled on all sides, poorly respected by petty clerical creatures and even by the principals themselves, condemned to crawling and cooling their heels in anterooms, to rudeness and the like; but necessity compelled him to venture on anything and everything. There was one commission that came his way, among others: to see about mortgaging several hundred serfs in the Tutelary Chamber. The estate was in the last stage of disorganization. It had been disorganized by a murrain among the cattle, by knavish stewards, poor crops, epidemics that had killed off the best workers, and, finally, by the senselessness of none other than the landowner, who had decorated a house for himself in Moscow in the latest style, and who for the sake of this decoration had drained the life out of his estate, squeezing out the last copper, so that by this time he actually had no money for food. For this very reason the necessity arose, at last, of mortgaging the last remaining property, the serfs. This form of mortgaging, conducted by the government, was at that time still a new business, and people resorted to it not without apprehension. Chichikov, in his rôle of agent,

having first predisposed everybody (without this preliminary of predisposing people one can't, as everybody knows,
make even a simple inquiry or verification—a bottle of
Madeira must, no matter how trifling the transaction, be
poured down each throat concerned)—having predisposed the proper people, Chichikov explained, among
other things, the following circumstance: half the serfs had
died off, henceforth he hoped there would be no objections
raised later on. . . .

"Yes, but they are listed in the census of the Bureau of
Audits, are they not?" asked the secretary.

"They are so listed," Chichikov told him.

"Well, then, why be so apprehensive?" asked the secretary. "There's a death and there's a birth, and each one has
a certain worth." The secretary, obviously, knew how to
talk in jingles. And in the meantime the most inspired idea
that ever entered human head descended upon our hero.
"Eh, but I am Simple Simon for sure!" said he to himself.
"I'm looking all over for mittens, and they're stuck right in
my own belt! Why, were I to buy all these souls that have
died, now, before the figures for a new census are submitted. . . . Suppose I were to acquire a thousand of them, and
also, let us suppose, that the Tutelary Chambers were to
give me two hundred rubles a soul on a mortgage, why, I'd
have a capital of two hundred thousand right there! And,
too, it's the most proper time now: there has been an epidemic recently; not a few common folk, glory be to God,
have died off. The landowners have lost their shirts at
cards, have been having their good times and playing ducks
and drakes with their money for fair; all of them have
crowded into St. Petersburg to work for the government;

their estates are neglected, run in any old way; it's harder and harder with every year to pay the taxes, so each one of them will be only too glad to let me have those souls, if only not to pay the poll-tax on them and every now and then I may even chance on a fellow whom I can actually charge a pretty kopeck for doing him this favor. Of course it's hard, there's a lot of fuss and bother, and there's always the fear lest, somehow, one get into hot water and land in a scandal over all this. But then, man hasn't been given his mind for nothing, after all. Yet the best thing of all is that this matter will strike everybody as improbable; no one will believe in its reality. True enough, one can neither buy nor mortgage serfs unless one has land. But then I'll buy them for resettlement—for resettlement, that's it! Tracts of land are now being given away, free and for the asking, in the provinces of Tabriz and Kherson, just so you settle there. And that's just where I'll resettle all my dead souls! To the province of Kherson with them! Let them live there in peace! And as for the resettlement, that can be put through in a legal way, all fitting and proper, through the courts. Should they want to certify those serfs, by all means, I'm not averse even to that. Why not? I will submit an actual affidavit of certification, signed by some Captain of the Rural Police in his own hand. The village might be called Chichikov Borough, or by my Christian name—hamlet of Pavlushkino."

And that is how this strange scheme was formed in the head of our hero, for which scheme I hardly know if the readers will be grateful to him; but as for how grateful the author is, that would be hard even to express, for no matter what anyone may say, if this idea had not come into

Chichikov's head, this epic would never have seen the light of day.

Having made the sign of the Cross over himself, after the Russian wont, he set about carrying out the scheme. Under the subterfuge of choosing a place of residence and various other pretexts he made it his business to drop in on various nooks and crannies of our realm and, by preference, those that had suffered more than others from calamities: poor crops, high mortality and the like; in a word, wherever he could buy most conveniently and as cheaply as possible the sort of serfs he needed. He did not tackle just any landowner at random but picked and chose those who were more to his taste, or those with whom one could put through such deals with the least difficulty, trying first to form an acquaintanceship, to predispose them in his favor so that, if possible, he might acquire the dead muzhiks through friendship rather than by purchase. And so the reader must not wax indignant at the author if the personae that have appeared up to now have not proven to his, the reader's taste: it's all Chichikov's fault; he is full master here, and wherever he may get a notion of going thither we, too, must drag ourselves. For our part, if we should really incur censure for the lack of color in, and the unprepossessing nature of, our personae and characters, we shall merely say that one can never see in the beginning all the wide current and scope of any matter. Entering any town, even though it be a capital, is always a bleak affair; at first everything is drab and monotonous: one comes upon sooty factories and workshops without number and endless fences stretching on and on, and only thereafter will one glimpse the angles of six-story houses, and shops, and signs, and streets with tremendous perspectives, consisting entirely of belfries, columns, statues, towers, with all of a city's glitter, din and thunder, and everything that the hand and mind of man have brought forth for man to wonder at.

How the first acquisitions had been consummated the reader has already seen; how the affair will go on in the future, what the fortunes and misfortunes of our hero will be, how he will have to resolve and overcome still greater obstacles in store for him, how colossal figures will appear, how the hidden springs of a far-flung narrative will move, while its horizon widens still further and it adopts a majestic lyrical flow—these things the reader will see later on. There is still a great distance lying ahead of this whole nomadic outfit, consisting of one gentleman of middle age, a light carriage of the sort that bachelors prefer to drive about in, Petrushka the flunky, Seliphan the coachman, and the trio of horses, which the reader is now thoroughly familiar with, from Assessor to that scoundrel of a piebald.

And so there is our hero, warts and all, just as he is! But perhaps the demand may be made to define him conclusively through a single trait: just what sort of man is he as far as moral qualities are concerned? That he is not a hero all compact of perfections and virtues is self-evident. What is he, then? He must be a scoundrel, in that case. But why a scoundrel? After all, why be so severe toward others? There are no scoundrels among us nowadays: there are only well-intentioned, pleasant people, while as for those who would risk general disgrace by doing something for which their physiognomies might be slapped in public, why, you find only some two or three such, and even they are talking about virtue nowadays. The most just thing of all would be to call him *proprietor, acquirer.* Acquisition is the root of all evil; because of it deals have been put through upon which the world has bestowed the description of *none too clean.* True, there is about such a character a something actually repellent, and the very same reader who on the road he pursues through life will be friendly with a man like that will gladly have him as a frequent guest at his hospitable board and will spend the time pleasantly with him, will start eying him askance if the same fellow turns up as the hero of a drama or an epic. But wise is he who does not contemn any character but, fixing him with a searching gaze, investigates him down to his primary causes. Everything transforms itself quickly in man; before one has a chance to turn around there has already grown up within him a fearful cankerworm that has imperiously diverted all his life-sap to itself. And more than once, some passion—not merely some sweeping, grand longing, but a mean, sneaky itch for something insignificant—has developed in a man born for great deeds, making him forget great and sacred obligations and see something great and sacred in insignificant gewgaws.

As countless as the sands of the sea are the passions of man, and no one of them resembles another, and all of them, the base and the splendidly beautiful, are in the beginning submissive to the will of man and only later on become fearsome tyrants dominating him. Blessed is he that hath chosen for himself the most splendidly beautiful of all passions: his bliss grows and increases tenfold with every hour and every minute and he penetrates deeper and deeper into the infinite paradise of his soul. But there are passions the choice of which is not of man's volition. For they were already born with him at the moment of his being born into the world, and he has not been given the powers to ward them off. They are guided by designs from above, these passions, and there is in them something eternally summoning, something that is not stilled all life long. A great earthly course are they fated to perform, it is all one whether in a sombre guise or flashing by as a radiant phenomenon that makes the world rejoice—they are equally called forth for a good that man is ignorant of. And perhaps, in this very Chichikov, the passion that is drawing him on is not of his choosing, and in his chill existence is contained that which will cast man down into the dust and on his knees before the wisdom of the heavens. And it is still a mystery why this form has arisen in the epic now seeing the light of day.

But it is not the fact that my readers will be dissatisfied with my hero which is heavy to bear; what is so heavy to bear is that there dwells within my soul an irresistible conviction that the readers might have been satisfied with that self-same hero, with that self-same Chichikov. Had the author not peered quite so deeply into his soul, had he not stirred up at the bottom thereof that which glides away and hides from the light, had he not revealed his most secret thoughts, such as no man will confide to another, but shown him as he appeared to the whole town, to Manilov and all other people, why, all my readers would have been mightily pleased and would have accepted him as an interesting fellow. There was no need to make either his face or his whole image to spring up so lifelike before the readers' eyes; had the author restrained himself the readers' souls would not be troubled by anything after reading the book through, and they would be able to turn anew to the card table, that solace of all Russia, in all equanimity. Yes, my good readers, you would rather not see mankind's poverty exposed. "Why all this?" you say. "What does it all lead to? For don't we ourselves know that there is a great deal of the contemptible and stupid in life? Even as it is, it often befalls us to see that which is not at all comforting. It would be better, then, to represent for us that which is splendidly beautiful, enticing. Better let us forget ourselves for a while!"—"Brother," says the landowner to his steward, "why do you tell me that things are going abominably with my estate? Brother, I know that without you; why, haven't you got anything else to talk about, now? You just give me a chance to forget all this, not to be aware of it, then I'll be happy." And so the money that might have mended matters to some extent goes for various means of inducing self-forgetfulness. The mind which perhaps might have come upon a sudden wellspring of great resources slumbers, and there goes the estate bang! under the hammer, and the landowner is sent forth into the world as a beggar to seek forgetfulness, with a soul which, out of extreme need, is ready to commit base deeds at which he himself would have been horrified once upon a time.

The author will also incur censure on the part of the so-called patriots who take it easy in their snug nooks and busy themselves with utterly irrelevant matters, accumulating tidy little bankrolls and arranging their life at the expense of others; but, should anything at all happen which in their opinion is an insult to the fatherland, should some book or other appear in which some bitter truth occasionally emerges, they will come scuttering out of all their crannies, like spiders on seeing a fly entangled in a web, and will suddenly raise their voices to shout: "But is it a good thing to bring this out into the light, to proclaim this aloud? Why, everything that is described herein—everything!—has to do with our own affairs! Is it the right thing to do? And what will the people abroad say? Is it so jolly to hear a bad opinion of our own selves? Do these people think this isn't painful? Do they think we aren't patriots?"

To such sage observations, especially touching on the opinion of the people abroad, there is but little, I confess, to be scraped up by way of an answer. Except the following, perchance. Once upon a time there were two citizens living in a remote little nook of Russia. One was the father of a family, by the name of Kipha Mokiyevich, a man of a mild nature, who passed his life in an easygoing, dressing-gown-and-slippers sort of fashion. He did not bother himself with his family much: his existence was directed rather toward intellectual speculativeness and was taken up with the following philosophical, as he called it, problem. "You take an animal, for instance," he would say, pacing the room. "An animal is born stark naked. But why, precisely, stark naked? Why isn't it born the way a bird is, why isn't it hatched out of an egg? Really, now, when you consider it, there's absolutely no understanding Nature, the deeper one goes into it!" Thus did the citizen Kipha Mokiyevich cogitate. But that is not the main point.

The other citizen was Mokiy Kiphovich, his own son. He was what is called in Russia a *bogatyr*, a man of might, and, at the same time that his father was preoccupied with how an animal is born, the son's broad-shouldered, twenty-year-old nature was simply straining to unfold. He did not know how to handle anything lightly; always, if he clasped anyone's hand, it would start cracking, or he'd raise a bump on somebody's nose; in the house and in the neighborhood every living thing, from the house wench to the house dog, would run off yelping at the mere sight of him; he had even smashed the bed in his room all to pieces. Such was Mokiy Kiphovich; yet, taking him by and large, he was a good soul. But that is still not the main point.

The main point is this: "Have mercy, our father and our master, Kipha Mokiyevich," he was appealed to both by his own domestics and by those of others, "what sort of man is this Mokiy Kiphovich of yours? There's never any rest for a body because of him, he's such a confounded pest!"— "Yes, he's playful, he's playful," his father would usually say in answer to this, "but then, what is one to do? It's kind of late to take the strap to him, and besides I would be the one to be accused of cruelty by everybody. And yet he's a sensitive sort of fellow: you upbraid him before two or three people and he'll quiet down; but then there's the notoriety, now—that's the trouble! The whole town will find out and call him a downright dog. Really, now, what do people think, that it doesn't pain me? Am I not a father? Just because I am taken up with philosophy, and occasionally have no time to bother with him, does that mean that I'm not a father? But, oh, no, never—I *am* a father! I am a father, the Devil take it—I am a father! I've got Mokiy Kiphovich enthroned right here, in my very heart!" At this point Kipha Mokiyevich would thump his fist on his chest quite hard and become downright aroused. "Well, if he's bound to remain a dog, then don't let people find it out from me, don't let me be the one to show him up!" And, having evinced such a fatherly feeling, he would let Mokiy Kiphovich keep right on with his mighty exploits, while he himself turned anew to his favorite subject, suddenly posing some such question to himself as: "Well, now, suppose an elephant were to be born in a shell? Why, I guess the eggshell would be mighty thick, then; there would be no breaking it through even with a cannon; one would have to think up some new sort of ordnance."

Such was the mode of life in their peaceful nook of these two citizens of Russia who have so unexpectedly peeked, as if out of a little window, at the very end of our epic, who have peeked out in order to furnish a modest answer to censure on the part of certain ardent patriots, who up to now have been quietly busying themselves with some philosophy or with increments in the sums acquired at the expense of the fatherland they love so tenderly, who are not concerned about avoiding wrongdoing but are only concerned lest people get to talking about their wrongdoing. But no, it is neither patriotism nor the desire to do no evil which is the true cause of their censures; there is something else lurking behind these apparent causes. Why hold one's speech back? Who, if not an author, is bound to tell the sacred truth? You fear a penetratingly fixed gaze, you yourselves dread to fix your gaze penetratingly upon anything; you like to glide over everything with heedless eyes. You will even laugh with all your soul at this Chichikov, you may, perhaps, even praise the author, saying: "However, he has observed a thing or two quite deftly! He must be a jolly sort of fellow!" And after saying this you will turn to yourselves with redoubled pride, a smug smile will appear upon your faces, and you will add: "And yet one must agree, one does come across the queerest and most amusing people in certain provinces—and quite considerable scoundrels, to boot!"

Yet which one of you, filled with Christian humility, not aloud but in silence, when you are all alone, during moments of solitary communion with your own self, will let sink deep into the inward recesses of your own soul this onerous question: "Come, now, isn't there a bit of Chichikov in me, too?" But there isn't much likelihood of such a thing ever happening! And yet, if at this point someone or other were to pass by you, even actually a friend of yours, a fellow whose rank is neither too high nor too low, you would at that very moment nudge the arm of the man next to you and say, all but snorting from laughter: "Look, look, there's Chichikov, there goes Chichikov!" And then, like a child, having forgotten all the decorum befitting your calling and years, you will start running after him, teasing him behind his back and calling his name: "Yah, yah, yah! Chichikov! Chichikov! Chichikov!"

But we have begun talking rather loudly, having forgotten that our hero, who had slept throughout the entire telling of his story, has awakened by now and may easily hear his name, so frequently repeated. For he is a fellow easily offended and is displeased if he is spoken about disrespectfully. It's little the reader will grieve whether Chichikov gets angry at him or not; but as for the author, he must under no circumstances quarrel with his hero; he still has to travel quite a long road arm-in-arm with him; there are still two long parts ahead of us, which is no trifling matter.

"Eh heh! What are you up to?" Chichikov asked Seliphan. "What are you—"

"What is it?" Seliphan asked, none too briskly.

"What do you mean—what? You goose, you! Is that any way to drive? Come, now, give the horses a touch of the whip!"

And really Seliphan had long been driving along with his eyes closed and half asleep, merely flipping the reins at rare intervals over the flanks of the horses, who were also dozing; as for Petrushka, his cap had long since flown off, no one could tell where, and he himself, having slumped back, had propped his head against Chichikov's knee, so that the latter had to give it a rap to make him sit up. Seliphan bucked up a little and, having clipped the back of the piebald several times, whereupon that horse set off at a dogtrot, and having flourished the whip over all of them, uttered in a high, singsong voice: "Don't you be scairt!" The nags bestirred themselves and dashed along with the light little carriage as if it were so much swan's-down. Seliphan merely kept brandishing his whip and adding the shouted encouragement of "Eh! Eh! Eh!" as he smoothly rose and fell on his box, depending on whether the troika was flying up a hillock or dashing with all its might down a hillock, with which hillocks the entire highroad was strewn, although it stretched away downhill in a barely perceptible slope.

Chichikov merely kept smiling, jouncing a little on his leather cushion, for he loved fast driving. And what Russian is there who doesn't love fast driving? How should his soul, that yearns to go off into a whirl, to go off on a fling, to say on occasion: "Devil take it all!"—how should his soul fail to love it? Is it not a thing to be loved, when one can sense in it something exaltedly wondrous? Some unseen power, it seems, has caught you up on its wing and you are flying yourself, and all things else are flying: some merchants are flying toward you, perched on the front seats of their covered carts; the forest flies on both sides of the road with its dark rows of firs and pines, echoing with the ring of axes and the cawing of crows; the whole road is flying none knows whither into the disappearing distance; and there is something fearsome hidden in the very flashing by of objects, so rapid that there is no time for each one to become defined before it disappears; only the sky in the infinity above and the light clouds and the moon breaking through these clouds seem motionless.

Eh, thou troika, thou that art a bird! Who conceived thee? Methinks 'tis only among a spirited folk that thou couldst have come into being, in that land that is not fond of doing things by halves, but that has evenly, smoothly spread itself out over half the world; therefore, try and count its milestones until they turn to specks before thy eyes! And far from cunningly contrived is the vehicle the troika draws; held together with no screws of iron art thou, but hastily, with a slam and a bang, wert thou put together and fitted out by some handy muzhik of Yaroslav, with nothing but an ax and a chisel. No fancy Hessian jackboots does they driver wear, he sports a beard and great gauntlets, and sits on the Devil knows what for a cushion, but let him rise in his seat, and swing his whip back, and strike up a long-drawn song and his steeds are off like a whirlwind, the spokes of each wheel have blended into one unbroken disk;

the road merely quivers, and a passer-by on foot, stopping short, cries out in fright, and the troika is soaring, soaring away! . . . And now all one can see, already far in the distance, is something raising the dust and swirling through the air.

And art not thou, my Russia, soaring along even like a spirited, never-to-be-outdistanced troika? The road actually smokes under thee, the bridges thunder, everything falls back and is left behind thee! The witness of thy passing comes to a dead stop, dumbfounded by this God's wonder! Is it not a streak of lightning cast down from heaven? What signifies this onrush that inspires terror? And what unknown power is contained in these steeds, whose like is not known in this world? Ah, these steeds, these steeds, what steeds they are! Are there whirlwinds perched upon your manes? Is there a sensitive ear, alert as a flame, in your every fibre? Ye have caught the familiar song coming down to you from above, and all as one, and all at the same instant, ye have strained your brazen chests and, almost without touching earth with your hoofs, ye have become all transformed into straight lines cleaving the air, and the troika tears along, all-inspired by God! . . . Whither art thou soaring away to, then, Russia? Give me thy answer! But Russia gives none. With a wondrous ringing does the jingle bell trill; the air, rent to shreds, thunders and turns to wind; all things on earth fly past and, eying it askance, all the other peoples and nations stand aside and give it the right of way.

VOLUME TWO

CHAPTER ONE

But why depict mankind's poverty, and more poverty, and the imperfectibility of this our life, digging up types from the backwoods, from the godforsaken nooks and crannies of our realm? Well, what's to be done if the idiosyncrasies of the writer simply run that way and, having sickened of his own imperfectibility, he actually can no longer represent aught else save mankind's poverty, and more poverty, and the imperfectibility of this our life, digging up types from the backwoods, from the godforsaken nooks and crannies of our realm? And so we once more find ourselves in the backwoods, once more have we stumbled upon a nook. But then, what backwoods and what a nook!

Like the titanic rampart of some unending fortress, with corner turrets and embrasures, the mountain heights stretched along windingly for hundreds upon hundreds of miles. Magnificently did they rear over the infinite expanses of the plains, now as fractures of lime and clay formation, looking like precipitous walls crisscrossed with hollows and gullies, now as comelily rounded, green-clothed convexities covered, as if with the skins of stillborn lambs, by young brushwood, springing up amid the stumps of felled trees, and, at the farthest point, by dark masses of forests, through some miracle still preserved whole from the ax. As for the river, though it remained true to its banks, it made its bends and turns in general conformance with the mountains, yet occasionally left them to go off into the meadows, only, after winding in and out there several times, to flash like fire in the sun, to disappear amid groves of birches, aspens, and alders, and finally race out therefrom in triumph, accompanied by bridges, mills, and dams which seemed to be running after it at every turn.

In one place the steep slope to the mountain heights abutted in denser masses against the green, curly foliage of the trees. Through artificial planting, owing to the unevenness of the hilly ravine, the North and South of the vegetable kingdom had come together here. Oak, fir, wild pear, maple, wild cherry, and blackthorn; broom and mountain ash, entwined with hopvines—all these, now helping one another to grow, now stifling one another, clambered all over the mountain, from its base to its summit. And above, near the very brow of the mountain, there were mingled with the green treetops the red roofs of manorial buildings and, hidden behind these, the ridges, and the weather vanes in the shape of little ponies, of the peasant huts, as well as the superstructure of the manor house itself, with a fretwork balcony and a great semicircular window. And over all this massing of trees and roofs, and highest of all, an ancient village church reared its five gilt domes that flashed in the sunlight. A gold, ethereally carved cross, held in place by chains of similar workmanship, was placed on each of its cupolas, so that from afar it seemed as if virgin gold, in sparkling, flaming, ruddy ducats, were suspended in mid-air, utterly unsupported. And all this, in an inverted view, with the treetops, roofs, and crosses pointing downward, was reflected with exquisite beauty in the river, where the misshapen, hollow-trunked willows, some standing near the banks, others altogether in the water, trailing therein both branches and leaves, entangled with slimy water growths that floated on the water together with yellow water lilies, seemed for all the world to be scrutinizing this wondrous image.

The view was very fine, but the inverted view, from the superstructure in the distance, was still finer. No guest or visitor could stand long on that balcony in indifference. From astonishment his breath would stop short, and he could but cry out: "Lord, how spacious it all is!" With never an end, without limits, the vistas opened up—beyond the meadows, with groves and water mills scattered over them, the forests showed their verdure in several green zones; through the air, by now becoming hazy, sands showed yellowly, and then forests anew, now bluish like seas, or like mist spread in a vast flood; and, anew, sands—paler now yet still showing yellowly. On the remote horizon chalky mountains sprawled in a ridge, gleaming in their whiteness even during inclement weather, as though they were illumined by an eternal sun. Over their blinding whiteness, near their bases, which in places were of gypsum, flickered blotches of a dark, dove-gray hue that seemed to be wisps of smoke. These were remote villages; but the human eye could not discern them by now. Only some gilt dome of some village church, a dome shaped like a poppy capsule, flaring up like a spark in the light of the sun, enabled one to know that some particular patch was a large, well-populated settlement. All this was enveloped in imperturbable stillness, which was not disturbed even by the echoes of the ethereal singers, lost in ethereal vastnesses— echoes that barely reached one's ears. In a word, the guest standing on the balcony, even after contemplating the view for two hours or so, could not utter anything else but: "Lord, how spacious it all is!"

Who, then, lived in and owned this village which one could not even drive up to from this direction, as if it were an impregnable fortress, but had to approach from another direction, where the oaks, growing far apart from one another, cordially welcomed the approaching guest, spreading their many-branched boughs like arms opening for an embrace, and escorting him to the façade of that very house whose roof-tree we had seen from the back and which now stands fronting us in its entirety, having on one side of it a row of huts, whose weather vanes and carved ridges we have glimpsed, and, on the other, the church, glittering with the gold of its crosses and the ethereal gold of the openwork of the chains pendent in the air? To what fortunate being did this nook belong?

It belonged to a landowner of the Tremalahansky district, one Andrei Ivanovich Tentetnikov, a fortunate young man of thirty-three, and unmarried to boot.

Who is he, what is he, then; what are his qualities, his attributes as a man? It is of the neighbors—of the neighbors, ladies!—that one should make inquiries. One neighbor of his, who belonged to the tribe of those adroit, retired field officers, as explosive as fire ships, a tribe now vanishing for good and all, commented on him with a single expression: "A low-down animal, if there ever was one!" A general who lived some seven miles away used to say: "Not a foolish young man, but he's gotten some big notions into his head. I could be useful to him, inasmuch as I am not without connections in St. Petersburg and even at—" The General always stopped short there. The Captain of the Rural Police gave his answer the following turn: "Wait and see if I don't call on him tomorrow for his arrears in taxes!" A muzhik in his village, when asked what his master was like, made no answer at all. It follows, then, that the prevalent opinion of him was not favorable.

Yet, impartially speaking, he wasn't a bad sort; he was simply a fellow crawling between earth and heaven. Since, after all, there are not a few people in this great world crawling between earth and heaven, why shouldn't Tentetnikov crawl thus as well? However, here is an abstract of a day out of his life, a day that is utterly like all the other days, and let the reader judge therefrom for himself what his character was like and to what extent his life was in keeping with the beauties of nature which surrounded him.

He would awake very late of mornings and, raising himself up a little, would sit a long while on his bed, rubbing his eyes. And since, unfortunately, his eyes were very small, the rubbing thereof lasted inordinately long, yet all this time his man Michailo was standing near the door, holding wash basin, ewer, and towel. Thus did poor Michailo stand there for an hour, then for another, then would go to the kitchen, then come back anew, and find his master still sitting in bed and still rubbing his eyes. At long last he would manage to get out of bed, wash himself, put on a dressing gown and meander into the dining room to drink tea, coffee, cocoa, and even milk fresh from the cow, taking a small sip of everything, crumbling bread unmercifully and unconsciously dropping the ashes from his pipe all over the place. And so he would sit for two hours dawdling over his tea. Nor was that enough; he would take a cup of cold tea and move over with it nearer the window which looked out on the courtyard, for there, under the window, the following scene would take place every day:

First of all there would appear Grigoriy, a house serf who did duty as butler, roaring away at Perphilievna, the housekeeper, in some such terms as: "Why, you scandalous little creature, you, what a worthless piece of insignificance you are! You, of all people, ought to keep your trap shut, you abomination, you!"

"Well, how would you like a taste of this?" the worthless piece of insignificance, or Perphilievna, would yell back at him, showing him a fig; she was a woman whose actions were rough and ready, despite the fact that she had a great fondness for raisins, fruit candy, and all sorts of other sweets which she kept under lock and key.

"Why, you'll be tangling with the steward himself soon, you storehouse sweepings, you!" Grigoriy roared.

"Well, the steward's just as big a thief as you are! Do you think the master ain't wise to the pair of you? Why, he's right here; he can hear everything."

"Where's the master?"

"Why, he's sitting right there by the window; he can see everything."

And sure enough, the master was sitting by the window and saw everything.

To make the bedlam complete, a little urchin, who had been heartily slapped by his mother, was bawling at the top of his voice; a borzoi hound was whining, sitting on his tail to cool it off after the cook, having looked out of his kitchen, had thrown some scalding water over him. In short, everybody was keening and caterwauling. The master saw and heard everything. And only when this became unbearable to such a degree that it hindered him from doing even nothing would he send somebody out to tell them to make less noise.

Two hours before dinner he would withdraw into his study to occupy himself in earnest with the writing of a work which was to take in all of Russia, in its every aspect—civic, political, religious, philosophical—which was to resolve the perplexing questions and problems which the times confronted the country with, and to determine clearly its great future; in a word, everything was to be done in such manner and form as contemporary man likes to impose upon himself. However, this colossal project was for the most part confined to profound cogitation; the quill would be chewed to pieces, little pictures would emerge on the virgin paper, and then all this was shoved to one side, he would pick up a book instead, and not let it out of his hands until the very dinner. This book was also read all through the soup, the roast, the various sauces, and even the pastry dessert, so that certain dishes grew cold and some others were removed altogether untouched.

Then followed the pipe and coffee, and a game of solitaire chess. As for what was done after that, right up to supper, really, it would be hard even to say. Nothing at all, apparently.

And thus, all by his lonesome in the whole world, did a young man of thirty-three pass his time, sitting like a bump on a log, a sloven in a dressing gown and without a cravat. No urge did he feel for a lark, or to go for a walk, or even to go up on the balcony, or as much as to open a window and let some fresh air into the room; and the beautiful view of his village, a view which no visitor could observe with indifference, was to all intents and purposes nonexistent for the very master of that village.

From this the reader can perceive that Andrei Ivanovich Tentetnikov belonged to that prolific human family whose members are never in danger of dying out in Russia and upon whom formerly were bestowed such names as afternoon farmers, lie-abeds, and mopes, but what names one could give them now I really do not know. Are such characters born that way, or are they formed subsequently as an engenderment of grievous circumstances harshly besetting an individual? Instead of giving an answer to these questions, perhaps we'll do better by telling the story of his childhood and education, and let the reader draw his own conclusions.

Everything, it seemed, tended to make something decent, something useful out of him. As a twelve-year-old lad, intelligent and clever, half-pensive by nature and half-ailing, he got into an institution of learning, the headmas-

ter of which at that time was an exceptional man. Idol of
the youths under him, a wonder among pedagogues, the in-
comparable Alexander Petrovich was gifted with an intuition . . . . . . [which enabled him to discern a man's nature].*
How well he knew how to impel and influence his boys!
There wasn't a mischievous boy who, after a prank, would
not come to him and voluntarily make a clean breast of
everything. But that was not all. The culprit would get a severe reprimand, yet he would leave the headmaster not
with his head cast down but holding it high in the air, with
an up-and-doing desire to atone for his action. In the very
reproach of Alexander Petrovich there was something in-
spiriting, something that said: "Onward! Get up on your
hind legs as fast as ever you can, and never mind the fact
that you fell." Ambition he styled a force that urged a man's
abilities forward, and for that reason made particular efforts to arouse it. He never delivered any speeches about
good conduct to his pupils. He would usually say: "I de
mand intellect, and nothing but intellect. He who aspires to
intellect has no time for mischief; mischievousness is
bound to disappear of itself." And it was verily so, the acts
of mischief did vanish of themselves. He who did not strive
to be intelligent was subjected to contempt. The grown-up
asses and dolts among the pupils had to endure the most
opprobrious nicknames from the most immature, yet dared
not lay a finger on them. "This is too much!" many people
said. "The bright pupils will become unbearable upstarts."

---

*An ellipsis indicates lacunae, undeciphered or incomplete words and
so on; brackets enclose carefully considered conjectures. *Trans.*

—"No, it isn't too much," he would say. "What can I do? I am partial to bright lads, and want everybody to see it. Those who haven't any aptitudes I don't keep long—one course of lectures is enough for them; but as for the intelligent lads, I take another course with them." And, true enough, all the capable lads kept to his course. There were many manifestations of high spirits which he did not curb, seeing in them the beginning development of spiritual qualities, and saying that they were as necessary to him as rashes were to a physician—in order to learn authentically just what a man had in his innards.

How all the boys loved him! Nay, there was never such attachment on the part of the children toward their parents. Nor, even in the mad years of mad infatuations was inextinguishable passion as strong as was their love for him. To the last days of his life, to his very grave, would the grateful pupil raise his glass in a toast on the birthday of his wondrous teacher, who had long been in his grave ... closing his eyes and shedding tears over him. His least approbation sufficed to set the pupil all aquiver with a joyous expectancy and spurred on his ambitious desire to surpass all his comrades. Those who had but little capacity he did not keep long, for them he had but the shortest of courses; but those who had the capacity had to undergo a double course of study at his hands. And his graduating class, which consisted only of the elect, did not at all resemble the graduating classes of other schools. It was then that he demanded from the pupil all that which some pedagogues ill-advisedly demand from mere children, that higher intellect which knows how to refrain from laughter yet how to endure every sneer; knows how to let a fool win the argument yet does not become irritated; how not to lose self-possession, how not to be revengeful in any case, and how to retain the proud tranquillity of an unperturbed soul. And everything that could form a steadfast Man out of a mere man was resorted to, and he himself put his pupils to incessant tests. Oh, how he knew the science of life!

He had many teachers under him, but he taught most of the subjects himself. Without pedantic terms, without pompous opinions and views, he was able to convey the very soul of a subject, so that even an immature scholar could perceive his particular need thereof. Of the subjects only those were chosen which were capable of forming a man into a worthy citizen of his land. His lectures consisted for the most part of telling each youth what lay ahead of him, and he could outline the entire horizon of the lad's career in such a way that the youth, while still on the school bench, already lived in thought and with his soul in whichever field he was to serve. He concealed nought; all the possible vexations and obstacles which are raised up in a man's path, all the ordeals and temptations in store for him, would he marshal before the pupil in all their nakedness, nought concealing. Everything was known to him, just as though he himself had gone through all the callings and posts. Whether it was because ambition had already become strongly developed, or whether because there was in the very eyes of this extraordinary preceptor something that said to the youth: "Onward!" (that potent word, so familiar to the Russian, which works such miracles upon his sensitive soul), the fact remains that the youth from the very beginning would seek only difficult things, yearning to act only in those fields where difficulty was to be encountered, where the obstacles were greater, where one had to evince great strength of soul. Not many emerged from this course of training, but then those that did were lads of great endurance, veterans who had been through the smoke of battle. If they went into the service of the State they would retain even the most precarious posts, even when many others, who were actually more clever than they, would drop everything, unable to restrain themselves because of some petty unpleasantnesses, or else, becoming torpid, growing lazy, would fall into the hands of knaves and bribetakers. But Alexander Petrovich's veterans remained steadfast and, knowing both life and man, and made wise by wisdom, exerted a strong influence even upon men of evil.

What an overwhelming impression this wonderful preceptor made upon Tentetnikov even in his boyhood! The ardent heart of the boy was long thrilled by the mere thought that he would at last get into his class. What, it would seem, could have been better for our Tentetnikov than this master! And at sixteen, having come out at the head of all his coevals, he was deemed worthy of promotion to this higher course for the elect, which good fortune he himself could not believe. But as misfortune would have it, just as this promotion which he so desired was about to take place, the extraordinary schoolmaster suddenly died. Oh, what a blow this was to the boy! What a fearful first loss! It seemed to him as if ... [everything were over and done with]. Everything was changed in the school. Alexander Petrovich's place was taken by a certain Fedor Ivanovich, a kindly man and conscientious, but whose point of view on things was entirely different from that of his predecessor.

He began to demand from children that which can be demanded only from adults. In their free-and-easy ways he imagined he saw something utterly unbridled. He initiated and emphasized certain outward observances of order among them, insisting that the youngsters spend all their time in some sort of speechless quiet, that all of them must in no case walk about otherwise than two by two—he even took to measuring the distance between the couples himself, actually using a yardstick. At table, just for the better looks of the thing, he seated all the boys according to height, so that the dunces got all the best tidbits and the clever boys only the leavings. All this created grumbling, especially when the new headmaster, as though out of deliberate spite for his predecessor, announced from the very first day of his coming that intelligence and good marks in studies didn't mean a thing to him, that he would take into account only good conduct, that, even if a pupil were a poor scholar, yet conducted himself well, he would prefer him to a clever lad. Yet, strangely enough, good conduct was the one thing that Fedor Ivanovich did not attain. Secret pranks of all sorts sprang up. Everything was drawn up as if for parade during the daytime, and the pupils marched two by two, but of nights revels became all the go.

Something very odd also happened to the curriculum. New instructors were imported, with new opinions and new points of view and new slants. They snowed their auditors under with a multitude of new technical terms and words; they evinced in their exposition of a subject both a logical coherence and an awareness of recent discoveries as well as a feverish absorption all their own; but, alas, the only thing lacking in the subject was life itself. The carrion of a subject reeked with a carrion smell upon their lips. In a word, everything went arsy-versy. Respect for superiors and authority was lost; the pupils began laughing both at the headmaster and at the instructors; they began calling the headmaster Fedka, Crummy, and sundry other names. The vice that sprang up was no longer childlike; the things that sprang up were of such a nature that it became necessary to expel or simply dismiss summarily many of the pupils. In two years it was impossible to recognize the institution.

Andrei Ivanovich Tentetnikov was of a quiet nature. He could not be drawn either into the nightly orgies of his mates (who had set up some lady or other for themselves, practically under the very windows of the director's home) or into their mockery at sacred things, merely because they had got a not overbright priest for a chaplain. No, his soul felt, even through its slumber, its divine origin. They could not draw him in, but he did become dispirited. His ambition had been aroused by now, yet there was no activity, no field of endeavor for it. It might have been better, perhaps, never to have aroused it. He listened to the professors as they flew into tantrums on their cathedras, but what he was recalling was the former headmaster who, never flying into a tantrum, knew how to talk so as to be understood. What subjects and what courses of lectures did he not listen to! Medicine, philosophy, and even law, and universal history of mankind, undertaken on such a grand scale that, in three years, the professor had managed to deliver only the induction, and to treat of the development of communes in some towns or other in Germany—and God knows what he didn't listen to! But all this would remain in his head in some sort of hideous scrapiana. Thanks to the mind that nature had given him he felt only that this was not the way things should be taught, but how they really should be taught he did not know. And often would he recall Alexander Petrovich, and such sadness would come upon him that he did not know what to do with himself because of his melancholy.

But youth is fortunate in that it has a future. His heart beat harder and harder as the time for his graduation neared. "For this is not life yet," he said to himself, "this is but preparation for life; real life lies in service: that is where one can perform great deeds." And, without looking in at the splendidly beautiful nook that so amazed every guest or visitor, without going on a pilgrimage to pay homage to the ashes of his parents, he, as is the way of all ambitious men, rushed headlong to St. Petersburg, whither, as everybody knows, our fiery youth streams from all the ends of Russia, to serve, to shine, to attain a career, or simply to skim the surface of a colorless, icy-cold, deceptive worldly education. Andrei Ivanovich's ambitious striving was, however, somewhat dampened from the very beginning by his uncle, Onuphrii Ivanovich, an Actual State Councilor. He announced that the most important thing was to have a good handwriting—that, and nothing else; that without this you'd never get to be either a Prime Minister or a statesman, yet Tentetnikov's penmanship was of the variety described as hen tracks. However, after taking lessons in calligraphy for two months and with his uncle's influence, he at last obtained a place in some governmental department or other.

When he was led into the magnificent, light-flooded

hall, with parquet floors and desks of lacquered wood, a hall that looked as if it were used as a conference room for the first grandees of the realm, deliberating the fate of that realm, and when he saw the legions of handsome gentlemen writing away, their quills scraping and their heads all bent to one side, and he himself was placed at a desk, with the suggestion that he transcribe a certain paper which, as if on purpose, was of a somewhat petty content (part of a correspondence which had been going on for half a year, and having to do with a matter of three rubles), an extraordinarily odd sensation came over the inexperienced youth: the gentlemen sitting around him appeared to him so much like schoolboys at their tasks! To complete the resemblance, some of them were reading frivolous translated novels, the book being thrust in between the folio sheets of some matter in progress, as though they were occupied with the matter itself, and at the same time guiltily starting every time a superior appeared. So strange did all this appear to him then, so far more significant did his former pursuits seem than the present ones, the preparation for service so much better than the service itself! He felt regret over having left the school. And suddenly, as if he were alive, Alexander Petrovich appeared before him and Tentetnikov all but broke into tears. The room swam before his eyes, the clerks and the desks became blurred and confused, and he barely held himself back from fainting away that very instant. "No," he thought to himself recovering his self-possession, "I'll tackle the work, no matter how petty it may seem at first." Steeling his spirit and heart, he decided to work, even as other men did.

Is there any place where no enjoyments are to be found?

They exist even in St. Petersburg, despite its austere, morose appearance. A cruel frost of thirty degrees may crackle through its streets; that child of the north, the snowstorm witch, squeals and whines as she sweeps snowdrifts over the sidewalks, blinding the eyes, powdering the coat collars of fur, and mustaches, and the muzzles of shaggy animals; yet invitingly, even through the crisscross flurry of the snowflakes, a small window sends its light from somewhere above, even from a fourth floor—there, in a cozy little room, by the light of unassuming stearine candles, to the hum of a samovar, a conversation that warms the heart and the soul is being carried on, a radiant page of some inspired Russian poet, one of those whom God has bestowed in reward upon his Russia, is being read aloud, and the young heart of some youth beats with such exalted ardor as is not to be found even under a sky warmed by a meridian sun.

In a short while Tentetnikov grew used to his work; the only thing was that it did not become for him his primary work and goal, as he had at first supposed it would, but something of a secondary nature. It served him in disposing of his time, making him treasure all the more the free moments that remained to him. His uncle, the Actual State Councilor, was already beginning to think that his nephew would amount to something, when suddenly the nephew made a nasty mess of things. Among the number of Andrei Ivanovich's friends, of whom he had a sufficiency, there proved to be two who were what is called embittered people. They belonged to that category of restless characters who cannot bear with indifference not only injustices, but even all that which in their eyes seems to be injustice.

Kindhearted to begin with, yet shiftless in their own actions, demanding forbearance toward themselves yet at the same time filled with impatience toward others, they had a great influence upon Tentetnikov both by their impetuous speech and through their noble indignation against society. Having stirred up his nerves and a spirit of irritation within him, they made him notice all those trifles which hitherto it had never even occurred to him to pay any attention to.

Fedor Fedorovich Lenitzin, the head of one of the divisions quartered in the magnificent halls, suddenly aroused Tentetnikov's dislike. He began finding a world of shortcomings in this superior. It seemed to him that Lenitzin, in his conversations with his superiors, turned instantly and wholly to cloying molasses, as it were, and to sharpest vinegar when a subordinate addressed him; that, apparently, running true to form like all petty people, he always made a note of those who did not pay him congratulatory calls on holidays, that he revenged himself on those whose names he did not find on his doorman's list of callers; and, as consequence of these things, Tentetnikov felt a nervous aversion for him. Some evil spirit was egging him on to do something unpleasant to this Fedor Fedorovich. He carried this chip on his shoulder with a peculiar relish, and he succeeded. On one occasion he talked with him so sharply that he received notice from his highest superiors either to ask Lenitzin's forgiveness or to submit his resignation. He did the latter.

His uncle, the Actual State Councilor, came to see him, frightened out of his wits and imploring him: "For Christ's own sake, have mercy, Andrei Ivanovich! What is this you're doing? To leave such an advantageously begun career simply because you didn't get the kind of a superior you wanted! Have mercy! What are you up to? What are you up to? Why, if one were to mind such things, then there wouldn't be a single soul left in the service! Come to your senses; cast your pride and your self-conceit aside; go and have an explanation with him."

"That's not it at all, Uncle," his nephew told him. "It wouldn't be hard for me to apologize to him. I am at fault—he is my superior, and I shouldn't have spoken to him like that. But the thing is this: I have other work to do, I have three hundred souls of peasants, the estate is all run down, the manager is a fool. There would be but little loss to the government if somebody else would sit down in the chancellery in my place to transcribe papers, but there would be a great loss if three hundred people paid no taxes. I—what do you think of that?—I am a landowner . . . who is a bureaucrat. Were I to concern myself with conserving, safeguarding, and bettering the lot of the people entrusted to me, and let the government see three hundred of most decent, sober, and hard-working subjects, wherein would my service be in any way inferior to service under some chief of a division, some Lenitzin or other?"

The Actual State Councilor remained standing there with his mouth gaping from astonishment. He had never expected such a torrent of words. After a little reflection he began somewhat as follows: "But after all . . . but then, how can you ever . . . how can you ever bury yourself away in a village? What sort of society can there be among . . . . . . [countrified squires?] Here, after all, you'll come across some general as you walk along the street, or some prince. You yourself will be an important figure as you pass by somebody ...... [or other.] Then, too, you have gas illumination here, and industrialized Europe; but over there, now, all you'll come across will be a muzhik or a country-wife. Why, then, why condemn yourself to a life sentence among boors and ignoramuses?"

But the earnest arguments of the uncle had no effect on the nephew. The village by now began to seem to him a haven of freedom and plenty, a foster mother of ideas and strivings, the sole field for useful activity. By this time he had even dug up all the latest books on agriculture. In a word, two weeks after this conversation he was already approaching those places where his childhood had sped so fast, approaching that splendidly beautiful nook which no guest or visitor could get his fill of contemplating. A new feeling had arisen within him. Former emotions, which had not emerged for long by now, were beginning to awaken in his soul. By now he had forgotten many of the localities and gazed curiously, like a newcomer, at the beautiful views. And again, for some unknown reason, his heart began to palpitate. And when the road was rushing away through a narrow ravine into the very heart of the enormous forest wilderness and he saw above and below, over him and under him, three-hundred-year-old oaks, each so big that three men with their arms extended could not clasp it around, interspersed with fir trees, elms, and black poplars that topped the regular species, and when, in answer to the question: "Whose forest is this?" he was told "Tentetnikov's"; and when, having made its way out of the forest, the road stretched away over meadows, past groves of aspens, young and venerable osiers and willows, with a view of the mountain heights going off into the distance, and flying over two bridges, crossed the river in two different places, leaving it now on his right, then on his left, and when, in answer to the question: "Whose meadows and lowlands are those?" he was told "Tentetnikov's"; when the road started going uphill and then went over a level highland, on one side past fields of standing grain—wheat, rye, barley—and, on the other side, past all the places he had traversed before, which now suddenly came into view in the foreshortened distance, and when, gradually growing darker, the road approached and at last entered the shadow of spreading double-trunked trees, scattered here and there over a carpet of green that extended to the very village, and the muzhik huts with their fretwork trim and the red roofs of the manorial stone buildings flitted in the distance, and the golden tops of the church gleamed, when his heart, beating vehemently, knew even without asking where it had come to, the emotions that had been incessantly accumulating burst forth at last in words of thunder: "There, have I not been a fool up to now? Fate meant me to be the owner of an earthly paradise, but I conspired to make myself a burrower among dead papers! Having been educated, enlightened, having acquired a fund of information necessary for the dissemination of good among those in my power, for the improvement of the whole region, for the fulfillment of the diversified obligations of a landowner, who personifies at one and the same time a judge and a director and a guardian of order, to entrust this place to an ignoramus of a steward! To prefer as one's own work the preparation of lawsuits between people whom I had never even set eyes on, neither whose characters nor attributes I know; to prefer to actual direction a fantastic, paper direction of provinces situated hundreds and hundreds of miles away, where I have never set foot and where I can create only mountains of absurdities and follies!"

But in the meantime another spectacle awaited him. Having learned of the coming of their master, the muzhiks had gathered near the front entrance. Varied colorful feminine headdress, peasant kaftans of homespun, and picturesquely large beards of the comely villagers surrounded him. When he heard the words: "Our provider! You have remembered us . . . . . ." and the gaffers and crones, who remembered both his grandfather and his great-grandfather, broke into involuntary tears, he himself could not keep back his own. And he thought to himself: "How much love there is here! And why is it bestowed? Because I never set eyes on them, have never concerned myself over them!" And he made an inward vow to share their toil and their tasks.

And he became a husbandman and a manager. He decreased the *corvée*, lessened the days the muzhiks had to work for the landowner, thus giving them more time to work for themselves. His fool of a steward he kicked out. He began to go into everything himself, to show up on the fields, on the threshing floor, at the barns where the crops were stored, at the mills, at the landing dock, at the loading and departure of the barges and scows, so that the sluggards actually began scratching their heads in perplexity. But this did not continue long. The muzhik is shrewdly perceptive: he understood in a short while that the master even though he was energetic, and also possessed of a willingness to tackle a great deal, yet still did not know the right way to tackle it, did not have the know-how; his speech smacked too much of book learning and you couldn't get what he said into your head. The result was, somehow, not that the master and the muzhik failed utterly to understand each other, but simply that they did not hit it off together, did not adapt themselves to striking the identical note in unison.

Tentetnikov began to notice that on the master's land everything came up poorer, somehow, than on that of the muzhiks. The grain on the master's land was sown earlier, yet came up later, although, apparently, the muzhiks had worked well. He himself had been present and had ordered a noggin of vodka to be served to each one, because they had all worked so diligently. Yet with the muzhiks the rye was long since coming up in ears, the oats had shot up, the millet was in thick bushes, whereas with the master the grain was barely beginning to tubulate, the ears were not forming even into nubbins yet. In short, the master began to notice that the muzhik was simply up to his old and usual knavish tricks, despite all the privileges granted him. He attempted reproaching the peasants, but all the answer he got was: "Sir, how could we ever fail to watch out for our master's good! You yourself were pleased to see how hard we worked at the plowing and the sowing—you ordered a noggin of vodka to be served to each one of us." What could he offer in contradiction to this?

"Yes, but why is the result so wretched now?" the master persisted.

"Who can tell? Looks like the worms have been eating away at the roots. And then look at what the summer's like: there haven't been any rains at all, at all."

But the master could see that the worms hadn't been

eating away at the roots of the muzhiks' grain, and the rain, too, fell in some sort of odd fashion—in streaks: it favored the muzhik, but hadn't let even so much as a drop fall on the master's fields.

Still harder for him was it to get along with the peasant women. Not a day passed by but that they tried to beg off from their tasks, complaining how hard the *corvée* was. A strange thing! He had done away altogether with all sorts of tributes of homespun cloth, berries, mushrooms, and nuts, had cut their other tasks in half, thinking that the women-folk would utilize the time thus saved for household work, would sew for and clothe their husbands, would make their truck patches bring forth more. But he had another guess coming: such idleness, hair-pulling matches, tittle-tattle and all sorts of feuds sprang up among the fair sex that the husbands were forever coming to him with such complaints as: "Master, curb my fiend of an old woman! She's like the Devil himself—there's no living because of her!"

He did, after steeling his heart, venture to try sternness, but how could one be stern? The woman would come to him so very much of a woman; she would set up such a caterwauling, she was so ailing, so sick, she wrapped herself in such vile, repulsive rags, God alone knew whence she had collected them! "Get you gone, get you gone, as long as you get yourself out of my sight! God be with you!" poor Tentetnikov would say, and right after that would see how the poor ailing creature, having gone out of the gates, would come to grips with some neighbor woman over a turnip and stave in her ribs in a more workmanlike manner than any husky muzhik could have done.

He conceived the notion of trying to set up some sort of

school for his people, but the result of this was such utter bosh that he had to cast down his head in shame—it would have been better never even to have thought of it! When it came to matters judicial and juridical, all those legalistic fine points to which his professors of philosophy had led him proved to be of no worth whatsoever. The plaintiff was lying, and the defendant was lying, and the Devil alone could do the trying! And he perceived that a simple understanding and knowledge of mankind was far more necessary than all the knotty points in the books on philosophy and jurisprudence; and he perceived as well that there was something lacking in him, but what it was God alone knew. And there ensued that situation which so often ensues: the muzhik did not get to know the master, and the master did not get to know the muzhik; the muzhik became the offending party, and the master became the offending party. All this considerably [cooled off] the landowner's ardor. When he attended their work in the fields nowadays it was without paying much attention to what was going on. If the scythes swished softly through the meadowlands, or the hay was being thrown up on the ricks, or the sheaves were being loaded on the wagons—if the rustic labors were being carried on near at hand, his eyes would be fixed on some point as remote as possible; if the work was going on at a distance, his eyes would seek out objects as near as possible, or would look to one side at some bend in the river where a red-beaked, red-legged martin was waddling along—an ornithological martin, of course, and not a featherless biped of a Martin. Those eyes watched curiously as the bird, having caught a fish near the bank, held it crosswise in its beak, as though deliberating whether to gulp it down or not, and at the same time keeping a watchful eye down the river, where another martin showed whitely which had not yet caught a fish but was eying fixedly the martin who had already done so.

Or else, with his eyes closed altogether and with his head raised up toward the heavenly void, he left it to his sense of smell to drink in the scent of the fields, and to his sense of hearing to be amazed by the voices of the singing denizens of the air when from everywhere, from the heavens and from the earth, they united in one harmonious choir, without one jarring note among them. In the rye the quail drummed, in the grass strummed the crake, [overhead] gurgled and tinkled the linnets flying by; the snipe, whirring up, sounded its bleating note, the lark trilled disappearing against the sun, and like the pealing of clarions there came the honking echoes of cranes forming their flights into triangles high in the heavens. All the region echoed, all of it transformed to sounds. How still fair is Thy world, O Creator, in the wildnerness, in some small hamlet, far removed from vile highroads and towns! But even this began to weary Tentetnikov. In a short while he desisted altogether from going out into the fields and planted himself indoors, refusing to see even the steward when he came with his reports.

Formerly, among his neighbors, a retired lieutenant of Hussars, a fellow so addicted to his pipe that he was permeated through and through with tobacco smoke, used to drop in on him, or a certain student of extreme leanings who had never finished his formal education and had gathered his wisdom from contemporaneous brochures and newspapers. But these calls, too, began to bore him. Their conversations began to seem to him somehow superficial, their continentally openhearted treatment of him, accompanied by pats on the knee, as well as their deep bows and free-and-easy ways, began to seem to him by now far too direct and openhearted. He decided to discontinue his acquaintanceship with all his neighbors, and brought this about even quite brusquely. To be exact, when the representative of that now vanishing tribe of colonels who were as combustible as fireships, who at the same time was in the vanguard of the then beginning new order of thought, and a most pleasant fellow when it came to superficial conversations on any and every subject, Varvar Nicholaievich Vishnepokromov, had dropped in on him to have his fill of talk that would touch upon politics, and philosophy, and literature, and morals, and even the state of finances in England, Tentetnikov sent a man out to tell the Colonel he was not at home, yet at the same time was incautious enough to show himself at a window. The eyes of the caller and the host met. One, naturally, growled: "Beast!" through clenched teeth; the other, in vexation, also sent after him something that sounded like "Swine!" And with that his relations with his neighbors ended. Since then nobody called on him any more.

He was glad of this, and gave himself up to meditating a great work on Russia. How he meditated over it the reader has already seen. A strange, disorderly order of life was established. It could not be said, however, that there were moments lacking at which he would, apparently, awaken from his slumber. When the post brought newspapers and periodicals and he would come across a familiar name in print, that of some former comrade who had already met with great success in the service of the State, or who, according to the best of his ability, was making his contribution to science and universal affairs, a secret, quiet sadness would come over his heart and a sorrowful, mutely sad plaint at his inactivity would involuntarily escape him. At such times detestable and vile did his life seem to him. With unusual vividness would his past schooldays come to life anew before him and his beloved schoolmaster would appear before him as if he were alive. Tears would spurt like hail from his eyes.

What did these sobs mean? Did his ailing soul reveal thereby the grievous secret of its ailment—that the exalted inner being which had begun to rise up within him had not succeeded in taking shape and growing strong; that, not having been put to the test in his youth by a struggle against fiascoes, he had not attained to the high ability of rising higher and becoming stronger by overcoming barriers and obstacles; that, having become molten like metal at great heat, the rich reserve of great emotions within him had failed to receive its final tempering; that the extraordinary preceptor had died too prematurely to benefit him, and that now there no longer was anybody in the whole world who had the power to raise up anew the forces shaken by eternal vacillations and the impotent will deprived of its resiliency, who could have called out to his soul as an awakening call that heartening word *Onward!* which the Russian thirsts after everywhere, no matter what rung of the ladder he may be standing on, of whatever station, calling, and pursuit he may be?

Where is he, then, he who would be able to tell our Russian soul in its native tongue this omnipotent word

Onward!—he who, knowing all the forces and abilities and all the profundity of our nature, could with a single thaumaturgic wave of his hand set us streaming toward the exalted life? With what tears, with what love would the grateful Russian repay him! But ages pass after ages; in ignominious sloth and the mad squirrel-cage activity of an immature youth will [the Russian's soul] be swathed . . . . . . yet there will not be granted of God a Man who will utter the word!

There was one circumstance which all but awakened him, which all but brought about an overturn in his character: something that resembled love came to him. But here, too, the matter ended in nought. In the vicinity, some seven miles from his village, there lived and had his being a certain General who, as we have already seen, did not speak very favorably of Tentetnikov. The General lived like a general, kept open house, loved to have his neighbors come to pay their respects to him; he himself did not pay any visits, had a hoarse voice, read books, and had a daughter, a strange being, such as the world rarely sees. She was something that was as alive as life itself.

Her name was Ulinka. Her upbringing had been a somewhat strange one. She had been taught by an English governess who did not know a single word of Russian. Ulinka had lost her mother in her childhood; her father had never had any time for her. As in any child that had grown up in freedom, everything about her was self-willed. Had anyone seen how sudden wrath made stern lines gather instantaneously on her splendidly beautiful brow and how fierily she argued with her father, he would have thought that this was a most capricious being. But her wrath flared up only when she heard of any injustice, no matter what it was, or any evil deed perpetrated against anybody, no matter who. For never did she contend for her own sake, or make excuses for her own self. This wrath would vanish in a moment if she saw that the very object of her wrath had been overcome by misfortune. At the very first request for alms, no matter from whom, she was ready to toss him her entire purse, no matter what its contents might be, without stopping to go into any considerations and calculations. There was something impulsive about her. When she spoke, everything within her seemed impelled to rush after her thought—the expression of her face, the expression of her thought, the motion of her hands; it was as though she herself would go winging at any moment in the train of her words. There was nothing secretive about her. There was nobody before whom she would have been afraid to reveal her thoughts, and no force could have compelled her to be silent when she wanted to speak.

Her bewitching, odd walk, which was hers and hers alone, was so fearlessly free that all would have involuntarily made way for her. It was as though the man of evil became abashed before her and fell mute; the man who was most free and easy with words was at a loss for words with her and became confused, while the shy man could talk a blue streak with her, as he had never yet in all his life talked with anybody, and from the very first words of the conversation it already seemed to him that somewhere and at some time he had known her, and as though he had already seen these very features of hers somewhere, that this must have taken place somehow in the days of immemorial infancy, in the house where he was born, some merry evening when a throng of children was at its joyful games, and for a long while thereafter to such a man the age of discretion would be a bore.

Precisely the same thing happened between her and Tentetnikov. An inexplicable new emotion entered his soul. His wearisome life was for an instant illumined.

The General received Tentetnikov at first rather well and cordially, but they could find no common ground between them. Their conversations would wind up with a dispute and some sort of unpleasant feeling on both sides, inasmuch as the General did not like contradictions and objections; Tentetnikov, for his part, was also a touchy person. Naturally, much was forgiven the father because of the daughter, and peace was sustained between them until some female relatives came for a stay with the General— Countess Boldyreva and Princess Uzyakina, maids of honor who had been left over from a former court, yet who had retained even up to now certain connections, in consequence of which the General crawled a bit before them. From their very arrival it seemed to Tentetnikov that the General had become cooler toward him, that he did not notice him, or that he treated him as a nonentity; he would say to him, somehow negligently, "My dearest fellow; look here, little brother," and would even *thee* and *thou* him. This at last made Tentetnikov explode. Steeling his heart and clenching his teeth Tentetnikov had, nevertheless, the presence of mind to say in an exceptionally respectful and gentle voice, although his face turned to red and white blotches and everything seethed within him:

"I thank you, General, for being so well-disposed toward me. By using *thou* you invite me to a closer friendship, obligating me as well to use *thou* in addressing you. But the difference in our years stands in the way of such a familiar treatment between us."

The General became confused. Collecting his thoughts and picking his words, he began by saying, even though somewhat incoherently, that he had not used the term *thou* in any derogatory sense, that *thou*'ing may be occasionally permitted to an old man when speaking to a younger (he did not mention a word about his rank).

Of course, from that time on the friendship between them ceased and Tentetnikov's love came to an end at its very beginning. The light which had gleamed before him for a moment expired, and the dusk that followed became still gloomier. Everything turned him toward that mode of life which the reader has seen at the beginning of this chapter—to lounging and inactivity. Untidiness and disorder reigned in the house. The floor brush would be left the whole day in the middle of a room, together with the sweepings. His trousers found their way even into the reception room. Upon the elegant table before the divan soiled suspenders would be lying, just as if they were a treat set out for a guest, and so insignificant and drowsy had his life become that it was not only the domestics who had ceased to respect him, but the very hens in the yard all but pecked at him. Picking up a quill, he would doodle senselessly for hours at a time, covering the paper with curlicues, little houses, huts, country carts, troikas. But at times, forgetting all things else, the quill would of itself, without the master's being aware of it, draw a small head with fine features, with a quick, penetrating look and an upswept lock of hair, and in astonishment he would see emerging a portrait of her of whom no artist, no portraitist could have limned a portrait. And a still sadder mood would come upon him, and, believing that there was no happiness upon earth, he would be left thereafter still more wearied and impassive. Such was Andrei Ivanovich Tentetnikov's soul.

And then one day, at the time when (as usual) he had seated himself at the window to stare out of it (as usual), to his astonishment he heard neither Grigoriy nor Perphilievna, yet there were nevertheless a certain stir and a certain bustle in the yard facing him. A scullion and a scullery maid ran to open the gates. Steeds appeared in the gateway, every whit the way they are modeled or limned upon triumphal arches: a horse's head to the right, a horse's head to the left, a horse's head in the middle. Above them, on the box, were perched a coachman and a flunky, the latter in a roomy surtout and with a handkerchief by way of a belt. Behind them sat a gentleman in a cap and overcoat, his throat swathed in a three-cornered muffler of all the hues of the rainbow. When the vehicle turned and drew up before the front entrance it proved to be none other than a light traveling carriage on springs. The gentleman, of an extraordinarily respectable appearance, jumped out on the steps with the briskness and adroitness of an almost military man.

Andrei Ivanovich turned a little poltroonish at first: he took him for a government official. It must be explained that in his youth he had been mixed up in an imprudent affair. Two philosophically inclined hussars, who had read no end of all sorts of brochures, and a certain aesthete who had never finished his studies, and a gambler who had lost his shirt, had started some sort of philanthropic institution, under the chief guidance of a certain old knave, a Freemason as well as a gambler and a drunkard, yet the most eloquent of men. The society was formed for a sweeping purpose—to bring substantial happiness to all mankind, from the banks of the Thames to Kamchatka. Enormous funds were needed; the contributions gathered from the magnanimous members were incredible. Where everything had gone was known to the director in chief alone. Tentetnikov had been drawn into this society by his two friends, who belonged to the category of embittered people, people who are kind enough, yet who, because of frequent toasts in the name of science, enlightenment, and future obligations to humanity, had in due time become patent drunkards. Tentetnikov had come to his senses in a short while and left the society. But by that time the society had already succeeded in becoming mixed up in certain other doings that were actually not quite proper for a nobleman, so that subsequently the police, too, had to take a hand in the proceedings. And, therefore, it isn't at all odd that, even after he had left this society and had severed all ties with it, Tentetnikov nevertheless could not remain unperturbed; his conscience was not altogether at ease. It was not without fear, even now, that he watched the door opening.

His fear was dissipated quickly, however, when his caller bowed with unbelievable adroitness, keeping his head in a respectful position, inclined somewhat to one side, and explained in a few brief but comprehensive words that he had been long traveling about Russia, impelled both by the needs of his affairs, and by curiosity, that our realm abounded most copiously with remarkable objects, to say nothing of the plentiful number of its industries and the diversity of its soils; that, nevertheless, despite the scenery, he would never have dared to disturb his host by his inopportune call, were it not that owing to the spring freshets and the bad roads his carriage had suddenly all but broken down, so badly that it required a helping hand from blacksmiths and other master mechanics; but that, even if nothing had happened to his carriage, he would not have been able to deny himself the pleasure of paying his respects in person.

Having ended his speech, the caller with an enchanting affability scraped his foot, shod in a dandified high shoe of kid, with mother-of-pearl buttons and, despite the corpulence of his body, immediately bounced backward, with the ease of a rubber ball.

Andrei Ivanovich, his fears set to rest, concluded that this must be some inquiring learned professor who was, perhaps, traveling about Russia to gather botanical specimens or, perhaps, to dig up archaeological artifacts. He immediately evinced every readiness to assist him with all speed; he offered him his master mechanics, his wheelwrights and blacksmiths, begged his guest to make himself perfectly at home, seated him in an exceedingly large and comfortable armchair, and prepared himself to listen to his talk about the natural sciences.

His guest, however, touched for the most part on incidents dealing with man's inner world. He likened his life to a vessel in the midst of the seas, buffeted from all quarters by treacherous winds; he mentioned that he had had to change many posts, that he had suffered much for the sake of righteousness, that even his life had been in danger more than once at the hands of his enemies; and he told a great deal more of such a nature as indicated him to be a practical man rather than anything else. And at the conclusion of his speech he blew his nose into a handkerchief of white cambric more stentoriously than Andrei Ivanovich had ever heard any nose blown before. Occasionally, in an orchestra, one will come across a horn so artful and rascally that, when it fetches a note, it will seem to have been blared forth not in the orchestra pit but in your very ear. Just such a sound pealed forth in the awakened chamber of the drowsing house, and immediately thereafter was followed by the fragrance of Eau de Cologne, imperceptibly spread by a deft flourish of the cambric handkerchief.

The reader has probably surmised by this time that the caller was none other than our estimable Pavel Ivanovich Chichikov, whom we have so long left neglected. He had grown a little older: as one could see, this interval had not been for him devoid of tempests and alarums. It seemed as if the very frock coat upon him had decayed a little; and his light carriage, and his coachman, and his flunky, and his horses, and the very harness upon those horses, had somehow become frayed through and worn out. It seemed as if even his very finances were in no enviable state. But the expression of his face, his decorum and his manners, had remained the same. Apparently he had become even more pleasant in his actions and ways, even more deftly did he catch one small foot behind the other whenever he sat him down in an easy [chair]. There was still more urbanity in the way he delivered his speeches, more of cautious moderation in his words and expressions, more of skill in the way he conducted himself and more tact in everything.

Whiter and purer than the driven snows were his collar and his dickey and, despite the fact that he was just from the road, there wasn't so much as a speck on his frock coat—you could have invited him to a birthday dinner that very minute. His chin and cheeks were so clean-shaven that only a blind man could fail to admire the agreeable convexity of their contours.

———

A transformation immediately took place in the house. That half of it which up to now had been in blindness, with the shutters battened down, suddenly opened its eyes and saw the light. Everything was shifted about in the lighted rooms, and soon everything took on a proper appearance: the room intended to be a bedroom took unto itself all the objects necessary for comfort at night; a room intended to be a study ...... [reverted to being a study] ...... but first of all the reader must know that there were three tables in [Chichikov's] room: one, a desk, in front of the divan; another, a card table, between the windows, before a mirror; a third, a triangular affair, fitted into a corner between the door into the bedroom and the door into an unused hall, cluttered with invalided furniture and at present serving as an entry, into which, for a year by now, no one had entered. Upon this corner table was placed the clothing taken out of the small trunk, to wit: trousers for a frock coat; another pair, new, another pair, grayish, two velvet waistcoats and two of satin, and a frock coat. All these were placed one on top of another in a neat little pyramid and covered over with a silk handkerchief. In the other corner, between the door and the window, the footgear was ranged in a row: one pair of shoes not entirely new, another pair entirely new, patent-leather high shoes, and bedroom slippers. All these, too, were demurely screened off with a silk handkerchief, just as if they weren't there at all. Upon the desk there were immediately disposed, in great orderliness, the traveling casket, a bottle of Eau de Cologne, a calendar and two novels of some sort, each being a second volume. The clean linen was distributed in the bureau, which by this time had been placed in the bedroom; as for the linen intended for the laundress, it was tied up in a bundle and shoved under the bed. The small trunk, after being emptied, was likewise shoved under the bed. The sword, which traveled over the roads to inspire fear in robbers, also found a place in the bedroom, hung up on a nail not far from the bed. Everything took on an air of unusual cleanliness and tidiness. Nowhere was there a loose scrap of paper, or a feather, or a grain of dirt. The very air became ennobled, somehow: the agreeable odor of a healthy, vigorous man, who does not wear his underclothes too long, who goes to the baths and has a sponge rubdown of Sundays, became fixed in the air. For a time the odor of Petrushka, his serving man, made an attempt to become fixed in the front hall, but Petrushka was soon shifted to the kitchen, which was as it should have been.

The first few days Andrei Ivanovich was apprehensive over his independence, apprehensive lest his guest constrain him, embarrass him by bringing about certain changes in his way of life, and lest the routine of the days, so successfully established by him, might be disrupted; but his apprehensions were groundless. Our Pavel Ivanovich evinced an unusually pliable capacity for adapting himself to everything. He approved the philosophical leisureliness of his host, saying that it held the promise of his living a hundred years. About his solitude he expressed himself quite happily, saying, to be precise, that it nurtured great thoughts in man. Having glanced at the library and having commented with praise on books in general, he remarked that they were man's salvation from indolence. The words he let drop were not many but weighty. And in his actions he showed himself still more adaptable. He appeared on time, he left in time; he did not embarrass his host with questions at those times when the latter did not feel talkative; he played chess with him with pleasure; he kept silent with pleasure. Whenever his host puffed smoke in wispy clouds from his pipe, his guest, who did not smoke a pipe, would, nevertheless, strike on some corresponding occupation—he would, for instance, take out of his pocket his silver-and-enamel snuffbox and, holding it securely between two fingers of his left hand, revolve it rapidly with a finger of his right hand, the way the terrestrial sphere revolves about its axis, or simply drum upon it with a finger as he whistled in time under his breath. In short, he did not interfere with his host.

"This is the first time I see a man whom one can live with," Tentetnikov would say to himself. "As a general rule, there is little among us of the art of getting along together. There are not a few among us who are actually intelligent, and educated, and kindly, but as for people who have invariably equable characters, people whom it would be possible to live with through a lifetime without quarreling—I don't know if we can find such people. This is the first time I see a man of that sort." Such was Tentetnikov's opinion of his guest.

Chichikov, for his part, was very glad that he had settled for a time with so peaceful and mild a host. He had become fed up with the life of a Gypsy. To rest up, if but for a month, in a glorious village, with a view of the fields and with spring at its beginning, was a beneficial thing, considered from the hemorrhoidal aspect alone.

It would have been hard to find a better retreat for a rest. The spring, long held back by cold spells, had suddenly begun in all its beauty, and life had commenced to ferment everywhere. The vistas appeared blue now, and over the fresh emerald of the first greenery the dandelion showed its yellow, the lilac-roseate anemone bowed its gentle little head. Swarms of midges and hosts of insects appeared over the marshes; the water spider was already dashing after them in pursuit, and, also coming after them, every sort of bird had flocked from everywhere to the dry reeds. And all living things were coming together to have a closer look at one another. The earth had suddenly become populated, the forests had awakened, the meadows resounded with song. Round dances began in the village. Merrymaking was in full swing. How vivid the greenery! How fresh the air! What clamor of birds in the garden! Paradise, joyance, and jubilation everywhere! The village rang and sang as if there were a wedding going on.

Chichikov walked a great deal. There were plenty of places for excursions and jaunts. Now he would set out for a stroll along the flat highlands, with a view of the valley spread out below, over which great lakes still remained everywhere from the spring floods, and the leafless forests still showed like dark islands among them; or else he would enter the thickets, the forest ravines, where the trees, bur-

dened with bird nests . . . . . . [crowded] one another . . . . . .
and the flocks of cawing ravens darkened the sky with their
crisscross flights. Where the earth had dried, one could set
out over the awakened earth toward the landing stage, from
which the first vessels, laden with peas, barley, millet, and
wheat, were pushing off, while at the same time the water
was rushing to fall upon the wheels of the mill, which was
beginning to operate. He went to observe the first farm
work of spring, to see how the freshly turned furrow passed
in a black strip over the greensward, and how the skilled
sower cast the seed in handfuls, evenly, true of aim, with
not a grain over on this side or that.

Chichikov went everywhere. He had talked everything
over and gone over everything with the steward, and with
the muzhiks, and with the miller. He had learned everything, and all about everything, and what was what, and
how it was, and how the estate was going, and what grain
was fetching, and what the charge was for milling the grain
in the spring, and what that charge was in the fall, and what
each muzhik was called, and who was related to whom, and
where did you buy that cow, and what do you feed your
pigs with—in a word, everything. He found out, too, how
many muzhiks had died off; not many, it turned out. Since
he was an intelligent man it took him no time at all to perceive that the estate was not getting on at all enviably under
the management of Andrei Ivanovich: everywhere one observed oversights, remissness, thievery, and not a little
drunkenness as well! And Chichikov thought: "What an animal this Tentetnikov is, though! Such an estate, and to let
it go to rack and ruin like that! One could get an income of
fifty thousand a year out of it."

More than once, in the midst of such strolls, the thought would come to him of himself becoming, at some time—that is, not now, of course, but later on, when the main enterprise had been carried through, and he had means on hand—of himself becoming the tranquil owner of some such manor as this. At this point, naturally, he immediately pictured to himself a little woman as well, who would be young, and fresh, and white of face, from a merchant family or belonging to some other well-heeled class, who might even know music on top of everything else. He pictured to himself a younger generation, too, whose duty it would be to transmit through eternity the line of the Chichikovs: a frolicsome little rascal of a boy and a beauty of a daughter, or even two little boys and two or even three little girls, so that it might be known to all men that Chichikov had actually lived and had his being, and not that he had merely flitted by like a shade or a spectre over the earth, and so that he, too, might not be ashamed before the spirit of his own father. Then he would begin to dream that it also might not be a bad idea to have his rank raised somewhat: State Councilor, for instance, was an honorable and respected rank. What ideas won't pop into a man's mind while he is strolling, which will so often bear him away from the dreary present moment, which tug at, tease, stir his imagination, and which he will love even when he himself is convinced that all this will never really come about!

The village proved to the liking of Pavel Ivanovich's people also. They, even as he, had settled down here. Petrushka in a very short time had formed a close friendship with Grigoriy the butler, although in the beginning they had both put on airs and puffed themselves up unbearably before each other. Petrushka threw dust into Grigoriy's eyes by telling him how many different places he had been to, but Grigoriy at once brought him up short by speaking of St. Petersburg, in which Petrushka had never been. The latter wanted to raise his stock and get out of his fix by citing the great distances between the places in which he had been, but Grigoriy named a place which could not be found on any map and reckoned that the distance to it would be twenty thousand miles and more, so that Pavel Ivanovich's serving man became utterly dazed, let his jaw drop, and was made the laughingstock of all the domestics right there and then. However, the matter ended with their becoming the closest of friends. Bald Pimen, who was uncle to all the peasants, kept a pothouse, the name of which was Akulka, at the end of the village, and in this establishment they were to be seen at all hours of the day. There they became bosom cronies, or what is called *burflies* among the common folk.

For Seliphan there was a lure of a different nature. Not an evening passed but that there was singing in the village and spring dances with the dancers weaving in and out of a ring. The pure-bred, well-built wenches, such as it would now be hard to find in the big villages, made him stand as motionless as a gaping raven for hours at a stretch. It was hard to say which one was the finest among them; they were all white-breasted, white-necked, they all had fiery, languishing eyes, a walk like a peacock's, and braids down to their waists. When, having taken a white hand in each one of his, he moved slowly with the wenches in a round dance, or came toward them, having formed a wall with the other lads, and the wenches, forming a living wall in their turn, came toward them, smiling and chanting their full-throated song: "Masters, show us your bridegroom!" and the whole region roundabout grew darker, and the refrain of the song, resounding far beyond the river, came back in a pensive echo, at such a time he himself did not know what came over him. Whether he slept or whether he waked, at morn or at dusk, he imagined thereafter that there was a white hand in each one of his hands and that he was moving in a round dance.

Chichikov's horses, too, found the new quarters to their liking. Not only the shaft-horse but Assessor and the piebald as well found their stay at Tentetnikov's not at all boresome, the oats excellent and the layout of the stables unusually convenient: each horse had a stall to itself which, although it was partitioned off, nevertheless actually allowed them to see one another over the partitions, so that if a sudden whim struck any one of them, even the one farthest off, to start neighing, any of the others could immediately respond in kind.

In a word, they all settled down just as if they were at home. As far as that necessary business which made Pavel Ivanovich ride up and down vast Russia was concerned (the search for dead souls, that is), why, he had become very cautious and circumspect on the subject, even when he had occasion to deal with out-and-out fools. But Tentetnikov, after all was said and done, read books, philosophized, tried to make clear to himself the causes of everything, all the whys and the wherefores. "No, it would be better to look around if he can't be approached from some other direction," thought our Chichikov. While indulging in small talk on frequent occasions with the domestics, he learned, among other things, that the master formerly had called not infrequently upon his neighbor the General, that the General had a young daughter, that the master had been *that way* about the young lady, and that the young lady, for her part, had felt the same way about the master ...... but then suddenly the master and the General had had a falling out over something and had drawn apart. And Chichikov himself had noticed that Andrei Ivanovich was forever drawing, whether he held quill or pencil, some little heads or other, and all of them looking alike.

Once, after dinner, turning the silver snuffbox on its axis, as was his wont, Chichikov spoke as follows: "You have everything, Andrei Ivanovich, yet there is one thing lacking."

"What is that?" asked the other, blowing rather curly smoke.

"A life mate," said Chichikov.

Andrei Ivanovich did not say anything. And with that their conversation ended.

Chichikov was undaunted; he chose another occasion, this time just before supper and, speaking of this and that, said suddenly: "But really, Andrei Ivanovich, it would not be at all amiss if you were to get married."

Not a word did Tentetnikov say in answer to this, just as if the very mention of this subject were distasteful to him.

Chichikov was still undaunted. On the third occasion he chose the time after supper and said: "Just the same, no matter how I turn your circumstances over in my mind, I still see that you ought to get married, otherwise you'll become a victim of hypochondria."

Whether Chichikov's words were so convincing this time, or whether Tentetnikov's spirits were on this day especially disposed toward frankness, on this occasion he sighed, sent up a puff of pipe smoke and said: "One must be born fortunate in all things, Pavel Ivanovich," and told him just how everything had happened, the whole story of the friendship and the rupture.

When Chichikov heard the whole story word for word, and perceived that the whole business had been over that one word *thou*, he was taken aback. For a minute or so he gazed fixedly into Tentetnikov's eyes, not knowing what decision to reach concerning him, whether he was an all-around fool or merely inclined to be a fool, and finally, "Good heavens, Andrei Ivanovich!" he said, taking both of the other's hands in his. "What sort of insult is that? Just what is so insulting about the word *thou?*"

"There is nothing insulting in the word itself," said Tentetnikov, "but it is in the meaning given to the word, in the voice in which it is said, that the insult lies! *Thou!* It means: 'Remember you are so much trash; I receive you only because there aren't any of your betters around; but, as soon as some Princess Uzyakina has arrived, you just know your place and stand on the threshold.' That's what it means!" As he said this, the meek and mild Andrei Ivanovich's eyes flashed; in his voice one could hear the irritation of offended dignity.

"Why, taking it even in that sense, what is there to it?" asked Chichikov.

"What! You would want me to go on visiting him after such an action as that?"

"Well, what sort of action is that? Why, that's not an action at all," said Chichikov coolly.

"What do you mean by that?" Tentetnikov asked him in astonishment.

"That's just a way generals have about them and not an action; they *thou* everybody. And, incidentally, why not even permit such a thing to a distinguished and estimable person?"

"This is a different matter," said Tentetnikov. "Were he old, and poor, not proud, not arrogant, not conceited, not a general, I would then permit him to *thou* me and would accept it with actual respect."

"He's an out-and-out fool," Chichikov decided to himself. "To permit such a thing to a ragged beggar, but not to a general!"—"Well and good!" said he aloud. "Let us suppose that he did insult you; but then, you actually paid him out for it; it was tit for tat. But to part forever over a trifle, to drop a matter so very personal, so very close to you, really, you must excuse me, but. . . . Once the goal has been chosen, you must forge ahead, letting no obstacles stop you. Why pay any attention if a man is offensive? Man is always offensive, for that's the way the good Lord created him. Why, you won't find a man in the whole world nowadays who isn't offensive."

"A strange fellow, this Chichikov!" Tentetnikov thought to himself in a quandary, disconcerted by such words.

"But what a queer stick this Tentetnikov is!" Chichikov was thinking in the meantime.

"Andrei Ivanovich, I'm going to talk to you as brother to brother. You are not a man of experience—let me set this matter to rights. I will go to His Excellency and explain that all this came through a misunderstanding on your part, because of your youth and your lack of knowledge of men and the world."

"I have no intentions of groveling before him!" said Tentetnikov, becoming offended. "Nor can I authorize you to do this."

"I am not capable of groveling," said Chichikov, becoming offended in his turn. "I can, being after all only a man like all men, plead guilty to some other shortcoming, but never to groveling. Excuse me, Andrei Ivanovich, I meant well; I did not expect that you would take my words in such an offensive sense." All this was said with a feeling of personal dignity.

"I am at fault, forgive me!" the touched Tentetnikov hastened to say, seizing both of Chichikov's hands. "I did not mean to insult you. I swear I appreciate your kind concern. But let us drop all talk of this. Let us never speak of this again!"

"In that case I shall go to see the General just so."

"Why?" asked Tentetnikov, looking into the other's eyes in perplexity.

"To pay him my respects."

"A strange fellow, this Chichikov!" reflected Tentetnikov.

"A strange fellow, this Tentetnikov!" reflected Chichikov.

"No later than tomorrow, Andrei Ivanovich; I'll be off to see him about ten in the morning. To my way of thinking, the sooner one pays one's respects to a man, the better. Since my carriage hasn't been put in proper shape yet, permit me to borrow a barouche of yours. I'd like to start off for his place about ten in the morning, let us say."

"Good gracious, what a request to make! You are full master here; not only a carriage but everything else is at your disposal."

After this conversation they wished good night to each other and went to bed, not without reflections on each other's quirks.

It was a wondrously curious thing, however! On the following day, when the horses were brought around for Chichikov and he hopped into the barouche with the ease of an almost military man, attired in a new frock coat with white cravat and white vest, and rolled off to pay his respects to the General, Tentetnikov underwent such spiritual agitation as he had not experienced in a long time. All the rusty and drowsy course of his thoughts now became turbulent and active. A nervous upheaval suddenly overwhelmed all the emotions of the sluggard who up to now had been sunk in uncaring sloth. By turns, he sat on the divan, walked up to a window, tried to settle down to a book, desired to think—a futile desire! No thought would come into his head. Then he strove not to think of anything—a futile striving! Snatches of something that resembled thoughts, the tag-ends and tailings of thoughts, crept into his head and stuck all over the inside of it gummily. "A strange state to be in!" said he and moved nearer the window, to gaze at the road that cut through a leafy grove, at the end of which road the dust, which had not yet had time to settle, still swirled like smoke.

But, leaving Tentetnikov, let us follow Chichikov.

CHAPTER TWO

The horses were in fine fettle and in a little more than half an hour carried Chichikov over the seven-mile distance, at first through a leafy grove, then along the fields of grain, beginning to show greenly against the recently furrowed land, then along the rim of the mountains, whence distant views were revealed at every moment; and finally, through a broad avenue of lindens that were barely beginning to burgeon, the horses carried him into the very heart of the village. Here the alley of lindens turned to the right and, transformed into a street lined with poplars with the bases of their trunks guarded by wattled enclosures, came to an end at a pair of barred, cast-iron gates through which one could glimpse the ornate and richly sculptured frontal, supported by eight Corinthian columns, of the General's house. Pervading everything was the smell of linseed paint, which renewed everything and would not permit anything to get weather-beaten and old. The courtyard was so spick-and-span that it looked like a parquet floor. Chichikov, duly impressed, hopped out of his carriage, ordered himself to be announced to the General, and was conducted directly to his study.

The General struck him by his majestic appearance. He was in a quilted satin dressing gown of magnificent purple. A frank look, a virile face, mustache and dundrearies grizzled, his hair cut short and, in the back, actually clipped; the nape of his neck fleshy, broad—three-storied, as it is called, or in three horizontal folds, with a deep vertical crease cutting through them down the middle; his voice a somewhat hoarse bass, his every motion and gesture a commander's. In short, this was one of those picturesque generals in which the famous year of '12 had been so rich. General Betrishchev, even like many among us, had within him, together with a host of good points, a multitude of shortcomings. Both the one and the other, as is usually the case with a Russian, were jumbled within him in picturesque disorder. At decisive moments you had magnanimity, valor, boundless generosity, intelligence in all things, and at other times an admixture of caprices, ambition, self-conceit, self-love, and those petty quirks of personality without which not a single Russian can get along when he is sedentary, without a thing to do and with absolutely no [goal]. . . . He disliked everybody who had got ahead of him in the service and expressed himself caustically concerning such people in needle-pointed epigrams.

Most of all did he rail against an erstwhile comrade-in-arms, whom he deemed below him both in mind and in abilities, but who, nevertheless, had left him far behind and by now was Governor General over two provinces and, as if on purpose, over those very provinces in which the General's estates were, so that he found himself in the other's power, as it were. In revenge he needled him at every opportunity, derided his every order, and saw in all his measures and actions the height of folly. Everything about General Betrishchev was somehow odd—as a first instance one might cite his notions concerning the enlightenment of the people, of which doctrine he was an ardent champion and a zealot; also, he liked to know that which others did not know, and did not like those people who knew anything at all that he did not know. In a word, he liked to show off with his intellect. Having received a semicontinental education, he wanted at the same time to play the rôle of a Russian grandee. And it is not at all strange that with such an unequal character, with such great, vivid contradictions, he was inevitably bound to encounter many unpleasantnesses in service, precisely because of which he had gone into retirement, blaming some sort of hostile cabal for everything and lacking the magnanimity to blame himself in the least. In his retirement he had preserved his unvaryingly picturesque, majestic bearing. Whether in full dress, in a frock coat, or in a dressing gown, he was always the same. From his voice to the least movement of his body everything about him was imperious, commanding, inspiring awe in those of lesser rank, if not actual respect.

Chichikov felt both the one and the other, both respect and awe. Inclining his head deferentially and with his arms stuck out, as though he were about to lift a trayful of cups, he bent his whole torso with an amazing adroitness and said: "I deemed it my duty to present myself to Your Excellency. Cherishing as I do a respect for the illustrious qualities of the men who have saved our fatherland on the field of battle, I deemed it my duty to present myself in person before Your Excellency."

Such an approach the General found, evidently, not unpleasing. Making quite a well-disposed motion with his head, he said: "Quite glad to make your acquaintance. I beg of you to be seated. Where did you serve?"

"My career in service," said Chichikov, seating himself in an easy chair, not plump in the center, however, but at an angle, and clutching an arm of the chair, "began in the Treasury, Your Excellency. Its further course I pursued in different posts: I was also in the Supreme Court, and on a Building Commission, and in the Customs. My life may be likened to a vessel in the midst of the waves, Your Excellency. In patience, one might say, have I been swathed and swaddled and am myself, so to say, patience itself personified. But as to what has befallen me because of my enemies, who have even attempted my life, why, that could not be conveyed either in words or pigments, or even by an artist's brush, so to say. And so, at the decline of my life, I am seeking but a nook where I may pass the remainder of my days. For the time being I am staying with a near neighbor of Your Excellency's—"

"With whom?"

"I am staying at Tentetnikov's, Your Excellency."

The General made a wry face.

"He is quite repentant, Your Excellency, because he had not evinced the proper respect—"

"Respect for what?"

"For Your Excellency's merits. He cannot find the words—he says: 'If only I could in some way . . . because,' he says. 'I certainly know how to appreciate the men who have saved our fatherland,' says he."

"Good gracious, why does he feel that way? For I am not angry at him," said the mollified General. "I had sincerely come to love him with all my soul and am convinced that in time he will be a most useful person."

"You have expressed it most fitly, Your Excellency; he is truly a most useful person, he possesses the vanquishing gift of words, and he knows how to write."

"But his writings are trifles, I guess—piffling verse, sort of?"

"No, Your Excellency, they are not trifles. He is engaged on something worth while. He is writing . . . a history, Your Excellency."

"A history? A history of what?"

"A history of—" Here Chichikov paused and, whether because there was a general seated before him, or simply to lend a greater importance to the matter, added: "A history dealing with generals, Your Excellency."

"What? With generals? What generals?"

"About generals . . . in general, Your Excellency. That is, properly speaking, about the generals of our fatherland."

Chichikov became utterly muddled and lost his head; he all but spat in disgust and said to himself: "Lord, what sort of rubbish am I spouting!"

"Pardon me, I don't understand quite rightly. What is it going to be, then—the history of some particular period, or individual biographies? And then, is it going to include all generals, or only those who took part in the campaign of eighteen-twelve?"

"Just so, Your Excellency, those who took part in the campaign of eighteen-twelve!" Having said this Chichikov said to himself: "If you were to kill me, I don't understand what all this is about!"

"Then why doesn't he come to me? I could get together quite a deal of interesting material for him."

"He hesitates to do so, Your Excellency."

"What nonsense! Because of some trifling word which he let drop between the two of us! Why, I'm not that sort of person at all. I am even ready to go to him myself, if you like."

"He would never let it come to that, he will come himself," said Chichikov, recovering himself and regaining his spirits entirely, and reflected: "What a lucky turn! Those generals surely came in pat! And yet it was just a fool slip of the tongue!"

A rustle was heard in the study. A carved walnut door leading into an adjoining small room opened of itself and revealed a living figurine, one of its exquisite hands holding the brass doorknob. If a transparency, brightly lit with powerful lamps behind it, had suddenly flared up in the dark room, it would hardly have stunned one with its sudden appearance as much as this figurine glowing with life, springing up as if to illumine the room. A ray of sunlight seemed to have burst in with her, suddenly lighting up the ceiling, the cornice, the dark corners. It was as though the General's frowning study had broken into a smile. Evidently she had come to tell her father something, but on seeing a stranger [had desisted]. . . . During the first moment Chichikov could not account to himself what was before his eyes. It would have been hard to say what land she was a native of. Such a pure, noble facial outline could not have been found anywhere save perhaps on small ancient cameos. Straight and light as an arrow, her stature seemed to tower over all men and things. But this was an illusion. She was not at all of great stature. It was all due to her extraordinary gracefulness and the harmoniousness of all the parts of her body, from her head to her toes. Her dress sat upon her as if the best dressmakers of both capitals had gathered in council as to how best to attire her. But this, too, was an illusion. She had fashioned the dress herself, apparently; the needle had caught up at random, in two or three places, an uncut piece of material of one solid hue and thereafter it had simply gathered and draped itself about her in such folds and pleats that, were they to be translated together with the girl to a canvas, all the misses tricked out in the latest mode would have looked like so many magpies tricked out in scraps of motley finery from some rag fair. And if one were to translate her, with all the drapes of the dress that clung to her, into marble, she would have been considered the work of some sculptor of genius. Despite the fact that her face was almost familiar to him through the drawings of Andrei Ivanovich, Chichikov gazed at her as if he were dumbfounded, and only later on did he note that there was one real defect about her: she was far too slim and slight.

"Allow me to introduce you to my spoiled darling!" said the General, turning to Chichikov. "However, I still do not know your family name, nor your first name and patronymic—"

"But then, is there any need of knowing the name and patronymic of a man who has not distinguished himself through any merits?" Chichikov countered diffidently.

"But after all, one must have that information—"

"Pavel Ivanovich, Your Excellency," said Chichikov, making a bow with the adroitness of almost a military man and bouncing backward with the buoyancy of a rubber ball, his head deferentially inclined to one side.

"Ulinka," said the General, turning to his daughter, "Pavel Ivanovich has just told me a most interesting bit of news. Our neighbor Tentetnikov isn't as foolish a man as we supposed. He is taken up with quite an important work, a history of the generals of the campaign of eighteen-twelve."

Ulinka seemed to flare up suddenly and became animated. "But whoever thought that he was a foolish man?" she asked quickly. "Except, perhaps, Vishnepokromov alone, whom you have such faith in, yet who is both a hollow and a vile man!"

"But why call him vile? Although he is sort of hollow, true enough," said the General.

"He is sort of vile and sort of abominable, as well as sort of hollow. Whoever has wronged his brothers the way he has, and has driven his own sister out of his house, is none other than an abominable man."

"Why, they are only saying that about him."

"People don't say such things unless there is some basis for them. I can't understand, Father, how with a soul as exceedingly kind as yours, and with such a rare heart, you can go on receiving a man who is as far from you as earth is from heaven, and who you yourself know is bad, tolerating him because he is a glib talker and knows how to get around you so well."

"There, now, you can see for yourself," said the General to Chichikov with a smile, "there, now, that's the way we're always arguing." And turning to the girl, he resumed: "Come, my soul, I can't very well drive him away, can I?"

"But why drive him away? Yet, at the same time, why bestow such attention upon him? And also, why love him?"

At this point Chichikov deemed it his duty to put in a word on his own account. "All living things demand to be loved, Madam," said he. "What can one do? Even a little animal loves to be stroked; it will thrust its snout out of its sty—there stroke it!"

The General broke into laughter. "There, just so! It will thrust out its snout—go ahead and stroke the animal! . . . Ha, ha, ha! Not only its snout but its whole body is black from living in soot all its life, and yet it, too, demands encouragement, as they say. Ha, ha, ha, ha!"

"According to the precepts of Christianity"—Chichikov nodded his head to Ulinka with a pleasant smile—"it's precisely such beings that we ought to love. Has Your Excellency ever heard"—he turned to the General with a smile that was now rather roguish—"has Your Excellency ever heard the story about 'Love us when we're dirty—anyone will love us when we're clean'?"

"No, I never have."

"It's a most spicy anecdote, Your Excellency," Chichikov went on with the same roguish smile. "Well, Your Excellency, on the estate of Prince Gukzovsky, whom Your Excellency undoubtedly knows—"

"Don't know him."

"—well, there was a German manager on that estate, Your Excellency—a young man, he was. He had to go into town, to attend to the recruiting of soldiers on the estate as well as other matters, and naturally, you know, he had to use palm oil on certain court officials. Of course they took a liking to him, too, and treated him in their turn. And so, one day at dinner, he says: 'Gentlemen, you must come out and see me some day on the Prince's estate.'—'We will that,' they told him. It so happened shortly thereafter that these same legal lights had to carry out an investigation about something that had occurred on the estate of Count Trehmetiev, whom Your Excellency undoubtedly also knows—"

"Don't know him."

"Well, they did not carry out any investigation but instead all that legal talent drove over in a body to the Count's old steward, and played cards for three days and three nights at his house, with never a stop. Naturally, the samovar and the punch bowl were never off the table, not for a minute. By that time the old man had become plenty fed up with them. So just to be shut of them he says, says he: 'Really, you ought to go and see the Prince's German manager; he lives not so far from here.'

" 'Sure enough. Why not?' they agreed, and so the whole lot and parcel of them, just the way they were, half drunk, unshaven, and sleepy, piled into their cart and started off to see that German. But the German, I must inform Your Excellency, had just gotten married. A girl just out of boarding school, his wife was, a young thing and most refined." (Chichikov's face at this point expressed how refined she was.) "There they were, sitting over their tea, with never a care, when suddenly the door flies open and the whole horde of them barges in."

"I can just imagine it—a fine lot they must have been!" said the General, laughing.

"The German was so upset, Your Excellency, that he hardly knew what he was about. 'What do you want here?' he asks. 'Oh, so that's the sort of fellow you are!' they tell him. And with that their faces changed and the whole matter took on a different complexion. 'We've come here strictly on business!' they tell him. 'How much alcohol is distilled on your estate? Let's see your books!' One thing led to another; the poor German didn't know which way to turn, or what to do or say. 'Hey, there, guards!' So they seized him, trussed him up, and carted him off to town, and there the German had to lie in prison for a year and a half."

"Well, well!" said the General.

Ulinka wrung her hands.

"His wife tried to get him out! But what could a woman do, and a young and inexperienced one, at that? Fortunately, some kind people turned up who advised her how to obtain justice in a peaceful way. The German got out, all right, and all it cost him was two thousand, besides a little banquet for the officials. And so, while they were at the banquet, and all of them, including the German, were full of fine spirits, if you follow me, they say to him: 'Aren't you sorry now for the shabby way you treated us? You wanted to see us only when we were all clean and shaved and all dressed up in frock coats. No, love us when we're dirty— anyone will love us when we're clean.' "

The General broke into ringing laughter. Ulinka moaned in pain.

"Ah, papa, I can't understand how you can laugh!" She spoke quickly, wrath darkening her splendidly beautiful brow. "As for me, these dishonest actions induce despondence, and despondence only. When I see a fraud being perpetrated before the eyes of all, and that such people are not punished by universal contempt, I don't know what comes over me, and for the time being I become wicked, downright evil; I keep on brooding and brooding—" And she all but burst into tears.

"My dear, I am not justifying them in the least," said the

General, "but how can one help laughing if a thing is funny? How did you put it? 'Love us when we're clean—'?" He turned to Chichikov.

" 'When we're dirty,' Your Excellency," the latter chimed in.

" 'Love us dirty—anyone will love us when we're clean!' Ha, ha, ha, ha!" And the General's torso began to sway from laughter; the shoulders that on a time had borne epaulets thick with gold braid were shaking as if they were bearing even now epaulets thick with gold braid.

Chichikov also broke into laughter, but it was merely interjected and, out of deference to the General, he pitched it on the letter *e: He, he, he, he!* And his torso, too, began to sway in laughter, although his shoulders did not shake, inasmuch as they had never borne any epaulets thick with gold braid.

"I can just imagine—that must have been a fine legal body—all unshaven!" the General was saying, still laughing.

"Yes, Your Excellency, for, after all, keeping ceaseless vigil for three days and nights is as bad as any fast; they were exhausted, simply exhausted!" Chichikov was saying, still laughing.

Ulinka sank into a chair and put her hand over her lovely eyes. "I don't know," she said, as if sorrowing that there was nobody whom she could share her indignation with. "I can feel only grief."

And really, the contrast in the feelings stirring the hearts of the three speakers was an extremely strange one. One was amused by the undeviating unresourcefulness of the German; the second was amused because the knaves had so deviously and amusingly turned the tables on the poor fellow; the third felt sad because an injustice had been perpetrated with impunity. All that was lacking was a fourth, who might have pondered over those very words which aroused laughter in one being and sadness in another. What, however, is the significance of a perishing, sullied man demanding love even in his fall? Is this an animal instinct? Or the faint cry of a soul stifled under the heavy burden of base passions, a cry escaping through the hardening crust of abominations and still wailing: "Brother, save me!"? There was lacking a fourth, to whom the perishing soul of a brother would have been the most harrowing thing to bear.

"I don't know," Ulinka repeated, taking her hand away from her face, "I can feel only grief."

"Only, please, don't get angry at us," said the General. "We aren't at all to blame in this instance. Isn't that so?" he turned to Chichikov. "Give me a kiss and go to your room, Ulinka. I'm going to dress for dinner right away. I hope," he said, looking directly at Chichikov, "that you are dining with me?"*

"If only Your Excellency doesn't mind."

"Come, now, why stand on ceremony! I am still in a position to offer a meal to a guest, glory be to God. There's plenty of cabbage soup!"

Adroitly crooking his arms, Chichikov gratefully and deferentially dipped his head so far that all the objects in

*From this point on the General begins *thee*-ing and *thou*-ing Chichikov. *Trans.*

the room disappeared from his view and he saw only the toes of his own high shoes. When, after keeping this respectful attitude for some time, he raised his head anew, he no longer saw Ulinka. She had vanished. In place of her there had appeared a giant of a valet, with bushy mustachios and side whiskers, bearing a silver basin and a ewer.

"Will you permit me to dress in your presence?" asked the General, throwing off his dressing gown and rolling up the shirt sleeves over his heroic arms.

"Good gracious! Your Excellency may not only dress but do anything Your Excellency pleases in my presence."

The General fell to washing himself, splashing like a duck and snorting; the soapsuds flew all over the room.

"How did you put it?" he asked, wiping his thick neck thoroughly. " 'Love us when we're clean'?"

" 'When we're dirty,' Your Excellency!"

" 'Love us when we're dirty—anyone will love us when we're clean!' Very, very good!"

Chichikov was in indescribably fine fettle. Suddenly inspiration swooped down upon him. "The General is a kindhearted and a jolly fellow—let's have a try at it," he thought and, seeing that the valet had left the room, he began: "Your Excellency, since you are so kind to everybody and so considerate, I have a most important request to make of you!"

"What is it?"

Chichikov looked all around him. "It's an amusing story, only it's not so amusing for me. I have, Your Excellency, a decrepit little dotard of an uncle; he has three hundred serfs and a couple of thousand rubles—and, outside of myself, no heir. He cannot, because of his decrepitude, manage the estate himself, yet he does not want to transfer it to me. And what a strange reason he offers for this refusal! 'I don't know,' he says, 'what my nephew is like; perhaps he's a spendthrift. Let him prove to me that he is a responsible person; let him first acquire three hundred souls of his own; then I'll let him have my three hundred souls too.' "

"Well, then, it looks as if he were an out-and-out fool!" said the General.

"It wouldn't be so bad if he were only a fool—that is his privilege. But consider my situation, Your Excellency!" At this point Chichikov, lowering his voice, began to speak as if he were imparting a secret. "The little old dotard has gotten himself some sort of a housekeeper, and the housekeeper has little ones. And so, first thing you know, everything will go to them."

"The stupid old man has outlived what wits he had, and that's all there is to it," said the General. "Only, I don't see how I can be of any help here," he said, looking at Chichikov in astonishment.

"Here's what I have thought of. Before the figures of the new census are submitted, there are bound to be on the large estates not a few souls who have run away or died, yet are listed on the same basis as the living. So if Your Excellency were to transfer all the dead souls in your village to me, just as if they were alive, putting through an actual purchase deed, it would enable me to present this purchase deed to the old man, and no matter how he'd twist and turn, he would nevertheless leave the estate to me."

At this point, the General burst into such laughter as hardly any man had ever before indulged in. He slumped, just as he was, into an easy chair; he threw his head back and almost choked. The whole house was aroused. The valet sprang up as if out of the ground. His daughter came running in alarm.

"Father, what's happened to you?" she asked in fright, looking into his eyes in bewilderment.

"It's nothing, my dear, don't worry about it. Ha, ha, ha! Go to your room; we will come to dinner right away. Calm yourself! Ha, ha, ha!"

And, after a few gasps, the General's laughter broke out again with renewed strength, resounding through all the lofty echoing chambers in the General's house, from the front hall to the attic.

Chichikov felt alarmed, waiting for him to be done laughing.

"Your uncle, now, your uncle! What a fool that will make of your uncle! Ha, ha, ha! He'll get dead serfs instead of living ones! Ha, ha, ha!"

"There he goes again!" thought Chichikov to himself. "Eh, what a ticklish fellow! It's a wonder he doesn't burst."

"Ha, ha, ha!" the General kept right on.

Chichikov was, to some extent, in an actually embarrassing position—the valet was still standing there, with mouth gaping and his eyes goggling.

"But that which makes you laugh, Your Excellency, has made me shed many a tear," said he.

"Excuse me, brother, but you've nearly been the death of me! Why, I'd give God knows how much to see your uncle when you offer him the purchase deed to those dead souls! Well, now, is he so very old? How old is he?"

"He's eighty, Your Excellency. But this is such a personal matter that I would like—" Chichikov glanced significantly at the General and then looked at the valet askance.

"You can go, brother. You can come later." The mustachioed giant withdrew.

"Yes, Your Excellency. This matter, Your Excellency, is of such a nature that I would like to keep it a secret—"

"Naturally, I understand that very well. What an ass the old man is! For he must needs, even at the age of eighty, get such a fool notion as demanding: 'Let him first acquire three hundred souls all by himself, out of thin air, then I'll give him three hundred souls!' Why, he's an ass!"

"He is an ass, Your Excellency."

"But then, the Devil himself must have put you up to such a trick—to gladden the old man by foisting dead souls on him! Ha, ha, ha! Well, now, what sort of man is he? What does he look like? Is he spry? For he must be pretty sturdy, at that, if he has a housekeeper staying on with him?"

"I wouldn't call it sturdiness! The sands of life are running out for him, Your Excellency!"

"What a fool! For he is a fool, isn't he?"

"He is a fool, Your Excellency."

"However, he visits around? Does he go to social gatherings? He still keeps on his feet?"

"He still keeps on his feet, but with difficulty."

"What a fool! But he's sturdy, just the same? Has he still got his teeth?"

"Two teeth, Your Excellency."

"What an ass! Don't you be angry at me, brother, but even though he is an uncle to you, he's an ass just the same."

"He is an ass, Your Excellency. Even though he is a relative of mine, and it is a hard thing to confess, yet what can one do?"

However, as the reader can surmise for himself, it was not at all a hard thing for Chichikov to confess this, all the more so since it was highly improbable that he had ever had any uncle.

"And so, if Your Excellency will be so kind as to—"

"To give you the dead souls? Why, for such a clever dodge as that I'll give them to you with land and dwellings! Take the whole graveyard for yourself! Ha, ha, ha, ha! The old man, now, the old man! Ha, ha, ha, ha! What a fool that will make of your uncle! Ha, ha, ha, ha!"

And the General's laughter went echoing anew through the General's chambers. [E]

CHAPTER THREE

"If Colonel Koshkarev is really a madman, it won't be so bad," Chichikov mused as he once more found himself amid the open fields and with wide vistas spreading before him, when everything had vanished and only the heavenly vault remained, with two clouds off to one side.

"Hey, there, you big fool!"

Both Seliphan and Petrushka turned around on the box.

"And where are you driving, now?"

"Why, just where you were pleased to order me, Pavel Ivanovich—to Colonel Koshkarev's," said Seliphan.

"And have you asked about the right way there?"

"I was so busy all the while with the carriage, now, Pavel

Ivanovich, if you please, that I had no time—the General's groom was the only one I saw. But Petrushka, now, he questioned the coachman."

"There's a fool for you! You've been told time and again not to rely on Petrushka: Petrushka is a blockhead; Petrushka is stupid; Petrushka, I guess, is drunk this very minute."

"There's nothing so very hard about it," said Petrushka, turning around halfway and looking at Chichikov out of the corner of his eye. "Outside of going down the hill and then taking to the meadow there's nothing to it."

"And as for you, you've taken nothing in your mouth outside of rotgut, I guess? And I guess you aren't sozzled right now, are you?"

Perceiving which way things were heading, Petrushka simply twitched his nose. He was just about to say that he hadn't taken a drop, but then he himself felt ashamed, somehow.

"A fine fellow you are, a very fine fellow! There's a fellow of whom one may say: 'He has astonished all Europe with his good looks!' " Having said which, Chichikov stroked his own chin and reflected: "I say, though, what a world of difference there is between an enlightened citizen and the coarse physiognomy of a flunky!" It must be pointed out that Pavel Ivanovich was firmly convinced that Petrushka was in love with his own beauty, whereas there were times when the latter forgot entirely whether he had a mug at all.

Seliphan commented to Pavel Ivanovich how smoothly the barouche was going—better nor any carriage; but Pavel Ivanovich rebuffed him, whereupon he flicked his whip

over the flanks of the horses and turned to talk to
Petrushka: "Have you heard, this Koshkarev gentleman has
made every muzhik he owns dress up like a German; from
a distance you can't even tell 'em apart; the muzhiks even
goose-step, the way all Germans do. And the womenfolk,
now, they don't walk around in no headdress, or with a kerchief tied like a three-cornered pie over their heads, but
each one sports a regular German *kapor,* the way German
fraus walk around in their *kapors,* you know; that's just what
they call it, a *kapor,* you know; a regular German *kapor.*" *

"Why, somebody ought to doll you up as a German and
clap a *kapor* on you to top everything off!" said Petrushka,
trying to be witty at Seliphan's expense, and smirked. But
what a phiz resulted from this grin! There was not even a
semblance of a grin; he looked, rather, like a man who has
caught a cold in the nose and, after trying to sneeze but not
succeeding, still remains on the verge of sneezing.

"You should really have thought, Pavel Ivanovich," said
Seliphan, turning around on the box, "of asking Andrei
Ivanovich for another horse in exchange for that piebald—
seeing how friendly he feels toward you he wouldn't have
refused; but that there horse, now, he's a sure-enough
scoundrel of a horse, also a nuisance."

"Get along with you, get along and stop gabbing!" said
Chichikov, and reflected: "Really, now, what a pity I didn't
think of it."

In the meantime the barouche had started going downhill. Again vast expanses unrolled, and meadows with

---

*Seliphan is trying to say *kappe,* a hood. *Trans.*

groves of aspens scattered over them. Vibrating gently on its tight springs, the comfortable vehicle went on staidly descending the imperceptible slope and finally raced along the meadows, flying past mills, rumbling like distant thunder over bridges, swaying slightly over the yielding, quaggy turf of the low-lying land. And if only one hummock or tussock would let your ribs know it was there, but no such thing! A sheer solace and no mere barouche, that one Chichikov was riding in.

Clumps of vines flew past them, and silvery-white poplars whose branches hit Seliphan and Petrushka perched up on the box. At every moment they knocked off the latter's cap; the morose servant would jump off the box, retrieve his cap, and curse out the stupid tree and the owner who had planted it, but just the same he did not want to tie on his cap or hold it down with his hand, hoping that this was the last time and that the thing would not happen again. Here and there, in the grass, one saw blue calamus and yellow forest tulips. Soon there were birches as well as alders and aspens; the trees grew closer and closer together, and soon formed a dense forest. The forest became darker and was on the verge of turning into night. But suddenly, from everywhere, gleams of light shot through, like so many flashing mirrors. The trees grew rarer, the gleams increased—and now lying before them was a lake, a watery plain about three miles across. On the opposite shore, beyond the lake, a village scattered forth its huts of gray-hued logs. There were shouts, apparently coming out of the water; a score of men, some in it as deep as their waists, others in up to their shoulders and even neck-deep, were hauling a dragnet toward the opposite shore. In their midst, swimming livelily, shouting and making enough fuss for all the others, was a man who was just as broad as he was long, as roly-poly as a watermelon or a keg. He seemed to be in desperate straits and was shouting at the top of his voice, but his fears must have been more over the possibility of the net tearing and the fish escaping than for himself since, because of his breadth, he could not possibly have drowned, and no matter how he might have twisted and turned, wishing to dive, the water would have always shot him to the surface; and even if a couple of men were to perch on his shoulders he would, like a stubborn inflated bladder, have stayed with them on top of the water, merely grunting a little under their weight and letting bubbles out of his mouth and nostrils.

"That, Pavel Ivanovich," said Seliphan, turning around on his box, "must be the master, Colonel Koshkarev himself."

"Why do you think so?"

"Because his body, if you will be pleased to look, is whiter nor that of any of the others, and the fat on him is of a more respectable sort, like a squire's."

The shouts in the meantime were becoming more distinguishable. The seigniorial watermelon was calling resonantly and in a patter: "Pass it on, Denis, you loafer, pass it on to Kozma! Kozma, grab that end from Denis! Thoma the Greater, you push right where Thoma the Lesser is pushing! Hold on, you devils, you'll tear the net! Get at it from the right, get at it from the right! Hold on, hold on, may the Devil take both of you! Now you've gone and tangled me up in the dragnet! You've caught me, I'm telling you, damn you—you've caught me right by the belly button!"

The men dragging at the right end stopped, seeing that an untoward occurrence had really taken place; their master was, believe it or not, all tangled up in the net.

"Look," said Seliphan to Petrushka, "they've started pulling in their master like he were a fish!"

The seignior kept floundering and, wishing to extricate himself, turned over with his belly up, thus becoming still more entangled in the net. Apprehensive of tearing the net, he swam along with the captive fish, having given orders for a rope to be tied around him. This having been done, one end of the rope was thrown up on shore. A score or so of fishermen standing there seized the rope's end and began cautiously hauling it in. Having made his way to a shoal, the master scrambled up on his feet, the meshes of the net covering all his body much as an openwork summer glove might cover a dainty feminine hand; looking up, he caught sight of the barouche, now beginning to cross the dam, and nodded his head to the occupant. Chichikov doffed his cap and respectfully bowed in response.

"Have you dined?" the master set up a shout, walking up on the shore, dragging the caught fish with him, shading his eyes from the sun with one hand while the other he held in the lower regions, in the manner of the Venus de' Medici emerging from the bath.

"No," said Chichikov, raising his cap still higher and continuing to bow as he stood up in the barouche.

"Well, in that case you ought to render thanks to God!"

"But why?" Chichikov evinced his curiosity, still keeping his cap poised over his head.

"Well, because of this!" said the master, who was now well up on the shore, in the midst of sundry carps and crucians that were threshing about his feet and leaping a yard from the ground. "All this is nothing, don't bother looking at it, but here's something for you to look at! Thoma the Lesser, drop that net and lift that sturgeon out of the tub. Kozma, you loafer, go and give him a hand."

Two husky muzhiks drew some sort of monster out of a tub.

"What do you think of that princeling? He must have strayed in from the river."

"Why, that's a prince and not a princeling!" said Chichikov.

"That's right, too. You drive on up to the house, now, and I'll follow you. Coachman, you take the lower road, through the truck garden, brother! Thoma the Greater, you muttonhead, run and take down the bars! He'll show you the way. I'm as good as there now; I'll be there before you can turn around."

"The colonel's rather odd," Chichikov reflected, having at last crossed the interminable dam and now approaching the huts, of which some, like a flock of ducks, were scattered on the slope of an elevation, while others were standing below on piles, like so many cranes. Nets, seines, dragnets, fykes were hung up to dry everywhere, for all the muzhiks were fishermen. Thoma the Greater, big, barefooted, ran just as he was, with only his shirt on, ahead of the carriage and took down the bars in front of one of the truck gardens; the barouche drove through several of these and at last came out on a square before an old, old wooden church. Beyond the church, some distance off, one saw the manorial buildings.

"Well, here I am!" a voice sounded off to one side.

Chichikov looked around and saw that the lord of the manor was already driving near him in a droshky, clothed in a grass-green nankeen frock coat and yellow trousers but with his neck innocent of any cravat, looking something like a cupid! He sat sideways, taking up the whole droshky. Chichikov was about to say something to him but the fat man had already vanished. The droshky reappeared on the other side, at a place where the fish were being handled, and all Chichikov could catch was: "You carry the pike and seven crucians to that muttonhead of a chef; as for that sturgeon, you let me have it here, I'll bring it myself on the droshky." Then, again, came the shouts: "Thoma the Greater and Thoma the Lesser! Kozma and Denis!" But when Chichikov drove up to the front steps of the house, to his utter amazement the stout lord of the manor was already standing on the top step, and took him into his embraces. How he had managed to fly thither was utterly incomprehensible. They kissed each other thrice, now on one cheek, now on the other, after the old Russian custom: this seignior belonged to the old school.

"I have brought you regards from His Excellency."

"From what excellency?"

"From your kinsman, Alexander Dmitrievich, the General."

"Who is this Alexander Dmitrievich?"

"General Betrishchev," answered Chichikov, not without a certain perplexity.

"Don't know him, Sir; I'm not acquainted with him."

Chichikov's perplexity increased. "But how is that? I hope, at least, that I have the pleasure of addressing Colonel Koshkarev?"

"No, you needn't hope that; you've come not to him but to me. I am Petr Petrovich Petuh—Petuh, Petr Petrovich!" the host quickly corrected him.

Chichikov was stunned. "There's a comeuppance! How did you ever manage to do it, you fools?" he said, turning to Seliphan and Petrushka, the former up on the box, the latter standing near the carriage door, both of them with their mouths gaping and their eyes goggling. "How did you ever manage it, you fools? Why, you were told: 'Drive to Colonel Koshkarev!' But this is Petr Petrovich Petuh—"

"The lads did right well!" declared Petr Petrovich. "For that you'll get a noggin of vodka each and fish pie to go with it. Unharness the horses and be off with you this very minute to the servants' quarters!"

"I am conscience-stricken," Chichikov was saying, bowing and scraping, "such a surprising mistake—"

"Not a mistake," Petr Petrovich quickly interposed, "not a mistake at all! You first try what the dinner is like, and then you'll ask whether you've made a mistake. I beg of you to come in," said he, taking Chichikov by the arm and leading him into the inner chambers. Chichikov, observing the proprieties, was passing through the door sideways, so as to give his host a chance to pass through together with him, but all his efforts went for nothing; first of all, the host could never have passed through any door together with any other man and, in the second place, he was no longer there. All one could hear was his diatribes out in the yard: "Well, where is that Thoma the Greater? How is it he's still not here? Emelian, you loafer, run over to that muttonhead of a chef and tell him to clean that sturgeon as quick as ever he can. Tell him to use the bream for a stew, and to serve

the crucians with sauce. Oh, yes—the crayfish, the crayfish!
Thoma the Lesser, you loafer, where are those crayfish?
The crayfish, I say, the crayfish?"

And for a long while thereafter all one could hear was
"Crayfish, crayfish."

"Well, my host is certainly going to a lot of bother,"
mused Chichikov, taking an easy chair and looking over the
walls and at every corner of the room.

"Well, here I am," said the host, entering and leading in
two young men in light summer frock coats; they were as
slender as willow wands, but they had shot up almost a
whole yard taller than Petr Petrovich.

"My sons, home from school for the holidays.
Nicholasha, you stay with the guest, while you, Alexasha,
will come with me."

And, anew, Petr Petrovich vanished.

Chichikov turned his attention to Nicholasha.
Nicholasha was talkative. He told the guest that the instructors in his school weren't so good, that for the most
part they favored those pupils whose mammas sent the instructors presents of the more expensive kind; that the In-
germandland Regiment of Hussars was stationed in the
town where the school was; that Captain Vetvitsky had a
better horse than the colonel himself, although Lieutenant
Vzyemtzev could ride a horse far better than the second
captain.

"I say, though, what condition is your father's estate in?"
asked Chichikov.

"Mortgaged," said the father himself in answer to this,
bobbing up in the drawing room again, "mortgaged!"

Chichikov felt like pursing his lips into the sort of expression which a man makes when he sees the little ivory ball spinning, spinning toward zero and finally landing there. "Things are bad!" he thought. "At that rate there soon won't be a single unmortgaged estate left. I ought to hurry."

"But why did you mortgage it?" he asked, with an air of commiseration.

"Why, just so. Everybody's doing it, so why be behind the others? They even say it pays. Besides that, I've been living here all the time, so I might as well have a fling at living a while in Moscow. There, my sons, too, are persuading me—they are after that enlightenment which a capital can give."

"What a fool! What a fool!" Chichikov was thinking. "He'll squander everything and will make his sons squanderers as well. That's a tidy little estate they have. Looks as if it were fine here, both for the muzhiks and for them. But when these three will become enlightened in the capital's restaurants and theatres, everything will go to the Devil. He ought to stay home, the bumpkin, in his own village."

"Well, now, I know what you're thinking," said Petuh.

"What?" asked Chichikov, ill at ease.

"You're thinking: 'What a fool, what a fool this Petuh is! He invited me to dinner, but the dinner still isn't here.' It'll be ready, my esteemed friend. It'll arrive before a shorn wench has time to plait her braids."

"Father, Platon Michalych is riding this way!" said Alexasha, looking out of the window.

"Where, where?" cried out Petuh, going to the window.

"On a sorrel horse!" Nicholasha chimed in, bending over to look out of the window. "Do you think our gray is any worse than that, Alexasha?"

"No, I wouldn't say he's worse, but he doesn't pace like that."

A dispute over the sorrel and the gray sprang up between them.

"Who is this Platon Michalych?" Chichikov asked Alexasha.

"Platon Michalych Platonov, a neighbor of ours, a splendid man, an exceptional man," Petuh himself answered.

In the meantime an Adonis entered the room, tall and well built, with light-ruddy hair, glossy and curling, and dark eyes. A hound with powerful prominent jaws, of such ferocious appearance that one felt frightened just looking at him, answering to the name of Yarb, with his copper collar rattling, came in at the visitor's heels.

"Have you dined?" asked Petr Petrovich Petuh.

"I have," said the guest.

"Well, now, have you come to make fun of me, or what?" asked Petuh, becoming angry. "What good are you to me if you've already dined?"

"However, Petr Petrovich," said the guest, with a slight smile, "I can console you with this—I didn't eat a thing at dinner: I have absolutely no appetite."

"But what a catch we had today—if you could only have seen it! What a monstrous sturgeon deigned to pay us a visit! As for the carps and crucians, we didn't even bother counting them, huge as they were."

"Why, one actually feels envious listening to you," said the guest. "Teach me to be as lighthearted as yourself."

"But why should anyone feel bored? Good heavens!" said the host.

"How can you ask why anyone should feel bored? Because everything is a bore."

"You eat all too little, and that's all there is to it. You just try dining rather well. Why, it's only of late that people have invented boredom. In former times no one felt bored."

"Come, that's enough bragging! Do you mean to say you have never felt bored?"

"Never! And besides, I don't even know what it is to feel bored; there's no time for boredom. You wake up in the morning—well, you have to drink tea, and then the steward is right there, and then it's time to go fishing, and then there's dinner. After dinner you hardly have time to put in forty winks when there's the chef, and you have to order supper. And after supper there's the chef again—one has to order the dinner for tomorrow. When, then, can one find time to feel bored?"

While this conversation was going on, Chichikov had been looking the guest over.

Platon Michalych was Achilles and Paris rolled into one: a graceful build, a painter's ideal in height, fresh vigor—he combined all these. A pleasant, slight smile, with a faint tinge of irony, somehow seemed to intensify his good looks. But, despite all this, there was something inanimate and somnolent about him. Passions, sorrows, and shocks had not engraved any wrinkles upon his untouched, fresh face, yet at the same time had failed to animate it.

"I, too," Chichikov declared, "I confess, cannot understand—if you will permit me to remark—I cannot understand how with such an appearance as yours one can feel bored. Of course, there may be other reasons: lack of money; persecutions by persons of evil intent, among whom one will find such as are ready even to attempt your life."

"That's just it, that there is nothing of the sort," said Platonov.

"Would you believe it, there are times I actually would like something like that to happen, to have something to alarm and agitate me—well, now, to have someone simply anger me? But nothing happens. I feel bored—and that's all."

"Strange, I can't understand it. But perhaps your estate does not bring in much, you have but few souls?"

"Not in the least. My brother and I have twenty-seven thousand acres, and a thousand peasants with it."

"And one can feel bored owning all that? It's beyond comprehension! But perhaps your property is not in good order? You have had poor crops, epidemics? You have had many of your male serfs dying off?"

"On the contrary, everything is in the best possible order, and my brother is a most excellent manager."

"I can't understand it!" said Chichikov, with a shrug.

"Well, we'll banish your boredom right away," said the host. "Dash over to the kitchen, Alexasha, and tell the chef to hurry up and send us some small pies as fast as he can. But where is that loafer Emelian and that thief Antoshka? Why don't they serve the cold snacks?"

But at this point the door opened. Emelian the loafer and Antoshka the thief came in with the napery, set the table and placed thereon a tray with six decanters of liqueurs of various colors. Shortly the tray and decanters were encircled with a necklace of plates: various caviars, cheeses, salted mushrooms (big and little, brown and golden brown), and then something new was brought from the kitchen in covered plates, and one could hear butter spluttering therein. Emelian the loafer and Antoshka the thief were good and spry serfs; the master was a kindly soul and had given them their bad names only because without epithets things sounded flat, somehow, whereas no Russian is fond of flat things, and simply can't do without a spicy word—it is as necessary as a little wine for your stomach's sake. However, Petuh's people themselves did not resent these nicknames.

The appetizers were followed by dinner. Here the host proved to be as utterly heartless as a cutthroat. No sooner did he notice that there was but one piece of something on anybody's plate than he would immediately add another, saying: "It is not good for either man or beast to live alone in this world." When the guest ate up both pieces, Petuh would underhandedly dump a third piece onto the plate, adding: "What sort of a number is two? All good things go by threes." The guest ate up the three pieces, whereupon Petuh would say to him: "Who ever heard of a cart on three wheels? And who would ever built a hut with only three corners?" In adding a fourth piece he had another proverb; and, for a fifth, still another.

Chichikov had eaten almost twelve slices of something and was thinking: "There, now my host won't pick out an extra helping, with a saying to match!" But he had another guess coming; the host, without a word, placed on his plate a whole saddle of veal, roasted on a spit, together with the kidneys—and what veal it was!

"For two years did I bring up that calf on milk," said the host. "Tended him as if he were a son of mine!"

"I couldn't eat another bite!" Chichikov protested.

"But you just try it, then say *I can't!*"

"I'm not up to it—there's no room."

"Why, there was no room in church, either, but the Chief of Police came there and room was found, and yet the crush had been such that there wasn't room to sneeze. You just try that morsel—it's the Chief of Police."

Chichikov tried; the morsel really turned out to be something like a Chief of Police: room was found for it, and yet it had seemed that there was no possibility of wedging it in.

"There, how is a fellow like that to get along in St. Petersburg or Moscow?" reflected Chichikov. "With his hospitable nature he'll lose his shirt there in two or three years!" Evidently Chichikov was not aware to what a pitch of perfection things have been brought by now—even without a hospitable nature one can let everything go down the drain not in three years but in three months.

The same thing happened with the wines. Having got his money for the mortgage, Petr Petrovich had laid in a stock of provender for ten years ahead. He did nothing but everlastingly keep adding to the glasses and then adding some more; but if anything was left unfinished by the guests, he gave the bottle to Alexasha and Nicholasha to finish, who put away glass after glass; one could tell at once to what branch of human knowledge they would turn their attention upon coming to the capital. Yet when they got up from the table it was as if they hadn't drunk a thing outside of a glass of water each, possibly. One couldn't say the same of the guests; they barely managed to fit into their arm-chairs. The host, the moment he had sat down in his own easy chair, which was big enough to seat four ordinary men, fell fast asleep. His corpulent substance turned into a blacksmith's bellows and his nostrils began to emit such sounds as are not to be found even in the new music. There was a complete philharmonic orchestra here—a drum, and a flute, and some sort of jerky sound, for all the world like a dog's yelp.

"Listen to him tootling!" said Platonov. Chichikov broke into laughter.

"Of course," Platonov went on, "if you dine like that, how can boredom ever come upon you! Slumber will come instead."

"Yes," Chichikov agreed lazily. His small eyes had become even smaller than usual. "Just the same, and you must really pardon me, but I can't understand how one can be bored. There are so many remedies against boredom."

"But just what are they?"

"Why, is there any scarcity of them for a young man? One can dance, or play on some instrument—or even get married."

"Marry whom? Tell me!"

"Why, do you mean to say there are no pretty and rich young ladies in the regions hereabouts?"

"Well, there aren't."

"In that case one can look for them in other places, one can travel about a bit." Here a magnificent idea flashed through Chichikov's head; his eyes widened. "Why, there's a fine remedy right there!" said he, looking straight into Platonov's eyes.

"What remedy?"

"Travel."

"Where is one to go, then?"

"Well, if you are free, you might come along with me," said Chichikov, and thought to himself, as he gazed at Platonov: "Why, that would be a good thing; then we can go halves on the expenses, while any repairs to the carriage could be footed entirely by him."

"And where are you traveling to?"

"There, how should I put it to you? For the time being I am traveling not so much for my own needs as for those of somebody else. General Betrishchev, my close friend and, I may say, my benefactor, asked me to call on his relatives. Of course, those relatives are one thing, but partly, so to say, I am traveling on my own, inasmuch as seeing the world, its constantly circling parade of people, is, no matter what anyone may say, like reading a living book, like going to school anew."

Platonov became thoughtful.

Chichikov, in the meantime, was weighing considerations of his own: "Really, now, it would be a good thing! One could even manage matters in such a way that he would foot *all* the expenses, and we could set out with his horses, while mine would be stabled and fed at his village, and we could use his carriage as well."

"Well, now, why not take a trip?" Platonov was thinking at the same time. "Like as not things will prove more amusing. There's nothing for me to do at home, anyway; the management is in my brother's hands even as it is, therefore there can be no detriment to it. Really, then, why not take a trip?"—"But would you agree," he asked, "to stay for a couple of days at my brother's? Unless we do, he won't let me go."

"With great pleasure—even three days."

"Well, in that case let's shake hands on it! We're going!" said Platonov, becoming animated.

"Bravo!" said Chichikov, and their palms smote each other as they clasped hands.

"Where are you off to? Where are you off to?" asked the host, waking up and staring at them with goggling eyes. "No, gentlemen; I've ordered the wheels taken off the carriage, and as for your stallion, Platon Michalych, he's ten miles away from here by now. No, tonight you stay over, and tomorrow, after lunch, you can be off on your way."

What could one do with Petuh? Platonov did not say anything, knowing that Petuh was stubborn in his ways. They had to stay.

But then they were rewarded by a wonderful spring evening. Their host arranged an excursion on the river. Twelve rowers, their four-and-twenty oars keeping time as one to their songs, made the boat fly over the unruffled surface of the mirrorous lake. From the lake they passed to the river, a boundless river, both its banks gently sloping. Not so much as a ripple stirred on the water! View after view unrolled before them, and copse after copse appeared, gladdening their eyes. They had tea on the cutter, passing every minute under ropes set with snelled hooks. Before the tea . . . . . . [their host] had found time to strip and dive into the river, where he floundered about and raised a rumpus for half an hour or so with the fishermen, upbraiding Thomas the Greater and Kozma, and, having had his fill of upbraiding, of fussing and of the chill water, bobbed up once more on the cutter with a wolfish appetite and drank his tea in such a way that one could but envy him. In the meantime the sun had set; all that was left was the clear light of the sky. Shouts came back in ringing echoes. In place of the fishers swimming urchins appeared everywhere near the banks, their splashing and their laughter echoing afar. The rowers after each stroke lifted their four-and-twenty oars on end as one, and the cutter yearned forward like a bird, of itself, over the unruffled, mirrorous surface. A stalwart, broad-shouldered, vigorous lad, the third from the rudder, would lead off with a song, resonantly, in a voice as pure as a nightingale's; five of the others chimed in with him, the remaining six swelled the chorus, and a song as boundless as Russia itself soared far and wide. And the singers, each with a hand cupped over his ear, seemed to be lost themselves in the boundlessness of that song. Petuh perked up, grunting and helping out where he thought the chorus was failing; one felt free at heart, and even Chichikov felt a surge of pride at being a Russian. Platonov alone was musing: "Well, now, what's so fine about this dismal song? One feels a still greater tedium coming over one's soul because of that song."

When they were returning it was already dusk. The oars in the darkness cleaved waters that no longer reflected the sky. One could barely see the little lights along the banks. The moon was rising as they beached their boat. Everywhere, in pots slung on tripods, the fishers were cooking fish chowder, of ruff and of other, still quivering, fish. All others save the fishers had already gone home. The geese, cows, and goats had already been driven to their sheds, and the very dust of their passing had long since settled and the herdsmen who had driven them were standing near the gate, awaiting a jugful of milk and an invitation to partake of fish chowder. Here and there one could hear subdued hubbub from the house-serfs' quarters, the yapping of dogs echoing somewhere in the distance, coming from villages belonging to others; the moon was rising and the dusk was suffused with its light, and at last everything became silvered therewith—the lake, the huts, the smoke coming out of their chimneys; the fishermen's fires paled.

Nicholasha and Alexasha dashed past the party on two fiery stallions, racing each other; the dust they raised in their passing was like that of a flock of rams. "Eh, really, I'm going to get me a hamlet of my own some day!" mused Chichikov. He envisioned anew the little woman and the little Chick-chickovs. Where could one find a man whose soul would not be aglow on such an evening?

And at supper they once more overate. When Pavel Ivanovich went into the bedroom assigned to him and, as he was getting into bed, patted his tummy, "A drum!" said he. "No room for any Chief of Police in there!" But, as is the way of things in this world, the combination of circumstances was such that the host's study was divided off only by a wall, that wall was thin, and one could hear every word that was being said on the other side. The host was ordering from the chef, by way of an early breakfast, a downright banquet—and how he was ordering! It was enough to make a dead man's mouth water. And as the host gave his orders he kept emphasizing them with sucking sounds and by smacking his lips. All one could hear was: "And brown it well, and baste it, and let it stew through and through!" And the chef kept chiming in with the highest of falsettos:

"Right, Sir! It can be done, Sir! We can do it that way, too, Sir!"

"And make the fish pie four-cornered. In one corner I want you to put in the sturgeon cheeks and the spine, the others you can fill with buckwheat groats, and small mushrooms with scallions, and also some sweet soft roe, and marrow, and you know yourself what else."

"Right, Sir! It can be done that way, too."

"And let it be nice and browned on one side—you understand?—but with the other side you can go easy. And the bottom, now—the bottom, you understand?—bake it so that the crust gets soaked through and through with the juices, you know, and so that it won't exactly crumble in the mouth, but rather, you understand, sort of melt away like snow!"

"May the Devil take him!" thought Chichikov, tossing. "He simply won't let a body sleep!"

"And I want you to make me a sow's belly stuffed with minced meat. Place a chunk of ice in it overnight, so's the belly will swell up good and proper. And when you serve the sturgeon, now, mind you don't overlook all the trimmings that go with it—the garniture, now, the garniture! Let it be really rich! You lay out crayfish all around it, and small fried fish, and trim the whole top of it with minced smelts, and add all sorts of finely chopped stuff—horseradish, and small brown mushrooms, and turnips, and carrots, and beans—and haven't you got some more herbs and roots around, of one kind or another?"

"One could dress it up with a large turnip or a sugar beet, cut into little stars," volunteered the chef.

"Dress it up with a turnip *and* a sugar beet. And here's how you will trim the roast—"

"My sleep is gone for good and all!" said Chichikov, turning over on the other side, burying his head in the pillow and pulling the blanket over himself. But even through the blanket he could hear incessantly: "And brown it well, and baste it right, and let it stew through and through!" Chichikov fell asleep only when they were discussing some tom turkey or other.

The following day the guests overate so that Platonov could no longer ride on horseback, and his stallion had to be sent on ahead with one of Petuh's grooms. Chichikov and Platonov seated themselves in the carriage. The big-jowled dog trotted lazily after the carriage; he, too, had overeaten.

"No, this is too much!" said Chichikov when they had driven out of the courtyard. "This is downright vile! Don't you feel uncomfortable, Platon Michalych? This barouche was as comfortable as could be, and now it has suddenly become uncomfortable. Petrushka, you haven't been shifting everything around by any chance, out of pure foolishness? There are all sorts of boxes sticking up everywhere!"

Platonov smiled slightly. "I can explain it to you," said he. "Petr Petrovich has shoved in all those things so you won't starve on the way."

"That's right," said Petrushka, turning around on the box. "We was told to put all them things in the barouche—pasties, and pies, and things like that."

"That's right, Pavel Ivanovich," said Seliphan, turning around on the box in his turn, with a merry face. "A gentleman one can look up to, the treatingest squire there is! He sent out a glass of champagne to each of us, and ordered dishes from his own table to be given to us—very good dishes, too, of a right delicate taste. There never was a gentleman one could look up to more."

"You see? He has satisfied everybody," commented Platonov. "However, tell me frankly, have you got time to turn in at a village about seven miles from here? I would like to say good-by to my sister and my brother-in-law."

"With great pleasure," said Chichikov.

"You won't lose anything by it; my brother-in-law is a remarkable man."

"In what way?" asked Chichikov.

"He is the greatest man at managing an estate that ever was in all Russia. In a little over ten years, having bought a run-down estate that barely yielded twenty thousand, he has improved it so that it now yields two hundred thousand a year."

"Ah, an estimable man! There's a man whose life ought to be set up as an example for all men. It will be a great, great pleasure to make his acquaintance. And what is his name?"

"Skudronzhoglo."

"And his first name and patronymic?"

"Constantin Fedorovich."

"Constantin Fedorovich Skudronzhoglo. . . . It will be a very great pleasure to make his acquaintance. It will be instructive to know such a man." And Chichikov launched into a series of questions concerning Skudronzhoglo, and everything that he learned about him from Platonov was truly amazing.

Platonov took it upon himself at this point to direct Seliphan, which was quite called for inasmuch as the coachman was barely able to keep himself upright on the box. As for Petrushka, he had twice gone flying from his high perch, so that at last he had to be tied there with a rope. "What an animal!" was the only thing Chichikov could say, but he said it repeatedly.

"There, look, his lands begin right there," Platonov was saying, pointing out some fields. "You will see the difference between them and the others right away. Coachman, take the road to the left here. Do you see that young forest there? It was planted. With another man it would not have come up in fifty years the way it came up with him in eight. Look, the forest has ended now, and the grainfields are beginning; and after a hundred and thirty-five acres will come another forest, also planted, and so on. Look at the grain, see how much thicker it grows than that of any of the others."

"I see. But how does he do it?"

"Well, you ask him, and you will see. He knows everything, you won't find another who knows as much. It isn't enough that he knows what soil each grain favors, he also knows what different grains should or should not be planted in adjoining fields, and what trees should be near each kind of grain. All the lands around his may crack from the drought, but not his; everybody around him may have poor crops, but not he. He calculates how much moisture he needs, and plants the trees accordingly; with him nothing goes to waste or is unused, everything plays not only a double but a triple rôle; the forest is all right in its own way, but the fields are improved by the dead leaves and the shade. And he does everything like that. It's a pity I know so little about such things, can't tell about them very well, but he knows such things! They call him a wizard. He knows such a great, great deal! And yet it's all such a bore—"

"An amazing fellow, really!" said Chichikov, and kept looking at the fields with curiosity.

Everything was in exceptional order. The forests were fenced in; the cattle pens they came across were also built not without forethought and maintained in an enviable condition; the stacks of grain were of a colossal height. Everything was plentiful, one felt the presence of full-eared grain everywhere. One could see right off that an acre of a husbandman lived here. Having gone up a slight rise......[they saw] opposite them a large village that had spread over three hillsides, like a very town. Everything had a well-to-do appearance here: well-beaten and well-laid-out ways, well-built huts; if there was a cart standing anywhere that cart was well-built and had a brand-new look; if one came across a horse, that horse was well-fed and good-tempered; the horned cattle seemed to be choice animals; the muzhiks one met had an exceptionally intelligent air, and even the muzhik's pig looked like a nobleman! One could plainly see that here lived those very muzhiks celebrated in song, who handle their silver with a shovel. There were no English parks here, no arbors and bridges with all sorts of fandangles, nor any special views before the manor house; from the huts to the owner's house stretched an old-fashioned succession of granaries and workshops. There was a turret with a large lantern atop the master's house—not for the sake of any views or appearances, however, but to see where everything was, what work was being carried on, and where it was carried on, and how, even though a field might be far off.

They drove up to the house. At the front entrance they were met by smart servants who did not at all look like that drunkard Petrushka and who wore Cossack coats of blue homespun instead of frock coats.

The mistress of the house herself ran out on the front steps. She was as fresh as strawberries and milk, as beautiful as God's daylight; she and Platonov were as like as two peas in a pod, with the sole difference that she was not languid as he was but talkative and merry.

"Greetings, brother! I'm so glad you came. But Constantin isn't home; he ought to be home soon, though."

"But where is he?"

"He has business down in the village with some commission merchants," she said, leading her guests into the house.

It was not the hostess, however, who drew Chichikov's attention. He was interested in beholding and studying the dwelling place of such an unusual person, who had an income of two hundred thousand a year. He looked over everything in the room, thinking he might find traces of the master's own nature, even as a savant may judge by a shell what sort of oyster or snail had been housed therein; but any such trace was the one thing lacking. The rooms were utterly without character, simple and spacious, and that was all. There were no frescoes, no pictures on the walls, no bronzes on the tables, no whatnots with pieces of porcelain and cups, no vases, no flowers, no statuettes, not even books; in short, everything was bare, somehow. Simple, or-

dinary furniture, and a grand piano standing off to one
side, and even that was covered: evidently the mistress of
the house sat down at it but rarely. The [door] of the drawing room [opened on the master's study]; but there, too,
everything was just as bare—simple and bare. It was evident that the master came home only to rest and not to live
in it; that his life was not at all passed within four walls but
out in the field; that for thinking over his plans he needed
no study, no armchairs with springs and sundry conve-
niences and comforts, and that his life consisted not of enchanting sybarite reveries before a flaming fireplace but lay
in his very work: the thought sprang directly from circumstances as they arose and was at once put into execution,
and had no need of being written down.

The only traces Chichikov was able to note in the room
were those of housewifery; upon the tables and chairs were
placed fresh boards of linden wood with petals of various
flowers drying on them.

"What sort of rubbish have you got all over the place,
sister?" asked Platonov.

"What do you mean by calling it rubbish! Those petals
are the best remedy against the ague. We cured all the
muzhiks with it last ...... [year]. And these are for cordials,
while those others are for jams. All you men laugh at the
idea of jams and pickles but, later on, when it comes to eating them, you're the first to praise them."

Platonov wandered over to the piano and began looking
over the sheet music.

"Lord, what ancient stuff!" he said. "Really, aren't you
ashamed of yourself, sister?"

"Well, now, brother, you must really excuse me, but

music above all is one thing I have no time for. I have an eight-year-old daughter whom I must educate. To place her in the hands of some foreign governess just so that I may have leisure for music—no, you must excuse me, brother, but that's something I'm not going to do!"

"But really, how boring you've become, sister!" said her brother and went over to a window. "Ah, there he is! He's coming, he's coming!" he exclaimed. Chichikov was already hastening eagerly to a window. A man of forty was approaching the front entrance, very much alive, of swarthy appearance. He had on a camel-hair surtout and a knitted cap. Evidently he did not waste much thought on dress. There were two people of inferior station walking with him, one on either side, with their caps doffed, talking with him as they walked, busily discussing something. One, apparently, was an ordinary muzhik; the other, in a blue Siberian greatcoat, was some traveling *kulak* and a cunning old fox. They all stopped at the front entrance, and their conversation could be heard in the drawing room.

"Give 'em your orders to take the stuff, then, father o' mine!" the muzhik was saying, with a low obeisance.

"Oh, no, brother, I've already told you over and over, a score of times, don't cart over any more of the stuff! I've so much building material piled up that there's no more place to put it."

"Well, now, Constantin Fedorovich, my father, you'll put all of it to use. Such another clever man as yourself ain't to be found in all the world. Your Honor will put every single thing in its right place. So please give 'em orders to take the stuff."

"Hands are what I need, brother; you supply me with workmen, and not material."

"Well, when it comes to workmen you won't have any lack of 'em. There's whole villages that will go to work—there's such a dearth of bread as we can't even recall ever happening before. It's a pity, now, that you don't want to take us muzhiks over altogether, for we'd serve you faithfully, as God is my witness. One can learn all wisdom from you, Constantin Fedorovich! . . . So please give 'em orders to receive the stuff, for the last time."

"Why you said 'for the last time' even the last time you were here, and yet you've brought the stuff once more."

"This really is the last time, Constantin Fedorovich. If you don't take it off me, nobody will. So give 'em orders to accept the stuff, father o' mine."

"Well, listen, now, I'll accept it this time, and even then only because I feel sorry about you carting the stuff for nothing. But if you bring anything another time, I won't take it, though you were to run whining after me for three weeks."

"Right you are, Constantin Fedorovich; you may feel easy I won't cart anything over again. Thank you most humbly!" The muzhik went off, gratified. He was lying, however; he would come carting the stuff over again—*Take a chance!* is a grand old adage.

"So then, Constantin Fedorovich, do me that favor, now, come down on the price," the visiting *kulak* in the blue greatcoat was saying.

"Why, I told you what the price was from the very beginning. I'm not fond of dickering. I'm telling you once more, I'm not one of those landowners to whom you'll drive up just when he's due to pay the interest on his mortgage at the government bank. For I know all you fellows. You have lists of all those who have to pay interest, with the dates when they have to pay it. What's so very clever about that? He's hard pressed, and so he'll sell to you at half-price. But what's your money to me? I can afford to have something lying around for three years; I don't have to be paying interest on mortgages."

"It's the downright truth, what you're saying, Constantin Fedorovich. But then I'm doing this . . . only so's to have connections with you in the future as well, and not out of any greediness. Here's three thousand by way of a little deposit, if you'll be pleased to take it." The *kulak* took out of the bosom of his coat a packet of greasy government notes. Skudronzhoglo took it imperturbably and, without as much as counting the notes, thrust the money into a back pocket of his surtout.

"Hm!" thought Chichikov. "Just as if it were a handkerchief!"

A minute later Skudronzhoglo appeared in the doorway of the drawing room.

"*Ba*, brother, you here!" he said, seeing Platonov. They embraced and kissed each other. Platonov introduced Chichikov, who reverently approached the master of the house and kissed his cheek, and came away with an impression that the other had kissed him in return.

Skudronzhoglo had a most striking face. One could perceive his Southern extraction. His hair was dark and thick, prematurely gray in spots and coarse; his eyes were eloquent, sparkling a great deal. Intelligence shone in every expression of his face, and there was decidedly nothing somnolent about him. But there was perceptible, however, an admixture of something jaundiced and embittered about him. He was not entirely of Russian extraction; there are in Russia many Russians who are not of purely Russian extraction, yet who, at soul, are Russians just the same. Skudronzhoglo himself did not bother much about what country his ancestors had come from or about his family tree, believing that such things were unimportant and that they decidedly did not matter so far as his work was concerned. He considered himself a Russian and, besides, did not know any other language save Russian.

"Do you know, Constantin, what I have thought of?" asked Platonov.

"No—what?"

"I've thought of taking a trip through various provinces; maybe that will cure me of my depression."

"Well, why not? It very probably may."

"And Pavel Ivanovich has suggested that I go with him."

"Splendid! What places," asked Skudronzhoglo, turning amiably to Chichikov, "do you propose to visit now?"

"I must confess," said Chichikov, inclining his head to one side and holding on to an arm of his chair, "that for the time being I am traveling not so much on my own account as for somebody else. General Betrishchev, my close friend and, one may say, my benefactor, has asked me to call on his relatives. Those relatives, of course, are one thing, but partly, so to say, I am traveling on my own, inasmuch as, to say nothing of the possible benefit to be derived from travel from the hemorrhoidal aspect alone, the mere fact that one is seeing the world, its constantly revolving parade of people, is surely, no matter what anyone may say, like reading a living book and as good as an education."

"Yes, it does no harm to look in on other nooks than one's own."

"The remark you were pleased to make is an excellent one," Chichikov concurred. "That is precisely, verily, and actually so—it does no harm. You see things you would otherwise never have seen, you meet people you would otherwise never have met. Sometimes a conversation with some man may turn out to be as good as a gold piece in your pocket, as for instance right now, when I am presented with such an opportunity as this. I appeal to you, most estimable Constantin Fedorovich, teach me, teach me; quench my thirst by making me understand the truth! I await your delectable words like manna—"

Skundronzhoglo became embarrassed. "Teach you what, however? Teach you what? For I myself acquired my education for coppers."

"Wisdom, most estimable Sir, wisdom! The wisdom to manage an estate the way you do; to be able to derive from that estate, the way you do, actual revenues and not visionary ones; to acquire, the way you did, an actual property and not an imaginary one and, having fulfilled the duties of a citizen in doing so, to earn the respect of one's fellow countrymen."

"Do you know what?" asked Skudronzhoglo. "You stay over with me for a day or so. I shall show you my whole system and will tell you about everything. There isn't any wisdom at all about it, as you'll see."

"Stay, by all means," said the hostess; then, turning to

Platonov, she added: "Do stay, brother. Where must you hurry?"

"It's all one to me," the other answered apathetically. "Whatever Pavel Ivanovich wishes."

"For my part I would stay and that with great pleasure. But here's a circumstance—it is necessary to call on a relative of General Betrishchev, a certain Colonel Koshkarev—"

"But then—do you know it?—he is a fool and touched in the head."

"I've already heard about that. I, personally, have no business with him. But since General Betrishchev, my close friend and, so to say, my benefactor ... well, really, it would be somewhat awkward to neglect the call."

"In that case, do you know what?" suggested [Skudronzhoglo]. "You go to him right now. My light droshky is all ready. It isn't seven miles to his place, so you can make it in one spurt. Why, you'll actually be back before supper."

"A splendid idea!" Chichikov accepted the proposal with delight and picked up his hat.

The light droshky was brought around and he immediately set out to see the Colonel, who amazed Chichikov as he had never been amazed before. Everything at the Colonel's was out of the ordinary. The whole village was higgledy-piggledy; building and rebuilding was going on everywhere; heaps of quicklime, brick, and lumber lay all over the place. Buildings that had quite an official look about them had been put here and there. One bore a sign in gilt letters: *Depot of Agricultural Implements;* another, *Chief Rural Bureau of Audits;* a third, *Committee on Rural Affairs;* a fourth, *School of Normal Education*—in short, the Devil knows what you couldn't find there! Chichikov was wondering if he hadn't gotten into a provincial capital.

The most incomprehensible thing of all was that the Colonel himself did not at all look like a madman. Chichikov found him standing at a pulpit-like high desk, a quill between his teeth. The Colonel was a finicky person, somehow; his face was prim, shaped like a triangle. His side whiskers were combed out till every hair was in place; his hair and the very fashion in which it was combed, his nose, his lips, his chin, all created an impression of having been kept under a press up to that moment. He was most delicate by the looks of him, his manners and ways were delicate—altogether a most delicate and most considerate person.

He began speaking like a most businesslike individual. From the very start he took to complaining to Chichikov about the lack of culture in his neighbors, about the great labors that lay ahead of him. He received Chichikov with exceptional affability and cordiality and took him entirely into his confidence, telling him with evident self-delectation how many, many efforts it had cost him to bring his estate to its present state of prosperity, how hard it was to make the simple muzhik understand the very existence of those higher impulses which enlightened luxury and ingenuity endow man with, or to make him realize that there is such a thing as art; he told Chichikov how much he had had to contend with from the ignorance of the Russian peasant in order to put trousers of a German cut on him and to make him feel, if but to some extent, the higher dignity of man; that up to the very present he had been unable, despite all his exertions, to make the countrywives wear corsets, whereas in Germany, where he had been stationed with his regiment in 1814, even a miller's daughter was able to play the pianoforte, speak French and make curtsies. With perturbation he told him about the lack of culture in his neighbors; how little they thought of those subject to them, how they actually laughed whenever he tried to explain to them how indispensable it was for the management of an estate to establish an office of correspondence, as well as offices in general, to form commissions, and even committees, in order to guard against any theft, and to inventory everything; also, that the corresponding clerk, the manager and the bookkeeper ought not to be men educated at haphazard but should be made to complete all the courses at a university; that, despite all his persuasions, he had been unable to convince his fellow landowners as to the advantages that would accrue to their estates if every peasant were so well educated that, even as he guided the plow, he would be reading the *Georgics* of Virgil or a book on Franklin's lightning rods, or a treatise on the chemistry of soils.

But Chichikov, as he listened to all this, was thinking: "A fat chance of that time ever coming! Why, I learned how to read and write, yet I haven't finished reading the *Duchesse de la Vallière* to this very day—can't find the time, somehow!"

"Their ignorance is dreadful!" Colonel Koshkarev said in conclusion. "The prevalent darkness is like that of the Middle Ages, and there are no means available to help them—believe me, there aren't! And yet I could help everything; I know one means, the most positive means of all."

"What is it?"

"To dress every muzhik in Russia, every last one, in the kind of trousers the Germans wear. That, and nothing more than that, and I'll stake my head on it that everything will go like greased lightning; education will spread, trade will boom, a golden age will come to Russia."

Chichikov kept on listening and listening, looking at him intently, and finally decided: "Well, now, there's no use in standing on ceremony with this fellow." Without letting any grass grow under his feet he explained to the Colonel right then and there just what was what: he had need of such and such souls, for which purchase deeds of this and that kind would have to be executed, with due observance of all the necessary forms.

"As far as I can gather from your words," said the Colonel, not at all taken aback, "this is a request, isn't that so?"

"Precisely."

"In that case, submit it in writing. Your request will be sent to the Commission of General Applications and Communications. The Commission of General Applications and Communications, having made its notation thereon, will forward it to me. From me it will go to the Committee of Rural Affairs, there all the necessary inquiries and investigations concerning the matter will be made. The Director in Chief, together with the Secretary, will in their turn—"

Chichikov was dumbfounded. "Mercy!" he cried out. "Why, that way the matter will be dragged out for God knows how long!"

"Ah!" said the Colonel with a smile. "But that's just where the advantage of paper work comes in! True enough, the matter will be dragged out a little, but then nothing will be overlooked, every little detail will be apparent."

"But, if you will permit me, how can one treat of such a matter in writing? For this business is of such a nature . . . for the souls are, in a certain way . . . dead."

"Very good. You just write it that way: that the souls are, in a certain way, dead."

"But then, how can one, when they're dead? You can't write that down. Even though they are dead, yet it is necessary that they should appear alive."

"Good. You just write it that way: 'yet it is necessary' or, 'it is required,' or 'it is desired,' or 'it is sought, that they should appear alive.' One can't do these things without paper work. Take England, for example, or even Napoleon himself. I will assign a Commissioner to you, who will show you through all the various offices."

He struck a bell. Some fellow or other appeared.

"I say, Secretary! Call the Commissioner here!"

The Commissioner showed up—a cross between a muzhik and a clerk.

"Here, he will show you all the indispensable offices."

What could one do with the Colonel? Chichikov decided, out of sheer curiosity, to go with the Commissioner and see for himself what all these most indispensable commissions and committees were like, and what he found was not only amazing but surpassed all understanding. The Commission of General Applications and Communications existed only on a sign and the door was locked. Its chairman, one Hrulev, had been transferred to the newly formed Commission of Rural Constructions. His place had been taken by one Berezovsky, who had been formerly the

Colonel's valet, but he, too, had been commandeered—by the Commission of Rural Constructions, to head an investigation that was to decide a dispute between Timoshka, that drunkard of a steward, and the elder of the village, a swindler and a knave. They tried the Committee of Rural Affairs, but this they found to be in the process of reorganization; they woke up somebody who was sleeping off his liquor, but couldn't get anything out of him. There was never an official in sight.

"But whom does one turn to here? How can one make head or tail of anything here?" Chichikov asked his escort, the Commissioner, who was also a Vice-President in Charge of Special Missions.

"Why, you won't make head or tail of anything here," said the guide, "because everything amongst us is at sixes and sevens. The Commission of Rural Constructions, you will be pleased to note, directs everything among us, tears everybody away from their work, sends 'em wherever it feels like. The only advantageous place among us is on this same Commission of Rural Constructions." (He evidently had it in for the Commission of Rural Constructions.) "Things amongst us are so run that everybody leads the master around by his nose. He thinks that everything is just as it should be, but that's just taking the word for the deed."

Chichikov did not want to see anything more and, having come back to the Colonel, informed him that his place was a holy mess and that one couldn't make head or tail of anything and that the Commission of Rural Constructions was robbing away right and left, while the Commission of General Applications and Communications did not exist at all.

The Colonel boiled over with righteous indignation, squeezing Chichikov's hand hard as a mark of gratitude; seizing paper and quill he dashed off eight of the harshest inquiries right then and there: On what grounds had the Commission of Rural Constructions so high-handedly utilized the officials not under its jurisdiction? How could the Director in Chief permit a Chairman to embark on an investigation without having first surrendered his post? And how could the Committee of Rural Affairs regard with indifference the fact that the Commission of General Applications and Communications was not even in existence?

"There, now the fur will fly!" Chichikov reflected, and began bowing and scraping in farewell.

"No, I'm not going to let you go! In two hours, at the most, you shall be fully satisfied. My personal pride has been touched. I will prove to you what organized, regular management means. I will entrust your business to an exceptional person who is worth all the others put together—he has been through a university. That's the sort of people I own! So as not to lose precious time, I respectfully beg of you to wait a while in my library. You'll find everything you need there, everything—you are full master of the place. Culture should be available to everybody!"

Thus spake Koshkarev, opening a side door into the book sanctuary. This was an enormous hall, its walls lined with books from floor to ceiling. There were even a few stuffed animals. The books dealt with every possible subject—forestry, animal husbandry, swine breeding (*Swine Breeding Considered as a Science,* proclaimed one title), horticulture; there were manuals and pamphlets presenting the latest improvements and developments in everything from stud farming to the natural sciences; there seemed to be thousands of all sorts of specialized periodicals—the sort one can never get except by going to the trouble of subscribing for them, but which no one ever bothers to read. Perceiving that all these were hardly meant merely to pass the time pleasantly, Chichikov turned to another case. But he had jumped out of the frying pan into the fire: all the books here dealt with philosophy. A set of six enormous tomes in a row confronted his eyes, under the general title of *A Preliminary Induction into the Realm of Thought; the Theory of Universality, Correlation, and Essentiality, as Applied to the Conception of the Organic Origin of Society, and the Reciprocal Partition of Social Productivity.* No matter what book poor Chichikov opened, he found on every page *manifestation, development, abstract, subjectivity,* and *objectivity,* and the Devil alone knows what else.

"No, this isn't my meat at all," Chichikov decided and turned to a third case, where the books all had to do with the arts. From there he pulled out some sort of elephant folio with immodest mythological pictures, which he fell to examining. These proved exactly to his taste. Such pictures are liked by middle-aged bachelors, and at times even by those little dotards who have acquired an exquisite taste by titillating themselves with ballets and suchlike spicery. Well, what can one do? Man likes spicy herbs. Having finished looking this book over, Chichikov had already pulled out another of the same sort when Colonel Koshkarev suddenly appeared with a radiant air and a paper.

"Everything is done, and done excellently. The man I told you about is a downright genius; he can do the thinking for everybody! Just for that I'll place him over all the others; I shall create a special, superior department and make him its Chairman. You'll see what a brilliant mind he has and how he has solved everything in a few minutes. Here is what he writes—"

"Well, glory to the Lord!" reflected Chichikov, and got all set to listen.

" 'Entering upon a consideration of the task entrusted to me by your Right Honorable self, I have the honor to report as follows: Firstly, there is in the very request of Pavel Ivanovich Chichikov, Collegiate Councilor and Cavalier, a certain misconception, inasmuch as, through an oversight, the souls listed with the Bureau of Audits are described as dead. Under this description the gentleman was probably pleased to understand those who are near to death, but not those who have died, inasmuch as dead serfs cannot be acquired. What is there to acquire, if there is nothing? Logic itself will tell us that, and the very designation indicates an empirical education, probably limited to a parochial school, for evidently the gentleman in question has made no great progress in the rhetorical sciences—' "

At this point Koshkarev paused for a moment and said: "In this passage the knave has . . . pinked you a little. But judge for yourself what a lively quill he wields; he has a style like a State Secretary's, and yet he didn't *quite* finish the university—he had only three years." Then he resumed:

" '—has made no great progress in the rhetorical sciences, inasmuch as he expressed himself concerning these souls as "dead," whereas it is a matter of common knowledge to anyone who has studied the humanities that the soul is immortal. Secondly, of the above-mentioned souls, listed with the Bureau of Audits, whether debited and credited (or, as the gentleman was pleased to put it, dead souls), or any other sort whatsoever, there are none at present available, inasmuch as all of them, collectively, have not only been mortgaged without recourse, but have been pledged as security on a second mortgage, for an additional sum of a hundred and fifty rubles a head, except those in the hamlet of Gurmailovka, the title to which hamlet and souls is in dispute owing to the litigation with the landed proprietor Predishchev, and which souls for that reason may neither be sold nor mortgaged, as advertised in Number Forty-two of the *Moscow News.'* "

"Then why didn't you inform me of that before? Why did you detain me over such trifles?" said Chichikov, heartily vexed.

"But then, how was I to know this at first? That's just where the advantage of paper work comes in; now everything has been explained as clearly as if it were on the palm of your hand. To do things just so is no trick. Even a fool can see something undiscerningly, but the thing to do is to see with discernment."

"What a fool, what a stupid animal!" Chichikov was thinking to himself. "You read many books, yet what have you learned?" Without observing any of the rules of amenity or politeness, he grabbed his hat and dashed out of the house. His coachman had kept the light droshky in readiness, knowing there was no use in unharnessing the horses, inasmuch as he would have had to put in a written request for the feed, while the decision to issue the oats would be reached only on the following day. But no matter how rude and impolite Chichikov had been, Koshkarev, despite all that, was unusually polite and delicate with him. He ran out, squeezed Chichikov's hand regardless of the latter's resistance and pressed it to his heart (even as Chichikov was seating himself in the droshky), and thanked him for the opportunity of showing just how productivity was carried on in practice; it would be necessary, he said, to have a shake-up and a general talking-to, because otherwise everything was likely to become dormant and the springs of administration would grow rusty and weak; he explained that, as a consequence of this eventful visit, a happy thought had come to him: to organize a new Commission of Supervision over the Commission of Rural Constructions, so that no one would any longer venture on any peculations.

"Ass! Fool!" fumed Chichikov, angry and dissatisfied during the whole return journey. He was performing that trip by the light of the stars. Night reigned in the sky. Lights gleamed in the village. As he drove up to the front entrance he saw through the windows that the table was already set for supper.

"What made you so late?" asked Skudronzhoglo when Chichikov appeared in the doorway.

"What were you discussing with him for so long?" asked Platonov.

"He's been the death of me!" said Chichikov. "Never in all my born days have I seen such a fool."

"What you have seen is really nothing," said Skudronzhoglo. "Koshkarev is a consoling phenomenon. We need him, because in him are reflected, as in a caricature and therefore all the more perceptibly, the follies of all wiseacres who, without having first learned what is good in their own land, fill themselves with fool notions abroad. There, that's the sort of landowners who have come to the fore now: they have set up offices and departments and commissions, and the Devil alone knows what they haven't set up, just as though each had an empire of his own to administer! How do you like that, I ask you? We had just recovered a little after the Frenchmen of eighteen-twelve, so now everybody has taken to ruining the country all over again. Why, they've ruined everything worse than any Frenchman could, so that now even some Petr Petrovich Petuh is actually considered an able landowner!"

"Why, even he has mortgaged his place," Chichikov volunteered.

"Well, now, everything will be mortgaged, everything!" Saying this, Skudronzhoglo grew angry, little by little. "You take a landowner who has plenty of tilth land and actually not enough peasants to work it, so what does he do? He sets up a hat or a candle factory; he imports master candlemakers from London and turns huckster! The calling of a landed proprietor is such an honorable one, so the landed proprietors turn into manufacturers, into mill owners! Or you'll find a still bigger fool, who will set up spinning machines—to turn out muslins for the city trollops and for country wenches!"

"But then you, too, have factories," Plantonov remarked.

"But who started them? They started of themselves. The wool accumulated, there was no market for it, and so I began weaving it into textiles, but those textiles are coarse, simple, and are quickly taken off my hands at a low price at the local fairs; the muzhik needs them, my own muzhik. The fishermen have been dumping fish offal and scales on my stretch of river bank for the last six years in a row: well, now, how and where was I to get rid of the stuff? So I started boiling it down into glue, and I took in forty thousand. For that's the way everything goes with me."

"What a devil!" thought Chichikov, watching him with all his eyes. "What a paw for raking in everything!"

"And I've gone in for those factories because there has been such an influx of workmen, all outsiders, flocking to earn a crust of bread, and who would have died from hunger otherwise; this is a year of famine, and all thanks to these mill owners, who've neglected to sow any grain. I don't import any master craftsmen from abroad, and I won't under any circumstances tear the peasants away from tilling the soil. Of such factories, brother, I can show you plenty. Every year another factory springs up, depending on what sort of leavings and refuse may have accumulated. You just look over your estate more closely and you'll see that every rag can be turned to account, every bit of rubbish will yield revenue, so that eventually all you can do is thrust it from you, saying: 'I don't need any more!' And I don't put up any special buildings for these factories; you won't find any palaces on my place with colonnades and pediments."

"This is amazing!" said Chichikov, overflowing with happiness. "Amazing! Amazing! But the most amazing thing is that every bit of rubbish actually yields revenue!"

"Hm! And that isn't all, either!—" Skudronzhoglo did not finish his speech; his gall had stirred within him, and he wanted to upbraid his neighboring landowners. "Why, good heavens! If only they would tackle things simply, just as they are; but no, every man is a mechanic; every man must needs open the coffer with a special instrument, when it isn't even locked. And so he'll make a special trip to England; that's what the whole business consists of for him! An awful fool!" As he said this, Skudronzhoglo spat. "But mind you, he'll be a hundredfold more stupid when he gets back from abroad!"

"Ah, Constantin! You've lost your temper again," said his wife, uneasily. "For you know that's bad for you."

"Well, what can one do but get angry? It would be all right if this concerned other nations, but this is near to one's own heart. For what's so vexing is that the Russian character is getting spoiled, that there has now appeared in the Russian character a quixotism which was never there before. You take one of these clever fellows: if he goes in for philanthropy he'll become a very Don Quixote of philanthropy. What do you think he'll set up on his place? Charitable institutions, stone edifices in a village! Good works for the love of Christ! If you do want to help, then you help each muzhik to fulfill his Christian duty, and don't tear him away therefrom. Help a son to warm his ailing father by his own fireside, but don't give him the chance to throw this burden off his shoulders. Better give him an opportunity to shelter his fellow man and brother in his own home, give him the money to do this with, help him with everything in your power, but don't draw him away from his work: he'll forsake his Christian obligations entirely. But they're simply Don Quixotes in all respects, these landowners! . . . It costs two hundred rubles a year to keep a man in a charitable institution! Why, I'll maintain ten men in my village for that! But no, one of these philanthropists will build you the most nonsensically run infirmaries and other institutions running into a million, with colonnades, will ruin himself, and let all his family out into the world to beg for bread— and there's your philanthropy!"

Chichikov was not interested in any charitable institutions; he wanted to turn the conversation to the subject of every bit of trash bringing in revenue. But Skudronzhoglo was now angry in earnest; his gall had risen, his words had turned into a very spate, and it would have been beyond him to stop.

"And then you have another sort: he conceives the idea of enlightenment, and so he becomes a Don Quixote of enlightenment; he'll set up such schools as even a fool would not conceive! There now, for instance, what can be more useful for a man than a knowledge of reading and writing? And yet how have they arranged things? The man turned out by one of these schools will be fit for nothing, neither for country nor town; he won't be anything but a drunkard, yet always standing on his dignity. For I have the muzhiks from such enlightened villages come to me. 'What's all this, father?' they ask me. 'Our sons have gotten out of hand entirely, they don't want to help us in our work, all they want to be is clerks, and yet all you need is one clerk to a village.' There's your result!"

Chichikov had no need of schools, either, but at this point Platonov contributed his mite to the subject: "Why, we need not be stopped because there are no clerks needed at present; there will be a need of them later. One must work for posterity."

"Oh, brother, you at least might be intelligent! Why have you all picked on this posterity? Every man thinks he's Peter the Great or something. You just watch your own step and don't keep your eye peeled on posterity so much. All this talk about enlightening the peasant! You just concern yourself with making the muzhik well-off and making him a good husbandman, and seeing that he has the time to learn of his own will, and don't be after him with a stick in your hand: 'Learn!' The Devil knows what end they begin with, always putting the cart before the horse! Why, you simply can't imagine how foolish the world has grown now, in this our day! What don't all these scribblers write now! One of them will put out a book and everybody just pounces on it. There, listen; listen, now, to what I'll tell you, and then judge for yourselves—" At this point Skudronzhoglo moved near to Chichikov and, so as to make him grasp the matter better, grappled the ship and boarded it, or, in other words, buttonholed him. "There, now, what could be clearer? You own your peasants because you're supposed to be their protector and the protector of their way of life. And of what does that way of life consist? Of what do the labors of a peasant consist? Of tilling the soil? Then do your best that he be a good tiller of the soil. Is that clear? But no; certain clever fellows have turned up, and they say: 'One can lead him out of that state. He leads too rude, too ordinary a life; one must acquaint him with articles of luxury, make him aware of needs above his condition.' It isn't enough that they themselves, thanks to this luxury, have turned into dishrags and are no longer men, and have gathered the Devil knows what diseases unto themselves, so that there isn't an eighteen-year-old brat who hasn't tried out everything there is—he not only has lost every tooth in his head but is as bald as a pig's bladder—but no, they are after infecting others as well. But glory be to God that we still have at least one wholesome class left to us, which has not become familiar with these vices. We must simply thank God for that. Yes, the tiller of the soil is the most honorable man among us. Why do you go after him? May God grant that everybody be like the tiller of the soil!"

"Then it is your opinion that cultivating the soil is the most profitable occupation of all?" asked Chichikov.

"Most legitimate, if not the most profitable. Till the soil in the sweat of thy brow—that was commanded unto all of us—and not in vain was it commanded. The experience of the ages has proved that when man follows the calling of agriculture he is purer, more moral, nobler, loftier. I'm not saying you're not to go in for any other productivity, but let agriculture be the basis of everything—that's what! The factories will come of themselves, but they will be legitimate factories, turning out whatever is needed locally, from material right at hand to the manufacturer on the spot, but not all these different wants which have so enervated the people of the present day. Not the sort of factories which eventually, to keep themselves going and to ram their goods down the public's throat, resort to all sorts of infamous devices and mountebankery, debauching and corrupting the wretched common folk. There, I'll never start up on my place, no matter how you may argue in their favor, any of those industries that instill the higher needs; I won't go in for growing and processing tobacco and sugar, not if it means the loss of a million to me. If corruption comes upon the world, let it not be at my hands! Let me be righteous in the eyes of God! I have been living for twenty years with the common folk, I know the consequences of these things. Where tilling the soil has formed the foundation of social life, there you will find plenty and content; there is no luxury, no poverty, but there is contentment. Delve the soil, man has been commanded; toil ... no use of trying to be cunning here! I tell the muzhik: 'No matter whom you toil for—for me, or for yourself, or for a neighbor—toil you must. When it comes to work I shall be the first one to help you. If you have no livestock, here's a horse for you, here's a cow, here's a cart. I am ready to supply you with whatever you need, but you must work. It kills me to see your homestead all run down, to see you living in shiftlessness and poverty. I won't stand for sloth: that's why I've been placed over you, so that you'll work.' Hm! People think they'll increase their revenues by institutions and factories! Why, let your first consideration be to have every one of your muzhiks well off, then you yourself will be well off without any factories and without any workshops, and without any fool schemes."

"To me the most amazing thing," Chichikov managed to put in, "is how all the refuse and leavings turn into wealth, and how every bit of trash yields revenue."

"Hm! Political economists!" Skudronzhoglo was saying, with an expression of jaundiced sarcasm and without paying any heed to Chichikov. "Fine political economists, they are! One fool mounted on another and using a third for a whip! Can't see further than his fool nose. Just an ass, yet he'll clamber up on a cathedra and clap spectacles on his nose. What a pack of fools!" And he spat once more.

"All that is so, and you're in the right about it, but please don't get angry over it," said his wife. "As though one couldn't speak of such things without losing one's temper!"

"The more one listens to you, my estimable Constantin Fedorovich," said Chichikov, "the more one's desire to listen to you grows; one penetrates, so to say, the meaning of life, one touches the very core of the matter. But, leaving things that affect mankind in general, allow me to direct your attention to something particular and personal. Tell me, my worthy and honored friend: were I, for instance, to conceive an intention of becoming a landed proprietor, in this province let us suppose, to what, in particular, ought I to pay particular attention? What is one to do, how is one to go about becoming rich in a short [time], thereby fulfilling, so to say, the obligation of a citizen to his fatherland?"

"How should one go about becoming rich? Why, this is how—" Skudronzhoglo began.

"Let's go in to supper!" said the mistress of the house, getting up from the divan and coming out into the centre of the room, as she wrapped her youthful chilled body in a shawl.

Chichikov jumped up from his chair with the adroitness of an almost military man, dashed up to the hostess with the genial air of a civilian who is considerate in ...... [all things], offered her his arm, crooking it so that it looked like the neck part of a yoke, and led her as if on parade through two rooms into the dining room, preserving throughout that certain agreeable inclination of his head, somewhat to one side. A servant took the lid off the soup tureen, and the delectable fragrance of a soup suffused with the fresh greens and the first herbs and roots of spring was wafted through the room. All sat down at the table. The servants dexterously placed all the courses on the table at once, in covered platters, as well as everything else necessary, and immediately withdrew—Skudronzhoglo did not like to have the flunkies listening to the masters' talk and, still more, he disliked having them staring at his mouth every time he took a bite.

Having done with his soup, and after following it with a glass of cordial (the cordial was an excellent one), Chichikov turned to Skudronzhoglo. "Allow me, my estimable Sir, to revert to the subject of our interrupted conversation. I was asking you what one could do, how one was to act, how one might best go about. . . ."*

". . . Such an estate that, if he were to ask forty thousand for it, I would count out the money to him on the spot."

"Hm!" Chichikov became thoughtful. "But how is it," he uttered with a certain hesitancy, "that you aren't buying it for yourself?"

"Well, one must know where and when to draw the line. I have enough things to keep me busy around my estates, without that. Besides, our gentry, even as it is, are yelling their heads off at me, saying that apparently taking advantage of their extreme difficulties and their ruinous situations I am buying up lands for a song. I've become fed up with that sort of thing at last."

"The gentry are so prone to say nasty things!" Chichikov sympathized.

"And especially among us, in our province. . . . You can

---

*Two pages are missing in the manuscript. In what is apparently the first recension of this part of *Dead Souls* the editor makes the following notation at this point: ". . . It must be supposed that Kostanzhoglo [Skudronzhoglo] had proposed to Chichikov that the latter acquire, through purchase, the estate of a neighboring landowner, one Hlobuev." *Trans.*

have no idea of what they're saying about me. They never call me otherwise than a first-class curmudgeon and skinflint. But they excuse themselves in everything. 'I, of course,' one of these gentlemen will say, 'have squandered my all, but I did so because I lived for the higher things in life, I must have books, I must live in luxury, so as to encourage our industries, but I'll grant you one could actually live out one's life without becoming ruined, if one were to live like a hog, the way Skudronzhoglo does.' For that's the way of things!"

"I would like to be a hog like that!" said Chichikov warmly.

"And it's all bosh. What higher things in life are they talking about? Whom are they fooling? Even though one of them may buy books, yet he never reads them; he always winds up playing cards or. . . . And they talk that way about me only because I don't give grand dinners, and won't lend them money. I don't give any grand dinners because they depress me, I'm not used to them; but if you drop in on me and are willing to try potluck, you are right welcome. And as for my not putting any money out on loan, that, too, is so much bosh. You just come to me if you really need money, and tell me in detail and sensibly what you're going to do with my money, and provided I gather from what you say that you're going to use it intelligently and that it'll bring you a clear advantage, I won't turn you down and I even won't take any interest for the loan."

"Well, now, I'll have to bear that in mind," Chichikov reflected.

"No, I'll never turn you down," Skudronzhoglo went on. "But I'm not going to scatter my money to the four winds.

They'll really have to excuse me from that. Why, the Devil take it—one of these fellows will stage one of those grand dinners somewhere for his mistress, or will start prettifying and furnishing his home on an insane scale, or will take some lewd creature to a masquerade, or arrange some sort of a jubilee to mark the fact that his life on earth has been lived in vain, and I'm supposed to lend him money!"

At this point Skudronzhoglo spat and almost came out with a few unseemly and violent words and curses in the presence of his wife. A morose shadow of dark hypochondria darkened his face. Horizontal and vertical wrinkles gathered on his forehead, witnesses to the wrathful rising of his agitated spleen.

Chichikov drank a glass of raspberry cordial, and began: "Allow me, my worthy and honored friend, to turn you anew to the subject of our interrupted conversation. Were I, let us suppose, to acquire that very same estate which you were pleased to mention, then how long would it take . . . how soon could one manage . . . to grow rich to such a degree—"

"If what you're after is to get rich quick," Skudronzhoglo, who was still in no amiable mood, caught him up sternly and abruptly, "then you'll never get rich; but if what you're after is to get rich without asking how long it will take, then you will get rich quick."

"So that's how it goes!" said Chichikov.

"Yes," said Skudronzhoglo abruptly, just as though he were angry at Chichikov himself. "You must have a love for work; without that you can accomplish nothing. You must come to love the management of your estate, yes! And, believe me, it is not at all tedious. People have invented the fiction that life in the country is a bore. Why, I would die of boredom if I were to pass one day in town the way those fellows pass it, in their clubs, taverns, and theatres! The fools, the pack of fools, the generation of asses! The husbandman must not be bored, he has no time to be bored. There is not a tittle of emptiness in his life; there is only fullness. One need merely examine the multiform cycle of the year's tasks—and what tasks! Tasks that truly elevate the spirit, to say nothing at all of their diversity. No matter what you say, here man marches side by side with nature, with the seasons of the year, the coadjutor and companion in all that is going on in Creation. Spring has not yet arrived, yet everything is on the alert and awaiting it, and the labors are already beginning: wood, and all things else, have to be carted before the roads become impassable; seed has to be prepared; grain has to be picked, measured, and dried in the granaries; new assessments have to be established. Everything is foreseen and everything is calculated in advance. When the snows are gone, and the rivers have lost their flood, and the ice has broken, and everything dries, the labors simply begin to seethe; there you have to load the barges, here you have to clear out the forest, to transplant the trees in the orchards, and everywhere the men have started turning up the earth: in the orchards and the truck patches the spade is at work; in the fields the plow and the harrows.

"Everywhere the planting and the sowing begin. Do you understand that? What a trifle! They're sowing a future bumper crop! They are sowing the blessedness of the whole earth! They are sowing subsistence for millions! Summer comes on: here you have mowing after mowing, the chief holiday of the tiller of the soil. What a trifle! There will be reaping after reaping; wheat will follow rye, oats will follow millet, and then you have to pull the hemp. Everything is seething, you must not let a minute slip: even though you had twenty eyes, there would be work for all of them. The hayricks are thrown up, and the grain is stacked. And there's half of August gone, and the carting of everything to the threshing floors has begun. Autumn has come, and you have plowing and the sowing of the winter crops, the repair of the granaries, of the silos and the cattle pens, the testing of the grains and the first threshing and, at the same time, all the tasks that are left to the women. The winter will come on, and here, too, the labors do not flag: there are the first loads going off to town, threshing on all the floors; the transfer of all the threshed grain to the granaries; through the forests there is the felling and the sawing of the trees; bricks and other material for building in the spring have to be carted.

"When I add everything up and see what has been done, why, I'm simply unable to take everything in. What a diversity of labor! Hither and thither you go for a look: to the mill, and to the work yard, and to the factories, and to the threshing floors; you go to look in on the muzhik, to see how he is making out for himself—all that is a mere trifle! Why, it's like a holiday to me to see how well a carpenter handles his ax; I'm ready to stand for two hours watching him, so much does work rejoice me! But if on top of that you see to what purpose all this is being wrought, how everything about you is multiplying and multiplying, bringing in fruit and revenue, why, I can't even tell you what a pleasure that is. And not because the money is ac-

cumulating—money is another matter—but because all
this is the work of your hands; because you see that you are
the cause of it all and the creator of it all, and that from
you, as if you were a veritable magus, plentitude and weal
are pouring forth upon everything. Why, where will you
find for me a delight to equal that?" asked Skudronzhoglo,
and lifted up his face; all his wrinkles had disappeared. He
was aglow, like to a king on the day of his triumphant coro-
nation, and it seemed as if his face were sending forth rays.
"Why, you won't seek out a delight like that in all the world!
It is here, precisely here, that man emulates God: God has
set Himself the task of creation as the highest delight, and
of man also He demands that he be the creator of benefi-
cence around him, and of an orderly progression of works.
And they call this boresome work!"

Chichikov was lost in listening to the mellifluous
speeches of his host as if he were listening to the singing of
some little bird of paradise. His mouth was watering; his
eyes had turned oleaginous and had a sugary look; he
would have listened without end.

"Time to get up from the table, Constantin!" said the
hostess, rising from her chair. Chichikov arose too, although he would have preferred to sit uninterrupted and
keep on listening. Crooking his arm again in a bow,
Chichikov led the hostess back to the drawing room. But
this time his head was not amiably inclined to one side;
adroitness was lacking in his ways. All his thoughts were
taken up with the substantial considerations of ways and
means.

"No matter what you may say, things are boresome just

the same," said Platonov, walking behind Chichikov and the hostess.

"My guest, apparently, is very far from being a stupid fellow," the host reflected. "He is attentive, careful of speech and no whippersnapper." And, after this reflection, he cheered up considerably, just as if he were jubilant over having found a man who knew how to listen to wise counsels.

When, later on, they disposed themselves in the small, cozy candle-lit drawing room, facing the french window into the starlit garden, Chichikov felt more content than he had felt in a long while, as though his native roof had received him after long wanderings, and he, after consummating every thing, had come into all the things he had desired, and had cast aside his wanderer's staff, saying "Enough!" That is how enchanting was the spiritual mood which the sagacious conversation of his host had brought upon his soul. There are, for every heart, such speeches, which seem nearer and more kindred to it than any others; and often, unexpectedly, in some godforsaken, forgotten backwoods, amid the most desolate desolation, you will come upon a man whose warming speech will compel you to forget the pathlessness of your way, and the heartlessness of your resting places, and the world of today, filled with human follies and with snares set by man for the ensnaring of man. And thereafter, forever and aye, there will abide with you the living recollection of the evening spent in such talk, and everything that may have happened and passed that evening will the faithful memory retain: who was present on the occasion, and who was standing where, and what such-and-such a person was holding in his hands, and the walls, and the corners, and every knick-knack in the room.

Just so everything made an impression on Chichikov's memory that evening; not only the charming, unpretentiously furnished small room, and the kindhearted expression that had come to reign on his clever host's face, but the very design of the wallpaper . . . and the pipe (with an amber mouthpiece) that was brought to Platonov, and the smoke that the latter began blowing into Yarb's thick-jowled muzzle, and Yarb's snorting, and the laughter of the endearing and comely hostess, interrupted by the words: "That's enough, don't torture him!" and the cheerful candles, and the cricket chirping in a corner, and the french window, and the spring night gazing at them from afar, leaning with its elbows on the summits of the star-strewn trees, among which the nightingales of spring were trilling.

"I find your speeches delectable, my worthy and estimable friend, Constantin Fedorovich," Chichikov declared. "I may say that I have not met in all of Russia a man who is your equal in intelligence."

Skudronzhoglo smiled: he himself felt that these words were not entirely unmerited. "No, Pavel Ivanovich," said he, "if you really want to know an intelligent man, why, we actually have one such among us, of whom it may truly be said that he is an intelligent man, whose shoelaces I'm not worthy of tying."

"Who could it possibly be?"

"It's our tax farmer, Murazov."

"This is the second time I hear about him!" Chichikov exclaimed.

"There's a man who could manage not only a landowner's estate but a whole realm. If I had a realm I would make him the Minister of Finance this very minute."

"I've heard about him. They say he is a man surpassing all belief; he's accumulated ten million, they say."

"Ten million, indeed! He must be worth more than forty by now. Pretty soon half of Russia will be in his hands."

"What are you saying!" said Chichikov, dumbfounded.

"Indubitably and infallibly. His wealth must be increasing by leaps and bounds now. That is self-evident. Only he who has some few hundred thousand gets rich slowly; but whoever has millions has a large radius; whatever comes within it doubles and trebles. The field, the arena, now, is far too vast. Here a man no longer has any rivals; there's none to contend with him. Whatever price he may set for anything, that's the price that will stick; there's nobody to top it."

As if he were rooted to the spot, with his eyes popping and his jaw gaping, Chichikov was staring into Skudronzhoglo's eyes. His breath was cut short. "It is beyond the power of the mind to grasp!" said he, coming to himself a little. "Thought becomes petrified with awe. Men are amazed at the wisdom of Providence when they contemplate some pismire; for me it is more amazing that such enormous sums can go through the hands of any mortal! Permit me to put a question to you concerning one circumstance. Tell me, all this, naturally, was not acquired without some transgression at the start?"

"It was all acquired in the most irreproachable manner and by the most just means."

"I won't believe that, most honored Sir, I won't believe it! If it were a matter of thousands, such might be the case, but when it comes to millions . . . pardon me, I won't believe it."

"On the contrary, it's the thousands that are hard to come by without transgression, but millions are accumulated easily. There's no need for a millionaire to resort to crooked ways. Just follow the straight road ahead, and take everything that lies before you. There'll be no other to pick it up; it isn't everyone who has the strength to tackle it."

"It's beyond the power of the mind to grasp! And what is most incomprehensible of all is that the whole business began with a copper!"

"Why, it never comes about any other way. It is the ordained order of things," said Skudronzhoglo. "He who has been born possessing thousands, who has been educated at the cost of thousands, will no longer acquire anything; such a fellow has already gotten fancy notions and there's hardly anything bad that you won't find in him! One must begin at the beginning, and not from the middle. It's at the bottom—at the bottom—that one must begin. Only there do you get a thorough knowledge of the people and customs in whose midst you will have to twist and turn later on. When you have borne this and that on your own hide, when you find out that every copper is nailed tight with a spike, and when you've been knocked about from pillar to post and survived, you will then have been made so wise and will be so schooled that you will never miss out in any undertaking and will not lose your grip. Believe me, that is the truth. One must begin at the beginning, and not from the middle. Him who says to me: 'Give me a hundred thousand and I will get rich right off,' I will never believe; he is going at things hit-or-miss, and not with certainty. It's with a copper that one must begin!"

"If that's the case, I shall get rich," said Chichikov, "inasmuch as I am beginning almost, so to say, with nothing." He meant the dead souls.

"Constantin, it's time to give Pavel Ivanovich a chance to rest and sleep," said the hostess, "yet you keep on chattering."

"And you will infallibly and certainly get rich," said Skudronzhoglo, without heeding the mistress of the house. "Gold, rivers of gold, will come pouring in upon you. You won't know where to put your revenues."

Like a man bewitched did Pavel Ivanovich sit there, in a golden realm of expanding visions and reveries. His thoughts were in a whirl. . . .

"Really, Constantin, it's time for Pavel Ivanovich to go to sleep."

"But why do you fret? There, go to sleep, if you feel like it!" said the host, and stopped short: loudly, through the whole room, came the snoring of Platonov, and right after him, Yarb set up still louder snoring. For a long time by now had the sounds of watchmen banging sheets of iron been floating in from afar. It was getting on past midnight. Skudronzhoglo, noting that it really was time to be going to bed, prodded Platonov awake, telling him to stop snoring. They all dispersed, after wishing one another sound slumber, and did not take long to avail themselves thereof.

To Chichikov alone sleep would not come. He was cogitating how he might become the proprietor not of a fantastic but an actual estate. After the conversation with his host everything grew so clear, the possibility of becoming

rich seemed so evident. The hard work of estate management now became so easy and comprehensible and seemed
so suitable to his nature that he began thinking seriously
about acquiring not an imaginary but an actual country
seat; he determined, right then and there, to acquire with
the money he would derive from mortgaging his phantasmal souls a country seat that would not be at all phantasmal. He already saw himself managing the estate and
acting precisely as Skudronzhoglo taught—smartly, thoroughly, not starting anything new without having first mastered all the old things through and through; he would look
into everything himself, would make a point of knowing
his peasants and all about them; he would thrust all superfluities and everything extraneous from him, giving himself
up only to toil and looking after his property. Even in anticipation he tasted of that delight which he would feel
when a smooth-running orderliness would be established,
and all the springs of husbandry, working in unison, would
move at a brisk pace. Toil would seethe, and even as in a
busy mill flour is briskly ground out of grain, so out of all
sorts of sweepings and oddments ready cash and more
ready cash would be ground out in a continuous stream.
His wondrous host rose vividly before his eyes at every moment. He was the first man in all Russia for whom
Chichikov had felt a personal regard; up to now he had respected a man either because of high rank or great possessions; he had never yet had regard for any man solely
because of his intelligence. Skudronzhoglo was the first
one. Chichikov comprehended also that there was no use
discussing dead souls with a man like that and that the
mere mention of them would be out of place. He was now

taken up with another project—the purchase of Hlobuev's estate. Ten thousand he had; the other ten thousand he proposed to borrow from Skudronzhoglo, since the latter himself had already declared that he was ready to help anyone who wished to get rich and to go in for husbandry. The remaining ten thousand he could assume as a subsequent payment, to be made after he had mortaged his dead souls. To mortgage all the souls he had bought up was as yet not possible, because so far he had no lands upon which he might resettle them. Although he . . . . . . [maintained] that he had lands in the Kherson Province, those lands existed largely as a hypothesis. He proposed to buy up lands in Kherson Province as well, inasmuch as they were going for a song there, and were even given away free, just so that they might be settled. Or he might simply stall off the last payment. Sure, that could be done; go and bother with the courts if you feel like it, if you don't feel like waiting. Chichikov was also thinking that he ought to hurry up and buy up whatever runaway and dead souls anybody had left, since the landowners were vying with one another in mortgaging their estates, and soon throughout all Russia there might not be a corner left not mortgaged with the Treasury. All these thoughts filled his head by turns and hindered him from [sleeping].

Finally sleep, which had for four hours by now held the whole house in its embraces, as the phrase goes, took Chichikov into those embraces as well. He fell asleep—fast asleep. [F]

CHAPTER FOUR

The next day everything was arranged in a way that could not have been bettered. Skudronzhoglo was only too happy to lend Chichikov ten thousand, without interest, without security, simply on his own signature, so ready was he to give a lift to anyone on the road to acquisition. Nor was that all; he took it upon himself to accompany Chichikov to Hlobuev's, so that they might look over the estate together. Chichikov was in the highest spirits.

After a filling breakfast they all set out, the three of them sitting in Pavel Ivanovich's barouche, the host's light droshky following them unoccupied. Yarb ran on ahead, scaring the birds off the road. For all of ten miles Skudronzhoglo's forests and tilled lands stretched along on both sides of the road. As soon as these came to an end, everything took on a different appearance: the ears of grain were light; instead of forests there were stumps. In a little more than an hour and a half they covered the twelve miles and saw the small village which, despite its beautiful situation, showed neglect even at a distance. A new stone house, big and uninhabited, which had been left unfinished for several years, was the first to appear; behind it was another, small and weather-stained but inhabited. They found the owner in disarray, still sleepy, since he had awakened only a little while before. He was forty; his cravat was tied all to one side; there was a patch on his coat, a hole in one of his boots.

He became as overjoyed at their arrival as though God

knows what good fortune had befallen him—just as though he was beholding his own brothers after a long separation. "Constantin Fedorovich! Platon Michailovich!" he cried out. "Fathers o' mine! There, you've favored me with a visit at last! Let me rub my eyes—I must still be dreaming. For really, now, I was thinking by this time that no one would ever drop in on me again. Everyone runs from me as from the plague—they're afraid I might ask for a loan. Oh, but things are hard, Constantin Fedorovich—hard! I can see that I myself am to blame for everything. But what's to be done? I'm a swine fallen into a swine's life. Excuse me, gentlemen, for receiving you in this getup; my boots are full of holes, as you can see. But what can I treat you to? Just tell me."

"Let's not beat about the bush, please. We have come to you on business," said Skudronzhoglo. "Here's a buyer for your estate—Pavel Ivanovich Chichikov."

"Glad to make your acquaintance, with all my soul. Allow me to shake your hand."

Chichikov gave him both his hands.

"I would like, my most estimable Pavel Ivanovich, to show you an estate that merits anybody's attention. But I say, gentlemen, may I ask if you have dined?"

"We have, we have," said Skudronzhoglo, wishing to have the business over and done with. "We won't put things off and can go right now."

"In that case let's go."

Hlobuev picked up his cap. The guests put on their caps and all set out on foot to look the village over.

"Let's go and look over the general disorderliness and my shiftlessness," Hlobuev was saying. "Of course you've done well to dine. Would you believe it, Constantin Fe-dorovich, there isn't a chicken on the place—that's what I've come to. I'm behaving like a swine, simply like a swine!"

With a deep sigh, and as though he sensed that there would be but little comfort forthcoming from Constantin Fedorovich and that the latter's heart was rather hard, he seized Platonov by the arm and, pressing it close to his breast, went on ahead with him. Skudronzhoglo and Chichikov lingered behind and, linking arms, followed at a distance.

"Things are hard, Platon Michailovich—hard!" Hlobuev was saying to Platonov. "You can't imagine how hard! No money, no bread, no boots! I wouldn't care a straw for all that if only I were young and single. But when all these troubles go to work on you when you're getting old, and you have a wife at your side, and five children, why, you lose heart, you can't help but lose heart."

Platonov felt sorry for him. "Well, now, if you'll sell the village, will that set you to rights?"

"Set me to rights, indeed!" said Hlobuev, with a hopeless wave of his hand. "Everything will go to pay the most pressing debts, and after that there won't be even a thousand left for myself."

"What are you going to do, then?"

"Why, God knows," said Hlobuev, shrugging.

Platonov was perplexed. "How is it, then," he asked, "that you aren't doing anything to extricate yourself from these circumstances?"

"Well, what am I to do?"

"What, are there no means?"

"None whatsoever."

"Well, look for a position, get some post."

"Why, I am a Provincial Secretary; yet what decent post could they give me? They'll give me an insignificant salary, and yet I have a wife and five children."

"Take a private position, then. Become a manager."

"Why, who would entrust an estate to me? I have lost my own through extravagance."

"Yes, but if starvation and death threaten, one must do something. I'll ask my brother if he can't get you a post through somebody in the city."

"No, Platon Michailovich," said Hlobuev with a sigh and pressing Platonov's arm hard, "I'm no good for anything any more. I have grown decrepit before old age has really come upon me, and the small of my back aches because of my erstwhile sins, and I have rheumatism in my shoulder. What's the use of my trying anything! Why go dipping into the public funds! Even without me there are too many on the public pay roll just for whatever there may be in it for them. God forbid that on my account any additional taxes should be put on the poor; things are hard enough already with all that multitude of leeches. No, Platon Michailovich, let it go."

"What a situation to be in!" Platonov was thinking. "This is worse than my lethargy."

In the meantime Skudronzhoglo, walking with Chichikov a considerable distance behind the others, was losing his temper. "Just see how he has neglected everything!" he was saying. "What poverty he has brought to the muzhiks," and he pointed. "Not a cart, not a horse! If your cattle get the murrain, there's no use watching out for your own good. You sell everything you've got and supply the muzhik with livestock, so that he may not be left even one day without the means of carrying on his work. Now you won't repair even in several years the damage that's been done: the muzhik has already grown lazy, fond of having his fling, and an out-and-out drunkard."

"It follows, then, that it isn't at all profitable to buy the estate now?" asked Chichikov.

At this point Skudronzhoglo looked at Chichikov as if he wanted to say to him: "What sort of an ignoramus are you? Must one start with you right from *a b c*?"—"Unprofitable? Why, in three years I could be getting twenty thousand a year out of this estate, that's how unprofitable it is! And what's the land like? Just take a good look at the land!" he said, pointing to the meadows that came into view a little beyond the huts. "It's all meadows, and meadows that are fertilized by the spring freshets. Why, I'll sow you flax, and rake in five thousand for the flax alone; I'll sow you turnips, and get four thousand out of those. And look over there—that's rye shooting up on that hillside. Why, it's all wind-sown. He didn't plant any grain—I happen to know that. And those ravines over there, why, I'll plant you such forests there that no crow will ever fly as high as those tree-tops. And to neglect such land, such treasure! Why, the value of this estate is a hundred and fifty thousand, and not forty!"

Chichikov became apprehensive lest Hlobuev overhear them and therefore fell back still more.

"Just see how much land he has let go to waste!" Skudronzhoglo was saying, by now getting downright angry. "If he had but let people know in time, plenty would have come willing to cultivate it for him. Well, now, if you have nothing to plow the land with, then take to the spade, spade it up for some sort of a truck garden, get your money in from truck. Take a spade yourself; make your wife, your children, your domestics work; die . . . . . . [but die] at work! You will die fulfilling your duty, at least, but not like a pig, from overstuffing your guts at the dinner table! He has made the muzhik go for four years without work—and that's no trifle! Why, by that thing alone you've already corrupted him and ruined him forever; he has already grown used to tatters and vagabondage!" As he said this Skudronzhoglo spat, and his jaundiced mood darkened his forehead as if with a sombre cloud.

When they drew nearer the others and stopped on the crest of a steep hill grown over with cytisus shrubs, and the river gleamed in the distance as it made a bend around a dark spur of the mountains, and the house of General Betrishchev, lurking amid its groves, appeared in nearer perspective, while beyond it showed a mountain clothed with curly woods and seemingly covered with a bluish dust cloud because of the distance, which mountain made Chichikov suddenly surmise that he must be gazing at Tentetnikov's estate, "If one were to plant forests here," he said, "why, this countryside could be of surpassing beauty—"

"Oh, so you're a lover of views, are you!" said Skudronzhoglo, suddenly looking at him sternly. "Watch out: you start running after views and you'll be left with neither bread nor views. Look for utility and not beauty. Beauty will come of itself. Take cities, for example: those cities are best and most beautiful to this very day which built themselves, where each man built accordingly to his needs and tastes; whereas those that were built along a surveyor's tapeline are nothing but barracks upon barracks. Away with beauty! Keep your eye on necessities! . . ."

"What a pity it is that one will have to wait so long; one longs so much to see everything already in the desired shape—"

"Why, what are you, a youth of twenty-five? A Petersburg bureaucrat? Patience! Work for six years at one stretch: plant, sow, till the soil, without neglecting it for even a minute. It's hard—it's hard! But then later on, when you have stirred up the land well, and it starts helping you of its own self, then it won't be like some . . . . . . [factory or other]. No, father o' mine, you'll have, outside of some seventy hands helping you, seven hundred helping hands that you can't see. Everything will multiply tenfold! The way I have things going now I don't have to raise a finger, everything goes by itself. Yes, nature loves patience—and that is a law, promulgated for nature by God Himself, Who favors the patient ones!"

"When one listens to you one feels an access of strength; one's spirit rises."

"Look how that land has been plowed!" Skudronzhoglo cried out with a caustic emotion of distress, pointing to the slope of a hill. "I can't stay here any longer; it's death for me to look at such disorder and desolation. You can now conclude the deal with him even without me. Take the treasure away from this fool as fast as you can. He merely dishonors God's gift."

And, having said this, Skudronzhoglo, already morose from his jaundiced and agitated mood, said good-by to

Chichikov and, overtaking Hlobuev, began saying good-by to him as well.

"Mercy, Constantin Fedorovich," said the perplexed proprietor, "you've just come and you're already going back!"

"Can't stay. I have most urgent business to attend to at home," said Skudronzhoglo. He said good-by, got into his light droshky, and drove off.

It seemed as if Hlobuev had understood the reason for his departure.

"Constantin Fedorovich could not stand it," said he. "I feel that it's no gladsome thing for such a husbandman as he to look on at such a shiftless way of running things. Would you believe it, Pavel Ivanovich, I can't do anything. I did not even sow any grain this year. As I am an honest man, I had no seed, to say nothing about my having nothing to plow with. Your brother, Platon Michailovich, is an excellent husbandman, they say; and as for Constantin Fedorovich, there's no use even saying anything! He is a Napoleon in his own way. Really, I often think: 'Well, now, why is so much sense put all into one head? Why, if but a drop of it were to be put into my foolish head, if only enough to enable me to run my house!' I can't do anything, I've no ability in anything. Watch out here, gentlemen, be as careful as you can going across that bridge, so you won't fall into the puddle. I gave orders this spring to have those planks fixed. . . . I feel sorriest of all for my poor little muzhiks; they need an example, but what sort of an example am I to them? What would you have me do? Ah, Pavel Ivanovich, take them under your guidance! I feel that I didn't know how—that I don't know how—to be demanding and stern. How can I teach them orderliness when I myself am disorderly? I would give all of them their freedom this very hour, but nothing sensible will come out of that. I see that first of all one must bring them to such a state that they would be able to live. What is needed here is a stern and just man, who would live with them a long time and set them an example through his own tireless activity. The Russian, as I can see by myself, is somehow so constituted that he can't get along without somebody to drive him on. If he hasn't he'll simply stagnate, simply drowse off—"

"Why, it really is odd," said Platonov. "How is it that among us the common man can stagnate and drowse off to such an extent that unless one keeps both eyes on him he'll become both a drunkard and a good-for-nothing?"

"It's due to the lack of enlightenment," said Chichikov.

"Well, God knows what it's due to. Come, now, we are enlightened, yet how do we live? Come, now, what have I learned? For I went to a university, and I listened to lectures on all sorts of subjects, but as for the art of living and an orderly way of life, well, I not only did not learn that but, what is worse, learned rather the art of spending as much money as possible on all sorts of new refinements and comforts, became acquainted, for the most part, with such things as demand money. Is it because I studied without much sense? By no means, for it was the same way with my fellow students. There may have been two or three who derived real benefit from their studies, and even that may have been due to their being intelligent anyway; as for the others all they did was try to find out the things that injure their health and pick their pockets. Why, they only attended to applaud the professors, to shower them with awards, instead of getting awards from the professors. So then, out of enlightenment we will after all choose that which is viler; we will seize the superficies of enlightenment but not enlightenment itself. No, Pavel Ivanovich, our ignorance of how to live is due to something else besides lack of enlightenment, but just what that something is I don't know, by God!"

"There must be reasons," said Chichikov.

"Really, it seems to me at times," poor Hlobuev said with a sigh, "that the Russian is somehow all done for. He has no will power, no courage to be steadfast. You want to do everything and can't do anything. You constantly think that on the morrow you will start a new life; on the morrow you'll tackle everything in the right way; on the morrow you'll go on a diet. Nothing of the kind. On the evening of the same day you'll stuff yourself so that all you can do is blink your eyes, and your tongue won't turn, and you'll sit there like an owl staring at everybody, actually. And it's that way with everything."

"Yes," said Chichikov with a slight smile, "things like that do happen. One must maintain a reserve of prudence, one ought to consult prudence every minute, hold friendly converse with it—"

"Well, now!" said Hlobuev. "Really, it seems that we haven't been born for prudence at all. I don't believe there is a prudent man among us. If I see that somebody is actually leading a prudent life, saving and accumulating money, I won't believe even in him; in his old age the Devil will trip him up too and he'll let everything go down the drain at one clip! And all of us are like that, both the no-

blemen and the muzhiks, both the enlightened and the un-
enlightened. You'll come across some intelligent muzhik;
he'll amass a hundred thousand out of nothing—but, when
he's accumulated it, he'll get the mad notion of bathing in
champagne, and bathe in champagne he will. But there, we
have apparently looked over everything. There's nothing
more. Unless you would like to take a look at the mill?
However, the water wheel is missing and, besides, the
building itself is unfit for anything."

"What's the use of looking it over, then?" said Chichikov.

"In that case let's go home."

And they all started back for the house. On their return
trip the views were the same as before. The only addition
was a new puddle in the middle of the street. Slovenly disorder thrust forth its hideous face simply everywhere.
Everything was out at the elbows and down at the heels,
with the muzhiks as well as with the master. A wrathful
countrywife in a greasy sackcloth dress had beaten a poor
little girl half to death and was cursing somebody out to a
fare-you-well in the third person and calling upon all the
devils in the catalogue. Farther on, out of a little window,
two muzhiks were watching with a stoical indifference the
wrath of the drunken harridan; there was a perfect division
of labor between them: one bearded fellow was scratching
his behind, the other was yawning through his philosophical beard. One could see that the buildings and everything
else were yawning; the roofs were yawning too. Platonov,
after a look at all this, yawned in his turn. "My future property, these peasants," mused Chichikov. "Hole upon hole
and patch upon patch!" And truly, a whole gate was lying
on top of one of the huts, by way of a roof; the tiny win-

dows, paneless and with the frames falling out, were stuffed with foot clouts and propped up with poles stolen from the master's granary. Obviously, the system of robbing Peter to pay Paul was followed throughout the economy of the estate, or on Trishka's method of patching his kaftan, as described in Krylov's fable: the cuffs and coattails were cut off to patch the elbows.

"Your domestic economy is not an enviable one," said Chichikov after they had seen everything and were approaching . . . . . . [the house].

They went inside. Chichikov was struck by the intermingling of poverty with certain glittering knick-knacks which were the last word in luxury. In the midst of tattered furniture and broken accessories stood new bronzes. A tiny bust of some poet (probably Shakespeare) graced the inkwell; lying on the table was a backscratcher—a tiny hand on a long stick, all carved out of ivory. Hlobuev introduced his wife. You couldn't wish for a more charming hostess; she would not have disgraced herself even in Moscow; she was dressed with taste and in the latest mode. She preferred to talk for the most part about the town and the theatre that had been started there. One could perceive by everything that she liked the country even less than Hlobuev did, and that she yawned even more than Platonov whenever she was left to her own devices. In a short while the room filled with children, enchanting little girls and boys. There were five of them, and a sixth was brought in on the arms of a nurse.

They were all beautiful; these boys and girls were a delight to the eye. They were dressed charmingly and with taste, they were playful and merry, and because of all this it was still sadder to look at them. It would have been better if they had been dressed poorly, in skirts and blouses of common striped ticking, if they were simply to run about in the yard and were in no way distinguishable from the children of the peasants!

A caller, some sort of giddy, empty-headed chatterbox, came to see the hostess and the ladies went off to the hostess's quarters. The children ran off after them. The men were left to themselves.

Chichikov got down to dickering. Like all buyers, he began by depreciating the estate he meant to buy and, after having depreciated it all around, said: "What will be your price, then? I am asking, I must confess, to hear your lowest and last price, inasmuch as the estate is in an even worse condition than I anticipated."

"In a most abominable condition, Pavel Ivanovich," Hlobuev concurred. "I'm not going to ask much, and besides I wouldn't like to do so, since it would be actually dishonest on my part. Nor is the vile condition of the estate the only bad feature; I will also not conceal from you the fact that of the hundred souls in my village listed with the Bureau of Audits there aren't even fifty among the living— cholera has seen to that; others have gone off without passports, so that you may consider them as good as dead, since if you were to go after them through the courts, the courts would get the estate in expenses. For these reasons I will ask only thirty thousand from you."

Chichikov, naturally, began to dicker. "There, now, how can you ask thirty thousand? The estate is neglected, the souls are dead or missing, and thirty thousand! There, take twenty-five thousand!"

"Pavel Ivanovich, I can mortgage it for that, if only I had . . . . . . [the expenses]. . . . In that case I get the twenty-five thousand and the estate is still mine. I am selling it for the sole reason that I need the money urgently, whereas the mortgage negotiations would drag along; one has to smear the clerks, yet I have nothing to smear them with."

"Well, you take twenty-five thousand just the same."

Platonov felt ashamed over the way Chichikov was acting. "Buy it, Pavel Ivanovich," said he. "The estate is worth . . . . . . [the price] he's asking for it, any time. If you won't give thirty thousand for it, my brother and I will put up the money and buy it together."

Chichikov became frightened. "Very well," he said, "I will give thirty thousand for it. I'll give you two thousand deposit right now, eight thousand next week, and the rest a year later."

"No, Pavel Ivanovich, that's something I absolutely cannot do. The main condition is that half the money be forthcoming as soon as possible. You give me at least half now, and the rest no further than two weeks hence."

"But really, now, I don't know how I can do it. I have only ten thousand right now, all in all," said Chichikov, and lied as he said it; he had twenty thousand in all, including the money he had borrowed from Skudronzhoglo; but somehow it was a pity to pay out so much at one clip.

"No, Pavel Ivanovich, please! I'm telling you that I absolutely must have fifteen thousand."

"Yes, but I am short five thousand. I myself don't know where to get it."

"I'll lend it to you," Platonov caught him up.

"Oh, in that case it's a different matter!" said Chichikov,

and thought to himself: "That's quite handy, his making me the loan! I can bring Hlobuev the rest tomorrow."

The casket was brought in from the barouche and the ten thousand were counted out for Hlobuev right then and there; as for the remaining five thousand, Chichikov promised to bring them on the morrow; that is, he promised, but really proposed to bring only three, the other two thousand would come two days later, or three, or even, if possible, be put off for some time longer. Somehow, Pavel Ivanovich did not like letting go of his money. But if there was an urgent necessity to do so, it nevertheless seemed to him better to hand the money out on the morrow than today. That is, he acted much the same as all of us do, for it is a pleasant thing to us to keep a recipient on tenterhooks. Let him cool his heels a while in the anteroom! Just as though he couldn't wait! What concern is it of ours if every hour is precious to him and that his affairs suffer? "You come around tomorrow, brother, I'm sort of pressed for time today!"

"And where are you going to live now?" asked Platonov. "Have you some other hamlet?"

"I have no hamlet, but will move to the city instead; I have a wretched little house there. I would have to move there anyway, not for myself but for the children. They will have to have instructors in religious matters, in music and dancing. For you can't get those things in the country for any money!"

"He hasn't got a crust to eat, and yet he wants to have his children taught to dance!" thought Chichikov.

"Strange!" thought Platonov.

"Well, what do you say? We really must wet the bargain," said Hlobuev. "Hey, there, Kiriushka! Bring us a bottle of champagne, brother!"

"He hasn't got a crust to eat, yet he has champagne!" thought Chichikov. As for Platonov, he did not know even what to think.

The champagne Hlobuev had gotten out of sheer necessity. He had sent somebody up to town to get bread cider, but the shop would not give out anything on credit. Yet he wanted to drink something, so what was he to do? But there was a Frenchman who had recently come from St. Petersburg and opened a wineshop; he extended credit right and left. There was no help for it; Hlobuev had been forced to take champagne.

The champagne was brought. They drank off three goblets each and grew jolly. Hlobuev relaxed; he became charming and clever, he showered them with witticisms and anecdotes. There was so much knowledge of the world and of people revealed in his speeches! So well and so justly did he see many things, so aptly and deftly could he sketch in a few words his neighboring landowners, so clearly did he perceive the shortcomings and errors of everybody, so well did he know the history of the ruined seigniors—for what reason, and how, and through what causes they had become ruined—so originally and amusingly could he convey their least traits, that both his listeners were utterly bewitched by his speeches and were ready to acknowledge him the cleverest of men.

"I am amazed, really," said Platonov, seizing Hlobuev's hand. "How is it that you, with so much intelligence, experience, and knowledge of life, cannot find ways and means of extricating yourself from your difficult situation?"

"Oh, there are ways and means," said Hlobuev, and right then and there unloaded a whole heap of projects before them. These were all so preposterous, so odd, so little derived from a knowledge of the world and of men, that all there was left to do was to shrug and say: "Lord God! What an unencompassable distance there is between a knowledge of the world and the ability to use that knowledge!" All these projects were based on the necessity of acquiring, somehow or other, but suddenly, one hundred thousand, or two hundred thousand. Then, it seemed to Hlobuev, all would be set to rights, and his estate would be a going concern, and he himself would be put in a position to pay off all his debts. And he would wind up his speech with: "But what would you? There isn't any such benefactor—there simply isn't—as would venture to loan me two hundred thousand, or even a hundred thousand. Evidently, God doesn't wish it."

"Of course!" thought Chichikov. "The idea of God sending two hundred thousand to such a fool!"

"Incidentally, I have an aunt worth three million," Hlobuev went on. "A pious little crone: gives money for churches and monasteries, but when it comes to helping someone related to her she's sort of tight. An auntie that belongs to a bygone age, worth while taking a trip to see. She has four hundred canaries alone, and such pug dogs, such female hangers-on and servants as you don't see nowadays. The youngest of these servants must be going on sixty by now, but she still calls him: 'Hey, there, boy!' If any one of her guests doesn't behave himself just right, she'll order the waiter to pass him over with a course, and passed over he will be. There, now!"

"And what's her name? Where does she live?"

"She's living in our town. Her name is Alexandra Ivanovna Hanassarova."

"Why don't you turn to her, then?" Platonov asked with concern. "It seems to me that if she were really to go into the situation your family is in she would find it beyond her power to refuse, no matter how tight she may be."

"Oh, no, it wouldn't be beyond her power! My auntie has a rather strong nature. She's a flinty-hearted little crone, Platon Michailovich! Then, too, there are plenty of willing hands besides me who are crawling around her. There's one in particular who's aiming at becoming a Governor. He has enrolled himself among her kin. God be with him! Perhaps he may succeed. God be with all of them! I didn't know how to get around people even before, but now all the more so—my back is no longer supple."

"You fool!" thought Chichikov. "Why, I would tend an auntie like that the way a nurse tends a baby!"

"Well, now, one's throat gets dry from such talk," said Hlobuev. "Hey, Kiriushka, bring us another bottle of champagne!"

"No, no, I can't drink any more," said Platonov.

"Same here," said Chichikov, and both refused in positive terms.

"Well, in that case, give me your word to call on me in town: I am giving a small dinner on the eighth to our town dignitaries."

"Good heavens!" Platonov cried out. "To be in a situation like that, utterly ruined, yet give dinners!"

"Well, what can one do? One can't do otherwise; it's a debt I owe them," said Hlobuev. "They have entertained me in the past."

"What's to be done with a fellow like that?" thought Platonov. He still was not aware that in Russia (in Moscow and in other cities as well) there are to be found certain ingenious individuals whose life is an unsolvable enigma. It seems as if one of these fellows has gone through his last copper, is in debt up to his chin, has no means anywhere, and the dinner he is giving seems to be the last one; and the diners think that no later than on the morrow their host will be hauled off to prison. Ten years pass after that dinner—the sage is still holding on (and out) in this world; now it's his ears he's in debt up to, and he is giving a dinner in the same old way, and everybody thinks that this is the last dinner, and all feel certain that no later than on the morrow the host will be hauled off to prison. Ten years pass—

Hlobuev was virtually that sort of ingenious individual. Only in Russia, and nowhere but Russia, can anybody get along like that. Having nothing, he entertained people and kept open house, and even extended patronage, encouraging whatever theatrical people came trouping to town, giving them both haven and lodgings. Were anyone to look in at his house in town, he would never have realized that the owner was living therein. Today a priest in chasubles would be saying mass there, on the morrow French actors would be holding a rehearsal; on some days some gentleman whom hardly anybody in the house knew would settle in the drawing room with all his papers and start a study in it. And all this did not perturb or inconvenience anybody in the house, as though it were all a part of the everyday routine. At times, for days on end, there wouldn't be so much as a crumb of anything in the house, but at other times they would stage such a dinner as would have satisfied the taste of the most exquisite gastronome, and the owner would appear in festal array, in jovial mood, with the bearing of a rich seignior, with the walk of a man whose life flows smoothly amid abundance and contentment. On the other hand, there were moments so depressing that anybody else in Hlobuev's place would have long since shot or hanged himself. But he was saved by a religious streak that in some strange way existed within him side by side with his shiftless way of life. At such bitter, oppressive moments he would read the lives of martyrs and workers in the vineyard of the Lord, who had trained their spirit to be above sufferings and misfortunes. His soul at such moments would soften, his spirit would be moved, and his eyes fill with tears. And—a strange thing!—almost always unexpected help would come to him from some quarter or other: either one of his old friends would recall him and send him some money; or some fair transient, some charitable being, having somehow chanced to hear his story, would, out of the impetuous magnanimity of a feminine soul, send him a rich gift offering; or else, somewhere, a legal suit would be decided in his favor, which suit he may never even have heard of. Reverently, gratefully, would he acknowledge at such a time the unencompassable mercy of Providence, have a mass of thanksgiving said—and begin his shiftless mode of life all over again.

"I feel sorry for him, really I do," said Platonov to Chichikov when, having said good-by to Hlobuev, they were setting out from his place.

"A prodigal son!" said Chichikov. "It's hardly worth while feeling sorry for such people."

And in a short time they both ceased thinking of him: Platonov because he regarded the situations human beings found themselves in just as apathetically and half-somnolently as he regarded everything else in the world; his heart commiserated and contracted at the sight of the suffering of others, but the impressions were not, somehow, impressed deeply upon his soul. In a few moments he was no longer thinking of Hlobuev. He no longer thought of Hlobuev because he did not think even of his own soul. Chichikov did not think of Hlobuev because his thoughts were taken up in all seriousness with his newly bought acquisition. Finding himself, after all was said and done, no longer the proprietor of a phantasmal estate but an actual, substantial one, he had grown thoughtful, and both his suppositions and thoughts had grown more sedate and were involuntarily bestowing a serious expression on his face. "Patience, toil! They're not so hard: I made their acquaintance in my swaddling clothes, so to say. They're no novelty to me. But will there be as much patience now, at my years, as there was in my youth?"

He calculated, he considered and weighed all the advantages of the estate he had acquired. But no matter how things stood, no matter how he examined everything, no matter which way he turned this aspect and that of his purchase, he saw that in any case it was a profitable one. He could work it so as to mortgage the estate, having first sold off the best pieces of land. He could arrange things so as to take the management of the estate upon himself and become a landowner in the style of Skudronzhoglo, availing himself of his counsels as a neighbor and benefactor. He could even manage things so as to resell the estate into private hands [if he should not want to manage it himself, of course], retaining the runaways and the dead souls for himself. And then another advantageous course appeared before him: he could slip away from these regions entirely and without at all repaying to Skudronzhoglo the money he had borrowed. A strange thought! Not that Chichikov had actually conceived it; it had, rather, sprung up before him abruptly, of itself, teasing him and smiling upon him, and winking at him. The wanton! The flighty little thing! And who is the creator of these thoughts that so suddenly swoop down upon us? He felt pleasure, pleasure because he had now become a landowner, not the owner of phantasmal castles in the air, but an actual owner, an owner who had lands and appendages of landed property, and serfs—serfs that were not dream-people, dwelling in his imagination, but having actual existence. And little by little he began to bounce in his seat, and to rub his hands, and to wink to himself; putting his fist up to his lips as if it were a trumpet he played some sort of a march, and even uttered aloud several encouraging words and names to himself, such as *little funny-face* and *little capon*. But then, recalling that he was not alone, he suddenly quieted down, trying to quell somehow his inordinate fit of exuberance, and when Platonov, having taken some of the sounds for speech addressed to him, asked him: "What is it?" he answered: "It's nothing."

Only at this point, looking about him, did he perceive that they had long been driving through a beautiful grove; an enchanting hedge of birches stretched along on their right. The white trunks of the forest birches and aspens, as gleaming as a snow-white palisade, reared up gracefully and lightly against the tender green background of the recently unfolded foliage. The nightingales were gurgling in the grove, in loud rivalry with one another. Forest tulips showed yellowly in the grass. Chichikov could give no account to himself how they had come to be in this beautiful place, when just a little while ago they had been driving through open fields. A stone church gleamed whitely through the trees, and, in another direction, a wooden wicket emerged from the grove. A gentleman appeared at the end of the avenue, coming toward them, wearing a cap and carrying a knobby stick in his hand. An English greyhound was loping ahead of him on long, slender legs.

"And there's my brother," said Platonov. "Stop, coachman!"

He leapt out of the barouche, Chichikov climbing out after him. They walked toward the gentleman. Yarb had already managed to lick the muzzle of the greyhound, with whom, evidently, he had been long acquainted, inasmuch as he accepted apathetically upon his thick chops the other's ardent kiss. The nimble hound, whose name was Azor, having kissed Yarb, ran up to Platonov and leapt at him, intending to lick his lips, but fell short and, pushed away, leapt at Chichikov, licking him on the ear, after which he ran anew to Platonov, trying to lick his ear at least.

Platonov and the gentleman who had been approaching them met at this point and embraced each other.

"Good heavens, Platon! What are you doing to me?" the gentleman asked with lively concern.

"Why, what do you mean?" Platonov responded apathetically.

"Really, now, what is all this? For three days there's been nor sight nor sound of you! A groom brought your stallion back from Petuh's. 'He rode off,' he said, 'with some gentleman.' There, now, if you had said but one word: where you were going, what for, how long you would be away. Good heavens, brother, how can anyone act like that? Why, God knows what I've been thinking these last few days!"

"Well, what can be done about it? I forgot," said Platonov. "We dropped in on Constantin Fedorovich. . . . He sent you his regards; sister did, too. Let me introduce you—this is Pavel Ivanovich Chichikov; Pavel Ivanovich, this is my brother Vassilii."

Brother Vassilii and Chichikov, having shaken hands, took off their caps and kissed each other.

"Who might this Chichikov be?" Brother Vassilii was thinking. "Brother Platon isn't very discriminating when it comes to forming acquaintances—probably didn't find out what sort of man he is." And, as far as politeness permitted, he looked Chichikov over and saw that, in appearance, he was a most well-intentioned person. Chichikov stood there with his head inclined somewhat to one side and maintaining a pleasant expression on his face.

For his part Chichikov also, insofar as politeness permitted, looked brother Vassilii over and saw that he was not as tall as Platon, darker of hair, and far from being as handsome of face, but that in the features of that face there was far more life and animation, more of kindheartedness. One could see that he did not pass his life in lethargy and slumber. But to that aspect of his character Pavel Ivanovich paid but little attention.

"Do you know, Vassilii, what I've thought of?" asked Brother Platon.

"What is it?" asked Vassilii.

"I have decided, Vassya, to travel about holy Russia with Pavel Ivanovich. Perhaps this will stir up and dispel my melancholy."

"How did you come to such a sudden decision?" asked brother Vassilii, wonderingly, and was on the very verge of adding: "And the very idea of traveling about with a man whom you're seeing for the first time, who may be trash and the Devil knows what!" Filled with distrust, he eyed Chichikov askance and saw a respectability that was truly amazing.

They turned to the right, into a gateway. The courtyard was of the old-fashioned kind; the house, too, was old-fashioned, such as is no longer built nowadays, with overhanging eaves and a high-pitched roof. Two enormous lindens grew in the middle of the courtyard and shaded almost one-half of it. Under them was a multitude of wooden benches. Blooming lilac bushes and birdcherry shrubs wound like a bead necklace around the yard and its hedge of birches, screening the lower trunks of the trees completely with blossoms and leaves and filling the whole yard with fragrance. They screened the whole manor house too, save for the doors and windows that charmingly peeped through. Between the arrow-straight tree trunks one caught glimpses of white-walled kitchens, storehouses and cellars. The whole place was in the midst of the grove. The nightingales shrilled loudly, filling the whole grove with their song. Involuntarily one's soul became filled with some sort of insouciantly pleasant feeling. The place was so reminiscent of all those carefree times when everybody lived in a kindhearted mood and everything had been simple and uncomplicated. Brother Vassilii invited Chichikov to be seated and they all sat down on the benches under the lindens.

A smart and deft lad of seventeen in a handsome shirt of pink bombazine brought several decanters of fruit ciders, of all colors and varieties, ranging from those that were as thick as oil to those that hissed and bubbled like carbonated lemonade. Having placed the decanters and glasses on a rustic table he seized a spade that had been leaning against one of the trees and went off into the garden. The brothers Platonov, even as their brother-in-law Skudronzhoglo, had no serving people, properly speaking; they were all gardeners who took turns in waiting on the masters. Brother Vassilii maintained that servants did not constitute a separate class: anyone could wait on table, and it was not worth while setting up a staff of servants. He also maintained that, apparently, the Russian was a good man and a smart one, and not a sluggard, only as long as he went about in shirt and sheepskin jacket; but just as soon as he got into a frock coat of a German cut he would suddenly grow clumsy, and lose all his smartness, and turn sluggard, and never change his shirt, and stop going to the baths altogether, and sleep in his frock coat, and an incomputable army of fleas and bedbugs would mobilize under that same frock coat of a

German cut. And perhaps he may have been right in maintaining this. In the village belonging to these brothers the
people dressed in a particular dandified way: you would
have had far to seek to find such handsome shirts and
sheepskin jackets; the women trimmed their picturesque
headdresses with gold thread, and the sleeves of their
blouses were every whit as elaborately embroidered as the
borders of Turkish shawls.

"Won't you please refresh yourself?" brother Vassilii invited Chichikov, with a wave of his hand toward the decanters. "These are ciders for which our house has long
been widely celebrated."

Chichikov poured out a glass for himself from the first
decanter that came to his hand; the drink was for all the
world like the linden-honey mead he used to drink in
Poland: it bubbled like champagne and the gas went from
his mouth and caught the nose with a pleasant shock.

"Nectar!" said Chichikov. He drank a glass from another
decanter; it was still better. "The drink of drinks!" he commented. "I can say that at your most estimable brother-in-
law's, Constantin Fedorovich's, I drank the very best of
cordials, while in your place I am drinking the very best of
ciders."

"Why, the cordial is also due to us, inasmuch as our sister is responsible for it. But where are you proposing to
travel, what places do you intend to visit?" asked brother
Vassilii.

"I am traveling"—Chichikov spoke, rubbing his hand
gently on his knee and accompanying his words with a
slight swaying of his whole torso and an agreeable inclina-

tion of his head to one side—"I am traveling not so much for my own needs as those of another. General Betrishchev, my close friend and, one may say, my benefactor, has asked me to inform his relatives about a certain event. The relatives are, of course, one thing, but in part, as it were, I am also traveling for myself, because—to say nothing of the benefit to be derived if one considers merely the hemorrhoidal aspect of things—to see the world and the procession of people passing by is of itself tantamount to reading a living book and getting a second education, so to say."

Brother Vassilii became thoughtful. "This man speaks in a somewhat flowery fashion, but just the same there's truth in his words," he reflected. "My brother Platon does lack a knowledge of people, of the world, and of life." After a certain silence he spoke up: "Do you know what, Platon? I am beginning to think that this trip really may arouse you. You're afflicted with nothing else but a spiritual coma. You've simply fallen asleep, and fallen asleep not because of satiation or fatigue but from a lack of living impressions and sensations. There, I'm just the other way. I would very much like not to feel things so vividly, and not to take everything that happens so much to heart."

"Well, why do you choose to take everything to heart?" said Platonov. "You dig up things to upset you and invent your own anxieties."

"Why invent them when there is unpleasantness at every step as it is?" asked brother Vassilii. "Have you heard what trick Lenitzin played on us while you were away? He has grabbed the wasteland with the little hill where we roll the eggs at Easter. In the first place, I wouldn't part with the wasteland for any money . . . . . . All the memories of the village are bound up with it, and since custom is for me a sacred thing I'm ready to sacrifice anything for it."

"He doesn't know it's yours, that's why he grabbed it," said Platon. "He's a new man hereabouts, he is just come from St. Petersburg; things ought to be pointed out to him, explained—"

"He knows, he knows right well. I sent somebody over to tell him, but his answer was very rude."

"You ought to go to him yourself and explain everything to him. Talk things over with him yourself."

"Oh, no! He's making himself far too important. I'm not going to go to him. By all means, you can go to him yourself, if you like."

"I would go, only I don't mix . . . [in the management of the estate] . . . . . . He can fool me and take me in."

"Why, if you like, I'll go," Chichikov volunteered. "Just tell me what it's all about."

Vassilii glanced at him and thought to himself: "Eh, how fond he is of gadding about!"

"You just give me some idea of what sort of a man he is," Chichikov went on, "and just what's what."

"I have compunctions about burdening you with such an unpleasant commission, inasmuch as I consider a mere explanation with such a man an unpleasant commission in itself. I must tell you that he belongs to the lower nobility, to a family of petty landowners in our province; he has worked himself up in the Civil Service at St. Petersburg, managed to scramble his way up by one means or another, and get in among the ranks of decent people, marrying somebody's natural daughter, and is making himself important. Putting on airs. But then, the people living in our province are no fools, glory be to God. Fashion is no decree to us, and St. Petersburg is not a holy of holies."

"Of course not," said Chichikov. "And what is the business all about?"

"Well, to tell the truth, the whole matter is so much nonsense. He hasn't got enough land—well, he up and grabbed somebody else's; that is, he figured it wasn't wanted and that its owners wouldn't [bother] ...... But it so happens that on this very piece of land our peasants, time out of mind, have gathered to celebrate their spring festivals. For that reason I am ready to sacrifice other, better pieces of land rather than give up this wasteland."

"Consequently, you are ready to yield other lands to him?"

"I would have given him land for nothing, if he hadn't acted toward me the way he did; but evidently he wants to try the courts. Why not? We'll see who'll win. Even though the matter is not so clear in the surveys, yet there are old men who can still remember and testify as to the boundary lines. But he walks about with a chip on his shoulder, and he'll think—"

"Hm! Both are men of spirit, I can see that," reflected Chichikov. Then, aloud: "In my opinion it would be better to talk things over; it seems to me that everything can be settled amicably. It all depends on the intermediary. I have been entrusted with negotiations before, and those who entrusted them to me did not regret having done so. There is General Betrishchev, for instance—"

"But I have compunctions because you will have to talk with a man like that."

. . . .

"......* and, above all, the utmost secrecy should be observed in the matter," said Chichikov, "since it is not the transgression itself which is harmful but the demoralization which it causes if known."—"That is so, that is so," said Lenitzin, tilting his head so that it almost rested on his shoulder.

"What a pleasure it is to find unanimity of thought!" said Chichikov. "I, too, have a certain business on hand that is both legal and illegal; it may appear illegal, but essentially is legal. I have to put through certain mortgages; at the same time I don't want to involve anybody in the risk of having to pay a two-ruble tax on each living soul. Well, now, should my affairs happen to go up the chimney— which God forbid!—the matter will be unpleasant to the previous owner; I have therefore decided to avail myself of runaway and dead souls, which have not yet been crossed off the census at the Bureau of Audits, so that I might at the one stroke perform both a Christian deed and relieve the poor owner of the burden of having to pay taxes upon them ...... [For instance, it seems to me] that it would be most advantageous to you as well to transfer all the dead souls on your estate to me. We will execute, merely between us, a *pro forma* purchase deed, as though the souls were still alive."

---

*At this point two pages have been clipped out of the manuscript. *Trans.*

"However, this matter is a most strange one," thought Lenitzin, and moved back, chair and all, finding himself in an utter quandary.

"But then, the matter, now . . . is of such a nature—" he began.

"I have no doubt whatsoever that you will agree in this matter," Chichikov answered him quite straightforwardly and frankly. "The business is of the same nature as the one we were discussing just now; it is between people of good intent, of prudent years, and, it would seem, of good social position and, with all that, it is undertaken in secrecy." And as he said this he looked with a frank and noble air straight into the other's eyes.

What was to be done? No matter how resourceful Lenitzin was, no matter how knowing a man in business matters, yet here he was somehow utterly perplexed, since, in some strange way, he had become entangled in his own snares. He could not have foreseen that the opinion which he had so recently expressed would lead him to actual performance. The proposal was extremely unexpected. Of course there could be nothing injurious to anybody in this transaction; the landowners would have mortgaged these dubious souls anyway on the same basis with the living, ergo, there could be no detriment to the public treasury in any case; the sole difference lay in that now these souls would be in a single pair of hands, whereas otherwise they would have been in many hands. He was versed in the law and a businessman, and a businessman inclined to do the right thing. No bribes could have made him decide a matter unjustly, and he would not have wanted to commit any injustice, even in secret. But here he paused, not knowing what name to give to this action—was it right or was it wrong? Had anybody else turned to him with a proposal like that, he might have said: "This is nonsense—what trifles! I don't want to tear paper dolls or to fool around." But his caller had already proven so much to his liking, he and Lenitzin had found so many points in common concerning the successes achieved by enlightenment and the arts— how could he refuse him? Lenitzin was in a most difficult predicament. "What an astonishing situation!" he reflected. "There, if you please, go and become intimate even with good people! And now you have a problem on your hands!"

But fate and circumstances seemed to be favoring Chichikov. Just as if on purpose to help in this embarrassing situation, the young hostess entered the room. Lenitzin's wife was pale, and a snub-nosed, thin, short little thing, like all St. Petersburg ladies, but she dressed with taste, like all St. Petersburg ladies, and had a great liking for people who were *comme il faut*. She was followed by a wet-nurse who brought in on her arms a baby, the first fruits of the tender love of the recently wedded couple. Chichikov, of course, immediately approached the lady and, outside of his deferential greeting, his adroit springy walk and the agreeable inclination of his head to one side would have been enough to dispose the St. Petersburg lady in his favor and to enchant her utterly. Next he dashed up to the baby. It began bawling but, through baby talk, through calling it darling and the like and snapping his fingers, as well as through the beauty of his carnelian watch seal, Chichikov succeeded in enticing it into his arms. Having succeeded in this, he began upsy-daisying it toward the ceiling and aroused a pleased smile on the baby's face, which delighted the parents no end.

But, either from pleasure or from some other cause, the child was moved to give vent to something else besides his aroused emotions, something not at all refined.

"Ah, my God!" Lenitzin's wife cried out. "He has spoiled your whole coat!"

Chichikov looked: the sleeve of his brand-new frock coat was ruined.

"I hope you get a fit, you little imp!" he muttered, heartily vexed, but he muttered inwardly.

The host, the hostess, the wet-nurse, all dashed for the Eau de Cologne, all began wiping him thoroughly.

"It's nothing, nothing, absolutely nothing," Chichikov was saying, trying to impart to his face, as far as he was able, a lighthearted expression. "Can an innocent infant spoil anything at that age?" he kept repeating, and at the same time thought to himself: "But just see how neatly the little beast did his work: he hit the bull's eye, may the wolves eat him up, the damned little canaille!"—"His is the golden age!" said he, when they had wiped him off at last and he had entirely recovered his pleasant expression.

"Yes, that is absolutely right," the host agreed, also smiling pleasantly as he turned to Chichikov. "What can be more enviable than the age of infancy? No cares, no thoughts of the future—"

"A state any man would immediately exchange his own for," said Chichikov.

"Without even stopping to think," said Lenitzin.

But apparently both of them were lying: had anyone offered them such an exchange they would have backed out on the spot. Yes, what fun is there, when you come right down to it, in being imprisoned in a wet-nurse's arms and spoiling frock coats?

The young hostess and the first-born withdrew with the wet-nurse, inasmuch as some things needed fixing on his own person as well: having bestowed something upon Chichikov he had not overlooked bestowing something upon himself also.

This apparently insignificant circumstance brought the host over completely to Chichikov's side. How could one refuse such an amiable, considerate guest, who had shown so many innocent endearments to his tot and had paid so magnanimously for them with his own frock coat? "Really, now, why not grant him his request, if he is so set on it?" was how Lenitzin put it to himself.

In order not to set a bad example, they decided to conclude the matter in secret, since it was not the matter itself that was so injurious but the demoralizing temptation connected therewith.

"Allow me, too, to repay you with a service in return for the service you have rendered me. I want to act as intermediary in the matter between you and the brothers Platonov. You need land, isn't that so? . . . ."[G]

· · · · · · · ·

CHAPTER —— *

Everything in this world works for its own ends. "You scratch where it itches," says the proverb. The tour through the coffers had been performed successfully, so that a thing or two from this expedition found its way into [Chichikov's] own casket. In short, everything had been prudently managed. Chichikov hadn't exactly *stolen* anything, he had rather *availed himself* of some things. For each one of us will avail himself of one thing or another: this one of government timber; the other of sums from the estate he is managing; a third steals from his children for the sake of some touring actress; a fourth robs his peasants to get fine carriages and furniture made by some famous cabinet-maker. What's to be done when so many seductions have sprung up in this world? And then there are the expensive restaurants with their mad prices, and masquerades, and pleasure excursions, and dancing with the Gypsy women. For it is a hard matter to hold oneself back when all men, on all sides of you, are all doing the same mad things, and fashion itself commands that they be done. Just try to hold yourself back!

It was high time for Chichikov to be leaving the town, but the roads had become impassable.

---

*The manuscript bears no chapter heading or number. All indications point to this being a fragment of one of the earlier recensions of this part of *Dead Souls*. Trans.*

—

At the very time that Chichikov, in a new Persian dressing gown of aureate brocade, was sprawling on a divan and dickering with a transient dealer in contraband, of Jewish extraction and with a German accent, and had already put aside the purchased bolt of the finest Holland linen for shirts and two cardboard boxes of excellent soap of the very best quality (this was the same soap he used to acquire at the time he was serving in the Customs House at Radziwill; it had, actually, the power to impart an unbelievable softness to the skin, and a whiteness to the cheeks that was truly amazing)—at the very time when he was purchasing, as a connoisseur, these products so indispensable to a cultured man, there came the thunder of a carriage driving up, making the windowpanes reverberate and the walls of the room shake, and His Excellency Fedor Fedorovich Lenitzin entered.

"I'll leave it to the judgment of Your Excellency—what linen that is, and what soap, and then there's this little object, bought only yesterday!"

As he said this, Chichikov put on a fez trimmed with gold and beads, and looked every inch like a Persian shah, filled with dignity and majesty.

But His Excellency, without answering Chichikov's inquiry, said: "I have business to talk over with you."

One could see by his face that he was agitated. The deferential trader with the German accent was immediately dismissed and Lenitzin and Chichikov were left alone.

"Do you know what unpleasantness we are faced with? Another will that the old woman has made has turned up, made five [years] ago. One-half of the estate goes to a monastery, the other goes to the two girls she was bringing up, and nothing to anybody else."

Chichikov was dumbfounded. "But that will is nonsense. It doesn't mean a thing—it is annulled by the second."

"But the second will does not state that it annuls the first."

"That's understood of itself; the last annuls each preceding one. This first will isn't any good. I know well what the deceased woman's wishes were. I was with her. Who were the witnesses to this old will?"

"It was properly witnessed, before a court. The witnesses were Burmilov, the ex-judge of the Court of Equity, and Havanov."

"That's bad!" thought Chichikov. "Havanov, they say, is honest; Burmilov is an old hypocrite and a bigot, and reads out the Apostles in churches of holidays." . . . . . "But it's nonsense, nonsense!" he said aloud, and at once felt resolute enough to try all dodges. "I know this matter better: I was present at the deceased's last moments. I know all this better than anybody else. I'm ready to take my personal oath on it."

These words and his resoluteness for a moment calmed Lenitzin.

He had been very much agitated and already beginning to suspect whether there had not been some fabrication on Chichikov's part concerning the will (although he could not even have imagined that the business was as bad as it really was). Now he reproached himself for having been so suspicious. Chichikov's willingness to take an oath seemed proof evident that he [was sincere] . . . . . . We don't know if Pavel Ivanovich would have had the courage actually to take his Bible oath in this business, but he did have courage enough to say he would.

"Calm yourself [and don't worry about anything; I'm going] to talk the matter over with a certain counselor-at-law. You must do nothing in the matter for your part; you must keep entirely out of it. As for me, I can now live in this town as long as I want to."

Chichikov immediately ordered his carriage to be brought around and set out to see the counselor-at-law. This counselor-at-law was a man of exceptional experience. It was fifteen years by now that he had been under fire, yet he had managed things so that there was no way of disbarring him. All knew that for his exploits he should have been sent away—and sent away six times over—to a penal colony. He was suspected all around and in every quarter, but there was no possibility of digging up any clear and incontrovertible proofs of his guilt. There was really something uncanny here, and one could boldly acknowledge him a wizard, if the story we have told had belonged to the Dark Ages.

The counselor-at-law struck Chichikov by his frigidity as well as by the soiled state of his dressing gown, which offered an absolute contrast to the quite good furniture of mahogany, the gilt clock under its glass bell, the chandelier that could be glimpsed through the muslin cover protecting it and, in general, to everything that surrounded him and bore upon it the vivid impress of a brilliant continental culture.

Chichikov, however, undeterred by the skeptical air of the lawyer, explained to him the embarrassing points of the affair and held out an enticing prospect of the inevitable gratitude he would feel after receiving his good counsel and assistance.

The counselor-at-law responded to this by dwelling on the uncertainty of all things earthly and also by artfully letting Chichikov understand that two birds in the bush didn't mean a thing; what was needed was a bird in hand.

There was no help for it; a bird in hand had to be produced. The skeptical frigidity of the philosopher vanished instantaneously. It turned out that this was the most kindhearted of fellows, most talkative and most pleasant in his talk, who did not yield in the adroitness of his ways even to Chichikov himself.

"Allow me to suggest this to you, instead of making a long-drawn business of it: you probably have not examined the testament itself; it has, probably, a bit of an addendum, a codicil, or something of that sort. You take it home with you for a while. Although, naturally, it is prohibited to take such things home, yet if one were to ask certain officials in a really fine way. . . . For my part, I shall use my influence."

"I understand," thought Chichikov, and said: "Come to think of it, I really don't remember very well whether there was any additional notation on the will or not," just as if he hadn't really written the whole thing himself.

"Look for that, above all. However, in any case," the lawyer went on, quite good-naturedly, "always keep calm and don't be confused by anything, even if something worse should happen. Never despair in anything: there is no such thing as an irreparable affair. Look at me: I am always calm. No matter how bad the charges brought against me, my calm remains unshaken." The face of the lawyer-philosopher really preserved an extraordinary calm, so that Chichikov [derived] much ... [comfort therefrom].

"Of course, calm is of the utmost importance," said [he]. "However, you must agree that there must be certain cases and affairs, certain affairs and calumnies on the part of one's enemies, and certain difficult situations, where all calm will fly out of the window."

"Believe me, that is pusillanimity," the philosopher-jurist answered very tranquilly and good-naturedly. "The only thing is, you must try to have the whole process of the case based upon papers, try to avoid anything oral. And as soon as you see that the case is reaching a dénouement and that it is ready for a decision, try not so much to justify and defend yourself as simply to confound and tangle it up with new interjections, new interpolated data, and thus—"

"That is, so as to—"

"Tangle everything up, tangle everything up, and that's all there is to it," answered the philosopher. "Bring into the case other extraneous circumstances, side issues which may implicate other people in their turn; make the case complicated, and that is all. And then let the official who has come especially from St. Petersburg try to straighten the matter out—let him straighten it out, let him straighten it out!" he repeated, looking with extraordinary pleasure into Chichikov's eyes, as a teacher looks at a pupil when he expounds to him a most enticing point in grammar.

"Yes, and it might also be a good thing if one were to pick out such circumstances as would becloud the issue," said Chichikov, also looking with pleasure into the eyes of the philosopher, like a pupil who has grasped the enticing point that is being explained by his teacher.

"Those circumstances will be found, they'll be found! Believe me, even the brain becomes resourceful from frequent exercise. First and foremost, remember that you will be receiving help all along the line. There is much to be gained by many people through the complexity of the case: there are more officials and clerks needed, and they get more remuneration. In a word, draw into the case as many people as you can. No need to hesitate if some may get into trouble for nothing at all; why, it's up to them to exculpate themselves—it's they who will have to answer the sundry papers, who will have to pay ransom. And that's one way of making a living. Believe me, the first thing to do when circumstances become critical is to tangle them up. One can so tangle them up, one can pile confusion upon confusion so that nobody will understand a thing. Why am I so calm? Because I know: let my affairs worsen, and I'll entangle everybody in my mess—the Governor, and the Vice-Governor, and the Chief of Police, and the Treasurer, I'll tangle all of them up. I know all their circumstances: who is feuding with whom, and who is peeved at whom, and who wants to put whom away. After that, by all means let them disentangle themselves. Why, while they're disentangling themselves, others will manage to put away something for themselves. For it's only by fishing in troubled waters that you'll catch any crayfish. Everybody is only biding a chance to entangle somebody else." At this point the philosopher-jurist looked into Chichikov's eyes again with the same delight with which a teacher explains to a pupil a still more enticing point in grammar.

"No, this man is a sage, beyond a doubt," thought Chichikov to himself, and parted with the counselor-at-law in the most agreeable, the finest, frame of mind.

Completely reassured and fortified, he threw himself with negligent adroitness on the springy cushions of the carriage, ordered Seliphan to draw back the top (when he had been on his way to the counselor not only had the top been up but the leather curtains were also tightly drawn), and sprawled out every whit like a retired colonel of the Hussars, or even like Vishnepokromov himself, one leg jauntily turned in under him, affably facing all the passers-by, his face beaming from under a new silk hat cocked somewhat over one ear. Seliphan had been given orders to keep going in the direction of the market place. The merchants, both the transients and the natives, respectfully doffed their hats as they stood in the doorways of their shops, and Chichikov, not without dignity, raised his own hat in response. Many of them he was already familiar with; others, although they were here only temporarily, were nevertheless charmed by the urbane appearance of this gentleman who knew how to carry himself, and greeted him as if they knew him.

The fairs in the town of Tphewslavl (Faugh-glory) were going on without a stop. The merchants who had come in wheeled vehicles proposed to return not otherwise than on sleighs. The previous fair had had to do for the most part with horses, cattle, raw materials, and all sorts of produce brought by the peasants and bought up by jobbers and *ku-laks*. But now a fair that was properly for the gentry was about to begin. Everything that had been bought up by the dry-goods merchants at Nizhegorod Fair, with an eye to fine gentlemen of a higher degree of enlightenment, had been brought hither. Frenchmen, those ravagers of Russian pocketbooks, had flocked hither, and Frenchwomen with their lines of bonnets, those ravagers of money got through blood and toil—those Egyptian locusts (to use an expression of Skudronzhoglo's) who, as if it were not enough that they devoured everything, also left their eggs behind them, burying them in the ground. Only poor crops and [other agricultural calamities] ... had kept many landowners in their villages. But then the officals, since they had not suffered at all from poor crops, had let themselves go all out and, unfortunately, so did their wives. Having read their fill of all sorts of books, disseminated of late for the purpose of inspiring humanity with the higher needs, there had been aroused in them an inordinate avidity to partake of all the new delights. A Frenchman had opened a new establishment, some sort of Vauxhall Garden, a thing hitherto unheard of in the province, where a supper was served that was said to be unusually cheap—and half the bill could be on tab. This was sufficient to make not only the high officials attend, but even all the chancellery clerks, who hoped to reimburse themselves with future bribes ...... A desire sprang up to show off before one another with their horses and their coachmen. Ah, this conflux of the various classes for the sake of diversion! Despite the foul weather, the elegant carriages dashed up and down the fair. Where they had all come from, God alone knows, but they wouldn't have disgraced even St. Petersburg itself ...... The merchants and the shop clerks, tipping their hats adroitly, were touting the gentlewomen to enter their shops. Only rarely could one see traders with great beards and rough fur caps.

All had a European look about them, with their chins clean-shaven, all [had bad complexions] ...... and decayed teeth.

"Right this way, please! Right this way, please! If you'll be so kind as to step in! Sir! Sir!" the shopboys were calling out here and there.

But it was with disdain that they were regarded by those merchants who had become acquainted with Europe [and its shopkeepery] ...... only uttering occasionally, with a sense of dignity: "St[andard grades of goods] ......" or: "Fancy, plain, and solid black materials inside."

"Right this way, please, right this way!" a German frock coat of Moscow tailoring was coaxing as he postured picturesquely at the entrance to his shop, holding his hat aloft and barely keeping up his rounded chin and an expression of refined enlightenment on his Russian face.

"Have you any cloths of a bilberry color, but scintillating?" asked Chichikov.

"I have excellent cloths," said the merchant, lifting up his hat still higher and indicating his shop with a wave of his free hand. Chichikov went inside.

The pleasant-faced shopkeeper made a passage for himself by lifting up a flap in the counter, and stepping in closed it after him, after which he turned around, thus having behind him the goods piled up bolt on bolt from floor to ceiling, and placing himself face to face with his customer. After once more greeting the latter by lifting his hat again, he put the hat on his head, and, placing his hands smartly on the counter and resting his weight on his hands, at the same time swaying his whole torso affably, got down to business: "What sort of cloth do you prefer, Sir? Of English manufacture or domestic make?"

"Show me the domestic make," said Chichikov, "but only of the better sort, which is styled English."

"And what colors would you like?" asked the merchant, still swaying amiably, resting his weight upon his hands.

"Scintillating; dark colors, olive or bottle-green—approximating bilberry-red, as it were," said Chichikov.

"You'll get the first sort of goods here, I may say, such as you would get only at our capitals. Boy! Let's have that bolt up there, Number Thirty-four. Why, brother, that's not it! Why are you forever climbing above your sphere, like you were a proletarian or something! Toss it here. There's a piece of goods for you!" And, deftly unrolling its end, he held it up to the light, bringing it so close to Chichikov's nose that the latter could not only stroke its silken sheen but actually smell the cloth. "Look at the play of that color! In the most fashionable and the latest taste!" The merchant had instinctively scented that he had a connoisseur of textiles standing before him, and had not wanted to begin with a cheap grade.

"This isn't bad, but still that's not it," said Chichikov, after stroking the cloth once or twice. "You see, I worked in the Customs, so I must have the best there is, and then it must lean more toward red rather than bottle-green; it must approximate bilberry-red, now. Tell you what, my dear fellow, you show me right now whatever you usually save to show last."

"I understand, Sir; what you really wish is the sort of color that is now in . . . that is now entering into vogue. I have the very thing, of the highest quality. I warn you that it is high in price as well as in quality."

The bolt plumped down on the counter. The European unrolled it with a still greater deftness (belonging to former days, forgetting that by now he belonged to a later generation), and actually brought it outside, to show it in the daylight.

"There, Sir, is the cloth for you, Sir!" he said, squinting against the light. "An excellent shade! The Navarino smoke-tint, with a flame shooting right though it!"[10]

The cloth proved to Chichikov's liking. They came to terms, even though the merchant maintained that he had one fixed price. An iron yard measure, like the wand of a thaumaturge, instantaneously measured off enough to make Chichikov a frock coat and trousers; after making a nick with the scissors, the merchant tore the cloth right across, as deftly as any prestidigitator, concluding with a bow of the most flattering amiability. The cloth was instantaneously rolled up and bundled, in the Russian way, in paper, with unbelievable rapidity; the bundle whirled under light string which encircled it palpitatingly, as if it were alive, and formed a knot; the scissors snipped the string, and the shopkeeper was raising his hat—since Chichikov was reaching for his money.

But at this point he felt his waist pleasantly encircled by somebody's most delicate arm, while his ears were greeted with: "What are you buying here, my most respected Sir?"

"Ah, a most pleasant and unexpected meeting!" said Chichikov.

"A pleasant encounter," said the voice of him who had

taken Chichikov around the waist. It was Vishnepokromov.

"I was just about to pass the shop by without much attention when suddenly I see a familiar face—how could I refuse myself so great a pleasure? No use talking, the cloths this year are incomparably better. Why, it's a crying shame! Hitherto I have been simply unable to find anything decent. I'll give forty rubles—charge me even fifty—but give me good stuff. In my opinion it is better to have nothing at all if you can't have the very best. Isn't that right?"

"Perfectly right!" said Chichikov. "Why should one work hard if it isn't to have good things?"

"Let me see some medium-priced goods," Chichikov heard a familiar voice behind him.

"There, the Devil take it, it's Hlobuev!" thought Chichikov, and turned his back still more so as not to see him, finding it imprudent on his part to enter into any explanation with him concerning the inheritance. But the other had already seen him. Everything about him testified that he was not buying the material out of any whim, inasmuch as his skimpy coat was painfully threadbare.

"What is this, really, Pavel Ivanovich—are you deliberately avoiding me, by any chance? I can't find you anywhere; I've been at your place several times, but you're never at home—never! But you must at last give me a chance to talk to you, for the matter is of such a nature that we must have a serious discussion about it."

"My dear, dear fellow," said Chichikov, taking both his hands and squeezing them, "believe me, I've been wanting to have a talk with you all this while, but I've been so busy, I swear, that I simply had no time!" In the meantime he was thinking: "If only the Devil would take you!" But, as he was looking around him for a chance to slip away, he saw Murazov entering the shop.

"Athanassii Vassilievich! Ah, my God!" said Chichikov. "There's a pleasant encounter!" And, after him, Vishnepokromov repeated: "Athanassii Vassilievich." And then Hlobuev chimed in: "Athanassii Vassilievich!" And, finally, the well-brought-up merchant, having lifted his hat as far off his head as his arm would reach, and leaning forward with all his body, uttered: "Our humblest respects to Athanassii Vassilievich!" On all their faces was impressed that doglike servility which erring mankind evinces toward millionaires.

"How is your health, Athanassii Vassilievich?" asked Chichikov.

"How are you?" said Murazov, taking off his hat.

"Well, now, the small of my back aches, and then my sleep is never what it should be. Probably because I don't move about enough—"

But Murazov, instead of going into the reasons for Chichikov's indispositions, turned to Hlobuev. "You must excuse me but, catching sight of you from a distance as you turned into this shop, I decided to intrude on you. If you'll be free [shortly] . . . . . . and going past my house, I hope you'll be kind enough to drop in for a little while. I have something I want to talk over with you."

"Of course, of course, Athanassii Vassilievich!" Hlobuev hastened to say. And the old man, after another bow all around, walked out.

"What in the world could they talk about?" [Chichikov]

wondered. Then, aloud: "My head simply goes 'round and 'round when I think that this man is worth ten million. Why, that's downright unbelievable!"

"It's against all norm, however," said Vishnepokromov. "There shouldn't be so much capital in any one man's hands. That's the subject of ever so many treatises now throughout all Europe. If you have money, well, pass it on to others; entertain other people, give balls, create beneficial luxury, which gives bread to master craftsmen and tradesmen."

"Athanassii Vassilievich is a most estimable and intelligent man," said the merchant, "and he knows his business, but there's no enlightenment about him. For a merchant is a man of enterprise, and not merely a merchant. You have the budget involved here, and reaction, for otherwise pauperism would result!"

Chichikov made a hopeless gesture. "I can't understand it," he said. "Ten million, and he lives like a common muzhik! Why, with ten million one can accomplish the Devil knows what! Why, one can run things so as to be in no other society than that of generals and princes."

"Yes, Sir," added the merchant, "there's really a lack of enlightenment. If a merchant gains respectability, he is no longer a mere merchant but a man of enterprise. I must then get a box at the theatre, and I won't marry my daughter off to any common colonel, no, Sir! I won't marry her off to anybody under a general. What's a colonel to me? And as for dinners, they'll have to be by a caterer, and not a woman cook—"

"What's the use of talking?" said Vishnepokromov.

"Good gracious! What can't one accomplish with ten million? Give me ten million, and you'll see what I'll accomplish!"

"No," reflected Chichikov, "I don't think you would do much of anything sensible with ten million. But if you were to give *me* ten million, I would, sure as you're born, show you a trick or two."

"Why, if you were to give me ten million!" thought Hlobeuv. "I no longer would act as I formerly did; I wouldn't run through my money so insanely. After such a dreadful experience as mine one learns the value of every copper. Eh, I'd no longer act the same way——" But then, after a few moments' reflection, he asked himself inwardly: "Come, now, would I manage things any more prudently now?" And, with a hopeless feeling, he added: "What the Devil! I think I would squander the money just as I did before," and, walking out of the shop, he set out for Murazov's, since he wanted to know what the other had to say to him.

"Pavel Ivanovich, I'm looking for you all over!" Lenitzin's voice resounded behind Chichikov. The merchant respectfully doffed his hat.

"Ah, Fedor Fedorovich!"

"For God's sake, come over to my place—I must talk things over with you," he said. Chichikov looked at him—Lenitzin's face was utterly distraught. Chichikov paid for the goods at last and they walked out of the shop.

———

"I've been expecting you, Semën Semënovich," said Murazov, as Hlobuev entered. "Please step into my room."

And he led him into the little room already familiar to

the reader; and one could hardly find a more uninviting room even in the house of a government clerk with a salary of seven hundred a year.

"Tell me—I suppose that now, surely, your circumstances are better? After all, you must have come into something after your aunt's death?"

"Well, what can I tell you, Athanassii Vassilievich? I don't know if my circumstances are better or not. All I got for my share was fifty serf-souls and thirty thousand, which I had to use to settle part of my debts, and now I again have exactly nothing. But the main thing is that this matter of the legacy is a most shady one. What swindles have sprung up in connection with it, Athanassii Vassilievich! When I tell you you'll be astonished at what's going on. This Chichikov—"

"Allow me, Semën Semënovich, before you talk of this Chichikov let's speak of what concerns you in particular. Tell me, how much would you consider sufficient to enable you to extricate yourself entirely from your difficulties?"

"My circumstances are embarrassing," said Hlobuev. "Why, to extricate myself from them, to pay everybody off in full, and to be able to live in the most moderate manner, I need at least one hundred thousand, if not more; in a word, it's an impossibility, as far as I am concerned."

"Well, now, if you had this money, how would you lead your life?"

"Why, I would rent a small apartment, I would busy myself with the education of my children. It's no use thinking any more of myself; my career is done, because I'm unfit for work, I'm no longer fit for anything."

"So after all your life would remain an idle one, and in

idleness temptations beset one, of which a man would never think if he were taken up with work."

"I can't work; I'm not fit for anything."

"But why aren't you fit for anything?"

"Why, where would I fit in? You have forgotten that I have a family; I am forty-five; the small of my back aches by now; I have become as dull as an owl, have grown indolent. Should I really enter the Civil Service? I couldn't take bribes, I couldn't keep up with Krasnonossov and Samosvistov."

"But still, and you must forgive me, I can't understand how one can do without a path before one; how one can go on otherwise than by following a path; how one can drive when there is no ground underneath, how one can sail if there is no water under the boat. For life is a journey. Forgive me, Semën Semënovich, but those gentlemen you speak of are, after all, following some sort of a path; they are, after all, working away. Well, now, let us suppose that they have turned aside, somehow, as may happen to any sinner; yet there is still hope that they'll find the right path again. It is impossible for anyone who keeps on going not to arrive at some destination; there is hope that he will eventually come upon the right path. But how is one to come upon any path when one remains idle? For the path will not come to you. And how can one live without any work? Mercy! Look at every creation of God: each one serves for some end or other, each has its function. Take even a stone, and it, too, is in this world to be put to good use—and is a man, the most intelligent of all beings, to remain useless? Is that a right thing?"

"Well, now, I am not without an occupation, after all. I can busy myself with the education of my children."

"No, Semën Semënovich. No! That is the most difficult work of all! How can a father educate his children when he has not educated himself? For one can educate children only through the example of one's own life. And is your life fit to be an example for them? Unless it be to learn, perhaps, how to pass their time in idleness and how to play cards? No, Semën Semënovich, give your children to me; you will spoil them. Think this over in all seriousness: you have been ruined by idleness, you must flee from it. How can one go on in this world without a post, without a place? No matter what the duty may be, yet fulfill some duty one must. You take any day laborer, and even his work counts. All he earns is a few coppers for bread! But then, he wins that bread himself, and he feels an interest in his work."

"I swear by God I have tried, Athanassii Vassilievich—I have striven to overcome myself! What is one to do, then? Well, how am I to act? Judge for yourself: how am I, at forty-five, to sit down at the same desk with chancellery scribes who are just beginning? And as for any of the more important posts, they won't give me one—I am not held so very highly. Besides that, I must confess that I myself would not take a post where one could line one's pockets. I may be a rubbishy sort of person, and a gambler, and everything you like, yet I am incapable of taking bribes—I will not only stand in my own way but will hinder others. For by this time they've already formed their own castes there in the Service. Believe me, Athanassii Vassilievich, I feel perfectly the justice [of what you say] . . . . . . but I'm telling you that all energy has absolutely perished within me; I can't see that I could be of any use to anybody in this world. I feel that I am an utterly useless log. Before, while I was somewhat younger, why, it seemed to me that the whole matter lay in money, that if I had had hundreds of thousands in my hands I could have made a multitude of people happy: I would have helped poor artists, would have founded libraries, started useful institutions, formed collections. I am a man not without taste, and know that in many things I could have managed far better than those rich men of ours, who do all such things so senselessly. But now I see that this, too, is vanity of vanities, and that there isn't much sense in such things. No, Athanassii Vassilievich, I am fit for nothing, just nothing at all, I'm telling you. I am incapable of the least trifling work. No, Athanassii Vassilievich, I've thought over all sorts of posts, have weighed them, have gone over them—in all cases I was unfit. Except, perhaps, for the poorhouse—"

"The poorhouse is [for those] who have worked; but those who have played and sung all through the heyday of their youth are given the same answer as the ant gave to the grasshopper; 'go and dance some more, now!' And even sitting in a poorhouse the inmates also toil and work; they don't play whist. Semën Semënovich," Murazov was saying, looking into his face intently, "you are deceiving both yourself and me."

Murazov kept looking at his face intently, but poor Hlobuev could not make any answer. Murazov felt pity for him.

"Look here, Semën Semënovich! You pray, don't you? You go to church; you miss, I know, neither the morning mass nor the evening. Even though you don't feel like getting up early, yet get up you do and you go, you go at four o'clock in the morning, when nobody is up yet?"

"That is a different matter, Athanassii Vassilievich. I know I am doing it not for man but for Him Who has ordained all of us to be in this world. I do that for the salvation of my soul, because I am convinced that thereby I will at least to some extent make up for my idle life, that no matter how [abhorrent I may be to myself], no matter how bad I may be, yet humble prayers and a certain compulsion over oneself do mean something in the eyes of God; I believe that He is merciful toward me, that no matter how abominable, how vile I may be, yet He may forgive me and accept me, whereas men will spurn me from them with kicks, and the best of friends will sell me out, and on top of that will say afterward that he sold me out only because of a worthy motive."

An aggrieved emotion found expression on Hlobuev's face. Tears appeared in the old man's eyes, but he [said] nothing . . . . . .

"I will also tell you this: that sometimes I pray even without faith, yet I pray all the same. All I sense is that there is a Master upon Whom all depends, even as a horse or a domestic animal senses a master who has all rights over it."

"Therefore, you pray so as to please Him Whom you are praying to, so as to save your soul, and this gives you strength and makes you get out of bed early. Believe me, if you were to undertake a post in the same way, you would thereby serve Him Whom you pray to; energy would come to you, and there would be nobody who would make you cool off about your work. Serve, then, Him Who is so merciful. Toil is just as pleasing to Him as prayer. Apply yourself to any occupation at all, but apply yourself to it as if you were doing it for Him and not for men. Well, now, simply bray water in a stoup, but keep thinking you are doing it for Him. If there were no other gain, there would still be the fact that there would be no time left for idleness—for losing money at cards, for playing around with parasites and gluttons for the sake of a social life."

"Athanassii Vassilievich! I say to you again, this is a different matter. In the first instance I see that I am doing something after all. I tell you that I'm ready to go to a monastery, and will carry out the heaviest tasks and great works which may be assigned to me, because I see for Whom I am doing them. It is not my business to reason why. There I am certain that [those] who have compelled me to do these things will be the ones held to account, there I submit, and know that I am submitting to God."

"But why don't you reason the same way in worldly matters? For in this world, too, we must serve God and none other. Even if we do serve some other we only serve him because we feel certain that God so wills it, for without that we would not serve. For what other purpose are all our abilities and gifts, which differ so from man to man? For these are the implements of our prayer; you have prayer in words, and these are for prayer in deeds. For you cannot go to a monastery; you are attached to the world, you have a family."

Here Murazov fell silent.

Hlobuev, too, maintained silence.

"So you suppose," Murazov resumed, "that if you had,

for instance, a hundred thousand, you would then be in a position to make your life secure and to lead it more prudently thereafter. . . . But suppose I were to tell you in answer to this, Semën Semënovich, that inside of two years you would again be entangled in debt as in a net?"

Hlobuev kept silent for a space, then began, slowly spacing his words: "However, after such experiences—"

"Why, what's the use of talking!" Murazov broke in. "You're a man with a kind soul: a friend will come and ask you for a loan, and you will let him have it; you will see a poor man, and will want to help him; an agreeable guest will come to see you, and you will want to entertain him with the best of everything; and so you will yield to the first kindly impulse and forget all about prudence. Then, too, your wife . . . even though she is kind at heart . . . is not at all educated in such a way as to educate the children. I even wonder—forgive me, Semën Semënovich—whether it may not be actually bad for the children to be with you!"

Hlobuev grew thoughtful; he began mentally scrutinizing himself on all sides and at last came to feel that Murazov was partly right.

"Do you know what, Semën Semënovich? Put all this in my hands—your children, your affairs; leave both your wife and your children: I will watch out for them. For your circumstances are such that you're in my hands; the way your affairs are headed now you're facing death from hunger. In a case like that one must venture on anything. Eh, Semën Semënovich! Do you know Ivan Potapych?"

"I know him, and respect him very much, despite the fact that he walks about in a peasant coat."

"Surely, he was a good trader; worked his way up to a

million; but when he saw everything bringing him in a profit, why, he just cut loose. Had his son taught French, married his daughter off to a general, lived like the Czar himself. After a while he wasn't in his shop much, or on the exchange, but mostly on the lookout to meet some friend and drag him off to a tavern for tea; spent days on end there. Well, naturally, he went bankrupt. What was he to do then? Now, you see, he is working for me as a shop clerk. Started all over again. It was no jolly matter for him to pass from dining off silver plate to supping out of a common clay crock. It looked as if he couldn't put his hand to anything, but he got to like the work. Now he could go into trade and make another million; he could eat off silver plate again, but he no longer wants to. 'I was a shop clerk once, and I want to die a shop clerk. Now,' he says, 'I've become healthy and spry, but at that time I was growing a belly on me, and was starting to get dropsy. . . . No fine living for me!' And he doesn't take tea into his mouth now. Cabbage soup and buckwheat groats is all he eats. Yes, Sir! And when it comes to prayer, he prays as none of us does; and when it comes to helping the poor, he helps as none of us does, for many another would like to help but he has gone all through his money. Ivan Potapych could have accumulated money again, but he says: 'No, Athanassii Vassilievich, I am not now serving myself or working for my own self, but working only because God so wills it. I don't want to do anything of my own will. I obey you because I want to obey God and not men, and because God does not speak save through the lips of the best men. You are more intelligent than I, and for that reason you are responsible and not I.' That's what Ivan Potapych says; and yet, if truth were told, he is several times more intelligent than I."

"Athanassii Vassilievich! I, too, am ready to [accept] your power over me. . . . I am your servant, and do as you will: I put myself in your hands. But do not place upon me a task that is beyond my strength: I am no Potapych, and I tell you that I'm not fit for anything worth while."

The old man took both his hands.

"It is not I, Semën Semënovich, who am placing a task upon you; but since you would like to serve, as you your-self say, here's a devout work for you. If you but knew how sorry I feel for you! I was thinking of you all the time. And now listen. You know that in the monastery there is a recluse, who never sees anybody. This man has a great mind—I do not know of a greater. [He doesn't say much] . . . . . . but if he does give you counsel at last, you may well heed it. I began telling him that I have a certain friend, but did not [mention] any name . . . that he is afflicted in such-and-such a way. He listened at first, but suddenly cut me short with the words 'God's work comes ahead of your own. There's a church being built: it's necessary to collect money for the church!' And he slammed the door of his cell behind him. 'What does it mean?' I thought to myself. He didn't want to give me his counsel, evidently. And so I went to call on our Archimandrite. No sooner had I stepped through the door than his first words to me were, did I by any chance know a man who could be entrusted with col-lecting money for the church, who might be a nobleman or from the merchant class, somewhat better educated than the others, and who would regard this work as his salvation?

At first I just stood rooted there. 'Ah, my God! Why, the recluse monk himself must have meant this work for Semën Semënovich! Travel would be good for his ailment. Going with his collection book from the landowner to the peasant, and from the peasant to the burgher, he will learn both how each one lives and what his needs are, so that later on, when he comes back after covering several provinces, he will know the locality and region far better than the men who spend all their life in cities. And there is a need of such people now.' There, the Prince was telling me that he would give a great deal to find an official who would know things not through papers but would get at their real gist, the way they really are; for, he says, nothing is to be got at from papers, everything having become so confused. And, outside of any chancellery promotions, you may attain a post where your life will not be useless."

Hlobuev was astonished by this totally new work being offered him. That he, who was after all a nobleman of an ancient, once wealthy line, should set out with a book to solicit funds for a church, jouncing along in a cart! And yet to squirm out of it and to decline was impossible—it was a devout task.

"Are you pondering and hesitating?" asked Murazov. "You will be rendering two services here: one service to God, the other to me."

"To you? But what service can I render to you?"

"Why, this: since you will be going through places where I haven't been yet, you will learn everything right on the spot—how the lowly muzhiks live, which localities are better off and which are in need of help, and what state all of them are in. I will tell you that I love the muzhiks perhaps because I myself come from them. But the thing is that a great deal of all sorts of abomination has sprung up among them. The Schismatics[11] and all kinds of vagabonds are stirring them up, some even arousing them against the authorities. For is it hard to egg on men who are really suffering persecution? But the whole thing is that redressing wrongs should not begin at the bottom. Things are bad when men take to fighting with their fists; there will never be any sense in that, for only thieves profit when honest men fall out. You are a clever man; you look around you, learn where men are really suffering because of others and where from their own turbulent spirit, and later on tell me everything. It won't be the same as with some official, whom everybody fears, and from whom everybody [conceals everything] ... but, since they know you are soliciting for a church, all will willingly talk with you and tell you plenty. In any event, I shall give you funds for distribution on your travels among those who really are suffering through no fault of their own. That way you can do a great many good deeds; you won't make any more mistakes this time—whomever you give anything to will really deserve it. For your part it will also be useful if you were to offer them a word of consolation and to explain to them as well as possible that God ordains man to endure without murmuring and to pray when he is unhappy, and not to riot and take the law into his own hands. In short, speak to them in such a way as not to arouse anybody against anybody else; if you should see in any man hatred against any other, exert all your efforts to reconcile the two."

"You have perplexed me, you have bewildered me completely, Athanassii Vassilievich," said Hlobuev, looking at the other in astonishment. "I actually can't believe that you are telling me all this in earnest; for this sort of work you need a tireless, active man. The work you would give me, Athanassii Vassilievich, is a holy work; yet recall to whom you are giving it. It can be entrusted only to a man of almost holy life, who would himself be able to forgive others. And besides, how am I to abandon my wife, my children, who have nothing to eat?"

"Do not worry about your wife and children, I shall take them under my care, and your children will have instructors. And I am not saying that you are to carry out everything I suggest, but as much as you possibly can. So you can put on a common peasant coat, for you are now a common mortal, a ruined nobleman, and the same as a beggar—why stand on ceremony? But rather than go wandering with a beggar's wallet begging alms for yourself, it's better to beg for God."

"I see that it is a splendid idea, and I would very much [want to] . . . . . . carry out even a part of it, but I am afraid it is beyond my strength."

"But then, what is not beyond your strength?" asked Murazov. "For everything is beyond your strength. Without help from above nothing can be done. But through prayer one gathers strength. Crossing himself, man says: 'Help me and be merciful, Lord!'; he leans on the oars and reaches shore. One should not even think upon this overlong; one must simply accept it as a behest from God. I'll get the cart for you right away—and don't be afraid of the jouncing: it will be good for your health! So go you forth with the collection book in your hand, and travel through town and village. The Archimandrite will give you not only the book but his blessing—and God go with you!"

"I submit to you and accept this task as none other than a behest from God. I shall try; I shall apply myself zealously, to the limit of my strength," said Hlobuev. And one could perceive a new spirit in his voice; his back straightened, and his head lifted up, as when a man sees hope glimmering in the distance. He felt vigor and strength penetrating into his soul; his mind began to awaken with the hope of an escape from his sadly unescapable situation. "I see that God has endowed you with understanding, and that you know some things better than we nearsighted ones do."—"Lord, help Thou me!" said he inwardly.

"And now let me ask you," said Murazov. "What's all this about Chichikov, and what sort of [affair] . . . . . . were you speaking about?"

"Why, the things I can tell you about Chichikov are unheard-of. He is up to such tricks! Do you know, Athanassii Vassilievich, that the will turned out to be forged? A genuine one has been unearthed, whereby the entire property goes to the girls my aunt was bringing up."

"What are you saying? But who engineered the forged will?"

"That's just the whole thing—that the whole thing is most abominable! They say Chichikov forged it, and that this will was signed only after my aunt's death; they dressed up some peasant woman as the deceased, and it was she who signed the will. In short, it's a most demoralizing affair. Certain officials also are under suspicion of complicity. They are saying by now that the Governor General knows about it too. They say that thousands of petitions have come pouring in from all quarters. Suitors are now fluttering around Maria Eremeievna; two individuals among the officials are fighting over her. There, that's the sort of an affair it is, Athanassii Vassilievich!"

"I have heard nothing about it, but the affair really seems to be not altogether innocent. Pavel Ivanovich, I confess, certainly strikes me as a most mysterious individual," said Murazov.

"I too have put in a petition on my own account, as a reminder that there exists an heir who is nearest of kin—"

"As for my part, let them all fight to their hearts' content," Hlobuev was thinking as he left Murazov. "Athanassii Vassilievich is no fool. He must have entrusted me with this task only after having carefully considered everything. It must be carried out, and that's all there is to it." He began thinking about his journey, while Murazov was still repeating to himself: "He strikes me as a most mysterious individual, this Pavel Ivanovich Chichikov! Why, if he were only to go after some worthy and honest enterprise with such will and persistence!"

—

But in the meantime petitions upon petitions were really swamping the courts. Relatives turned up of whom nobody had ever even heard. As scavenger birds flock to feast on carrion, so all swooped down on the incalculable property the old woman had left behind her. Secret information and denunciations were lodged against Chichikov, against the forged nature of the last will, and against the forged nature of the first will as well; evidence of one sort or another as to theft and secreting of funds was submitted. There even bobbed up evidence against Chichikov in the matter of his buying up dead souls, in the matter of the smuggling transactions during the time of the same Chichikov's service in the Customs. Everything was dug up, all his past history was ferreted out. God knows how they had smelled all this out, whence they had come to know all this. But the fact remains that there was evidence of such things the knowledge of which Chichikov thought was shared only by himself and his four walls. For the time being all this had been a juridical secret and nothing had come to his ears, although a confidential note from his counselor-at-law which he shortly received gave him to understand, to some extent, that the pretty kettle of fish would soon be coming to a boil. The note was brief in content: "I hasten to inform you that there will be quite a row over the affair; but remember, one should never be alarmed. Calm, that's the main thing. We shall manage everything." This note completely reassured Chichikov. "This man is absolutely a genius," said he, after reading the note.

As a crowning happy touch, the tailor brought his new suit at this juncture. Chichikov experienced an intense desire to behold himself in his new frock coat of Navarino flame-and-smoke. He pulled on his trousers, which fitted him in such a marvelous way at every point that you could just go ahead and draw him for a fashion plate. Those thighs, gloriously fitted, and the calves too; the cloth seized upon the least details, imparting a still greater resiliency to them. When he pulled in the belt strap in the back, his belly became just like a drum. He immediately tapped it with a clothesbrush, saying: "What a fool thing the belly is, yet on the whole it rounds out the picture!" The frock coat, it seemed, was tailored still better than the trousers; there wasn't even one teeny-weeny wrinkle; it clung at the sides, it had an outward sweep at the waist, setting off the smart curve of his figure. To Chichikov's remark that it was a little tight under the right armpit the tailor merely smiled: because of that it clung still better to the waist. "You may rest assured about the workmanship, you may rest assured," the tailor kept repeating with unconcealed triumph. "There's no place except in St. Petersburg where they could tailor a suit that way." The tailor himself was from St. Petersburg, and he had put on his sign: *Costumier—Late of London and Paris.* He did not like to do things by halves, and by using the names of two cities he meant to shut the mouths of all other tailors, so that in the future no others might bob up and lay claim to them, having to content themselves with putting on their signs that they came merely from Karlsruhe or Copenhagen.

Chichikov, left alone after magnanimously paying off the tailor, began studying himself leisurely in the mirror, like an artist, with aesthetic emotion and *con amore*. It turned out that everything was even better than before, somehow: his darling little cheeks more interesting, his chin more enticing. The white collar gave tone to the cheek; the blue satin cravat gave tone to the collar; the pleats, in the latest vogue, of the dickey, gave tone to the cravat; the rich velvet vest gave tone to the dickey, while the frock coat of Navarino flame-and-smoke, as shimmering as silk, gave tone to everything. He turned to the right—fine! He turned to the left—still finer! The curve of his figure was better than that of a court chamberlain or an attaché of the foreign diplomatic corps, or even that of one of those fine gentlemen who spout French so well as to put down any Frenchman, and who, even when they lose their tempers, will never disgrace themselves with a common Russian oath but will curse in French. How refined he looked! Inclining his pretty head to one side, he tried to assume a pose as if he were addressing a lady of middle age and up to the last word in culture: the result was simply a picture. Artist, take your brush and limn away! He was so pleased that he performed a light leap right then and there, something like an *entrechat,* or gambado, or caper. The bureau shuddered and a bottle of Eau de Cologne crashed to the floor, but this did not upset him in the least. He called the silly bottle a she-fool, which was only right, and mused: "Whom shall I call on first, now? It would be best of all—"

When suddenly, from the entry, came something like the scrape and jangling of spurred boots, followed by a gendarme, fully accoutred, who seemed to personify a whole body of troops all by himself.

"You are commanded to appear at once before the Governor General!"

There it was! Chichikov was simply stunned. Towering before him was a horrendous mustachioed bogey, a horsetail on his helmet, a bandolier over one shoulder, a bandolier over the other shoulder, and the most enormous of sabres swinging at his side. It even seemed to Chichikov that a rifle, too, was swinging at his other side, and the Devil alone knows what else: this was a one-man army! He was about to protest, but the bogey answered him rudely: "You are commanded to appear at once!" Through the door into the entry he saw that another bogey was flitting about there; he glanced out of the window, and saw an official-looking vehicle. What could he do? And so, just as he was, in his frock coat of Navarino flame-and-smoke, he had to get into the vehicle and, his whole body shivering, ride off to the Governor General's with the gendarmes.

He was not given a chance even to come to in the foyer at the Governor General's.

"Go ahead! His Highness is already expecting you," the official on duty told him. Before him, as in a haze, flashed the entry, with couriers carrying packages, then a hall, which he traversed thinking only: "There, he'll nab you and, without any trial, without anything, hustle you right off to Siberia!" His heart began to pound with greater force than even that of the most love-crazed swain. Finally the door of doom opened before him, revealing a study with portfolios, closets, and books, and the Prince himself, as wrathful as wrath itself.

"My destroyer, my destroyer!" said Chichikov to himself. "He'll destroy my soul!" Here he all but swooned. "He'll slay me, even as a wolf slays a lamb!"

"I had spared you, I had permitted you to stay on in town, when by rights you should have been put in prison; but you have besmirched yourself anew with the most dishonest knavery with which any man has ever besmirched himself!" The Prince's lips were quivering with wrath.

"What dishonest action and knavery, Your Highness?" asked Chichikov, his whole body shivering.

"The woman," said the Prince, taking a step closer to Chichikov and looking into his very eyes, "the woman who signed the will at your dictation has been seized and will be confronted with you."

Everything grew dark before Chichikov's eyes and he

turned as pale as a sheet. "Your Highness! I will tell you the whole truth of this matter. I am guilty, I am truly guilty, but not as guilty as you think—my enemies have traduced me."

"No one can traduce you, because your abominations are several times as great as the greatest liar could invent. You have not, I believe, performed a single action in your life that has not been dishonest. Every copper you have acquired was acquired in the most dishonest manner; it testifies to thievery and most dishonest activity, meriting the knout and Siberia! No, you have done enough by now! From this moment on you will be led off to prison and there, side by side with the lowest villains and cutthroats, you will have to await the decision of your fate. And that is actually showing you mercy, inasmuch as you are several times worse than they; they are in shoddy coats and sheepskins, but you—"

Here he glanced at the frock coat of Navarino flame-and-smoke and tugged at a bellpull.

"Your Highness!" cried out Chichikov. "Have mercy! You are the father of a family: spare not me but my old mother!"

"You lie!" the Prince cried out wrathfully. "That's the very way you appealed to me last time, asking me to spare you for the sake of your children and your family, which you never had; and now it's your mother!"

"Your Highness! I am abominable, I am a villain and the lowest of scoundrels," said Chichikov in a [heart-rending] . . . . . . voice. "I was actually lying then, I had neither children nor family; but, as God is my witness, I always longed to have a wife, to fulfill the duty of a man and a citizen, so that eventually I might earn the respect of my fellows and of those in authority. But what a disastrous combination of circumstances! With blood, Your Highness, with my heart's blood did I have to win my daily bread. At every step there were pitfalls to lure one and temptation lurking everywhere ... and enemies, and men ready to ruin you, and to rob you of your winnings. All my life was tempest-tossed, like a bark in the midst of the ocean, at the whim of the waves. I am only human, Your Highness!"

Tears suddenly spurted in streams from his eyes. Just as he was he threw himself down at the feet of the Prince— frock coat of Navarino flame-and-smoke, velvet vest, satin cravat, marvelously tailored trousers and all, his hair, dressed in the latest style, diffusing the fragrance of Eau de Cologne.

"Get away from me! Call somebody to take him away! Call the guards!" the Prince commanded the clerks who had entered in answer to his call.

"Your Highness!" Chichikov shrieked, and threw his arms around one of the Prince's boots.

A shudder of disgust ran through the Prince's every fibre.

"Get away from me, I'm telling you!" said he, straining to extricate his leg from Chichikov's embrace.

"Your Highness! I shall not stir from this spot till I am shown mercy!" said Chichikov, not only without releasing the Prince's boot but clasping it harder to his breast and slithering with it over the floor in his frock coat of Navarino flame-and-smoke.

"Get away, I'm telling you!" the Prince kept repeating with that inexplicable feeling of revulsion which a man feels at the sight of a most hideous insect which he nevertheless has not the heart to crush underfoot. He shook his leg so hard that Chichikov felt a kick on his nose, on his pleasantly rounded chin and his teeth, yet he did not release the boot and hugged it with still greater force. It took all the strength of two stalwart gendarmes to pry him loose, after which, taking him under the arms, they led him through all the chambers. He was pale, crushed, in that unconscious, fearful state of a man who sees before him black, ineluctable death, that frightful monster so repugnant to our nature. . . .

Near the front entrance he saw Murazov coming toward him. A gleam of hope glided before Chichikov. In an instant, with a preternatural strength, he tore himself loose from the arms of the gendarmes and cast himself at the feet of the astonished old man.

"Pavel Ivanovich, father o' mine, what is the matter with you?" Murazov cried out.

"Save me! They're leading me off to prison, to my death—" The gendarmes seized him again and led him away, without giving Murazov a chance to hear Chichikov.

A dark, dank hole-in-the-wall cell, reeking of the odors of the boots and foot clouts of the garrison soldiers, with an unpainted deal table, two miserable, rickety chairs, an iron-grated window, a decrepit stove, whose cracks emitted only smoke and no heat—such was the habitation assigned to our Chichikov, who had already been beginning to taste of the delights of life and to attract the attention of his compatriots, in his fine new frock coat of Navarino flame-and-smoke. They had not given him so much as a chance to take the most necessary things with him, to take his traveling casket with the money, the small trunk that contained his wardrobe. His papers, his purchase deeds to the dead souls, everything was now in [the hands] of the officials! He slumped to the ground, and grief, grief fearful and hopeless, coiled itself around his heart like a cankerworm. With increasing tempo that grief began to gnaw at his utterly defenseless heart. Another such day, another day of such grief, and there would have been no Chichikov at all left in the world. But some vigilant being, ready to extend the all-saving hand, must have been watching even over Chichikov. An hour after he first found himself in this dreadful plight the door of his prison cell opened and Murazov entered.

Had someone poured a draught of spring water into the parched throat of a weary, fainting wayfarer, covered with the grime and dust of the road and perishing from fiery thirst, that wayfarer would not have found as much new strength and life as our poor Chichikov did at the sight of his visitor.

"My savior!" he cried out, suddenly springing up from the ground on which he had cast himself in his [heart]-rending misery, quickly kissing the old man's hand and pressing it to his breast. "God will reward you for visiting an unfortunate!"

Chichikov was inundated with tears.

The old man was regarding him with grieving commiseration and could only say: "Ah, Pavel Ivanovich! Pavel Ivanovich, what have you done?"

"What's to be done? My accursed nature has ruined me! I did not know moderation, was not able to stop in time. Satan, the accursed one, tempted me, leading me out of the bounds of reason and human prudence. I have offended, I have offended! I have done everything that the vilest of men could have done. But then, judge for yourself, how can they do this to me! To throw a nobleman—a nobleman!—into prison, without any hearing, without any investigation! A nobleman, Athanassii Vassilievich! Why could they not have given me a chance to drop in at my place, to see to my things? The casket, Athanassii Vassilievich, the casket! Why, all my money is in that casket, all my property. In the sweat of my brow did I acquire it, sweating blood, through years of toil, of privations! The casket, Athanassii Vassilievich! For they will steal, will carry off everything! Oh, my God!"

And, without the strength to hold back the paroxysm of grief attacking his heart anew he broke into sobs, so loud that they penetrated through the thickness of his prison walls and echoed in the distance, and snatching off his satin cravat he clutched the collar of his Navarino flame-and-smoke frock coat and ripped the whole garment apart.

"Ah, Pavel Ivanovich! How this property has blinded you! Because of it you did not perceive your desperate situation."

"My benefactor, save me, save me!" poor Pavel Ivanovich cried out in despair, falling down at Murazov's feet. "The Prince loves you, he will do anything for you."

"No, Pavel Ivanovich, I can't do anything, no matter how I might wish and desire it. You have fallen under an inexorable law and not under the power of any man."

"Satan, the fiend, the enemy of mankind, tempted me!" Chichikov struck his head against the wall, and fetched the table such a blow that his fist became bloody, yet he felt no pain in his head, nor did the cruel blow pain his hand.

"Calm yourself, Pavel Ivanovich, think of how to make your peace with God and not with men."

"But what a fate is mine, Athanassii Vassilievich! Has any man ever met with such a fate? I have ruined myself, I feel that none other is the author of my ruin but my own self. But why such a dreadful [chastisement], Athanassii Vassilievich? For am I a brigand? Has anybody suffered because of me? Have I brought misfortune upon anybody? With toil and sweat, with bloody sweat, did I acquire each copper; it wasn't as if I had robbed anybody, or looted public funds. Why did I acquire it? So that I might finish out the remainder of my days in comfort, and leave the rest to my wife, to my children, whom I planned to beget for the good, for the service of my fatherland. I went astray, I won't dispute it, I went astray—what's to be done? But I went astray upon seeing that one couldn't get anywhere or anything by following the direct path, and that cutting a corner was the shortest way. But when I worked, I used my ingenuity. If I took anything, I took it from the rich. But what about those abominable villains who get theirs through courts, perfectly legally, and not from the public funds, mind you, but who rob the poor, who fleece those who have nothing of their last copper! Athanassii Vassilievich, I was not dissolute, I did not drink. [Have I not redeemed myself?] . . . . . . Why, how many efforts I have made, how much iron fortitude I have shown! Why, one could say that I have paid for every kopeck with sufferings, sufferings! What misfortune is it, then, which dogs me? Tell me! Every time when a man begins to see his efforts beginning to bear fruits and, so to say, to stretch his hand toward them, a storm unexpectedly springs up, or he strikes an underwater reef, or his ship is smashed to smithereens. There, I had a capital of nearly three hundred thousand at one time; I already had a three-story house; twice, by now, have I bought a country estate. Ah, Athanassii Vassilievich, why such [misfortunes]? . . . . . . Why such blows? Show me anybody who has suffered as much as I have! For what does my whole life represent? A cruel struggle, a bark in the midst of the waves. Where is the justice of Heaven? Where is the reward for my patience, for my unexampled steadfastness of purpose? Why, three times did I begin all over again; having lost everything, I began again with coppers, whereas anyone else in my place would have taken to drink from despair and rotted away in a pothouse. Think how much I had to overcome, how much to endure! For every copper was, so to say, earned with all the forces of one's soul! Others, perhaps, may have come by their money easily, but for me, as the proverb goes, every copper was nailed down with a spike. And to be suddenly deprived of everything that I have earned, Athanassii Vassilievich, that which I have acquired through such a struggle—"

He did not finish and burst into loud sobs because of his unbearable heartache, and slumped on a chair, and tore off completely the hanging skirt of his coat, and threw the rag away from him, and, plunging both his hands into his hair, about the preservation of which he had formerly been so solicitous, tore it mercilessly, enjoying the pain wherewith he wanted to stifle the unbearable, the unquenchable pain in his heart.

Murazov long sat watching this extraordinary . . . . . . [display of emotion], such as he had never beheld before. But the unfortunate, embittered man, who had only so recently been fluttering around with the free-and-easy adroitness of either a worldly or a military man, was now dashing about all disheveled, unpresentable, in a torn coat and unbuttoned trousers, his hand battered and bleeding, upbraiding the inimical forces which barred a man's path.

"Ah, Pavel Ivanovich, Pavel Ivanovich!" Murazov was saying, looking at him sorrowfully and shaking his head. "I am always thinking of what a man you would have been if, with the same energy and determination which you have shown, you had exerted yourself for honest work and toward a better end. My God, how much good you would have done! If only some one of those men who love the good were to expend so many efforts for that good as you have for the acquirement of your coppers! And if they had been able to sacrifice both their self-love and their love of advancement, without sparing themselves, as you have not spared yourself in the acquisition of your coppers, my God, how our land would flourish! Pavel Ivanovich, Pavel Ivanovich! One does not feel sorry so much because you stand guilty before others, but one does feel great sorrow because you are guilty before your own self, before the rich powers and gifts which had fallen to your share. You were meant to be a great man, but you have been the cause of your own perdition and ruin."

The soul has its mysteries: no matter how far the errant one may have strayed from the narrow path, no matter how hardened the feelings of the incorrigible offender may have grown, no matter how inured he may have become to his warped and thwarted life, yet should you reproach him with his own good qualities, which he has disgraced......

[everything] within him is swayed against his will and he himself is all shaken.

"Athanassii Vassilievich!" said poor Chichikov, and seized both his hands. "Oh, if I could but succeed in getting free, in getting back my property! I swear to you I would henceforth lead an entirely different life! Save me, my benefactor, save me!"

"But what can I do? I must contend with the law. Let us say that I might even decide to do it, but then the Prince has justice on his side; he will not retreat from his stand, in any circumstances."

"My benefactor! You can do everything. It is not the law which frightens me—I shall find means to protect me there—but that I am cast into prison without a hearing, that I shall perish here like a dog, and that my property, my papers, my casket, are taken from me . . . . . . Save me!"

He embraced the old man's legs, watering them with his tears.

"Ah, Pavel Ivanovich, Pavel Ivanovich!" old Murazov was saying as he shook his head. "Because of your worldly goods you do not even hearken to your poor soul."

"I shall think of my soul too, but save me!"

"Pavel Ivanovich!" old Murazov began and paused. "Saving you is not within my power—you can see that for yourself. But I will exert myself to ease your lot and to free you. I don't know if I'll succeed in doing so, but I will try. But should I succeed despite my expectations, I shall ask a reward from you for my efforts: that you abandon all this itch for acquisition. I tell you, upon my honor, that were I to be deprived of even the whole of my property—and I have more of it than you—I would not break into tears. For, I swear it, the importance does not lie in this property, which may be confiscated, but in that which none may steal and take away! You have lived long enough in the world by now. You yourself style your life a bark in the midst of the waves. You already have the wherewithal to see you through the remainder of your days. Settle down in some quiet nook, as near as possible to a church and good, simple folk; or, if you have so urgent a desire to leave descendants, marry some good, not at all wealthy girl, used to moderation and a simple household, and really, you won't regret it later. Forget this noisy world and all its seductive whims, and let the world forget you. There is no tranquillity in it. You see for yourself, not a man in it but is an enemy, a tempter or a traitor."

"How right, how right! I had already intended and wanted to lead a proper life, I was planning to manage an estate, to moderate my life. But the demon tempter seduced me, led me astray—Satan, the Devil, the misbegotten!"

Chichikov grew thoughtful. Something strange, some emotions hitherto unknown, which he could not explain to himself, came to him, as though something were striving to awaken within him, something that had been crushed since childhood by a harsh, dead discipline, by the dreariness of his bleak childhood, by the desolateness that had reigned in the house where he had been born, by his lonesome life without a family, the niggardliness and poverty of his first impressions; it was as though something within him which had been made to cower under the harsh gaze of a destiny which had regarded him so dourly, as through some turbid snow-drifted window, was now striving to win to freedom.

"Only save me, Athanassii Vassilievich!" he cried out. "I shall start leading a different life, I shall follow your counsel! I give you my word!"

"See to it, then, Pavel Ivanovich, that you do not go back on your word," said Murazov, holding onto Chichikov's hand.

"I might, perhaps, backslide, were it not that this lesson has been far too dreadful," said poor Chichikov with a sigh, and added: "But the lesson is too painful; painful, painful is the lesson, Athanassii Vassilievich!"

"It is a good thing it is painful. Thank God for that; pray to Him. I'll go and see what I can do."

Chichikov was left alone. He no longer wept, no longer tore his frock coat or his hair; he had calmed down.

"There, enough of this!" he decided at last. "A different life, a different life! It is high time, really, to become a decent man. Oh, if I were only to extricate myself somehow and leave this place even with a small capital, I would settle far from here.... If I get my papers back, however ... And what about the purchase deeds? Well, now," he reflected, "why drop this matter, over which I have worked so hard? I'm not going to buy any more souls but I will have to mortgage those I already have. For their acquisition cost so many exertions! I shall mortgage them, mortgage them to get an estate with the money they'll bring. I shall become a landowner, because then one can do a great deal of good." And in his thoughts awakened those emotions which had come over him at the time when he had been at Skudronzhoglo's, and he recalled the soothing, intelligent conversation of his host at the hour when the evening candles had been lit, of how fruitful and useful the management of an estate was.

The country suddenly appeared before him in such a beautiful light, just as though he were capable of feeling all the beauties of living there.

"We are foolish, we run after worldly vanities!" he decided at last. "Really, it's all due to idleness. Everything is near us, everything is right at hand, but we must go seeking things that are far removed. Wherein is life any worse even in the backwoods, if one is occupied? For there is actually pleasure in work. Skudronzhoglo is right. And surely there is nothing sweeter than the fruit of one's own labors. Yes, I will settle in the country and start working, and I will work honestly, so as to have a good influence even upon others. Really, now, am I altogether useless? I have an aptitude and inclination for management; I have good qualities, such as thrift, and enterprise, and prudence, and even determination. All I have to do is make a resolve. Only now do I feel truly and clearly that there is a certain duty which man must fulfill on earth, without running off from that place and niche in which he has been placed."

And an industrious life, remote from the bustle of cities and all temptations which man, having forgotten toil, has invented out of idleness, began to appear before him in such sharp outlines that by now he all but forgot the entire horror of his situation and, perhaps, was all set to thank Providence for this heavy blow, if only they would let him out and give him back but a part of what was his own. But ... the thick door of his noisome cell opened and an official person entered—Samosvistov, the epicure, a dashing fellow, just a few inches short of a yard across his shoulders, with well-turned legs, an excellent friend, a reveler, and an out-and-out scoundrel, as his own friends spoke of him. In time of war this man would have done wonders; had he been sent to some sector to make his way through impassable, dangerous places, or to steal a cannon from under the enemy's very nose, that would have been his very dish. But since he had no military arena to display his talents in, he had tried what he could do in the civilian field and, instead of exploits for which he really might have merited decorations, he indulged in snide and nasty tricks. An incomprehensible thing! He had strange convictions and a strange code of honor: he treated his friends well, never sold any of them out, and once he gave his word he kept it; but he regarded his superiors as something in the nature of an enemy battery, through which one must smash one's way, availing oneself of every weak spot, every breach or oversight.

"We know all about your situation, we've heard everything!" said he when he saw that the door was shut tight behind him. "It's nothing, it's nothing! Don't be afraid—everything will come out right. We shall all be working for you and we are all your servants. Thirty thousand for everything, and not another copper."

"Really?" Chichikov cried out. "And I shall be fully acquitted?"

"All around! You'll even receive compensation for the damages you have suffered."

"And for your efforts? . . ."

"Thirty thousand, as I said. That covers everything and everybody—our fellows, and the Governor General, and the secretary."

"But wait—how can I do it? All my things . . . the casket . . . all this is now under seal and guard—"

"In another hour you'll get everything. What do you say, shall we shake hands on it?"

Chichikov held out his hand. His heart was pounding, and he could not believe that this was possible. . . .

"For the time being, good-by. Our mutual friend instructed me to tell you that calm and presence of mind are the chief thing."

"Hm!" thought Chichikov. "I understand; it's that counselor-at-law."

Samosvistov disappeared. Chichikov, again left alone, still did not put much faith in what he had heard; but hardly an hour had passed after this conversation when the casket was brought; the money, the papers, everything was in the best order. Samosvistov had come to Chichikov's quarters as one in charge of the case; he reprimanded the guards on duty for not being very vigilant, ordered the inspector to station extra soldiers to guard the place, took not only the casket but even extracted all such papers as might compromise Chichikov, tied all these things together, sealed them, and ordered none other than one of the soldiers there to carry all this without any delay to Chichikov himself, as things he needed for the night, so that Chichikov, together with the papers, received even the warm clothes he needed to cover his frail body. This quick delivery of his effects rejoiced him unutterably. He was inspired with a strong hope and certain visions began to glimmer before him: going to the theatre of evenings, a danseuse whom he was dangling after. The country and a peaceful life took on fainter hues; the city and its bustle again became clearer, more vivid. . . . Oh, life!

But in the meantime a case of infinite scope had begun in the courts and the chancelleries. The quills of the clerks worked away and, taking pinch after pinch of snuff, the casuistical minds toiled away, admiring with the pride of artists each line of pothooks they brought forth. The counselor-at-law, like a magician in the wings, operated the whole mechanism unseen; he entangled absolutely everybody, before anybody had a chance to turn his head. The snarl increased. Samosvistov surpassed himself in audacity and unheard-of impudence. Having learned where Chichikov's female accomplice was being kept under guard, he went straight there and entered the place with so much swagger and authority that the sentry saluted him and drew himself up as if on review. "Are you standing here long?"—"Since morning, Your Honor!"— "Is it long till the change of guards?"—"Three hours yet, Your Honor!"— "I'll need you. I'll tell your officer to send somebody to replace you."—"Right, Your Honor!" And going home, without losing a minute Samosvistov dressed himself up as a gendarme—so as not to implicate anybody and hide all clues; he even put on false mustachios and side whiskers, so that the Devil himself would not have recognized him. He called at the place where Chichikov was incarcerated, seized the first peasant woman that came handy and entrusted her to two clerks, slick fellows of the same kidney as himself, while he, properly uniformed and with a gun, went directly to the sentry he had left a while before.

"You can go . . . . . . the commandant sent me to relieve

you." The other sentry left and Samosvistov was left on guard. That was all he needed. Within a few minutes the prisoners were switched, the peasant woman, knowing nothing and understanding nothing of what was going on, replacing Chichikov's female accomplice, who was spirited away and hidden somewhere, so effectively that even later on nobody found where she had gone to or what had ever become of her.

At the same time that Samosvistov was play-acting as a warrior, the counselor-at-law had done wonders in civilian quarters; he let the Governor know indirectly that the Public Prosecutor was making up a secret report against him; he informed the official in charge of gendarmes that another official, living in town incognito on an undercover mission, was sending in secret reports concerning him; he convinced the official on an undercover mission that there was another official on a mission still more undercover who was informing against him; and he placed all of them in such a situation that they had to turn to him for advice. The resultant hodgepodge was so senseless that the secret reports poured in one on top of another, and there was a ceaseless succession of exposures of such things as have never been seen under the sun, and such as had never even existed. Everything was turned to account and put to use: So-and-so's being an illegitimate son, and this one's origin and calling, and that one's having a mistress, and the fourth man's wife carrying on with a fifth. Scandals, demoralizing situations, and everything else were so mixed and tangled with the *affaire* Chichikov and with the dead souls that there was no possible way of understanding which one of all these matters was the most nonsensical: all seemed equally worthy of that honor.

When at last the papers came pouring in upon the Governor General, the poor Prince couldn't make out a thing. The quite intelligent and shrewd bureaucrat who had been assigned to make an abstract of the case almost went out of his mind: there just wasn't any way of catching hold of the thread of the business. The Prince was at this time taken up with a multitude of other matters, each more unpleasant than the preceding one. Famine began in one part of the province. The officials who had been sent to distribute grain somehow had not managed the business right. In another part of the province the Schismatics were up to their old tricks again. Someone had spread the rumor among them that an Antichrist had come to birth who would not let even the dead rest in peace, but was going around and buying up certain dead souls. The Schismatics did penance first and then sinned and, under the pretext of trying to catch the Antichrist, had done in some non-Antichrists. In another place the muzhiks had risen up against certain landowners and Captains of the Rural Police. Certain vagabonds had spread rumors among them that a time was coming when muzhiks must be landowners and put on frock coats, while the landowners would put on drab overcoats and become muzhiks, and a whole district, without stopping to figure out that in such a case there would be far too many landowners and Captains of the Rural Police, had refused to pay . . . . . . taxes. It had been necessary to resort to forceful measures. The poor Prince was in a most distraught state.

At the very height of his misery he was informed that the tax farmer had come to see him. "Let him come in," said the Prince. The old man entered.

"There's your Chichikov for you! You stood up for him and defended him. Now he has been caught in such a business as the lowest thief would not venture on."

"Permit me to say, Your Highness, that I do not understand very clearly this business [in which he is implicated]."

"The forgery of a will—and what a forgery! He ought to be publicly flogged for such a thing!"

"But, Your Highness—and I am not saying this to defend Chichikov—this matter has not been proven yet; the trial has not yet been held."

"There is proof: the woman who impersonated the deceased has been seized. I purposely want to interrogate her in your presence." The Prince pulled the bell rope and gave orders to the man who entered to bring the apprehended woman.

Murazov said nothing further.

"A most infamous affair! And, to our shame, be it said, the foremost officials of the town, even the Governor himself, are all implicated. He shouldn't be in the same mob with thieves and good-for-nothings!" said the Prince with heat.

"Why, the Governor is an heir; he has rightful claims; and as for all those others who have latched on from all sides, why, that, Your Highness, is human nature. A rich woman died, without having made an intelligent and just disposition of her goods; fortune hunters have come flocking from all sides—it's human nature—"

"But then, why commit such heinous deeds? The scoundrels!" said the Prince, with a feeling of indignation. "I haven't a single official who's any good; they're all villains!"

"Your Highness! But if it comes to that, which one of us is really good? All the officials in our town are only human; they have their good points and many of them know their work; and as for sin, it is always lurking around the corner."

"I say, Athanassii Vassilievich, tell me this, since you are the only honest man I know: what is this passion you have for defending all sorts of abominable villains?"

"Your Highness," said Murazov, "no matter who the man may be whom you call an abominable villain, he is after all a man. How, then, can one help defending a man if half the evils he commits are due to grossness and ignorance? For we commit injustices at every step even without any ill intent. And you yourself, Your Highness, have also committed a great injustice."

"What!" exclaimed the Prince, taken entirely aback by such an unexpected turn in the conversation.

Murazov paused, kept silent a while, as if considering something, and finally said: "Well, take even the case of Derpenikov—"

"What, I was unjust? A crime against the basic laws of the realm, tantamount to treason against one's own country!"

"I am not justifying him. But is it just for a youth who, because of his inexperience, was tempted and led astray by another, to be given the same sentence as the one who was one of the instigators of the affair? For the same punishment was meted out both to Derpenikov and that fellow Voronoi-Dryanoi."

"For God's sake—" said the Prince, with perceptible agitation. "Do you know anything about it? Tell me! That's the very case I recently sent a note about directly to St. Petersburg, asking that his punishment be mitigated."

"No, Your Highness, I am not saying any of this because I know of anything that is not known to you. Although, to be sure, there is one circumstance which might benefit him, but he himself would never consent to reveal it, because another man would suffer if he did. No, I am merely wondering if Your Highness was not overhasty at the time. Forgive me, Your Highness, but it seems so to my weak reasoning. You have commanded me several times to speak to you frankly. A man's past life should also be taken into consideration. For one should examine everything coolly. If you begin by shouting, you will only frighten the man, yet get no real admission out of him; but when one asks him with sympathy, as brother to brother, he will come out with everything himself, without even asking for mitigation, nor will he be embittered against anybody, because he perceives that it is not I who am punishing him but the law."

The Prince became thoughtful. At this point an official entered with a portfolio and paused at a respectful distance. There was a worried and overworked look on his youthful and still fresh face. One could see that he deserved being entrusted with special missions. He was of that small number of men who do secretarial work *con amore*. Consumed neither by ambition nor by a desire of acquisition, nor by a longing to ape others, he followed his calling only because he was convinced that he was needed here and not elsewhere, that is what his life had been given to him for. To study the most entangled affair, to analyze it and, having captured all its elusive clues, to explain it clearly—this was his work and his toil, his efforts, and his sleepless nights were bounteously rewarded if the affair would at last begin to clear itself up before his eyes, if its hidden springs would begin to expose themselves, and he felt that at last he could convey the whole business in a few words, distinctly and clearly, so that it would be evident and understandable to everybody. One could truly say that no scholar rejoiced as much when some exceedingly difficult phrase disclosed its sense, and the real meaning of a great writer's idea was revealed to him, as this young man rejoiced when the most entangled case disentangled itself before him. But then ......*

——

"...... with grain to the places affected by the famine; I know this work better than the officials: I shall look into this matter myself, to see just what is needed. And, if you will permit me, Your Highness, I will also talk with the Schismatics. They will be more willing to talk freely with my kind, with one of the simple folk, so that, with God's blessing, I may help in settling things with them peacefully. But as for money, I shan't take any from you, because I swear by God that it's a shame to think of one's gain at such a time, when people are dying because of famine. I have grain available in storage; also, a short time ago I sent to Siberia for some more, and by this summer there ought to be a new shipment."

"God alone can reward you for such a service, Athanas-

———

*A considerable hiatus follows this break in the manuscript.

sii Vassilievich. But as for me, I'm not going to tell you a single word, because—you can feel that yourself—all words fail me here. But permit me to say one thing concerning the request you made. Tell me yourself: have I the right to drop this matter without any further attention, and would it be just, would it be honest on my part to pardon such abominable villains?"

"Your Highness, I call upon God that one cannot bestow that name upon them, for among them are many who are quite worthy people. A man's circumstances may be very difficult, Your Highness, very difficult. There are instances where you may have what looks like an open-and-shut case against a man, yet when you really go into the matter he turns out not to be the guilty one at all."

"But what will they themselves say if I let the whole thing drop? For there are among them such as will stick their noses up still higher after this and will be actually saying that they scared me. They will be the first not to show any respect—"

"Your Highness, permit me to give you my opinion. Get them all together, tell them that everything is known to you, and place before them your own position in exactly the same way as you were pleased to place it before me just now, and ask their advice: what would each one of them do if he were in your position?"

"Come, do you think that they are prone to any impulses more noble than those of chicanery and lining their pockets! Believe me, they will laugh at me."

"I don't think so, Your Highness. The Russian, even one who is worse than his fellows, has, after all, a sense of right and wrong. Unless he is some alien and not a real Russian.

No, Your Highness, you don't have to conceal anything. Speak to them in the same way you were pleased to speak before me. For they criticize you as an ambitious, proud man who does not even wish to listen to anything, who is self-opinionated; therefore let them see everything just as it is. What have you to fear from them? For you are in the right. Speak to them as if you were confessing not before them but before God himself."

"Athanassii Vassilievich," said the Prince thoughtfully, "I will think this over, and in the meantime I thank you exceedingly for your counsel."

"As for Chichikov, Your Highness, do order him released."

"You tell this Chichikov to make himself scarce as fast as he can, and the further he gets away from here the better. For he is the one fellow whom I would never have pardoned."

Murazov bowed and, immediately after leaving the Prince, set out to see Chichikov. He found Chichikov in better spirits by now, quite calmly busied with a rather decent dinner, sent over in faïence containers from some fairly good eating place. From the opening phrases of their conversation the old man perceived that Chichikov had already contrived to talk things over with one or two of the fine legal minds among the officials. He comprehended that the unseen participation of the knowing counselor-at-law was involved here.

"Look here, Pavel Ivanovich," said he, "I have brought you your freedom, upon condition that you leave town at once. Get all your belongings together and be off, and God go with you, without putting matters off for one minute, because your affair is worse than ever. I know, Sir, that there is a certain man who is encouraging you; I will therefore inform you, in secret, that there is still another case about to be brought out into the open, of such a nature that no powers on earth will save this individual. He, of course, is glad to drag others down, just to have company as he drowns, but his affairs are about to be wound up. I left you in a well-disposed mood, better than the one you are in now. I am advising you in all seriousness. Verily, verily, that which matters is not this property, which people are fighting over and killing one another for, as if one could arrange a well-ordered life here on earth without giving thought to another life! Believe me, Pavel Ivanovich, that until such time as one abandons everything over which people fight with fang and claw and devour one another for here on earth, until one thinks about putting in order one's spiritual property, earthly property will never be put in order either. There are times of famine and of poverty coming, for all the nation as well as for each one of us . . . . . . That, Sir, is clear. For no matter what you say, it is upon the soul that the body depends. How, then, without heeding it, can one expect to have everything go right? Think not of the dead souls, but of your own soul and take a different road, and God go with you! I, too, am leaving town tomorrow. Make haste. Otherwise, while I am away, calamity may overtake you."

Having said this, the old man left. Chichikov became thoughtful. The meaning of life again became not insignificant. "Murazov is right," said he, "it is high time to take another road!"

And, in his turn, he walked out of his prison. The sentry

dragged the casket out after him . . . . . . Seliphan and Petrushka rejoiced over the liberation of their master as over God knows what. "Well, my dear friends," said Chichikov, addressing them graciously, "we must pack and be off."

"We'll go rolling along, Pavel Ivanovich," said Seliphan. "The road must be well beaten by now; there has been enough snow. And high time, really, we were getting out of this town. It has grown so wearisome it's like an eyesore."

"Go to the coachmaker and tell him to put the carriage on runners," said Chichikov, while he himself went into the centre of the town; not because he wanted to pay any farewell visits to anybody, however. After all that had happened that would have been actually awkward, all the more so since there was a multitude of the most unsavory stories about him going the rounds of the town. He avoided even chance encounters and only dropped in, as unobtrusively as possible, into the shop of the merchant from whom he had bought the Navarino flame-and-smoke cloth, and obtained nine yards more, enough for another frock coat and pair of trousers, and then set out to see the same tailor who had made the first suit for him. For a double price the master tailor undertook to intensify his zeal; he set the tailoring population of the town to toiling all night by candlelight, plying their needles, flat-irons, and teeth, and the suit was ready the next day, even though somewhat late.

The horses were harnessed and waiting, but Chichikov nevertheless tried the suit on. It was a good suit, every bit as good as the previous one. But, alas, he noticed in the mirror a smooth white patch now gleaming on his head, and he said, sadly: "Why did I have to give myself up to such despair? And as for tearing my hair, I shouldn't have done that at all." Paying off the tailor, he left the town at last in an undefinably strange mood. This was not the former Chichikov; this was but some ruin of the former Chichikov. One might have compared the inner state of his soul with that of a structure that had been pulled down, but only for the purpose of putting up a new building from its materials; the new building had not been started yet, because a definite plan had not yet come through from the architect, and the builders are left without knowing what to do.

Old Murazov had set out an hour before him, in a cart covered with matting, accompanied by Potapych, while an hour after Chichikov's exodus an order was issued that the Prince, on the occasion of his going to St. Petersburg, wanted to see all his officials, without any exception.

All officialdom in town gathered in the grand hall of the Governor General's mansion, from the Governor down to the secretary of a titular councilor; there were directors of chancelleries and administrators, councilors, assessors; there were Kisloyedov, Krasnonossov, Samosvistov; there were those who took bribes and those who did not, those who had larceny in their souls, those whose souls were larcenous only halfway, and some with no larceny at all in their souls. All of them, with an interest not entirely free from uneasiness, bided the coming of the Governor General. When the Prince appeared he was neither morose nor radiant; there was a calm firmness in his look and step. The gathered officialdom bowed to him as one man; some of them even bowed from the very waist. With a slight bow in response, the Prince began:

"Before leaving for St. Petersburg, I thought it would be

the right thing to see all of you and even to explain to you, in part, the reason for my journey. A very demoralizing affair has sprung up in our midst. I suppose that many of those standing before me are aware what case I have reference to. This affair has brought about in its train revelations of even other affairs, no less infamous, implicating at last even those men whom up to now I have considered honest. The hidden purpose of confusing everything in this manner so that there might be absolutely no possibility of deciding the case by due process of law is also known to me. I likewise know who is acting as the mainspring in all this, and who cherishes that most secret [desire to confuse everything] . . . . . . even though he has most artfully concealed his machinations. But the point is this: I intend to investigate this affair not through any formal examination of papers, but through a summary court-martial, as if in time of war, and I hope the Emperor will grant me this right when I have placed the whole matter before him. In a situation where there is no possibility of trying a case through civil law, where whole files of papers catch fire, and where, finally, attempts are made to obscure through an excess of false irrelevant testimony and false secret information a matter that is sufficiently obscure in itself, I propose that a court-martial is the only means of solution, and wish to know your consensus of opinion."

The Prince paused, as if waiting for an answer. All stood before him with their eyes cast down. Many had turned pale.

"There is still another affair, although those who participated therein feel fully certain that it cannot possibly be known to anybody. This affair also will not be handled through papers, inasmuch as the plaintiff and petitioner will be none other than myself, and the proofs I am going to present will be incontrovertible."

Here and there among the gathered officials a man shuddered, and some of the more timorous ones became flustered.

"It goes without saying that deprivation of rank and confiscation of property must follow for the chief instigators; for the other accomplices, removal from their posts. It also goes without saying that, among the number, a host of the innocent will suffer. What are we to do? The affair is far too infamous and cries out for justice to be done. Even though I know that this will not serve as a general lesson, since other evildoers will appear to replace those who have been cashiered, and that those who have hitherto been honest will become dishonest, and that those who have been deemed worthy of confidence will turn into deceivers and Judases, despite all this I will have to act harshly, for the very reason that this affair does cry aloud for justice to be done. I know that many will accuse me of harshness and cruelty . . . . . . yet all of you ought to regard me merely as an impassive instrument of justice, which is fated to descend upon your heads . . . . . ."

All faces were involuntarily convulsed.

The Prince was calm. His face expressed neither wrath nor spiritual indignation.

"And now," he went on, "the very same man in whose hands lies the fate of so many, and whom no appeals could have been strong enough to move, that same man now throws himself at your feet and appeals to all of you. Everything will be forgotten, expunged, forgiven; I myself will be the intercessor for all, if you grant my appeal. Here it is. I know that through no means, through no intimidations, through no chastisements, can one root out wrongdoing; it has rooted itself all too deeply. The infamous business of bribetaking has become a necessity even for such men as have not been born dishonest. I know that it is almost impossible for many to go against the all-prevailing current. But now I must, as at a decisive consecrated moment when one is faced with the necessity of saving one's fatherland, when every citizen endures all and sacrifices his all—now I must send forth a clarion call to those who still have Russian hearts beating within their breasts and to whom the words *nobility of spirit* are to any extent comprehensible. What will it avail to discuss who is the guiltiest among us here! I, perhaps, am guiltiest of all; I, perhaps, may have received you too austerely at first; may have repulsed, by excessive suspiciousness, those of you who may have sincerely wished to be useful to me, even though I, for my part, might also have [been too reserved] . . . . . . If such men had a real love of justice and of the welfare of their own land, they should not have been affronted even by the haughtiness of my treatment of them; they should have crushed the self-love within them and have sacrificed their individual feelings. It would have been impossible for me not to have noticed their self-sacrifice and their high love for the general good, and not to have accepted at last their useful and intelligent advice. After all, it is rather for the subordinate to adapt himself to the temperament of his superior than for the superior to adapt himself to that of the subordinate. That is more in keeping with the general nature of things, and easier, since the subordinates have but one chief, whereas a chief has a hundred subordinates. But let us put to one side now the question of who is more to blame than another. The point is that the time has now come for us to save our native land; the point is that by now our country is perishing not because of any invasion by nations speaking twenty alien tongues, but because of our own selves; the point is that, outside of a legitimate government, another government has formed itself, far more powerful than any legitimate one. It has established a code of its own; a scale of prices covering every form of civic corruption has been set up, and these prices have actually been made a matter of common knowledge. And no administrator, even if he were wiser than all the lawgivers and administrators who have ever lived, is strong enough to rectify this evil, no matter how he may curb the actions of the corrupt officials by appointing other officials to watch over them. Nothing will succeed until each one of you comes to feel that he must rise up against wrongdoing even as [every man] armed himself during the epoch when all the nations rose up against [a common enemy] ...... As a Russian, as one bound to you with kindred blood-ties, I now turn to you. I turn to those among you who have any conception at all of what nobility of ideas means. I call upon you to recall your duty, that duty which faces every man, no matter where he may be placed. I call upon you for a closer scrutiny of your duty and obligations, whatever your work upon this earth may be, for by now our duty is but dimly perceptible to us, and we can hardly ....." [H]

[1842–1852]

To the Reader
From the Author

Foreword to the Second Edition of Volume One

No matter who you may be, my reader, or what your station, or what your calling, whether you have been honored with the highest rank or are one of common estate, as long as God has taught you to read and write and my book has already come into your hands, I ask you to help me.

The book before you, which you have probably already read in its first edition, depicts a man who is taken from no other realm than our own. He journeys up and down our land of Russia; he encounters people of all conditions, from noblemen to commoners. He has been taken chiefly to show the shortcomings and vices of the Russian and not the Russian's merits and virtues, and all the people around him are likewise taken to show our frailties and shortcomings; the better people and characters will come in the other parts.

In this book many things are described incorrectly, not the way they really are and as they occur in the land of

Russia, inasmuch as I could not learn everything: a man's life would not suffice to learn by himself even an hundredth part of what goes on in our land. In addition to that, due to my own blundering, immaturity and haste, a host of all sorts of errors and slips occurred, so that there is something on every page to correct.

I ask you, reader, to correct me. Do not disdain such work. No matter how highly educated you may be and no matter how high in life, and no matter how insignificant my book may appear in your eyes and how petty may appear the work of correcting it and jotting down remarks concerning it, I ask you to do it. And as for you, the reader who is not highly educated and whose calling is but a simple one—do not consider yourself such an ignoramus as to be unable to teach me a thing or two. Every man who has lived and seen the world and encountered people has observed something or other which a different man has not observed, and has come to know something or other which others do not know. And for these reasons do not deprive me of your observations: it is impossible that you should not find in the entire book something or other to say concerning some passage, if you will but read that book attentively.

How fine it would be, for example, if but one of those who are rich in experience and comprehension of life, and familiar with the society of such people as I have described, were to make his notes so thorough as to cover the book in its entirety, omitting not a single page of it, and if he were to set about reading it not otherwise than with pen in hand and a sheet of notepaper placed before him, and if after reading several pages he were to recall to himself his whole life and all the people he had met, and all the happenings which had taken place before his eyes, and all that he himself had seen or heard from others which is similar to what is depicted in my book, or else that which is contrary thereto—if he were to describe this in exactly that form in which it arises in his memory, and were to send me every sheet as soon as it is finished, until the book has been read through in this manner! What a kinsmanly service he would render me! There is no need here to be concerned over style or beauty of expression: the matter here lies in the *matter itself* and in the *truth* of the matter, and not in the style. Nor need he stand upon ceremony should he feel like reproaching or upbraiding me, or pointing out to me the harm instead of the good I may have wrought by an unconsidered and inexact depiction of anything whatsoever. I shall be grateful to him for everything.

It would be a fine thing also were there to be found some person of a higher estate, far removed in all things—both in his very mode of life and in his education—from that social circle which is depicted in my book, yet who, on the other hand, knows the life of that class in the midst of which he lives, and if he were to decide to read my book anew in the very manner I have suggested, and were to call to mind all the people of higher estate whom he had encountered in his time, and were he to observe closely if there be not some point where these two estates approach each other, and if occasionally the very same thing is not repeated in the higher estate which goes on in the lower? And if he were to describe everything which would come to his mind in regard to this—that is, every incident in the higher social circle which might serve to confirm or refute such an approach—if he were to describe such an incident just as it happened before his eyes, without passing over either the people with their manners, tendencies, and habits, or the inanimate things about them, from their garments to the very furnishings and walls of the houses they live in. It is necessary for me to know this higher estate, which is the flower of the people. I cannot issue the last volumes of my work until such time as I learn, to some extent, life in Russia in all its aspects, even if but in such measure as I need know it for my literary creation.

It also might not be a bad thing if someone endowed with the ability of imagining or of forming for himself lively conceptions of the different situations in which people find themselves, and with the ability of pursuing them mentally in their various fields of endeavor—someone, in short, who is capable of penetrating deeply into the general thought of every author he reads, or of developing that thought—it might not be a bad thing if such a one were to trail closely every personage delineated in my book, and were to tell me how that personage ought to act in such and such circumstances; what, in keeping with his beginnings, ought to befall him subsequently, what new circumstances may confront him, and what it may be well to add to that which has been already described by me: all this I would like to take into consideration at the time when a new edition of this book, in a different and better form, may ensue.

One thing do I ask fervently of him who may wish to bestow his observations upon me: not to think at the time when he may be penning them that he is doing so for a man

who may be his equal in education, who has the same tastes
and ideas as he, the reader, has, and is therefore able to surmise a great deal even by himself, without any explanations; let him imagine, rather, that standing before him is a
man incomparably inferior to the reader in education, a
man who has studied practically nothing. It would be better still if, instead of me, he would picture to himself some
rustic savage whose whole life has been passed in the backwoods, in whose case it is necessary to enter into the most
particularized explanation of every circumstance and to be
as simple in speech as with a child, being on guard at every
moment not to use expressions above his comprehension.
If he who will undertake to make such observations on my
book will bear this constantly in view his observations will
prove of greater significance and interest than he himself
thinks possible, while at the same time they will prove of
genuine benefit to me.*

As for all others, the journalists as well as littérateurs in
general, while thanking them sincerely for all their previous comments on my book, which comments, despite a certain intemperance and tendencies toward passion which
are natural to man, have nonetheless brought great benefit

---

* At this point, after saying: "And so, should it come about that my heartfelt request is honored by my readers, and that there should actually be
found among them such kind souls as might wish to do everything as I
desire it to be done," the author gives very precise instructions for the
transmission of their "observations" as enclosures directed "either to
... the Rector of the University of St. Petersburgh ... or to" Prof. S. P.
Shevyrev, of the University of Moscow, "depending upon whichever
city happens to be nearer" the correspondent—a thoughtful suggestion, since postal rates at the time depended on the mileage involved.
Trans.

both to my head and my soul—I ask them too not to leave me without their observations on this occasion as well. I assure them sincerely that everything which they may say for my better understanding or instruction will be accepted by me with gratitude.

1846

A GLOSSARY OF
NAME MEANINGS

Not Given in the Text

Names whose lack of a particular meaning is in itself a stroke of peripheral characterization, and those which, while utterly juste *in the original, simply do not lend themselves either to translation or to interpretation, are not included.*

BEGUSHKIN: Run-along.
BEREBEDOVSKY: There is more than a soupçon of balderdash, of being in hot water, about him.
BEREZOVSKY: *Bereza* is *birch.*
BLOHIN: Fleasome.
BOBROV: Beaver.
BOLDYREVA: Mongrel.

CHEPRAKOV: Saddle-cloth.
CHICHIKOV: Although utterly apt, the name is not based upon an actual word; it nevertheless does convey the notion of a *dickey-bird,* of a bird's chick-chi-*lick´*-ing.

DROBYAZHKIN: Birdshot.

HANASSAROVA: Derived, one feels, from *khan,* implying descent from one of the Golden Horde invaders; also based on *han* [*zha*], a word of Turkish origin, meaning a *sanctimonious hypocrite.*

HLOBUEV: Slap-dash.

HVOSTYREV: From *hvosty*, or tails—almost certainly equine.

KARIAKIN: More than a hint about him of *straddling*, of *stubbornness.*

KISLOYEDOV: One who feeds on sour stuff, one who fares but poorly.

KOLOTYRKIN: Son of a She-Tattletale, of a She-Tittletattler.

KONAPATIEV: Nearest basis is *konopat´*—oakum, or tow.

KOPEIKIN: Based on *kopeika*, usually spelled *kopeck* in English.

KOROBOCHKA: Little Box, or Small Coffer. Now a byword in Russian.

KOSHKAREV: *Koshka* means *cat.*

KRASNONOSSOV: Red-of-nose.

KUVSHINIKOV: Descended from a maker and seller of pitchers.

LENITZIN: Name hints at indolence.

LIHACHEV: A *lihach* is a dashing, smart fellow; usually applied to driver of a fine carriage with a spirited team.

MANILOV: Based upon *maneet´*, to beckon, to lure, to entice; in short, Manilov is he whom a will-o'-the-wisp hath possessed. *Manilovism*, meaning ineffectual idealism, sentimentalism, is as current in Russian as *quixotism* is throughout the world.

MILUSHKIN: Based on *milusha*, a darling, a lovely person.

MYLNOI: Soapy-fellow.

NOZDREV: Achieved through *nozdrya*, nostril, and *nozdrevatost´*, sponginess. *Nozdrevshchina* is a byword for lying-cum-bragging-cum-bullying.

ODNOZOROVSKY: Implies who keeps his eye peeled on one thing.

PEREKROEV: One who has been recut and resewn; a fellow who has been in a fix, who was put through a wringer.

PERHUNSKY: Has a hint about him of clearing the throat—and of dandruff.

PETRUSHKA: Diminutive of Peter, but also means parsley, and the Russian Punch.

PLESHAKOV: Bald-patch.

PLIUSHKIN: He is *plushy* only to the extent that mildew or mold is; most of the revulsion he inspires is due, one feels, to the *pliu* sound in Russian: of the dozen purely Russian words with this beginning in my dictionary, only one is not unpleasant or downright nasty, or sinister—like *pliushch:* the deadly, the strangling ivy. There is, in all of Russian literature, perhaps only one other comparable feat of single-stroke characterization: that of Turgenev who, by the insertion of a *p* in the marvelously apt name of his Chertopkhakhanov, added to the traits of devilish daring and Asiatic imperiousness, the notions of arrogance and a violent temper. Pliushkin has long since become as living a character in Russia as Harpagon in France, and Scrooge in England—and America.

POBEDONOSNOV: Victorious-nose, or Bearer of Victory.

POCHITAEV: Guess-so.

PONOMAREV: There must have been a sexton or a sacristan among his forebears.

POPLEVIN: The name insinuates that he is a bit of a weed.

POPOV: Of a family of priests. Calling a man a *popovich*, or a son of a priest, was a sure-fire way to start a fight, even though bastardy was not implied, since Russian priests could marry.

POTSELUEV: *Potselui* is a *kiss;* also the imperative of the verb.

PROTOPOPOV: Somewhere along the line there was an archpriest in this character's ancestry.

SAMOSVISTOV: Blow-your-own-whistle.

SHAMSHEREV: Mumbler.

SKUDRONZHOGLO: The *zhoglo* ending is a very common one in Turkish surnames. Here, despite all his efforts to create a *balturish* paragon of a Free Enterpriser, Gogol shows a flash of his old self with the first syllable of the name, creating an impression of weakness, of insufficiency, of the barrenness of a New England field whose only bumper crop consists of morainial stones.

SOROKOPLEHIN: Son of Forty Sluts.

SVINIIN: A *svinya* is a *swine.*

TELIATNIKOV: *Teliatnik* is a stall for calves; also a cattle dealer.

TREHMETIEV: One who aims at three targets simultaneously.

TREPAKIN: A gadabout; dancer of a very lively peasant dance; one at the receiving end of a thorough beating.

TRUHACHEVSKY: *Truha* means *dry-rot, trash.*

UZYAKINA: *Uz* hints at narrowness.

VETVITSKY: Ramose, or Many-branched.

VISHNEPOKROMOV: Cherry-selvaged.
VORONOI-DRYANOI: Raven-black–trashy-stuff.
VZEMTSEV: Conveys the idea of a small-towner.

ZOLOTHUA: Scrofula.
ZYABLOVA: Chilled woman; one who hasn't too hot a time of it in life.

GOROHOVAYA: Pea Street; equivalent of Fifth Avenue, Regent Street, or Rue de la Paix.
LITEINAYA: Foundry Street, its prominence belying its name.
TORZHOK: Means Flea Market, but is the actual name of a town famous for its leather goods, just as Tula was for samovars and firearms, or Orenburg for woollen goods that were impervious to time and wear.
TRUHMACHEVKA: Dry-rot–Stepmother Village.
ZAMANILOVKA: Outer Manilovka.

Addenda and Variants

A (p. 312). In another version Sobakevich is (probably due to pressures of censorship) well nigh milk-and-honeyish (at least as much so as a Sobakevich can ever be) and is shown as an outright prevaricator and practically an accomplice of Chichikov's, answering the officials to the effect that Chichikov, in his opinion, was a good man, and that the peasants he had sold him were a choice and a truly lively lot in all respects, but that he could not vouch for what might befall in the future; that if these souls should chance to die on the way, owing to the hardships incident to resettlement, it wouldn't be his fault—it was all the will of God, and as for fevers and sundry other afflictions, there were not a few of them in this world, and there were cases, now, where entire villages had died out therefrom.

B (p. 315). In variant it is not merely the Chairman but all the officials who cannot draw much out of Korobochka:

Chichikov had, now, bought fifteen dead souls from her, and he was a traveling feather merchant [!], and a down dealer, too; and he'd promised to buy up a slew of all sorts of things; he also supplied the government with lard on contract, and therefore must be a sure enough knave, for there had been a fellow like that around before, who bought up feathers and down and supplied the government with lard on contract, and he'd taken everybody in, while the Dean's wife he had diddled out of more than a hundred rubles. Everything she said from then on was practically a repetition of the one and the same thing, and all that the officials gathered was that Korobochka was a foolish old woman.

This is followed by a characteristic passage:

Manilov answered the inquiries of the officials by stating that he was as ready to vouch for Pavel Ivanovich at any time as he was for himself; that he would be willing to forego all his estate if he might but have an hundredth part of the good qualities of Pavel Ivanovich and, in general, spoke of him in the most flattering terms adding, with his eyes by now sweetishly puckered, several thoughts on friendship. These thoughts, while they of course satisfactorily explained the tender motivation of his heart, nevertheless failed utterly in explaining to the officials just what was what.

C (p. 319). An interesting variant:

Messieurs the bureaucrats had recourse to still another expedient, not quite gentlemanly yet one which is, nevertheless, resorted to on occasion: that is, they tried to pump Chichikov's help through various backstairs acquaintances among the servants, to find out whether Pavel Ivanovich's domestics knew of any particulars concerning the former life and circumstances of their master, but they did not get much. All they got out of Petrushka was a whiff of stuffy living quarters and, out of Seliphan, that Chichikov "had worked for the government and at one time had served in the Customs," and nary a thing more. People of this class have a very strange way about them. If you ask one of them outright about something he'll never recollect the matter, won't get everything straight in his head, and may even simply answer that he doesn't know; but, should you ask him something else entirely, he'll instantly blab out whatever it was you wanted to know about, and will go into such details as you mightn't even want to listen to. All that the secret inquiries conducted by the officials revealed to them was merely that they didn't know with any degree of certainty what Chichikov was but that, just the same, Chichikov must inevitably be something.

D (p. 339). I have found three versions of *The Tale of Captain Kopeikin* and have, in the main, followed the suppressed one and, to a lesser extent, a supplemental one, both of which vary widely from the one usually available. I must have examined at least a baker's dozen (or so it seems) of English translations of *Dead Souls*, and can recall only one translation of the story—or, rather, a very flat synopsis; all the other translators gave the poor pegleg the widest of berths—except for one forthrightly Briton who frankly admitted that it was impossible to English the raciness of the original story. The censors were not at all slow about construing the *Tale* as an attack on fat-cat bureaucrats and, to save his book from being banned altogether, Gogol re-wrote the story in five days. Captain Kopeikin was transformed into "an empty-headed fellow, as hard to suit as the very Devil; he'd been in plenty of guard-houses and under arrest time and again; he'd had a taste of everything." The Prime Minister is incredibly sweet; Kopeikin never has any trouble seeing him; on the second call the grandee digs into his own pocket to keep the disabled veteran going. But "the Peterburgh way of life had already worked on him; there was a thing or two he had already tried"; the dissolute half-man had tasted of the flesh-pots, and had an Englishwoman and other dissipations and luxuries on his mind. " 'Well, now,' thinks he, 'let 'em do what they like, but as for me,' he says, 'I'll go and stir up the whole Commission, all the heads of it, and I'll tell 'em they have to do something!' And really, he was such a pesky fellow, a regular nuisance, with but little sense in his head, you understand, yet no end spry." When the Prime Minister asks him what he wants, Kopeikin says: " 'I can't get along from hand to mouth like this. I've got to sink my teeth into a good piece of meat every now and then,' he says, 'and have me a bottle of French wine; then, too, a man needs a little diversion once in a while, theatres and the likes of that.' " Naturally, the Prime Minister cannot see his way clear to pampering the veteran. "But my Kopeikin, as you can imagine, didn't give a hoot in hell. Those words, you understand, bounced off him like peas off a wall. What a hullabaloo he raised—how he sailed into all of them! All those Directors there, you understand, and the Secretaries, he started dressing them down and nailing up their hides. 'Why, you,' he says, 'are this,' says he, 'and you,' he says, 'are that! Why,' says he, 'you don't know your bounden duties! Why,' he says, 'you peddle justice at so much and so much!' he says. He let them all have it good and hot. There was some General there who had turned up from an altogether different department, actually—well, my dear Sir, he pitched into him too. What a ruckus he raised! What would you have done with a devil like that?" What happens to Kopeikin thereafter the reader already knows.

E (p. 481). There is a long hiatus at this point. Arnoldi, who was present at some of the readings of chapters from the second part of *Dead Souls* which Gogol gave for his intimate friends, has recorded his recollection of the missing chapter which followed, describing an entire day in the General's mansion.

Chichikov stayed to dinner. Ulinka came to the table with two others: the Englishwoman who was her governess, and some Spaniard or Portuguese who had been living on at the General's since time out of mind, for what purpose no one knew. The Englishwoman was a middle-aged spinster, a colorless being of homely appearance, with a big thin nose and unusually quick-darting eyes. She held herself erect, kept silent for days at a stretch, and merely kept shifting her eyes incessantly in all directions with a foolishly questioning look. The Portuguese, as far as I remember, was called Expanton, Xitendon, or something of the kind, but I do recall positively that everybody on the General's estate called the man Esquadron. He, too, kept silent all the time, but after dinner it was his duty to play chess with the General.

Nothing unusual happened at dinner. The General was in a gay mood and joked with Chichikov, who ate with great appetite; Ulinka was pensive, and her face became animated only when Tentetnikov was mentioned. After dinner the General settled down to chess with the Spaniard, incessantly repeating the point of Chichikov's story about "Love us when we're dirty; anyone will love us when we're clean,"* but constantly getting mixed up, with Chichikov obligingly correcting him every time. The General proposed a couple of games to Chichikov, and here, too, Chichikov evinced his extraordinary adroitness. He played very well, making things difficult for the General by his moves, yet would lose in the end; the General was very much gratified by overcoming such an expert player, and came to like Chichikov still more because of this. When Chichikov left, the General begged him to come again soon and bring Tentetnikov with him.

On returning to Tentetnikov, Chichikov tells him how sad Ulinka is, how the General misses him; also that the General was thoroughly repentant and that, to end the misunderstanding, the General had intended to take the initiative and call on Tentetnikov to ask his forgiveness. Chichikov has, of course, invented all this but, naturally,

---

*This has become a folk-saying in Russia. *Trans.*

Tentetnikov is glad to avail himself of this pretext, saying that he would never allow the General to take the initiative and that he was ready to start off on a visit tomorrow to forestall the General. Chichikov encourages him and they agree to go to the General's on the morrow. That evening Chichikov confesses to his fabrication about Tentetnikov's writing a history of the generals. Tentetnikov cannot understand why Chichikov had invented this story and does not know what to do if the General should broach this subject. Chichikov explains that he himself does not know how he had come to make this slip of the tongue, but since the harm has already been done he earnestly asks Tentetnikov, if the latter does not wish to lie in his turn, to say nothing about the story, at least to refrain from denying it categorically, so as not to compromise Chichikov before the General.

The visit to the General is a sort of reunion with him and his daughter. The description of the dinner which follows is, in my opinion, the best part in the second volume [of *Dead Souls*]. Tentetnikov was seated at the General's right hand, Chichikov at his left.—All seemed in a gay and contented mood. The General was content because of the reconciliation and the opportunity of chatting with a man who was writing a history of the generals who had fought for the fatherland; Tentetnikov, because Ulinka was sitting almost facing him, their eyes meeting from time to time; Ulinka was happy because the man she loved was again with them and because her father was again on good terms with him; Chichikov was satisfied with his rôle of peacemaker in this distinguished—and rich—family. The Englishwoman rolled her eyes to her heart's content; the Spaniard kept his eyes fixed on his plate and lifted them only when the waiters brought in a new course. Having marked down the best piece, he would not let his eyes stray from it all the time that the platter was going around the table, or until the desired tidbit was put on someone's plate.

After the second course the General began a conversation with Tentetnikov about his projected book and touched upon the campaign of 1812. Chichikov was thrown into a bit of a scare, anxiously waiting for Tentetnikov's response, but the latter parried skilfully, answering that it was not up to him to write a history of that campaign, of the individual battles and the individual commanders who had played a role in this war, that it was not so much through their heroic exploits that the memorable year was noteworthy, that the historians of this period were numerous enough even without him, but that one ought to regard this epoch from a different angle: what mattered, in his opinion was that the whole nation had risen as one to defend the fatherland; that all considerations, intrigues, and passions were stilled for the duration—what mattered was that all the social strata united in the single emotion of love for their fatherland, that every man hastened to give up all he owned and to sacrifice everything for the winning of the general effort. These were the things which mattered in that war, and that was what he would wish to describe in a single vivid picture, with all the details of the unseen exploits and the lofty but secret sacrifices!

Tentetnikov spoke rather lengthily and with passion, all imbued, at that moment, with his emotional love for Russia. Betrishchev was listening to him in rapture; this was the first time such a living, ardent speech was coming to his ears. A tear, clear as a diamond of the purest water, was caught on his gray mustache and trembled there. The General was magnificent, splendid at that moment. And what of Ulinka? Her eyes were fixed on Tentetnikov; she seemed to drink in his every word avidly, his speech was like music to her; she loved him, she was proud of him! The Spaniard was looking at his plate more intently than ever; the Englishwoman was staring at everybody with a stupid air, unable to understand anything.

Silence reigned when Tentetnikov had done; all were stirred. Chichikov, desirous of contributing his bit, was the first to break the silence. "Yes," he said, "there were frightful frosts in eighteen-twelve!"—"The frosts have nothing to do with it," the General remarked, looking at him sternly. Chichikov was abashed. The General extended his hand to Tentetnikov and thanked him in a most friendly manner, but Tentetnikov felt happiest merely because he had read approbation of himself in Ulinka's eyes. The history of the generals was forgotten.

Arnoldi does not remember the order of the next chapters. He does remember, however, that on the day of the momentous dinner Ulinka decided to have a serious talk with her father concerning Tentetnikov. After praying at her mother's grave she talks with her father, begging his consent and blessing for her marriage to Tentetnikov. The General hesitated for a long while but finally consented. Tentetnikov was called in several days after the reconciliation and told of her decision. Tentetnikov, delirious with happiness, longs to be alone and rushes out into the garden.

Here Gogol had two wonderful lyrical pages. On a sultry summer day, at noon, Tentetnikov is in the dense, shady garden, amid profound silence. With a master's hand was this garden drawn—one saw every branch, felt the sultriness in the air, heard the grasshoppers and all the insects in the grass and, finally, experienced all that Tentetnikov was going through: happy, in love, and with his love requited! I remember that this description was so vivid that I had to catch my breath. Gogol read superbly. In the excess of his emotions, in the fulness of his happiness Tentetnikov wept and vowed on the spot to devote his life to his bride. At this moment Chichikov appeared at the end of the garden path. Tentetnikov threw his arms around Chichikov's neck and thanked him: "You are my benefactor—it is to you I owe my happiness! How can I show you my gratitude? All my life would be too short to prove it to you—"

At that instant an idea all his own flashed through Chichikov's head:

"I haven't done anything for you—it was merely chance," he answered. "I am very happy. However, you can very easily show me your gratitude!"

"But how? How?" Tentetnikov kept repeating. "Tell me as quickly as you can and I'll carry it all out." At this point Chichikov told him the story of the supoosititious uncle and the need for three hundred serfs, even if they exist only on paper.

"But why must they necessarily be dead?" asked Tentetnikov, who had not grasped very well what kind of serfs Chichikov was after. "I'll give you the whole three hundred of my souls on paper and you can show our agreement to your uncle, and later on, when you come into his estate, you'll destroy the purchase-deed."

Chichikov was petrified from astonishment: "How is it you're not afraid to do this? Aren't you afraid that I may take you in—may misuse your confidence?"

But Tentetnikov would not let him finish. "What!" he cried out. "Would you have me doubt you, to whom I owe more than life?"

They embraced and the matter was settled. Chichikov's slumber was sweet that night.

A council was held at the General's house the next day, as to how all the relatives were to be informed of the betrothal. Evidently Betrishchev was very much concerned how Princess Zuzukina and his other high-born kinfolk would receive the news. Here, too, Chichikov proved to be very useful. He volunteered to make the rounds of the General's relatives. Naturally, he had in mind those eternal dead souls of his. His proposition was gratefully received. "What could be better?" reflected the General. "He's a clever, respectable fellow; he'll be able to announce this marriage so that everybody will be gratified." He offered Chichikov an imported traveling barouche, while Tentetnikov offered him a fourth horse. Chichikov was to set out in a few days. From that moment on he was considered by everybody as one of the family, as an intimate. On returning to Tentetnikov's Chichikov summoned Seliphan and Petrushka and told them to get ready to leave. Seliphan had grown lazy and was logy with drink and did not look like a coachman at all; the horses had been neglected; Petrushka had turned into a perfect ladies' man because of the village wenches. But when the barouche was brought over from the General's and Seliphan saw what a roomy box he would sit on and that he would be directing a team of four, all of a coachman's impulse awakened within him; he examined the vehicle closely, with a connoisseur's eye, and demanded from the General's people all manner of spare parts, some of which did not even exist. Chichikov, too, was thinking with pleasure of his proposed trip; how he would sprawl out on the resilient cushions, and how the team of four would tool along with the feather-light barouche.

I have given this recollection not only to fill in, to some extent, the gap in the story, but to show that Gogol did not violate the seemingly irrefragable law of the picaresque: that every scoundrelly hero must offer the Dostoevskian redemptionary onion, must perform one redeeming good deed during his motley career. Even Yushkevich's nefandous Leon Drey was not immune from that law!

F (p. 545). In another version Platonov's sister is "flaxen-fair, white of face," with a frank, thoroughly Russian air, as exceptionally good-looking as her brother, but just as semi-somnolent as he. She seemed but little concerned over the things which usually concern people, either because her all-absorbing activity left nothing as her own share, or because she belonged, because of her very nature, to that philosophical category of people who, while endowed with emotions and thoughts and intellect, look at life only through half-closed eyes and, witnessing its agitating alarms and struggles, say: "let the fools rage! So much the worse for them."

As Skudronzhoglo first appears on the scene the muzhik is not pleading with him to accept the load of building materials he has brought but imploring him to take over a whole village of serfs. Skudronzhoglo tells him that they would still be in bondage, since he insists, above all, on toil.

Incidentally, this paragon of all the *bourzhui* virtues goes by at least two other names in the various recensions (Kostanzhoglo, Gorbozhoglo); toward the end Gogol seems to have had more trouble in keeping this character in focus than with any other.

G (p. 580). The conjectural reconstruction of the missing portions of *Dead Souls* apparently offers as fascinating a literary problem to Russians as the completion of *Edwin Drood* does to the English. One anonymous reconstruction fills in the gaps in this chapter most logically: Chichikov, after his talk with Vassilii Platonov, calls the next day upon Lenitzin, quickly ingratiating himself with the gentleman. Lenitzin turns out to be the man who aims at a governorship and is seeking to inherit the property of Hanassarova, Hlobuev's aunt. Lenitzin denies that the latter ambition is really true; besides, the old woman has willed most of her estate to monasteries and churches. These, as Chichikov points out, are rich enough as it is; why doesn't he try to make her change her mind? Why not actually write out a new will, all ready for her signature, if she should decide to annul the present one? Chichikov is going to stay in town for some time; he offers to see what he can do in this matter.

Lenitzin is afraid she will never consent. Chichikov is aware that old people are strong-headed; he intimates that a signature is a relatively small matter to stand in one's way. Lenitzin is frightened, but the reader gathers that he and Chichikov concoct a scheme between them.

After the episode with the inconsiderate baby Chichikov acquires some dead souls from Lenitzin and persuades him to return the seized wasteland to the Platonovs in exchange for another piece of land. He returns to the Platonovs, buys some more dead souls from Vassilii; Platon falls ill, and Chichikov sets out alone for the town. There he concludes the purchase of Hlobuev's estate, incidentally deferring the final payment for a considerable length of time.

Through a letter of introduction Chichikov gains the confidence of the wealthy Hanassarova and shortly ingratiates himself to such an extent that he becomes practically her right-hand man. He cannot, however, persuade her to change her will. In the meantime Chichikov makes no attempt to pay the note he has given to Hlobuev, which is by now long overdue. Rumors spread about his trying to sell the estate—and about his buying up dead souls, the latter launched by an official who chances to pass through the town and hears about Chichikov's stay there. Hanassarova dies; her house and effects are sealed up; gossip is rife: the old woman's death is alleged not to have been reported for forty-eight hours; Chichikov is considered to be the only one who could say how she had died—he had been hanging about until her last breath, practically running her household.

The Governor General makes due allowances for gossip; nevertheless he summons Chichikov for an interview and then gives him twenty-four hours to get out of town. However, our hero persuades him it's all a matter of small town gossip, it seems—and is allowed to stay.

The promissory note to Hlobuev is very shortly thereafter paid off by Chichikov. The late Hanassarova's house is unsealed and a will is found, leaving everything to Lenitzin, with the exception of a few small legacies—one of them to Hlobuev. Lenitzin, incidentally, is informed that several caskets and some jewelry and other effects are missing, but he merely shrugs this matter off. And our Chichikov proves, somehow, to be sitting on top of the world.

H (p. 644). The following recovered fragment from Part Two was, according to an editorial note, written in the latter half of the 1840's. A great deal of bracketed conjecture is necessitated by the prevalent incoherence. It is presented here not only for the sake of completeness but as a clinically classic example of what inevitably befalls a writer of genius when he gets religion and tries to write *haltura*.

...... All [try] to live at the expense of public funds, to make their posts into good things for themselves, to turn the entire government into a philanthropic institution which is obligated to feed all of them! ...... This striving on the part of officials and administrators to get into the [higher] ranks is after all, if I may say so ...... [utterly insufferable!] ...... Let us see, then, just who will be left in the ranks of those who are administered? And will those who are administered have sufficient means to support the enormous mass of those who do the administering? The [region] is deprived of working hands. The land goes uncultivated. Russia remains to this day in its primitive desolate state. No, it's impossible for all of us to turn into fishermen and to fish. It is fitting to abandon solicitude for one's own private and personal [life] and it is necessary to call poor Russia to mind. If we do not call Russia to mind by ourselves, if we ourselves do not, by a united effort, raise [the general level] ...... then no genius-inspired ideas from above [will avail] ...... no matter what resources and energies we expend ...... Nay, it is fitting that we turn our attention to the evil which is the origin of all [this] ...... Nay, it is fitting to consider at last in all seriousness how to start living a simple life, which ...... All can see—even the blind—that bribes are due to a desire to live somewhat better, somewhat more in [keeping with those of a

higher station] ...... to avail oneself of all the conveniencies and enlightened superfluities of the present [times]. ..... Embezzlements,
too, are due to this desire, and to it, too, are due all the impulses to
establish posts supposedly indispensable—on the supposition that it
isn't at all hard to fool people! [Such] were the projects presented for
the establishment of new posts, and so touchingly was their indis-
pensability presented, that even I confirmed them and presented
them for [further] confirmation; I had used my trust for bad ends,
and only quite long afterward did I see that I had deceived my benefactor, the Sovereign, and that I had become a deceiver in my turn!
And how many phenomena of that sort turn up at every step! ......

No, this cannot be! It is necessary to put an end to this at last; it is
necessary to abandon at last a life of this sort which [can lead] to no
good ...... [we must realize] that men cannot attain through embezzlements and bribes the fulfillment of all their luxurious whims,
and status, and a position in the world. Even with the acceptance of
bribes and the commitment of embezzlements for the sake of your
miserable daughters you are hardly able to give them that stupid,
miserable education demanded by the conditions of that stupid
mode of [life] which none of you feels like abandoning. I address
myself, first of all, to those who are rich and well-to-do. It behooves
you to [set] an example. Do away with furnishings and all luxurious
whims. Go after simplicity, if only until such time when circumstances in general improve ...... you will all be gainers thereby; you
will have enough money left over to help [others] and go in for philanthropy—something that I know you are not in a position to do
now; you can do no good because everything has been [used up for
your own selves]. As for me, I give you my word not to set up an elegant carriage for myself, and even during the [most] formal gala occasions I will appear not otherwise than in a hired hack, and my wife
will not put on anything save the most ordinary clothes, and my
daughters will never be in anything which comes to more than ten
rubles in printing-press money, and they will wear their things till
there's no more wear in them, no matter what fashion plates may be
published, and even though the mode may turn everything inside
out. And as for you, Petr Nicholaievich, I am instructing you to get
used to a club of another sort than [your present one], a club [which]
all may get into without ruining themselves. You might ask Murazov's advice about that. He will find an honest restaurant. In a
province where provisions sell in the market for next to nothing it is
disgraceful [to be paying exorbitant prices to restaurants] ...... [You

should order] *table-d'hôte* dinners . . . . . . *table-d'hôte* . . . . . . [to cost] no more than a printing-press ruble [a person]. I know very [well] that for a sum like that three—even four—courses [can be prepared] from fresh provisions, such as are right at hand, without any imported condiments. . . . . . . As for the French [restaurateur], I beg of you to drive him out. You'll be doing him a good turn, actually—if he stays on for long he'll go bankrupt, the fool. Nobody will pay the bills run up with him. It's all his own fault—charging ten times the real price! It's no concern of mine if he needs to accumulate money enough to enable him to [live] well in Paris later on. He may be bribing the police. . . . . . but, as one in authority, I shan't permit this, since those bribes are at the expense of wretched intemperance. Also, in general, I would request you to exert all your efforts to have the master craftsmen turn out their goods as cheaply as possible. I request you to talk this over with Murazov. At present he is particularly taken up with the class of burghers and artisans and has already educated many of them.

I feel confident that if certain pickings are done away with, if pickings which are paid over to the police are not permitted, things will [improve] considerably all around . . . . . . Would it not be better if policemen, without waiting [for compulsory measures], were to curb their extortions, inasmuch as I now appeal to them also as being Russians [at] heart to whom, I think, Russia is still near and dear. There has to be sacrifice on all our parts, and not merely from some single individual. For then prices and the cost of living will inevitably decline, and consequently it will be cheaper for each one of us to support himself. Finally, I implore you to terminate all lawsuits among [yourselves peaceably], without calling in the administration and without encouraging pettifogging and the multiplication of lawsuits and, together with them, the multiplication of new posts and new officials who, poor fellows, must willy-nilly be parasitical plants. You would do better by having recourse to the old Russian way of common arbitration and, choosing from among yourselves persons known for their honesty and fair dealing, letting them judge; no matter what their decision, even the loser will be a gainer if he considers what he would have lost in legal costs and being knocked about from pillar to post through the courts, which process could drag out matters even to his hoary old age and poison his life for [ever]. But, I hope that [such] a trial will not lead to hard feelings. However, should any case be a difficult one, I advise submitting it to the judgment of a man whom I shall not name, but whose identity you will surmise—a man of irreproachable life, and an activity filled with good deeds which will speak for [itself]...... It may very well be that we will thus imperceptibly attain such a state as cannot be attained through any administrative measures, even the most intricately wise—that is, we may attain to doing away with all those temporary Commissions and Committees which, through all sorts of intrigues, we have striven to make permanent ones. This, at the least, is our duty: we must all exert ourselves as one to fulfill it as the sons of [our] land, as loyal men who have taken an oath in the name of God to serve [our] land faithfully. And it may very well be that even now, after our firm resolve, the number of lawsuits and all that mountainous paperwork will decrease. Nevertheless I ask you to be punctilious in the performance of your duties: to arrive at your office on time and to leave your office on time. However, I request the directors of chancelleries not to inaugurate that pedantry, that outward hypocrisy, of everyone *seeming* busied with some work. No! It is enough if the man is present. No, if there is no work, let the man read some useful book, and let the office be his study—let it, at least, be a place where those books are read which make a man more temperate, more prudent, preparing him to be a future statesman and a son of [his] land. No later than tomorrow there will be delivered to every division of the administrative office a copy of the Bible, a copy of a history of Russia, and three or four classics, the works of the greatest universal po[ets], of faithful chroniclers of their own lives. I am glad to have [the wherewithal] to make this offering, at the cost of certain [personal] privations. I feel that this is important. Of late your heads have had everything within them wind-scattered by this frivolous reading of ephemeral books and by [watching] musical comedies— [reading which] has been perverting [and turning] inside out life, thoughts, opinions, and general conceptions. Come, really, it is high time to read that which should be read before everything else. To our shame be it said, perhaps there is hardly a man to be found among us who has read the Bible through, and yet this book [exists] to be read perpetually—no, not out of any religious consideration, but out of curiosity, as a memorial of a people which has surpassed all peoples in wisdom, in poetry, in law-giving—a book which even unbelievers and pagans consider the loftiest creation of the intellect, instructing us in life and wisdom. How can we demand, then, that we produce men capable of prudent influence and of action! Yet how astonished we are because we are forever producing rareripes, upstarts, weathercocks, lightweights, irrespressible bunglers, headlong innovators, weaklings who have no control over their passions! . . . . . .

No, I am addressing myself to you. Let us not feel sorry for ourselves but for the children, whom we have abandoned into the hands of [others] . . . . . . and whom we have no wish to know—yet who could be a better mentor for a son than his own father? Yes, it would require nothing more than reading books together with your children intelligently, reading works which, even from earliest youth, mould strong character, bestow a knowledge of life, a knowledge of one's land. If nothing else this course would be several times more useful than all that heap of money spent on teachers with varying points of view. . . . . . conceptions which clog up the mind so on all sides that in the end [the learner] does not find out [even] in his hoary old age whether he ever had an opinion or a thought of his own and is ready, like a submissive sheep, to follow the first loud-mouth, the first unconsidered pamphlet. Just as if a father who has himself gone through both [a military school] and a university could not prepare his son for an institution [of learning], when the curriculum and [all] are printed all over as common knowledge. . . . . . . There is no time! However, we do have time for cards. Why, in two evenings, in the midst of one's family, one can convey without a book an idea of any subject, or at least what it consists of and what our need of it is; in short, arouse a consciousness of it, so that your wife and daughters will hear [you] out, while a desire and a curiosity to read and fill out his knowledge of that subject will be engendered in your son. . . . . . . And it must be owned that such evenings would afford nothing but pleasure to our own selves and nothing but instruction to our own selves. No, we. . . . . . With a dreadful, insulting reproach will indignant posterity insult us, and a righteous wrath will smite [us] because in addition [to all else]. . . . . . while toying with the sacred word *enlightenment* as if with a toy, we were ruled by dressmakers, hairdressers, modes, we dared to place [ourselves] above our manly [forefathers]. . . . . . I am saying these things because that is how I feel and consider it my duty to tell you everything that I feel. At this moment of farewell, which is after all a solemn moment—perhaps we may see one another again and perhaps we may not—one should not say frivolous things. My speech and I may be laughed at—by whoever has the heart to do so. But I know that those to whom the happiness of [our] land is dear, who are still Russians to the core and have not yet had everything within them scattered to the winds—

those will agree with a great deal of what I say. I repeat once more: "I shall exert myself for all and shall endeavor to entreat pardon for all, every single one—consequently I have a certain right to demand from you that you weigh [my words] rather carefully and ponder upon them.

TRANSLATOR'S NOTES

1. Kotzebue, August Friedrich Ferdinand von (1761–1819). In Russia from 1781 to 1795; from 1798 to 1800 Court Dramatist in Vienna; on his return to Russia in 1800 sent to Siberia for one of his dramas but was shortly recalled and appointed Director of the German Troupe in St. Petersburg. In 1819 was sent to Germany, where he was put to death on suspicion of espionage. Wrote more than 200 plays, sentimental, rhetorical—and enormously successful in their day.

2. Golenishchev-Kutuzov, Michail Ilarionovich (1745–1813), Prince of Smolensk, General-Field Marshal; filled several important government posts. Fought in every Russian war from 1764 to 1812; made Commander in Chief against the French in August, 1812, and in November of the same year won the Victory of Smolensk over Ney and Davout. Peer of Suvorov as a military genius; was most popular with the army and common people—and anything but popular with Alexander I.

3. *"Thetiuk* [pronounced phetiuk]," Gogol explains in a footnote, "is a word insulting to a man; it is derived from θ, a letter which is considered the indecent letter." Ranking among the achievements of the Russian Revolution as second in importance only to the czarectomy is its expulsion from the Russian alphabet of several notoriously featherbedding characters, whose sole visible means of support was in making life miserable for generations of schoolboys. And ranking

second in parasitical uselessness only to the abominable *yat'* (Ѣ) was the *theta*, which occurred only in words of Greek origin but, since the Russians find the *th* sound of the *theta* at least as difficult to negotiate as Americans do the *ch* sound of the *chi*, the indecent letter was pronounced as *f*—with, of course, the few inevitable exceptions where it was sounded as *t*. It has now been uniformly supplanted by the less suggestive φ, to the regret of none save the irreconcilable codgers among the émigrés who do not find their *hlebnoi kvass* at all palatable unless the bottle label spells it *hlyebnoi kvass*.

4. The first name and patronymic bestowed by the Russian folk on its totem animal, in both affection and respect; when the bear is trained or a pet he is usually called Misha, or even Mishka. He has a surname, too, Toptyghin (Tread-Heavily), and Nekrassov, for one, has made him a general, in *General Toptyghin*, a gem of Russian humorous verse.

5. Maurocordato, Prince Alexander (1791–1865); Greek patriot, statesman; fought in the Greek War for Independence. —Kolokotronis, Theodoros (1770–1840); leader in Greek War for Independence. — Miaoules, Andreas Vokos (1768[?]–1835), naval commander in Greek War for Independence; defeated Turkish fleet in 1822; destroyed his fleet to keep it from capture by the Russians. Kanaris, Konstantinos (1790–1877); naval commander, performing daring exploits in sea fights against the Turks (1822); statesman.

6. Bagration, Prince Petr Ivanovich; Russian general of noble Georgian family; served under Suvorov; warred against Napoleon; mortally wounded at Borodino during the French invasion of 1812.

7. The Lancasterian system, named after Joseph Lancaster (1778–1838), an Englishman, who introduced it in primary schools, with advanced students teaching those in lower grades. Some of the contempt felt for this system by the higher society of Russia can be gathered from a discussion in the third act of Griboyedov's immortal comedy, *'Tis Folly to Be Wise*.

8. Gogol specifies that the signature was that of Prince Hovansky. The only prince of that name who has made his way into several works of reference is Ivan Andreivich who, interestingly enough—but quite unsuitably—was made a head shorter (in 1682) for his suspected aspirations to put his son on the Russian throne. What we have here is, most probably, a pure Gogolism, based upon the Ukrainian verb *hovat'*, meaning to hide, to put away carefully.

9. *Whitey, red*, etc.: from America to Zanzibar, popular speech seems mostly concerned with affectionate and ridiculous designations for Women and Money, in that order—and one doesn't have to be a Dar-

win to figure out the reason for such concern. The only point in this monetary slang, or cant, in which the Russian differs from and surpasses all others is the extreme *colorfulness* of folk expressions for his paper money. When an American sneers "Let me see the color of your money!" the poor, drab fellow has in mind only the *long green;* the Russ, however, had during the days of serfdom (and even up to the Revolution) an exuberant monetary palette of *whiteys* plain, *trompe-l'œil* whiteys watermarked with delicately detailed and genuinely beautiful portraits of Peter the Great, Catherine the Great, Paul the Mad, and so on, exquisitely calligraphic whiteys, and whiteys overprinted with gray; *grays* in monochrome, *grays* iridescent on the face, *grays* iridescent on the reverse; *blues, sky-blues, brownies, pinkies; reds, little reddish darlings, little all-rainbow sweeties, et* so many *al.*

All of this may sound like picayune pendantry or (I hope) simple conscientiousness. I would have little regard for a Russian translator who Russianized *a continental* literally, and still less for one who rendered *a shinplaster* not only literally but without making clear *where* the shinplaster was issued, or whether it was issued during the American Revolution, or the American depression *ca.* 1837, or the War Between the States. Such fellows simply let their authors go hang and leave their readers dangling in midair, whereas I have always felt that my writing muzhiks turned out honest wares and that it was up to their literary middleman to see that their foreign trade got a fair shake for its money. Craftsmen like Turgenev, Leskov, Shchedrin-Saltykov, Gogol don't resort to slang or cant merely to be smart Alexeis, but for the sake of the succinctness and effectiveness of cant and slang in the presentation of the telling fact, the knacker's-mallet detail. Telling the reader of *Little Judas* in English that a town cabby was paid off with a crumpled *little yellow* is meaningless, unless the stark actuality is also brought out that in the late 1850's, coachman, coach and team could be hired to drive fare and baggage miles out into the country, in the cruelest of Russian frosts, for the paper equivalent of sixteen cents in hard cash; nor does it make much more sense merely to state that an average provincial professional woman could be bought for either as high as a *greenie* or a *little greenie* of one variety, or for as low as a *little greenish* of another variety—the reader must also be made to realize that the range was from a five-ruble bill to a three-ruble one, or from all of eighty-three cents to practically six bits—a truly spectacular tariff, incidentally, for female hacks, when compared with the hire of the male ones.

In the case of Gogol it would have been neither excessively hard nor too time-consuming, I suppose, to give merely the colors of the notes; I could not help feeling, however, that the reader was entitled to somewhat more fair and rather less indeterminate agiotage than that. Since friendly Russian-born bankers and economists are no longer available for brain-picking, this required a refresher course in monetary spectroscopy, and the spending of an entire working day (not at all unpleasantly) in an ensorcelled yet practically unknown oasis of specialized scholarship in the upper reaches of Broadway, examining an extensive, and bewildering, collection of Russian paper money, with a time range of 1769 to the late 1920's, and a range of denominations from one ruble to 1000 rubles, in order to form educated estimates of what the going prices on government clerks and officials were in Chichikov's day. Let the reader (or, I hope, readers) bear one very important factor in mind: that Gresham's law (the only law that has never been broken by anybody, anywhere) was operative in Russia long before Chichikov and long after him; hence Russians were in general buying and selling one another for the Russian version of the French *assignats*, or printing-press money, worth about one-third of its face value in hard money, which was silver. Thus, while the payoff of the mere quill-drivers was in 25-kopeck pieces (worth 12 1/4¢ each—considerably less than the hire of even cab-drivers), it was at least in silver; the usual 10-ruble *red* tendered to a single higher-up in the good old days amounted to no more than $1.63 in hard cash—just about double what a professional woman fetched; while each of the 25-ruble *whiteys* represented, in hard cash, all of $4.17.

10. Navarino (Neocastro, or the ancient Pylos): a port in Messenia, Greece; scene of the victory of the Anglo-Franco-Russian fleet over the Egyptian-Turkish fleet on October 20, 1827.

11. In the overlong, never-ending chronicle of human idiocy a history of the Russian Schismatics (Raskolniki, Splitters, Dissenters, Old Faithers, Sectarians, Heretics) would make by no means the least fascinatingly imbecilic section in the multivolumed division tagged Religion. For a more comprehensive note on these Old Time Religionists, the more or less eager reader is referred to page 250 of *A Treasury of Russian Literature* (Vanguard Press, New York).

A NOTE ON THE TYPE

The principal text of this Modern Library edition
was set in a digitized version of Janson, a typeface that dates
from about 1690 and was cut by Nicholas Kis, a
Hungarian working in Amsterdam. The original matrices have
survived and are held by the Stempel foundry in Germany.
Hermann Zapf redesigned some of the weights and sizes for
Stempel, basing his revisions on the original design.